A CAT'S
ALMANAC
OF MAGIC AND
DRAGONS

DRAGONCAT OMNIBUS 1

CHRIS BEHRSIN

Editing by Wayne M. Scace
(www.facebook.com/Editor.Scace)
Proofreading by Carol Brandon

CONTENTS

A CAT'S GUIDE TO BONDING WITH DRAGONS

DRAGONCAT BOOK 1

CHRIS BEHRSIN

To Lion. Betcha never expected you'd inspire a novel.

THE TOWER

M y story doesn't start, unfortunately, in the hills of South Wales where I once had a good life, dashing through the long dry summer grass chasing butterflies with the heat from the sun beating against my fur.

It doesn't start eating salty tuna straight out of the can every Sunday morning, and the remains of roasted chicken in the afternoon.

Nor does it start with me propped up against a velvet cushion that was tossed onto the sofa as I watched Tom chasing Jerry on television, amazed and slightly offended at how stupid the creators made Tom.

Instead, it starts on a muggy day, where the only way of telling the weather was the pressure on the sides of my head and the moisture I could sense in my whiskers.

It starts in a stone tower with no windows, built of roughly hewn stones, sealed together with magic rather than mortar.

It starts trapped under the service of an evil warlock who teleported me into a world and back to a time where humans only kept cats like me to chase mice and rats.

I'm not a usual cat, either in these magical lands or my original home.

I'm a Bengal, meaning I'm larger than your average house cat. But not as large as a Savannah cat, two of whom inhabited my previous neighbourhood. Nor am I as large as that beast of a cat called a Maine Coon that I saw once on television – that was the biggest domestic cat I'd ever seen. But I am a descendant of the great Asian leopard cat, which makes me special in my own right.

My fur is a kind of amber colour, and I have these black patches on me. If you caught a leopard cub in the warm light of sunset, maybe I'd look a little similar. Except I'm not quite as lazy as a leopard, and not quite so stupid as to start a fight with a wildebeest. Also, don't mistake me for a tabby, a calico, or a tortoiseshell – those are the three worst things you can call a Bengal. I'm proud of my heritage and the way I look.

I have a name, but there's no way you'll be able to pronounce it in your language. You think Russian's hard, then try hissing and sputtering and mewling out one of our long names. The humans called me Ben as I'm a Bengal, imaginative as they were. The younger kid had a little more imagination and decided that because of my breed I should be called Bengie.

He was cute, that one, when he didn't try throwing me around the room.

I won't tell you much more about my life back in Wales, because it's probably uninteresting to human ears. Instead, I'll tell you about the evil warlock who whisked me away across time and space from a nutritious breakfast of milk and salmon trimmings right into the centre of a pentagram drawn in red chalk on his floor.

His name was Astravar, though I only learned of his name later. Like many men of misery, he liked to keep himself neat, not letting a single bobble of fluff grace his purple cloak, and always ensuring his collar kept as straight as still water. He had a long face, so gaunt you could see the bones underneath his eyes, cheeks, and chin. He had cruel grey eyes without a tint of colour in them – incredibly unnatural for a human.

At first, I looked up at him in shock. Then I thought, *might as well make the most of it.* Maybe at least I could get this strange man to pet me. So, I mewled for a little comfort, and you know what he did? He slapped me in the face.

I was quick to react, and I swiped at him with my right paw, scratching through his trousers. That was when he dragged me over to this tiny and cramped cage, and he locked me in there for two days straight without food and water. At least I think it was two days – there was no way of telling when day moved to night in that place.

When Astravar went out, I remained there in complete darkness, so cramped I couldn't even pace, my paws cold against the floor, without a blanket for comfort; where I could just feel the cockroaches crawling all over my paws and I couldn't do anything about them.

Those were the worst two days of my life.

You can probably imagine the rest of my life there wasn't easy, either. Astravar eventually let me out of the cage, but he never let me outside, and he kept the room so pitch black when he went out during the day, that I couldn't see a thing, even with cat vision.

Meanwhile, I would lie there on the thin mattress on the bedstead in this circular room, mewling away, hoping someone would pass by this tower, take pity, and knock down the door and steal me away. All the dust in here just made me sneeze all the time. Astravar didn't leave food in a bowl on the floor. Not even that cheap processed meat stuff – not that they had it in his day – and I couldn't help but long for the tuna, salmon, and roasted chicken and other delicious feasts that my previous owners would spoil me with every day. He didn't even leave proper water down, just some algae infested swill from the bottom of some dirty pond.

In all honesty, I don't know where he got the water from. Maybe it had magical properties. Maybe if I drank enough of it, I'd be able to grow wings and fly. But where would I go? Like I said, this tower didn't have any windows, so I couldn't even sit on the sill and gaze out at the wilderness.

Astravar often went out foraging during this time, and he'd come back with a bag full of things like mandrake roots, deadly nightshade, and all kinds of other plants you wouldn't dare touch with a paw, let alone a whisker.

Other days he'd bring back heavy shiny rocks like the one that hung above his enchantment table. Each time, he'd bring home all this stuff for who knows what nefarious intention, and he didn't even think to throw in a sprig of catnip.

Then, he'd work under the light of a transparent crystal above a stone table, engraved with red, yellow, and purple runes. This crystal hung too far out of reach for me to access, unfortunately. It would shine bright white, allowing him to get to work grinding his herbs with a mortar and pestle, etching more runes into the table, and hammering at shiny rocks; making a racket far too intense for my sensitive ears.

It wasn't terrible living in Astravar's tower for the first week or so. There were mice here, lots of them. Mind you, with the way this place had been put together, with stones thrown one on top of the other, there were plenty of places for mice to hide.

They hid in holes underneath the spinning wheel, behind the cold obsidian stone of the enchantment table, underneath the bed frame – full of nasty splinters, that one. There was even one in the pantry, which is the worst place to have a mouse hole, if you ask me. Particularly in a world where they haven't yet invented tin cans.

That's probably why Astravar summoned me here and, being a good cat, I got rid of them pretty quickly. I even ate a few of them, because I was hungry. Mouse tastes okay, but I can't stand all those sharp bones in awkward places. To be honest, I also prefer my meat cooked.

You would have thought a wizard would be selective about who he brought into his abode. Well, he was really, other than the mice, and the cockroaches, and the single rat who made it up there one morning. The rat didn't find his way through a hole, a window – because I already told you there weren't any – or even the front door. It found its way through a portal that Astravar summoned in that same pentagram he'd brought me through, bang in the centre of the tower.

Oh, and I didn't tell you it was a demon rat. That's right, a demon rat that I had to kill nine times. But that demon rat was only the first of them. After I had killed it, Astravar seemed to think it a good idea to summon more of them from his portals. Each day, after returning from his foraging, he'd enter his pentagram and mutter some strange words. Then the portal would open up, only for a few seconds mind, but it was enough for those infernal rats to swarm out of them. Then, I'd have to go chasing after them, and beating them down. It was exhausting, I tell you. By the end of it all, I just wanted to collapse on the bed.

Then, Astravar would sweep them all into some kind of open closet that he never let me anywhere near. Really, he must have picked up thousands of those demon rats after a while, and their bodies never seemed to decay.

I got no rewards for my efforts, no extra smoked salmon or chicken liver or anything like that. Trust me, I really didn't want to be eating any of those demon rats.

Anyway, here I am rabbiting on – don't you just love rabbits? – about the terrible life I had in the tower, when I have so much else to tell.

My story really starts one day when Astravar came home from his foraging. He'd just been picking some kind of mushrooms from a nearby cave, and the spores must have made him a little drowsy. So, he neglected to close the door properly.

I admit it, I thought twice about sneaking out the door, as I wasn't sure how long the mushrooms' spell would last on Astravar. If he woke up and saw that his prized Bengal was missing, he might hunt me down and turn me into a mouse or a frog, and then feed me to another cat.

Perhaps even one he teleported across time and space to hunt the demon rats he accidentally let through his portals. He'd probably pick an even bigger cat, just because Astravar liked to be ironic. I'm guessing he'd choose a Maine Coon.

But then it would be an equally fitting end to die of starvation in some conceited warlock's tower, and that thought made me bat open the heavy wooden door with my paw, slide out the gap, and make my way down the cold, stone, spiral staircase. I squeezed through the cold iron bars of the gate at the bottom of the tower, and I sprinted out into a cruel and unfamiliar world.

THE SPRINT

I didn't just run; I sprinted like a jaguar. I let my two hind legs carry me across the ground, imagining myself back in the jungles my ancestors came from, or dashing across the plains like the cheetahs the Savannah cats from my South Wales clowder claimed inhabited their ancestral lands. I didn't halt once to look over my shoulder, mind. There's no better way to kill momentum than to stop looking where you're going and then tumble into a rock or trip over a lump in the ground.

A strange purple mist enveloped the land, smelling more of death and decay than anything natural. The air here felt almost choking, and I found it difficult to breathe. But still, I soldiered on.

The ground beneath me wasn't great for running. It was marshy and cold. The water came up to my knees in places. Under normal circumstances, I wouldn't go near such a place, even if I knew a vast field of catnip lay on the other side of it. But then, anywhere was better than that tower.

My legs got tired after a while, but I didn't stop. I doubted that the mage could outrun me, but he might send something after me that could – a demon cheetah, perhaps. Or he could even use that portal to cross time and space and materialise right in front of me. I didn't know which possibility I feared more.

Fortunately, nothing came, and soon enough I managed to get out of the terrifying place. The sun also broke out of a thick grey layer of clouds. The sensation of warmth against my fur and naked nose, after so long without it, caused me to slow a little. I found myself on much firmer ground, thick with long dry grass and rich in pollen. Dragonflies buzzed around overhead, and I spent a little while chasing some of them. But, after running for so long, I tired quickly, and so I lay down to have a little snooze in the sun.

It was then that I noticed something wheeling by overhead. Now, back in South Wales, our little clowder had a rule. Everything that flew was good for hunting as soon as it landed. We didn't have eagles or hawks or anything like that in South Wales, so nothing in the sky would get us into any danger, except perhaps an occasional aggressive seagull.

But the thing that cast a shadow over me was enormous, to say the least. Even being whiskers knows how many miles up in the sky, it still looked bigger than me.

It had these long wings like those of a goose, but much broader and webbed rather than feathered. As it passed by, it let off a roar that cut apart the sky. The creature had come from a snow-capped mountain range in the distance, much more impressive than the Brecon Beacons back in Wales.

I yawned, deciding that as long as that creature didn't mind me, I wouldn't mind it either. So, I closed my eyes, and I slept fitfully, occasionally waking from nightmares of Astravar dropping out of a portal and putting me in that horrible cage again. But after a while, the dreams also faded away, and I awoke underneath the amber glow of the setting sun, which caused the high strands of grass around me to cast long shadows.

That was when I decided it was a good idea to go hunting. I wasn't sure what I was in the mood for then. But regardless, there was no running water nearby so I wouldn't have a chance of catching any fish. Unless I went back to the marshland, of course, which I wasn't going to do for obvious reasons. I tried chasing some starlings, but they lifted themselves up from the ground whenever I got within a few yards of them. Instead, I scouted around for voles or mice.

That's the thing though – small rodents are easy to hunt indoors. You just trap them inside their holes and scoop them out with a paw. But outside, they had places to run to, so the tiny critters would just scramble away.

After a while of stalking across the land looking for food, I came across a rock over what looked like moist ground, just next to an oak tree. I was desperate, so I turned it over, to find it crawling with earthworms and woodlice. They didn't make for a particularly appetizing meal – I hated eating creepy crawlies. But they satisfied the hunger pangs somewhat.

That was how I lived for the next several days or so. Eating insects and worms from underneath the earth, carrying on across the land hungry and tired, but at least grateful to once again be able to see the sun rise and set. I tried to travel and hunt at night. But the night didn't reward my hunting. I could swear there was something about the mice and rabbits here – they just knew to stay well away from me, as if they had greater dangers to deal with than a mere cat. They dug deeper into their burrows and curved their holes down into the ground so I couldn't reach into them successfully.

During the day, I slept in the long grass. Occasionally, one of those strange and massive beasts flying overhead would wake me from my slumber – always either going to or coming from the mountains, and always flying in the same direction.

When I saw them from the right angle, I would imagine something was sitting on top of them. Perhaps a human in bright clothing. But I thought it must be my imagination. I was hallucinating, and it wouldn't do me any good.

After a while of living this way, and the intense hunger pang in my stomach, I could literally feel my ribs pressing out against my chest. I realised my problem then. I needed to be around humans, and I'd lived without them for far, far too long.

It was ridiculous, I know. A great beast like me – a Bengal – not being able to hunt for himself. But I had to face the facts I was domesticated, not bred to live in such a wild world.

Yet there was no way I would turn back to the marshlands to live with Astravar. Whiskers, if I returned there asking for food and a ticket back to my owners in South Wales, he'd probably skin me alive. Still I had no idea where I would find a town, or a city, or any place where I could find a nice family to feed me. I only had one lead – the massive creatures that flew overhead, always coming from one direction towards the mountains in the morning and returning the other way in the evening.

It was then that I decided that I'd follow their trail and find out where they were all returning to.

THE CASTLE

The trail led me to a mound, with what looked like a castle on top of it. Back in South Wales, we had a castle nearby on top of a hill. But while the one back home was in ruins, with stones that had crumbled apart hundreds of years ago and no one living there save for the occasional badger and hedgehog, this castle was teeming with life.

It wasn't ruined for a start, and had these tall towers, six of them, in fact, that rose up into the fluffy grey clouds, vanishing behind them. Those flying creatures wheeled around the towers and, once I was close enough, I saw them to be massive flying lizards with long necks and tails. They were like nothing I'd seen before, really, not even on the television.

Some beasts were red, some yellow, some green, some purple, some black, and some white. They flew in these brilliant aerobatic patterns that I could swear would put a swallow to shame. They dived through the clouds, almost touching the castle walls with their claws, before sharply veering upwards in the air.

It was then, watching from a slight rise with a cooling breeze passing through my fur, that I saw humans were riding these things. They carried long staffs across their backs, with crystals just like the ones Astravar used to collect, affixed onto the top of them. Sometimes, they took their short swords out of the sheaths at their hips, raised them up in the air, and swooped down with them. Other times, one of them would lift the staff off of their back, point it at the ground, and bathe the earth in brilliant displays of lightning, fire, and ice.

I'd never seen anything that could do that. I mean, back in South Wales, they had blocky machines that could create ice and blocky machines that could create fire. But they had to be closed to do so, and these staffs were creating brilliant effects all by themselves. I had to be dreaming.

I also found the behaviour of these people incredibly strange, even for humans. I mean, if you wanted to fly a creature like that, I would think you'd use it to get food. But they didn't seem to be trying to kill anything, but just attacking the ground and making pretty patterns on it. They brought nothing back from their hunts, not even a mouse.

None of it made any sense.

I tried to ignore them, as I realised a place with so many people in it would also likely have a kitchen with lots of food. In fact, I could smell the aroma of some smoked fish coming from somewhere within.

I sprinted towards the castle. The grass shortened as I approached, and I passed a stable with horses grazing outside. A scruffy-looking man was outside with the horses, tossing hay to one side of the wooden fence with a pitchfork. He had a strand of straw in his mouth, with smelly smoke rising from the tip.

The man glanced at me as I passed and uttered something. Not being human, of course, I didn't understand. I imagined he said something like, "Not seen too many of you fellows lately. We need a good mouser in the kitchens." But I have no evidence to suggest whether or not that is true.

For all I know, he could have accused me of being one of the demon incarnations that Astravar had summoned up from his portals. Although the man didn't seem afraid of me or anything like that.

I passed over an open drawbridge, and I stopped before I stepped underneath the portcullis. There was water in the moat, and I hadn't drunk a drop all day. I lowered myself down the bank – steep for humans but not for cats – and I lapped up several mouthfuls of the freshest water I'd tasted for months. It had a tint of rose in it and was strangely warm.

Several moments later, thoroughly hydrated, I found my way into the castle proper. There were people in there, hundreds of them. Some of them were sitting on a stone wall eating apples. Others, in pairs, sparred with each other with wooden swords – for who knows what reason. A man stood in the centre of the sword-wielders, shouting out at the top of his voice in a punctuated rhythm.

He was loud, and so I didn't want to go anywhere near him. Instead, I passed through the courtyard and pushed my way through a heavy looking door which was only slightly ajar. The corridors were cold and dusty, but I could smell my goal. The aroma of food was more intense than a chicken roast fresh out of the oven.

There was fish, there was chicken, there was pork, there was beef, and I swear I even caught the whiff of rosemary. I entered the kitchen, ducking between the feet of men and women scurrying around. I found a rather stout looking woman stirring something in a pot over a fire. I mewled at her, purring deep within my chest, and she turned and looked at me. Her expression suddenly turned to one of disdain, and she shouted out something at me.

She kicked me, and I shrieked back at her, and swiped with my paw, ripping through the fabric of her trousers. She shouted out at me again, and lurched at me with the spoon, dripping hot specks of a yellow mustardy sauce. But I darted away before she could hit me, finding my way between tangled feet and under the table.

I couldn't find any scraps of food on the floor, so I scurried out of the kitchens, and around the castle, looking out for a plate of something, sniffing around as I did. I stopped to spray a few times, of course, to let other cats know that a Bengal was now interested in this territory.

Soon enough, I found another door, with some steps leading up a thin spiral staircase. I followed this upward and took the next room out, to find another straight and dusty corridor. Along the left-side edges of it, the stone peeled away into massive chambers. I turned into the first one, and I found a massive deer's carcass half-eaten on the floor, set in front of an opening, looking out towards the mountains in the distance. The brown roasted meat emitted this amazing smoky scent that drew me towards it like a magnet draws iron filings.

I was so hungry I didn't even bother to check what else might be in the room. I sprinted over to the meat, tore an enormous chunk off one of its ribs and started chewing it apart on the floor.

Then, there came a clear voice in my head. I'd never heard such a language before, but I understood it as clear as bowl-water. It was as if a human was speaking inside my mind, and I could put meaning to every single word.

"What in the Seventh Dimension do you think you are doing, youngling?"

But that voice couldn't have belonged to anything, surely. I was starving and clearly hearing things.

"You dare ignore a creature of magic... Look behind you, you fool." I felt a sudden searing sensation of heat passing over my head, and a jet of flame hit the wall right in front of me.

I shivered, and then I turned around and shrieked out of shock, as hackles thrust out of my arched back. I looked right into a massive yellow eye, set into a red reptilian head which must have been around five times the size of me, if not more.

"Finally," the voice said. It sounded like a female human, yet still low-pitched at that. *"Now, I'm starting to see some well-deserved respect."*

4

AN UNEXPECTED FIND

I didn't know how to react to the beast that had somehow just spoken to me in my head. Up close, it was like a creature out of nightmares I'd never imagined possible. It looked even more terrifying than the demon cheetah I'd imagined Astravar might have sent hunting me.

The only lizard-like creatures I'd seen before were the newts and salamanders back in my former owners' garden back home. I would chase them through the grass sometimes, never really intending to kill them – they didn't look particularly appetizing, and so I'd release them and let them scurry back into the water, and then I'd go back to chasing butterflies instead.

But I'd seen crocodiles on television, with their macabre grins and ability to lurch out at people from the water. This beast was like a crocodile, except worse. She had sharp teeth along the side of her mouth, eyes that glowed bright yellow like miniature suns, huge front-loaded nostrils that didn't just steam but smoked, a breath that stank like rotting meat, and this strange fire burning at the back of her throat whenever she opened her mouth.

Not to mention her sheer enormity. My first thought upon seeing her was that she must have had enough of the deer and now wanted to eat me for dinner. What I didn't consider at the time was that she would probably hate eating me for the same reason I hated eating mice.

I backed up all the way to the drop and looked down at the landscape below. I was far too high up to jump down without injuring myself – even with my ability to land on all fours.

"*Oh, come on, I can't surely be that scary,*" the creature said, again inside my mind. "*I'm only a Ruby, after all.*"

But what was I meant to say back? I mean, normally I shouldn't understand another species' language. Yet, here I was hearing her in my head as if she was now part of my train of thought. I hissed back at her, looking for a way to dart back out the door. But she had blocked off any chance of escape.

"*You know, cats aren't usually allowed outside their cattery,*" she said, and she raised one of her massive brows. She was hairless and had these harsh red scales that seemed to converge towards her eyes. "*Sometimes, the humans let them out in the kitchens. But no one in their right mind would enter a dragon's chambers. So how, might I ask, did you end up here? Or is this your first time visiting Dragonsbond academy? Perhaps you're a stray from outside.*"

I arched my back even higher than I thought possible, and hissed again at the creature, baring my teeth. In hindsight, I don't know how I was expecting to scare her. But then the fact I hadn't eaten for days meant I was a little grumpy and wasn't thinking straight.

"*I've never known your kind to be so unfriendly. Don't you speak at all? I've given you the honour of having access to my mind, and I thought you'd at least say something.*"

Well, I'd never spoken to any creature that wasn't a cat before. But surely it was just the case of putting one word after the other in my mind. I tried it.

"What are you?" I asked. Really, given the circumstances, she couldn't expect me to be a creature of many words.

The massive lizard tossed her head forward and let out a massive roar that almost sent me stumbling off the wall. "*What am I? How dare you suggest you've never heard of a dragon.*"

"*A what?*" Come to think of it, I think they had called the Maine Coon 'Dragon' on television, funny as humans were with names.

"*A dragon... you know, fearsome creatures who knights used to hunt down with lances and swords. Or at least they did until the warlocks rose to power and became both ours and the humans' arch enemies.*"

I opened my eyes wide at the creature. For a moment, I didn't feel threatened but rather utterly confused.

"*Are you really telling me you've never heard of a dragon? You don't have nightmares of us in the night? You don't tremble when you see us, the fiercest of all the creatures known to man?*"

"*I... Are you like a hippopotamus?*" Word had it from the two Savannah cats in my old neighbourhood, that these were the fiercest of all the creatures. The two cats had never seen a hippopotamus, of course. Such creatures didn't roam the wilds of South Wales. But their ancestors had passed down the wisdom to fear the hippopotamus, monsters of the mud with razor sharp buck teeth.

The dragon creature bellowed out again, and this time a little heat came out with the roar, making me think it might finally cook me as it had probably done the venison. "*How dare you compare me to a hippo – a hippa – sorry, what was that word, again?*"

"*A hippopotamus,*" I replied.

"*How dare you compare me to a hippopotamus.*"

"*Do you even know what a hippopotamus is?*"

She raised one of her massive eyebrows, and steam puffed out of her nose. "*No... Enlighten me.*"

I explained to her exactly what the Savannah cats had told me. As I did, I kept glancing over at the ground below, wondering if I could survive the leap, because this insult would probably be the straw that broke the dragon's temper. Now, she would likely tear me to shreds.

She puffed out a second plume of smoke from her nostrils, this one much thicker than the first. It hit me right in the face. I coughed, then I sneezed, and I prepared myself to jump. But instead, the dragon made some strange low-pitched noise. After a moment, I recognised this as laughter.

"*Is that what you think dragons do? We wallow about in the mud all day? I've never heard anything so ridiculous in over fifty years.*"

"*Then what do you do?*" I asked.

She shook her head. "*You know, you've been quite entertaining, and I hear that you cats have quite good balance. Why don't I take you on a little ride?*"

The dragon lowered her head to the ground, and then the arch of her back followed. This was the first time I saw the spikes running along her back. They followed two thin rows on either side of her spine, curling out and then back in as if part of a second ribcage. But fortunately, they were so close together, it didn't look like I'd tumble out from between them.

"*What are you doing?*" I asked. She'd gone from wanting to eat me to now deciding to go to sleep in front of me.

"*I've only just come of age as a dragon,*" she continued, "*and I've reached the time of my life where I'm due to choose a rider. But these spikes present a problem. With them, I can't hold a saddle. They're such a nuisance to the humans, that they've threatened to cut them off. But I'm proud of my spikes and I don't want to have them cut off. Now, maybe, you could be a solution.*"

"*What the whiskers are you talking about?*" I asked.

"*Just hop on my back, and we'll go for a little ride. If it goes well, maybe I'll let you have a little venison for supper.*"

Now that was an offer I couldn't refuse. I looked over at the carcass, the delicious smoky scent of it wafting into my nostrils. "*Let me have a bite first. Then I'll consider.*"

"*You drive a hard bargain,*" the dragon replied. "*So let it be. But only a bite, unless your tail wants to see the end of my flames.*"

I cautiously approached the deer, eyeing the dragon on the way. It seemed to pose no threat, so I took hold of a bite of the roast in my teeth and sequestered it away to the other end of the room.

After I'd eaten it from the floor, I decided that maybe this dragon creature wouldn't be so bad after all. So I did what she said. I leaped over her nose, landed on her forehead, and then I nestled myself between the spikes on her back.

Suddenly, the ground lurched underneath me, although this ground wasn't composed of earth but dragon flesh. But her spikes held me firmly in place, as she walked me over to the edge.

Presently, the dragon unfurled her massive wings, sending up a massive gust of wind around me. Then, I almost tumbled backwards down the corridor between her two rows of spikes, but I found my footing before I rolled off onto the floor.

"*Keep steady,*" the dragon said.

"*Of course I'm steady. I'm a cat,*" I replied.

"*We shall see,*" the dragon replied, and before I knew it, the skin underneath me spasmed in a sickening way that made me want to vomit. Presently, her feet lifted off the ground, and she carried me up into the sky.

5

DECISIONS

I had never seen the ground beneath me so far away. It was so distant it looked unreal, as if it was part of a painted floor, so flat that I could just leap on to it. Fortunately, other parts of my body told me that this wasn't a good idea. My balance centre told me to stay nestled safely in the corridor between the dragon's rows of spikes. Then, there was the noise of the wind whooshing around me, creating an intense chill that cut right through my short fur coat.

Part of me wished I hadn't leapt on this massive creature's back. I thought that within a minute, or perhaps even thirty seconds, I'd be a pancake on the grasslands below. Perhaps that was how dragons liked to eat cats – break all their bones first to tenderise the meat a little.

I also didn't like the way the dragon sent me tumbling between her spikes with every sudden sharp manoeuvre. Cats are made to stay on their feet, not to be flung around like a hamster that had just fallen unconscious on its wheel.

After a while, she stopped whirling around so much, and I felt sick. I tried to find some balance, but with each step I was incredibly dizzy. I tried to jump up on the dragon's head to at least get a good view of the horizon. But the wind roared even louder up there, and the way the ground moved below just didn't look right. That feeling in the back of my head told me to stay well away from the edges. So, I retreated down the dragon's neck and cowered within her corridor of spikes.

"*My name is Salanraja,*" the dragon said after a while, "*and I'm a creature born of magic.*"

"*You say some strange things,*" I replied. "*Can't we have a conversation about food?*"

"*Not until you've told me your name.*"

I tried to swallow down the nausea and vertigo spinning inside my head and put some word to thought. "*My name's Ben,*" I said.

"*What a mundane name.*"

"*You wouldn't be able to pronounce my actual name.*"

"*And you wouldn't be able to pronounce my magical name either, and I wouldn't give it to you before a thousand suns had burned. But, for your common name, you could at least have thought of something with a little appeal. Perhaps you have another name?*"

"*Don't tell me you want to start calling me Bengie too...*"

"*Bengie...*" Salanraja paused for a moment. "*That at least is passable.*"

"*But I hate that name.*"

"*It's far better than Ben,*" Salanraja said.

I hissed at the dragon, and I tried to dig my claws into her back, but its skin was far too leathery between the scales to even injure her. I don't think she noticed, to be honest, which was probably fortunate for me. "*I didn't pick my name,*" I said after a moment.

"*Oh, so who did?*"

"*The humans.*"

That was when I felt her belly rumble, and out of her mouth came that maniacal laughter again. "*You let the humans name you? I never realised cats had so little self-respect.*"

"*What does a name matter? All I need is a familiar word the humans can call so I know when I'm getting food.*"

"*It matters more than you can imagine,*" Salanraja replied. "*A well-chosen name will make you remembered to both your enemies and your friends. You don't hear people saying, 'Excuse me, which Salanraja was that', do you?*"

"*To be honest, I've never heard anyone use the name Salanraja at all.*"

"That will change. Once I strike my legacy into the hearts of men and dragons. It will become a name remembered throughout the history textbooks. One that all sentient creatures on this planet will utter in both fear and respect."

I yawned. At least when Salanraja talked to me, she stopped those crazy flight manoeuvres. So, it seemed better to keep the conversation going.

"You really are full of yourself, aren't you?" I said.

"I'm a dragon. The greatest creature in the lands. What do you expect?"

"A little modesty, perhaps. It would go a long way."

"And what do you know about modesty?"

I licked my beautiful, silky fur. *"Look. I know that you're big and strong, and all that. But also, quite frankly, you're ugly. Fair enough, you might scare people, but somehow I doubt you have the grace or intellect of a cat."*

"Grace?" Salanraja's body rumbled from beneath my feet and she let out a massive roar once again. *"I shall show you grace."*

Just when I thought I had my balance mastered, Salanraja's body lurched once again. She threw me to the left, and then she spun me around and around as if I was trapped in a washing machine. I don't know how long the dragon had me tumbling around in that corridor within her spikes. But, once she levelled out, I felt as if every bone had broken in my body. I also wanted to throw up.

"That's not graceful," I pointed out. *"It's no wonder none of the humans ever want to ride you if you keep behaving like that."*

The dragon turned her massive head back to me. Her leathery top lip had curved upwards in a snarl, displaying a long fang-like incisor that was yellowing a little at the top. *"And you're probably now going to show me what graceful is,"* Salanraja said.

Whiskers! She would have to make such a request after beating me around so much. *"I can show you graceful. If you promise not to drop me out of the sky."*

"Be my guest."

I stretched out my limbs and back, feeling my bones creak as I did so. Then, I tested the spot in front of me on Salanraja's back first, before climbing up her neck and onto her head. I perched myself there, half worried that the dragon would throw me off at any second, but instead she made a deep rumbling sound that almost sounded like a purr.

I looked down at the ground rolling by below, the fields arranged in uneven squares of green and yellow, trees dotted between them. A layer of fluffy clouds passed by overhead. I didn't particularly want to be up here in the cold wind, and I tried not to pay attention to the ground whirling by below.

"*You are sitting on my head,*" she said.

"*I don't intend to stay up here,*" I replied. "*I just wanted to prove my point.*"

"*Which is?*"

"*That I made it up here without causing you any pain at all. Grace is all about being able to pass through an environment without disturbing it. That way, we can sneak past even the scariest of dogs undetected. It's about elegance, not breaking every bone in your passenger's body.*"

"*My flight might have felt ungraceful to you, but it would have looked spectacular to an observer on the ground.*"

"*And do you see any observers down there? I see a few sheep. But their eyes are for the grass they're munching, and not you.*"

Salanraja laughed again, but this time it came out as a low chuckle, probably because maniacal laughter would result in throwing me right off my perch. "*You know, I never thought I'd meet someone suitable. But you've changed my mind. Get down from there,*" she said. "*I want to show you something.*"

I scratched my head with my hind leg. "*Tell me what it is first.*"

"*Would you rather I threw you off my head and caught you on my back? I'm not always the best catch, I might warn you.*"

"No," I said, and I stalked back down her neck, nestling myself in the corridor of her back. "*Just don't do any of that rough flying again. It's not good for my spine, flexible as it is.*"

She didn't seem to hear me. "*Hold on for now,*" she said. "*This is going to be a rough landing.*"

"*Hold on to what?*"

"*Anything you can find.*"

Though the air was cold before, it now carried icy blasts and I felt like my fur was going to freeze. Ahead, the snow-capped mountain range I saw before was approaching, the sun glistening off the glazed tops of it, with eagles – and this time I mean birds and not dragons – wheeling over a blanket of mountain mist.

Salanraja roared up to the sky, and then she reeled backwards. She used the momentum to pull herself upwards, and the chill in the air intensified. Suddenly, she decelerated. I shrieked as I rolled down the corridor of spikes towards Salanraja's head. Beneath that was a blanket of caked snow, coming at us faster and faster.

"*Stop!*" I said to her in my head.

"*I said, hold on,*" Salanraja replied.

I had no choice but to comply, because I almost tumbled off her neck. But I caught myself last minute. The spikes that ran up the back of her neck were made of a soft kind of ivory, and I managed to dig my claws into one, and hold myself there with all my strength, as I dangled above the snowfield. I thought for a moment that I would plummet with such a force I'd cause an avalanche.

Salanraja thudded into the ground with such impact, I got thrown off her neck into the snow. Luckily, of course, I landed on my feet. But once I felt the cold, powdery stuff against them, I shrieked and ran leaped right back up onto Salanraja's back.

"*What's the matter?*" Salanraja asked.

I shuddered. "*I hate snow,*" I said. "*I hate it more than I hate rain.*"

Salanraja barked out a laugh into the icy wind. "*Don't be such a wimp. You have that thick fur coat. What about me? What do I have to keep me warm?*"

"*Dragon fire?*"

"*True that,*" Salanraja replied. "*Well, we're here.*" She lifted up a claw and pointed to a cave mouth tall enough to accommodate nine stacked elephants.

"*And where is here, exactly?*" I asked.

"*This is the source of our world's magic. It's a place where all dreams are first born before they travel through the ley lines of the land into the minds of mindful beings. Here dragons first get their fire, and dragon riders first get their gifts. This is only one of thousands of entrances in a place we guard against the warlocks and dark creatures that wish to use it for ill.*"

I yawned widely and scratched my neck with my hind paw. *"Okay, okay, it's special. I've got that. But what is it? Get to the point, will you?"*

Salanraja shook her head. But this time, she decided not to complain about my rudeness. *"It's the Versta Caverns of the Crystal Mountains, and here you shall learn of your destiny. Because I don't know why, but my gut is telling me to choose you as my next rider. I think we are destined for great things together, Bengie, and legends say that we dragons can foretell the future."*

6

MADE OF CLAY

The Versta Caverns were perhaps the most spectacular thing I'd ever seen. I used to think birds were fascinating to watch. But these caverns, which seemed a massive passageway into the bowels of the earth, contained gems as large as houses and which shone out in every single imaginable colour. Within them, the swirling patterns of light seemed to depict images so surreal they might as well be dreams. If I stared at one long enough, I imagined I was seeing myself in a familiar world that I'd seen in the Land of Nod.

In one of them, I saw myself from a distance, running through long grass, chasing dragonflies like I had been only days ago. I caught one in my paw until it bit me, and then I yelped out in pain. But after that, I was soon out there chasing another dragonfly, and this time I caught it and examined it, and it didn't seem to be a dragonfly at all, but a small red dragon. The dream zoomed in, to make the dragon bigger, until I could see myself flying on that dragon's back. The corridor of spikes had gone now, and I looked as comfortable there as I would on a garden fence.

I saw an enemy down below, something skeletal, with hollow ribs. I pointed downwards at it with my paw, and a column of fire came down from the sky, charring both creature and earth beneath.

"Dragons aren't the only entities that can foretell the future," Salanraja told me, clearly realising what I was staring at. *"Sometimes these crystals display a creature's dreams. Sometimes they display premonitions. Sometimes, they show the past. And sometimes, rumour has it, they can even see across dimensions."*

I sat on her back, as she stalked carefully through the cavern, as if with reverence for the crystals that lay within. Though the passage was wide enough for her to walk through, the ceiling came down too low for Salanraja to take off into the air and fly through the passageway, although I didn't discount the possibility there might be taller chambers as we ventured further through the caverns.

There was no snow in here, so I probably could have continued on foot. But I had reached the point where I, admittedly, was quite enjoying the ride. There was no snow on the red-packed earth that supported the crystals, and I could taste the clay in the air.

"You can sit on my head if you want a better view." Salanraja said.

"But won't it get hot up there if you decide to breathe fire?" I replied.

"Oh, you won't have to worry about that here. The crystals prevent me from using my magic."

I mewled, and ran up Salanraja's neck onto her head. Now, I could see everything in panorama. We'd already passed quite a way into the caverns and the entrance was getting increasingly smaller behind us. The crystals seemed to not just emanate life, but a glow that warmed me from the bones out. There was something about this place that I liked, and I didn't want to leave.

But then, Salanraja jerked to a halt. She wasn't going fast to begin with, but she was so massive that her sudden motion sent me tumbling forwards. Fortunately, I caught myself, so I didn't end up hanging off one of her nostrils. I didn't want to end up swinging right into her mouth.

"Don't make a sound," Salanraja said. *"Not even a purr."*

How she could ever expect me to stop purring, I don't know. It was like asking a dog to stop wagging its tail. *"What is it?"*

"There's something there, just around the corner..."

I craned my head over Salanraja's top mounted horn to get a better look. But I couldn't see what she was fussing about.

"*Wait until it comes into the light of the crystals,*" Salanraja continued. "*It's camouflaged against the earth.*"

It didn't take me long to notice something out of place. On the draught came a whiff of rotten vegetable juice, as if someone had painted it over the clay.

I zoned in on the smell. Then I detected motion. True enough, something was slithering around down there, almost concealed. It moved in the shadows the crystal cast against the rocks in front of it, sliding over the ground, without making a footstep. It seemed as if it was part of the earth itself, growing out of it to move forward, and then shrinking back into the ground. It turned toward us and then I saw its two eyes. They were glowing, just like the crystals.

"*A golem,*" Salanraja said. "*Made of clay.*"

"*A what?*"

"*Do you know nothing of magical creatures?*"

"*I knew nothing of this thing you called magic until today, and I still don't know exactly what it's meant to do.*"

Salanraja lowered her head to the ground, very slowly. "*A golem is a creation of man, a part of the earth given life through a magical crystal. It's probably here to mine crystals for a warlock's dark plans.*"

"*I thought you said that we couldn't use magic in here.*"

"*We can't.*"

"*Then how can a magical creature survive here?*" I asked.

"*Because it would have been conjured outside. Those eyes are just one of a warlock's ways of seeing. The warlock in question is unlikely to notice us unless we do something to alert him or her to our presence. But its very existence here means that there is a warlock nearby.*"

"*A warlock? Astravar...*" The man had never told me his name, or if he had, I hadn't understood his language at the time to register it. But he'd burnished it into my memories through some kind of magic. Now, I could see his long face and cruel grey eyes inside my mind each time I remembered his name.

"*It could be Astravar,*" Salanraja said, "*or it could be any of the other six known warlocks to inhabit the Darklands.*"

"*And what does he want with us? We're not doing him any harm...*"

"*Our kingdom of Illumine is at war with the warlocks whose souls have* been consumed by dark magic. They strive for the destruction of all non-conjured life in this world. Humans, cats, and every other creature that you hunt and cherish would be annihilated if they had their way."

I glanced around at the shining massive gems, trying hard not to be mesmerised by their beauty. He'd had one of these swinging above him as he worked, filling his tower with light. Others he'd used to summon demons from portals. Whiskers, he'd probably summoned me from a portal using one of the crystals.

"There's a crystal here for you, Bengie," Salanraja said. "As soon as I decided to choose you as my dragon rider, one of the crystals here called me. Now, you must find the one that knows you well, and it will give it your ability."

"My ability?"

"Of course. All dragon riders have a kind of magic about them, and as you grow as a dragon rider your crystal will grant you more abilities."

"I—" I couldn't believe my pointy ears. I hadn't even learned of magic before today. Now this 'dragon' was telling me I could use it. "What abilities will it give me?"

"You will only gain one for now, and you won't know what it is until you've gained it. Now, go and find your crystal, and do so silently, because we don't want to attract the attention of that golem."

I looked down at the morphing clay creature again, its form twisting from one wicked shape to the next. It kept moving forward in a direction, and its arm had moulded itself into the shaft of some tool. A metal blade had morphed out of the top of this, looking something like a pickaxe. The golem was shifting towards the crystal that I'd seen my dream in before. The one that seemed to know me well…

"I think I know which one's mine," I said.

"Oh?"

"The one with my dreams in it… It's that purple crystal over there."

"What?" Salanraja said, and her head tossed back all of a sudden, almost throwing me off it. "No! The golem!"

I could feel Salanraja was getting irate, and so I scrambled down her neck, so she didn't throw me on to the cold floor in her rage. Then, I turned around to see what she was screaming at. The golem now had that pickaxe-like tool raised over the crystal, and it looked like it was about to bring it down in a wide arc.

It was about, in other words, to smash my crystal to pieces.

7

SINKING

Salanraja bellowed out a roar, and the golem turned in a broad circle. It bent over backwards, then let out an ear-piercing screech that sent my head spinning for a moment.

"*You can't let it destroy your crystal. You have to fight it,*" Salanraja said.

"*How? It's bigger than a human, and it moves funny.*"

Salanraja lowered her head back to the floor. "*Knock out its eyes – and you'll destroy its magical energy.*"

"*Easy for you to say... Why don't you just eat it?*"

"*I can't, you fool. Just do it. We don't have much time.*"

Salanraja shook her head, like a dog shaking off water, sending me tumbling onto the floor. I landed right next to the golem, and I gazed up at it. The thing was massive, twice as large as a human perhaps, and twice as wide too. It stared down at me with its two crystal eyes – one red, one blue. It also had the pickaxe extension on its arm raised, which was swinging down towards me.

I screeched, and then I scrambled out of the way, as the pickaxe buried itself in the earth. It got stuck there for a moment, giving me time to recover myself. I tried scratching at the golem's leg, but my claws just went right through its body, bringing off some sticky clay that I tried to shake off but couldn't.

"*Do something, Salanraja,*" I said.

"*Like what? My claws will just go right through it, and they're much too large to dislodge his eyes. If I try eating it, it will just reform in my stomach and rip me apart from the inside.*"

"If it's made of clay, can't you just breathe fire on it? It might harden the thing, securing it in place."

"*I can't use magic in here, remember, and even if I could, it would be disrespectful to the crystals. This is your job, Bengie. Accept it.*"

By the time Salanraja had finished explaining things, the golem had its pickaxe raised again, and was lifting it up into the air. Meanwhile, its other hand had grown into a scythe-like blade, also metallic. It swept this around in a low arc, and I leapt over it just in the nick of time and then stumbled over towards the wall.

"*The eyes, Bengie. Go for the eyes,*" Salanraja said.

I snarled up at her, then darted behind a tall column of stone. I used that spot as my cover as I arched my back and hissed at my opponent. But this didn't stop it coming at me. It took a high swing with its scythe blade and cut right through the column. Then, the golem charged into the column with its shoulder, rocking it slightly, and then bringing it crashing down. I scampered out of the way to avoid getting flattened into the floor.

I ran in a circle, trying to get around the golem. It bent down towards me, evidently preparing itself to sweep that scythe blade around once again. I lowered myself, ready to pounce on it, but the golem's legs melted into the earth and rose again so fast I couldn't work out where to leap.

"*You won't weaken it, Bengie,*" Salanraja said. "*It will just tire you out if you keep trying to evade it.*"

"*Can't we just run away?*"

"*No. Watch out!*"

I turned to see the pickaxe almost upon my head. I rolled out of the way at the last second. Then I turned again and bared my teeth and I saw an opening. The golem's arm was right there on the ground, the pickaxe stuck in there. I darted forwards and leapt onto its shoulder and, before I slid back down, I swiped away the red crystal. It fell to the floor.

But before I could go for the other crystal, the golem's shoulder melted away underfoot. Its entire body dissolved into the earth. Next moment, it had formed a puddle with me at the centre. I started sinking down into the thick viscous pool. I tried to swim out towards the edge, but I just ended up getting dragged further and further down.

"It's eye, Bengie. Stop struggling, the eye's right in front of you."

I kept my head above the surface and tried to focus on what Salanraja was talking about. There was a crystal in front of me, glowing blue. I pawed at it, but the motion just sent me further into the puddle of clay. I was down to my neck at that point, just inches away from not being able to breathe.

Ah well, it had been a good life with more roasted salmon and chicken than I'd get in the wild.

"Bengie!" Salanraja called out.

She readied herself to roar, then she lowered her head into the clay and tried to lift me up using her front horn. But it was too slippery, and I couldn't get any purchase on it. I could still see the blue gem right in front of my eyes now. My claws were underneath the surface of the clay now. So, instead, I ducked my head forward, and I took a massive mouthful of earth and gem.

I'd never tasted clay before, but I'd had a few mouthfuls of soil in my kitten days when I'd needed to chew grass to help me bring back up furballs. This clay had the taste of soil, but not the texture. It was pretty gross.

My head sank underneath the surface of the clay. I tried not to breathe down there – the last thing I wanted was nostrils full of that stuff – and I kept my lips firmly shut.

But soon enough, my breath gave out, and I felt intense pressure on my eyes, as if I was going to black out. Then the earth shuddered beneath me. Next thing I knew, I was shooting out of the clay like a cannon. Or at least I thought I was.

What had actually happened was that Salanraja had reached down again and tossed me out with her horn, just as the clay started to harden around me. I flew across the passage, legs flailing, and then I hit my head against the wall.

"*Quick Bengie, get on my back.*"

I tried to come to my senses, pretty dizzy. "*I thought we'd killed it,*" I said.

"*We did, but the warlock will be after us. There'll be more of them.*"

I didn't need further instruction. Finally, we were getting out of here. I scrambled up onto Salanraja's back, trying to ignore the intense throbbing where my neck met my spine. Before we left, Salanraja lurched forward and wrapped her mouth around the crystal that had my dreams inside of it and charged away.

I ran down to the tail-end of her corridor of spikes to see what was going on behind me. I could only vaguely make out the shapes morphing against the rock in the background, but they seemed to be getting closer and closer.

But they didn't reach us in time before Salanraja was back out in the icy wind. She lifted herself up into the sky, and I almost fell off her tail, being so close to the end of it. I caught myself and scurried back up towards her neck.

From my vantage point, I looked down below, and I could see around a dozen golems against the snow, no longer camouflaged within their natural terrain. My head was spinning, and I couldn't look at them for very long.

That was the first time I'd ever heard him speak in a language I could understand. It was Astravar, speaking in my head. I recognised him from the voice's timbre...

"*You!*" he said. "*You ran away from my tower, you destroyed my golem, and now you steal away my magic. You may be just a cat, but I never let insults go unforgotten. Soon, I shall hunt you down, and then I will make you pay!*"

8

GIFT

I didn't pay too much attention to the journey. My head was absolutely spinning. It ached like it had never ached before, and any time I tried to move it in one direction, an intense thumping would cause me to lower my head back down again as a deep groan came out of my chest. But I remember the colours I saw – white segueing to yellow and green, blue sky rolling overhead, and the bright light from the sun exacerbating the pain in my head.

That journey felt like hours, and I didn't even have the energy to ask Salanraja where we were heading. Meanwhile, I kept remembering Astravar's voice in my head. It hadn't been my imagination, and it hadn't been the stuff of dreams, I was sure. Rather, his presence there had been much like Salanraja's – as if he could read what I was thinking and had known my very location. He must have been in the crystal that I'd swallowed – the eye of the golem – which already contained the warlock's magic.

Eventually Salanraja thudded against the ground. Because of my headache, I didn't have a great sense of balance, and so she ended up bashing me into the side of her corridor of spikes.

"Wake up, Bengie," she said.

I didn't move from my position. Instead, I yawned widely. *"I told you that I hate that name,"* I replied.

"Bengie, this is important. Get off." The body underneath my chest shuddered like an earthquake, and I felt it starting to warm.

I growled at Salanraja, then I stood up and stretched, shaking every muscle in my body at the same time. It wasn't just my head that hurt, but my back and legs, and I couldn't take one step without some kind of pain lancing through my knees. I knew that if I didn't get off Salanraja, she'd shake me off. So I sauntered lazily down her tail to the ground, feeling every single stride within my joints.

"Why can't we just rest?" I asked.

"Just go to the crystal. It will sort out your ails and give you your gift. You've worked for this Bengie. Don't waste the opportunity now."

"Can't it give it to me later?" I asked. *"I'm tired. And, if you could bring me that venison you promised, I'd much appreciate it."* I lay down in the long grass. It wrapped around me, providing an extra blanket of warmth.

"No!" Salanraja let out a gigantic roar, causing me to leap to my feet in shock. I stared up at her and blinked, and she lowered her massive head to me and enveloped me in a plume of smoke from her nostrils. *"I didn't bring you all this way to show disrespect to the crystals. This is not just your future on the line, but also mine."*

"But the future is the future, like tomorrow is tomorrow. Now, this hour, I need to sleep."

Salanraja bared her sharp teeth at me, and a rumble came out from her belly. I could just imagine the fire burning within there. Her nostrils flared and her yellow eyes took on a brilliant glow.

"Fine," I said, and I walked around her towards the tall crystal she'd left on the ground. It was standing on its point, balancing there as if upheld by an invisible force. It was even taller than the statue I remembered on the roundabout back in South Wales – a weird metallic creature, formed of ribs that curved out from its centre like sickle blades.

My joints continued to ache with each step. My throat was also dry; probably all the moisture in it had been wicked away by that foul-tasting clay, and I imagined the feast of venison I could be eating right now.

But as I approached the crystal, these thoughts washed away, and I instead became mesmerised by the images flashing by behind the facets once again. My eyes fixated on the light emanating from within. The images displayed a version of me looking so much stronger than I'd ever imagined. I was atop Salanraja again, carrying some kind of staff in my mouth. Dark-winged creatures – that looked like a cross between a bat and a buzzard – flitted around us, and I had my eyes closed as purple tentacles of light lashed out from the glowing stone of the same colour at the staff's head.

The bats swooped down, extending out talons that were almost as long as their wings. But before they could get close, the tentacles whipped at them, and knocked them out of the sky. Hundreds of the creatures fell to the earth. Another swarm approached from the front, and Salanraja tossed back her head and let out a column of amber flame at them. When the light from the flame subsided, the creatures were nowhere to be seen.

"*This is your destiny, Ben,*" a voice said in my head. It sounded like a female human voice, but one I could understand. Just like the mistress back home in South Wales, it had a soft lilt to it, which drew me even further towards the crystal.

"*You have weaknesses, and you have fears; we all do. But the difference between those who live up to their callings and those who don't is that we don't let the weaknesses control us. Pride, sloth, reliance, and gluttony are transient. Yet, if you let them, they will stop you from becoming who you are meant to be.*"

I mewled, and I rubbed up against the crystal. When I touched it, its warmth seemed to cleanse away the muscle pains and my headache. I suddenly became aware of everything around me – the distant bird sounds, the swishing of the cool wind as it brushed through my fur, the slow rhythmic sound of Salanraja's breath, the clouds, the light flowing out of the crystal and soothing everything it touched.

Of course, because I was a cat, being aware of my environment was nothing new to me. But this was different. Before, I would react to every sudden movement, unable to control my instincts. Now, I could disconnect from it all, and focus on what I chose to be of value. I could decide consciously what was a threat and what was not.

I was completely in control of my own mind and body.

"*Why do I need this?*" I asked the crystal. "*Salanraja makes me think this is important, but I'm not sure what I'm meant to do.*"

"*That's because you don't know the fate of the world to come,*" the voice in the crystal said. "*It's not just our world, but many, including your own.*"

"*What do you mean?*"

"*Close your eyes, and I will show you.*"

I did as the crystal bade me to. I could still feel its presence, feel its warmth washing over me, and I turned into it as if turning my face to the sun. Then, I felt a slight pressure on my eyelids – not enough to be painful.

Behind them, the tapestry of the future began to unfurl.

❧ 9 ❧

A CAT'S PURPOSE

At first, I didn't think I was looking at the real world, but rather a moving painting. Still I recognised the setting – the crystal had taken me back to my home in South Wales. I didn't traverse it like a normal cat would, nor was I being carried on a dragon's back. Instead, I floated over the land, as if dreaming.

It was different to the world I'd grown up in and come to love. The landscape was charred; the rolling hills beneath contained no grass or trees, only settled dust. The sky wasn't blue but a deep blood red, spattered with a layer of purple cloud, from which came an occasional flash of lightning.

The vision floated me into the town. The streets had immense cracks in them, out of which fronds of spiky ochre weeds waved in the odorous breeze. The houses and bungalows, usually decorated with shiny quartz, were all reduced to rubble. I floated into my former owner's house, past the broken television set in the living room, into the kitchen where my food and water bowls lay shattered on the kitchen floor. In the bedroom were my owners, all three of them as skeletons huddled together on the master bed.

"*If all good creatures succumb to superficial desires,*" the crystal said, "*this is what shall come to pass. The warlocks' greed won't just stop on this world, but it will cross dimensions. We crystals cannot control how creatures use our magic, but we can give you the powers to stop the evil of this world spreading across dimensions like a blight."*

I had nothing to say to that. I just wanted to wake up from this dream. I didn't want to have to stare down at the skeletons of my former owners. Here, they could no longer call me back from the garden for meals of roasted salmon and chicken. They could no longer cuddle and pet me when I felt down. They could no longer bring me wonderfully scented sprigs of catnip from the garden and throw dry treats to me out of a foil-lined bag. None of this seemed to exist now.

No, this couldn't come to pass.

"Get me out of here," I said. *"Please, I can't take this..."*

"Then take responsibility," the crystal said. *"And do what you have to do."*

The dream took me upwards, and the landscape beneath me faded to white. I found myself back inside my true mind once again, as the light intensified. Once it was bright enough, my eyes opened. I felt something pressing at my temples, almost as if it was trying to get in.

"Will you take your first gift?" the crystal's voice asked in my mind. *"Doing so will complete your union with your dragon, and you will be accepted as her rider."*

I took a deep breath, then looked back to Salanraja, who had one of her massive eyebrows raised. I guess I didn't have much of a choice in the matter. If I didn't do it, she'd probably eat me alive.

If I did though, she would probably feed me and look after me, just like my owners did in South Wales. But I was sure she'd make me have to work for that food. My previous owners would just dish it out into my bowls, on schedule three times a day.

"I accept," I said. *"Though, I wish you would at least tell me what this gift was."*

"You shall learn soon enough. Now, open your mind."

"How—" I didn't have a chance to finish my question, because a sudden pain seared into my temples at both sides as if someone had suddenly thrust a huge iron spike through my head. It came so quickly

that I didn't have time to yelp out. I only could grimace, and then the pain was gone.

Presently, the light from the crystal got brighter again, until it burned as intensely as a sun. But I couldn't close my eyes against it. It felt as if my lids had been glued to my brows, and the magic from the crystal bored right through my skull.

At the same time, I felt something leaving me. It floated out of my chest, where a faint and very thin blue thread of light emerged. A similar effect came from Salanraja – both threads connecting right to the centre of the crystal, which started spinning on its own axis.

More visions flashed through my mind's eye. I saw my past – the glorious bowls of food, resting on the sofa as my owners petted me, fighting other cats out of my territory, chasing squirrels along the garden fence, and then leaping into the hawthorn to scare away a sparrow. Then, I saw my future. Although, I should say, I saw many possible threads of my future. One had me dying through hunger due to days of roaming, looking for food that didn't exist on the dusty earth. Another had one of those bat-buzzard creatures slashing me off a dragon's back. In others, I was confident and powerful – swiping gems out of golems' eyes, or I commanded a dragon over a battlefield, armoured soldiers lined up like matchstick men below as I battled against a warlock, a blue beam of energy from my staff meeting head on with a red bolt of energy from his.

The visions flashed faster and faster through my mind until I saw nothing but a fluid and constant blur. A buzzing sound emerged in my ears, so loud it was painful. The sound intensified, increasing in pitch as if building to a climax.

All the time, the light got stronger and stronger in front of my eyes, and it seemed to emit an intense heat, as if I was sitting there cooking under Salanraja's flame. Whiskers, for all I knew, this might be her way of eating me. Using the crystal to hypnotise me like a frog in water slowly coming to the boil.

Either I was in the afterlife, or I'd survived, because all of a sudden, the images, the heat, and the terrible buzzing vanished. I opened my eyes to stare right into the facets of the crystal. But they were now a dull grey, slightly yellowed by the light from the sun.

"Is that it?" I asked Salanraja. *"I thought I was meant to get a gift?"*

I felt strangely empty not having the crystal's voice in my head anymore. It felt like those times my owners had gone on holiday and left me to stew with the other cats in the cattery. I could never understand the moggies you met there, and they didn't seem to understand me either. Many of them had lost their grace, their pride for the hunt, their sense of uniqueness, their wild side. They just seemed to want to sleep all day, and many of them didn't even care so much about food.

They'd become fully domesticated. They'd forgotten who they were – descendants of the great beasts of the plains, the jungles, the mountains, the forests. It was as if their ancestry had leached out of their very bones.

Salanraja lowered her head to me and studied me beneath her thick eyebrows. *"You are different,"* she said. *"I can see it in your eyes."*

"What? How?" I examined my paws, extending my paws and then my claws, looking for even a minor alteration. Then, I craned my neck and licked the fur on my side, wondering if I tasted any different. Everything was exactly the same.

Salanraja opened her mouth, and I darted out of the way, thinking she was about to breathe fire on me. Maybe she thought my new superpower was invulnerability. Instead, she spoke out loud in a remarkably clear and deep voice. "You can understand me now, can you not?"

I looked up at her with wide eyes. "You speak cat?" I said, and I thought I said it in my own language.

"No, I speak the dragon tongue," she replied. "Now, it appears you do too."

"What's the point of doing that when I can talk to you in my head?" I had the sinking feeling of being cheated. All those promises of being able to shoot fire out of staffs and cast intense beams of energy at warlocks. Now, this crystal had given me an ability that I already had.

"I also prefer to communicate with you that way," Salanraja said, still out loud. "It will help preserve my voice for when I need it the most."

I growled at her. "You didn't answer my question."

Salanraja let off a deep and loud sigh. She continued to speak, as we had been previously, inside my mind. *"I will tell you what abilities you've gained, because you seem too ignorant to work it out yourself. Firstly, now we're bonded we can communicate like this across vast distances. But it's not just me you can speak with, but any sentient creature. The crystals have gifted you with the magic of language. Do you realise how powerful that can be?"*

I yawned, and I turned away from the dragon. *"I still think it's pretty lame."*

"I'm sure you'll find good uses for it," Salanraja replied.

"I wonder how long that will take."

"That is surely up to you. Now hop on, it's time to return to Dragonsbond Academy."

I mewled, remembering the venison Salanraja had promised me. After everything that had happened, admittedly, I was famished. Salanraja turned her tail towards me, and I ran up it into the corridor on her back. She took off into the cerulean sky, and then she swooped down again to pick up the crystal with her talons.

"One more thing," she said. *"We must now defend this crystal at all costs. It is now the medium of our bond."*

"And what does that mean?"

"It means that if anyone destroys it, then both of us shall die."

KINSHIP

My mouth was watering by the time the castle, or Dragonsbond Academy as Salanraja styled it, came into sight. I couldn't imagine anything but that wonderful tender venison that she'd promised me.

I'd been pretty sleepy on the way through, and I'd drifted in and out of dreamland several times. Fortunately, Salanraja had kept her flight gentle. She was probably tired too, after everything. This made the corridor of Salanraja's spikes feel like a cradle that could rock me gently to sleep. My dreams were sweet, of venison and the gamey and majestic taste of it.

Soon enough, I woke up to see the castle getting ever bigger, and the tower containing Salanraja's chamber speeding towards us. She touched down with a soft thud, and I lifted myself up and stretched and yawned. I looked down Salanraja's corridor of spikes towards the shiny castle floor.

Guess what? There was no venison there, and the floor had a polished look, as if someone had just swept and scoured it clean.

I shrieked out loud, and I tried to tear my claws into Salanraja's flesh. But her skin was still tough, and it probably hurt me more than it hurt her. Before she could retaliate, I ran down her back and off her tail. I turned to the dragon.

"*There's no venison,*" I said. "*Salanraja, you promised.*"

Salanraja glanced over at the spot where the carcass had been. She then turned to me and gave a devilishly wicked grin. "*So there isn't,*" she said. "*They must have given it to another dragon. We can't have meat going off in this place. It will attract crows.*"

I felt the rage burning in my chest. "*Eaten by another dragon? That was my venison, Salanraja. You promised it to me.*"

"*I did nothing of the sort,*" Salanraja replied, shaking her head slowly. "*I only said that I might let you have some of it, which you did. You can't claim someone else's hunt as your own. What are you, a scavenger?*"

"*A scavenger?*" I took a step forward and then arched my back to make myself seem as big as possible.

"*Well, isn't that what you do? You eat the food that others have hunted and farmed after all.*"

"*That doesn't make me a scavenger... How could you call me such a thing?*"

"*You're the one accusing me of breaking promises. If there's one thing you should know about dragons is that we always keep our word. It's our code, and it keeps us noble.*"

But I wasn't listening to her nonsense. "*You promised me venison, and you lied to me. For that, I shall make you pay!*" I turned around, strolled back up to the corner, and then I angled my behind towards the wall and sprayed there.

Salanraja let out a deep threatening growl, and smoke rose from her flared nostrils. "*What in the Seventh Dimension do you think you're doing?*" she asked.

"*That should teach you,*" I replied. "*This is my territory now, and any food that enters it I claim as my own.*"

"*You just urinated in my home!*"

"*But it's mine now. I've just marked it so.*"

"*What are you talking about?*"

I lowered my back and scowled up at the dragon. "*Don't you know how to mark territory?*"

"*What do you mean, territory?*"

"*Have you forgotten what it's like to be wild? Pah, you're just like the moggies in the cattery.*"

"You're insane. Now get out the way, before that stuff you've just put there starts to stink."

"*I'm not moving,*" I said, and I lowered my front to the ground and growled, ready to mark the wall again.

"*Move, or you shall burn!*"

Salanraja lifted her neck, and her glands started to swell there. More smoke seeped out of her nostrils, like steam does a kettle. Then, she pulled back her head, and a jet of flame leaped out towards me.

I darted just out of the way in time, and I turned to the dragon, screeching and hissing out swear words in my own language. "*You could have killed me!*"

"*Oh, you're nimble, you would have got out of the way in time. Now, never do that again, because I hate having to clean up after smelly creatures.*"

I wanted to give her some more of my mind. But before I could even put word to thought, a scratchy voice coming from the doorway interrupted me. It belonged to an old man.

"What in the Seventh Dimension is going on here?" he said.

MEETING THE ALCHEMIST

The old man was huddled over a staff with a blue crystal on top of it, polished and ground into a smooth bevel at the edges. I actually couldn't tell how old he was. He had a multitude of wrinkles set deep into his skin, but he didn't look sallow or pale, as a lot of incredibly old humans might. Rather, he emanated a sense of vitality – not only through the colour of his skin but also out of his brilliant blue eyes.

Salanraja turned to him. The way both the old man and the dragon looked at each other, told me they were talking telepathically. I felt a little jealous, admittedly, to have Salanraja talking to someone in my own presence, without having a clue what they were saying. I mewled, trying to get some attention, but that didn't distract either of them. So, I looked at the scorched stone where I had sprayed and considered remarking it. But I thought better of the idea and instead put my nose to the floor and tried to sniff out a scrap of venison that whoever had cleaned this place might have overlooked.

Eventually, the old man hobbled over to me on his staff. He stooped over it and put down his hand to pet me. His skin was dry and wrinkled but he didn't seem scary in any way. I rubbed my face against his hand, then looked up to him and mewled again, thinking he might have food.

I let him tickle me underneath my chin, as I tried to find out what he and Salanraja had been talking about.

"Can you talk to anyone like that?" I asked Salanraja.

"Like what?"

"Like you do with me, in my head."

"Not now I'm bonded to you," Salanraja said. *"Now you're the only non-dragon I can connect to telepathically."*

"Then how did you just speak to him? And don't try to tell me you were just staring at each other like lovers."

"I talked through his dragon. He's a dragon rider too, you know."

"Oh," I said.

Meanwhile, the old man had now started to scratch behind my ear. It tickled a little, so I gently pushed away his hand with my paw. The old man smiled.

"We can talk, you know, Bengie?" he said. "The crystals gave you that gift."

"Not Bengie," I said. "Bengie is an awful name. Call me Ben."

The old man turned to Salanraja, and she chuckled from deep in her belly. *"Bengie is a much better name, so much more elegant,"* she said to me.

"It's a childish name," I said.

"Ben sounds like a commoner."

"Better that than what a child might name a stuffed toy."

I mewled at the old man again, jealous of the attention he was giving Salanraja. He turned back to me.

"Salanraja refuses to use the name I prefer," I said. "But you seem to have much more respect..." I licked my paw, which had picked up a little of the taste of the venison from the floor.

"Very well," the old man said. "Ben it is. Meanwhile, I am Aleam. A dragon rider and also an alchemist and healer here at the academy. It's a pleasure to make the acquaintance of such a fascinating creature."

"The pleasure is all mine to be so fascinating," I said. "Now, do you have any food?"

The old man chuckled. "Yes. I heard Matron Canda complaining about the starving cat who tried to steal from her kitchens. That must have been you. You must be famished."

He reached into a leather pouch on his hip and produced out of it a chicken drumstick, yellowed with turmeric on the outside. I looked up at him, unable to distinguish between the rumbling sound in my tummy and my purr.

Aleam reached down and scratched me under the chin again, and then he threw the chicken on the floor. I picked it up in my mouth by the thigh bone and sequestered it over in the corner which I had marked. I ripped into the meat with my teeth, savouring a taste I hadn't experienced for months. The chicken was cold, admittedly. But it still tasted fresh, and slightly herby – the way I liked it.

"Well," Aleam said. "This is certainly going to rile up the Council of Three. They wanted to cut the spikes off Salanraja to make her saddleable again, but Salanraja wasn't having any of it."

I glanced over my shoulder at Aleam. "Yes, you humans have a habit of cutting off our body parts." The number of times they'd trimmed my claws, and there was something else their 'vet' had done to me when I was younger too – I won't go into that one.

"Thank you," Salanraja said to me. *"I'm glad to hear there's someone here who understands these things."*

Aleam shook his head. "I guess we do. If only they could hear you talk, maybe they'd think a little differently about cats. But for now, you're only here to catch mice. Except for Ta'ra, that is. But many don't believe Ta'ra is actually a cat at all."

I finished the last scrap of meat off the chicken and then licked the remaining taste off my lips. So, it wasn't as good as venison, but chicken was still a great tasting classic.

I walked up to Aleam and rubbed my nose against his knee. He smelled like someone I could trust. I don't know how to describe it, really, but his scent had a certain cleanliness about it. Unlike Astravar, who smelled of dark things that set off thoughts of decay and despair in my mind, Aleam smelled of lavender perhaps, or like pollen drifting upon a warm summer breeze. It's these kinds of subtle things that tell a cat whether a human can be trusted from the start.

"Who's Ta'ra, anyway?" I asked. Where I came from, South Wales, the humans liked to say 'ta-ra' to people all the time. It meant goodbye.

"Ta'ra is quite a character, if I say so myself," Aleam replied. "But really, you should meet her for yourself. I think you two might get on well – if Ta'ra can get on with anyone, that is."

He turned on his heel and hobbled away on his staff. I turned around to Salanraja, who had already folded herself up on the floor. "*Go with Aleam,*" she said. "*I need a rest anyway, and I don't want you urinating all around this place while I sleep.*"

I growled back at Salanraja. In all honesty, I didn't like her tone of voice. I turned back to Aleam and mewled again – kind of hoping he had more chicken.

"Come on, Ben," Aleam said. "Let's go and meet our friend."

He hobbled off, and I followed him into the corridors of this cold, unfriendly castle.

12

CAT SIDHE

I couldn't believe my eyes when I first saw Ta'ra. If it weren't for her size, she would have looked like a standard black cat, with a tapered face and wide round green eyes. But she was absolutely massive, and she didn't quite smell like a cat. Instead she had a wild scent about her. She sat propped up by a few cushions on a mahogany bench, licking her fur.

As soon as I entered Aleam's workshop, she stared at me and her eyes, I swear, started to glow. Her gaze had a kind of intensity that seemed able to measure the worth of my soul. But she didn't seem to think it worth very much at all, because she soon broke off her examination, yawned, and returned to grooming herself.

"Bengie, will you stop thinking so loud?" Salanraja said in my head. *"I'm trying to get some hard-earned sleep."*

"But she's ginormous," I said. *"She's even bigger than a Maine Coon."*

"Who?" Salanraja replied. *"And what in the Seventh Dimension is a Maine Coon?"*

"A Maine Coon is the biggest cat in the world. I thought everyone knew that." Although, to be honest, the Savannah cats often disagreed with that fact. They claimed that their grandfather was much, much bigger than the Maine Coon some of us saw on television. To which our old

neighbourhood Ragamuffin, perhaps the wisest of our clowder, pointed out that crossing a domestic cat with a serval of the Savannah to create a massive domestic cat is cheating. No domestic cat, he said, was bigger than the Maine Coon.

Salanraja laughed. *"I think you'll find the Sabre-Tooth tiger is the biggest cat in the world. Or, debatably, it might be the chimera."*

"Never heard of them."

"Well, if you don't quieten your thoughts a little, I might decide to drop you into a chimera's lair. Now, let me sleep."

I didn't know how I was meant to think quieter. But, although I didn't know what a chimera was, I honestly wasn't enthusiastic to find out either. I imagined myself whispering with each thought, and that seemed to do the trick. A moment later, something went quiet in my head, as if a voice nattering in there had shut itself off. Had that been Salanraja's thoughts?

The massive cat, Ta'ra, had now put her head down against a cushion and her eyes had sealed shut. Around her, a load of dusty looking books peered down from the high mounted bookshelves. The humans back in South Wales used to read much more glossy looking versions of these, but I'd never worked out what any of those funny symbols meant.

I wondered if I could also read the human language, now I could speak it. I tried to find a way up onto the shelves, but I couldn't see one. So instead, I sauntered over to see what Aleam was up to.

He stood over a complex glass alembic – and I wouldn't have known the word for that if the crystal hadn't granted me the gift of language. It was a collection of tubes and bulbs with green and yellow liquids bubbling within. Aleam peered over, studying the apparatus through a pair of glasses he had balanced on the bridge of his nose. After a while, he nodded as if in satisfaction, raised his staff to the apparatus, said some words I didn't quite understand – even with my gift – and turned to face the bench.

"Ta'ra," he said. "You have a guest, and you haven't even said a word to him. Show some respect, for goodness' sake."

Ta'ra opened her eyes again, blinked slowly at me, and yawned once more. "He's a common house cat," she said, and I recognised her to be speaking in the human tongue.

I responded in my language, screaming out feline expletives that would have disgusted Aleam if he could understand them. "I'm no common cat," I told her in the same language. "I'm a Bengal. The greatest of all domesticated cats. A descendant of the great Asian leopard cat."

But the massive cat seemed nonplussed by this. "See what I mean. He speaks cat language. He should be out hunting mice and not bothering me here."

Aleam shook his head, and he opened his mouth as if he wanted to say something. But I decided it better to butt in and try to deflate this cat's ego, which seemed almost as large as its bulk.

"What in the whiskers are you?" I said in the human language. "You look like a cat, but you don't look like a cat."

Ta'ra snarled at me. "I'm a much more spiritual creature than you can ever imagine. I can also look smaller, if it intimidates you less?" She stood up, and then for the first time I noticed her fur wasn't completely black. She had a single white diamond on her chest, neatly arranged as if someone had painted it there.

Then, the air seemed to shimmer around her, and she literally started to shrink in her chair. She went from being larger than a Maine Coon to the size of a normal cat within the space of seconds.

"What are you?" I asked again.

The cat let out a loud, desultory laugh. "If you were as intelligent as you like to think, you would know. Those versed in the ways of magic would call me a Cat Sidhe. I'm of the Faerie Realm, once a princess, but fate changed my form. You don't have a clue what I'm talking about, do you?"

I tried to blink off my disbelief. I must have been dreaming; this couldn't have been real.

"Ta'ra," Aleam said. "Don't be so judgemental. Ben is not of this world. Astravar teleported him here from another dimension, and he would still be under the warlock's thrall now if he hadn't managed to escape."

"Judgemental? I'm the most misunderstood fae of them all. Don't you think I have a right to be judgemental sometimes?" The black cat stood up, slinked off the bench, and then she walked up to examine me.

"So, tell me, Ben... How did you come to speak the human tongue, and why did you end up under the service of someone as foul as Astravar?"

"He brought me here," I said. "I was eating the best dinner of salmon trimmings I'd tasted in a long time, and I was just about to lap up some milk, when I got flung out of his portal right on to his hard stone floor." I thought being a cat, Ta'ra might understand what a travesty it was to be suddenly separated from a good meal.

She stared at me, blinking. I might have known she wouldn't quite get it.

"Why aren't you in the cattery like the rest of the cats?" I asked. "Don't you get along with them?"

"Because I'm not a cat, I'm a fae," she snapped back. "Once a fairy with a 'y', until I got banished from the kingdom because of my new form."

"A what?"

She growled from deep inside her stomach. "Do you really know so little about the magical worlds?"

"I didn't even know magic existed until I met Astravar."

Ta'ra shook her head like a human would. "And I didn't know that cats existed either until Astravar summoned me away from my wedding ceremony to Prince Ta'lon and decided that he would change my life completely. Gone were my wings, replaced by this furry body and my claws. It was horrible."

"So, you don't enjoy being a cat?" Such a notion seemed utterly unfathomable to me.

Ta'ra looked over at the bubbling solution. "Astravar gave me the ability to turn back into a fairy eight times. I've used up six of them, three because of my own stupidity. Aleam has been trying all this time to find a cure for my curse, but I fear that only the curser can reverse it. I can transform twice more, only for a day mind, then I'll be stuck with this terrible form for life."

"Terrible?" I really couldn't understand this lady. "Cats are the greatest creatures alive."

"No, you're not," Ta'ra said. "You just think you are. But you don't have wings, you don't have magic, and you can't even look after yourselves. Cat-hood is the pinnacle of reliance, and none of you seem to understand how demeaning it is." She examined her paw.

I was starting to feel attacked. I arched my back and circled around Ta'ra, baring my teeth as I did so. She did the same, looking at me with those bright green eyes.

"We can hunt," I said.

"Can you? I've heard of cats who tried to run away from Dragonsbond Academy. They didn't last two days out there, before they came back to the kitchens mewling for food."

I felt the hackles rise on my back. "They're merely useless moggies. But I'm different, I'm a Bengal, a descendent of the great Asian leopard cat. And I can hunt. In fact, I killed thousands of mice for Astravar."

"Ooh, big deal. You reached into a hole and scooped out defenceless mice with nowhere to go but their holes. There's a difference to catching mice in a human dwelling and hunting in the wild. My instincts tell me you wouldn't be very good at the latter."

"Oh yeah," I said. "I'll show you what a wild cat I am."

I lunged forward at Ta'ra, scratching with my claw. I hit her on her shoulder, and she responded with a loud shrieking sound as she batted back with her claws. Then, she grew in size until she was almost as big as a human child. I didn't let that scare me, and I clawed at her leg, a primal part of me wanting to do much damage.

How dare she imply I was a poor hunter. How dare she imply I was useless.

Ta'ra continued to grow until she was towering above me, and then she pinned me underneath her massive paws. I tried to scratch her off me, but she kept me pinned, with a wicked grin on her face. "I'm a witch, you know. That's what they call me, a witch!"

Aleam had been so busy with his experiment, that he'd been completely oblivious to what was going on. But I guess the two of us screeching so loudly caused him to turn his attention towards us.

"What, in the Seventh Dimension?" he said, and he quickly hobbled over on his staff. He used it to take a swipe at Ta'ra. She batted at it and then clutched onto it with one paw while she kept me pinned down with the other.

"Ta'ra," Aleam said. "Let go at once."

Ta'ra hissed at him, but Aleam glared back with his cold blue eyes. Ta'ra had the bottom of the staff in her grasp, and the top of it glowed bright yellow.

"He started it," Ta'ra said.

Aleam turned to me, and a stern look stretched across his eyebrows. "Is this true, Ben?"

I snarled at Ta'ra. "She provoked me," I said.

Aleam turned on Ta'ra. "What have I told you about your moods? You really have to work on this."

The angry green glow in Ta'ra's eyes faded, and soon enough she let go of the staff and let off an apologetic meow. She lifted her paw from me, and I immediately wriggled free, hissing at the cat. But she looked at me, an abashed, guilty look in her wide eyes, as if she'd just stolen chicken off of a human's dinner table.

"I'm sorry, Ben," she said. "It's just... Astravar did this to me. Sometimes, my emotions... I just hate it!"

"We will find a cure, eventually." Aleam took hold of a cloth on the table, and he began to polish his crystal that had now stopped glowing. "We may not be able to turn you back to a normal fairy, but I think we'll find a way to stop the episodes."

Ta'ra meowed again, and she then shrunk back down to normal cat size and slinked back over to the bench and leapt back onto it. She was soon yawning, and then she closed her eyes and was quickly fast asleep.

I heard footsteps, and I smelled a human approaching the door. I darted under the table and hid behind the leg, remembering how that woman had treated me in the kitchen. But it wasn't the chef who arrived there, but a spotty faced teenager, no older than sixteen, with a scroll in his hand. He had a short sword in a sheath hanging off his hip, and a staff with a blue crystal head fastened to the back.

"Driar Aleam," he said. "I'm sorry to disturb your work, but I'm looking for a moggie. Apparently one with unusual leopard like spots. Have you seen him anywhere?"

"He's right here," Aleam pointed down to where I was crouched, trying to make myself as small as possible. "Ben, don't be shy. Why don't you come out and say hello to your dragon rider peer?"

I mustered up a little courage, and I moved out from under the table. The dragon rider boy had blond hair, and a hard jaw behind his spots. When they eventually cleared away, humans would probably see him as handsome.

The boy looked down at me, contempt evident in his eyes.

"Well, Ben, this is Initiate Rine," Aleam said.

I opened my mouth to say something, but the boy scoffed and then turned on his heel. He glanced back at me over his shoulder. "Come on, you'll be late. You really don't want to keep the council waiting."

He marched off, leaving me no option but to follow on his heels. As he walked, I could swear I heard him mutter under his breath, that he couldn't believe I was a 'bleeding cat'.

13

THE COUNCIL OF THREE

The dragon rider boy led me to a courtyard, and he walked so fast, it was hard even for a cat to keep up. He had quite a stride about him, as if he regarded himself in a higher station than he actually was. Meanwhile, he didn't turn his head to look at me even once.

We walked past the kitchens, and I could smell bread baking in there. I was half tempted at one point to abandon this Initiate Rine character and instead give the woman who had attacked me earlier with a spoon – who I think Aleam had called Matron Canda – a piece of my mind. She would be surprised to have a cat talking to her, for sure. Maybe it would even scare her away for a while, leaving me alone to enjoy some food.

But despite the hunger still rumbling in my tummy, I continued onwards. I hadn't heard from Salanraja yet, and I wondered if she'd end up joining us in this special meeting.

"What does this Council want with me?" I tried asking Initiate Rine. But my question didn't seem to warrant an answer from him. Rather, he just sped up.

He dashed through the corridors, and we passed a group of young adults making a racket and laughing as they moved forward in a crowd. I had to concentrate to stop myself getting trampled as I weaved my way between their legs. Really, half of them didn't even seem to notice I was there.

Soon, we found ourselves inside the bailey of the castle which was surrounded by tall crenelated castle walls. Those walls looked fun to climb, and I imagined myself running along them chasing birds and butterflies. But then all I saw flying around here were dragons and crows, and I didn't fancy chasing either of those. We reached an archway in the wall that led into an inner courtyard.

"In here," Initiate Rine said, and he gestured with his short sword. "I shall wait outside."

Alone, I entered a cloistered section of the castle, surrounded by an outside corridor raised up by columns. Doors led into the castle, but most of these were closed. A neatly mown patch of lawn covered the centre of the courtyard, cut off by a raised semi-circular platform built from a chequered pattern of rough red and white stones.

Four pillars led up from this platform, supporting a domed roof. Underneath this stood two women and a man behind three wooden lecterns. Each had short swords sheathed on their hips, staffs hanging from their backs, and mustard coloured shoulder pads, with golden thread woven through them in an ornate floral pattern. They were all old, and I could see that without even needing to be close to them. The gems in their staffs were red, blue, and green respectively.

I approached them slowly at first, wondering which of them posed the greatest threat. I'd seen the dragon riders use their staffs from their dragons, and right now I didn't doubt that one of them might have wanted to scorch me alive. They all wore these white robes, secured with cords that hung down above the floor. Something about the way they frowned at me told me they weren't really on my side.

The first of the women, the one on my left, had the red staff and her grey hair was swept back and tied in a bun. She also had wrinkles at the corners of her eyes so deep, they looked like fruit flies could use them for flight training. She was as thin as a scarecrow, with long arms and legs that almost looked as if they didn't fit her body.

"I am Driar Yila," she called out to me. "Approach, cat."

As I got even closer, the second woman opened her mouth to speak. "We are the Council of Three," she said. "And I am Driar

Lonamm." She was a little plumper than the first – meaning she probably liked food and that we had something in common. Though her face also displayed many wrinkles, her fiery wavy red hair made her look a little younger.

The third elder was a good two feet taller than the women, a giant by any measure. He had a bald head, a pockmarked face, and thick corded hands that made me think his bulk was largely muscle.

"My name is Driar Brigel," he said. "And it is time to test your worth."

Once I got close enough, I noticed a white crystal hanging from rafters on the underside of the dome. The three elders lifted their staffs off of their backs and pointed them at the crystal. Beams of their respective colours shot out of the staffs, and they soon merged to infuse the crystal with a powerful light.

It glowed brightly, bathing the courtyard with a blinding light. Whiskers, it seemed almost as bright as the sun. But soon, the light faded a little to display an image. It showed a view of my own crystal, with my dreams once again running through it – me on Salanraja's back with a staff clasped firmly in my jaw, as I shot fireballs out of it into those massive bat-like creatures.

But that wasn't all the crystal showed. It also showed the inside of Salanraja's chamber, with the dragon sleeping on the polished stone floor, her massive eyelids clasped so tightly shut that it didn't look like she'd be waking soon. Her nostrils flared as her lips vibrated, as if letting out huge snores. Plumes of smoke rose out of her nose, and drifted over towards my crystal, almost as if it was sucking them in.

"There she is, sleeping during important affairs," the thin elder, Driar Yila said.

"Typical Salanraja," the male, Driar Brigel said. "When is she going to learn?"

"I thought she'd soon let us make her saddleable," Driar Lonamm said with a slow shake of the head. "Then she pulls this stunt."

Driar Yila turned a hard stare on to me. "And now here is the specimen she chose as a rider. Not a human, or a dwarf, or even a lowly troll. No, he's your run-of-the-mill cat!"

When I heard them speak about me this way, I couldn't help but arch up my back and hiss at Driar Yila. But she didn't even blink, her stare seeming to bore right into my soul. The other two elders, whose gazes had drifted up towards the crystal, also turned their heads back towards me and met my gaze with equally probing stares.

"I'm not just a cat," I said. "I'm a Bengal, a descendant of the Asian leopard cat."

A smile crept across Driar Brigel's lips. "Ah, so the rumour is true. You can speak our language. But we still don't understand why the dragon chose you."

"Driar Brigel," Driar Yila said without taking her eyes off me, "we shouldn't be having this conversation without the dragon. Wake her up, cat. I presume you can at least do that."

"What? You want me to just run over there and stamp on her head? She won't be happy."

Driar Yila raised an eyebrow. "I thought you were bonded?"

"We are, but—"

"Then you should be able to wake her from here."

"I..."

Driar Yila opened her mouth to say something more, but Driar Lonamm raised a hand to stop her. "We can't just expect a cat to know what humans do. He's not had the same education as us, and he has a much smaller brain. Cat—"

"I have a name," I cut in.

Driar Lonamm froze and she gave me a stern look. She twisted her staff, and I waited for her to throw some magic at me. But after a moment she said, "so tell me that name."

"Ben," I said.

She smirked. "Very well, Ben. Talk to your dragon loud enough, and she'll wake."

"Are you crazy? She'll break my bones first, and then she'll eat you alive."

"She won't," Driar Yila snapped back. "Now do it!"

"As you wish," I said. "It's your funeral." Just as I'd imagined myself whispering before, now I imagined myself screeching as if I'd just landed in the same garden as an unfamiliar dog. To put some extra flare into it, I arched my back and let the hackles shoot up. Then, I felt Salanraja wake, and she wasn't happy.

A loud roar resounded out from one of the towers behind me. In the crystal above, I saw her rise on her two hind legs, charge out into the sky, and then she screamed in my mind.

❧ 14 ❧

A MISSION

"I warned you not to wake me, or you'd find yourself in a chimera's lair," Salanraja said. She was certainly angry.

"I had no choice," I replied.

"What do you mean you had no choice?"

"The Council of Three," I said. "A spotty faced boy came to look for me, and then he told me to go and see them. These people, they're so rude. They think they're the greatest things that ever lived."

I felt Salanraja calm down a little. It was as if the same dragonfire burning within her also burned within my chest. "Humans. They will always be arrogant. But they are in charge here."

I couldn't help but laugh, at least inside my mind. I didn't want to end up fried by the magic that these elders were spewing out of their staffs. "I thought you said dragons were the most powerful creatures to have ever lived, and yet you are subject to humans."

"They don't control us," Salanraja said. A shadow passed overhead and a moment later, Salanraja thudded onto the ground, shaking the earth a little.

I looked at her, unimpressed, and yawned. "If they don't control you, why are they waking you up?"

Salanraja lowered her neck to me and examined me with those

massive yellow eyes. *"They are bonded to their dragons, remember? All Dragon riders are. Their dragons are part of the Council too, and right now the humans will be communicating with their dragons to work out what to do next. So, I'm not answering to them, but their dragons."*

"So why aren't the dragons here too?"

"The Council deemed it would be less intimidating to have massive dragons looming over potential Initiates."

"I see. Also, what's a Driar?" I asked. I had so many questions.

Salanraja examined one of her claws, extending it slightly. *"A Driar is a dragon rider who has graduated from Dragonsbond Academy. Either they work at King Garmin's castle, or they are stationed here as teachers or lookouts."*

She then turned to the council, and I felt the rage flare in her chest again. She opened her jaws wide, displaying those tremendously long teeth, and she let out a loud roar. I could swear that she was about to breathe fire on the elders and roast them there and then. Well, they couldn't say I didn't warn them.

The three elders examined her for a moment. They raised their staffs, and the crystal above us flashed bright white.

"Calm yourself, Salanraja," Driar Yila shouted. "That is a command."

Salanraja continued to rage. She gnashed and clawed at nothing in particular. Really, she looked as if she'd caught rabies, and I half expected her to start foaming at the mouth.

As she raged, the elders in front raised their staffs ever closer to the crystal above their heads, feeding it with more and more energy. The intensity inside brightened so much that I thought it might explode.

Yila said something out loud. It was in a language I couldn't understand at first, very similar in cadence to what I'd heard Aleam speaking before in his study. I would have thought that I could understand all languages because of the crystal's gift. But then, I guessed they were speaking in the language of the crystals, and crystals weren't technically creatures.

Suddenly, everything went quiet. It was as if someone had just smashed a wineglass at a party, and everyone was looking around wondering who broke it. Salanraja let out a whimper, and she backed away. She buried her head in her front claws for a moment, almost as if she was crying. It took her awhile to emerge from that position.

"Salanraja," Driar Brigel said after a long moment, his muscles flexing underneath his robe. "I must say that we're disappointed. For a long time, we've tried to find you a suitable rider, and you only needed to trim your spikes to hold a saddle. But instead you go and choose this mangy creature as a rider. What were you thinking?"

Salanraja let out a low and quiet growl, but this soon turned into a soft whimper.

"*Aren't you going to say something to them?*" I asked.

"*I can't,*" Salanraja replied. "*I'm not bonded to them.*"

"*Then speak to their dragons.*"

"*I'd rather not,*" Salanraja replied. "*They'll just remind me what a misfit they've always thought I am. This is an argument that I've never managed to win. Just tell the Driars that I think you are the most suitable candidate, and that you have as much strength of character as any human rider. And tell them that you're descended from a Sabre-Tooth tiger or something. Not one of those puny leopard cat things.*"

I did as she told me, leaving out the descendant from a Sabre-Tooth tiger part, as I'd already told them what I was descended from, and I saw absolutely no reason to mock my heritage.

"You never did quite get on with the other dragons," Brigel replied, directing his voice at Salanraja. "It won't hurt to cut off the spikes, you know. Once they've been gone a few days, you won't realise you ever had them."

"*No!*" Salanraja replied, and it took me a moment to realize that the shout only echoed in my head. Salanraja also let out another long roar. The elders reacted by lifting up their staffs towards the crystal again.

Salanraja corrected herself.

"*Look, stop getting all angry all the time,*" I said. "*I don't know about you, but I don't want to be on someone's plate for dinner.*"

"*I'm sorry,*" Salanraja said. "*But this is quite personal. This isn't just about my spikes. I can't have a human rider. I've never wanted one. I've*" *never trusted any humans around here to want one as my rider. Apart from Aleam, but he's already bonded."*

"So, what do I tell them?" I asked.

"Tell them that you are ready to prove your worth. Tell them that we will serve honourably the Kingdom of Illumine, and the king, pompous as he is."

"Fine," I said. I turned back to the council and told them exactly what Salanraja had told me, not omitting a single detail. Yila scowled at the bit about the king being pompous and banged her staff loudly against the floor.

"I didn't ask you to say that part. Gracious demons, the Dragon Council will roast me alive if you're not careful."

"I said exactly what you asked me to."

"You, Bengie, it seems, have a lot to learn."

The elders at this point were conferring amongst themselves. While the two ladies continued to speak, Brigel turned back towards us. "Salanraja," he said. "Are you sure you want this? Despite your rebellious streak, we want to protect you. Having an incompetent dragon rider might cost you your life."

"But what's the alternative," I asked, and I didn't wait for Salanraja's permission to speak this time. "She's already bonded to me, isn't she?"

"They don't want us to unbond anymore," Salanraja explained. *"Now they want me to serve as a transport dragon for royal passengers and you as a regular rat-catcher. But I knew when I bonded with you that there was no turning back."*

"So, what do I tell them?"

"Tell them I've made up my mind."

I did just that, and Driar Lonamm sighed as she pivoted around back towards us. She examined Salanraja for a moment, then turned to me. "Well, I guess we'll have to learn to accept it at Dragonsbond Academy. Although for now we wish to keep this a secret from the palace. You'll need to prove your worth to us before news of your existence is published in the royal papers. Or, if you get yourselves killed, we could easily just cover this one up."

"What are you talking about?" I asked. "We're not going to die."

"Aren't you?" Driar Yila said. "You will eventually. No magic can stop fate."

"I will die when I'm old and have lived a good life," I said.

"So be it," Yila replied. She turned to Brigel, who nodded.

"Remind us of your name, again?" he said.

I stepped forward. "My name is Ben, because I'm Bengal, a descendant of the great Asian leopard cat."

Salanraja growled quietly. *"Not that again."*

I hissed at her. Driar Brigel all this time, was watching our exchange with intent, as he leaned toward us. "Well, Ben," he said. "Do you promise to swear fealty to Dragonsbond Academy and the King of Illumine? Do you promise to serve as a loyal subject, and to put the fate of your kingdom before your own life? The truth now if you please."

Well, if he wanted the truth, I might as well give it. "I came from a pleasant house in South Wales where I could eat salmon every day. Here, I've eaten nothing in days except bugs, a tiny scrap of venison, and a bit of chicken. You want to know what I want? I want to go home."

I mewled as I spoke that last sentence, giving my best cat like cuteness that had won humans over so many times. I hoped that they'd know of some magic that could send me back through a portal across time and space. Tomorrow, I could be in South Wales, sleeping on the plush sofa in the conservatory, the sun coming through the windows. Later, I would chase birds and butterflies around the garden. I would feast every day like a cat should, and I would get food when I wanted it.

I was interrupted from my reveries by Driar Yila's staff banging against the floor. "You have no choice, you selfish creature," she said. "Either you do what we ask, or you'll spend the rest of your life chasing rats."

I hadn't expected that response. I mewled again, to try to get at least some of their sympathy for my plight, but they weren't having any of it. Eventually, I realised that this harsh mistress, Driar Yila, wouldn't bend one bit.

"Very well, I promise to serve your kingdom." But I also told myself I'd find a way to go home. There had to be some way back.

That grin returned to Brigel's face. Really, even though he was the bulkiest of the three, he also seemed the kindest. "Then, I think it's time to give you your first mission," he said. "Prove yourself at this, and we will accept the pairing into Dragonsbond Academy."

"What in the Seventh Dimension are they going to send us after now?" Salanraja said, and I mewled quietly, not liking the sound of danger. But I noticed the three elders were now looking at me, as if expecting me to say something.

"Go on," Salanraja said. *"Ask them what the mission is. Show some interest in helping out and things will be a little easier here."*

I looked at Salanraja, and she cocked her head towards the council. So, I turned back to them.

"What do you wish for us to do?" I asked, reluctantly.

Driar Lonamm reached down into a hidden pocket at the front of her robe and pulled out a scroll. She fumbled with this a moment, struggling to open it with one hand, as she gripped her staff tightly in her other hand.

"Let me see," Lonamm said. "Yes, here it is. There's a bone dragon terrorising Midar Village on the edge of the Wastelands. Go there and stop it. Once you come back with proof that this has been done, then we will reconsider your application."

"Thank you," I said.

"That's not enough," Salanraja said. *"You need to bow."*

"I need to what?"

"Bow..."

"How the whiskers can a cat bow?"

"I don't know, just lower yourself on your front legs or something."

But I wasn't listening to this idiocy, and so I gave another meow instead. It wasn't so much to say thank you, but more to remind them that I still wanted to go home, and that if they could kindly open a portal back to the Brecon Beacons after this mission, I'd greatly appreciate it.

"Very well," Yila said, the harsh look not leaving her face. "Then be off with you, and remember, only return once the mission's complete."

"Fine," I said.

She glared at me as if expecting something.

"You don't just say 'fine' here," Salanraja explained. *"You say, yes ma'am."*

But I wasn't listening. I kept staring back at Driar Yila and then I yawned, licked my paw, and started grooming myself.

Driar Lonamm shook her head. "Go on, be off with you." She made a gesture as if shooing away a cat. But then, come to think of it, to them I was just that – a cat.

I slinked away, back towards the bailey. But before I could take a few steps, Salanraja gnashed her teeth loudly behind me, and made a sound like an angry dog.

"Get on my back, you impudent fool," she said. *"Gracious demons, how did I end up choosing you?"*

I let out a deep growl, then I turned back to her. I really didn't feel like going anywhere after how these humans had treated me. But I guess we had a bone dragon to destroy. So, I ran up Salanraja's tail and secured myself in the corridor of spikes on her back.

As Salanraja lifted herself off the ground, I cursed at the three elders in cat language, safe in the knowledge that they (probably) wouldn't understand what I said.

15

MASTERY OF FLIGHT

I was getting the hang of flying. This was my third time in the air with Salanraja, and I was starting to enjoy the sensation of it. The sun beat down from the sky, bringing a pleasant warmth that offset the cool breeze. The clouds rolled by overhead, so far away they looked like massive balls of candy floss floating up in the sky. The yellow and green fields had been arranged so neatly beneath us that they reminded me of the board from that silly game that humans liked to play.

You must know which one I mean. The one where humans took it in turns – that sometimes could last for hours – to shuffle pieces around from one black or white chequered square to the next. The master and mistress of the bungalow used to love playing this in the winter besides the roaring log fireplace, the heat from it warming my soft fur. They would have salami and olives on the table, one which made me intensely hungry, and the other which made me just think, yeuch!

But honestly, this game was so boring that I would go over and sit on the master's lap and pretend to watch them for a while. Then, while he wasn't watching, I'd knock off the tallest of the pieces closest to me – the one that had the cross on it. The master would get so angry then, but the mistress would start laughing so loudly she'd spill her wine. Because she found it funny, I found it funny, so I continued to keep playing that way. Over time, the master would try to stop me getting anywhere near the pieces, blocking them off with his forearm, and so that became part of the game.

Of course, I always won.

As I watched the fields passing by beneath me, like a forever-moving floor, I purred from deep within my chest. I'd momentarily forgotten about those idiot humans back at Dragonsbond Academy. That was the beauty of being a cat. You didn't need to have any worries. You could just put everything behind you and focus on being in the moment.

But, at the same time, I could hear Salanraja growling and groaning from her chest somewhere beneath my feet. Occasionally she'd open her mouth, and out would emerge a ring of smoke that would drift off behind us, dissipating into the sky.

She was trying to get my attention, but I was having none of it. This was the first flight I was enjoying, even when my memories of home left a sinking feeling of wistfulness inside me.

Eventually, Salanraja must have realised she wasn't doing a great job of communicating her anger. So, she lurched to her side, and had me tumbling within her cage of spikes. My ribs made a nasty cracking sound as I bashed against the wall. Whiskers, that hurt.

"Ouch," I said. "Fly in a straight line, will you?"

"I'm sorry," she said, with a tinge of irony in her voice. "But sometimes I need to turn."

"Then turn gently. It's not as if we're navigating through a canyon."

"You don't get to tell me what to do," Salanraja said, and she did a few rolls in the air, sending me around and around again, like the proverbial cat in the washing machine.

I couldn't really focus on staying alive in there and talk to her at the same time. I thought I was going to throw up, and this time I'd do so on her back. But she stopped eventually, and the ground beneath my feet no longer looked like a chessboard, but rather was spinning around like a kaleidoscope.

"What is wrong with you?" I asked her.

"What is wrong with me?" She growled. *"It appears to be you who wants to get us killed. How could you behave so impudently in front of the Council of Three? Have you any idea how powerful they and their dragons are?"*

"I thought it was the warlocks who were the bad guys," I said. "Isn't the Council meant to be on your side?"

"They are," Salanraja said, and paused. She beat her wings rapidly a few times to lift us up higher in the air and then lowered us into a glide. A large crow with a great grey beak soared alongside at the same level as us for a moment. But then, it noticed either Salanraja or me, and probably her. It cawed out and then dived back down towards the ground.

"They are," Salanraja said again, *"and you're right, they probably would never kill us. It's just..."*

"What?" I said gently, thinking better to keep her calm than to aggravate her back into stunt mode.

Salanraja shook her head slowly, causing her body to sway slightly underfoot. *"Dragons aren't usually born with spikes like these on our backs. Usually we have horns that come out of our heads, and sometimes a line of spikes along our spine. The other dragons call me Double Ribs, and they ask me what I'm keeping inside my cage. Some dragons understand why I don't want to change myself, but others feel I should just get rid of these spikes."*

"So why don't you?" I asked.

"Would you ever want to get rid of your claws and your teeth? These things are a part of me now. I was born with them, and I've learned to fly with them. They make me strong, and I can even use them to knock other dragons out of the sky. It's an extra defence mechanism."

I turned my head to the side. The crow had come back up to join us now, albeit at a much more cautious distance. Its black eye watched me, as if trying to assess if I was friend or foe. I lost interest in it and turned to look at the horizon, appreciating the cool wind swishing through my fur.

"Isn't there like a human who could ride you without a saddle?" I asked. *"A small lady, perhaps, who would be happy to lie in this 'ribcage'?"*

Salanraja groaned. *"You would never find any human willing to ride a dragon without a saddle, and even if you did, the elders would never allow it."*

"Why not?"

"Because they're human, and they're all about keeping safe. That's what this war against the warlocks is about for King Garmin, creating a world that is safe."

"And they don't care about my safety?" I asked, remembering what Driar Yila had said about covering up my death.

"I guess not," Salanraja replied. *"You're just a cat to them. Which makes you expendable."*

Salanraja flapped her wings a few times, gently this time. The crow was still there, and it was now edging a little closer to us. But Salanraja paid it no heed. The sun hid behind a cloud, and the world went darker for a moment.

That was when I noticed a thin purple line emerging from the horizon.

"There it is," Salanraja said. *"The Wastelands."*

I licked my paw. *"What are the Wastelands, anyway?"*

"No man's land," Salanraja replied. *"A land full of magical creatures, some of them serving the King's mages, while others are machinations of the warlocks. It's a vast battlefield that separates the Kingdom of Illumine from the Darklands where the Warlocks reside. You must have passed through them when you came to Illumine, as Astravar's tower is right on the edge of them."*

I remembered that yucky boggy land that I'd sprinted through before reaching Illumine. Though I hadn't seen any magical creatures in there, I had contended with that suffocating purple gas.

My tummy rumbled. *"Can we stop for a bite to eat before we get there,"* I asked. *"They mentioned a village. Perhaps they might have a kitchen and a chef willing to at least donate a fish or two."*

Salanraja laughed. *"Do you ever think about anything else?"* she asked. *"It's like everything I've heard from you since I met you has been food, food, food, food, food..."*

"That's because I've not eaten for days," I said.

"What about that chicken Aleam gave you?"

"It was one drumstick. Do you really think one drumstick is enough to feed a busy Bengal?"

"Busy?"

"Yes, you've made me busy. My life before I came to this place was eat, groom, sleep, play. Now, we're off chasing a bone dragon through some disgusting lands which I really wanted to see the back of."

"Oh, quit moaning," Salanraja said. "I tell you what. When this is all over, I'll hunt you something nice, and we can feast together."

"Like that venison you promised?"

Salanraja let out a plume of smoke. "Venison if you like. Or pheasant, or a nice roasted mutton."

"How about salmon?" I asked.

"No, we're not going fishing. It's got to be real hunting."

"Fine," I said. "Just make sure you stick to your promise this time, or you'll be sorry."

I had been so curious about this strange world I'd been thrust into that I hadn't even realised how much greyer the ground beneath had become. The sky was truly darkening around us, and a purple haze floated over the ground below. I looked down at it, truly not wanting to go back to that land. I really didn't want to have to meet Astravar again, whether I had a dragon or not.

"Just one more question," I said. "What's so special about warlocks, anyway? How are they any different from the king's mages?"

"It's to do with the crystals they use," Salanraja replied. "Warlocks use dark crystals; mages use light crystals."

"So, there are only two types of crystals."

"Yes," Salanraja said. "Something like that. Dark crystals drain life and draw off its power, while the magic of white crystals focuses on creation. Mages can readily use white magic, but dark magic is now banned in Illumine after how it completely corrupted the minds of the warlocks. That's the thing about dark magic – you use too much of it and it darkens your soul."

"Then what about the dragon riders," I asked. "What kind of magic do we use?"

"Really, dragon riders and dragons use a mixture of light and dark through a very special kind of crystal. It's the bond between dragons and their human riders that stops dark magic corrupting us. In most cases, anyway."

"You mean there are dark dragon riders?"

Salanraja lowered her head, and I felt a tinge of sadness in her soul.

"Out there somewhere," she said, *"yes, there are. But they are a story for another day, because it looks like we've arrived."*

Now the land beneath us smelled intensely familiar. I don't know how to describe the sensation. It wasn't a physical smell, as such, but rather one that emerged in the mind. It reminded me of memories rooted in my primal ancestry. The fear of not being at the top of the food chain, knowing there were things in the sky that might swoop down and lift you up in their claws and tear your flesh away from the bone. The fear of great lizards roaming the land on two legs. The fear of death, and the fear of living forever alone. This fear smelt like death and decay and all the rotten things of the soul.

The purple mist was thick below us now, seeping all over the ground. It wove its way through the red reeds sticking out of the swamps. This wasn't a place for cats. In fact, it wasn't a place for any living creatures. No wonder I'd found it so hard to find food here.

"There," Salanraja said. *"Do you see it?"*

"Do I see what?"

"Our quarry... The bone dragon."

I lifted myself up onto my front paws and I climbed up to the top of Salanraja's external ribcage and peered out from between the spikes. Then I saw it, streaking across the sky. A great skeletal beast, long and terrifying, similar to what the crystal had shown me.

The creature veered towards us, and then it tossed its head up to the sky and roared.

16

BEDSHEET OF LIGHT

S alanraja was gliding closer and closer to the ground. She didn't seem to want to lift herself up again, perhaps worried that the bone dragon might hear her if she flapped her wings even once. Or perhaps she had decided that we weren't going to fight the bone dragon at all, that instead we would hide in a swamp until it flew away, Salanraja submerged like a crocodile. I have to admit, I preferred that latter solution.

"*That's no normal bone dragon,*" Salanraja said. "*I wish the council had told me we were dealing with one of those.*"

"One of what?" I asked.

"*Shh!*" Salanraja whispered. "*Don't make a sound. Not even a purr.*"

"What is it? What's so dangerous about that thing?"

"*Are you telling me you'd be happy to meet this thing on a dark night and a new moon? Would you invite it to a party?*"

"You're a dragon, and it's made of bone. Just throw some flame at it and burn it out of the sky."

Salanraja turned back to me and looked at me with one eye. "*You really think you're smart, don't you? You've got it all figured out. As long as the Manipulator is there on the ground, then its summoned creature can't die.*"

"*A what?*"

"*A Manipulator.*" Salanraja landed softly on the ground, kicking up some dust that glistened purple in the waning light. "*It should be around here somewhere. You've got sharp eyes haven't you, Bengie? Look for a change in patterns. A shimmer in the air.*"

I tried to peer through the murk, but I could see nothing. "*I don't think there's anything even there,*" I said, "*and I don't believe in ghosts.*"

Salanraja scoffed. "*It's not a ghost, it's a Manipulator, as I said.*"

"*But you haven't even told me what a Manipulator is.*"

"*It's a warlock's conjuration that allows him to cast spells from a safe position. Anything under the Manipulators' control is invulnerable until you kill the Manipulator. Gracious demons, can't you smell the thing?*"

"*No, I smell the land.*"

"*Just follow your nose. Once you find it, you'll know.*"

"*I—*" I trailed off when I sensed something moving in the distance. One moment, it was as if the purple mist was swirling around in strange patterns, and the next I could see the gas taking on a form of its own. Faintly, beneath the patterns, I thought I could make out a shape as I might make creatures out of clouds. Then, the swirling gases started to glow, first purple, and then they brightened towards a shade of white.

I said I didn't believe in ghosts, but that's exactly what this creature looked like. Or rather like the kind of ghost that the child of my owners would dress up as every year during the autumn. He'd put a sheet over him, covering him completely except for the two slits he had cut out for eyes. This thing looked much the same, like a trailing bedsheet of light dragging along the ground.

"*Ah, you've found it,*" Salanraja said.

"*So, you can see it too, now?*"

"*Of course, I can. We're bonded, remember. What you see, I can see.*"

"*You mean you can see through my eyes?*"

"*Not quite. I only know instinctively what you're focusing on. If you listen to your senses, you'd be able to do the same thing with me.*"

The bone dragon roared out into the sky again, causing the ground to tremble. At the same time, a putrid smelling wind washed over the land. I turned up my nose, wanting to retch. Then, the Manipulator turned towards us, and I felt the sudden sensation of being watched, as if the thing was examining my very soul and trying to measure its worth in magic. The conjuration slinked forwards holding something in its hand. On closer inspection, I noticed it to be a staff just like the kind the dragon riders carried around with them. Except this one didn't have any physical shape, twisting and writhing in form alongside the rest of this wraith's body.

Meanwhile, the bone dragon wheeled around to face us in the sky. It opened its mouth and out came this strange purple flame. Strange, in the fact that it didn't glow like flame but instead looked like one column of roiling gas. Yet still it burned the reeds it touched underneath it, quickly withering them into ash.

"*Get off,*" Salanraja said.

"What? No! It will kill me."

"*Do as I say. You must fight the Manipulator, while I distract the bone dragon.*"

I screeched, then I realised that I had no choice. If I didn't jump off, Salanraja would throw me off, and the latter would hurt much more. I growled as I ran down her tail and leapt off it, just as Salanraja lifted herself up into the air.

I stalked towards the Manipulator, keeping down low, trying to work out where its arms and limbs were as I moved. It saw me and pointed its staff at me, tendrils of light leaking back from its body into the head. Something then shot out of it, a bolt of purple lightning, emitting no light.

It missed me by inches and hit the ground beside me. Out of it grew these red stems and brambles shooting out in all directions. One of these brambly stems lashed out at me, and I ducked out of the way. I looked up to see that the plant had now grown a head which looked like an elephant-sized tulip with sharp white teeth that gnashed up at the sky. It lurched down with this head, in an attempt to eat me whole.

I rolled out of the way, then looked back to see it take a massive chunk of dirt from the ground. It spat it out, sending it scattering in large chunks. Then, it turned to me and let out an incredible shriek, so high-pitched it hurt my sensitive ears.

"Bengie, stay away from that thing!" Salanraja said.

"State the obvious, why don't you," I said. I dared to look up into the air to see that Salanraja was now fleeing from the bone dragon. She rolled to avoid a jet of flame coming at her tail, and it looked like it almost grazed her. I'd seen what that flame had done to the reeds in the swamp, and I was pretty sure that Salanraja wouldn't fare so well against it either.

"Hurry up and go for the Manipulator and avoid its magic!" Salanraja said. *"I can't hold on like this forever."*

Back on the ground, the Manipulator had shot out more of those bolts in random directions, and a forest of these terrible plants had risen all around me. They'd created a foliage so thick I couldn't see the Manipulator through them anymore.

That was when I heard Astravar's voice. It boomed out from somewhere behind the thorny foliage, sending a shudder down my spine.

17

A WARLOCK'S RAGE

"You fool," Astravar said, his voice filling the sky like thunder. "You're a cat, a rare breed, I admit, which is why I summoned you into this world. But now you think you can go up against an all-powerful warlock. You're just a common moggie against one of the greatest mages who has ever lived."

I tried to find a way through the thorns, keeping down low so at least I could see the manipulator. I thought I caught sight of Astravar then. His skin was blue and was cracked just like the earth beneath him. His head had replaced the head of the Manipulator, bathing within its spooky glow.

I had to get through to him, but those thorny stems still twisted all around me, lashing into the earth and ripping it apart. That terrible purple gas was now seeping out from the base of these plants. It smelled like petals rotting in a compost bin – so overwhelming and powerful it made me want to faint.

The warlock's voice boomed out again. "What should I do with you, I wonder? You might make a nice taxidermy on the wall. But no, why should I let such a supple body go to waste? You can serve as a shade, hunting the rats I summon out of the Seventh Dimension. I have a need for their husks still. Although, I think I may have found a creature to replace you."

I hissed at him and then, suddenly, a sharp pain lanced through my flank. It wasn't from those flailing thorns in front of me. I had managed to evade them thus far. Instead, I felt the end of a long skeletal claw, tearing right between Salanraja's scales. Great, I could feel her pain like it was my own. That was all I needed. I yowled out, and Salanraja let out a deep bellowing roar at the same time.

"Hurry, Bengie," Salanraja said.

"I can't get through the thorns."

Salanraja paused a moment. *"Hang on, stay low."*

A moment later, a shadow passed over me, and then an intense heat flared out from the landscape in front of me. A bright, amber fire filled the forest there, and I felt it scorching at my skin beneath my fur.

"Ow!" I said.

"Just go, you fool."

I swallowed and focused on the flames roaring in front of me. The plants writhed and thrashed within their midst. They no longer whipped out towards me, but rather at the sky in a dying effort to survive.

I had to get through them. But the flames were so hot.

But I would die if I didn't. Or worse, Astravar would have me serving under him as one of his awful minions. Maybe I'd be like that bone dragon, unable to eat because I didn't even have a stomach inside my body. I shuddered at the thought.

The flames were extending even lower now, and I knew I only had a moment before I'd be unable to pass underneath them. So, I ran forward, keeping my shoulders loose so I could squeeze through the slightest gaps. The flames dashed across my back, and I grazed something. It was a thorn belonging to one of those toxic plants. I yelped out. But I couldn't lose focus.

Astravar had now left the Manipulator, which again had the staff raised, facing the bone dragon. It was feeding some kind of energy into it, sending up a purple gaseous stream laced with tendrils of white light.

In the sky above, Salanraja had now found her way behind the bone dragon. She had a crimson gash on her flank, right where I'd felt myself get hit. Salanraja opened her mouth and let out a stream of flame, bathing the bone dragon in amber. But the flames weren't enough to kill the bone dragon. Not while the Manipulator remained.

Salanraja glanced down at me from above. *"Gracious demons, focus on the Manipulator. Distract it, and maybe I can kill this thing."*

I turned back towards the Manipulator. But it didn't seem interested in me anymore. I heard something whip from behind me, and a fiery branch was sent spinning towards me. I dived out of the way, just in the nick of time.

But with that scratch I'd taken on the leg, I felt weak and nauseous. Astravar again appeared inside the body of the manipulator, staring down from behind his cracked blue face with cruel purple eyes. "You cannot defeat me. The poison will kill you, eventually."

Yet, he didn't turn the Manipulator's staff towards me, instead focusing all its attention to casting energy towards the bone dragon.

"Take it!" Salanraja screamed out in my mind. *"While you have the opportunity."*

"Take what?"

"The crystal, you idiot! The source of its power."

I readied myself down low, and I didn't hold my position too long. The light from the Manipulator was so bright now that I couldn't see where that crystal was. But judging from the way it moved, I guessed the crystal I needed was somewhere within its chest. I crouched, then I pounced, leaping as far as I could into the Manipulator's body, which seemed to have no physical form. I'd calculated it well, and I clasped my jaws around something solid.

I landed, then continued to sprint forwards. Something tugged back at me, as if I was running against a strong gale. I could hardly breathe, but still I continued. A stream of white light surrounded me, and I found it hard to see what was beyond me.

I didn't look back.

Then, there came a whoosh of wind from above me, and some claws closed around me like a vice. They didn't belong to Salanraja. I whined out as they lifted me into the sky.

18

CAT SANDWICH

I watched the ground spin away in front of me, then I looked back at my waist to see myself gripped in a skeletal claw. It was crushing me so hard that I thought it would squeeze all the life out of me.

"*Don't let go,*" Salanraja said. "*Whatever you do, don't let go.*"

Of course, I still had the crystal within my grasp. A white stream of light trailed out from it towards that wraith-like Manipulator that slid along the ground at the same speed as us. It was as if I was pulling it along with my own mouth, and the force of it pulling back against me seemed to want to rip me in two.

"*Keep it together,*" Salanraja said. "*Hold it for long enough up there, and the bone dragon will die.*"

I didn't have the will in my mind to respond. All I could feel was the life force leaching out of me. My vision went red, and I wondered for how long I'd be able to breathe. The muscles in my mouth had by this time gone completely numb, but I didn't drop the crystal.

I felt sick, and my head was spinning, and I didn't know if it was from vertigo, or from whatever poisons that thorn had injected into me back on the ground. I mewled, and I growled, and I groaned, but still I didn't let go.

The bone dragon was now lowering itself back down to the ground. If it stayed low enough, I realised, then the manipulator might regain its energy giving the bone dragon enough strength to crush the life out of me.

Suddenly, an intense orange fire raged up from below. It burned my dangling paws, and the searing pain that rushed up made me want to open my mouth and yowl. But I had to hold on. I couldn't let go of that crystal.

"Incoming," Salanraja said.

"I wish you'd said that earlier—"

But she wasn't talking about the fire, which the bone dragon instinctively lifted itself away from. Salanraja suddenly emerged underneath us. Then, she flapped her wings so hard that she pressed her back against the bone dragon's underbelly, sandwiching me in place. It felt like being squeezed in a vice, as she pushed upward, and the bone dragon fought with its dwindling strength to push back towards the Manipulator again. I genuinely thought I'd run out of air, and my eyes went blurry. I swear that I almost blacked out.

But Salanraja's voice brought me back to the present. *"Hold on, Bengie. Don't die on me."*

I wasn't dead. I was hyperventilating in the bone dragon's grasp that was no longer so tight on me. I could wriggle slightly now. My skin within its claws had started to tickle. I looked up to see that each bone was fragmenting into oblivion, drifting away like embers of burnt charcoal on the wind.

"We... Did we make it?" I asked.

"Conserve your strength," Salanraja replied. *"And just never do that again."*

"Never do what?"

"Never make me think you're going to die on me Bengie. We're bonded now, and I can't lose you. It would tear apart my soul."

The last vestiges of the bone dragon drifted away into the void, and the pressure lifted off of my back. I looked up into the cloudy sky, amazed to be alive. I ambled over to the edge of Salanraja's body, every muscle aching with every step I took. Down below, the forest that Astravar's Manipulator had created lay charred and dead. Those wilted stems now looked like black mummified claws sticking out of the ground.

Finally, it seemed safe to put the crystal down, and so I dropped it in between two of Salanraja's external ribs, then pawed it into a corner so it wouldn't end up falling to the ground. I was surprised how big it was. No wonder my jaw had ached carrying it.

"If you don't want me to die, don't put me in a situation where you might kill me," I replied. *"Simple solution."*

Salanraja groaned, sending a soft rumble through my legs. *"You never learn, do you? We're in this together, and it means we both need to take equal responsibilities. We'll both have to risk our lives sometimes if we're going to save this world."*

"But why should I care about your world? I wasn't born here. All I want is food, and a good rest after all that happened here."

"Because you saw what your crystal revealed, did you not? It's not just this world, but the fate of all worlds at threat. Once warlocks like Astravar control this planet, they won't stop there. Their lust for power has no bounds, and only brave souls like you and I can stop them."

I examined one of my paws and shuddered when I saw the char marks on it. *"But he's so powerful,"* I said. *"You've seen what he can do."* I tried to lick my paw so I could groom myself. But it hurt too much.

"He can be beaten," Salanraja replied. *"We have to believe that. They cannot win."*

"Whatever you say. Now, I remember you promising some food."

"Can't you ever think about anything else?"

"No..."

Salanraja laughed. But this time it sounded like a laugh of endearment rather than one of mockery.

"Fine," she said. *"Let's report our conquest to the village, and then I can hunt you something nice."*

19

MIDAR VILLAGE

Mutton was on the menu for the evening. A whole sheep, can you believe it? Though Salanraja didn't steal it or anything like that. We got it from Midar village for free.

The village elder came out to greet us as soon as we landed. It looked completely different to Dragonsbond Academy, and also completely different to the village I'd lived in, in South Wales. There were no stone houses here; everything was built of wood and straw. Honestly, with these dragons flying around that could flame these buildings and roast villagers in their sleep, it surprised me they'd be so stupid as to use flammable materials for building. Still, I'd never claimed humans were smart.

The village elder was an old man, no different looking than any other old man I'd seen. He hunched over a walking stick as he hobbled over on his two feet. This time, it was a regular old walking stick, and not a magical staff like Aleam's. It didn't have any crystals on it or any of that nonsense. Honestly, it felt good to meet someone normal for a change, so I jumped off Salanraja's back, as I rubbed myself against the side of his leg, purring away.

The old man looked up at Salanraja. "Where's your rider, dragon?" he asked.

"I am the rider," I replied, and then the man jumped up in surprise and almost toppled over.

"Oh," the man said after he'd recovered himself. "You can talk... Well, with the things that come out of the Wastelands, you're not the strangest thing I've seen by far."

"And what do you mean by that?"

"Nothing." The old man shook his head and laughed nervously. "Just beings of magic and all that."

"I'm not a magical being," I said. "I'm a Bengal. A descendant of the great Asian leopard cat. You should have some respect."

The man's jaw dropped, and Salanraja let off a loud groan. *"Will you stop it with that Asian leopard cat nonsense? None of us even know what it means."*

I ignored her and instead tried to glare the old man down.

He chuckled and then reached over to scratch me under the chin. I let him, but I didn't react with any signs of endearment. I still was unsure whether or not to trust him. He smelled funny.

"So, are you the dragon rider who defeated the bone dragon? Shepherd Rala, my granddaughter, bless her, saw it die while she was out grazing her flock. Before that, it had already taken the lives of most of the flock. I'm just glad Rala got out alive." He glanced over at a small pen containing several sheep, no more.

"I am that dragon rider," I said. "You got a problem with that?"

"No, not at all," the elder replied. "So, I guess, you'll be wanting a reward. We've got a good stash of gold in our village treasury reserved for incidents like this. Or maybe, if it would please the king, he'd rather have a few hundred yarns of our Midar wool?"

I growled, softly. He just wasn't getting it. "I'm starving, and I want food." I said.

The man paused a moment, looking at me with an expression of incredulity. "You want food?"

I looked back at the pen. The sheep in there looked fat and tasty. Though they weren't lambs, I could still make do with a bit of mutton. "One of your flock should do the trick," I said.

"Bengie, are you crazy?" Salanraja said to me.

"Shut up," I replied. "*I'm the one who speaks his language, so I'll make the necessary negotiations.*"

"*But they'll skin us alive at Dragonsbond Academy. We should take back some payment as a reward for the mission. It can help fund the academy and secure its future. Then they'll give you as much food as you like from the kitchens once they make you an Initiate.*"

"No," I said. "*I don't trust them, and you never seem to deliver on your promises either.*" I mewled and then rubbed my head up against the old man's leg.

Salanraja grunted, and the old man flinched, then looked at her sheepishly.

"Just ignore her," I said. "She's having a bad day. But I can tell that your village isn't the best stocked, and you need to recover from the terror. One sheep or lamb, if you have one, will do just fine."

The man tugged at the skin on the front of his neck. "Yes, well, that can be arranged, I guess." He turned back to the village and cupped his hand over his mouth. "Rala, take your fattest sheep to the slaughterhouse."

"Oh, no need," I said. "Salanraja will slaughter it herself."

"*Will I now?*"

"*You did promise to hunt something nice for me,*" I replied. "*I just thought I'd make it a little easier on you.*"

"*Gracious demons, you're an idiot...*"

The elder's granddaughter had now arrived, a tall thin woman with blonde hair, wearing a long white shepherd's frock. They were whispering between themselves. I adjusted my ears so I could hear them a little better.

"I think we can give them Colos," she said. "He'll make a fine meal, I guess." She rubbed her eyes with the back of her hand and let off a slight sniffle.

"Just point to the sheep you wish to donate, and we'll be on our way," I said.

Rala turned back to me and pointed over to the pen. "That one, eating grass by the fence. She'll be the tastiest, I think. Take her and thank you. I was so worried when I saw the bone dragon, I thought our village would be the next to fall to the Wastelands." She sniffled again.

"You're welcome," I replied, and I walked over to her and pushed my head against her shin.

But she seemed stiff and didn't really want to stroke me. So, I ran back up onto Salanraja's back. "You heard them. Take that sheep closest to the fence."

Salanraja grunted again, and then she beat her wings and flew up into the sky. The way she was behaving, I thought she was going to fly away without the sheep, but she swooped after a moment and took up the defenceless farm animal in her talons.

The sun was setting on the horizon, and it stretched across the green and yellow fields, casting its warm rays of protection as its own way of saying farewell.

A FEAST MOST FINE

A fter dropping the sheep from a great height and roasting it to mutton, Salanraja had left me to guard our meal while she went off in search of firewood. We'd camp for the night, she'd told me, and I was okay with that idea as long as we had food. Though I asked why we needed a fire when I had a fur coat to keep me warm.

But she said it was traditional on these kinds of journeys. If I was a human, I'd appreciate it. Admittedly, now darkness had fallen, the night was getting pretty cold, even for a cat.

Salanraja soon returned with a tree trunk in her claws. I looked up from my feast of mutton, which I'd already started, and licked my lips.

"*Couldn't you just hold on for one minute?*" she asked. "*The dragon should always get first bite of her hunt.*"

"*But you didn't hunt it,*" I said.

"*I killed it. Because, I seem to recall you saying that it was far too big for you to kill yourself.*"

"*Will you be quiet? I'm trying to enjoy my food here.*" I turned back to the carcass and ripped another chunk of tasty mutton off of its belly.

There came a rush of wind against my fur and I saw something massive falling fast towards me in my peripheral vision. I screeched and darted out of a way of the tree trunk, right before it thudded against the ground, sending up tufts of grass and soil.

"*What the whiskers do you think you're doing?*"

"*I said we needed firewood,*" Salanraja replied. "*And here it is.*"

"*But you could have crushed the life out of me with that thing...*"

"*Oh, I was quite careful where I dropped it, thank you very much.*" Salanraja landed on the ground next to the log and tore off some strips of bark with her teeth and claws. She moved fast, and she soon had a tall pile of loose wood on the ground between us and the mutton. She turned to this and let off a fast jet of flame at it, which ignited at once.

I watched her cautiously for a moment, but she didn't seem to be in the mood for roasting me as well as the mutton. So, I approached the carcass, tore off another strip of meat, and then I took it over in my mouth towards the fire.

Now the warmth was there, I realised how much I appreciated it. It reminded me of being back in South Wales in winter, curled up on the mistress' lap in front of the fireplace as she rocked gently back and forth on her armchair, a book in her hands. I missed that place and I couldn't help wishing that all this was a bad dream. That I'd wake up tomorrow back in my cushioned bed on the living room floor, with a breakfast of salmon trimmings waiting for me in the kitchen.

But how could I be thinking about salmon when this mutton tasted so wonderful?

"*I hope you're enjoying that,*" Salanraja said. "*Given how you damaged a poor family's livelihood to take it.*"

"It's good," I said, and I licked my lips. "*What was that you said about livelihood?*"

"*Didn't you hear them say? The bone dragon slaughtered most of their flock. They had, as I counted it, six sheep left. Before that, they probably had at least sixty.*"

"*So?*"

"*So, they now need to rebuild their flock and taking one of their sheep away when they have so few is going to make it much harder for them to do that. You may have ruined that family, and you don't even seem to care.*"

I dropped the mutton on the ground. Suddenly, it didn't taste so good anymore. *"Why didn't you tell me?"* I asked.

"Would it have made any difference? You would have acted the same, anyway."

"I'm not sure I would." I said. *"And I think I've had enough mutton for one day."*

"Well..." Salanraja looked into the distance. *"This is what happens when you go around acting on a whim all the time. You need to put some thought into your actions, Bengie."*

"Whatever," I replied, and I yawned. The heat from the fire was reminding me how tired I was. *"I'll know better next time."*

"That's the thing. There might not be a next time. If word gets back to the Council how you behaved there, there will go your chances of becoming an Initiate. You'll be stuck in the cattery while I'll have to ferry the king's pompous relatives across the land."

"And how long will it take for them to hear?"

"Probably when the next tax collector comes."

"Which will be?" I asked.

"At the end of the year, I should think."

"So, we've got plenty of time then, because it's not even winter yet."

"That's not the point, it's the principle of it."

"Well, my principle is I need a good night's sleep so I can present our mission's success respectably before the Council tomorrow..."

Salanraja snorted, but she said nothing more on the subject. Even though I was pretending to be nonchalant about the whole mutton incident, I did feel terrible about it. Really, though, I didn't know why. These humans had given me food when I'd needed food, and that was the way the whole cat-human relationship was meant to work.

There was a cool breeze in the air, which added a pleasant sensation to the warmth coming from the fire. Underneath this breeze, I soon drifted off to sleep.

21

A NIGHTMARE MOST FOUL

My body still ached from both the burns and being crushed before, and I kept tossing and turning as I slept. But eventually, I found a comfortable spot to dream, and I saw myself in a long meadow, chasing dragonflies underneath the shade of a sad willow. The air was warm, and my master, mistress, and their son were nearby. The adults sat on a picnic blanket while the son was laughing and rolling through the grass.

Suddenly the air became chilly, and the sky took on a purple hue. A massive blue head arose from the horizon, its skin cracked like an eggshell. It looked down on me, emanating a glow like the rising sun, except this glow washed away any warmth left in the air, rendering me shivering and helpless.

I wasn't in the valley anymore. I was in a land of swamps and a purple, lifeless gas. No one was around to keep me company, other than those wisp-like creatures, the Manipulators. There must have been thousands of them scattered out across the landscape, filling it with ghostly pockets of white light. Each of them looked up as if in reverence towards Astravar's cruel face that was growing and growing in the sky. Soon, it got so large that it stretched from one end of the horizon to the other. His lips curled upward as he glared at me with those cruel grey eyes.

Then he laughed. But it wasn't a laugh of joy, it was a laugh with one sole purpose, to instil terror into the soul of anyone who heard it. To communicate that there was no greater power in this world than him. Then his gaze spun downwards and focused on me, and I had the sensation of being watched not just by him but by thousands of different creatures at once.

"You were a fool when I met you, and you remain a fool. Do you think by bonding with a dragon I won't be able to find you? Do you think you can truly escape the power of a warlock?"

My legs felt heavy and rooted to the spot, as if someone had put my feet in special manacles designed for cats. As Astravar continued to stare at me, his eyes gained a pale shade of blue, and my body felt colder and colder. I felt like I was stuck out in the snow with no shelter to hide in. I thought for a moment that I might die.

But I could not die here. I had to run. So, I mustered up strength, and pulled my legs off the ground. I didn't have my normal agility, and each step felt like I was dragging my feet through a pool of thick honey.

I trudged between the Manipulators, who each turned their heads to look down at me as I passed. I looked up at one and saw Astravar's face where the manipulator's head should be. His pale blue eyes glared down at me. His gaze seemed able to strip my life force away from me, as if he could reach inside me with his mind and yank out my soul.

I continued dragging myself along the ground, not knowing where I was going. I didn't care. I just wanted to escape. But each time I even thought I'd made some progress, I'd be right in front of a Manipulator again, staring up at it, the warlock's cruel gaze boring into me.

"Stop!" I screamed out. "Stop, stop, stop, stop, stop!"

I looked back up at the horizon. Nothing had changed. Astravar's head was still there, massive and unforgiving.

"You cannot escape me, Dragoncat," he said. "You swallowed my magic at the Versta Caverns, and now I exist burrowed inside your body where you'll never find me. Eventually I'll hunt you down, and I'll claim you back as my own."

I stopped trying to run. I had to face up to him. I had to speak my mind. "What do you want with me?" I asked. "Why did you have to bring me into this world? I had a good, comfortable home. And now you hunt me when all I want to do is live my life."

Astravar again roared out that terrible, derisive laugh. "You are such a pathetic creature," he said. "You're a scavenger who thrives on the service of others. What would your life be if I took everyone you relied on away from you? No creature that cannot survive alone deserves to live on this world, or any world for that matter."

"I'm domesticated," I said. "It's not my fault. I was born that way."

"Were you?" Astravar replied. "Because I believe you were born to be feral, and I shall make you feral again once I find you. And your dragon, she will serve me too."

I whimpered inside my throat. I hated this man. But I couldn't fight him. He was too strong.

"What do you want of me?" I said again. "Why are you here, visiting this dream?"

"I came to tell you you've failed. You disrupted an experiment when you killed my Manipulator. But if you meddle again, I will come out and destroy you with my own hands."

"An experiment?"

"A demon dragon," Astravar said. "The first one to have been brought forth from the Seventh Dimension for thousands of years. I will bring it into this world, and it will hunt down all of the dragons that protect Illumine Kingdom and convert them to my cause. You shall serve me once again, Dragoncat. Do you like the new name I've assigned to you? It's ironic, don't you think?"

An intense chill washed over me, as if an icy wind had just appeared from nowhere. It rushed past my face, and it was so strong and in my face that whichever direction I turned, I couldn't escape it. I couldn't breathe. I was going to die here. This was the end, and my life would come to nothing.

As the wind rushed past my ears, I heard him laughing in my head.

He wouldn't shut up. He wouldn't go away. "Farewell, Dragoncat. Until we meet again."

I awoke into a night blanketed by cold darkness, suddenly aware of how cruel life was.

22

A TERRIBLE SICKNESS

I wasn't sure if it was because of Astravar finding me in my dream, because of the poison, or because of the crushing I'd taken when sandwiched between two dragons, but I got increasingly ill on the journey back. My fur, and probably the skin beneath, was literally turning green, and I vomited on Salanraja's back at least three times, much to her chagrin.

Eventually, she turned her head back to me nestled in the cage. *"What is wrong with you?"* she asked.

"I don't know," I replied. I couldn't help feeling queasy.

"Probably the mutton didn't go down too well with you," she said, and barked out a laugh. *"Talk about irony."*

I wasn't in the mood for joking around. *"No, it's not that. The thorn from those toxic plants the Manipulator created. You told me not to get scratched by one, but I did. It must have gone much deeper than I thought."*

Part of me wanted to tell her about Astravar and that horrible dream. But I knew such a conversation would also lead to admitting to swallowing the golem's crystal back in the Versta Caverns. Somehow, I didn't think she'd react well to that.

It bothered me though, because what Astravar had said about the demon dragon sounded somehow significant. It really sounded like something I should tell her. But Salanraja had already said that I was in trouble with the Council of Three, and I didn't want to give her information that might make things worse.

"*You should see Aleam when you land. He'll fix you up. He's good with healing and stuff,*" Salanraja said.

"*Maybe I will,*" I replied. "*Or maybe I'm just going to die soon. It's been a good life, Salanraja. I had lots of salmon and roast chickens. And that mutton, even though I shouldn't have asked for it... Now, I feel complete.*"

"*Stop it,*" Salanraja replied. "*You're not going to die on me, you idiot. You've still got a lot in you yet.*"

"*What do you care?*" I said, licking my paw.

"*Because we're bonded now, and that means I care about your wellbeing, believe it or not. And I should hope you also care about mine.*"

But by that point, I was getting all bleary-eyed, and I soon drifted off to sleep.

I was woken up by the thud of Salanraja landing on cobblestones. I rolled down her tail before I could open my eyes, and then I yowled out when I hit the floor.

"*Sorry,*" Salanraja said.

"*Couldn't you have landed a little more softly? I was having pleasant dreams.*"

"*No. Now just get up and see Aleam.*"

I picked myself up to see that we'd landed inside Salanraja's chamber. On the other side of the room, half a cow had been skinned and laid out for her. It wasn't roasted yet and, in all honesty, I didn't feel so hungry. I just felt dizzy, and a little nauseous.

"*I thought you'd at least drop me off outside Aleam's door.*"

"*What? Are you crazy? Dragons can't land inside the bailey. It's against the code.*"

"*Why? It's not as if you'll eat anyone.*"

"*We might,*" Salanraja replied. "*It hasn't been unknown.*"

I groaned, and picked myself up on all fours, my legs wobbling as I stretched. I half thought they wouldn't hold me, and I'd just collapse here and die. My fur still had that green sickly hue, and it was getting even greener. What kind of disease did this, anyway? Ailments might affect a cat's eyes, nose, and ears, but I'd never known of anything to attack the fur.

But maybe Astravar was delivering on his promise early. He already had his magic inside me, and he'd injected me with his poison. Soon, if he had his way, my skin might slink off my bones and my soul might drop out of me. By tomorrow, I could be reduced to a feral skeletal cat that skulked about Dragonsbond Academy by night, murdering every living cat that I encountered.

Then, the rats here would multiply, and Astravar would work even more magic to turn them into demon rats. Dragonsbond Academy could be doomed.

It was probably the fear of what I might become that kept me padding through the bailey, following the path that Aleam had led me over just a couple of days ago. As I walked, I passed men and women, some of them in common clothes, others in uniform. All of them stared at me disdainfully as I passed. Then they backed away as if I was carrying some kind of plague.

For all I knew, I might have been.

I kept my head low as I went, half expecting an arrow to take me down from one of the walls. Then I heard some shouting from the guardhouse at the gate, and three heavyset men in shiny armour stormed over to me, shouting something. But my head was spinning so hard, I couldn't understand a word they said.

One of them lifted a sword into the air, and I was ready for it to come down on me and chop me in half. But a door opened behind me, and out of it stepped an old man in a brown robe, carrying a staff. Aleam, I recognised his voice, and he said something to the guards which calmed them down.

Aleam took me up in his arms, and he whisked me back into his study.

"What happened, Ben?" he said softly, as he stroked me under my chin. He lifted my leg and examined the cut there. "This is a Mandragora's work. You poor thing. Don't worry. The spell can be reversed if we act fast."

He dropped me onto a rug, next to the warmth of a roaring fire-place. I glanced across the long room and I caught a glimpse of Ta'ra lying on the bench. She saw me, and stood up, then jumped over the top of the sofa and hid behind it. She peeked out from behind the edge of it.

Aleam turned to look at her. "Don't worry, it's only Ben. Not a demon. He's been hurt."

"Ben?" Ta'ra said, and she walked out from behind her sofa, but still kept a safe distance. "What happened to you, you idiot?"

But I wasn't in any state to answer, because I felt a sudden wave of queasiness. The world around me was spinning, and I vomited on the floor. Shortly afterwards, I blacked out.

23

FOOD IS NOT FOR SHARING

I woke up to the smell of salmon, and for a moment I thought that I'd awoken from this terrible dream and returned home. But I hadn't, as it was Ta'ra's breath I smelled. She lay snuggled up beside me on the rug, her face right next to mine, seemingly appreciating my warmth as the fireplace had run out of fuel. I leapt right on to my feet.

"What the whiskers are you doing there, Ta'ra?" I screamed out in the cat tongue. She opened her eyes and blinked at me. I remembered then that she didn't speak cat, so I said it again in the human language.

Ta'ra yawned and then lifted herself up on all fours. She stretched, shaking as she did so, and she sat back down and gazed at me lazily.

"Oh relax," she said. "Don't you like having a pretty lady next to you?"

I arched my back. "Last time we were fighting, and now you think we're chums?"

Ta'ra yawned once again and snapped her mouth shut. She shook her head, which meant that she either had problems with her ears or she hadn't quite lost the need for that pointless humanoid gesture.

"Such a typical cat. I thought you were having interesting dreams, and I wanted to watch them for a while. I had no idea so much could go on in that little head of yours. You're very unlike the other cats here."

I snarled at her, then I said, "Weirdo."

"Whatever," Ta'ra said and stalked towards her bench.

Aleam was standing over his desk, gazing into his alembic as the solution boiled within. It had more of a green hue to it today. He was so engrossed in whatever he was doing that he didn't notice me approach until I meowed at him. He turned towards me and examined me over his glasses.

"Oh, you've awakened. Thank gracious. I thought for a while we might lose you. Salanraja looked so worried, you know. She hasn't eaten since dusk yesterday."

"Dusk," I said. "How long was I out?"

"The entire night and the morning after." Aleam said. "But after a bit of sage balm and a little white magic, I managed to get the poison out of you. Fortunately, it didn't go so deep. Just be more careful next time you ever have to fight anything like that again."

"I don't intend to," I replied. "All I want is to find a way home."

Aleam laughed. "I'm sure you will one day. Although you have to accept that it might take some time."

The alembic apparatus whistled at him and some steam rose from a pipe at the top of it. Presently, some green solution dripped out of the tap at the end into a vial. Aleam picked this up and took it over to Ta'ra who was now sitting on the sofa. "Here, drink this," he said, offering it to her.

She looked at the vial. "I'm not sure I want to. I'm starting to quite enjoy being a cat."

"What? Nonsense. You were moaning about it yesterday."

Ta'ra glanced at me, then looked away when she noticed me glaring at her. "Fine," she said. "One drop won't make much difference."

Aleam raised the vial to her mouth, and I took the opportunity to jump up on the table. The alembic was the only reflective object in sight, and I wanted to get a good look at myself. I found a spot that had plenty of liquid behind the bulb, and I examined my reflection.

Aleam had done a good job. I had my leopard-style markings back, and my skin had that beautiful amber colour to it again.

"Hey, get down from there," Aleam called out and shook his staff at me. "That's Ta'ra's cure. We can't have anything happen to it."

Ta'ra licked her lips and then examined her paw. "Whatever," she said. Something had certainly changed about her.

I jumped down from the table and I walked over to her, then I looked up at her, licking my lips. "What?" she asked.

"You, you just seem different. What's got into you?"

"I just thought that it's not that bad being a cat, that's all," Ta'ra replied. "The food's good. The humans think you're cute. As long as I can talk to them, I can be their advisor or something. I'm sure they won't assign me to catching rats."

I couldn't help but laugh, and I did so in a very human and mocking voice. "You think you'll ever learn to be a cat? You don't have it in your genes."

"Don't have what in my genes?"

"The grace. The ability to balance. You don't even know how to walk like a cat."

"Of course I do," Ta'ra said, and she jumped off the sofa and walked along the straight line between the floorboards in a particularly inelegant way. "See?"

"That's not how you do it," I replied. "Your feet don't meet."

She scowled at me. "What do you mean they don't meet? I don't want to be tripping over myself."

I groaned, then I showed her how it was done. "Your back paws should hit exactly where your front paws land, like this see?" I walked in a straight line with my head held up high. I didn't even need to focus on it – I'd been doing this since I was a kitten.

Ta'ra looked at me and blinked. "What's the point of that?"

"It makes us harder to track," I said, proudly. "It also makes us quieter. Although..." I looked down at her feet. "... you're not going to be stealthy if you don't learn to stand on your toes."

Ta'ra tucked her head inwards. "Fine, I'll practice," she said. "Maybe you can teach me to be more ladylike." She approached me and rubbed her head against my cheek. Then, she pattered over to Aleam, who was now focusing again on the alembic, and she meowed.

Aleam scratched behind her ear. Then he walked over to a high cupboard, reached inside, and tossed down some fish for Ta'ra. The aroma from it assaulted my senses. It was smoked trout!

"Hey," I called out. "What about me? I haven't eaten for ages." I didn't mention the feast of mutton that I'd gorged on before my flight back. Though, at least this fish wouldn't taste of bitter guilt.

"Very well," Aleam said. "You too." He tossed some more pink fish down on the floor, a little away from Ta'ra. As soon as he did, though, Ta'ra walked over to protect it.

I hissed at her, arching my back. "Hey that's my food," I said.

Ta'ra laughed. "No it's not. It came out of my cupboard, and so it's mine."

"What do you mean, your cupboard? Is this your floor too?" I scowled at Ta'ra.

"Will you cats stop fighting?" Aleam said. "I'm trying to concentrate."

Ta'ra looked down at the food, then she touched it with her paw. "Fine," she said. "You eat it then. But remember, I'm doing you a favour."

"And I'll teach you how to eat it properly someday," I called after her as she stalked back over to her pile of food.

Just as I'd taken a good mouthful of the fish and was starting to chew down on it, there came a banging from the doorway. The young Initiate Rine – that spotty-faced teenager – was standing there hammering the base of his staff against the floor so hard that it hurt my sensitive eardrums.

Aleam spun around from his alembic and glared at the boy. "Do you have to make such a racket?" he said. "I'm trying to work."

Rine had a grin stretched across his face that was so smarmy that I wanted to slash it off, if only I could reach that high. "I'm sorry," he said. "The Council of Three wanted me to alert you that they need your presence. Not you, Driar Aleam, the cat."

He looked down at me with that same grin and a knowing look, as if to tell me he had learned of a secret of mine. But what that secret might be, I had no idea.

"Fine," I said. "Just let me finish my food." I took another mouthful of the delicious moist fish.

"No," Initiate Rine replied. "I'm afraid they want to see you immediately, no time to eat." He walked forward and shooed me towards the door with the base of his staff.

"Hey, what do you think you're doing?"

"I said now!" Initiate Rine said.

I realised I had no choice but to follow him out of the room.

It seemed so familiar – being whisked away from my breakfast of smoked fish by an arrogant magic user. The sounds of Ta'ra's laughter followed me out the door. I didn't look over my shoulder, but I could swear she'd moved in at the first opportunity so she could go back to eating my fish.

24

FRESHCAT BEN

Salanraja was already waiting in the Council of Three's courtyard when I ducked underneath the arch to meet them. She hadn't spoken to me since I'd recovered, and I figured she was angry again about the mutton incident. Why she had to let things stew so much, I had no idea. Now, she had her nostrils flared out, was growling from the base of her chest, and I could feel her rage burning there as if it was my very own.

Really though, I didn't understand what she was so upset about. We had completed our mission, so she would look great and get the praise she wanted. Then I would become an Initiate and I'd gain the favour of the Council of Three. After that, all I needed to do was find a nice man or woman somewhere in this castle who could summon a portal for me to go home.

"Why didn't you just call me?" I said. *"Why did you have to send that annoying Initiate Rine?"*

"Because," Salanraja replied. *"All I could hear going on in your mind was food, food, food, food, food, and I knew I didn't have a chance of drag-ging you away from your gluttony using just my mind."*

I turned up my head. *"I would have come. The food will always be there later."*

"Will it?" Salanraja asked. *"Because I don't think you ever quite believe that."*

I whined and then turned away from the dragon. I was having a good day so far, and I didn't want her dragging me down with her negativity. This would be my moment of glory, and my opportunity to finally return home.

Driar Yila, Driar Lonamm, and Driar Brigel already had their staffs raised up to the crystal over their heads, and they were feeding their energy into it. The three Driars watched me as I moved further forward, and I looked at each Driar in an attempt to work out what they were thinking. But their faces didn't register much emotion.

"You summoned me," I said to them once I was standing right in front of their raised platform. "Here I am, and I'm sure you've heard that our mission went well. Now, if you—"

Driar Yila's sharp voice cut me off as her expression melted into a frown. "We've heard very well about your mission, and it was a complete failure as far as we're concerned."

"What?" I said, and my eyes opened wide in shock. "But we defeated the bone dragon..."

"We defeated the bone dragon, Ma'am."

I blinked at her.

"Say it," Driar Yila said. "It's about time you learned to speak respectfully."

"Fine," I said. "We defeated the bone dragon, Ma'am."

"Good. Now, from now on, remember that you shall refer to all other superiors as ma'am and sir. Is that understood?"

"As you wish," I said.

"As you wish, Ma'am."

"As you wish, Ma'am." I accompanied this with a reverent and sorrowful meow. Then, I walked up to the platform and put one foot on it, hoping that I could at least cheer them up by being cute.

"Get down off there, you filthy mongrel," Driar Yila said, and she swung her staff forwards and pointed it at me, cutting off for a moment her stream of white light that fed the crystal. I didn't want to be at the receiving end of whatever magic would be at the end of that, so I growled and then moved out of the way.

"You really know how to make a name for yourself, don't you?" Salanraja said.

I turned to her. *"I'll make it right,"* I replied. *"Where's the Manipulator's crystal?"*

"It's on my back where you left it."

"I'll get it," I said, and I sprinted around the back of her and then ran up her tail. I reached the corridor of her back, and I clasped my mouth around the crystal, then returned to the ground and dropped it right beneath the council's platform.

"You don't seem to believe we defeated the bone dragon, but I brought proof. Here is the source of the Manipulator responsible for controlling the creature. Once I stole the crystal away from the source, the bone dragon ceased to exist."

"There you go," Salanraja said. *"Take all the credit, why don't you?"*

I ignored her. I was focused on making the council happy, not her.

"So, tell us, little one," Driar Lonamm said. She leaned forward, and her broad frame cast an ominous shadow over me. "What did you do after you'd defeated this bone dragon? We know the story, but we want to hear it from the horse's mouth."

"I'm not a horse," I snapped back. "I'm a Bengal, a descendant of the great Asian leopard cat... Ma'am."

"Do you ever stop?" Salanraja chimed.

"Shut up!"

Driar Lonamm was watching me with narrowed eyes. "Fine. We heard it right from the Bengal's mouth," she said with a smirk. "Now answer my question. And before you think of lying to us, cat, know that we sent a shadow dragon rider to Midar Village to assess your eligibility as a fledgling Initiate. He followed you and he has already returned and delivered his report."

Whiskers, they knew something. I lowered my head. "I claimed my reward, Ma'am," I said. "The villagers offered me what I wanted, and so I took it."

"They offered you what you wanted?" Driar Brigel said. He no longer had that kind look on his face, but instead a rather disappointed one. "Why didn't you take what would be good for the academy and the kingdom? Tell us, do you want to serve this kingdom, or do you want to serve yourself?"

I groaned, frustrated at the idiocy of these people. "I want to go home," I screamed out. "Why is that so hard for you people to understand?"

"That's never going to happen," Driar Yila shot back. "You're a mangy, uneducated cat, and no one in this realm is going to waste powerful magic and energy on helping you cross dimensions."

Now that hurt, and not so much the part of being called mangy – even though that was an insult to my pride – but rather because I knew in my heart of hearts that Driar Yila was right. I didn't have a chance of returning home.

I lowered myself to the floor. I didn't know what to say, but I had to say something.

"Does that mean I can't become a dragon rider now?" I turned back to Salanraja, and some smoke rose out of her nostrils. She really looked like she wanted to toast me alive.

"You see, that's the problem," Driar Brigel said. "The crystal did choose you, and we can't just ignore its request. But none of us present can quite understand the reason for it."

"Because I'm a Bengal," I said and slinked out from behind my cover so I could raise my head up high. Maybe they were finally starting to understand. "But I'm not just a Bengal. From what I've learned about this place, it sounds like I'm the only Bengal in the world."

"I don't doubt you are," Driar Brigel replied, and he placed one hand on his chin. "But you are also selfish, arrogant, and unsuited for the role that has been chosen for you. Or at least, right now, it seems that way."

"So, what will you have me do? Will you send me out on another mission?" I shuddered at the thought of fighting another one of those bone dragons, or one of those golems I'd fought in the Versta Caverns. I still had that horrible taste of clay in my mouth.

"No," Driar Brigel said. "This isn't about what to do next, but your attitude about it all. Do you know what the consequences could be about the way you behaved in this village?"

"I don't," I replied.

"I believe Salanraja gave you some hints. But it's not just about the villagers. Fortunately, our Driar replaced that sheep for them."

I purred. "So, all's well that ends well."

"No," Driar Brigel snapped back. "Because unless you learn from your mistakes, you will continue to make them. Imagine what would happen if every dragon rider behaved like you did. Villagers would stop supporting the kingdom, meaning the king's realm would dry up from the inside. We'd lose funding to this academy, meaning dragon riders wouldn't get trained. That would weaken the king's forces and allow the warlocks to gain power. Negligence costs lives, you see. You need to think big in a position of responsibility, not just about yourself."

I lowered my head. When he put it that way, maybe he was right. Though I still had no idea how I could put my wishes of my tummy behind the needs of a kingdom. "I'm sorry," I said.

Driar Brigel nodded. "Admitting that is the first step, and for the first time I believe you." He looked at Driar Yila, then at Driar Lonamm, and they both gave him a nod. "So, we have decided what to do with you. You need to prove yourself to us before we even consider your schooling. We will therefore assign you a rank no one has had since we created this academy. From this day, until we feel you're ready, you will be a freshman."

"A freshman?" I said, and it wasn't the sexist nature of that rank that I objected to. "But I'm a cat."

"Fine," Driar Brigel said. "From this day on, you'll be assigned the rank of Freshcat."

"Freshcat?" Whiskers, I was making it worse. Now, I sounded like something you might order from an illegal butcher.

"Freshmoggie?" Driar Lonamm offered.

"No, no," I said. "Freshcat will do just fine."

"Very well," Driar Brigel said. "Freshcat Ben it is... Actually, I quite like the sound of that. So, from this day you can attend classes, eat in the dining hall, and you must obey the needs of any prefect or Driar on campus, as well as Initiate Rine who will serve as your temporary guardian. Is that understood?"

"Yes, sir," I said, and a cold shiver ran down my spine. Perhaps I wouldn't so much mind taking orders from the Council of Three – though they weren't particularly nice, they also didn't seem particularly needy.

But when I thought about the smarmy attitude of that Initiate Rine, someone like him would have me delivering newspapers to his feet like a dog. That was if they even had newspapers in this world, I have to admit in South Wales I always found them a little peculiar. They seemed to serve no purpose at all other than to be good for tearing up and as a cheap lining for my litter tray.

In all honesty, I couldn't understand how dogs could wrap their mouths around something that would end up in a litter tray. It was almost as bad as drinking toilet water. Dogs were disgusting creatures, really.

Anyway, I digress.

Driar Brigel stood watching me for a moment, and his look of kindness had returned to him. "Let's get this ceremony out of the way then," he said.

"Agreed," Driar Lonamm said, and Driar Yila nodded once slowly, but didn't say anything.

The three Driars raised their staffs high above their heads, and the light that streamed out of their crystals got brighter. The streams converged at a point on the front face of the crystal, and then they reflected off that point right into my chest. At first, I thought I should flee, but I was rooted to the spot, unable to move.

"Wait," Driar Yila said, and she narrowed her eyes to slits and looked right at me. "I sense something in there." The beam from her staff became red, and it suddenly felt as if something was trying to pull me back towards the crystal.

A headache pounded against my skull, and I felt like I was being searched, as if something was invading my mind and prying out all the private things in there. The pull intensified, and the surrounding air took on a strength of its own. I reached out with my claws and dug them into the stone beneath me to try to stay rooted to the spot.

Driar Lonamm's eyes shot open, and her light turned blue. "A warlock's crystal. Inside him. He's a creation of Astravar's. We've been tricked. We must kill it at once, before he does any more damage."

Driar Brigel opened his eyes a little more slowly. "Oh, I don't think he is," he said, and his light turned green. The magic lifted me into the air until I was suspended inches from the ground. The air swirled around me, becoming a strong whirlwind that beat against my sides. I felt like I was going to throw up. "See, this memory? The cat swallowed the crystal on his own will."

That was when I saw it in the crystal above my head. It was showing flashes of my memories, just as I visualised in my head. I could see myself up there, clawing clumsily against the golem as I slid around on his arm and then knocked the crystal out of his eye. Really, I'd thought I'd executed the manoeuvre more elegantly than that. It was strange seeing me from the outside.

Then I was sinking and sinking into the mud, and Salanraja lunged in to save me. But before she could reach me, the vision showed me lurching out with my head so I could cover the crystal with my mouth.

"*You fool,*" Salanraja said. "*You swallowed the crystal, and you didn't tell me about it. Gracious demons, we're finished.*"

But I didn't have the will to answer. I was just floating above the ground, pinned in place by the Council of Three's magical energy, and I couldn't wriggle, let alone think.

Suddenly the light cut off, and I fell back to the floor. I landed on my feet, fortunately; thank the whiskers for my flexible spine. But still, the landing sent a jolt of pain up through my legs and right down my back.

"What do we do now?" Driar Lonamm asked.

Driar Brigel shook his head. "We can't get the crystal out, unfortunately, as the warlock's magic has lodged it inside his body. We also can't undo the crystal's assignment and I think it would be unwise to do so."

"Still," Driar Yila said, "the cat must be kept under strict guard."

"We'll instruct Initiate Rine not to let him out of his sight," Driar Brigel said. "He's a promising young student, that one. I'm sure he'll stop any signs of the warlock trying to take control."

"Very well," Driar Lonamm said. She looked at me. "Freshcat Ben, congratulations on your new rank. However, you should have told us about this rather dire complication." She then cupped her hands over her mouth and shouted out in such a loud volume that I scurried behind Salanraja's leg.

"Initiate Rine!" she called.

There came a scuffling sound from behind me, and the spotty-faced teenager appeared at the entrance to the courtyard. "Yes, Ma'am."

"We need you to keep this cat under guard, and if you see any sign of him becoming evil, you must terminate him at once."

25

GOOD HYDRATION

After my beating from the Council, the three Great Driars dismissed me and told me to spend a little time with Initiate Rine. The spotty-faced kid didn't look too happy about it, and stared down at me with an expression of contempt. Honestly, I didn't get what his problem was. To him, I could be a useful sidekick. Having a cat around him might cause the girls around him to forget about his spots and focus on his sensitive nature. That was, if he had anything to him underneath his pompous exterior.

He walked over to the archway while the Council cut off the streams of the light from the crystal and then shuffled in their robes towards a door at the back. Brigel and Lonamm entered it, while Driar Yila turned to regard me with her harsh, scornful frown, and then she shooed me away with the back of her hand and lifted her staff slightly.

Scared of being turned into a dog or something, I decided it better to follow Initiate Rine. He was waiting for me by the archway, playing a game where he tossed a coin in the air, then landed it on the back of his hand. I followed the movements of the coin for a moment, wanting to bat it off its flight path. But it was too high up.

The young Driar looked down at me and laughed. "Whatever they say about you, you're still a cat, aren't you? I guess nothing will change that."

I narrowed my eyes. "I'm not just a cat. I'm a Bengal, a descendant of the great Asian leopard cat."

"So I've heard," Initiate Rine said. "And I'm an Alterian, descendant of the great King Zod." He flashed me an ugly, toothy grin.

I didn't like the mocking tone in his voice. "You are nothing compared to me," I told him. "You have no grace, you can't even walk in a straight line, and if I dropped you from the top of the tower you wouldn't land on your feet."

He scoffed, then looked up at the tower above us. A green dragon flew out of one of the openings high up in the tower and roared out into the sky. Driar Brigel was on the dragon, his head shining in the sun and his green-gemmed staff swinging on his back. He had managed to climb up the tower pretty quickly, and I wondered if he did so using magic.

Another dragon flew after him on its tail. This one was as yellow as lemon and had two long spikes that stuck out from both corners of its jaw. A young man sat on a saddle on its back, wearing a tabard with the symbol of a sun and moon on it over a burnished coat of silver armour. He had long black hair that whipped back behind him in the wind, and a faceted face that reminded me of one of those crystals.

"Where are they going?" I asked.

"Why's that any of your business?" Rine replied.

"Because I'm a freshcat now, one of your club."

"Exactly, which means you have to do exactly what I say, remember. To answer your question, there are rumours of something terrible out there, and Driar Brigel has probably gone to check it out."

"What exactly?" I asked. But the boy didn't reply, and so I sat down and groomed myself.

"That's right, just wait there and don't go anywhere." Initiate Rine walked over to a stone fountain and drank from the steady stream of water. I watched him for a moment, then I realised that I hadn't drunk anything for a while. I jumped up on his back and darted across it until I got to the stream. Before he could lift himself up, I perched myself on the rim of the fountain, and I caught the drops in my paw and tossed them into my mouth.

"Who said you could touch me?" Initiate Rine said, and he brushed himself off vigorously as if he thought having a strand of fur on him might kill him.

"I'm thirsty," I replied, "and you're meant to be looking after my needs."

"Wrong. I'm meant to be making sure you don't get up to no good. You've got a warlock's magic inside you and I don't want you tainting me with his evil touch."

I didn't have to listen to this nonsense. I blinked at Initiate Rine and yawned. "I'm hungry."

"How convenient," Initiate Rine replied, and looked up at the sun in the sky. "Because it's just about time for dinner. Maybe if you look at some of the younger Initiates with wide enough eyes, you'll be able to get a few scraps."

He walked off, and I followed him, the thought of food pulling at me like a leash. I'd already smelled the fish, and smoked meat, and gravy, and butter, and all the wonderful things in the kitchen here. Finally, I was going to have a chance to sample this food. I was sure at least some humans would give me some. They always did.

26

ALLERGIES

We walked through the bailey and passed Aleam's quarters. I wanted to go inside and gloat to Ta'ra that I was finally going to get a chance to dine amongst the humans. But with Initiate Rine moving with such urgency, I didn't have the chance.

He quickly turned into the corridors underneath the parapets, and he led me through them until we reached a set of double doors that led into a massive hall. A woman stood at the door, and I recognised her immediately. She was that same woman who'd attacked me with the serving spoon back in the kitchens a day or so ago.

She glared down at me over her folded arms as she tapped her huge foot on the ground.

"Matron Canda," Initiate Rine said to her with a nod.

She scowled at him. "No cats in the serving hall, Initiate Rine," she replied. "You know the rules."

"I'm sorry. But this is the Council's order. We need to keep a watch on him at all times." Rine pushed his head up to Matron Canda's thick ear and whispered in it. I turned my ears towards them. "He's got a warlock's magic inside him."

"I can hear you, you know." I told them, out loud. "I've got particularly sensitive ears."

I don't know what caused Matron Canda to jump more – what Rine had just told her or the fact that the cat by her feet could speak in the human tongue. She backed away towards one of the doors and flattened herself against it. "Go," she said. "And make sure you don't touch my plates or cause any trouble, or I'll come after you with a hot ladle of oil."

I mewled, but my action didn't seem to make her think me any less of a freak. I didn't get it, really. How could these people have such contempt towards such a cute and innocent cat? Humans are strange creatures, sometimes.

The hall had three long tables across it, each of which must have had room for feeding one hundred people. Students had gathered at the tables, sitting on the long benches as they tucked into mouth-watering plates full of turkey legs and gravy. Of course, they also had the human yucky stuff on them like potatoes, and broccoli, and carrots.

Initiate Rine moved to the table on the left, and a couple of girls his age shuffled aside to make room for him. He said something, but I didn't quite catch what it was, being so mesmerized by the plates of food. One of the girls laughed and put a hand over his shoulder, as she brushed his cheek with other.

I wasn't interested in those weird human antics. I had work to do. I just had to figure out which of these humans was most likely to give me food, and then show them the widest eyes and the saddest face. It worked every time, even with the harshest of humans, excepting Astravar.

I approached the girl who'd brushed Rine's face first, thinking if she was friendly with him, she'd also be friendly with me. I meowed up at her, and she edged away from me.

"What in the Seventh Dimension?" she said. "Rine, there's a cat in here." She sneezed, and her face went a shade of light red, which stood out quite comically against her bright blonde curls.

Rine looked down at me. "Hey stay away from Bellari," he said. "She has allergies."

The girl on the other side of Rine turned her head to me. "Aw, he's so cute," she said. "Here, kitty, kitty."

I moved over to her, and she reached down and stroked me on the back of my head with a thin finger. She was a brunette with shiny and smooth hair and a small, snub nose.

"Why, thank you," I said, purring. "Now, if you could kindly donate some turkey…"

Her jaw dropped, and her eyes went wide. "What, you talk?"

"Be careful, Ange," Rine said. "He has warlock magic inside him."

"You're kidding, never? Well, you know the rules, talking or not. We can't give you food, otherwise you'll be less effective as a ratter."

"I'm no ratter," I replied. "I'm a Bengal, descendant of the great Asian leopard cat."

"He seems proud of that," Initiate Rine said. "Such an oaf."

"Rine," the first girl, Bellari said. "Get him away, I'm not joking. Really, I could swear the warlock's magic is making it worse."

"Fine," Rine said. "Shoo, cat. Be off with you. And remember I'm keeping my eye on you."

"Oh, don't be so cruel," Ange said, and she cast Bellari a hard look. "But yeah, cat, she does have allergies, so maybe you'd be better over there." She pointed to a corner, and I looked at it, despair sinking in my chest.

"Rine's not going to tell you twice, you stupid creature," Bellari said, flailing her arms wildly in front of her. "Scat!"

I mewled, then I groaned, then I growled deeply from the stomach. Finally, I turned slowly away and slinked over to the corner they'd banished me to. I kind of wish I hadn't understood them – it would have been easier that way. I would have just sat there looking up at the food, begging until either my eyes fell out of my sockets or I got a scrap of turkey.

But I was in the wrong world. No one here respected cats. No one here gave us food or looked after us. Nobody here cared about anyone but themselves.

Time passed as I watched the students carve scraps of meat off the dwindling turkeys at the centres of the table and lift them onto their plates. They laughed, and they chattered, and occasionally one of them squealed so loudly I wished I could cover my ears. All the while, my tummy rumbled, and I felt so sad.

What had I done to deserve this torture? It was as if I was living through the worst nightmare of my life.

That was when there came a clanking of metal against the floor, and a massive young man walked into the room. I recognised him as the same man I'd seen on the citrine dragon before. He'd taken off his armour, but he still wore his metal boots and the tabard with the symbol of the sun and moon emblazoned on its front. His long black hair flowed over two heavy-looking yellow leather shoulder pads.

An older boy at the far end of the room stood up and called out, "High Prefect Lars has entered the serving hall. Please stand up and show him your respect."

27

HIGH PREFECT LARS

Q uickly the rest of the students stood up, and they all clapped together. The young man known as High Prefect Lars bowed his head, and then he put his hand out, stretching out his fingers towards the room. Everyone quietened down. This prefect, whatever a prefect was, had a tired look in his eyes and though his face had lots of hard edges to it, it was also long. He took a place at the head of the central table, next to a group of students who also had yellow shoulder pads.

Given no one even seemed to realise I was here, I thought I'd listen to his conversation. This Lars figure looked important, and I figured that if I gained some information from him, I could use it as a bargaining chip for food. A young woman and a young man sat on either side of him, but they didn't look the playful, youthful type like Rine and his two girlfriends. The young woman had short red hair, and the man had his hair cropped so short, I couldn't make out the colour.

"What news is there of the demon dragon?" the woman asked. She had her back turned to me, so I couldn't see her face.

Prefect Lars paused a moment, and he gazed towards the other end of the table, shaking his head. "It's true," he said. "Our dying Driar at Colie Town confirmed. He saw it with his own eyes."

The short-haired man lowered his head. "Will Driar Forn survive?"

"He passed just before we left," Perfect Lars replied, and he took hold of the young man's hand. "I'm sorry, Calin. I know what he meant to you."

"But, what of his dragon?" Calin replied.

"Callandras barely managed to get Driar Forn to the town before the burn on her flank took her."

Calin's face went white, and he let go of Prefect Lars' hand and turned away from the table. He wiped his face with his sleeve and then turned back to Lars, bowed, and walked hastily out of the room without even touching any turkey.

The woman leaned forwards towards Lars and put a hand on his knee. "I'm sorry, Lars," she said. "It must have been hard for you."

"We just need to stop Astravar," he said. "But no one knows where he might be right now. He flew off on a bone dragon right after he'd almost killed Driar Forn."

"But where's he getting his power from? He can't use the life force of anything in this realm."

"Demon rats," Prefect Lars replied.

"What?" the woman replied.

I backed away from their table and hid under the adjacent table. It was me who'd summoned the demon rats, and so I felt partly as if I was to blame.

"Driar Brigel told me all about it on the way back. Astravar's been experimenting in using creatures from other dimensions. He summoned a cat from the Fourth Dimension, which I believe is somewhere in this castle. Then he used that cat to kill the rats he summoned from the Seventh Dimension. They're tough rats, as you probably know, but I hear it's also a tough cat. After Astravar gained a large enough stack, he could use them for an even greater summoning."

"It's terrible," the woman said, shaking her head.

"That's not all," Lars said. "Driar Forn discovered on his mission that Astravar has enough summoning power to call up a demon dragon."

"A demon dragon? But you can't kill them, can you? It will destroy us all..." the woman lifted her hand to her face.

"I fear a war is coming, Asinda," Prefect Lars replied, then he lowered his voice to almost a whisper. "And, yes you're right... It's not one that we can win. Not if the warlocks have a dragon like that at their disposal."

Whiskers, I'd heard enough. All those demon rats I'd killed, and at the time I thought I'd been doing someone good service. Not only did they taste disgusting, but Astravar was planning to use it to conjure the demon dragon that would destroy this world. Then, if they were right, the creature would also destroy my world.

But not just that, it would destroy the entire universe's supply of food, and here I was, the creature who assisted Astravar in this deed. Really, I wasn't surprised that these humans hated me so much.

I pulled myself out from underneath the table, brushing against a female student's bare calf who shrieked as if she'd just seen a hippopotamus. The young lady talking to Lars, Asinda, turned sharply around and glared at me through two intense cornflower blue eyes. I regarded her a moment, and then I remembered that I was the enemy here.

So, I dashed to the other end of the room, and I retreated back to the corner that I'd been banished to. I watched with sadness as the students devoured the rest of the turkey. I wanted to eat some, but at the same time I knew I didn't deserve it.

Eventually, the students finished up, and they filed out of the room, leaving their plates bare on the table. An army of serving maids came in and quickly whisked the plates away. Soon, it was just me, Initiate Rine, and his girlfriend Bellari left in the room.

He kissed her on the mouth, and then he stood up and moved towards me.

"Not him again," Bellari said.

"I've been assigned to look after him," Rine replied. "What can I do?"

"Please, just don't get any of him on you. You know it's not good for me. I'll see you tomorrow, okay?" She kissed Rine on the lips again, and then rushed out the door.

Initiate Rine approached me, the sound of his footsteps echoing off the walls. "What are you looking so sad about?" he asked.

"Don't you humans think cats always look sad?" I hadn't known facts like this before I came to this world. But along with the language, the crystals had gifted me with a little knowledge of how humans think.

"You do," Rine replied, "and I've never known why. So, did you manage to get any food out of anyone?"

"I didn't feel like it," I replied. "Besides, your girlfriend said no one was allowed to feed me. Aren't I meant to be chasing rats or something?"

"Yes, about that. Don't let Bellari get to you. She's harsh some-times, but once you get to know her she's sweet, and she's so beautiful, don't you think?"

I blinked at Rine. "Are you really doing this?" I asked.

"What?"

"Apologising to me."

Initiate Rine glanced over his shoulder towards the door. "I just thought you'd appreciate it."

I meowed, and then I brushed my cheek against his trouser leg. It finally felt good to have some sympathy around here, and I thought that maybe if I could appeal to Rine's soft side, maybe things would be a little easier. Plus, given how horrible his girlfriend had been to me, it made sense to get as much of myself on his clothes as possible. That would teach her a lesson.

He chuckled and then reached down and tickled me at the back of my neck. I rolled over on my back, and he rubbed my tummy. Maybe this boy wasn't so bad after all.

"You know," I said. "Maybe that Bellari girl isn't as great a potential mate as you think."

"I don't think any of the other boys think that." Rine winked at me.

"But what about the other one, Ange? I think she's much more suitable. Her genes are better."

Rine raised an eyebrow at me. "What are you talking about?"

"Think about it. Do you really want your children to grow up with cat allergies? You never know, first it might be cats, then dragons."

"Don't be stupid. No one's allergic to dragons."

"That's what you think."

He laughed again, then he lifted himself up and reached into a pouch on his hip. "You know, you're quite entertaining. Say, I don't usually do this. But seeing you over there, I couldn't help but feel sorry for you."

Out of the pouch, he produced a massive scrap of turkey, with the skin on it and all. I looked up at it and started meowing. He dangled it above my head, and I tried to bat it out of his hands with my paw. But he raised it out of reach whenever he saw me move.

Whiskers, it was so annoying when humans did that.

"Please," I said. "I'm starving."

"Okay," Rine replied. "You said the magic word." He dropped the turkey on the floor. I pounced upon it and tore it up into pieces with my tongue and my teeth. It tasted so good – the best meat I'd had for days. I don't mean to say anything bad about Salanraja or anything, but she wasn't much of a chef.

"Hey," I heard someone call out from the doorway, and heavy footsteps stomped towards me. It was that horrible woman, Matron Canda. "I thought I told you not to feed the cats."

Initiate Rine put his hands on hips and turned to her. "No," he replied. "I believe what you said was not to let him eat off any of your plates. But look at this… He's eating off the floor."

"Fine," Matron Canda replied. "Just hurry up out of here. I want to lock up and get a nap."

It didn't matter, because I'd pretty much finished eating. Initiate Rine shrugged, and I followed him out of the door.

28

DORMITORY

I t's strange, I'd been so hungry back at the kitchen that I'd completely forgotten about that conversation Prefect Lars had had with his friends. But as I strolled with Rine through the corridors, at first looking up in pride as the boys and girls pointed at me and giggled, I started to feel guiltier and guiltier and I sank my head in shame. Like the mutton had previously, the turkey now left a sour tang on my tongue. Food just didn't taste the same when you didn't feel you deserved it.

Rine led me through the corridor and down a stone spiral staircase with steep steps into a dark corridor lit by lights that reeked of oil. By the time we reached the boy's chambers, I found it hard to drag one foot in front of the other, I was so demotivated. My head, and my legs, and my stomach all felt like lead, and I wanted to curl up in a corner and have a good sulky sleep.

Initiate Rine took a key from his pouch. It was the size of his hand – much bigger than anything I'd seen my master and mistress use in South Wales. He put the key into a wide keyhole, and the door creaked open to reveal his dormitory room.

We stepped inside, and I started to explore Rine's territory, sniffing out every nook and cranny, as you should when you first discover a new place.

One thing I could say about my old place in South Wales was it had so much room for running around in. Even the child's bedroom had a nice armchair for scratching and a tall double bed I could hide under. But Rine didn't have any of that.

His room was boxy and as soon as I felt the air flowing out from the darkness against my whiskers, I could taste the mould in there. He had a single bed, neatly lain with a woollen grey blanket. There wasn't much else in the room except a bookcase, a small round table with a candle on it, a heavy wardrobe, and a rack for placing his staff. Rine took a match from a box on the table and lit the candle, suffusing the room in a warm flickering light.

"You don't have a bathroom?" I asked.

Initiate Rine cocked his head. "The bathhouse is upstairs. But I thought cats hated water."

"Not a bathhouse. A bathroom. You know, a place where you can have a shower but also go to relieve yourself."

"The latrine's down the corridor. But it's for humans only." Rine shut and locked the door.

"But where am I meant to go if I need to relieve myself? You don't even have a litter tray."

"Don't tell me you need to go already? I would have thought you'd do so outside."

I groaned, and then I found a spot under the table that looked suitable. I rubbed against the wall there to mark it with my scent, so I'd remember it later.

Meanwhile, Initiate Rine had opened the wardrobe and was rummaging around inside it. He threw a few clothes out onto the bed, and then he produced a second blanket, looking just as dull as the first. "Here. You can use this as a bed. I think it will be comfortable enough."

I purred and brushed against his leg, and he reached down and stroked me. He then placed the blanket underneath the table. "Not there, for whisker's sake," I said.

"Why not?" I wanted to tell him that litter spots were meant for cockroaches, not cats. But I thought it wiser to keep my trap shut.

"Nothing," I replied. "It's just I prefer this spot by the wardrobe. It's cooler, and I have less chance of burning to death if someone knocks that candle over."

"And why might someone do that?"

"I don't know... They might get a little bored." I licked my paw.

"You're a funny creature," Rine said, and he kicked out the blanket with his foot and then shuffled it over to the place by the wardrobe. I yawned as I watched him iron out the creases with his foot. I was starting to see a new side to Initiate Rine, and I liked it. When he wasn't showing off around the girls, he seemed to know how to care for cats. If I could only find a human like him outside of this castle, maybe I could have a good life in this world.

I found I was so tired that I just stepped over to the blanket, padded the creases back into it again, and then I lay down for an afternoon nap. I dreamed sweet dreams of running through a field of long grass towards Salanraja and then jumping on her back. She took off into flight and we sailed through the sky.

Part of me expected to see Astravar in every cloud we passed. I expected to hear his voice in my head and listen to him gloat about how he was summoning a demon dragon using the otherworldly rats that I killed for him. It was strange. Part of me felt that Astravar belonged in that dream. But he wasn't there. It was almost as if someone was protecting me from him entering my mind.

Still, my guilt caused me to sleep fitfully. I woke to see that the candle had been extinguished. But I could still see in here, due to a little light spilling in beneath the bottom of the door. Initiate Rine lay in his bed, fast asleep. But now I couldn't sleep, and so I looked around for something I could use to sharpen my claws.

I tried scratching at the blanket, but I didn't like the way it felt. I tried the wardrobe, but the wood there was too solid for me to gain any traction. Same with the table, and the chair, and the rack for the staff I could only just reach the bottom of. It felt unnatural almost, as if everything in the room had been augmented with magic to make it undamageable.

"You are so loud at night," Salanraja said. *"Why can't you just stay asleep?"*

"I can't help it, I'm nocturnal."

"Then learn not to be. It's not as if there's anything to hunt in Initiate Rine's room."

I scented a cat outside the door, and I heard it stalk by. In a way, I wished I was out on duty hunting rats with it. Maybe I belonged out there. After all, that's what the descendant of the great Asian leopard cat should be doing at night, hunting. But instead, I was here unable to do a thing – the cat that had contributed to the inevitable annihilation of the universe.

"You're so negative lately," Salanraja said. *"Can you not think about something a little more motivational?"*

"What? You can hear my thoughts?"

"I can hear the ones that you shout loud enough. They're full of all kinds of little secrets. Which is one of the reasons I'm so frustrated with you. Humans trust dragons to share their worries and help them through problems. But you seem to want to keep everything bottled inside."

"So, you know about the demon rats?" I asked.

"I do... You should have told me. The more information I have, the more I can communicate to the Dragon Council about what to do next. But you kept that part about swallowing that crystal a little quiet inside your head. You didn't even seem to want to think about it."

I curled up into a ball. *"So, what am I going to do about it?"* I asked. *"Astravar can just take control at any time, can't he? What if I lose control of myself completely? What if he turns me into a demon cat?"*

"Don't be stupid, he can't turn you into a demon. Demons were born in the Seventh Dimension and they must be summoned from there." Salanraja sounded frustrated. *"I don't know what it means. You're dangerous, yes, we know that. But you're going to have to learn to deal with it by yourself. Now let me get some sleep."*

I growled, and then I went back to whispering in my thoughts. That seemed to be the way to stop her prying, and also for me to let her get the sleep she 'needed'.

Really though, I didn't want her to cotton on to what I was planning. Because I knew I couldn't stay in Dragonsbond Academy any longer. I didn't belong here. I belonged in the wild, like my great Asian leopard cat ancestors. Either I would learn to survive there or die.

I walked over to the door and tried scratching at it. If Rine hadn't locked it properly, maybe I could paw it open and sneak out. But I wasn't so lucky. I had to revert to Plan B instead.

Initiate Rine was now facing towards me on his bed. His mouth was wide open, and he was snoring from the bottom of his throat. I meowed so loudly you could probably call it a yowl. Then I jumped on to a spot on the mattress right by his stomach, and I crawled on top of Rine and put my mouth to his ear.

"Initiate Rine," I said and meowed a couple more times. "Wake up, it's important."

He pushed me away. "More sleep," he said. "No, not there, Ange... Please, Ange..."

"Now Rine," I said, and I walked back up to his ear and then licked it. When a cat wanted to wake you up, he meant it.

Rine opened his eyes, and I dropped down in front of him and looked right into them. "What in the Seventh Dimension?" he asked.

"I need to go to the toilet," I replied.

"Oh, just go under the table or something. The cleaner will clean it up in the morning."

"Please," I said. "I can't hold it in any longer."

Rine raised his voice. "I said just go underneath the table."

"But I can't do it there. I must do it on something soft. This bed looks perfect..."

"No!" Rine replied, and he slung his legs around and put his feet on the floor. "Oh, you are such a pain in the bum."

I jumped off the bed and stood by the door. "Oh, thank you, Rine," I said. "But if you would hurry up, I'd be so eternally grateful. Really, I'm not sure how long I can hold on. It's a matter of life and death."

"Give me a moment." Rine rubbed his eyes with the back of his hand and yawned. He put his slippers on and walked over to lift the key off a hook on the side of the wardrobe. He took hold of his staff at the same time.

"Stay with me," he said as he unlocked the door. "I wish I had a leash or something."

I followed him obediently into the light of the corridor, looking up at the cold blue crystal on his staff as we walked. I didn't want to find out what he could do with that, and so I didn't plan on trying to run away from him. Or at least not while he was looking.

He led me out into the bailey, and then he stopped and leaned against the wall. The air had a breeze on it which was frigid enough to create frost. I looked up at Rine, and I licked my lips.

"Come on," Rine said, tapping the butt of his staff against the cobblestones. "Or are you telling me you don't want to go after all?"

I turned towards the thin crescent of the moon. The silhouette of a cat stalked in front of it over one of the walls. A rat scurried down the stone, but it wasn't fast enough for the cat which caught it within its claws and then squealed in delight.

"Ben," Rine said. "You're really making me want to cook you alive."

I turned back to him. "I can't go while you watch. I need at least some privacy."

"What?" Rine said. "You're a cat for demons' sake."

"I'm not just a cat," I replied, and I almost used the great Asian leopard cat line, but I realised just in the nick of time it probably wouldn't work.

"I'm a talking cat," I continued. "Which means you should treat me with more respect than a normal cat. I mean it. Turn away. Otherwise, we'll be here all night."

"Fine," Rine replied, and he turned his eyes upwards and whistled.

"No peeking, now," I said.

"I'm not looking."

"Not even from the corner of your eye?"

"Not one bit," Rine said.

I didn't believe him. But this was the best chance I was going to have. So, I crept slowly towards the wall, looking out for a shadow I could use to my advantage. But Rine had been smart and taken me to a place fully covered by the moonlight, and there wasn't a cloud to be seen in the sky.

I started scratching at the ground, behaving very catlike as if I was preparing the terrain to receive its offering. All the while, I kept one eye on Rine as I scanned the wall for a way up with the other. Clearly it wouldn't be easy for a human to climb. But I wasn't a human.

"Rine, are you sure you're not looking?"

"I'm not," he replied. He had his staff clutched in both hands now, and I could see his arm muscles were tense underneath the folds of his clothing. Whiskers, he was expecting me to try something. Fortunately, I remembered a little something he said in his sleep.

"I thought I said I didn't want anyone looking," I said.

"I'm not..."

"Not you. Ange."

"What, where?" Rine sharply turned his head away from me.

"Over there by the fountain," I replied. "Fooled you!"

I scarpered up onto the wall and caught the stone rim at the top, which I grappled with all the strength I had in my paws.

29

TO SWIM OR NOT TO SWIM?

T he wall wasn't as easy to climb as I thought it would be. I must have lost a lot of my strength, because I'd had plenty of practice climbing up the loose stones of the castle on the hill back in South Wales. Us cats used to gather there and have all kinds of competitions. I won most of them until the Savannah cats arrived in the neighbourhood.

The moonlight and the long shadows had made the stones on this wall in Dragonsbond Academy seem to stick out much further than they actually did. So, when I got to the top, my shoulder muscles were screaming out at me in pain. But I made it and pulled myself over.

But by the time I did, Rine had worked out that I'd created a decoy and there was no Ange waiting nearby ready to steal his affection.

"Hey!" he yelled, and he raised his staff. Something cold and blue shot out from his crystal. I ducked behind a parapet so it didn't hit me, and shards of ice erupted from the stone.

I continued to run along the wall, hoping that I could just jump down the other side. But the moat was down there, and I really didn't want to have to leap into water, particularly given how cold it was. From this height, I wouldn't have a chance of catching myself on the steep bank, even with the balance of a cat.

So, I darted my way along the parapets. A guard blocked my path. He wore shiny armour and a cone shaped helmet with a ridiculous looking nose-guard protruding from it. Really, those helmets made the guards look like elephants with half their trunk missing. But I didn't have time to stop and mock. I weaved my way between the guard's feet and carried out along the *chemin de ronde*. It wouldn't be long until he realised the commotion that Rine was causing below the wall was about me.

I found a staircase at the end of the *chemin de ronde* and I sprinted down it. I reached the bottom. The door was open in the guardhouse, but I wasn't interested in that. Instead, I sprinted towards the portcullis, hoping to squeeze underneath it.

But when I narrowed my shoulders and pushed as hard as I could, I couldn't make it past my belly. Whiskers, I had far too much mutton and turkey inside me. It was as if Salanraja and Rine had planned this to trap me in here. If they fattened me up, I'd have no chance of escape.

I growled, and I groaned and pushed even harder. But my efforts achieved nothing.

"Stop right there, Ben," Initiate Rine said from behind me. "Take one step further and I'll freeze your bum."

I froze stock still, and I listened to the clanking metal boots and armour coming from the guardhouse. "Captain Onus here," a man with a gruff voice said. "Am I to understand, young Initiate, that you've woken up the entire guard because of a cat."

"That isn't any old cat," Rine replied. "He's a descendant of the great Asian leopard cat."

"What?" Onus said.

"He's special. And the Council of Three have ordered that he must not leave this castle. This is a matter of great importance, Captain." The whole *swallowed a warlock's crystal* thing must have been top-secret, as he didn't mention it. This was probably for the best, really.

"It's a cat," another guard said, this time female.

"Just seize him," Rine said. "I know I'm a kid, but these aren't my orders."

"Fine," Onus said. "I'll do it myself. I'm good with cats."

Rough hands grasped me from behind, and they tugged me out of the portcullis, with such force I thought he would rip my shoulders off. One thing was clear, this man wasn't as good with cats as he claimed.

His hands moved up to my waist, and he lifted me up to examine me from below. The guard captain had a pockmarked face, with lips far too big for it and a nose that looked like someone had twisted it at a right angle and then put it back again. I kept my cool and didn't wriggle and scratch, despite how much his tight grip was hurting me. I needed time to work out what to do next.

"I'd be careful," Rine said with an undertone of cheekiness. "I only brought him out here because he needed to go, and he hasn't done so yet."

The captain pursed his massive lips at me. "Here, kitty, kitty. I guess the moat makes a good toilet, does it?"

Rine sighed from behind me. "I doubt it. Tell him, Ben. In fact, tell us all why exactly you wanted to escape?"

But I kept quiet. I wanted to save the element of surprise for the most apt moment. The guard captain moved me to the side a little so he could look at Rine. "Initiate, did the chef give you the wrong kind of mushrooms today?"

"This cat talks," Rine replied. "That's one reason he's so important to us. Ben, say something."

"There have been rumours of talking cats in this castle," the female guard pointed out.

"And I've already told you that this rumour is nonsense," Onus replied. "Besides, how could something so cute cause so much trouble?"

The captain moved me a little closer and tickled me under my chin. Unfortunately, even with my special language abilities, I didn't seem able to fake a purr. But it seemed Captain Onus didn't need one to assume that I liked him. "He might be crazy, but you don't seem crazy, do you?"

"Okay, that's enough," Initiate Rine said, and I turned to see him extend his arms. "Here, hand him over. Ben, I won't let you out of my sight again."

"What do you think, little kitty? Do you think this man is safe?"

But I could see that Rine had the authority here. So, I didn't have much time.

I hissed at the guard. "I think both your name and your face are only one vowel away from looking like a bottom," I said, and I swiped at him hard with my claw. I hit him on the cheek before he shouted out in shock and dropped me on the cold stone ground. Of course, I landed on my feet.

"You buffoon," Initiate Rine said. "Stop him!"

But the guards weren't fast enough to react as I darted between their legs and scrambled back up the staircase to the *chemin de ronde*. I passed the first corner tower, and then I took a sharp right and balanced myself on the crenel. Heavy footsteps resounded from behind me, clanging urgently against stone.

I looked down at the water, and I shivered as I imagined the cold of it. But I really didn't have much choice. Something icy and sharp whizzed by me, just as I leapt off the wall. I didn't land in the water. I landed on the steep bank, hurting my knee as I rolled down.

The water was freezing and shocking, and it tasted like mud. But still I swam towards the opposite bank, rage and adrenaline pushing me forwards. I didn't look back as I scrambled up the side and then I ran into the darkness, the moon now hidden behind a cloud.

Some arrows followed in my wake alongside some sharp looking icicles. But through speed, and darkness, and the fact I wasn't exactly the largest of targets, I escaped out into the wild world.

30

ROAMING THE WILDS

I don't know for how long I continued to run. It must have been for hours. As I did, the clouds continued to build in the sky, and I could feel the humidity on my whiskers threatening rain.

I had a stitch in my side because of all the food I'd eaten lately. But I needed to get far away from Dragonsbond Academy. For all I knew, there could have been dragons up there, hunting me from the sky. I had no doubt that with their massive eyes, they could see well in the dark. But I couldn't see anything hovering above.

Ages later, I found a forest. I couldn't see the trees, but I could sense them. The way the wind rolled through forests felt different against my whiskers than it did over the plains. I continued onwards until I knew I was underneath the tree cover. It was warmer in the forest, though I listened out for wolves or anything that might want to take advantage of a smaller cat. Here, I felt naked and vulnerable. There was bound to be something bigger than me here, ready to tear me apart.

Salanraja had mentioned all kinds of dangerous beasts – chimeras, Sabre-Tooth tigers. All the while she would be back at Dragonsbond Academy, dreaming away, not realising what danger I might be in. Whiskers, knowing my luck, I might come face to face with a hippopotamus. It would tear me apart with its razor-sharp buck teeth before I even saw it.

I decided it better to put all my worries behind me, because I was tired, and I really needed rest. I searched around for soft underbrush, which I then patted down with my paws. Once I lay down, I fell asleep almost instantaneously.

Astravar watched me in my dreams.

In them, I was once again running through the darkness. I couldn't quite see it, but I could sense it in the sky, a massive grey eye blinking the rain and the wind away. It rolled around and watched me wherever I stepped. No matter where I went – behind trees, into caves, through swamps, it was always there. I couldn't escape him.

There was no sunrise to wake me, only a sombre wall of grey cloud and a chilling drizzle in the air. It seemed to seep into my bones, and so it was hard to lift myself onto all fours and get moving again. But after all the exercise, I was also famished.

I started by eating woodlice. It was absolutely disgusting, and I knew I wouldn't go far on such tiny bugs. But they were easy to find under logs and stones, and they gave me enough energy to continue onwards.

Soon, I was ready to stalk the land for larger prey. But no rabbits or birds or even mice wanted to come out and play in this disgusting weather. I couldn't see anything. I couldn't hear anything. Whiskers, I couldn't even smell anything. So, I continued to walk through long, cold, and wet grass, looking out for even the slightest movement.

"It doesn't matter where you go, Dragoncat," his voice said in my head. "You will always need help. You will never learn how to survive alone."

I tried to ignore the voice, but it droned on and on through my head, telling me how useless and pathetic I was. It was as if, through some kind of magic, the warlock was causing every single living creature to hide away. Maybe he was even causing this terrible weather. But was he that powerful?

After I'd hunted for what must have been a couple of hours, without success, all I wanted to do was collapse. I lay down in the grass, meowing to no one in particular. I was just about ready to curl up and die.

That was when Astravar decided to throw me a bone. *"What would you like to eat little one,"* he asked. *"Perhaps some rabbit?"*

My eyes were so bleary that I wasn't sure if I saw it for real or imagined it. But, all of a sudden, a purple tiny creature that looked something like a sparrow except with butterfly wings and a human-looking face appeared on my nose. She laughed so loudly that her voice seemed to ring in my ears, and she fluttered away, a trail of purple glowing dust streaking behind her.

Then, she sprung up into the air like a rocket, and came back down again. She dived right into a hole in the ground. A rabbit hole...

The ground shook, and a white rabbit came out and gazed blankly ahead. I didn't even care where it had come from. I crouched down and readied myself. It twitched its ears and sniffed at the air, but it didn't seem to notice me stalking through the long grass.

I curled up my hind legs, then I pounced forwards. It tried to run away at the last minute. But it was too late. I kept it pinned with my claws, and I don't know what happened next. I remember wild thoughts going around my mind. I saw red, I tasted iron on my tongue, and my nostrils filled with the scent of something sweet and, in retrospect, sickly. I tore into the flesh with claws and teeth, and the grass bowed around me as a strong and icy wind rolled through the vale. Clouds boiled in the sky, thunder booming out of them. Soon, the fields became sodden with virgin rain.

I woke up from my trance feeling strong, satisfied, a powerful beast of the wild. My ancestors, at that moment, must have stirred in their graves.

The rain had stopped by that point. Beneath me was a carcass, almost completely stripped of flesh. Flies buzzed around it and vultures wheeled overhead. But they wouldn't dare come down until this beast of the wild, the great Bengal of South Wales, had abandoned his feast.

I gave them permission by turning away from the carcass and walking through the wild grass. *"That's it, Dragoncat,"* Astravar said in my head, and I wanted him to be there. *"This is truly what it means to be wild and free. Now come, and we shall explore the world together."*

I didn't feel afraid. Nor did I feel ashamed to have abandoned my friends and my dragon back at the academy. After all, humans were worthless creatures who tried to exploit cats like me for their own benefit. But what they never realised was that it was actually the cats that exploited them.

I felt truly complete, as if I was pursuing my destiny as a hidden force inside me pulled me onwards. It was as if there was something solid in my head, right in front of my nose that was acting as a compass. It told me exactly where I needed to go, and I only needed to follow it.

I crossed over into a swampland where a purple gas rose from the reedy plants and the water. There was something about this that was absolutely intoxicating. This was where a wild Bengal truly belonged.

But all this while, the world was gaining clarity, as if I was just emerging from an incredibly vivid dream.

31

SCORPIONS AND SPIDERS

The intoxication wore off eventually as I delved deeper into the Wastelands, and a sinking realisation came over me that I shouldn't have gone so far. I wanted to turn around and go back. But that was the thing, I'd lost that directional compass at the front of my nose and I really didn't remember the way I'd come.

What a fool I'd been. How had I allowed myself to get tricked like this? But Astravar had used my mind to get me here. He was leading me into a trap which I was sure I'd spring any moment now, and without knowing exactly where the tripwire might be, I had no chance of escape. I should have listened to Salanraja. I should have listened to the Council. But instead, I just had to go around doing things my own way.

Astravar had stopped talking in my head by that point, and so I was completely alone as I continually cursed myself for my stupidity. The purple gas didn't just rise out of the ground, but it seemed to follow me. It twisted into shapes as I went, almost as if it had magic inside it. Every so often, I'd get the creepy sensation of something watching me, and then I swear I would turn around and see something humanoid dissolve into the mist.

After a moment, I could hear the sounds of skittering feet and then a chittering that sounded like magpies cackling at ten times their normal speed and volume. I spun around in circles until I was dizzy, trying to identify the source of the sound. But the purple mist was getting denser all around me, and I could see nothing.

More chittering came out of the murk, as if the sound had formed a cloud itself. When I thought I could hear it coming from one direction, another sound would emerge behind me. It's as if there were evil creatures in the mist that wanted to toy with me. They wanted to see how much they could agitate poor Ben.

That was when I saw the first of them. A bulky arthropod armoured with interlaced plates of slimy chitin, and a tail that towered up as high as a telephone pole. A massive purple bulb teetered at the top of the tail, with a long black sting shooting out of the front of it. The creature had two fat pincers on either side of it, with sharp blades on them, making them look like incredibly sharp scissors. Although I couldn't see any eyeballs within the creature's narrow jet-black eyes to show where it was looking, I knew it had its gaze affixed on me.

It sped forwards on its long spiny legs. I didn't even think about it. I darted away before it could plunge its sting into me. It hissed, and I ran as far towards the horizon as I could, not caring anymore where I was going.

But another of these creatures blocked my path. I turned to be again blocked by another, then another. They seemed to be crowding around from all directions, the ethereal purple mist swirling around them as if it belonged to them.

"You know," Astravar said in my head. "These were such fun to conjure. In my land, you call them serkets. But oh, how I've studied your world from afar. Once upon a time there, I believe a desert princess summoned one, and the people worshipped it as a god. Alas now, all you have on your planet is measly little scorpions. You are used to a world that's so tame."

The serkets continued to close in around me, their massive stings wavering in the air. I tried to look for a gap through them. I might have been able to make it past one, but many more were closing in from behind the front row. The monsters continued to shuffle around until they had me surrounded in a horseshoe formation, opening at a massive crag that rose high into the sky. There was nowhere to go but a cave mouth, shrouded in complete darkness.

I backed into this darkness, shivering at a sudden wave of cold washing over me. The serkets continued to chitter and snap their pincers, ever more unnerving as I couldn't see them now.

It was so dark in the cave that I couldn't navigate by sight. But I had my sense of smell, and I had my whiskers to detect the variations in the air currents. I didn't want to run as the ground was slippery. But I kept my ears attuned to the serkets behind me, making sure they kept their distance.

The cold air flowed through the cave, and I knew there must be an exit somewhere further in. But not a sliver of light came from within. I heard bats squealing away, and I wondered if some of them were those horrible vampire bats that the Savannah cats had told me about. Those things, they said, could tear off your flesh in your sleep. They weren't as scary as the hippopotamus but terrifying all the same.

Suddenly, something sticky brushed against my nose. Yeuch, a cobweb. There would have to be spiders in here. I'd been bitten by a wolf spider once, and it hurt so much I thought I was going to die.

I turned around, considering backing back into the serkets. But I could hear them inside the cave now, and I didn't fancy my chances of ducking away from their stings in the dark.

I swiped the cobwebs away with my paw and continued onwards. But the stickiness got worse and worse, and before I knew it, I couldn't move forwards. I struggled in the dark, trying to claw away the cobwebs, but I ended up getting further entangled. Soon, I found myself half suspended off the ground, and I couldn't budge a muscle.

I mewled, and I groaned, as I waited for the horrible sting of a serket to pierce my flesh. Those things looked like they'd have so much venom inside them, they'd kill me in an instant. I just hoped it would be painless. There was no point struggling anymore. This was finally my time to die.

Then, a light came on, green and witchlike. It wasn't coming from a crystal, or a torch, or an oil lamp, or anything like that. It belonged to the body of something massive and swollen. The light emanated out of a creature's abdomen, which was even bigger than each of the serkets that had now crowded around as if part of a religious congregation. This glowing belly belonged to a spider with eight hairy legs as big as tree trunks, eight eyes that looked like polished stones, and two raised fangs which dripped with a glowing green substance.

This wasn't a wolf spider. This was the biggest spider I'd ever seen. It smelled of all the things that nature shouldn't smell of – like a dustbin full of food that had been left alone in the heat for months.

"*You really were a disappointment to me, Dragoncat,*" Astravar said in my mind. "*I thought you might even put up a small fight. But don't worry, my pets will strip the flesh off you and then we'll reanimate you in a new form. You shall soon become the creature you were meant to be. Wild, and undead, and so powerful that you won't even need a soul.*"

I thought the spider was going to tear me apart with one of those massive fangs. But instead, it crawled a little along the web, and then it spat some venom in my face. It burned so much that I soon lost consciousness.

32

COCOONED

I woke up cocooned in spider's silk. My skin felt numb, and I wondered if it was even there. I couldn't feel any sensation in my whiskers, I couldn't smell, I couldn't taste. All I could see was the ground far below me now, lit by the hideous green light from the spider sitting in its web, and the serkets skittering around below it.

The web stretched out in all directions, emanating a slight green, spooky glow. I couldn't see the cocoon I was in, as I couldn't move my head, but I imagined it looked much the same. This stuff was probably eating me alive. Tenderising my skin, perhaps so I'd be tastier for the serkets and the spiders when they decided to feast.

I wanted to shudder, but I couldn't even do that. I knew only one thing, that I was completely and utterly doomed.

I'd been stupid, and I deserved it.

As if the spider had sensed that I'd awoken, it climbed up the web towards me, and then regarded me with its ugly eyes. I could smell something terrible on its breath, and if I could have turned my head away, I would have. But instead, I could only feel sick. But I couldn't even move my diaphragm to throw up.

The spider edged closer to me, and then it let out a shriek, and it raised one of its fangs. I didn't even close my eyes, waiting for the final moment of death to come.

Suddenly, there came a bright blue flash followed by an even more intense white light. I didn't see it directly, only the reflection off the serkets and the spiders. Below me, the serkets screeched out as another orange light filled the cavern. A pleasant warmth arose from somewhere, followed by a loud and bellowing roar.

"Gracious demons, it's a good job we're bonded, otherwise I wouldn't have had a chance of finding you." I couldn't tell you how glad I was to hear Salanraja's voice inside my head. But I was so delirious that I couldn't even put words to thought. Whiskers, I wasn't even sure if what I saw was real, or just some hallucination caused by the spider's poison.

Another blue light streamed through the cavern, this time attached to some kind of glowing ball. This hit me, or at least it hit the cocoon I was entangled in. An intense wave of cold spasmed down my body, as if someone had just thrown me into a bucket of icy water.

Well, it certainly woke me up. *"I'm freezing,"* I said back to Salanraja.

"Good," Salanraja said. *"You deserve a little suffering after what you pulled. You know, when I finally woke, I couldn't reach you for a long time. There was this voice in your head, mumbling something about rabbits over and over again. Then when you started talking about giant scorpions and spiders, I'd pretty much worked out where you'd gone. I don't know if I can forgive you for this, Bengie..."*

"Salanraja..."

But she said nothing else. Instead, another bright orange light came from the entrance, followed by a crackling sound. Then, I heard the frozen web I was in begin to crack. I couldn't feel the venom on my body and leaching into my blood anymore. Instead, I felt strangely refreshed.

The serkets had now turned to face the entrance, gathering in one closely knit crowd. This wasn't the smartest idea, because a wide flame reached out right into the cavern. The walls became laced with terrifying screeches, and the serkets skittered about randomly, many of them turning on their backs with their legs kicking up into the air. Initiate Rine appeared at the entrance, and he shot out icicles from his staff at some serkets that remained standing. The momentum sent them rolling across the ground as they curled up in balls. Rine sent more icicles after them, pinning them against the wall.

Another human figure then entered the cave but, before I could see who it was, he reached up with his staff and let out these brilliant flashes of light. Yellow and white streaks of lightning shot out from his crystal, connecting one adjacent serket to the next.

If Initiate Rine was powerful, this man was a master. I waited for the light to subside and I only just made out the wrinkles on the familiar face before the cocoon underneath me shattered to pieces.

I hit the ground with a thud, sending up splashes of water from a stream at the bottom of the cave. I rolled over, forgetting that my muscles were still weak and full of poison. I shook off the water in my fur, and then I looked back towards the cave mouth.

Aleam stood there hunched over his staff. He looked left and right across the cavern, assessing the state of a crowd of dying serkets. Many of them had stopped and were motionless. Others still moved their legs, but they did so very slowly, as if on the verge of death.

There came this high-pitched noise like a circular saw grating against metal. A massive shape thudded down in front of me, separating me from Aleam. I was staring right at the massive terrible eyes of that spider, and its huge dripping fangs.

It raised its fangs and charged, shooting a strand of web at me as it did so, as if it was that silly man in the tight red costume the little one liked to watch on TV back in South Wales. I ducked before the web could hit me in the face, and then I dodged under its fangs, trying not to touch that dripping venom.

The spider turned around and reared up on four of its hind legs, as it tried to swipe at me with the front four. I dodged them, hoping that either Rine and Aleam would hurry and work some of their magic on this beast. But I then realised that I might not have that much time. I had to try to take it down by myself.

The spider raised another of its fangs high in the air again, and I waited for the right moment. Just as it came down towards me, I rolled out of the way, and then jumped onto the spider's head. I sprinted across the creature's back, as it screamed and tossed and turned, trying to throw me off. But after those flights Salanraja had taken me on, trying to stay steady on this spider rodeo was nothing in comparison.

That was when I spotted a crystal nestled between two plates at the peak of the spider's bulbous back. It glowed green, much as the rest of the abdomen.

The spider shuddered like an earthquake, sending me tumbling back down its back again. I rolled as if falling down a hill, and I only just caught myself on the chitin of one of the spider's hairy legs. It lifted another leg in front of me and tried to spear me with the single claw at the end of it. But I twisted in the air, and then I pulled myself back onto the back. I ran towards the crystal.

I tried to swipe it out of its socket, but it was a lot harder to dislodge than the crystals in the golem and the Manipulator had been. As the spider screeched and wriggled underneath me, I suddenly realised that it was backing me into one of its webs.

I had another go with my claw again, trying to get underneath the green crystal. It was wedged between two thick layers of chitin that were pressing against each other like a vice. I tried once more, then I swallowed my fears about swallowing this venom and clasped my teeth around it.

Just as I felt the stickiness of the web against my back, I managed to pry out the crystal. I felt the bitter, rancid taste of spider venom on my tongue, and some wetness trickled down my throat. At the same time, there came a bubbling sound from beneath me, and the venom on the spider's skin boiled as if it were lava. This happened for a few seconds, before the spider exploded, throwing me up into the air together with spatters of green, yucky goo. I yowled out as I hit the wall.

Before I could even turn towards my friends, I was greeted by a grating chittering noise from behind. I could sense the serket right behind me, and I turned to look at its black and lifeless eyes. It had me cornered within a slimy and cold alcove. I tried to scramble up the walls of it, but they were too slippery. There was absolutely no escape.

The serket charged and lunged its stinger forwards. I closed my eyes and prepared to die. What irony – especially right after I'd killed that massive spider.

"Oh no you don't," Ta'ra said from somewhere nearby. The serket hissed, then turned to engage her. It lunged downwards with its sting, but Ta'ra ducked out of the way, shrinking in size as she did. She led the serket away for a moment, then she turned on the charging beast and grew again, until she was three times the size of the arthropod.

Whiskers, she was larger than a lion at this point. She was as large, in fact, as a dragon. The scorpion stuck its sting into her paw, but she looked down at it and yawned. "Is that all you've got, you stupid critter?"

With her other paw, she swiped underneath the serket and knocked it flat on its back. There was something glowing red on its underbelly – another crystal. "You might as well do the honours, Ben," she said. "But be quick, we haven't got all day."

I mewled, and then I ran over. Or more, I should say, I hobbled over. I was still incredibly weak with whiskers knows what chemicals I had inside me. I swiped at the red crystal with my claws. The serket had an unusually soft underbelly, and I managed to knock the crystal away with ease.

The serket lashed at me one more time with its sting, but I was quick enough to get out of the way. Then, it went still, and shrivelled up within its own shell. I looked at Ta'ra, who was now the same size as me, licking the paw the serket had just stung. I mewled once more, and then I rubbed my nose against hers to say thank you.

She laughed. "Flaming demons, Ben," she said. "Why do I have to like you so much?"

The answer to that one was obvious. "Because I'm a Bengal, descendant of the great Asian leopard cat."

"Nah," Ta'ra said with a yawn. "It's just the hormones. I'll get over them in a few days."

She got up and stalked towards the front of the cavern, a certain feline and seductive sway to her hips. As she walked, her back feet landed in the same position as her front feet. She'd clearly been practising.

Initiate Rine and Aleam were busy at the front of the cave mouth knocking the crystals out of the serket's underbellies with the butts of their staffs. Ta'ra went over to help them. I watched them for a moment, thinking that I was too tired to work and that I needed some time to groom myself. But then, I realised that they had come all this way to help me, and I should at least help out a little.

So, I moved towards the front of the cave and helped with the arduous task of knocking the crystals out of the serkets. There were a lot of them, and so it took us an awfully long time.

33

AFTERMATH

I could tell Salanraja was angry, as she'd said nothing to me since my battle with the spider. So, by the time we'd reduced all the serkets to shells on the cave floor, I dreaded going outside.

Aleam, Rine and Ta'ra had already left me there, and I half worried that they might fly off without me. But then, at the same time, I worried that Salanraja would flame me as soon as I left this cave.

After a while, I mustered up the courage to leave. Salanraja had joined a couple of other dragons, each of them feeding upon a carcass of roasted goat. One of these dragons was an emerald with bright red eyes and two charcoal lines of spikes that ran across both flanks. The other was a brilliant white, the colour of snow – and by that I mean proper snow, the type I saw outside the Versta Caverns, and not the yucky type that falls in thin quantities in South Wales once or twice a year.

Both dragons wore saddles and had panniers on either side of them so wide that each bag looked like it could fit a large animal. The humans had created a campfire a little off to the side of the dragons, and they also had another goat roasting on a spit. Really, with all the delicious smells mingling with the air, I should have been starving.

But I don't know if it was because of the spider's poison, or just my general mood, but I'd really lost my appetite.

The sun had set low in the sky, and though that same purple gas was still here, the presence of dragon riders and dragons seemed to push it away. So, the air had a certain freshness to it. Not the kind you'd get in the forest, but it didn't taste stale, at least.

"*So, you finally came out to join us,*" Salanraja said.

"Salanraja," I replied. "*I really don't know what to say. I'm sorry. I shouldn't have run away like that. It was stupid.*"

Salanraja turned to me and snorted. A plume of smoke rose from her nostrils. "*It really was...*"

"*But the warlock,*" I continued. "*Astravar is in my head, and I don't know what to do about him.*" I glanced at the humans and Ta'ra. They hadn't yet seemed to notice that I'd left the caves.

"*I've been keeping Astravar out of your mind, you fool. But if you run away, I won't be able to watch what he's doing in there. Until we find a way to get that crystal you swallowed, Bengie, you need to stay close to me.*"

"*You mean to say that you can protect me from him?*"

"*Usually,*" Salanraja said. "*And I can do it in my sleep as well. It's a by-product of us being bonded – we protect each other. Only once did I let my attention slip. I was so exhausted after battling that bone dragon, I may have let him into your dreams. But as long as I'm close and protecting you, the warlock won't be able to take control.*"

This mind control stuff was so much to take in. Before I'd come to this world, I hadn't even conceived that people could talk to me in this way. It was all rather strange.

"*I'm sorry,*" I said again. "*I really am.*"

A deep rumbling sound came from the base of Salanraja's stomach. "*Just don't do it again. Remember, we're a team, and we need to work together. From now on, you're going to have to accept that.*"

"*Okay,*" I said.

"*Good. Now go and get some food; you really should eat something.*" I looked over at the goats that the dragons were munching into. "*Gracious demons, not here. Go over with the humans. After all we've been through, I don't want to see the other dragons tear you apart.*"

I groaned, and then I pulled myself over to the humans. Each step felt like I was trying to drag my feet through molten lead. My muscles not only ached, but they also burned as if that venom was still raging inside them. I didn't think it would kill me. Luckily, I don't think I'd taken enough of it. But my body still needed to break it down.

I approached the campfire where Initiate Rine and Aleam sat on a long stone ledge jutting out of the crag. Ta'ra sat opposite them, already with a good several scraps of goat in front of her. They must have brought the wood for the fire over in the panniers, because nothing around us looked good for burning.

"*Why don't you get panniers?*" I asked Salanraja.

"*Please shut up,*" Salanraja replied. "*Don't mention that idea to anyone.*"

"*What? Why?*"

"*Because no one who has any power has had that idea yet, and I'd rather fly light, thank you very much. My dragon friends, Ishtkar and Olan here agree it's for the best. If they had any choice, they'd lose the panniers too.*"

I glanced back at the two dragons, who had their heads tucked into their food, without seeming to have a care in the world. "*Which one's which?*" I asked.

"*Ishtkar's the green and Olan's the white. Ishtkar and Rine are bonded, as are Olan and Aleam. Now haven't you got some apologising to do?*"

I meowed, then I jumped up next to Initiate Rine on the ledge. Rine turned to me and turned up his nose. "Come to cause more problems, have you?" he asked. "Because you have no idea how much trouble you almost got me in."

"I came over for..." And I suddenly realised how hungry that the smell of the goat on the spit was making me feel.

"What, you want food now?" Rine said.

"No," I said. "I came to say sorry." Then, I pushed up to him and I let off a soft purr as I sat down next to his hip.

"I guess we're always going to be different," Rine said. "You're a cat, and I'm a human."

"I guess."

Aleam turned to look at me. "You know, Ben. Even if you're new here, you've caused quite a stir at the Council of Three. I'm sorry to say this, but I'm not sure they'll accept you as a dragon rider when we get back. There will be a trial, and the fate for you and Salanraja they were threatening might come to pass."

"But it was me who stepped out of line," I pointed out. "She doesn't deserve to get punished for it." Whiskers, no wonder she was angry with me.

"It doesn't matter," Aleam said. "You're bonded and your responsibility is also Salanraja's. You get rewarded together for your good deeds, and you get punished together for your bad. That is the law."

"Not just that," Rine said as he tore a thick strand of meat off a bone. "But you got me into trouble too. There's a reason why I brought Ishtkar out here. Fortunately, Driar Aleam had the heart to help too, because I'm not sure I could have handled these creatures alone."

"And me," Ta'ra said, and slinked around the fire. "Don't forget about me." She jumped up and sat on Aleam's lap.

"You were the bravest of all, Ta'ra," Aleam said with a chuckle, and I don't know why, but something about that was funny. I couldn't help but laugh. Like a human...

34

AN EPIPHANY

After we'd all eaten and had some time to chat the evening away, Initiate Rine and Aleam put out the fire then strapped up the panniers and tightened the saddles on the dragons. I had remained silent through the rest of the meal, as I kind of realised that I had an ordeal ahead of me. I felt awful, I really did. Both Salanraja and I would be punished, me probably locked up in the cattery and not even let out on rat duty in case I ever tried running away again.

Meanwhile, I couldn't imagine what they might do to Salanraja. They might clip her wings or something, which is what I heard they did to those nasty swan birds that every cat but Adam knew not to go anywhere near.

There was also something else bothering me. I remembered that conversation that High Prefect Lars had had with his friend, Asinda in the dining hall. He'd mentioned something about a demon dragon.

I walked over to Aleam as he tightened the straps on Olan's saddle to try and find out some more. "Aleam," I said. "Can I ask you something?"

Aleam turned to me and raised an eyebrow. "Go on..."

"I heard about the demon dragon," I said. "High Prefect Lars was talking about it in the dining room."

"Terrible thing," Aleam said, shaking his head. "I just hope the king can send enough forces in time to stop it. Otherwise, no dragon rider or mage on this world will be able to kill it. It will hunt all dragons down and then it will destroy cities, and after a year there might be nothing left of civilisation on this world."

I thought about it a moment. Then, I remembered what the crystal had shown me. How South Wales had become a barren landscape, my owners lying down as skeletons on the master bed. Could it be the demon dragon that caused this? All because of the demon rats I killed...

"How long until he summons it?" I asked.

"The problem is that we don't know," Aleam replied. "Nor do we know exactly where the warlocks will perform the ceremony, or which warlock will be involved."

"Astravar..." I said.

"How do you know?"

"He told me his plans in a dream," he said. "And he wants me to be part of them."

"If only we knew where he was," Aleam replied. "Then maybe we could put a stop to this. We have scouts out hunting the Darklands for him. But I fear we don't have enough time."

I left Aleam to finish checking the saddle on his dragon, feeling as if I'd failed everyone. If I hadn't come to this world, none of this might have happened. But I was just part of Astravar's nefarious plans.

That was when I felt a force in my head. It felt as if there was a stone just behind my nose, and someone was pulling it gently. A sudden image entered my mind. I saw Astravar in the middle of a massive pentagram, set in the centre of a shallow crater in the grey earth. He had tiny bodies arranged all around him – the husks of dead rats. He stared right into a crystal on a pedestal, which fed light into a massive hole in the sky. This shimmered like the surface of a lake, reflecting the putrid landscape that surrounded the warlock.

Suddenly, he turned his head as if he knew I was watching him, and I batted my eyelids and blinked him away.

I turned around to see that Initiate Rine and Aleam had already mounted. Ta'ra was sat on Aleam's lap, strapped into a belt that the old man had wrapped around his legs.

"*Come on, little one,*" Salanraja said. "*It's time to face our punishment.*"

"*Wait,*" I replied and I sprinted right past Salanraja and then in front of the emerald and the white dragon. They had their legs lowered, as if they were ready to take off. "Wait!" I shouted out loud.

Rine pulled on the reins in front of me and then looked down from his dragon. "What is it now?" he called back.

"It's Astravar. He's starting to perform the ceremony to summon the demon dragon, and I know exactly where he is."

FLIGHT TO ASTRAVAR

After I'd delivered my news that I knew where Astravar was, Initiate Rine and Aleam had told me not to be fanciful, and Salanraja had called me an idiot inside my head. But I informed them that since I'd swallowed the golem's gemstone, somehow it worked as a compass between me and the warlock. That caused them to become more interested. Aleam put his hand to his chin, scratching it, then he gazed off towards the purple horizon.

"We should go," he said. "I think the young cat is right." Aleam also instructed his dragon to call for reinforcements from Dragonsbond Academy. But he didn't think they'd get there in time to stop Astravar summoning the demon dragon. We had the advantage of distance, and so it was down to us.

Hence, we took off into the sky.

We had a long flight ahead of us, through the Wastelands and into the Darklands. Fortunately, we took a sharp right at some point, as we wanted to minimise the encounters with griffins and harpies and other horrible minions of the warlocks that I couldn't remember the names of.

I'd been tripping out on those purple gases so long, that the green and the yellow hues of Illumine's fields didn't look so vivid and straight as they should. Rather, they spun by below, whirling and dancing in my vision, as if they were alive. Though, this might have been a side effect of the venom, admittedly.

After a while the effect wore off. The air tasted fresh again. The grey layer of clouds had lifted by this point, and the sun had passed through, casting its warm rays upon the farmers and sheep down below. It also helped allay the effect of the strong and cold wind, somewhat.

We passed by Midar village, and I looked down at the sheep pen. The young lady – Rala the shepherdess – was down there shearing the wool off her flock of six sheep. She turned up to look at us, shielding her eyes as we passed.

After that, the sun set, and we flew under the cover of night without stopping. As we progressed, the weather got colder, and the air took on a smell of rotten eggs. We didn't have time for camping. Astravar could complete the ceremony at any time.

I was still worried. This could easily be another trap. Astravar could have faked my visions for all I knew. Maybe the portal wasn't to summon a demon dragon, but to suck us all into the Seventh Dimension. Then, from what Salanraja had told me, we'd have to deal with demon beasts of all kinds.

"We're all fully aware of what we might be flying into," Salanraja told me. "But we don't have time to wait for reinforcements to arrive. Nothing can kill a demon dragon once it's out of the Seventh Dimension. If Astravar succeeds in summoning it, it will eliminate anything that we send at it and eventually destroy everything upon this world."

I guess she was right, but I couldn't help but shudder at the thought of a massive invulnerable dragon from another dimension. Whiskers, Salanraja was scary enough.

The thought of it all made my skin itchy, and the only way to calm the stress was to groom myself with my paws and tongue. But then I recalled that I had just been wrapped in a venomous cobweb, and so licking myself didn't seem such a good idea.

We turned back into the Wastelands, just as day approached. There was a beautiful sunrise that brought farmers out from their huts to watch. The massive orb in the sky cast brilliant red rays over the fields, and it made me feel good to be alive.

"*This is the best part of flying,*" Salanraja said. "*To experience sights like these.*"

But unfortunately, this sight was short-lived, because that odorous purple horizon was approaching and the mist there was thicker than I'd seen it before. We soon hit it like one hits a wall, and with it an intense chill washed over me. That dense purple fog had taken over the land and sky, and I imagined how a massive demon dragon might jump out of the murk and swat us down in one fell swoop.

I felt a sense of emptiness from the absence of the sunrise. Everything that I'd lived for, the good life full of milk and salmon trimmings for breakfast in the morning, running over my owners' lawn in South Wales trying to bat the butterflies out of the air. All this, I'd now had to leave behind so I could face my destiny.

"*Do you have to be so melodramatic?*" Salanraja said. "*I think I prefer the old Bengie.*"

"*Well he's gone,*" I said, clenching my jaw. "*This time, we're going to stop that evil warlock and then you and I will force him to send me back through the portal.*"

A slow and sonorous rumbling came from Salanraja's chest underfoot. "*Do you really want to go home? Does our bond matter to you so little?*"

I hesitated as I lowered my head. Of course, the bond was important to me. But then, I didn't ask for any of this.

"*I don't know,*" I replied. "*Let's just take this one step at a time.*"

The mist soon cleared a little, and I could make out some shapes through the murk. There was a tall tower there, which I presumed to be Astravar's. It's funny, when I was running away from it, I never turned around to look at it. But now, I could see how menacing the thing looked. With the mist drifting around it, it looked almost like a ghost flickering in and out of existence. On the top of it, it had what looked like a raised crown, with thorns like spades sticking out the top instead of parapets.

Seeing it now, part of me wondered if I could just summon the portal myself. Maybe I could just climb off Salanraja, run to the top of Astravar's tower that would be conveniently unlocked for me and then step into the centre of his portal. Shazam, it would open up for me, and the next moment I'll be looking right into my bowl of milk and salmon trimmings. None of this would have happened and everything could go back to normal.

But then, such a portal could take me to the dangerous Savannah. A land full of hippopotamuses that would tear me up with their razor-sharp buck teeth or take me down underneath the mud and suffocate me. The worst deaths, I had heard, happened underneath the belly of the hippopotamus. Oh, those Savannah cats were such storytellers.

"Will you stop daydreaming your nonsense," Salanraja said. *"We're almost there."*

I'd been in such a reverie, I'd lost track of what was going on around us. We'd taken a sharp turn away from the tower and were now heading towards a shallow mountain range.

"There," I heard Initiate Rine call out from Ishtkar's back on my right. He pointed off into the distance with his staff.

I looked where he was pointing, at a white glow coming up from the horizon. "Is that it?" I called out, struggling to raise my voice over the loudness of the wind.

"Yes," Salanraja replied. *"Now brace yourself. It's now time to find out what that warlock has in store."*

36

BONE DRAGON BATTLE

W e saw the bone dragons first, and this time we didn't have only one to contend with but a good dozen of them. They were wheeling around in a circle above the ground created from the dried husks of all the demon rats I'd killed. There must have been thousands of them – I never realised I'd killed so many. That then made me wonder how much of my stay in Astravar's tower I remembered. Maybe the warlock hadn't needed me to swallow the golem's crystal for him to take control of my mind. Maybe he'd had dominion over me all along.

Manipulators stood outside of the circle feeding energy into the bone dragons. Each had a dragon of their own, and they slithered around on the ground as they tracked the position of their minions.

Astravar stood in the centre of the circle, with a crystal on a pedestal in front of him. He was bent over this with his arms stretched out wide, and his lips were moving as if chanting a ritual. But we were too far away to hear what he was saying.

The crystal cast a bright light out from the circle, almost as bright as the sun had been before. It seemed to be feeding its energy into a massive oval as tall as a castle. It shimmered white around the edges, and the reflection of our world faded, to display a land full of fire and magma. The Seventh Dimension. It couldn't be anything else.

There was also something standing next to Astravar, that looked rather feline and slightly overweight. It had red skin, with cracks running down it that looked like they were on fire. Black smoke rose from the beast as it stared up at me with red glowing eyes, as if challenging me to come down and fight it. As Salanraja got closer, I also saw the thing was massive, perhaps four times the size of me. But we were moving so fast I couldn't quite make out what it was.

My major concern wasn't the massive beast or the massive portal thingy, anyway. It was the bone dragons that screeched up into the air in unison, and then wheeled around in the sky to face us. One of them was coming at Salanraja head on.

"Hold on..." Salanraja called out in my mind.

"You keep saying that when I've got nothing to hold on t—"

Before I knew it, purple flame was spewing out of the bone dragon's mouth. Some of it brushed against my fur, withering it on touch. Presently, Salanraja performed a barrel roll and swooped out of the way, sending me spinning around in her second rib cage again. All this time, when I'd stood in front of the washing machine in South Wales, watching clothes spin round and round, I never thought I'd end up in one. But at that moment, I couldn't help but feel sorry for the clothes.

I scrambled up Salanraja's back to stop myself falling off. I reached the top just as Salanraja reached her apex, and all seemed still for a moment. I caught sight of Aleam and Rine flying side by side on their dragons. They had their staffs stuck out in front of them as they headed towards two bone dragons while another three chased them on their tails. Flashes of lightning came out of Aleam's staff, while Rine tossed out a stream of water that quickly froze and then shattered in the air.

But they only knocked the bone dragons out of the way, which soon corrected themselves and flew back off into the distance, ready to strike again.

Salanraja started to climb again, and I ran back up to her neck, doing everything I could to stay there without falling off. I turned to see that we had another two bone dragons on our tail, but Salanraja veered quickly to the right, to throw them off target.

"*What are we going to do, Salanraja?*" I asked, as the turning force pushed me into one side of her corridor of spikes.

I felt Salanraja's back muscles tense underneath my skin. "*I've already talked to the other dragons about it, who of course have discussed this with their riders.*"

"*And their conclusion is?*"

Another roar came from behind and some purple flame swooped over my head. It wasn't hot, but rather felt like a spray of concentrated acid. Some of it touched the back of my ears, and it really stung.

Salanraja executed a loop-the-loop, and I cursed as I thought I'd fall right out of the sky. She got on top of the bone dragon that had assailed us, and as I lay on my back pressed against the top of Salanraja's second ribcage, I wanted to throw up. Then, she came back down, so she was behind the thing, and she opened her mouth and let out a loud roar mixed with a jet of fire. Of course, it didn't do much damage.

In a way, I didn't see much point in fighting these things if they couldn't be defeated without first destroying their Manipulators. But I guess dragons and dragon riders enjoyed making pretty patterns in the sky with their magic.

"*Just get down on the ground, and fight,*" Salanraja said. "*We need Aleam's and Rine's magic up here to fight the bone dragons.*"

Memories of the battle with the previous bone dragon flashed across my mind. I remembered the thorns, and the sting, and almost dying in my sleep. "*I can't take all the Manipulators,*" I pointed out.

"*No, don't stop them. Stop Astravar's ceremony. Winning this battle is much more important than our own lives.*"

Salanraja dived towards the ground, and she jerked into a hover, throwing me towards her tail. Instead of trying to grasp on for my dear life, I submitted and let myself roll down it. I landed on the cold and dusty ground.

I lifted myself up to see that massive beast standing right before me. It opened its mouth and let out a terrible hiss as it displayed a fine set of incredibly sharp teeth.

37

MEET THY NEMESIS

I couldn't believe what I was looking at. I had never seen one in my life before, even if I knew them to be the king of domesticated cats. I scanned the cavernous, pointed ears that rose high above its head, its menacing glowing eyes set into a flat face, and a mane and beard that extended far below its chin.

It was massive. It was hideous.

I was standing face to face with a Maine Coon. Except this wasn't a normal Maine Coon, it was a demon Maine Coon, presumably summoned from the Seventh Dimension. So maybe I hadn't killed as many demon rats as I thought, because this thing looked like it would be great at killing things. Forget about the demon dragon. With this thing at Astravar's disposal, every cat in this land was doomed.

I could feel the heat coming off it, as if I was facing a pile of burning embers. If not for the fiery cracks in its skin, the beast would have been a flat charcoal colour. It was also big – I hadn't gathered the true scale of it from the air. But it was certainly bigger than a lion. Perhaps it was even bigger than Ta'ra had been when she'd knocked the senses out of that serket.

Whiskers, why wasn't she down here instead of me? Surely that would have been a fairer fight. I glanced upwards to try and catch sight of the Cat Sidhe on the white dragon. But I couldn't see her and Olan now had four bone dragons on its tail.

The demon cat opened its mouth and yawned. Red slaver run out from its mouth and fell towards the ground. This sizzled when it hit the rock, leaving a black char mark. Around it, the purple gas danced and swayed, and I noticed then that the cat's eyes weren't just glowing. They were like windows looking into a raging furnace inside the Maine Coon's head, as if fire had replaced its brain.

"NO CAT CAN DEFEAT HELLCAT," it said incredibly loudly, hissing out the cat language that I'd not heard for so long.

It arched its back and circled me, and I followed its path, wondering how I had any chance of taking this thing down. I tried to see behind it, so I could ascertain the position of the crystal. But my enemy blocked any possible path I had through.

So, I arched my back just like him, and hissed back at him. I don't know what I was thinking, really. It was just natural instinct kicking in, really. But there was another feeling in my gut that was telling me to run, Ben. Get as far from this place as I could and leave the fate of the world in the dragons' and the dragon riders' hands.

A roar came from the sky, just as the demon cat crouched down and then leaped at me. I rolled out of the way, feeling the heat from it searing against me. Whiskers, I really didn't want to touch that thing. But it was quick to turn around, and I was soon facing it again. I thought of charging for the crystal, but I had no time before it pounced again. I lifted myself on my hind paws to parry the blow. It was stupid, because the demon cat caught me by the shoulders and pinned me to the ground.

I wriggled and tried to free myself from the demon's grasp. My shoulders burned as if I was pinned underneath two red-hot iron pokers. I wanted to cry out in pain, but it was too much for me to even move my mouth. I struggled, and I gasped for breath, and I thought I was going to pass out.

That's when the Maine Coon suddenly rolled off me along the ground. Salanraja's skin brushed against my legs, and she took back off into the air. I stood up, and I finally took an opportunity to yowl out my pain.

"*You can't kill it, Ben,*" Salanraja said. "*Don't even try. Go for the crystal!*"

The demon Maine Coon lifted itself up and spun around to face me again. It opened its mouth and hissed and growled as it looked up at Salanraja, who was now doing a loop-the-loop to avoid a purple flame coming from a bone dragon approaching from her side.

"*The crystal, Ben!*" Salanraja said.

I turned and looked at the pedestal. Astravar was facing away from me, his arms now stretched above his head. I heard the demon cat scuff the ground behind me, and I took the opportunity to run. I sprinted faster than a greyhound chasing after a lump of steak. Or at least that's how it seemed at the time.

But the massive demon cat was close on my tail, and I had to dodge to the right to stop it barrelling into me and pinning me back to the ground. I felt the heat from it as it brushed against me, but I had too much adrenaline in me, which propelled me forwards towards my target.

There it was, in front of me, so much white light glowing from the crystal that it almost blinded me. I leapt up onto the pedestal, and I heard Astravar shout out from behind me.

"You!" he screamed.

But he was too late, because I readied a huge swipe and I knocked at the crystal with all my might. It was much steadier on its perch than it looked, and the impact sent a shudder up my paw to my shoulder that was already screaming at me from the burn. So, I used more strength than a cat could possibly have to push the heavy crystal towards the edge, putting my head, shoulder, and back into it. Eventually, it toppled to the floor, making a loud crashing sound.

It shattered, sending up shards of whatever it was made of into the air and filling the sky with a prismatic display of light.

"*You did it, Bengie,*" Salanraja said, and there came a great bellowing from the sky. The victory cries of not one dragon, but three.

But that's when I noticed something was wrong. Because Astravar was nowhere to be seen, and the demon Maine Coon was sprinting to a point where a bright white light shone out of the horizon. Around me, the circle of dead demon rats had completely disappeared off the ground.

OUT OF THE PORTAL

The Manipulators tossed their wispy heads into the sky, looking like they wanted to scream out. But they were silent, as their energy leeched out of them, and dissipated into the earth. The bone dragons also withered away in the sky, turning into flakes of what looked like black charcoal. Surprisingly, no crystals dropped out of them, nor did any crystals fall from the Manipulators onto the ground.

The portal had completely vanished as well, almost as if it had never been there at all.

"*Gracious demons,*" Salanraja said. "*We've been tricked.*"

"What, how?"

"*That crystal you knocked out was only summoning an illusion. No time to explain. Follow now!*"

Above, Olan was already heading towards that glowing spot on the horizon, and Ishtkar and Salanraja wheeled around in the sky and dived, using gravity to their advantage to catch up with the white dragon. I groaned from deep inside the belly, part of me wanting to turn around and go back to being wild again.

But we all know how that turned out last time. I needed to help my friends.

I could still see the demon Maine Coon, and so I summoned up some remaining threads of energy and sprinted right after him. My legs felt like jelly at first, and my body really wanted to give up. I panted as I went, and I pushed myself so hard that all of my muscles burned.

I arrived at a circle made of the same demon rats that I'd seen before. In fact, everything looked so similar that I realised what I'd just battled must have been a mirror duplicate of this scene. Except that there were no Manipulators. It was just Astravar and the demon Maine Coon.

There was also a massive white portal, just like the first one. Except it now had a fiery red centre to it, which rippled as I moved. It looked almost as if I was staring through a pool of water into another world. Which, in retrospect, I guess I was.

Astravar had a staff in his hand with a dark purple crystal set into the head of it. He pointed this at the crystal on the pedestal, feeding it with purple energy, which turned into white energy that fed the portal proper.

The dragons swooped down as one and tried to flame Astravar. But he just raised his staff into the air and swept it from the floor over his head in one fluid motion. A purple barrier of light blossomed out of him, and the flames met that and didn't go any further. The dragons continued their dive, and they hit the barrier head on. They ended up bouncing off it, and all three of them struggled to recover in the sky.

Whiskers, I don't know how the dragon riders managed to stay on their mounts. But then, I guess they had the luxury of being strapped into their saddles.

As the dragons swept around for another pass, Astravar's voice boomed out so loudly that I thought he had one of those funny shaped devices that humans used in carnivals and the like to amplify their voice. "You are too late," he said. "The ritual is complete, and the world will soon belong to us."

That was when there came an intense flash of red light from the portal. It felt like the entire world burned with flame for just a moment, and I thought I was going to get scorched alive. Then, the ground shook underfoot, and a roar ten times louder than thunder filled the sky.

It all happened in less than a second, after which the red light faded, and there was the demon dragon flying out of the portal from its previous world.

It was five times the size of the dragons and had those same cracks in its skin that I'd seen on the demon Maine Coon's body. The air around it seemed to shimmer, almost as if it was getting sucked into what burned beneath the demon dragon.

"*No!*" Salanraja screamed out in my head.

The dragons had turned around to face the demon, and they were already charging in once again. But the mighty demon dragon opened its mouth, and the ground trembled so violently I was knocked off of my feet. A spherical pulse of energy shot out of the dragon, looking very much like the surface of a bubble lined with veins of fire. Salanraja, Olan, and Ishtkar flew right into it, and then the energy field swept them away.

It was as if they'd just been hit by a cricket bat the size of a cloud, and soon, all three dragons became lost to sight.

A voice thundered out, so deep it sounded like that man who played the father lion in that cartoon the kid in South Wales used to love to watch. "I AM DEMON DRAGON," it bellowed. "CONJURATION OF THE WARLOCK ASTRAVAR. THIS WORLD SHALL SOON BE HIS."

A little voice inside me wanted to call back, "Big deal, I'm a Bengal, descendant of the great Asian leopard cat." But an even bigger voice told me that this creature probably wouldn't be so impressed.

The demon dragon flew off in the direction it had knocked the other three dragons. It wasn't travelling particularly fast, I noticed. But then it was a great lumbering beast.

I turned to Astravar, now looking down on me with his pale face and lifeless grey eyes. Like in my dream, his skin had taken on a certain blueness and had started to crack a little like an eggshell. This dark magic addiction was changing him in most unnatural ways.

I wanted to approach Astravar and at least scratch him with my long claws and show him how much I hated him. I took a step forward, but his pet demon Maine Coon, my replacement, blocked my path. It raised its back and hissed at me.

Astravar looked down at him and laughed. "Cats will always be cats," he said. "No matter what realm I summon them from."

"And humans will always be humans," I replied. "Who are meant to live in servitude of cats."

"Not in this world," Astravar replied. "Although, it would seem that if I let it have its way, then humans would eventually let that happen. But they will never have a chance. Once this world is my own, I shall seize control of all dimensions. I don't need the other warlocks now. I can do this alone."

I growled at him. "What do you want of me, Astravar?" I said. "I had a good life, and you had to bring me here. You deserve to die."

"Maybe I will one day," Astravar said with a grin that chapped his lips, "and then I shall come back a greater being. I thought of doing the same to you. But I'm not sure you deserve it anymore. It's a shame. I brought you here thinking you might be interested in becoming one of the most powerful beings across the dimensions. But it looks like you're not as opportunistic as I first thought."

"I just want to live my life," I said. "Eating and sleeping and grooming and playing..."

"No, you don't. You want to survive like any creature upon this world. But that's the irony of it all, you have never been powerful enough to survive alone. Just like the humans... Or at least the ones who don't claim power for themselves." He pointed his staff in my direction, and he shot a bolt of purple energy out of it. The beam hit the ground right next to me and caused a rock there to shatter into pieces. Astravar curled up his mouth and laughed, entertained by his cruelty.

He was a bad man that one, of the kind that liked to tease and torture cats.

I stared back at him, licking my lips. If he was going to kill me, he might as well do it here and now. At least I wouldn't have to deal with this world anymore, and I wouldn't have to witness the destruction of all the wonderful food within it.

The warlock sighed wistfully, and then he jumped on the demon

Maine Coon. I couldn't help but hope that doing so gave him a burnt bottom. He pointed his staff off into the distance.

But before he had gone far, he stopped the Maine Coon, and he twisted around and let off another bolt of purple energy. This fizzled as it hit the ground next to me, and sparks flew out from the impact point in all directions. These created more impact points, and the ground seemed to melt for a moment. Then, red sprouts shot out of it in all directions, and out of these grew hideous thorns and those snapping heads that I'd had to deal with during my first encounter with a Manipulator.

Astravar's voice boomed out once again.

"This world will teach you, Dragoncat, how you are truly incapable of survival," and he rode off into the distance, his maniacal laughter trailing in his wake.

39

TOSS UP

The forest of Mandragoras grew and grew, and the thorns became thicker and thicker. Their heads snapped into the air as if feeding on a flock of sparrows. Everywhere I looked, I could see thickening stems and thorns that I knew were tipped with venom. I couldn't see any way out.

Astravar had kindly left a large circle around me that kept me safe from this forest. But it was slowly closing in on me, as the plants continued to grow on their own accord. I could try running through. But I'd get stung so many times, it would kill me.

"*Salanraja,*" I called out in my mind. "*Salanraja, are you out there?*"

I heard no reply, and I could only assume her to be unconscious. She'd probably been stupid enough to fight the demon dragon, even though she knew she couldn't kill it.

I tried to find a path through the plants. I saw a glimmer in the distance between the thorns, indicating sky. I was probably going to die anyway, so I might as well try something.

That's when I noticed the purple mist creeping in from the outside. It was getting thicker, and as it moved more and more stems seemed to grow out of it. It was as if the mist fed the plants and gave them life.

I stood meowing from the back of my throat and feeling hopeless. The gas soon reached me, and I found myself unable to breathe. I was weak, and I fell down on the ground, my legs collapsing under me. Thorns writhed above me, and my vision went red and blurry.

A roar came out from the distance, faint now, but still like thunder. I knew what it was, the demon dragon creating even more carnage.

"*Salanraja,*" I cried out again. "*Please, I need you.*"

Her voice came back to me faint. "*Hold on, Bengie. Hang in there...*"

"*Salanraja... I can't breathe.*"

"*Just one more moment...*"

The branches of these terrible plants were now almost close enough to touch me. They didn't seem to want to lash out like before, as if they knew that I was rendered helpless and there was no point in spending energy on sudden movements. I closed my eyes, ready for them to pierce my skin and inject their deadly poisons into me.

But then, strong claws grappled around my waist, and lifted me up into the sky. I opened my eyes, wondering if this was one of those angel creatures that sent you up to cat heaven. In that place, our old Ragamuffin mentor had said, you could have as much salmon and chicken liver as you wanted. Apparently, angel cats had wings, but I don't think they had long scaly talons like the ones that were gripped around me.

I came to my senses pretty quickly. "*Salanraja you came,*" I said, my eyes a little bleary.

"*Of course,*" she replied. "*We're bonded, and I won't let you die. Now get up onto my back.*"

"*I—*" But I didn't have a chance to even start my thought, because Salanraja shot suddenly upwards. She gained momentum, so she could open her claws, tossing me out of them. I rose, and then I started to fall, looking down at the forest of those terrible thorny plants and purple gas that had formed around them.

I plummeted, and I shrieked out into the wind, although I'm sure nothing heard me. I landed on Salanraja's back and tumbled down her corridor of spikes before I caught myself on one outer rib with my claws. I lifted myself up to safety, then I sat down, breathing heavily.

I couldn't believe it. I was alive. But I felt sick...

So, I threw up on Salanraja's back.

"What in the Seventh Dimension?"

"I couldn't help it," I replied. *"And it's me who should be complaining. You almost killed me."*

"What? I saved your life, and then you thank me with the contents of your stomach for it."

I growled. *"Just never do that again."*

"Fine, I'll abandon you in the warlock's forest next time."

"Not that. Never toss me up in the air and catch me like that again. What if I'd hit the ground?"

"Bengie, we haven't any time for your moaning right now. We need to meet up with our friends."

She turned sharply in the air, and I watched the forest disappear below. It wasn't long before we broke out into Illumine again, and I breathed the fresh air as if I'd just emerged from my mother's womb and was tasting it for the first time.

40

SO MANY WASTED FISH

Salanraja didn't seem to want to take time to slow down and appreciate the scenery. We flew over a forest – this time a normal one with pine trees in it. There was a glade down there, with a long blue lake that stretched across it. We approached a silver beach where Olan and Ishtkar were waiting. Salanraja landed so heavily on it, that I ended up tumbling off her back onto the sand.

"Ben," I heard Aleam say. He was there in the distance, setting up a load of fish bones in a circle. In the centre of this there was a wooden pedestal, with a massive crystal on it just like the one Astravar had used to summon the dragon.

I soon spotted Rine and Ta'ra out on a small raft on the lake. Rine had a rod raised over the water whilst Ta'ra was crouched over the side of the raft, her head lowered to the surface as her head rolled from side to side.

I jumped up from the sand, forgetting about the injuries from my scrap with the Demon Maine Coon. I moved over to Aleam, purring, and I rubbed my cheek against his knee. "Please let it be salmon," I said. "Finally, are you about to find salmon?"

Aleam didn't turn to me, as he continued to concentrate on getting the exact arrangement of fish bones. I didn't like being ignored, so I moved over to one of the bones right next to him and knocked it out of the way.

"Don't do that," he said. "We must get it in exactly the right position."

"But it's fish. I've not tasted salmon in ages."

"Just..." Aleam shook his head. "This is much more important than your stomach. We've found a lake abundant in fish, and we're using their bones to summon up an offering to the Seventh Dimension. I'll need to concentrate, because I don't want to have to deal with a demon tetrapod as well as a demon dragon."

I blinked at him. "A what?"

"An ancient demon fish," Aleam said. "Now, let me get back to my work."

I growled, and I moved over to the water, watching as Rine and Ta'ra lifted fish after fish from the water. As they did, I wondered which ones would be salmon and which ones wouldn't. Come to think of it, I had absolutely no idea what salmon looked like in the wild. The fish they lifted out seemed rather small, and I'd heard from the Savannah cats that a salmon could be as large as an Asian leopard cat. Which meant they had to be massive.

"*Don't you want to know what Aleam is doing?*" Salanraja asked me.

I yawned. "*I guess you're going to tell me, anyway?*"

"*Of course. We don't have a chance of killing the demon dragon. But we might be able to lure it back. If we can trick it back to where it came from, then we only need to close the portal.*"

"*What? That's a suicide mission!*"

"*If we don't,*" Salanraja said. "*Then it will kill us eventually, whether we like it or not. That beast has only one purpose, to destroy any mortal life it finds. Or at least that is the task Astravar has set for it.*"

I crouched down in the sand and gazed out into the distance. Rine and Ta'ra had gathered a sackful of fish, and Rine was rowing the raft back towards shore. "*How does Aleam know how to do this stuff, anyway? Is he some kind of warlock himself?*"

"*Kind of,*" Salanraja replied, and she lowered her head to the ground and looked at me with her yellow eyes. I turned to meet her gaze, now not at all scared of her massive head. "*Several years ago, King*

Garmin of Illumine Kingdom decided that he wanted to train up eight powerful mages to help protect the kingdom from its enemies in other lands. Use of dark crystals for magic had been banned by his ancestors long before him. But he decided to bring their use into the realm. Aleam was one of those mages, and the others became the seven warlocks."

"You mean to say the other seven turned on the king?"

"Yes," Salanraja replied. *"The power in dark crystals corrupts the mind of those that use it, just as the power in the light crystals brings them closer to their souls. But dragon riders are immune to the effect dark magic has on the mind. It is we dragons who protect you from the darkness that seeks to taint your souls, which is how I managed to keep Astravar out of yours – most of the time, anyway."*

"So, what you're saying is that Aleam could have turned out just like the other warlocks?"

"Exactly. If he hadn't found Olan and bonded with him, then he probably would have. Dark magic is now once again banned within the Kingdom of Illumine. But the warlocks betrayed King Garmin long ago and tore apart a large part of his kingdom which they claimed as their own. This was the Darklands. Soon after, the Wastelands became a battlefield, where the king's Mages of the Light fought against the warlocks, each trying to gain power for themselves."

"But what does this magic from crystals of the light do, exactly?" I asked.

"Not much that's useful in war, unfortunately. It helps build cities and wealth and heal those in need. It's focused on growth, whilst the warlock's magic is focused on decay."

Rine and Ta'ra had almost reached the shore now. Rine lowered his oar down into the sand and pulled the raft in. I looked in awe at the massive sack they had on that boat, imagining its tasty contents. The bag was literally wriggling, with all those poor fish inside trying to escape. Perhaps I should have felt sorry for them, but I was too hungry to care.

Rine hefted up the sack and lugged it onto shore. He placed it just outside the circle that Aleam had created, but he didn't open it. Rine turned to Aleam, then he lifted up his staff off his back. Aleam did the same.

"Are you ready?" Rine asked.

"Yes," Aleam said.

I was already at the sack, sniffing at its contents, relishing the smell of something I'd not eaten for so long.

"Stand back," Rine said. "Unless you want to be a fried cat."

I didn't need to be warned twice. I dashed out of the way and then turned around to see what the humans were up to. A massive bolt of blue shot out of Rine's staff. It hit the sack in the centre and immediately froze the material on the outside. Then, Aleam took his turn to send out a cascade of yellow lightning. His magic hit the sack and then the sparks danced over its surface, as Rine added more and more of his ice to the recipe.

"What are you doing?" I cried out. "Stop, you'll waste all that lovely food."

"Oh, can't you stop worrying about your stomach all the time," Ta'ra said, stepping up to me. "We've got a demon dragon to stop."

"But the food," I protested, and I watched with wide eyes as the sack shrunk under the power that Aleam and Rine fed into it. My heart sank in my chest, and I realised that I wouldn't be getting any salmon today.

After a while, the sack tore apart and shrivelled under the forces that Rine and Aleam were putting upon it. Fish bone after fish bone tumbled out of it, all of them devoid of flesh.

"That should be enough," Aleam said. "Now, it's time to get on with your duties, Rine. Ben, you and Salanraja shall accompany him."

I wasn't listening. I was just staring in shock at the smouldering pile of fish bones that didn't even smell like fish anymore.

"*Ben, will you stop being so selfish for once?*" Salanraja requested. "*And jump on my back.*"

"*But why do you need me there?*" I said. "*What use am I going to be against a demon dragon?*"

"*Just get on,*" Salanraja said, and she fixed a stern gaze upon me. Ta'ra was staring at me too, looking at me in a cat's expression of what I could only describe as disappointment. For some reason, I didn't want to let her down.

"Fine," I said out loud, and I turned and ran up Salanraja's tail. She took us up, up, and away in pursuit of the demon dragon.

THE DEMON DRAGON

Rine was soon flying alongside us on Ishtkar's back. Aleam, Olan and Ta'ra meanwhile stayed on the ground. From up high, I watched Ta'ra help lift the fish bones with her mouth and drop them in the right position. Aleam had them all neatly arranged, and from this height it all looked like an intricate clock pattern. The wind was warm, but this soon chilled as we gained altitude.

"*Why does she get to stay?*" I asked Salanraja, as I felt a little jealous for the fact she could wrap her mouth around the fishbones and get a slight taste of them, even if Rine and Aleam had completely destroyed the food.

"*Because she isn't bonded to a dragon,*" Salanraja replied. "*And you are.*"

"*But I still don't understand what use I can be up here. I can't shoot jets of ice like Rine can. I don't have any of that useful battle magic.*"

"*Do you know how to summon a portal?*"

"*No...*"

"*Then even the tiniest use you can be up here,*" Salanraja said, "*is better than making mischief on the ground.*"

She had a point, I guess. The demon dragon was flying slowly, and Salanraja and Ishtkar seemed to be putting all their strength into catching up with it.

This, we soon did. I saw the air shimmering on the horizon before I saw the great lumbering beast. Black smoke drifted up from the huge rents in its skin and trailed behind it in the sky. It didn't seem threatened by our arrival and didn't turn to knock us out of the sky. It just carried on its path, as if no force upon this world could stop it.

"*What do we do now?*" I asked Salanraja.

"*Well, we've not quite worked that one out yet.*"

I felt the hackles shoot up on my back. "*You've not worked it out? I thought you said that Aleam had it all planned out.*"

"*We had up to the how do you make a demon dragon turn around, bit.*" Salanraja said. "*Now, all we have to do is annoy it so much that it abandons its orders to destroy Dragonsbond Academy and instead comes chasing after us.*"

"*And how do we do that?*"

"*We try everything we can, and we don't give up,*" Salanraja replied.

Great, I thought. I'd never even imagined such idiocy would be possible.

"*I heard that.*"

"*Good,*" I said.

Beside me, Ishtkar let out a massive roar and sprayed fire out of his muzzle. Salanraja joined in the battle cry, and they were both casting amber jets of flame at the demon dragon, as if trying to set something on fire that was already on fire. See what I mean by idiocy.

Then, Initiate Rine tried something which seemed a little smarter. He turned Ishtkar around in the air and lifted his staff up high. It seemed to suck in blue light from all around it, and it was soon glowing with an intensity almost as bright as the moon. He opened his mouth and screamed with an energy I never imagined he'd had.

His ice beam hit the demon dragon right on the flank, and it might have shifted the beast by a fraction of a claw. But even trying to cool fire with ice didn't seem to make any difference, as the demon dragon didn't sway from his path.

"*You know nothing,*" I said to Salanraja. "*That's not the best way to taunt something.*"

A rumbling came from Salanraja's chest under my feet, and she let out a deep growl. "*Do you have a better idea?*"

I licked my paw. "*As a matter of fact, I do,*" I said, and I used my superior cat perception to judge Salanraja's current trajectory, as well as the distance between us and the beast and the speed at which both dragons were travelling. Satisfied, I leaped up onto Salanraja's head. "*Get right next to its head. I want to be able to reach.*"

"*I won't be able to do that without barrelling into it,*" Salanraja said.

"*Then do that,*" I said.

"*Are you going to explain why?*"

"*No... We have no time.*"

"*Fine. As I said we need to try everything.*"

Salanraja flapped her wings to get slightly above the demon dragon. From the other side of it, Rine tried sending off another stream of icy energy which this time hit it on the head. But that didn't seem to do anything, either.

Salanraja soon entered a slight dive, and we accelerated towards the demon dragon's head. I crouched down and watched it, ready to swipe at the most opportune moment. Then, I swatted the demon dragon right on the nose with my paw.

Because everyone knew, surely, that there was nothing more annoying than just appearing out of the blue and bashing you in the face. Salanraja then lurched to the right so quickly that I almost fell off of her head. I caught myself on one of the horns sticking out of her neck, and then I pulled myself to safety and retreated into her corridor of spikes.

Meanwhile, the demon dragon turned its head slightly and let out a horrendous roar that seemed to shake both the sky we were in and the earth beneath it. It turned around and followed Salanraja.

"*See,*" I said. "*You don't need magic to get underneath somebody's skin.*"

"*I've lived through that, since the time I met you,*" Salanraja replied. She tossed her head around to look at the demon dragon behind her. "*Now, what do we do next?*"

I rushed back towards Salanraja's tail to see the demon dragon right on it. It opened its jaw wide and let out a roar that almost deafened me, I swear. Fires burned from inside its cavernous mouth, as if that great open gap was itself a portal to the Seventh Dimension. "*Fly away,*" I said. "*Fly away very fast.*"

"That shouldn't be a problem," Salanraja said, and she flapped her wings hard. She gained a little distance, but then the demon dragon made its counterattack. From its mouth came another roar, and then out came a vortex that was spinning around so fast it engulfed Salanraja's flight path, and we started to get sucked in towards the demon dragon's maw.

"Fly away faster," I instructed. I could feel the tug and the burning, and I couldn't even see the demon dragon now – only the fires that wanted to consume me whole. The wind beat against my fur. I was using my claws to keep a grip on Salanraja's scales. But the pull was so strong that they felt like they were going to rip out of their sockets.

"I can't get any speed," Salanraja said.

"You've got to do something," I replied. *"We'll die otherwise."*

"All in good service," Salanraja said. *"As you said, it's been a good life."*

"No," I replied. *"We can't give up after coming so far."* I looked around for any sign of Initiate Rine. But all I could see was the grey air whirling around me so hard and so fast, and that great raging fire, so hot, so consuming.

"Hang in there, Salanraja," I said, and I crouched, and then leapt upwards as high as I could. I put my whole spine into it, bending backwards, and then I stretched up my paws and extended my claws as far as possible. I found something, and I clung on with all my might. There was a large hole there, in fact two of them, and I soon realised these were the demon dragon's nostrils. I pulled myself up and scrambled onto the demon dragon's head.

Then, I swiped downwards once again at the beast's nose, and it let out another great roar. Instead of eating Salanraja, it swiped at her in the air with its foreleg, sending my dragon tumbling away.

❧ 42 ❧

SPEAKING THE LANGUAGE

"*S*alanraja!*" I cried out in my mind.

I watched her fall for a moment, wanting to dive back down and do something to stop her. The vortex coming out of the demon dragon's mouth had cut off now, and Salanraja fell into a wall of grey and cold clouds. Another cloud hit us dead on, blanketing me in cold and sleety darkness.

"*Salanraja!*" I called again.

No response.

"*Salanraja...*"

"*I'm alive, Ben,*" she said. "*Do what you have to do.*"

Ben... She'd finally called me by my real name. But I didn't have time to dwell on the victory because, just as we emerged from the cloud, the demon dragon let out another roar, and it jerked its head around sharply. I tumbled down its neck, thinking I was going to fall off this thing, then I found myself on the back of the beast. I almost fell right into one of the cracks in its skin, just managing to stop myself with my claws at the very last moment.

These gaps looked even more massive up close. Each one looked like gaps into the centre of the earth, with fires and magma raging beneath. I picked myself up and tried to get my bearings. But the demon dragon shook its body again, and I slid towards another gap. I leapt over it, and turned around, orienting myself.

I ran up the demon dragon's neck again and looked down to see the lake and the beach and Aleam moving on the ground so far below now, I couldn't see what they were doing. I needed to get the demon dragon down there. But it didn't look like the portal was there yet.

"*GET OFF ME, INFIDEL!*" the demon dragon said, and its voice was so loud and booming inside my mind, that I thought for a moment I'd heard it in my ears.

It shook its head again, and this time I dug into the skin with my claws. It wasn't leathery like Salanraja's, instead having the texture of porous rock, and I could feel the intense heat rising from it through the pores in my skin. If I tried staying in place for too long, it would scorch me to death. So, I ran down the demon dragon's neck again, and navigated my way across its back. But it shook its back again, throwing me around like an unwanted child's toy. I found it hard to keep purchase and not fall into any of the cracks.

Initiate Rine on Ishtkar levelled out next to us, and he let off more magic, which this time came out of his staff as a block of ice. It hit the demon dragon right on the side and shattered. Some of the ice went inside its body and rose as steam from the vents. A few of the other shards broke off around me, and one hit me right between the eyes.

"Ouch," I shouted. "That hurt, Rine!" But I wasn't sure whether he heard me. Whiskers, I wasn't sure he even knew I was here.

Then, the demon dragon had the smart idea of rolling, keeping its wings outstretched as it went. It sent me sliding down, and I tried to grasp on with something, but the skin on the wings was smooth like hardened obsidian. I managed to catch myself on some kind of spike that stuck out from the end of it, and from there I dangled. The demon dragon had brought itself down low towards the forest, and he was about to send me smack into a pine tree.

I pivoted out of the way just in time and kept holding on with all my strength, while the dragon lifted me back into the air, going up and up. It lifted me so high my ears wanted to pop. That was when I realised what it was up to. Up there, there wouldn't be enough air for a poor Bengal cat to breathe. But this creature didn't need air, it seemed. Even as it rose, the fires still seemed to rage out of the cracks in its body.

The air became thinner, and my ears hurt even more, and I felt faint. I imagined myself floating even higher in the air, finally carried up by the wings of two beautiful angel cats.

"*You can't,*" a voice came in my head. It wasn't Salanraja. It wasn't the demon dragon. It wasn't Astravar. It was that melodic and lilting female voice that I'd heard in my crystal. "*I gave you your gift for a reason. Trust yourself.*"

I hesitated, as I tried to understand exactly what the crystal was getting at. Then, it became clear what I had to do.

I had the gift. The ability to speak to all creatures. I could speak the language of any sentient creature. I could command this demon dragon. "*STOP!*" I screamed out in my mind. I knew the language instinctively. I just needed to work out what to say.

"*I AM DEMON DRAGON,*" it replied in my head. "*THE WARLOCK ASTRAVAR IS MY MASTER... MY PURPOSE IS TO DESTROY ALL LIFE UPON THIS WORLD...*" I wasn't sure whether it was speaking in my mind or out loud anymore. My vision had already gone completely blurry and the world around me was spinning from lack of good air. But I let my instinct guide me. I had to trust something.

"*NO,*" I said. "*I AM YOUR MASTER. NOW, LOWER YOURSELF SO I CAN GIVE YOU YOUR COMMANDS.*"

"*I AM DEMON DRAGON...*" it replied, then it paused a moment as if uncertain. "*I AM DEMON DRAGON... AND DRAGONCAT IS MY MASTER... ASTRAVAR THE DRAGONCAT IS MY MASTER... MY PURPOSE IS UNCERTAIN.*"

Well, whatever I'd done, I'd certainly confused it. I held on for dear life, hanging from the horn at the end of the demon dragon's wing. My vision got less bleary, and I could breathe again. I panted hard, and then I checked down below to see Aleam pointing up at me with his staff. Next to him, glared an oval-shaped eye with a white cornea and fire and magma burning within. The portal. Aleam had summoned the portal. Now, all I had to do was bring the demon dragon back to it.

Now, I could hear the demon dragon's primitive thoughts in my own mind, and I knew exactly what Salanraja meant about screaming these thoughts in her mind. Because that is exactly what the demon dragon did.

"*I AM DEMON DRAGON...*" it continued. "*WHO IS MY MASTER? DRAGONCAT... ASTRAVAR... MY FUTURE IS UNCERTAIN...*"

It sounded like it needed a little identity reassurance. "*I AM YOUR MASTER,*" I said in the hideous language of the Seventh Dimension. "*THE WAY BACK TO YOUR WORLD IS NOW OPENED. RETURN AND NEVER COME BACK AGAIN.*"

"*RETURN... PORTAL VISIBLE... ASTRAVAR... I SERVE ASTRAVAR... BUT ALSO DRAGONCAT...*"

I knew that this ruse wouldn't last forever. I didn't have the powerful magic that Astravar had to control this thing. But all I needed to do was fool it for long enough to get it inside.

The demon dragon spiralled downwards towards the portal. As we got even closer, it felt like the portal latched on to us like a vacuum. It was almost as if the Seventh Dimension felt that I belonged in there. Meanwhile, the demon dragon had started to work things out.

"*DRAGONCAT... ASTRAVAR... DRAGONCAT IS AN IMPOSTER... YES, ASTRAVAR.... I HEAR YOU, ASTRAVAR, MY MASTER... DESTROY DRAGONCAT... DESTROY THE WORLD...*"

Whiskers, he'd woken up out of his state. Just as I was about to bring him down to the portal.

"*Just hold him a little longer,*" Salanraja said.

"*I don't know how,*" I said, and it was as if I could feel someone prying inside my own head. Something was trying to stop me speaking, and to take control of my thoughts. It was as if the vengeful eye of Astravar was watching me from inside the portal. I could see it, I swear, hovering above those raging fires. That cruel grey eye that knew nothing of comfort. The one I'd seen in my dreams.

The demon dragon started to lift, as my consciousness continued to rouse. At the same time, the portal was closing, and we were so close to being sucked in. But if the demon dragon continued its current course, we would miss the portal by a paw's span.

"Ben," Salanraja said. "*Don't lose control. You can do this.*"

Then, I heard the voice of the crystal in my head again. *"Remember your destiny,"* it said. *"You must save the world."*

Those words were enough. The language, the commands, what I needed to do, it came to my mind as clear as lightning. "I, DRAGONCAT, COMMAND YOU!" I screamed, and I screamed it out loud. "RETURN TO THE SEVENTH DIMENSION!"

My thoughts took control of its mind. They snapped on to it, and it felt like I'd leashed invisible reins around the creature's muzzle. The demon dragon's mind suddenly went quiet, and it turned its lumbering form back towards the portal.

I prepared to get sucked in and to join my new world, the Seventh Dimension. I would probably die in there. If everything in there was a demon, then there was absolutely no way I'd find the food I needed to survive. I felt as if I was passing through an incredibly hot waterfall. It seared my skin, and I was prepared to accept my own fate.

"No, Ben," Salanraja said in my mind, and her voice snapped me back to the present. *"Choose life!"*

I screeched and remembered who I was. I wasn't a Dragoncat, whatever a Dragoncat was. I was a Bengal, descendant of the great Asian leopard cat. I was wild, and I was free. Those thoughts gave me enough power in my hind legs to leap off the demon dragon and roll over in the sand.

I turned to face the portal then, the great eye with the raging fires within. It led to a horrific place, one I never wanted to remember seeing, even in nightmares. The demon dragon flew towards a burning sky and then seemed to realise it had been duped. It turned its head, and it looked at me with those empty eyes of fire.

It flew faster in there, or maybe life inside that place was accelerated, because it did a half loop-the-loop and barrel roll within seconds, and for a moment it looked like it would fly right out again. From the direction it was heading, I could tell it wanted to eat me whole.

But Aleam was watching it with one eye, his staff raised as the portal leached energy from a crystal on a pedestal made from a tree trunk. He knocked his staff to the side, to send the crystal toppling to the floor. This cut off the portal just before the demon dragon could emerge.

All that remained was an ear-piercing roar. It sent a massive gust of wind out through the forest, and it shook the trees and brought the sand up from beneath my feet as if it were dust. It whisked it up into suffocating eddies, and it caused the air to howl through the trees. The noises and the crying winds built to a climax as if calling out from the oblivion beneath the world. It screamed out like a massive and very, very angry hippopotamus.

And then, all was still.

I blinked twice, and then I looked back at my fur. It looked charred; it looked beaten. But I was alive, and I couldn't believe it. We'd defeated it. We'd won.

I turned to Aleam, and I meowed and I brushed up next to him. I was purring so loudly, happy just to be alive. He laughed, and he reached out and scratched me under the chin.

"Now," I said. "Maybe Initiate Rine would be so kind as to go out there and catch me a fish." And Ta'ra leapt down from a rock and also looked up at Aleam with wide eyes, as if to tell him she quite fancied fish too.

INVISIBLE FISH

I t took a while to return back to Dragonsbond academy, and we took the journey slowly. We had plenty of stop-offs, which gave me time to talk with Rine, Aleam, and Ta'ra about their adventures. They told me about the experiences they'd had throughout the world, and for the first time I gained stories that would make the Savannah cats back in South Wales weep in disbelief.

Salanraja was right, the hippopotamus was nothing compared to the chimera.

We arrived in Dragonsbond Academy later that night, and I'm not sure anyone saw any importance to our return. Aleam suggested that I could spend the night in his study, and Rine seemed to think that was a good idea.

It definitely was a good idea, because the next day I awoke lying on Aleam's sofa, snuggled up next to Ta'ra. I woke naturally, not because of the light, but the delicious aroma of chicken liver coming from two bowls on the floor. They were both white. One had a black cat painted on the front, with a tiny, winged human perched on her shoulder. The other had a cat that didn't look too different from me, with a red dragon flying over his head.

I rushed over to the bowl, purring, and I gobbled up the chicken liver. It tasted so good, and I'd forgotten how much I liked liver. I was so hungry that I was tempted to eat from Ta'ra's bowl as well. It would have been her own fault, really, for wanting to sleep through such a tantalising aroma. But somehow, I resisted. She needed to eat as well, and it took all my willpower, I'm telling you, to pretend that the food wasn't there and to sit in the corner and groom the dust off my fur instead.

Soon, heavy footsteps approached the door. Initiate Rine stood at the entrance. He scanned the room, then his gaze fell on me in the corner. Meanwhile, Ta'ra opened her eyes and yawned.

"Freshcat Ben," Rine said. "You have been called by the Council of Three, and you are to come to see them immediately."

"What do they want?" I asked.

"It doesn't matter," Rine said. "Once the Council summons you, you must come at once."

I looked over at Aleam, who was working away at his alembic apparatus, as if he did anything else. He peered down at me over his glasses. "Initiate Rine is right, I'm afraid," he said. "But once you become an Initiate here, you will be able to apply for a small amount of paid holiday, with the number of days increasing as you rise up the ranks."

I lifted myself up on all fours. "Does that mean I'm about to be promoted?"

Aleam looked at Initiate Rine, and he shook his head. "Just go, will you?" he said. "And don't tell them I said anything."

I stalked towards the door, even if my legs were hurting so much that I thought I would collapse. Aleam had applied some of this so called white magic, but he said it could only cure the bone and it wouldn't soothe the bruises.

I followed Initiate Rine out into the bailey, which was empty. There wasn't a servant, a cat, or even a rat in sight. But after looking around a bit, I noticed a few guards on the *chemin de ronde*, and two stationed by the portcullis.

A light wind rushed through the castle, sending fallen leaves up from the ground. Rine led me across the yard, and then underneath the archway that led to the courtyard.

Which was exactly where the rest of the residents of the castle had gathered, with the exception of Aleam, Ta'ra, the cats in the cattery, and the stationed guards. Everyone had gathered in two clusters, leaving an aisle at the centre which Rine led me through. The servants and the kitchen maids stood at the back, including Matron Canda who turned to regard me with stern eyes. Then we passed the guards, and then the students. Rine's girlfriend, Bellari, was near the aisle, and she backed away from me as I passed, looking down at me with wide eyes. Ange was on the opposite aisle, and she gave me a cute pout, then looked up at Rine and smiled.

Closer to the front, we passed some older dragon riders I'd not even met yet. Some of them looked close to Aleam's age. Prefect Lars and his two friends – Calin and Asinda were also there. But only Asinda turned and looked at me, an expression of mistrust in her narrowed eyes.

We were soon standing right in front of the platform and the lecterns at which the three Driars of the Council of Three – Yila, Lonamm and Brigel – stood in their usual positions. They all had their staffs raised, feeding energy into the crystal. But their gazes were firmly fixed on me.

There came a murmur from the crowd, until Driar Yila raised her free arm and shouted out, "Quiet!" in a voice nearly as loud as a demon dragon's. Then she turned her head sharply toward me and her harsh gaze latched on to mine.

"I hear you've caused quite a commotion, Freshcat," she said. "What do you have to say for yourself?" She banged her staff down against the ground, and I backed up against someone's leg, and hid behind it, remembering what had happened the last time that she'd used that staff's power on me.

Driar Brigel bellowed out a loud and deep laugh from the other side of the platform. "Oh, don't be so cruel to him, Yila," he said. "This pussycat is a hero."

"Indeed, he is," Driar Lonamm said. "Come forward, little one. Don't worry, we won't eat you."

What? Why would they think of eating cats? They didn't do that where I was from. Although I'd heard rumours in my clowder, that they did eat cats on the other side of the world.

I peered out from my hiding place. Driar Lonamm was hunched over her stocky frame and she beckoned me forward. "You'll need to come up to our level if you're to claim your prize," she said, and she tapped on her lectern. "Here, up here."

Well, if I didn't do what they said, they'd probably fry me with their magic. I leaped up, and Driar Lonamm reached out and took something from her pouch. It was a small round disc, connected to some kind of thin chain. It looked just like a cat toy meant for batting around in the air, and I can't imagine it served any kind of functional purpose.

"This is your medal," she said, and she reached out and she placed the thing over my neck.

Yeuch. Collars were bad enough, but this thing felt horrible. I tried to claw it off with my back paws, until Salanraja protested about it in my mind. *"What are you doing, you fool?"*

"I don't like it."

"Leave it there. It's an honour. You don't want to insult the Council of Three."

"Fine," I replied, and I calmed myself down and tried to get used to how wearing this impractical thing impeded my flexibility. Hopefully, I wouldn't have to wear it forever.

Driar Brigel stepped forward, and he stopped the light flowing from his staff to the crystal for a moment, by turning the staff around. He lifted the base and tapped me on each shoulder with it. I flinched, expecting it to hurt. But this man was a lot gentler than he looked.

"Congratulations, Ben," he said. "From this day, you shall be known as Initiate Ben and you will enjoy the full privileges of a student at Dragonsbond Academy. Also, for your heroic deeds, a feast will be made in your honour. Now, let us give our young hero a round of applause."

The humans did that weird thing where they clapped their hands together as if they had suddenly decided they wanted to eliminate a scourge of flies. Some of them even whooped out. Then all went quiet as Driar Yila approached me.

"Much as I hate to do this," she said, not showing any emotion on that cold face, "I am going to give you a grand privilege for your heroic deeds. You, Initiate Ben, shall choose the dish of the day for our feast. Choose wisely, mind, because you can only choose one dish."

Wow. I had never thought I'd have such an honour. Today, I actually got to choose what I had for dinner. I don't think that had ever happened in my life. Of course, the answer was easy.

"I choose salmon," I said.

Driar Yila frowned, and then she looked at Driar Lonamm. "Uh…" she said.

"*Gracious demons,*" Salanraja said. "*Trust you to choose something that doesn't even exist in this world.*"

"*What? You don't have salmon?*" My heart sank, and I suddenly remembered home.

"*And what is a salmon?*"

"*It's a fish, a big one that's pink.*"

There must have been some communication that went on between Salanraja and Great Driar Brigel's dragon, because he immediately boomed out. "I'm sorry, Initiate Ben. But we don't have salmon in this world, and we can't summon one from another dimension."

With that, my heart sank even more. If they couldn't pluck a salmon out of my world, they probably wouldn't be prepared to send me home either. "So, what do you have?" I asked.

"Well, we can offer a rather magical fish," Driar Brigel said. "Something you've never tried before."

My ears perked up. "Really?"

"Yes, it's called Invisible Fish," Driar Brigel said, raising an eyebrow. "It's quite a delicacy."

"And what's it like?"

Driar Brigel shook his head with a grin. "I don't know," he said. "In all honesty I've never seen one."

He turned to the crowd and lifted up his arms. The crowd responded with a round of laughter, followed by another round of applause.

EPILOGUE

I n the end, we settled on roasted duck as the dish of the day. I had a lot of it, and I even asked Matron Canda to take some over for Ta'ra too, which she did. That night, I slept with contentment. For the first time, I slept in Salanraja's chamber as a celebration for reaching a new rank. I lay curled up next to her chest, where her dragonfire kept me as warm as if I was lying next to the fireplace back in South Wales.

I dreamed strange dreams that night. At the start, I stood peering into a fast-flowing brook. I was looking for fish, as the spray off the water tickled my nostrils, and cooled me against the warmth of the sun. But after a while of finding nothing, I decided that it would be better to dive into the water and find the fish for myself.

So, I plunged into the depths of the river, and the next thing I knew I was swimming upstream, my tail and fins propelling me at great speed. Because I wasn't a cat anymore, I was a fish. In fact, I believe I was a massive salmon swimming my way from the Atlantic Ocean towards our breeding grounds. I had joined a school, and we stayed in close formation. There was safety in numbers should a badger try to fish us out of the water.

But soon, we came to a tributary, and I felt a tug in my head – something telling me to swim in another direction. The rest of the school turned left, but I turned the other way and arrived at a quiet lake, away from the roar and the rush of survival. There was a waterfall in the distance, and I swam towards the bubbles pushing down into the water. Then, once I was close enough, I leapt up into the cascade.

I landed on my feet in a cave behind the waterfall, now a cat again. I shook the water off, then I went on to see what might be inside. There came the squeals of bats, and the cave was lit by a floating light that hovered close to my head, pushing away the darkness. It led me into a chamber, hot like an inferno. Streams of lava seeped down the cave walls, and a white crystal stood at the centre of the chamber.

It glowed brighter as I approached, and I rubbed myself against it to thank it for its help fighting the demon dragon. For a while, my fur brushed against something solid, until the crystal suddenly changed.

I stepped back in alarm, because the crystal had vanished, and Astravar's head instead hovered where it had been. "So, there you are, Dragoncat," he said. "I've been trying to find a way through to you all night."

"What do you want?" I asked. "I defeated you."

"Correction. You sent one of my minions back home. But you will never defeat me, because you are worthless. And you fail to understand now that we warlocks have summoned one demon dragon, we can summon many more."

I tried to ignore him. I didn't want him to ruin my warm feeling of victory. "*Salanraja*," I tried calling out. "*Salanraja, where are you?*"

"She won't help you," Astravar replied. "Not in this dream. Because you chose to come here yourself."

I considered running. But I knew that wherever I fled to, Astravar would find a way to follow me. What I needed to do was wake up, but I had no idea how. "What do you want with me?" I asked Astravar again. "Why are you here?"

"Because I underestimated you," Astravar said. "You can control demons, and that's an incredibly powerful gift. Join me, and we can rule this world together."

The vision that I'd seen of my owners flashed back into my mind. All three of them lying as skeletons on the bed. I could never let that come to pass. "No," I said. "You are our enemy, and we will find a way to thwart your plans."

Astravar frowned. "I thought you'd say that. Well, it doesn't matter, because I'll find a way through to you one way or another. Believe me, Dragoncat, I will hunt you down and I will make you join me whether you want to or not."

I didn't run. I turned slowly around to send a message to Astravar that I was now in control and could move as I wished. I could hear the roaring of the waterfall somewhere in this cave, and I had to get out from this place – to wake from this dream.

But first, I wanted to return to swimming in the stream, because for a while I could go where I wanted and pretend that I was free.

A CAT'S GUIDE

TO MEDDLING WITH

MAGIC

DRAGONCAT BOOK 2

CHRIS BEHRSIN

To Mitzi, a belovedly remembered feline friend.

NEFARIOUS DREAMS

There he was again, his head floating in the sky, his face with blue skin like a cracked eggshell, looking down upon me with grey lifeless eyes. Astravar... The man who brought me into this world; the evil warlock who hated cats and didn't treat us well.

All around me, purple stalks whipped and flailed, sending up a thick purple mist that stretched across the horizon. If I got close to the plants, they could tear my skin – shred it off my very bones.

I stood there, looking up at the head without a body, paralysed. It wasn't that I couldn't run. But if I did run, then he'd just materialise in front of me, with that wicked grin and expression of dire hatred for any living creature in the world. I couldn't escape him.

This land smelled of death and decay, and each time I came here it became worse. At the same time, I had a metallic taste upon my tongue – a taste of raw meat and of being as wild as wild comes.

I watched, and I waited as the words rolled out of his mouth.

"Join me, Dragoncat..."

Then, I opened my own mouth to say something in his own language, but no words came. It was terrible. I didn't belong here. My stomach burned with hunger, and I felt the urge to hunt down something and slaughter it. A rabbit, perhaps, or something bigger. Something that would pose a challenge for a great mighty Bengal like me.

It wasn't right. I had to wake up from this dream. I didn't belong here. If I stayed here too long, he'd consume my soul and I'd become feral.

"Join me, Dragoncat..." he said again. "You know it is your destiny."

But I'd promised myself, and I'd promised Salanraja, that I wouldn't let him talk to me for long enough to drag me over to the other side. So, though my muscles wouldn't let me, I tried to move my limbs and stand up. Not in this world, but back in the real world – the world of the living. Even if it wasn't my home.

I tried to open my eyes, but I couldn't. Astravar had too much of a hold on me. If I didn't do something, I'd never wake up again.

I turned to see a strange girl in a long chiffon dress. She looked like a young teenager, with long straight and platinum blonde hair. She rolled her gaze down towards me, and it was then that I noticed her red eyes, the irises looking as if they were burning.

"Wake up," she said.

It was Déjà vu. I'd met her many times, I was sure. But I couldn't place where I'd seen her last.

"I said, wake up!"

My eyelids shot open, and a sudden shudder ran down my spine. A bright white light filled my vision, which soon faded to show a world I knew well enough. It wasn't quite the world I wanted to live in.

But I was much safer here than in Astravar's domain.

2

WHERE IS PERSIA?

Dawn had already broken, and warm light streamed through the gauze curtains of Aleam's abode. I lay on Aleam's sofa, nestled into the warmth of Ta'ra's furry chest, my mouth now dry and a bitter ferric tang on my tongue. Aleam slept in the next room, the door ajar from where his soft snores emanated.

I stirred, and Ta'ra pushed me away with her feet. I leapt down to the cold stone floor, and I yawned. I went over to lap up some water, imagining it was the soft taste of milk that rolled over my tongue. After that, I wolfed down some dried mackerel, working my way around the thin bones.

How I missed those days of comfort and freedom in South Wales. Now, stuck in the kingdom of Illumine, I imagined I'd never return home. But at least I was safe and not trapped in some warlock's abode as he tried to coerce me into executing his nefarious plans.

"The dreams again?" my dragon, Salanraja, asked in my mind. I'd come into this world through a portal created by Astravar, and after escaping I'd stumbled upon Dragonsbond Academy and bonded with her.

"Every night, now, it seems," I replied. *"Why can't that warlock just go back to playing with his crystals and leave me alone?"*

Salanraja hesitated. *"I'm dreaming of him recently too, remember. He's clearly up to something."*

"If his demon Maine Coon isn't enough for him, then he can summon another cat from another dimension. Maybe a good Persian would be stupid enough to do his bidding."

"A what?"

"A Persian. You know... from Persia?"

"Where?"

I lowered my head. *"I don't know, exactly. Never been there."*

"You're an odd one," Salanraja said. *"I keep saying it, but I really, really think it's time to tell the Council about your dreams."*

"I'll tell them when I'm good and ready... In other words, when I consider them to be a threat."

"Suit yourself..." Salanraja said, and her voice cut out of my mind. She didn't sound pleased with my decision.

Since Salanraja had learned of my dreams of Astravar, she'd started nagging that I should go to the Council of Three about them. But, in all honesty, I didn't think the Council would be too pleased to hear of them. The Council of Three consisted of the three humans and three dragons who ran this place – three rather than six, because each human was bonded with a dragon.

Last time I'd told them something about Astravar, they'd pinned me up in the air with their magic, probed around inside my head, and then sent me on a near death mission against a bone dragon and one of Astravar's elusive Manipulators. It wasn't so much that I was afraid of what the Council would do to me, but rather that they'd order me to go out and do something about it.

It had been a good month since I defeated Astravar's demon dragon, and I really didn't want to have to face the evil warlock again. I also didn't want to have to encounter my nemesis, his pet demon Maine Coon.

There came a mewling sound from the sofa, and Ta'ra woke up. She looked down at me, blinked, and then stretched herself on all fours. At the moment, she was the same size as me, but she could change her size whenever she wished. She hadn't done this, though, for quite a while.

She jumped down on the floor, then she strolled over to her food bowl. When she got there, she turned to me and growled. "Ben, you ate my food," she said, and she arched her back, hackles shooting up out of it.

"I did not," I replied. "I've been good, and I only touched my own bowl."

"Then where did it go?"

"I don't know. You must have eaten it." I really was telling the truth. But Ta'ra had seemed a little forgetful as of late.

"Liar!"

She looked like she wanted to pounce, and I readied myself for a fight.

"What is this commotion about?" Aleam asked from the bedroom door. He wore his nightgown and sleeping cap and looked like he'd not slept all night.

Ta'ra turned to him. "He stole my food."

"I did not."

"Did so!"

I groaned, and Aleam sighed at the same time. His gaze jerked from me to Ta'ra, and then he shook his head. "There's plenty more mackerel where that came from, Ta'ra. Though I saw you eating something last night while I was up working on the cure."

He hobbled over to us, leaning on his staff for support, picked up Ta'ra's bowl, took it over to the cupboard, and opened it. As he dished out more minced mackerel from a larger bowl, there came a knock on the main door.

"Come in," Aleam shouted. "We're all awake now."

The door opened to reveal Rine standing there. He wasn't as spotty as when I'd first met him. I guessed it was because he was kissing Bellari less.

"Initiate Rine," Aleam said. "What can we do for you this fine morning?"

He scanned the room, and then he noticed me staring back up at him on the floor. "There you are, Ben. I thought you might be sleeping in Salanraja's chambers."

But that's what so many humans fail to understand. One thing that's great about being a cat, is that you have complete liberty about where you sleep. In truth, it's also entirely political. The more you endear someone to you, the more likely they are to give you food.

Which is why, in South Wales, I chose to sleep in the master's bedroom most of the time. They were the ones with access to the food.

Back in Dragonsbond Academy, I had multiple subjects I needed to keep on my side. The first was Salanraja, the ruby dragon I'd bonded to. I'm not sure she appreciated my company that much. But then who was I to judge? In all honesty, I liked sleeping in her chamber, warmed up by the dragonfire boiling in her stomach. It was just like sleeping by the fireplace in the world where I'm from.

Sometimes I also slept in Initiate Rine's room as well, although less and less since his girlfriend, Bellari, had complained that he was getting too many of my hairs on him. She was allergic to me, you see. Although given her temper, I often wondered if she was allergic to everyone but Rine.

For the last few days, I'd slept here, but given Ta'ra's recent outburst, I'd already decided to try somewhere else for a few days.

Right now, though, I couldn't be bothered to explain this all over again to Initiate Rine. "What is it now?" I asked, because the look in his eyes told me he had a task for me he didn't think I'd like.

He gave me a knowing look. "The Council of Three has summoned you," he said. "They want to talk to you about your dreams."

3

DREAMWATCHER

W inter had come to the Illumine Kingdom, and for the last five days, a thick blanket of snow had settled on the ground. I wasn't human, and so I wasn't foolish enough to want to go out in the snow. Things froze in such conditions, and animals died if they stayed exposed to this stuff too long.

As you've probably gathered, therefore, I don't particularly like snow. In fact, I absolutely hate it. 'Bah humbug to it', as you might say in the human language.

With each step through the snow, I sank into it, leaving my paw prints trailing behind me in two neat lines. Rine's footprints followed a much wonkier pattern beside them. Fortunately, we only had to trudge for a little way before we reached the Council's courtyard, behind which, I'd learned by this point, stood the keep that housed the most important rooms of this castle, including the council room and treasury.

Two snowmen waited for me at the archway leading into the courtyard. Both of them had eyes made of raisins and courgettes as noses. The guards had built these on watch, apparently, and then they had put two helmets on them to make them look like guards. Apparently, they thought it might help scare away the crows.

Rine stopped by the archway and pointed at one snowman. "Handsome fella, isn't he?"

"I have absolutely no opinion of him," I said.

Initiate Rine looked down at me and smiled. "Apparently, Captain Onus decided how he should look."

"Then I've changed my mind. This snowman is much better looking than Captain Onus."

"I thought you'd say that."

I peered around the snowman and looked into the courtyard. The three elders hadn't arrived yet, it seemed, but there was a girl with light blonde hair standing at the bottom of the dais, her back to me. She seemed to be staring up at the crystal, though I couldn't see enough of her to read her expression.

"What exactly does the Council want of me?" I asked. "And what do they know of my dreams?"

Rine tutted and smirked. "Tut, tut, Ben. Been dreaming things you shouldn't?" He gave me a wink.

"I'm not going to tell you about my dreams."

"Why not? I've always wondered what a cat might dream."

"Because they're personal. Why, would you tell me yours?"

Rine gave a curious frown. "I don't see why not."

"Fine, what did you dream last night?"

"Well, I dreamt that..." Rine scratched his chin as his words trailed off. "Actually, you're right, I probably shouldn't tell you any of that at all."

"Typical adolescent boy stuff, then. I can imagine."

"Probably better than dreaming of fish and chicken all day," Rine said.

"That's not all I dream of. I'll have you know that I have very intelligent dreams."

"Yeah, right."

I opened my mouth to say something else, but a tinny female voice shouting out from the other side of the bailey interrupted me.

"Rine, there you are." Rine's girlfriend, Bellari, stepped up to us. Her long blonde hair framed her face which was red, perhaps because of the cold or perhaps because of her allergies to me. "I've been looking everywhere for you. We start our shift in five minutes. Come on, we'll be late."

She tried to pull Rine away, but he broke free from her grasp and turned back to me. "Bellari, I was ordered to deliver him to the Courtyard. The Council told me to keep close to him at all times."

Bellari sighed and stepped around Rine, keeping as far away from me as she could. She peered around the snowman. "Ben," she said. "What are you waiting for? Go on... They want to see you. And the new student's there already."

"New student?" I asked, starting to get curious. I had thought there was something about the girl I'd just seen in the courtyard. I moved towards the archway. As I did, I closed the distance between me and Rine's girlfriend. Bellari backed away and hid behind Rine.

"Ben, I told you to stay away from me. Rine, do something. Oh, that cat, they should never have Initiated him."

Rine shrugged, and then he lifted his staff off his back. It had a blue crystal at the top, glowing slightly, meaning it was full of magic.

"Okay, Ben," he said. "Either you do as you're told, or I play a game of cat cricket. Which will it be?"

Before I'd come to this world, my reaction might have been to run away shrieking. But I knew if I did that, Rine would send an ice-spell from his staff right after me and freeze me on the spot. Frozen, I might make a suitable cricket ball.

I growled deeply, then I slinked towards the archway that led into the courtyard. The student still stood there, now with her head turned slightly so I could see the side of her face. Her skin was white and unblemished, and she couldn't have been older than thirteen, if that. She had long straight platinum blonde hair that cascaded over a fur collar attached to a thick beige coat.

I turned back to Rine, as I caught a gust of cold air that washed away the taste of the morning's meal on my tongue.

"Go," he said again with a sly grin, and he made a low sweeping motion with the bottom of his staff, which glowed blue slightly as it moved.

I mewled, unhappily, and then I walked into the courtyard. The snow here was even thicker than in the bailey, and I hated the sensation of my paws pressing into it. I groaned as I went, then I thought that maybe if I approached the girl, she could pick me up so I wouldn't freeze.

My only other option was to step onto the dais, but if the Council of Three saw me doing that they might turn me into a frog or something and I'd spend the night trying to work out how not to get eaten by a cat.

I stepped up to her brown leather boot, and I meowed.

She looked down at me. "You!"

When I saw her eyes, I immediately shrieked and scuttled behind the dais for cover. Her eyes were red – I could swear they were – and they glowed like embers.

"I've seen you, many times," she said.

"And I've seen you," I rasped back. "Somewhere..." But I couldn't quite put a claw on where.

"It isn't your place to know who I am... But I know you and your dreams all too well."

Her eyes stopped glowing and took on a lifeless grey colour just like Astravar's. I assessed this girl, unsure whether I should flee or stay put. A creaking sound came from my side, and instinctively I fled to the other end of the courtyard.

But it was nothing to be afraid of yet, as the three Driars of the Council of Three – Driar Yila, Driar Lonamm, and Driar Brigel shuffled onto the dais and took their places by their lecterns. Well, I say nothing to be afraid of, but they were all pretty scary, being powerful magic users and all that.

"Typical Initiate Ben. Always scared of something." Driar Yila bawled out. She was the tallest and thinnest of the three Driars, with long grey hair and a staff that could shoot fire.

I took a deep breath, then I composed myself. I walked back with my head held high towards the dais. "I don't have magic to protect myself, Ma'am. And what do you expect when you leave me to contend with this witch!"

"Seramina is no such thing," Driar Brigel said. He was the only male in the Council of Three – a gentle giant with thick, muscular arms hidden underneath his tunic. "She's our new dreamwatcher among other things. We've been bereft of one for a good ten years."

"What the whiskers is a dreamwatcher?" I asked. Then I remembered myself. "Sir…"

Brigel smiled and glanced at Driar Lonamm, who lowered herself on her stout frame to peer down at me. "Initiate Ben, you promised us you'd inform of all strange going's on. And yet, here you are holding a tremendous secret from us."

"A secret?"

"Your dreams," Driar Yila said. "Your dragon told me all about them… Ben, you must be punished for this. You know the rules. You've risked letting Astravar inside Dragonsbond Academy by not telling us this."

"But it was a dream!"

"It doesn't matter. There are many ways to penetrate a castle. Young one, it appears you still have a lot to learn."

That caused me to stop in my tracks. I felt the rage boil up in my chest all of a sudden, almost as if I had dragonfire burning within. *"Salanraja,"* I said in my mind. *"You promised you wouldn't say anything to them."*

"Correction," Salanraja said. *"I told you I would give you time to tell them yourself. But once the dreamwatcher told me what had happened in your last dream, I realised I didn't have a choice."*

"And what exactly is a dreamwatcher?"

"Exactly what the name says. She walks around at night watching people's dreams."

"So, when does she sleep?"

"She sleeps as she walks…"

I looked back at the girl who was staring up at the massive crystal above the three Driars as if nothing else existed in the world. Her eyes had that red glow to them again. Another gust of wind came, kicking up the snow around her feet. It whipped her hair into her face, but she didn't even flinch.

The three Driars were watching the girl, each of them with their heads cocked and expressions of curiosity on their faces.

"He's here again," she said. Her mouth moved, but she didn't even blink or change her expression. It was as if she was channelling the words from another dimension.

Driar Lonamm cocked an eyebrow. "Astravar? But who would be sleeping at this time?"

"Not a student," Seramina replied. "The fae. The Cat Sidhe."

"Ta'ra?" I asked.

"She's moving," the girl said. "She's on the walls... With Astravar inside her head."

"Go," Driar Yila shouted out. "Ben, go after her and wake her up at once."

"What, why me?"

"Because you're the only one fast enough," Driar Lonamm said. "Ta'ra is under our protection, and we can't risk losing her to the warlocks. Go!"

I growled at the Driars for making me move in such cold weather, when all I really wanted to do was curl up by Aleam's fireplace and sleep.

"Don't test us, Initiate," Driar Yila said, and she banged the butt of her staff against the floor. That was enough to startle me out of the courtyard. I heard Seramina's feet pattering behind me, but she wasn't as fast as me.

In front, a crow lifted into the air, cawing loudly. It joined a flock of other screeching crows wheeling above the academy. Ta'ra was already on the castle walls, looking up at the flock. She turned to me and yawned with her eyes closed. Then, without opening them, she jumped down off the other side of the wall.

4

SLEEPRUNNER

"Ta'ra!" I shouted as I sprinted after her. I jumped up onto the *chemin de ronde*, using the gaps between the stones as pawholds to pull me up. A couple of the archers on watch looked at me disdainfully. Last time I had done this, they had tried to shoot me down with their arrows.

But now they had their bows pointed up at the crows and they were loosing their arrows at them. A couple of crows plummeted from the sky into the moat.

Ta'ra was already emerging from the other side of the moat which must have been freezing at this time of year. I shuddered just thinking of crossing it, but I had no choice. So, I dived right into the water, and I went under for a moment, before I surfaced again on the other side and scrambled up.

I didn't even have time to shake myself off. Ta'ra was already running fast, tracking the flock of crows that were flying above her. The birds seemed to be following a bright purple light that they circled around. Ta'ra also seemed mesmerised by it, because she didn't watch the landscape ahead of her, but rather the flock as she ran.

This meant she should have been easy to catch up to.

But the snow slowed me down a bit. I was a Bengal, descendent of the great Asian leopard cat, and I'm sure my ancestors never had to deal with this disgusting stuff. Ta'ra, however, seemed fleet footed on it. So much so, in fact, that I still had to sprint to have any chance of keeping up with her.

Fortunately, she hadn't tried growing to five times her size or anything like that, because if she did, I was sure she would outpace me.

"Ta'ra... Stop! Wake up! Don't let Astravar into your dreams!" I shouted.

Maybe she could hear me, or even see me in my dreams. But then, although I seemed to vaguely recall another figure in my dreams, I could only vividly remember Astravar.

I was just a couple of spine-spans away from Ta'ra when the crows cackled loudly into the sky above me. They shot down like they had rabies, pecking their beaks into the ground and creating thin dents in the snow. I rolled out of the way of one, which I swear almost speared me right through the head.

They were going crazy. What the whiskers was causing this? Crows don't attack the living. Especially not a mighty creature like a cat.

"*Ben,*" Salanraja called out in my mind. "*Hold on, I'm coming for you.*"

"*I can handle a few birds. I'm a Bengal, descendant of the great mighty—*"

My words were interrupted by a loud roar that cut through the sky and made the ground shudder. A gust of wind came from above, and a shadow passed over me. I raised my head to see Salanraja letting off a jet of flame at the flock, which scattered in the dragon's path. Some of them fell to the ground, and some of them managed to break free and continue to plummet down and attack me.

But Salanraja had given me enough space to continue after Ta'ra who had gained quite a distance on me. I readied myself at a crouch, and then I sprinted at full speed to catch up with her. I overshot a little, and I turned around to see her frozen on the spot.

Her eyelids covered her eyes completely, but still she had her head turned to me, as if she was looking right at me. I tried to move to the side a little, and she tracked my movements with unnerving accuracy.

"Ta'ra, wake up!"

She didn't respond to me in any way. Instead, she turned her head up to the sky, and let out a whining sound as if she was after a fly. The purple light up there floated over to her, and the crows that Salanraja had disrupted had started to gather around it. Salanraja was much further away in the distance, coming in at them for another pass.

"Whiskers," I said. "I'll have to wake you up through more conventional means." I moved in towards her, and I struck out to bat her on the cheek. But she caught my paw and knocked me away with unbecoming strength.

"Ta'ra... It's me... Stop this!"

She growled back at me, her eyelids still sealed shut.

"Ta'ra? What's happened to you? Wake up."

Still nothing. The hackles shot up on the back of my neck as she opened her mouth to hiss at me. She grew to the size of a panther, and then she leapt at me. I rolled out of the way, just missing another crow trying to spear me from the sky.

I considered fleeing, but I knew Ta'ra would outrun me, and so I turned to face her. She launched herself off her haunches to pounce at me. I shrieked as I clawed at her, but she pinned me to the ground, baring her teeth and growling angrily. Her eyes were still fastened shut, and I tried to shriek as loudly as I could to wake her up, but it had no effect.

She stopped then, as if to regard me from behind those sealed eyelids. "How disappointing, Dragoncat," she said. "I would have thought a great mighty Bengal like you would have put up more of a fight. Perhaps, your ancestry isn't as great as you claim."

"Astravar," I said through bared teeth. "Release her..."

"Or what?" Ta'ra asked. Or at least Astravar asked through Ta'ra's mouth.

I said nothing.

"You know, maybe I don't have a need for you after all, Dragoncat. I had forgotten about this specimen whom I'd transformed so long ago. But she could be a useful tool in my plans."

"Let her go!"

"No," Astravar said, and then he brought Ta'ra's mouth down

towards my neck. I tried to flinch out of the way, but she had me pinned to the ground with one paw over my chest. I thought that she'd eat me then, but instead she licked me using her long tongue.

It isn't pleasant being licked by a cat, and particularly a big one. The chitin at the back of her tongue, meant for helping to mash up her meals, scratched through to the skin and brought some fur off the side of my face, as if it were sandpaper.

"Oh, what fun this is," Astravar said.

I didn't have a clue where Salanraja was right now, but I really needed her. *"Salanraja, get her off me. She'll kill me!"*

"I can't," she said. *"So sorry."*

"Why not?" I asked, as I squirmed relentlessly under Ta'ra's grasp.

"Because we have other plans."

"What?"

I was answered by a roar, and not Salanraja's. It came from the direction of the castle, followed by the sound of great beating wings. Ta'ra turned towards it, her eyes still fastened shut. I also strained my head to see what we faced.

There was a charcoal dragon, so much smaller than the other dragons I'd seen that I thought it must only be a fledgling. On the back of it sat that weird girl with the flaming red eyes and long straight blonde hair. She carried a staff raised above her head with a glowing white crystal affixed to the top of it.

"That meddling witch," Astravar said through Ta'ra's mouth. "What wasted potential." The Cat Sidhe lifted her paws off me and started to sprint away. Before she could get far, though, Salanraja swooped down from the sky and thudded down on the ground in front of her, blocking her path.

She tried to turn to evade, and a narrow beam of white energy from Seramina's staff hit her on the side of the head. Ta'ra started to run again, but it was like her body didn't want to follow her legs, as if she was physically in battle against herself.

Soon, she skidded to a halt, and then her head turned towards me. Still, her eyes didn't open. "This isn't the end. I will find another way." As she spoke, she shrank until she became a normal cat size again. I was pretty sure that Astravar was trying to reduce her further, maybe as a ploy to steal Ta'ra away.

Another narrow beam of bright white energy came from Seramina's staff, this time hitting Ta'ra right between the eyes. It lasted for a few seconds before her eyes shot open.

I gazed into the bright green eyes of a very confused black cat.

5

LESSONS IN DRUDGERY

Two days later, I was lying, comfortably sleeping, in Salanraja's chamber, nestled up against the warmth from the dragonfire burning in her chest, when the bell rang to signal the start of class. Admittedly, there wasn't much else to do in winter other than studying, and Driar Aleam had pointed out that I had a lot to learn.

The sun hadn't even risen yet. Mind you, I usually liked to wake up when it was still dark. Nights were far better for hunting and sneaking up on your prey while it slept.

I lifted myself up and stretched out, yawning. A crescent moon hung high in the sky, and I looked out at the place that I'd awoken Ta'ra from her dream.

I stalked down the spiral staircase, and onto the cobblestones, everything lit by flaming torches of the kind I really didn't see much of in South Wales. Much of the snow had melted the previous day, reducing it to puddles and slush. Some guards eyed me suspiciously from the walls, and I hissed back up at them to communicate that if they tried shooting me down, the Council of Three would eat them for breakfast.

Astravar's attempt to capture Ta'ra had put the whole of Dragonsbond Academy in lockdown. The Council of Three had ordered the archers on the wall to shoot anything that left on sight. That included cats – especially cats, Driar Yila had said.

Of course, it takes a lot of effort to imprison so many cats in such a large space. You have to make sure every nook and cranny is covered. Which is what the humans did – they greased the walls so me, my brothers, and my sisters couldn't scramble up them, and they put these tall spiky wooden barricades around the staircases leading onto the walls, so high and sharp looking that no cat would dare even try to climb them.

I admit, I did scout the grounds a few times to check for any ways out. But the guards and carpenters here had done their jobs well and sealed the place off tight. Meanwhile, Ta'ra was locked in a small room in the guard's tower, the cats here were now let out into the bailey at all times, instead of being confined to the cattery during the day. If there was one thing Dragonsbond Academy needed right now, it was efficient crow-catchers.

A few of them, including a white cat with pink ears, had gathered around Captain Onus who dangled a ball of wool that apparently resembled a crow from a fishing rod. The white cat was so agile, she leapt up to catch the ball of wool in both her paws, and then pinned it to the ground.

In response, Captain Onus laughed, and he produced a piece of dried beef from his satchel and threw it on the ground in front of the white cat. It looked so delicious.

In a way, I wanted to join in the fun. But I knew I had a classroom to fall asleep in.

Just as the sun began to rise, the bell rang again to remind all of the students not to be late to their allotted lessons, and several throngs of students came out from the dormitory doors on the other side of the bailey. Some of them laughed away in conversation, while others stopped to drink from the water fountain.

I watched the students for a while, looking out for that platinum-blonde haired teenage witch with the power to watch dreams. I couldn't find her anywhere, but then she seemed the type to get to class well before everyone else.

Instead, a familiar voice came from the side of me. "Initiate Ben," it said. "Aww, it's been so long."

I looked up to see one of my favourite students, Ange, looking down at me, smiling a little goofily. She brushed a few strands of short brown hair away from her eyes, and then she leaned down and tickled me under the chin.

"Here, kitty kitty," she said, and she laughed.

"You know, I'm around three times the age of a kitten," I said. "In human terms, I'd be much, much older than you."

"Well, aren't you the wise one?" she said, and she bent down and lifted me up into a nice soft cuddle. "Come on, we'll be late for class."

I liked Ange; I really did. She was one of the few humans in Dragonsbond Academy who seemed to grasp how much we cats deserved pampering. I also still held that she was a much better suitor for Initiate Rine than Bellari. Her perfume, I swear, even had a whiff of catnip in it, which said a lot about her character.

I purred as she carried me along in her warm embrace, keeping her gaze down on me and ignoring the harsh, disapproving stares she got from some of the other students. Really, I don't know why so many of them still hated cats so much. I mean, humans worked the cats like horses here.

Really, it was meant to be the other way around – the cats should have been working the humans. I couldn't get over, sometimes, how messed up this world was.

The bell rang a third time, much louder than the other two. This was the final warning to get to class, which sent all the students into frenzies of panic.

Ange hurried too, but I didn't mind because I wasn't doing the walking. She waltzed me across the bailey, into the stone corridors, past the kitchen that smelled of herby goose, and into the dusty classroom. She placed me down in a custom-built chair – built higher than all the other chairs – and then she took the seat just next to me. Initiate Rine stumbled in and smiled at Ange, then sat in front of her. Bellari came in shortly afterwards with a red face and sat deliberately three desks away from Rine, letting out an incredibly loud huff as she plonked her bottom down on the stool.

Driar Brigel was the teacher for today. The gentle giant watched the students file in, with his bare arms crossed, showing the thick muscles on his forearms. "Come on, come on, you're all late again. How we're running a military academy here when none of the students are on time, I don't know."

A goose-feather quill lay on the desk in front of me. "Hello Ben," it said to me, and it stood up on its tip, and then dipped itself in the inkwell containing concentrated beetles' blood. The inkwell glowed from within, giving it a blue tint. This wasn't due to the ink, but the white magic crystal inside there that apparently allowed me to put my thoughts to paper. It made a lot of sense really, because in my whole life I've never seen a cat that can write with their paws.

The quill moved over to the aging parchment already on the desk in front of me and inked something down at the top of the page. It didn't matter to me what it said – my crystal had given me the ability to speak languages and not to decipher writing. But then I wasn't going to be the one reading it – it would be our Driar teachers who examined the thoughts that came to my mind which the pen, consequently, knew how to read.

I ignored the pen, scratching away, and turned my attention to the front of the classroom where Driar Brigel had started to deliver his lesson.

Cats aren't meant to sit in classrooms and watch the teacher scratch arcane symbols on the blackboard in different colours of chalk. Though, fortunately, most of the teachers didn't just rely on writing but said things out loud too. The problem was that Driar Brigel, it turned out, had an incredibly boring teacher's voice.

The lesson today was on alteration, or in other words the kind of magic that allows you to change your form. Of course, because the Cat Sidhe, the cause of the lockdown, was on everyone's mind right now, Driar Brigel decided to use her as an example to explain the concept.

Alteration spells were interesting to me, because they always came with a catch. If you turned into something too much, then you eventually became it. It all depended on the power of the crystal and the ability of the caster. Astravar, apparently, had cast a dark alteration spell on Ta'ra, which turned her from fairy to cat. But he'd done something – and no one quite knew what – to make it so that when Ta'ra used her ability to turn back into fairy form, she could only do it for a day, and then she'd turn back into a cat again. Once she'd turned back eight times though, she'd be permanently a cat, because that was the way that alteration worked.

Driar Brigel also surmised that Astravar had cast the spell this way, so he could take advantage of Ta'ra's fairy magic sometimes, but he wouldn't risk her accidentally casting anything when she was in cat form. If she did become problematic, he wouldn't have to deal with her fairy form this way for anything more than eight days.

When Ta'ra took on her final cat form, she would also lose things like the ability to speak the human and fairy languages, and her taste for certain foods. Around me, everyone seemed to shudder when Driar Brigel said this. But I personally didn't see why this was so scary. I mean, it seemed normal not to like things like vegetables and bread and to instead focus on the good stuff like meat and eggs and dairy. Whiskers, humans were so strange.

As Driar Brigel droned on, I found myself less and less able to focus. Alas, although I was curious what Astravar had done to Ta'ra, Driar Brigel's dry voice eventually sent me to sleep.

6

A CALL FOR COURAGE

The wind soughed through the needles in the pine forest all around me, and the ground felt crunchy underfoot. The sun shone down from the sky, adding extra warmth to the heat coming from a roaring fire.

I was expecting to see Astravar in my dream, but he wasn't there, and instead I found myself looking at a massive salmon roasting on a spit. It sent off delicious smells, scented with tarragon and lemon, neither of which I minded, so long as they were only used as mild flavouring.

Salmon, oh how I missed it. There was none of it in this world, and often I wondered if I would taste it ever again. A man was sitting by the fire, wearing a brown cloak. His face wasn't visible through the shadow of his hood, and part of me wondered if I was looking at Astravar. But he didn't smell like Astravar – and trust me, I'd know because that warlock carried the odour of rotten vegetable juice with him wherever he went.

The man didn't move like Astravar either. I watched, and I waited as he turned the salmon around with a solid branch. I meowed to tell him that I was hungry, and that I hadn't eaten for a long time. But that didn't cause him to stir one bit, almost as if he didn't realise I was there.

Suddenly, there came a rustling from the forest behind me, and I jerked around, expecting to be looking at the sharp teeth of a wolf or something. Nothing was there, only the crackling and the heat coming from the fire behind me.

And a stench, this time of rotting meat coming from behind the fire. Suddenly, the heat disappeared, and everything felt so cold. Day quickly fell to night, and I felt the presence of something much larger than myself behind me. The hackles shot up on the back of my neck, and I turned towards a face three times the size of mine.

I'd seen it on the television, and the Savannah cats back home had told me this beast was almost as dangerous as a hippopotamus. A mane surrounded its yellow face like a picture frame. It regarded me in a characteristically catlike way. Except its catness wasn't like any cats I knew.

A lion – the king of the Savannah. The greatest hunter in the world from which I'd come. The beast that every cat wanted to be.

"Can I have your autograph?" I asked.

The lion didn't give me an answer, or at least an intelligible one. Instead, it opened its mouth and let off both an incredibly smelly and incredibly loud roar – the stench and amplitude of it meant to paralyse, I was sure.

It was then that I noticed that this wasn't any normal lion. It had another head – one of a goat – protruding out of its neck, and a third one coming out of its tail – that of a venomous-looking snake.

I'd never seen anything like it in my life.

I'd had my moment of freeze, and now it was time for either fight or flight, and one of those options seemed much more appealing than the other. I spun around and sprinted off into the forest, not looking back once. I brushed past thorny branches and nettles, but I didn't let the pain from the scratches deter me. As I went, I turned my ears behind me, listening for that beast's footsteps crunching over the forest floor. The wind sounded like voices whispering through the trees, and I was expecting to see Astravar's face at any moment

Eventually, I came into a clearing, and realised nothing was following me. I spun around, looking for that thing, but it had assumedly decided it didn't want to eat me for supper.

I had emerged in a glade, with a lake stretching out in front of me, the surface as clear as bowl-water. I could see the orange and yellow fishes swimming around as if they didn't have a worry in the world.

But they should have been worried because a cat had just entered their domain. Intently, I studied their movements as I tried to work out how I could catch one while avoiding getting wet.

"*What you need is a good fishing net,*" a voice said to me, and it took me a moment to realise that it hadn't spoken out loud but in my mind. "*Maybe attached to a simple rowing boat.*"

The words sent a shudder down my spine.

Astravar had found his way to me finally, and he was going to try to possess me like he had Ta'ra. But the voice didn't sound like Astravar. Instead, it was female and had a nice soft lilt to it. She sounded much like the mistress back home in South Wales.

I looked up to see a crystal spinning above the water. In it, I could see images of myself kneeling over the side of a rowing boat and chasing fish. I was looking right into the facets of my crystal, meaning that what it was showing was one possible thread of the future. But all of a sudden, I didn't fancy going fishing anymore. I didn't want to get my paws wet.

"*It has been a while now, young Ben,*" the crystal said. "*And what progress have you made in pursuing your destiny?*"

Her question caught me off guard. After defeating Astravar and his demon dragon, I'd been so busy just surviving in this world, that I hadn't really had time to think about any of that 'pursuing my destiny' palaver.

"*I've used my gift of language to talk to a lot of people,*" I said after a moment. "*And I managed to command a demon dragon and return it to the Seventh Dimension.*"

"*I do not ask about the past,*" the crystal said. "*I ask about the present. What are you doing right now to improve yourself and make sure you're on the right path?*"

"*Improve myself?*"

"We're all on a path of either growth or decay, and your actions now will determine how you will grow."

I thought about it for a moment. *"I'm eating a lot of good food,"* I said. *"That helps me grow and become strong. But if I ate rotten food, I'd surely decay."*

"I'm not talking about your physical form," the crystal said. *"I'm talking about becoming the hero who can face and defeat your nemesis. If you don't become stronger, then the warlocks will destroy all life in all dimensions. This is the fate that I have foretold."*

I groaned. I didn't like the sound of this self-improvement stuff. I'd seen humans do it on television sometimes. It seemed to involve lots of painful stretching and listening to dull and repetitive music.

"What the whiskers do you expect of me? Because right now I'm utterly confused."

"You need to learn courage," the crystal said. *"Or in other words, the ability to circumvent your instinct in the face of fear and keep a level mind. You must face the chimera and win, young Ben. Then, it will be time for your second spell."*

"My second spell?"

But the dream was already fading to white. The fish went first, then the lake, then the ground and the surrounding trees. The crystal blinked out last, leaving me facing a wall of whiteness.

Then I awoke.

7

GOOD EDUCATION

I don't think it was the dream that woke me, but the bell ringing out indicating the start of our lunch break. An immediate commotion exploded from the classroom, as the Initiates all around me leaped up from their desks. They left their parchments and inkwells on the table and made towards the door – creating a bottle-neck at the entrance.

"Don't forget your homework," Driar Brigel shouted out as he rubbed his writing off the board. "I expect all parchments back on my desk at this time tomorrow."

No one seemed to hear him. I also had a bit of a problem, as I'd never heard what the homework was. Once Driar Brigel had wiped the board clean, he looked around the classroom and then strolled up towards me.

Ange was still sitting at her desk, her nose buried in her parchment as she wrote down some notes. Driar Brigel looked over her paper, and she glanced up at him, then returned to whatever it was she was studying.

"Always a dedicated student, Initiate Ange," Driar Brigel said.

Ange didn't look up from her parchment. "Just give me a minute, sir."

Driar Brigel smiled. "No problem. You can have as long as you need."

I yawned as he approached and leaned over my desk. He peered down at my paper, a slight gleam in his eye. "Now I wish I could say the same of Initiate Ben. What's this long line, here? It looks like your thoughts went blank for a while. Did you drift off again, Ben?"

I growled. "I'm a cat, what do you expect? We're not meant to do stuff during the day."

"But you still need to study like everyone else. Tell me, what did you learn today?"

"I learned of the dangers of alteration."

Driar Brigel raised an eyebrow. "Oh, and what might they be?"

"Never to get involved with it," I said. "Because I might end up turning into a human or something and never being able to turn back..."

"Or a dog," Driar Brigel said with a chuckle.

I shuddered. "Definitely not a dog. Nothing's worse than turning into one of those."

"Worse than a cockroach?"

"Yes," I said. "At least cockroaches find it easy to hide."

Driar Brigel shook his head. Then, something on the paper seemed to catch his eye. "What's this? Transmutation into a chimera? What were you dreaming, Ben?"

"Nothing."

"Was the warlock there?"

"No..."

The Driar studied me for a moment. "Fine. Just try harder to concentrate. I don't want to have to fail you at the end of the year."

"Yes, sir," I said. The crowd had now dispersed at the door, and so I leapt down to leave Ange to her studies and Driar Brigel to whatever he wanted to do.

"*Bengie,*" Salanraja said in my mind after I was through the door.

"*Yes?*"

"*It appears it's time.*"

"*Time for what?*"

"I know you had a dream too. The crystal contacted us, and it seems you have a mission from the source of magic itself."

I growled, causing a couple of students waltzing down the corridor to jump out of my way and then look at me funny. *"I'm not sure I want to. Besides, we're on lockdown here. We can't leave."*

I was outside now, weaving my way around the puddles created by the melted slush. The air smelled of wood smoke, and the students had gathered in the bailey, playing a game where each player had a piece of string stretched across the span of their arms. One student would use this to throw an hourglass shaped cut of wood up in the air to be then caught by another student on their string.

The bell rang again, signalling lunch was ready. The students dropped their toys and immediately rushed back into the corridors towards the kitchen. I started to follow them, until Salanraja said, *"You know, I've got a whole cow up here. Roasted by my own breath."*

My mouth immediately began to water. I mean the food from the kitchens was good, but they'd not had much beef recently, which was exactly what my stomach wanted right then. *"I guess when I visit, you'll be giving me another lecture."*

"Beef, Bengie. Just think of the beef!"

Whiskers, when she put it that way, I couldn't think of anything else. *"Fine, I'm coming."*

Hence, I made my way towards Salanraja's tower – not quite sprinting, but at least with some urgency in my steps. On the way, I passed a lady with raven black hair spilling down both sides of her face in waves. She wore a black woollen cloak, unbuttoned near the top to reveal a white frilly shirt underneath it. She wasn't a student but looked more to be in her thirties.

"Hello, Ben," she said as I passed. "Fancy seeing you here." She raised her hand to her mouth and giggled.

But my stomach was rumbling too much by this point to pay her much heed. It wasn't until I reached the staircase that I realised I'd never seen her before in Dragonsbond Academy. I turned back to look for her, but she wasn't anywhere to be found.

8

LUNCHING WITH THE
DRAGON

Salanraja, as promised, had prepared a delicious feast of flamed beef. My dragon didn't put any herbs on her cooking, but still her dragon flames imbued the meat with a smokiness that I'd become quite partial to.

Obviously, there was no way I could eat a whole cow, but with Salanraja there I wouldn't have to. Though, I did hope that she would leave some leftovers.

The roast carcass spanned the unexposed corner of Salanraja's chamber, where I had once sprayed and never would do so again, given I'd almost got scorched in the process. Next to this was a wide opening that looked out over the open world. Out there, a murder of crows had gathered in the distance, flying in a loose formation around and around. It was as if they were waiting for something to happen. But they didn't seem to dare come anywhere near Dragonsbond Academy.

Crows were weird – I'd always thought that. Mind you, they were one of the birds that no cat back home wanted to pick a fight with – vicious things that they were. I turned back to Salanraja, who was munching on a massive chunk of beef that she'd torn off the ribcage. I also had a pile of beef that I'd chewed off into chunks. I took hold of one in my mouth and munched.

"*Have you heard about a new Driar here in Dragonsbond Academy?*" I asked Salanraja in my mind.

"*No one told me that the Driars were recruiting.*"

"*Well, I saw someone. A woman just now. She looked a little odd.*"

Salanraja chuckled. "*She's probably one of the guards. Or a student you've not noticed yet.*"

"*No. She was far too old to be a student, and she wasn't wearing armour.*"

"*Then you were hallucinating, Bengie. Maybe the hunger was getting to you.*"

I growled, and I bit into another piece of beef. Then I turned towards the crystal placed by the opening from Salanraja's chamber to the outside world. It displayed a vision of that hideous beast I'd seen in my dreams.

I really didn't want to have to face off against that thing. It would eat me. Forget about destiny and all that. It was fierce, and it had three heads for fighting with, while I only had one. Salanraja could have beaten it perhaps, but she was adamant that it was me that had to fight it.

"*You don't have a choice, you know,*" she said. "*When your crystal chooses for you to do something, you have to do it.*"

"*But we're in lockdown. The Council said no one can enter or leave.*"

"*That's where you're wrong. Any requests from a crystal take precedence over orders even from King Garmin himself. We'll go after we finish our feast.*"

"*And where exactly are we going to find a chimera?*" I asked.

"*Trust me, I know of a place.*"

Suddenly, I didn't feel so hungry. Or rather, I wanted to delay eating it all for as long as I could. This was ridiculous. I shouldn't have to go and fight something I wouldn't stand a chance against. I mean, had Salanraja seen the size of that beast? It was even larger than Astravar's demon Maine Coon.

I glanced towards the entrance to the chamber, but Salanraja had strategically placed herself in front of the archway, blocking it off. The only other way out of here was out from the side of the tower. But we were so high up that if I jumped, even if I'd land on my feet, I'd break all of my bones doing so. If only there was a bed or something I could hide under. Though, knowing Salanraja, she'd probably then set the bed on fire to force me out.

"*Is that why you invited me here?*" I asked.

"*Say again...*"

"*You invited me to a delicious feast so that you could trap me here so I wouldn't have a chance but to fly with you on your stupid mission.*"

"*It's not my mission,*" Salanraja said. "*As always, Bengie, you seem to fail to understand how important this is.*"

"*What, to walk straight up to death's door, also known as the jaws or fangs of a chimera?*"

"*You won't kill yourself...*"

"*How do you know?*"

Salanraja stood up and edged towards me. She moved her head so close that I could smell the fumes from her dragonfire seeping out of her nostrils. "*Because the crystal can predict the future,*" she said, "*and it would never set a mission for someone that can kill them. Gracious demons, you can be impossible sometimes, Bengie.*"

Salanraja moved even closer to me, revealing a gap small enough underneath her for me to squeeze through. I picked up another piece of beef in my mouth to make sure I had a fair serving of the lunch that Salanraja had invited me to. Then I squeezed underneath her belly, through her back legs, and out of the doorway. I sprinted down the spiral staircase, and across the slushy ground towards the water fountain. I hid underneath the stone there, going so deep that no one would be able to see me. No students were around now – everyone was in the dining hall eating roasted goose.

"*You can't escape me, Bengie,*" Salanraja said. "*I can still speak in your mind.*"

"*I'm not going,*" I said.

"*Then you leave me no choice...*"

"*What? What do you mean, Salanraja? What are you going to do?*"

All went quiet inside my mind for a while, and I stared out at the empty bailey, not particularly wanting to come out from my hiding hole. Eventually Salanraja's voice came back in my head.

"It is done," she said.

"What is?"

"The Council of Three wants to see you. You are to go to their offices. Now!"

Whiskers, the traitor! I wasn't going anywhere. Instead, I edged even further underneath the fountain, as I listened to the crows cawing in the distance, and the wind howling through the castle.

9

HOW TO SHOW AFFECTION

After several minutes of sulking underneath the fountain, I decided that the worst thing that I could do was stay in my hiding spot. This strategy would have worked in my own world – I was too far underneath for anyone to reach me. But the Driars in Dragonsbond Academy had magic that they could use to pull me out with ease.

The Council of Three had already demonstrated how they could raise me up in the air using beams of light from their staffs and pin me there, completely paralysed. I was sure that they would do a lot worse to me if I didn't heed their summons.

I walked through the open archway to the Council's Courtyard. But the Council hadn't asked to meet me here. For the first time in my life, I'd actually meet them in their own office.

I had thought that the door might present a problem. The heavy walnut-oak door to the keep was usually closed with one of those round handles that cats didn't have a chance of opening. The door had a knocker on it, but that was far out of reach.

Fortunately, the door was slightly ajar this time, and I pushed it a little further using all my strength. It wasn't easy, I tell you. Tasks which often seem simple for a human are a lot harder for a cat. But saying that, there's also an awful lot of things that cats can do that humans can't.

The door creaked open a little more, and I pushed my way around it. I entered an office – a wide and tall room with a curved standing reception desk at the centre of it. Two red-carpeted staircases flanked the room leading up to a mezzanine. Doors led off in all directions.

Each staircase had a bench underneath it, and Bellari and Rine sat on one of these, their mouths wrapped each around the other's. I have to say that I didn't get this whole kissing thing that lovers – if I could call Bellari and Rine that – did to show affection. It wasn't just gross, but also utterly pointless.

The two were so engrossed in what they were doing that they didn't seem to notice me enter the room. I thought that I could have some fun with this, and so I took a deep breath, then I bawled out in the mightiest voice I could muster, "Initiate Rine!"

Rine jumped up off the bench and spun around. "What? Who?" He looked around the room in confusion, and then he turned down and glared at me. "Ben!"

His girlfriend, Bellari, sneezed. "Rine, it's that cat again. Get him out of here."

I growled. Initiate Bellari was perhaps my worst enemy in the whole of Dragonsbond Academy, including some of the more ignorant cats who didn't seem to appreciate a Bengal, a descendent of the great Asian leopard cat I might add, marking what they considered their territory.

"You know," I said. "I don't think you're allergic to cats at all, Bellari."

"How dare you. Of course I'm allergic. I sneeze whenever I see one."

"And do you sneeze when you don't see one?"

Her face went a bright shade of puce. "I—What in the seventh dimension are you talking about?"

I moved over to her, and she backed up against the bench. Her eyes were red as if she'd been crying. She and Rine must have been making up after an argument.

"You know, I learned quite an interesting word when I gained the ability to speak your language," I said. "Psychosomatic."

"Psycho-what?"

"Oh, your civilisation will learn that word when you decide you have a need for psychology."

Bellari's nostrils flared. "Who do you think you are? And what in the Seventh Dimension are you talking about?"

I jumped up on the bench and pushed up to her, rubbing my nose against her elbow. This, you see, is the proper way to show affection, even if Bellari didn't really deserve it. She immediately shot up out of her seat and backed up against the wall. "I told you not to go anywhere near me. Rine, do something..."

I leaped off the bench, and I followed her towards the wall until I had her backed into a corner.

Rine was watching the whole encounter, and he looked as if he was trying to stop himself from laughing. "He's right, you know. Ben's an Initiate now, and you've got to start treating him like one of us."

Bellari sneezed again, and I flinched but stayed in my spot looking up at her. I let out a meow for good measure.

"I do hope you're joking," Bellari said.

"There's no need to be so cruel to him, sugarpot. He saved us from a demon dragon, remember. He's a hero."

"He's a cat. Rine, I swear, get this cat away from me, or I'll—"

"You'll do what?"

"Don't test me," Bellari said. Really, she looked so funny when her face went red like this, contrasting boldly against her rich blonde curls.

Rine sighed. "Fine." He walked over, scooped me up in his arms, and carried me to the other side of the room. I nestled myself into the warm folds of his cloak, purring deeply. I got on much better with Rine now than when I'd first met him. I admit, he still seemed a bit of a snob. But his girlfriend was much, much worse.

Bellari crossed her arms. "Make sure you change clothes and bathe before you come near me again, Rine."

Rine sighed and looked down at me, turning away from his girlfriend. "So... What brings you here, Ben? I heard you were scheduled to have lunch with your dragon."

"I've already eaten. Then the Council of Three summoned me here."

"Really?" Rine took me over to a dusty smelling open book on the desk with what looked like names scrawled on after the other on the page. "You're not on the list."

"Probably because they only just summoned me."

"Oh," Rine said. "Well, there's a meeting in there right now." He turned towards the large double doorway underneath the mezzanine.

"A meeting? About what?"

"Aren't you the nosy one," Rine said with a chuckle. "I don't know much, and I'm not allowed to tell you what I do know."

"I guess I'll wait then," I tried to pull myself out of Rine's arms and jump down towards Bellari to annoy her some more. But he held me there with a firm grip.

"Oh no," Rine said in a hushed voice. "Come on, Ben, you've already got me in enough trouble today. Don't go causing more."

"Fine," I said with a growl. But I didn't push it. Instead, I watched the double doors to the Council Room, wondering when the meeting would finally finish inside. I didn't wait long. After a few minutes, perhaps, the doors swung open and they stayed open. No one was standing by the door, so I guessed someone must have opened them through magic.

Rine dropped me down on the floor. "Go on in, it's your turn I guess."

I considered going over to annoy Bellari even more, fun as the game was. She returned a sneer at me and made a shooing motion towards the Council Room. Well, it was probably better to not keep the Council of Three waiting.

Behind the double doors to the Council Room, I could already see the three Council members sitting at their desks. I raised my head high, and I strolled into the room.

10

COUNCIL BUREAUCRACY

The three desks were arranged in the Council Room, much as the lecterns were outside. Each was made of sturdy looking hardwood, with papers and ornaments scattered all over them. The room was much warmer than outside, too – which I greatly appreciated. Heat roared out of two fireplaces stacked with burning logs on either side of the room. The air also had a much cleaner taste to it than it did in any other room in the castle, as if someone dusted here three times a day.

Driar Yila sat at the left desk, her head resting in her cupped hands as she peered at me inquisitively. Driar Lonamm was at the centre desk, shaking her head, and I wasn't sure if this was due to what had happened in her previous meeting with Prefects Lars and Asinda or because I was in a lot of trouble. Driar Brigel was gazing up at the ceiling nonchalantly. Three high arched windows stood behind each desk, with a stained-glass depiction of each of the Driar's dragons at the top of each window.

Apparently, you got summoned here when the Council of Three didn't even deem it worth their while to step outside. Their staffs were propped in racks within easy reach of them, at the sides of their desks. I was sure that if I tried anything funny, they wouldn't hesitate to punish me with their magic.

From here, I could also see there was far too much stuff on the desks, and some of it belonged on the floor. I turned my head from desk to desk, wondering which bit of paper or trinket I should knock off first.

"What are you doing, cat?" Driar Yila asked.

"I thought you knew my name now, ma'am," I said, drawing out the last word slightly to demonstrate my annoyance.

"I shall use your name while you're in our good graces. When you aren't, I shall call you what I please. Now answer my question."

"I'm merely examining your papers…"

"Why?" Driar Lonamm asked.

"They look interesting…"

"If you knock anything off the desk, I'll skin you alive," Driar Yila said, and she leaned forwards and wrapped her hand around her staff. The red crystal at the top of it glowed at her touch.

I growled, and I sank down onto my haunches. "Fine," I said. "I'll be good."

Driar Lonamm was shaking her head. "You've got a lot to learn. Now a little bird told me that you've been refusing your crystal's calling."

"By 'little bird', do you mean 'rather big dragon'?" I asked.

"I mean that my dragon told me what your dragon told him. Now, it's meant to be us that's asking the questions. What reasons have you for refusing the call?" She glared at me as she asked the question, looking no less fierce than Driar Yila.

I turned to Driar Brigel, hoping for a little sympathy. But he also had a massive frown on his face. I tried to give the Driars a wide-eyed look – a kind of magic 'cuteness' spell that always worked in my world – but none of them were having any of it.

"Initiate Ben," Driar Brigel said. "I don't think you understand the responsibility of being a dragon rider. The crystal gave you a gift not so you could do what you please, but so you could work for the future of the kingdom."

"But I have to face a beast that's bigger than me and could eat me for breakfast, dinner, or supper. There's no way I can defeat a chimera."

"That's where you're wrong," Driar Lonamm said. "The crystal wouldn't reveal to you a destiny that leads to your death."

"Unless such death could save the entire kingdom," Driar Yila added.

I swallowed hard as my heart started thumping in my chest. I just couldn't believe what I was hearing. These people, they'd grown up with these crystals and they'd based their entire belief system around them. But I didn't come from their world, and so I couldn't trust a massive gem, magical or not.

"No," I said. "I'm not doing it. I don't want to die."

I must have said that extremely loudly or something, because my words reverberated off the room's walls, decaying into silence.

"You have some nerve," Salanraja said in my mind. *"Don't you think it's less scary to just go on this mission than deal with the punishments the Council of Three can enact on you?"*

"They can do what they like," I said. *"Because they won't catch me."*

I turned and sprinted towards the open doors. But I could only take a few steps before a massive gust of wind came from the doorway and a green glowing light exploded from the centre of the opening. Then the doors slammed shut in my face. I turned back to see that Driar Brigel had his staff pointed at the door, his staff's crystal glowing green.

One thing I'd learned in his classes was that the leaf magic in his crystal gave him the power to manipulate nature. That included, I guessed, the ability to telekinetically swing wooden doors on their own hinges.

"You have to learn to rise above your instincts, Ben," Driar Brigel said. "Fear always wants you to take the easy way out, but more often than not that path isn't good for you."

"My instincts? I'll have you know I consider my actions quite carefully. It's just I'm an extremely fast thinker."

"If your thoughts were that fast," Driar Lonamm said. "Then you'd have realised there was no point in running. With this entire castle on lockdown, you have nowhere to go."

Suddenly there came a banging at the door, startling me for the second time.

"Yes," Driar Yila said, and I skittered out of the way of the opening door.

Captain Onus, the head of the guards here, stood at the entrance, together with a female guard. The captain looked down at me with his ugly face, pursed his lips and made a sucking sound as if he wanted to endear himself to me.

"Yes, Captain," Driar Yila said again.

Captain Onus seemed to remember himself. He stood to attention and then gave a bow. An expression of alarm returned to his face. "It's the Cat Sidhe. I really don't know how, but she's escaped."

WHERE DID SHE GO?

W e didn't waste any time leaving the Council Office. The three Driars were immediately up on their feet and storming out of the doors. There must have been a good reason why Astravar had wanted Ta'ra so badly, but no one had told me exactly why yet.

Outside, in the bailey, a thick fog had settled on the academy. Though I couldn't see them, I could hear the crows high above the castle, screeching into the air. The cats, my brothers and sisters, crouched watching where the sounds came from, waiting for a crow to emerge from the cover. Everything was cold now – the ground, the fog, the howling wind that cut through it, and the sinking feeling that Astravar had stolen Ta'ra away from us. What did he want of her? Was he using her as a trap to try to get hold of me?

I saw something falling from the sky, and I leaped out of the way of a crow-dropping that splattered on the ground. Thank goodness I still had my wits about me, because the last thing I wanted was the excrement from those ugly birds ruining my beautiful silky fur.

The Driars had ordered me to stay close to them, and after what Driar Brigel had done to those doors, I didn't think it was a good idea to argue with them. They led me over to the gate tower where Ta'ra had been locked away. A guard was waiting outside there, his posture sunken, and I guessed he was probably the culprit. I wanted to scratch him to teach him a lesson, but every inch of his body from the neck down was covered in light armour.

"What happened here?" Driar Yila asked the guard. "I thought you had her under lock and key."

"I did," the guard replied. "We sealed off any gaps underneath the door, and I had one of the prefects make sure there was nothing on the ground she could have crawled through."

"So how could she have escaped?" Driar Brigel asked, one hand on his hip, the other on his chin. "I checked the wards Initiate Ange had set and all of them were sound."

"We have no idea," Captain Onus said. "That's what we're trying to work out."

A door creaked open behind me, and Aleam came out of it. He quickly hobbled over to us, using his staff for support. "I've just heard the news," he said, coming to a stop next to the three Council members.

Everyone turned towards Driar Aleam.

"Do you have any idea how she might have escaped?" Driar Lonamm asked him.

"No," Aleam said. "But we need to examine all possibilities. The crows are still up in the air," – he pointed at them with his staff – "and I don't think any of them would have got past our cats."

"What can a crow do?" I asked.

"You have no idea…" Aleam said, looking down at me and shaking his head. "But I think the major question right now, is what does Astravar want with Ta'ra?"

Aleam and the Council of Three continued to interrogate the guards. Meanwhile, I looked up at the crows, and I wondered if Ta'ra could have been there among them. Maybe Astravar had somehow turned her into one of those foul birds. She could get shot down by an arrow, without the guards knowing who she was. Then, the cats might come in and try to eat her – even though crow tastes disgusting. But some of my brothers and sisters looked so malnourished, they probably wouldn't even care.

"Ben?" Aleam asked me.

"Huh?" I said, and I realised that I'd been daydreaming, perhaps even almost dozing off.

"Did you see anything funny around here? You were in the courtyard just moments ago, and Ta'ra must have escaped around the same time."

I didn't know. I pressed the rewind button on my life for the last hour or so, and I remembered the council being mean to me, annoying Bellari just before I caught the two kissing, Salanraja nagging me about fighting the chimera, and the delicious beef. Then what was before that? Oh, it was always so hard to remember anything before the food.

Then I remembered climbing the staircase, following that delicious aroma of smoky beef, mesmerised. Before the staircase there was that woman – the one with the raven black hair, dark coat, and the white blouse.

"I saw someone," I said. "Just before I went up to see Salanraja."

Aleam raised an eyebrow, and he leaned towards me on his staff. "Go on…"

"There was a woman. I'd never seen her before."

"What did she look like?" Driar Lonamm asked.

"Well, she had a black robe, a white shirt underneath it, and black hair. Come to think of it, her clothing looked a bit like…" I trailed off, as the implications dawned on me.

"You're kidding," Driar Brigel said.

"No," Driar Lonamm said. "Astravar can make her do that?"

"She's used one of her nine transformations," Aleam said. He examined the door. "A fairy, small enough to fit through the keyhole. Did anyone put any wards on the lock?"

Driar Brigel lowered his head. "I didn't think to tell Initiate Ange to do that… I'm sorry, Aleam."

"No time for apologies," Aleam said. "We must go out there and find her. But where might she have gone?"

That was a mighty good question. Of course, I wasn't really the best creature to ask. I'd never even heard of fairies until I entered this world and met Ta'ra for the first time, and that hadn't been so long ago.

The four older Driars had now turned towards the keep tower. That building apparently contained the most powerful of the dragons, including Olan – Aleam's white dragon.

"I'll go now." He walked off towards the keep.

"Me too," I called after him, but Driar Brigel put out a hand to stop me.

"You have a mission, young one," he said.

Whiskers, I'd hoped they'd forgotten about it. Even if searching for Ta'ra might have turned out to be more dangerous, I'd rather do that than face a chimera.

"*Bengie,*" Salanraja said in my mind. "*Has Aleam gone yet?*"

"*No,*" I replied. "*Why?*"

"*Stop him now!*"

"*Why?*"

"*Just do it.*"

Aleam had already travelled halfway across the bailey towards the Council Courtyard. I tried to shout out, but he didn't seem to hear me. So, I sprinted after him, half expecting Driar Brigel to cast a magic spell to stop me.

"Stop!" I shouted.

Driar Aleam turned around. "Ben, we haven't got time for this. You must respect your crystal's wishes."

"It's not me that's telling you to stop, it's Salanraja."

He paused a moment. "Why? What is it?"

I asked Salanraja the same question.

"*It's the crystal,*" she said. "*It's giving us a little bit more information on our mission to fight the chimera, which seems to involve Ta'ra and Astravar...*"

I groaned from deep in my stomach, because I really wasn't sure I liked the sound of that. Battling a chimera was one thing. But having to battle a chimera, Astravar, his demon Maine Coon, and whatever horrible creatures he might have summoned from the Seventh Dimension sounded a lot, lot worse.

But still, I knew we needed to discover what the crystal knew. So, I told Aleam exactly what Salanraja had said.

12

THE VISION

Inside her own chamber, Salanraja watched our crystal from the entranceway. The three dragons belonging to the Council of Three and Aleam's white dragon, Olan, hovered outside, flapping their wings every several seconds to keep them aloft.

Unusually, each of the Council had dragons that matched the colour of their staffs. Driar Yila had a ruby dragon called Farago, just like Salanraja except Farago had no spikes on his back. Driar Lonamm's dragon was a sapphire, known as Flue, with exceptionally long teeth. And Driar Brigel had an emerald dragon called Plishk that, just like the gentle giant, carried a lot of extra muscle bulk.

The three Driars and Aleam had huddled closest to the exposed opening, as if ready to mount their dragons at any moment. I had taken a place by my meal of beef, and I chewed on a piece of it for comfort, even if I didn't feel like eating. It had dried out, anyway. Knowing Salanraja, she'd probably roasted it a second time deliberately evaporating any tantalising moisture out of it to express her anger for my disagreement before.

The crystal emanated a warmth that felt like the setting sun. It was spinning slowly on its vertical axis, just by the opening. This meant that it had something important to say. Last time it did this, it had wanted to gift me my ability to speak multiple languages. But this time it didn't bring good news.

Instead, two of my fears had combined to create an even greater fear. When I'd last faced off against Astravar, I'd had to battle a massive beast he'd summoned from the Seventh Dimension. And I'm not talking about the demon dragon.

I'd gone up against a beast of nightmares, something no cat should ever have to face. I shuddered every time I thought about how Astravar's demon Maine Coon had pinned me to the ground and almost killed me.

But now, beneath the facets of the crystal, I could see Astravar riding the beast. Except, this wasn't the Maine Coon I'd last encountered – but then the old Ragamuffin in South Wales had always said that you never encounter the same cat twice. As before, it had cracks all over its body, revealing the lava boiling underneath its skin. The Maine Coon also had that same face, with its ashen lion-like mane. But it now had gained a snake for a tail and a second neck with a goat's head sticking out of it.

In other words, the demon Maine Coon was now a demon chimera, and I couldn't believe my eyes.

The snake tail of the beast was covered in flames and lashed out violently into the air as Astravar gripped the goat's horns like handles and rode it onwards. The view in the crystal zoomed out to show his companions – thousands of black cats, twice the size of panthers, with white tufts on their chests.

They had a massive crystal with them too. This was purple and hovered in the air above Astravar and his demon chimera. Thin tendrils of light emanated from this crystal, each of them connecting with a Cat Sidhe below.

Together Astravar and his companions sprinted, and the purple crystal floated, towards a massive city that stretched across the horizon. This was Cimlean, the capital city of Illumine, residence of King Garmin and what I'd heard was an opulent palace. It looked so innocent there, its marble walls lit in a brilliant, almost blinding white and

the golden towers glinting in the sunlight. Around the city, the whiteness of the snow on the ground and the pine trees added to this image
of pureness.

But this snow would soon dissolve, I realised, once the purple
acrid mist that Astravar and his army of black cats carried around
them seeped into the city and slowly choked it of life. Still, the city
wasn't defenceless, and I could already see the archers standing like
dominoes upon the city's walls.

"An invasion," Driar Lonamm said, "but how could Astravar get
such a large army, and what is that beast he's riding?"

"I don't know," Driar Brigel replied. "He's clearly learned a new
spell."

"They're Cat Sidhe," Driar Yila said. "All of them. He must have
stolen them from the Faerie Realm."

"Which is why he wanted to capture Ta'ra," Aleam said. "To open a
portal."

If you'd asked me a year ago, I wouldn't even have known what a
magical portal was. As far as the cats in our South Wales clowder
knew, there was only one world, with oceans and deserts and great
plains like the Savannah, and the jungles from where my powerful
ancestors, the great Asian leopard cats, came. More recently, I'd
learned from my lessons with Driar Brigel that there were actually
seven worlds, or dimensions, interlinked, with the seventh being the
scariest of all. That was where the demons lived.

The first was this one, the second the Faerie Realm, the third the
Ghost Realm, and the fourth the Earth I knew so well and longed to
return to. The fifth and the sixth dimensions were more mysterious,
as no magician – not even Astravar – had learned to open them yet,
and so no one knew what lived within them.

"Still, we've not yet completely answered my question," Driar
Lonamm said. "How did Astravar obtain such powerful magic? We're
talking about alteration powerful enough to convert an entire fairy
city population to his cause. What channel could he possibly be
using?"

Everyone turned to Aleam. He was the oldest, and the only one
here who knew dark magic as well as the warlocks. If it weren't for his

dragon, Aleam would have also been corrupted by dark magic. But Olan saved him, so the legend goes, from his darkest hour.

"It's that crystal," Aleam said. "In all my time when I was dark mage for the king, we never even imagined a dark crystal that large. It has a lot of power in it, and I'm guessing Astravar plans to use it to capture the fairies' souls. Somehow, though, Ta'ra must be the key."

"The key to what?" Driar Yila asked.

"Perhaps he's using her love to channel the power…" Driar Brigel said as he gazed out towards the horizon. "Didn't you say, Aleam, that Ta'ra was betrothed to a prince before Astravar turned her into a cat?"

Aleam nodded. "She was cast out of that society long ago. Branded by the fairies as a fae because she had dark magic nestled within her. After Astravar summoned her from her wedding ceremony, she tried to return. But once Prince Ta'lon, her betrothed, realised what she'd become, he cut off all ties with her. From what I've heard about that prince, I'm not sure he ever loved Ta'ra in the first place. Although admittedly I've only heard the story from one source."

Driar Brigel nodded. "I guess she still loved him. And we all know from the fairy tales that unrequited love can spawn the worst type of magic."

Aleam sighed but said nothing.

I remembered the crystal that I'd swallowed back when Salanraja and I had battled the golem. It still was lodged within me, apparently, now nestled within the creases of my brain. In all honesty, it wasn't because I was a cat but rather because of the existence of that dark magic within me that made so many students here wary of me. So, I kind of understood how Ta'ra must have felt.

Inside the display on my crystal, Astravar and his army had now reached the city, and the archers fired their first volley. As the army moved, the purple mist around them seemed to seep into the land, melting the snow and sending up smoky steam. Arrows fell all around the warlock who had his staff raised up in the air, glowing purple at its tip. He cast a spell that created a bubble around him. Some arrows hit this but bounced off. Others hit the sides of the cats, some of which collapsed on the battlefield.

Presently, Astravar reached down into his pouch and lifted out a handful of small crystals. He threw these in the direction of the city, and they followed his trajectory for a moment, before lighting up in blue and then following a much straighter path of their own. As they shot forwards, they split up into more and more trails of light, creating a display that looked like those scary fireworks that humans liked to let off back home.

The view, kindly, followed the path of one of these crystals so we could see their effects up close. They continued in a straight line, not even seeming to waver, until they found their way right into the archers' heads. But the magic didn't kill them. Rather, the archers' eyes filled with white, and a blue spot glowed at the top of their head. Soon, they turned their bows away from the ground towards the sky. The view panned upwards and around to show dragons soaring in from the distance.

There must have been hundreds of them flying in from Dragons-bond Academy. The archers loosed their arrows at the dragons. In flight, these arrows took on a purple hue, sending out a trail of that magical gas behind them. Many of them hit the riders and knocked them off their mounts. Others buried themselves into the dragons' flanks and wings.

Despite the onslaught, still some dragons broke through and unleashed fire upon Astravar, who had a massive blue energy shield all around him to ward off the flames.

The view panned around to show a wide angle across the battle-field, the dragons now flying away from Astravar and starting to regroup. Suddenly, the air around these dragons began to twinkle, and then it filled with a flowing yellow powder. On the ground, the number of Cat Sidhe had reduced to around half.

"As I thought," Aleam said. "Astravar has the fairies completely under his control. He must be using the ones he's sent into the sky as conduits for his dark magic."

I didn't want to watch the rest of the scene, but my eyes seemed glued to what was happening, and I couldn't turn my head away. Everywhere around the dragons, explosions blossomed – brilliant displays of fire and light. I couldn't hear anything that was happening in the crystal, as it didn't seem quite as sophisticated as television back home. But still I could feel the dragons' anguish as they tossed their heads to the sky and gnashed and roared before they came crashing down to the ground.

The battlefield was presently reduced to ash, rubble, and smoke, with that horrible purple mist surrounding Astravar and his demon chimera Maine Coon, who were both protected by their shield barrier. Soon, the glistening wisps in the air came back down to ground. But they didn't transform back into the Cat Sidhe. Rather, they settled there on the ground, as if their life force had been extinguished.

"He's going to kill them," Driar Yila said. "He's sacrificed those fairies' lives to kill our own dragons."

"Ta'ra," I muttered, then, my breath caught in my throat before I could say anything else. Ta'ra could have been one of those fairies. He would just send her out to sacrifice her. Is that all her life, or all any of these fairies' lives meant to Astravar? A weapon to take down his enemies.

Astravar pulled back his magical bubble-shield, and then he pointed at the city walls with his staff. Together, the remaining Cat Sidhe and the warlock charged at the city, with nothing to protect it. The archers on the walls also turned their arrows upon the city and rained down volleys of fiery arrows upon their own kind.

Soon Cimlean went up in flames. The light from the fires became an intense white light glowing out from the crystal, which then spoke inside my head.

"This is the fate that will become of this world," it said. "If you fail to face up to your destiny, Initiate Ben. Soon after, Astravar will take his battle across all worlds, and everything shall be destroyed."

Every single muscle in my body was trembling, and I needed to sit down. I don't know what I feared more – the demon chimera, Astravar destroying all sources of food across the dimensions, or what he might do to Ta'ra.

I couldn't let it happen. I couldn't let Astravar take control. But I hated it. Part of me just wanted to go home back to my normal world where I didn't have to worry about anything.

Growling, I turned back to the four Driars whose faces were so white that they looked like they'd just seen a thousand ghosts.

13

AN UNLIKELY VOLUNTEER

The crystal had now dimmed to a dull grey, displaying nothing more. The entire scene had sent the four Driars into agitation, and they were currently discussing how to react.

"The portal Ta'ra came through to get to his world is in the Willowed Woods," Aleam said. "And so, I'm guessing that's where Ta'ra is heading now."

Driar Yila bristled, and her face blanched. "We sent Prefect Asinda and High Prefect Lars out there yesterday. We heard there was an anomaly in the area, and we needed someone to investigate. Now, it sounds we may have sent my niece and her boyfriend into grave danger."

I often forgot that Prefect Asinda was Driar Yila's niece, which might have explained why the younger woman acted so angry around me all the time – because, simply put, that anger ran in the family.

Aleam shook his head. "We'll find a way to help them. But we must go out there at once."

"But who should we send?" Driar Brigel asked.

"I'll go," I said.

That sent the room into silence. The Council of Three looked down at me, each of them with surprised looks on their faces. From the corner of the room, Salanraja let out a croon which sounded almost like a mewl.

"*You've changed your tune,*" she said to me. "*What happened to being scared of the chimera?*"

An image flashed into my mind of the demon chimera that Astravar had managed to acquire, one head roaring, another bleating, and the third lashing out towards me with a venomous hiss. I hadn't a clue how I was meant to fight that thing. It had almost slaughtered me without effort the last time I'd encountered it, and that was before it had grown two extra heads. "*I'm not letting that evil warlock destroy all the fish and mutton and venison and delicious things in this world,*" I said. "*What will there be left to eat then?*"

Salanraja chuckled in my mind. "*Are you sure it's nothing to do with Ta'ra?*"

"*What are you talking about? She's a fairy and I'm a cat.*"

"*But she won't be if she changes into a fairy one more time. She'll then become a cat forever.*"

"*Salanraja, this is nonsense.*"

"*We will see... We will see,*" Salanraja said, and she chuckled in my mind once again.

While Salanraja spoke in my mind, the three members of the Council were studying me. Probably, they also wanted some time to talk to the dragons about my sudden decision. I could imagine that they were trying to work out what to do if I took the first opportunity I had to run away from this lockdown. But I wasn't going to run away. I didn't want to risk being eaten by spiders and serkets again.

Aleam also watched me, but his expression was so passive, I didn't know what he was thinking. Eventually, it was Driar Yila who spoke.

"It makes sense to send the cat, I think," she said, though since she'd first mentioned Asinda her face hadn't regained its colour. "There's no better creature to track the Cat Sidhe across the land. You'll know her scent, I guess?"

"I'm not like a dog," I said. "I don't hunt creatures down for sport."

Driar Yila frowned. "But when push comes to shove, you'll be able to track her." Her voice was flatter than usual.

"Of course I can. Cats can smell better than dogs. In fact, we have one of the best senses of smell of any creature alive." I didn't know, in all honesty, if the last sentence was true. But I thought it sounded good enough to say. Then I added for good measure, "Oh, and because I'm a descendant of the great Asian leopard cat, that makes my olfactory sensibilities even greater than your typical moggie."

"Good," Driar Lonamm said, "But we're going to need to put a team together. This isn't just about stopping Ta'ra but also about sending reinforcements to help Prefect Lars and Prefect Asinda."

"I agree," Driar Brigel said. "This isn't a task for Initiates or Prefects anymore. We must send some of our Driars out there, even if it means putting classes on hold."

"Surely, none of you three are thinking of going out there?" Aleam said.

"Oh no," Driar Yila said, shaking her head. "Though I feel I should help my family, it's probably unwise for me to go out and face Astravar at my age. I'm sure Driar Lonamm and Driar Brigel feel the same." She looked at each of them and they each returned a nod.

"I understand," Aleam said. "But you probably realise that I will have to go."

"I thought you'd say that," Driar Brigel replied. "And we also need to send Seramina. After what happened with Ta'ra, we need to look after Initiate Ben's dreams."

I was already regretting my decision to go. There are some people that cats just don't like, and that weird blonde-haired teenager was one of them. I looked out at the dragons hovering outside. They were watching our conversation with intent, and I had no doubt that the Council of Three was also asking them for ideas.

Then I wondered. Maybe I could take another of those dragons, rather than Salanraja. They might be a little gentler with me in flight after being so experienced carrying old people across the land.

"*I heard that,*" Salanraja said.

"*Well, don't you feel you need a holiday?*"

But Salanraja didn't have time to answer before the crystal cut into our conversation. Suddenly, it glowed white, though this time it didn't display any mysterious scenes. And, instead of speaking in my head, it pulsed out light to the rhythm of its words. It was strange – I'd never heard it speak out loud before.

It still had that beautiful Welsh sounding voice though. I had no idea why this crystal liked to speak just like the humans back home. I wondered if there was a human in a room back in my world somewhere controlling it all.

"The cat must choose the team," the crystal said.

Driar Brigel was the first to spin around and stare at the crystal in surprise. Then, the other two members of the Council cast their gaze upon it. Aleam was the last to turn around. No one said anything – they had great deference for the crystal, almost as if they saw it as some kind of religious deity.

"This will be another test," the crystal continued. "Initiate Ben will one day lead armies into battle, and so he must learn to make such decisions for himself."

Driar Yila grimaced at these words, Driar Lonamm frowned, and Driar Brigel crossed his arms. I started purring and rubbed myself against the crystal. It did, after all, have that pleasant warmth to it that combated the icy breeze coming from the exposed opening. I just wished its predictions didn't involve getting me into danger all the time.

Soon, the warmth died down from the crystal, and the light faded once again. Salanraja was glaring at me from the corner of the room, clearly insulted that I'd considered riding another dragon. I don't know why she took these things so personally.

"*Because I'm bonded to you,*" Salanraja said to me. "*And flying another dragon is worse than adultery in a relationship. Unless, doing so might save your life, that is.*"

"*Well, flying a more able dragon might decrease my chances of getting thrown off from miles high.*"

"*And what's that meant to mean?*"

"*Nothing...Fine, you can come. I wasn't ever going to not take you. But I need to work out the rest of the team. It sounds like quite a task the crystal has set for me.*"

"*Then tell the Council that. Show them you can act responsibly, because right now the Council of Three and their dragons think we're all doomed.*"

I opened my mouth to say just that. But before a single word came out, Driar Yila raised her hand. "Don't say anything. Just gather your team, and then we'll meet you down at the Council Courtyard to brief you on your mission."

I glanced at Aleam, who shrugged. Then, I slinked off down the stairway, and I went to search out my team.

⚜ 14 ⚜

BELLARI OR ANGE?

I went first to the fountain, and there I found Rine once again kissing Bellari. The students were on their break and they laughed and danced and played that strange game with the string and the hourglass-shaped wood.

It had warmed now, with the sun shining down from the sky. This melted the snow off the parapets, which drip-drip-dripped onto the stone below. From the kitchens came the aroma of smoked trout. It seemed a shame that we'd have to fly away and miss this meal, although maybe I'd be able to convince Matron Canda to pack some of it for our journey so we could eat it for supper.

Rine and Bellari seemed oblivious to everything going on around them. Which was a shame, because I'd hoped that I'd caused a bit of tension between them before, as I really wanted to push Rine towards Ange. I'd said it before, and I'll say it again – she was a far better mate for Rine. Ange wouldn't only teach him a lot about magic, but also about how to care for cats.

Maybe, if I didn't find my way back to my own world, I could one day convince Rine and Ange to settle down in a pleasant cottage somewhere, away from scary things like wolves and serkets and demon chimeras. Then they could feed me nice food, perhaps hunted and cooked by Salanraja.

Ta'ra could be there too once we rescued her. She only had one more transformation left, after all, before she became a cat forever. I could look after her, and teach her how to roam the village, how to hunt for sport, and how to mark and guard territory.

But, as tempting as it was to do so, I didn't have time for daydreaming right now. I only had an hour to recruit my team, and I already knew that Rine and I fought well together. He'd helped me bring down the demon dragon, and though his ice bolts had done little against it, I was still sure he'd be able to help in a pinch.

The first thing I had to do was put a stop to their pointless displays of affection, and there was no better way to do so than jump up on the fountain and rub myself up against Bellari's back.

"What?" Bellari said, spinning around. As soon as she saw me, she leapt up off her perch. She turned away from me to sneeze, and then she backed up. "I thought I told you to stay away from us. Why do you keep ruining our private time, you stupid cat?"

I looked around at all the teenagers talking and playing in the bailey. "It's hardly private."

"That's because we're banned from doing such things in the corridors. Rine, remember what we talked about? Get him away!"

Her screaming was damaging my sensitive eardrums, and so I flattened my ears against my head. I looked up at Rine, purring, and mewled for some affection. He sighed, shaking his head.

"Ben, Bellari wanted to kindly request that you don't come near her. She really doesn't react well to you. It's nothing personal, but these are medical reasons. You should respect that."

I growled. "I didn't come to annoy her. I came because you've been requested on a mission."

Rine raised an eyebrow. "By who?"

"By me. My crystal deemed that I was to pick a team to go out and find Ta'ra and also rescue Prefect Asinda and Prefect Lars."

"I don't think those two need rescuing," Rine replied with a chuckle. Then he looked at me incredulously. "Wait, you're serious, aren't you?"

"I need to pick a team of four dragon riders and four dragons. We're to meet in the Council Courtyard before the next strike of the clock. It's very important, Rine. If we don't act soon, all the food in every single dimension could get destroyed."

I looked over at Bellari, who had placed her hands on her hips. "If you're going out into danger again, Rine, I'm coming with you."

"But your allergies might get in the way," I pointed out.

"I won't go anywhere near you on my dragon," Bellari said. "Besides, you might need a good fire mage." She put her hand on the staff affixed to her back.

"It's me who chooses the team, not you," I said. "And the way you've treated me lately, I see no reason to choose you."

"I'm allergic to you, you stupid cat. What am I meant to do?"

"See, that's what I mean." I tucked my head into my neck. "You could try being a bit nicer about things."

Her face went red, and she opened her mouth, clearly ready to scream out more insults. But a voice calling out interrupted her.

"Ben," Ange said as she skipped across the bailey. "I've been looking everywhere for you."

"What does she want?" Bellari asked as she folded her arms. When I'd first met these two, they'd been good friends. But I guess now Rine's spoilt girlfriend saw Ange as a bit of a threat.

I leaped down off the fountain, and I went over and rubbed myself against Ange's foreleg, purring. She smiled and then tickled me underneath the chin.

"I hear you're going out on an important mission," Ange said.

"Well, doesn't news travel fast? Do you want to come?"

"That's why I'm looking for you, silly. In fact, Driar Brigel just told me about it and he recommended I should pop along, if possible. He said it would be good for my studies to understand some fairy magic. Particularly given I'm a leaf magic user."

Leaf magic was the reason that both Brigel's and Ange's staff were green. They had the ability to manipulate nature. Although, according to Brigel's classes, it wasn't really manipulation, but rather nature made the choice to help the magic user out. Apparently, only those who were kind of heart could use leaf magic.

Nature just didn't trust everyone, in much the same way as I didn't trust Bellari.

I meowed to Ange, and she reached down, and picked me up, and carried me over to the fountain. Rine edged a little away from Ange, nervously, as Bellari scowled at her. He looked as if he wanted to stand up and move back to Bellari. But he seemed unsure if this was the best move.

"So that's it," Bellari said. "Ben, you have your team. Me, Rine, and Ange, and maybe Driar Aleam can come too, or one of the prefects."

Ange looked down at me, and gave a curious frown, as if expecting me to say something.

"I'm sorry, Initiate Bellari," I said. "But there's only room for two, and Ange would make a much better asset to the team than you will."

It wasn't just about going after Astravar, but though Ange's leaf magic might come in useful, I already had dragons to breathe fire and cook our food for us. Plus, I really didn't want Bellari there. Rine and Ange were suited for each other, and this was a perfect opportunity to finagle them together. I'd reserved the other two places for Aleam and one of the prefects. I wanted someone who was an accomplished swordsman, because I'd need all the strength possible to take down that demon Maine Coon chimera.

"I know what this is about, Ange," Bellari said. "You're trying to get between me and Rine, aren't you? I told you to stay away from him."

Ange looked at Rine, and it was his turn to look embarrassed.

"I…" he said.

But Ange would not stand for this aggression from Rine's girl-friend. She stood up, dropping me by the fountain. I went over to sit on Rine's lap.

"I've told you, Bellari. Really, there's nothing between me and Rine. I'm too busy for that kind of stuff. I've got my studies to worry about, and you know why I need to get those good grades." This, honestly, didn't sound good. I had assumed that I only needed to work on Rine to get him to realise who was better for him. But now, I clearly had to work on Ange too.

Bellari huffed. "You can't fool me. Rine, I refuse to let you go on this mission. Not without me, anyway."

"I don't think he has any choice," I said. "The crystal told me to choose, and that's what I'm doing. If he refuses, the Council will punish him severely."

Bellari was breathing heavily through her flared nostrils. She glared at me a while, then she turned her gaze on Rine. "Rine, say something. You can't let this happen. You need me there, Rine." Her breath was catching in her throat as if she was about to cry.

Rine shook his head. "You need to go and cool down, sugarpot. We'll talk when we're back, okay?"

But she didn't seem to want to hear this, because she was already storming across the bailey, and I could swear she almost tripped over a clump of snow.

"She'll get over it," Rine said with a shrug.

I walked away, satisfied that I'd made the first move in bringing Ange and Rine together. Before I went far, I looked over my shoulder and said, "Remember, be in the Council Courtyard before the clock strikes the hour."

Ange smiled and gave me a mock salute. But I'm not sure Rine even heard me, as he was watching Bellari hurrying away.

15

AN OBVIOUS CHOICE

B efore I'd learned to speak the human language, the concept of time hadn't concerned me. Back then, it wasn't measured by a clock, but specific moments like when my former mistress in South Wales scooped food into my bowl, put me out of the door to go for a run, and called me back in again. If I was late for any of those things, it was their problem, not mine.

When I gained the ability to speak the human language, I also learned certain human sayings. There was one that particularly intrigued me: 'time waits for no man'. Honestly though, if we cats had a concept of time like humans did, I'm sure we would say something like: 'cat waits for no time'.

So, deadlines like this one seemed a little unnatural to me. Time also seemed to move faster than it should when I was on a mission, and by the time I reached Aleam's abode, I'd already wasted twenty minutes.

Aleam's door was ajar, and so I squeezed my way inside and found the old man to be doing what he always seemed to do nowadays – working on Ta'ra's cure. A yellow solution bubbled away inside his alembic apparatus. The soft sunlight streamed through the window, reflecting off the surface of the glass and suffusing it in an almost mystical light. Or maybe the solution was also glowing slightly. I wasn't so sure.

I meowed to let Aleam know that I'd entered the room, but he didn't quite seem to hear me. So, I took the next best measure for getting attention – I jumped right up on the desk in front of him. Aleam pushed me away.

"Ben, how many times have I told you not to jump up here? I don't want you damaging Ta'ra's cure."

"But I'm a cat and I won't knock anything off the desk that I don't want to." Admittedly, though, I quite fancied smashing this whole apparatus to pieces. I would have done, perhaps, if I didn't fear the repercussions. Aleam seemed quite gentle on the surface, but I'd seen him cast magic and I didn't doubt his wrath would be just as dangerous as that of any member of the Council of Three.

I jumped back on to the floor, growling. I didn't want Aleam to give Ta'ra the cure. I wanted her to be a cat forever, so I'd have a companion here who understood what it was to exist between worlds, a concept that no other creature knew.

"You know," Aleam said, studying me, "this time I think I've finally found the right ingredients. Really, I don't believe anything is irreversible. In the end, I guess time will always revert things back to their original state."

Now he was getting philosophical, and I knew exactly what he was getting at. Life crumbling to ash and returning to the soil and feeding the plants and all that stuff, creating a circle. It wasn't just humans who wondered what happened to us after death.

It didn't matter anyway, because once I'd fulfilled my destiny, I was going to cat heaven where I would get fed as much food as I wanted. I didn't have a clue what this food would be like, I just knew that it would be better than anything I'd tasted before.

"I don't think Ta'ra should take the cure," I said. "I think it's better that she stays a cat forever. That's what she wants."

"How can you be certain what she wants, Ben?"

"She's said so."

"Of course she says it while you're around. But when you're not there, she tells me how she misses her home and Prince Ta'lon and all her family. Those ties aren't easy to break."

I thought back to my own mother – a Bengal and descendant of the great Asian leopard cat, of course. I hadn't known her so well, really. I'd left her when I was a kitten and never actually visited her again. Family was another human concept I'd always failed to grasp. You moved on from your ancestors, and became better and more powerful versions of them, and you never looked back to the past. That was how it worked.

"She's already changed back into a fairy seven times now," I said. "If she changes back one more time, there's no going back for her, right?"

"Unfortunately, yes," Aleam said. "Which is why I want to offer her the cure as soon as we rescue her. She should have the chance to choose for herself."

Time, time, time, time, time. I realised suddenly that while we were having this conversation, I was 'wasting' it. "Well, you can offer it to her sooner," I said. "Because I also want you on this mission."

"I thought you'd say that. Who else did you choose?"

"Initiate Rine and Initiate Ange. And I told Initiate Bellari that she's not welcome."

"I'm sure she would have loved that."

"Not really. Now after you, I only need to find the strongest prefect who's agile and good with a sword. If another cat could ride a dragon, I'd choose them for sure."

Aleam frowned. "Ben, I think you're forgetting something."

"No, I'm not."

"Yes, you are. Your dreams, Ben. Astravar can control them. The Council of Three wanted to send Seramina with you for a good reason. She can stop the warlock reaching into your mind. Because it's reached the point that not even Salanraja can keep him out."

I didn't like the sound of that at all, and the noise I made from the base of my stomach expressed this. There was something about that young woman that I just didn't trust. There was this aura bristling around her that made me want to stay away from her. Then, there was the way that she stared at me with those terribly fiery eyes. Part of me wondered if she was from the Seventh Dimension, like the demon dragon and demon chimera.

"I know you don't like it, Ben," Aleam said. "But don't forget the crystal is testing you. It wants to see that you can make the right decisions so it will help you in the future."

"But I'm afraid of her."

Aleam laughed. "Of a thirteen-year-old girl?"

"Yes. It's the way she looks at me. She just seems evil. Plus, you've got to remember, she may be slight by your standards. But she's still much, much bigger than me."

"We can't understand everyone, Ben, much like many students here don't understand you. But that doesn't mean she's a bad person."

I growled again, and then I moved back towards the door. Before I left, I turned my head over my shoulder to say one more thing to Aleam.

"I'll consider your opinion," I said to placate the old man, even if I had given that opinion all the consideration it needed. "Now, don't forget to be at the Council Courtyard before the clock strikes the hour."

"I won't," Aleam said. "Just let me get this cure together and I'll be right over."

Presently, I squeezed out of the door. The next task was to find the strongest prefect for the task. Someone, I hoped, with a very pointy sword and the ability to use it. Someone who could fell a demon chimera, with one mighty swoop.

He would have to be strong, and muscular, and an excellent hunter, and probably also a decent cook. I knew the perfect young man for the task.

16

THE PREFECT OR THE WITCH?

Fate had it that the bell went off as soon as I left Aleam's study. The students went from chatting and laughing and playing games outside, to scrambling over each other in a mad-dash panic to get to the next class. I scanned the bailey for the red robes that denoted students as prefects. All of them were all heading in one direction – towards the training field in the far corner of the bailey.

I navigated through the tangle of legs and rushing students. I had to be careful in this place; everyone's eyes were always on the destination and never on the floor. Fortunately, as a Bengal and descendant of the great Asian leopard cat, I was faster than them, and so they never tripped over me – which probably would have hurt me more than it would hurt them.

It wasn't long until the stampede had passed. Given I had an all-important mission, I didn't have to worry about going to class, so I decided instead to watch from a distance, until I found who I was looking for.

The prefects had gathered around a sandy training ring that had been dug out of the snow. They chatted amongst themselves, making a racket and hurting my poor feline eardrums.

After a while, a wiry-looking man with a long salt and pepper beard and scraggly hair, whom I knew as Driar Gallant, the castle's quartermaster, stepped to the centre of the ring and shouted out at a volume that belied his slight frame. He called two students forward. One of them was a massive, heavily muscled prefect, almost as large as Driar Brigel. The other was a young man with a lithe body, cropped hair and a pockmarked face.

It was the second young man I'd been looking for – Prefect Calin, who I believed was High Prefect Lars' best friend.

Driar Gallant walked up to a weapons rack, and took from it two wooden swords, which he handed to the prefects. The giant's sword was twice the size of Prefect Calin's, which he wielded with two hands and a lumbering posture. Calin had more of a one-handed sword, which he held out in front of him in a sideways stance, with his other arm crossed along his chest, as if he was holding an imaginary shield.

The quartermaster stepped out of the ring, then he blew into a whistle that dangled from his neck. The prefects around the ring fell silent, and the giant charged forward, sending out a whiff of testosterone behind him. He roared as he went, red fury flashing in his face, and for a moment it looked like he'd flatten Calin with his attack. But the giant put too much weight into it to keep control, and Calin nimbly pivoted out of the way and put his foot out as his opponent rushed by. He waited until the giant went crashing to the floor, and then he brought his sword around towards his back.

It looked so fast that I thought Calin might break the giant's spine. But at the last moment, he slowed the sword, so it only tapped the massive student's back. It caused the giant to flinch a little, but I was sure this was because of the pain of being defeated so quickly than anything physical.

"He's quite an accomplished fighter, isn't he?" The voice came from right beside me, causing me to bristle and scarper away. When I was far enough, I turned to see that same scary teenager, the one they called Seramina. Her eyes again had that raging fire behind them as she stared at me, her face expressionless. "Although, I've heard during sparring, he's no match for High Prefect Lars. Only Prefect Asinda is rumoured to have ever beaten Lars."

I realised then what unnerved me so much about her. Every single human I'd known had a smell to them. Astravar smelled of rotten vegetable juice, these prefects in the ring smelled of human sweat, Ange smelled of catnip, and Rine smelled of whatever cologne he'd put on as a special of the day.

But Seramina had absolutely nothing I could detect on her. That wasn't normal at all.

"What are you doing here?" I asked. "Shouldn't you be in class?"

"I go where destiny takes me. It seems to have led me here. Fate told me I had to come to this spot, where you will choose me for an important mission. Thus, I am here."

I blinked off my disbelief. Something really was odd about this woman. She can't have possibly known that I was here, could she?

"I will take Initiate Rine, Initiate Ange, Driar Aleam, and now I only need to gather Prefect Calin and I have my team," I said. "I've made my decision and not you, nor destiny, nor fate, nor whatever fancy word you use to describe utter nonsense, can change that."

Her lips didn't move, but still in her tone of voice I could detect the slightest sliver of a grin. "Do leaders truly make decisions? Or do the right choices choose them?"

I really didn't want to be having this conversation with her right now. I turned away from her, back towards the ring where Driar Gallant shouted out an order once again. Prefect Calin stayed in the ring to face a young woman with dark skin, curly black hair, and high cheekbones. She looked at Calin with wide eyes, and I could smell fear upon her. Driar Gallant handed her a training sword from the weapons rack – this time the same size as Prefect Calin's. She assumed much the same stance as Calin, with her legs placed slightly wider apart.

Part of me didn't want to break up the games here, even if the clock tower said I only had twenty minutes left on the clock. So, I decided to let them have one more round, and I waited for Driar Gallant to blow his whistle.

Neither prefect charged this time. Instead, they circled each other in a kind of slow dance, with hard gazes locked on each other. They touched swords a few times, but they were merely simple parries, each move designed to test the other's mettle. This woman, whoever she was, clearly was a better fighter than the giant before. But still, she didn't look or smell like she believed she could take him down.

Eventually, Calin lunged forwards, and the female prefect pirouetted out of the way. But Calin had already predicted her move and brought his sword around in a low and narrow circle. He touched the flat of his blade to her bare kneecaps, and the female prefect puffed out her cheeks and let out a forced breath through her puckered lips. Driar Gallant blew the whistle again. He then clapped his hands, and Driar Calin left the ring, to be surrounded by a good half-dozen cheering prefects.

"How will you wake up from your dreams?" Seramina asked me. "Who will protect you from Astravar when not even your dragon can anymore?"

I growled at her to tell her I wasn't even going to entertain that thought. I stalked casually over to the prefects who had gathered around Prefect Calin and I shouted out as loudly as I could.

"Excuse me, prefects," I said, pushing through their legs. "Excuse me..."

They parted slightly, and I spun around to apprehend their expressions of wide-eyed surprise for a moment, before I turned to the man I'd been looking for. "Prefect Calin, I wish to request your presence for a mission of utmost importance. Your friends Prefect Asinda and High Prefect Lars, and also the Cat Sidhe, Ta'ra, are in grave danger. We must go out to rescue them at once."

I heard the prefect's breath catch in his throat. "That's terrible," he said. "I wish I could go, but—"

"You will do this," I interrupted, and I didn't care if he was a prefect and could order me to spend my next break in a classroom copying out the school rules. It's not as if I had hands to write with anyway, and I couldn't even read anything to copy it out. "My crystal has ordered me to choose a team, and you seem to be the strongest fighter of them all. I need you to defeat a demon chimera."

I expected Prefect Calin to be a little taken aback by my directness. But instead the features sank on his face and his gaze became distant. "You don't understand... My dragon, Galludo, has been injured for a long time. She can't fly far, and so instead we defend the academy when any threats arise nearby."

The teenager, Seramina, floated over our way as Calin talked. She looked down at me with those freaky fiery eyes. Strangely, no one around here seemed scared of her. It was almost as if they didn't acknowledge her existence, making me wonder if she was really there, or just a figment of my imagination. She did have the power to control dreams. Could she perhaps also enter my mind when I wasn't dreaming?

Or maybe I was actually dreaming, and I would wake up to Ta'ra's fishy breath, snuggled up next to her. I'd discover that she hadn't really run away, and Aleam had put down a tantalising meal of roasted duck for us, and we were going to eat to our hearts' content.

"Do leaders make decisions?" Seramina said again, interrupting my daydream. "Or do good decisions choose them?"

She was definitely annoying; I would give her that.

I looked up at the clock tower. I only had ten minutes left now, and my stomach had started to rumble. If I didn't fill up my belly, then I would go hungry while flying for a long, long time. Alas, I knew it wouldn't be wise to go face to face against a demon chimera on an empty stomach.

In desperation, I scanned the prefects, wondering if any of them might fit the bill. But I'd seen how readily Calin had defeated the two of them, and I also saw how Seramina had used her powers to wake Ta'ra from her strange dream.

"Fine," I said. "You can come. Make sure you're at the Council Courtyard when the clock strikes the hour."

"I'm already there," she said, and I only needed to blink once, and she'd vanished from view.

The prefects were looking at me oddly, probably wondering who the whiskers I'd just been talking to. I let out a low growl, then I made my way to Salanraja's chamber, knowing that I had very little time left to eat my meal before our briefing was due.

17

COUNCIL BRIEFING

I arrived at the Council Courtyard with the soft taste of beef on my tongue, my stomach now content that I had eaten a good meal. Salanraja had been sleeping in the tower, and I'd let her rest because I wanted her as alert as possible when we fought Astravar and the demon chimera.

Beneath the dais that jutted out from the keep, the grass was cold and wet underfoot from snow melt. Seramina stood on my right, and I could smell her now, which meant she was present for real this time and not just a product of my mind. She wore this kind of light perfume that reminded me of snowdrops and early spring. Driar Aleam stood next to her, leaning on his staff, which he used as a walking stick as he moved around.

Rine and Ange stood on my left, an awkward distance apart from each other, even for friends. I looked over my shoulder at least once, expecting Bellari to be standing at the archway glaring at them. She wasn't. But still, I'd driven a solid thorn into their relationship, and this was going to take a while for Rine to undo.

In fact, I wasn't even sure he could undo this one. I felt that I'd done enough to push Rine into Ange's arms, and I was proud of my accomplishment. I felt proud of all of my accomplishments, really. I'd also almost picked the perfect team, with Seramina being the only part that didn't quite work in it. But at least now she smelled of something normal and sweet and not just emptiness. Everyone should have a smell, just as everyone should have a shadow.

The double doors opened to the keep behind the dais, and the Council of Three emerged. Driar Brigel came out first and took his position at the lectern on the right, which he rested his arms against while leaning forwards. Driar Lonamm came next, waddling like a penguin over to her position. She adjusted the blue-gemmed staff on her back and glanced over her shoulder at the crystal on the ceiling. Driar Yila came out last, scanning the ground in front of her like an owl as she moved forwards. She cast her gaze first on Aleam, then on Seramina. Her gaze then passed right over me before she saw Ange and Rine and shook her head.

"This is the team, you picked, Initiate Ben?" she said. "I thought you would have had at least one prefect..."

I growled back at her. "I tried, ma'am. But Seramina here convinced me out of it."

She spun around to face Seramina and stared at her for a moment. Seramina returned an incredibly passive gaze, her eyes looking almost glazed. Still, she didn't show any emotion, and she didn't seem at all scared of the most terrifying Driar in the whole of Dragonsbond Academy.

"Is this true?" Driar Yila asked her.

Seramina spoke without even moving her head. "This is the optimal team, ma'am."

Yila frowned, and then turned back to look at Driar Lonamm, who nodded at her. She looked at Driar Brigel, who also smiled.

"Very well," Driar Yila said, "then I guess we should begin the briefing."

She reached out behind her back and produced her staff. I flinched, thinking she might want to cast some magic at me. I'd learned not to trust her with her magical staff since she'd used it once to pin me up in the air and paralyse me. Fortunately, this time, she didn't seem to want to do this.

Instead, she pointed her staff at the crystal, and relief washed over me. A red beam shot out of her staff and hit the crystal at its centre, where it created a warm orange glow. Driar Lonamm then took her staff off her back and also pointed it at the crystal, creating a blue beam that melded with Driar Yila's. Shortly after, Driar Brigel also sent out a beam of green energy.

The crystal reacted to these beams, sucking up their light, glowing ever brighter. Soon enough, it had become filled with enough energy to project an image in front of it. It was just like the picture on a television. Still, there was no sound, which made it feel just a little disappointing.

My master and mistress back home had their television set up so that I could hear sounds coming from all directions at once. The master would play this trick on me sometimes, where he'd put a moving picture of lots of birds on the screen. I could hear them not just in front of me, but behind me, almost as if they had found a spot behind the sofa. It drove me nuts at first, as I scampered around the room trying to hunt down the birds which were clearly singing so close to me. That was until I realised they weren't real, but just a part of the show. After that, the joke got old pretty fast.

The image projected from the crystal displayed a wood, with trees with long droopy branches, and thin leaves projecting out of them. Willows, that's what I believe humans called them. Which is why I guess this place was called the Willowed Woods. Really, I wish humans had more imagination with certain names. I mean, when I learned the human language, I discovered there was a place in my home country called Green Park. But when is a park not green?

The canopy hung over the entire terrain, blotting out the sky, and casting deep shadows over the ground. It didn't look like a particularly friendly place, and I immediately regretted my decision to go out and rescue Ta'ra.

"The Willowed Woods," Driar Brigel said. "This is where fairies come into this land when they choose to do so, and where they leave the same way."

"It looks dark and scary," I said.

"That's because it is," Driar Yila said. "Waigs lurk within these woods, which is why the fairies chose it as their entryway. It's a land where no hunter dares tread."

Now I was getting confused. "What's a warg?"

"A creature like a wolf, but much bigger," Driar Lonamm said. "A massive lumbering beast, with red eyes and evil intent. Some say that the warlocks can control them. Others say that they just live to kill anything that crosses their path that moves."

"Which is why you mustn't camp in the Willowed Woods," Driar Brigel added. "They will hunt you for sport, and unlike wolves, they don't care if you're in a group or alone."

"And they also sometimes hunt during the day," Driar Yila added.

I didn't like the sound of any of this at all. A bitter howling wind came out of the sky and passed through my fur, causing me to shudder. "We better stay in the air then," I said.

"You may need to go on the ground to stop Ta'ra opening the portal," Driar Yila said. "You see, the only way to enter the Faerie Realm is for a fairy or fae to open the portal themselves. They can open it in this dimension, or they can open it from the Second Dimension."

"And we suspect," Driar Brigel said, "that Astravar is using Ta'ra as a tool to enter the fairy realm."

"Which we cannot let happen," Driar Lonamm said.

I let out a long mewl to express my fear of this situation. Knowing that I might have to battle the demon chimera was bad enough. But now, it looked like I would also have to deal with oversized wolves as well.

"Now," Driar Brigel said. "Does anyone have any idea how you're going to track the fairy?" He turned to Aleam with a smile. "Aleam, you're banned from answering this one."

Ange's hand immediately shot up. Driar Brigel glanced at her, but then turned his gaze towards her companion. "How about you, Rine?"

Rine shook his head. "Sorry, sir. I didn't have time to do any research." He gave Ange a nervous look.

"Very well. Seramina?"

She nodded. "I know, but you would rather the answer came from someone else."

"True, true," Driar Brigel said. "How about you, Ben?"

"Wait," I said. "I've seen this one on television. We listen out for tinkling bells, and then we walk anticlockwise around a ring of toadstools and the little people appear."

Driar Brigel shook his head. "Not quite," he said. "Okay, Ange, what's the answer?"

Ange relaxed her arm, which had been stretched up towards the sky as if she'd been trying to reach a cloud. "Fairy dust... We look for signs of it glittering in the light."

Brigel nodded. "Always the diligent student, Initiate Ange. But that is the key, light. You look for golden glimmers in the sky when sunlight passes through it. You can't detect it when it's cloudy, and you can't detect it when it's dark."

"So what happens if it's cloudy then, sir?" I asked. "What do we do then?"

Driar Yila looked up at the sun and shielded her eyes. "It won't be, cat. We've had our snow, now the days ahead will be clear as spring approaches."

"But how can you be so sure, ma'am?"

"Because we have mages across the realm," Driar Yila said, "who can accurately predict the weather. You ask too many questions, Initiate Ben, when you should be taking action."

I growled, and I turned away slightly. "So, the plan is to fly out, find Ta'ra, bring her back again, and not get eaten by wargs. Have I got that right?"

"You're a fast learner. Now, get out there and find Ta'ra." Driar Lonamm said, with a slightly cheeky grin. Although Driar Yila was still her harsh self, I think the other two members of the Council were warming to me.

I didn't waste another minute. "Come on then," I said to the others, and I sprinted off towards Salanraja's tower. As I went, I screamed out in my mind at my dragon, "*Wake up!*"

She wouldn't be happy to be jerked awake like that, but clearly time was of the essence.

FLIGHT OUT

I sprinted across the bailey and up the stairs to the tower, faster than anyone could run in this academy. None of the humans had flexible spines like mine which allowed me to leap in long strides across the terrain, and none of the cats here were as spry as old Ben. I didn't look around to see if any of the cats on crow-catching duty took notice, but I'm sure they all stopped in their tracks in admiration at my work. Here, the Bengal from another world, descendant of the great Asian leopard cat, was showing his abilities in full stride. They all, I was sure, had a lot to learn.

Salanraja was already awake in her chamber, her tail lowered to the ground, her weight on her haunches, ready to run forward out into the open air. I scrambled up her tail and took my position on her back. She ran out of the opening of her chamber, dropped ever so slightly and then unfurled her wings. We were soon soaring over the fields outside Dragonsbond Academy.

Finally, I'd escaped the lockdown. But instead of flapping her wings to gain momentum, Salanraja continued in a glide, circling slightly.

"Why are you flying so slowly?" I asked in my mind.

"Have you forgotten, Bengie?" she replied. *"We're flying as part of a team."*

"But why? We're not even close to our destination yet. Isn't it better to get there as fast as we can? We need to beat Ta'ra to the Willowed Woods so we can stop her."

"Which is why we need to fly in formation," Salanraja said. *"We'll be faster that way."*

I didn't know what the whiskers she was talking about, and I assumed it to be some kind of magic or something. Still, I guess this way Salanraja wouldn't try to pull all kinds of stunts, sending me tumbling around in her 'ribcage' of spikes that jutted out of the top of her body. I hated that.

I looked behind me to see Seramina's charcoal dragon launch itself from the bottom of the tower that rose above the keep. Unlike other dragon riders, she seemed to prefer to carry her staff in one hand by her side, rather than on her back. She brought her dragon around in a circle and then had him fly back up until he was level with Salanraja.

She glared at me from the saddle, without expression on her face, but still the fire burning in her eyes seemed to display their own kind of anger.

"Her dragon, Hallinar, wants to express Seramina's disappointment in you," Salanraja said.

"What did I do?"

"Seramina thinks she needs to watch over you in case Astravar finds his way into your head. You shouldn't venture too far from her."

I growled from deep within my stomach. I tried to stare back at her, but that gaze was too intense, and even from here I could see how that fire danced within her eyes.

"I don't like the way she stares at me. It freaks me out."

"But she needs to do that. Seramina needs to know when Astravar is trying to get into your mind. We can't risk losing you to him. Not after what the crystal foretold about Astravar's demise."

"But why can't you protect me from Astravar anymore? Didn't you say that was your job?"

Salanraja lowered her head from in front of me. *"I don't know. My bond should be powerful enough. But there's something else about your connection with Astravar that none of us can quite work out."*

"And Seramina can see inside my mind and know when Astravar is in there."

"That's the gift the crystals gave her," Salanraja said. *"Some say that when she becomes a Driar, she'll be one of the most powerful dragon riders of us all."*

From behind, there came a sudden roar, and two dragons shot out of the tower above the dormitories. The first was Initiate Rine's emerald Ishtkar, the other Ange's sapphire dragon, Quarl.

The two dragons rose into the air, corkscrewing around each other playfully. They swooped and dived, creating a display even more impressive than I'd seen during air shows in South Wales. You probably know the ones I mean, when those fast flying machines shoot through the air, making lots of noise and then swooping around, before they disappear again.

The two dragons soon reached us and took their places on Seramina's and Hallinar's left. That put Ishtkar and Rine on the left wing of the formation, and Salanraja and I on the right.

"I thought we were meant to be the leaders," I said.

"Far from it," Salanraja said. *"The strongest flier takes the front, meaning it's less work for the weaker fliers to cut through the air stream to keep up."*

"So, who's the strongest flier?" I asked, trying to work out whether it was Hallinar or Quarl. But it was neither, because soon a magnificent beast rose out of the keep tower. The famous white dragon, the only one of that colour in Dragonsbond Academy – Aleam's dragon, Olan.

She flew in a straight line without wavering one bit, as precise as a hawk towards her target. Her wings kept a fluent rhythm that kept her at a steady height, and she pushed her way between Seramina and Ange to lead the formation.

Aleam looked back from his saddle at each of us in turn. While he always hobbled on the ground, in flight he looked like a young man in posture. It was almost as if he'd been born for the saddle.

Olan let out a roar, and the other dragons replied with an equally noble cry. We then turned west towards the setting sun. I kept on looking out for glimmers of gold, but it was quite hard to see anything with the sunlight burning in my sensitive eyes. Still, although I admittedly had the sharpest eyes out of anyone here – and that included the dragons – everyone else also kept watch for Ta'ra. But no one reported any sign of any fairy dust, and it wasn't long until day fell into night.

By that point, we were approaching some woods. These weren't the Willowed Woods yet, but instead contained silver birch and beech trees. Olan led the formation down to the ground, and I bristled as I watched us descend. *"What are we doing?"* I asked Salanraja. *"We can't stop now. We've not found Ta'ra yet."*

"And we certainly won't find her under cover of darkness," Salanraja replied. *"Plus, I'm sure you don't want to be camping out in the Willowed Woods."*

I remembered what the Council of Three had said about those evil wargs, and I shuddered when I thought about the huge evil wolves that hunted through day and night and killed everything that crossed their path. With them and the chimera of this world, I'd learned of two scarier beasts than the hippopotamus of the Savannah. When I returned home, I'd have some grand stories to tell the Savannah Cats, I was sure.

"Fine, we should land," I said.

"That's what we are doing," Salanraja replied.

"But aren't I meant to be the one in charge here?"

"No, the crystal told you to choose the team, not to lead us all into darkness and get us killed. Trust Driar Aleam and Olan, Bengie. They know what they're doing."

I said nothing more, as I watched the ground approach through the darkness. The sky was dark now, but I could still see the ground through superior vision. Salanraja thudded against it, jolting me against her corridor of spikes. We landed just on the edge of the tree-line, which gave us suitable cover from the wind coming from that direction.

"Ow," I said. *"I thought you said you'd get easier on the landings."*

She chuckled in my mind but said nothing else. So, I thought I'd leave that dragon to converse with her own kind. I scurried down her tail and onto the ground.

I decided to patrol the area and spray everywhere I could, just in case any cats in the area thought this territory was their own. Seramina continued to watch me as she climbed down the side of her dragon, who had flattened himself against the ground. With the way her fiery stare bored into me as she descended, I guessed it wouldn't be smart to go far.

19

LOVE LESSON

I t was winter and the night was cold. But this wasn't such a bad thing, because it meant it didn't take Rine and Ange long to set up the fire. They'd already brought firewood in the panniers on their dragons. The two older Initiates did all the work, while Seramina just stood as close to me as possible, with that same smell about her again of snowdrops and early spring. She continued to stare at me, but I tried not to let her weirdness get to me, and instead I curled up on the ground and tried to get some sleep.

But that was the thing – even in the land of dreams she was there, still staring at me with those fiery eyes. Except here she wore a white chiffon dress rather than her fur-collared coat. There was no escape. It was worse than having Astravar following me. At least the warlock gave me some moments of respite.

"Can't you just pretend not to be there?" I asked her. "You're going to turn me into a loony cat at this rate."

I'd seen a cat like that before – one of the strays in the neighbourhood who couldn't stand her loneliness. She would yowl into the night while she chased her tail around and around, and she would not stop yowling and chasing her tail until the day broke.

Humans would throw things out of the window at her, forcing her to scurry away to a different spot and yowl some more. But though humans couldn't hear her at her new location, I could from my sleeping spot in the utility.

On those rare nights when the master and the mistress let me roam outside – or should I say I failed to come in when called – I'd watch the mad cat dancing around beneath my perch on the garden fence, as if she had nothing better to do in the whole wide world.

In my dream, I realised I was chasing my tail, just like that loony cat. I stopped myself, slightly embarrassed. Then I wondered what I had to be embarrassed about. It was only me in the dream and this weird teenager who stood stonelike, not even blinking.

"You don't say much, do you?" I said, and I wondered for a moment if she was frozen in time. I couldn't smell her. Instead, I could smell raw lamb coming from somewhere.

"I know you don't like me," she replied, and only her lips and the muscles of her cheeks moved as she spoke. She had her hands folded below her waist, her chiffon dress blowing in the light breeze. "But this is what I have to do. To observe and protect you."

I growled, and then I realised I didn't even want to be in this dream. Besides, something was pulling me out of it, and I don't know if it was the roar of the campfire, the heat coming off it, or the rich scent of smoky lamb seeping into my nostrils.

I awoke to the brightness of the flames, and I turned to see Seramina looking down at me, standing in exactly the same posture as she had in her dream. I wasn't sure what I saw in her fiery eyes – was it the reflection of the fire, or were they just burning on their own accord?

A little away from the fire, the five dragons had all gathered in a circle and they were toasting massive lamb sausages on the ground using their flames. From behind us, the wind swished through the woods.

I turned around again to see Rine and Ange sitting next to each other, laughing as they held large sticks with their smaller sausages at the other end of them over the fire. They didn't have that awkward distance between them anymore, so at least something good was coming out of this trip. Aleam sat next to Ange, watching his sausage as it sizzled over the fire.

I stood up and shook myself off, and then I walked over to Aleam. I meowed at him, because that sausage just smelled so good. He laughed.

"Well, I thought you might want some as well, Ben," he said. He had one already prepared on the log just next to him, and he threw this down to me.

I mewled again in appreciation, and then I devoured the sausage. It must have gone down in five mouthfuls, before I was licking my lips and looking back up at Aleam.

"What? You're not telling me you want another?" he asked.

I gave Aleam the cute wide-eyes treatment and meowed again. Honestly, it was great to be able to speak the human language, but endearing gestures were often much better ways of getting what I wanted. Aleam laughed, and he took another sausage from a basket placed beside him and threw it to the ground.

Two grand lamb sausages were enough for a great mighty Bengal like me. I stepped away from the few morsels I'd left on the ground, richly satisfied. I turned back to Rine and Ange, purring. For a moment, I wanted to go over and sit on Ange's lap. But I could see they were getting on so well now I didn't want to ruin the moment for them.

Thing is, with Aleam sitting next to them, and Seramina not far away, they didn't really have enough privacy to get romantic. If only I could find a way to get Aleam and Seramina away. I could demand that I needed a toilet break perhaps. But that wouldn't get both of them away. Or perhaps I could think of another good reason as to why Aleam, Seramina I should go for a walk in the woods. Honestly, I was out of ideas.

Fortunately, though, this time Rine took the initiative and stood up, stretching his arms up to the sky. Firelight danced in his eyes, and I could see the joy in them. "I'm going to go for a walk," he said, and he picked up his staff from the floor. "Want to come, Ange?"

Ange looked around, and then her gaze fell on me. I made a motion with my head to tell her to follow him. Only good things could come from it. She looked a little sheepish and then turned back to Rine and shrugged. "I guess it's always good to walk off our meal before bedtime."

They didn't hold hands as they walked off into the darkness, but there was a certain skip in Rine's step, and I could hear in Ange's tone of voice how much she was enjoying herself. I moved over to the spot where Rine had sat – kept nice and warm for me, and I perked up my ears so I could listen to what they were talking about.

I could hear Rine's and Ange's footsteps rustling over the crunchy frozen leaves, as Ange chatted away. She was talking about Rine's and Ange's life back in Cimlean city. His mother had been the royal seamstress, apparently, and Ange's father was a baker in town. Rine and Ange had known each other for a long, long time, and they shared anecdotes from their childhood far too boring for me to recite.

Seramina glided over to stand next to me. "You shouldn't eavesdrop, you know."

"Shhh," I replied. "This conversation is very important. The fate of the world depends on it."

"No, it doesn't," Seramina said.

I glared at her. "You're only thirteen, I wouldn't expect you to understand."

"And how old are you? Five?"

Whiskers, how did she know? It didn't matter. "I said be quiet… Please."

Fortunately, Seramina's rude interruption didn't get in the way of the important part of their conversation.

"You know, Rine, it's been a while since we could talk like this," Ange said after a moment. "I forgot how fun it is, talking to you."

"You've been so wrapped up in your studies, Ange," Rine replied. "I think you've forgotten what it's like to have fun."

Although Rine's tone sounded jovial, it caused Ange to let out a sigh. "I guess you're right, in a way," she said, and she hesitated. "But if I don't get good grades, I won't be able to help my father pay off his debts to the moneylenders."

"I told you before," Rine said. "My parents can give him the money."

"No... We've talked about this. I wouldn't want that, and neither would my father."

"Fine," Rine said, and the conversation paused for a while.

"You know," Ange said after a moment. "I remember the days that you, me, and Bellari used to be good friends. I don't know what happened to them."

"It's not your fault," Rine said. "Bellari has just become a little insecure as of late. But she's a good person underneath it all."

"I know. I just wish she'd see I wasn't a threat to her."

Well, I knew exactly why Bellari saw her as a threat. They might have been old childhood friends, but they were both growing up and seeing each other in a new light. Unfortunately, neither of them seemed to realise this. I'd seen the way Rine looked at her, and I'd seen that demure expression on Ange's face when he did. But no matter how much I'd tried telling Rine that he actually liked Ange more than he liked his girlfriend, he never seemed to believe me. Perhaps, he thought me a little biased, which, in all honesty, I was.

"I'll talk to her," Rine said. "She'll come around, I'm sure she will."

The moon took the opportunity to peek out of the clouds just at that moment. It shone through the trees, framing the two in a silhouette as they stood facing each other. They were still standing too far apart. Things weren't working as they should.

"Why aren't they holding hands?" I asked Seramina. "They should be holding hands."

I saw her shake her head from the corner of my eye. "Maybe it's because they don't love each other."

"Of course they love each other. Why can't you see that?"

"You're a strange one," Seramina said.

"Shh. This is the moment. Ange is about to tell Rine what she feels about him."

She took a step towards him and put her hand on his arm. Rine didn't step away, which was a good thing. "Rine," she said. "There's something I wanted to ask you."

"What is it?"

"Are you happy? With Bellari, I mean..."

"Of course I am," he replied, and he didn't even take the time to think it through. "Bellari's so beautiful, and I'm the envy of all my friends. Plus, we get on well together, I think…"

My heart sank as I heard Rine say those things, and my dreams of living in a nice country cottage with Rine and Ange shattered into oblivion.

No! That wasn't how you did it, Rine. I'd seen the way these things work on those trashy soap operas that the mistress liked to watch back in South Wales. You spoke in soft voices. You complimented the lady. You smiled a lot. You moved closer and closer until it was time to secure your bond.

But you didn't, on all accounts, let her know there was another lady you were interested in. Otherwise, instead of kissing you, she'd end up screaming at you, and might even end up throwing something at you. And then there would be tears, and then the credits and the music would roll.

Human affairs were so complicated, which consequently made me happy to be a cat.

In the distance, Ange took a step back from Rine, and lowered her head. "I thought so," she said. "She is beautiful, I guess." She turned back towards us. "Come on, we should get some rest. We need to be sharp for the search tomorrow."

I'd seen enough of Rine messing things up completely. I took a mental note to have a word with him one day. Aleam was now sitting by the campfire, reading a book, clearly letting teenagers, cats, and dragons get on with their own affairs. I walked up to him and snuggled up beside him.

There was nothing else I could do for the humans this night and, more importantly, there was nothing else they could do for me.

20

THROUGH THE UNDERBRUSH

I didn't usually sleep so well through darkness. We cats are nocturnal after all, and our bodies have been designed for hunting at night. But that night, for some reason, I slept without waking. I don't think I even dreamed.

Dawn woke me as the sun came up bright and refreshing. It washed away the chill in the air. Though the snow had melted, frost limned the ground, evaporating under the spell of the sunlight. Aleam was the first to get up, and he handed out some breakfast of bread and sausages from the previous night. I didn't eat the bread, of course, but I wolfed down another sausage before we were on our dragons and flying out in formation again, Olan at the front, Ishtkar and Salanraja on both wings.

By this point, it had been around a day since Ta'ra had trans-formed into a fairy. Given her transformation only lasted a single day, she probably had reverted back to her normal form. Which meant that we also had to look out for a black cat. Saying that, though, she also might have used her final transformation. So, we had to look out for magical gold dust as well.

We weren't guaranteed to see either the traces of fairy dust or Ta'ra in her Cat Sidhe form en route. But Aleam knew the exact place

Ta'ra had emerged from the portal. To return to the Second Dimension, she would need to either enter at the same spot, or have another fairy open the way on the other side for her. She would have no way of asking the fairies to open the portal on the other side, of course. So, we knew the only place she could possibly get in.

"*I saw you meddling in Rine's and Ange's affairs, last night,*" Salanraja said to me as we flew.

"*That's because they're going to be our master and mistress. The four of us will retire to a cottage, and we will have good lives without conflicts and warlocks.*"

A rumbling came from Salanraja's back beneath my feet. "*You do realise that they'd also need to keep their dragons outside that cottage.*"

"*So, we can all live there. In the countryside, with Ta'ra too once she becomes a cat, and lots of room to explore and hunt.*"

"*Really? And how will a small village in the countryside support three dragons?*"

I growled at her. Why did she have to be so practical all the time? "*I haven't any idea.*"

"*That's because your dream isn't particularly realistic, Bengie. Anyway, I thought you wanted to return home.*"

"*I do... If I can find anyone to open a portal, to my world. But I don't think that's going to happen.*"

"*It won't,*" Salanraja said. "*Meanwhile, you have a duty to Dragonsbond Academy, as do all the students here. By signing up, you pledged to serve them for a long time. Do you remember that?*"

I did, and I didn't particularly like it. Instead of answering Salanraja, I moved over to the gaps in between her spikes, and looked down from ahigh. Everything looked so insignificant from here – the sheep grazing in the fields, the scarecrows waving in the wind, the farmers cutting the grass with scythes, and that one black shape bounding through a yellow canola field, the crops rippling away from it as it ran.

"*Wait... Salanraja, do you see that?*"

"*What?*"

"*There's something there, running through the field.*"

"*You think it might be...*"

"*Let's go down for a closer look.*"

"I'll let the others know," Salanraja said, and then she swooped down away from the formation.

"Grasp her in your talons, Salanraja," I said.

"But it could be anything. Maybe just a goat skipping through the fields."

"No, that's a cat all right. Trust me, I know how cats move."

"I guess you would, being one."

"Exactly... You're so smart."

Salanraja soon caught up with the cat which had grown to be the size of a panther. It was Ta'ra all right. She was running so fast. But we'd both been so focused on the ground, that we hadn't noticed what she was running towards. A great forest of thorny, twisting plants loomed ahead of us.

"The Briared Woods," Salanraja said.

"Great... Another wonderfully original name."

Salanraja wasn't listening. *"Gracious demons, we have to act fast."*

"Then hurry."

"I'm doing so..." Suddenly her body lurched forward, throwing me against her back. I couldn't watch the ground coming so fast towards us, and so I held on with my claws for support. Salanraja never minded when I scratched anyway – her skin was so thick that I couldn't hurt her.

I peeked out from between the spikes, to see that the brambles were awfully close now. Salanraja suddenly jerked around, throwing me against the other side of her corridor of spikes.

Then she thudded against the ground, creating an awfully rough landing.

"I thought we'd talked about the bad landings," I said to her.

"Shut up, and go after her," Salanraja said. *"She's in the Briared Woods."*

I didn't waste another moment. I scrambled down Salanraja's tail and ran across the field she'd landed on, into the underbrush. The thorns scratched, and they scraped, but I didn't have time to avoid them as I weaved my way through the thicket. I couldn't see Ta'ra, but I could smell her. The thick tangle of branches cut off the wind, meaning her scent hung in the air.

I took the straightest path I could, and I must have been running for about a minute, when I heard his voice in my head. Astravar was laughing like a maniac. Seramina had stopped him doing this in my dreams for quite a while. But I guessed she now didn't have a line of sight to me through the underbrush, so she couldn't protect me anymore.

"*Dragoncat,*" the warlock said in my head. "*You can't stop fate, you know. I will destroy this world, and the others, and you will be my aide.*"

"Never!" I replied to him. "You can't take Ta'ra away from us."

"*Oh, but I already have. She will open the door to me to the Faerie Realm and through clever magic all the fairies shall become my pawns.*"

I really hadn't missed Astravar, and the last thing I wanted to listen to right now was his ugly voice. So, I blocked him out, trying to ignore him, to pretend he wasn't there. Those hideous cackles followed me everywhere though, and they made me want to halt in my tracks and give up the chase.

Still, I found my way through the brambles to the other side. Scratched and tender, I emerged into a clearing framed by willow trees. Ta'ra stood by a thick bole, a good minute's sprint away. Dark, sleepy shadows filled the gaps between the trees, twisting as if they had a life of their own. From the distance, in all directions, the icy wind carried a grating chorus of deep howls, barks, and growls. I shuddered, as the realisation came over me. I was surrounded by those hideous wargs. I could hear and smell that there were a lot of them, circling us from somewhere beyond the distant trees.

But I didn't have time to worry about them now. If I woke Ta'ra, she and I could fight them together. She could change her size and become a massive cat and toss them into the air. Thus, I summoned the energy I needed and dashed towards Ta'ra at full sprint.

"Ta'ra," I shouted. "Wake up, will you?"

As I got closer, she turned to me and looked at me with her eyes closed. She had shrunk to the size of a normal cat and I thought I might be able to swipe her out of her sleep with my paw. But I was sprinting so fast, and she just stepped away. I barrelled into the tree trunk and whined as I hit it head on.

I saw stars and my head thumped as I turned around. I tried to see behind the blotches of blue that marred my vision. They faded away after a moment, and then everything fell to silence. The absence of noise, the opening of a portal – I'd experienced it more than once. Static pulled on the hairs of my back, and the shimmering oval revealed a world as verdant as this one, except each tree, each strand of grass, the sky, and the clouds, were all painted in richer, much more vivid colours.

"Dragoncat, you seem great at survival," Ta'ra said, although she wasn't speaking her own words. "Let's see how well you do with my friends, the wargs."

"Ta'ra, no!" I screamed as she leaped into the portal, but it was too late to stop her. I summoned up my remaining energy and I bounded after her.

The portal closed before I could pass through it. The frozen willow leaves crunched underfoot, and then I heard the howls. I spun around, trying to identify the nearest threat, wondering where the wargs would emerge first. A purple mist enveloped the horizon behind the farthest trees. All around me, I could see shapes passing through this. They would flicker by like ghosts that only wanted to make their presence known for the briefest of moments.

But it wasn't long before I saw the first of the beasts, slaver dripping from its fangs. It approached me with a wicked grin, and the fury in its red eyes told me only one thing. It wanted to eat me whole.

21

WARGS AND WHIRLWINDS

M y legs held me in place, not understanding what I wanted them to do. It was as if those red eyes of the massive beast had the power to paralyse. Yet it wasn't magic holding me in place, but my own fear.

A long crimson tongue lolled from the warg's mouth as it approached me. Its grin seemed frozen. It didn't charge yet, but rather sauntered up to me, its gaze affixed on mine. Then, as if to taunt me, it let out a loud bark, and snapped its jaws at me. That finally caused my legs to spring into action, and I scampered away.

I ran through the woods, Astravar's laughter echoing in my mind. *"Such a show, Dragoncat... Such a show..."* I sprinted faster than I'd ever known until my legs burned with acid, but I didn't let that stop me.

Another beast crashed through the woods ahead of me, blocking my path. I rolled to the side, tumbling over the crackling leaves. The purple mist creeped in ever faster, and I only just evaded the jaws of another warg that had emerged as if from nowhere.

How many of them were there? How would I stand a chance?

Then I remembered. I was a cat, and they were dogs. Which meant I had something they didn't have. I turned to see another warg charging at me. I ducked out of the way at the last minute, and then I made for the nearest tree. It didn't have low branches, but I didn't care at this point. I readied myself on my haunches, and I leaped up at the tree. I caught it with my claws, and I used all my strength to pull my lower legs away from a warg's gnashing teeth.

I scrambled away from the hideous growls, pulling myself up to the lowest branch. From there, I found a perch, as I looked down at what must have been a good two-dozen wargs, angrily circling the tree.

"*You'll never escape from me, Dragoncat,*" Astravar said in my mind. "*No matter where you are, I will always find you. I claimed you when I brought you into this world, and you'll end up serving me again with or without your own soul.*"

Beneath me, the purple mist seeped around the wargs. Wherever that mist went, dark magic also roamed. Which meant that Astravar or one of his more powerful minions was nearby.

Could the demon chimera climb this tree? I wondered. Had I just trapped myself with nowhere else to go?

I listened out for the dragons. They had to be nearby somewhere. "*Salanraja,*" I called out in my mind. "*I need help!*"

It wasn't my dragon that replied, but Astravar.

"*Oh, did I fail to mention that little oversight? I've worked the magic inside you to create a little loophole. Now, whenever I'm in your mind, your dragon can't reach you. I'm afraid, right now, she has no way of knowing where you are.*"

Whiskers, I really was in a fix. Beneath me, on the ground, the wargs had stopped gnashing and trying to find their way up the trunk. Instead, they had arranged themselves in clusters of three forming a larger circle all around me.

One cluster had themselves crouched, as if ready to pounce. They charged and rammed the trunk with their thick heads. Though the tree was sturdy, these beasts were also massive – even bigger than Great Danes – with an enormous bulk. Their combined weight rocked the tree like an earthquake, and I would have tumbled out if I hadn't had my claws fixed firmly into the wood. Still, the branches of the willow creaked, and they swayed slowly yet unnervingly.

Another cluster of wargs charged the tree, and the tree rocked again. I felt my branch begin to creak under my weight, and I scrambled further up the tree.

I looked back down at the wargs, feeling absolutely hopeless. Whiskers, this just wasn't fair. It was siege warfare, and I was the only creature remaining in the keep, absolutely defenceless.

Next, the wargs charged two clusters at a time. They hit the trunk from opposite directions, creating an impact that nearly jolted me off the tree. That was when I noticed something strange. Beneath the curtain of purple mist, I could faintly see the leaves moving. After a moment, they gathered momentum and seemed to rise as if whipped up by whirlwinds. More and more whirlwinds soon appeared, rising as great columns above the purple mist, which coalesced into the rough shape of a bulky humanoid. The mystical creature gathered even more power, snapping branches off the surrounding willows, gaining form as it spun towards me.

This must have been the anomaly which the Council of Three had sent Prefect Lars and Prefect Asinda out to investigate. Whatever it was, it seemed able to rip apart and gather substance from anything natural around it. It wouldn't be long, I realised, until it tore up my own tree, sending me tumbling to the ground.

The wargs crashed against the trunk again, and I groaned, not knowing whether I should scramble down and try to flee. Maybe, I could at least try to find the magical crystal that I guessed powered the magical creature behind those leaves. But I had no idea where to look for it, and if I returned to the ground, the wargs would tear me to pieces.

"This is the power you are up against," Astravar chimed in my mind. *"And still, you have the arrogance to think you can beat me in mortal combat."*

The stupidest thing right now would have been to let him taunt me. I needed to think of a way out of this. But Astravar was right, I didn't stand a chance. The branch beneath me creaked even more, and I knew it would be only minutes until it snapped.

If only I could fly like the dragons, then I could glide right over all of this. But then, this strange creature of leaves and wind could suck me into its centre where I would surely suffocate. It still was largely made up of whirling air, but it seemed to be gaining more and more mass sucked in from the forest. I would soon be part of that, compacted between a tangle of tree branches and leaves and soil.

I felt the branch snap, and then I felt it getting sucked in towards the golem. At the same time, I fell, and I caught myself with my claws as I dangled from the branch. As I struggled, the branch whirled towards the creature that had now become as big as one of the trees. I closed my eyes and prepared for the end.

"*Drop,*" Salanraja's voice came into my mind.

I didn't need to be told twice. I released my claws and fell, half expecting myself to tumble right into the merciless jaws of a warg. But at the very last moment, Salanraja swooped by underneath me. I landed right in her corridor of spikes and I grasped at her leathery hide with my claws.

I scrambled up to her neck to see that she was heading right into the centre of the forest golem. "*Salanraja, you'll kill us!*" I screamed out in her mind.

She ignored me and instead unleashed a torrent of flame. It lashed out all over the eddying tangle of leaves and branches and ignited the thing as a whole. Salanraja veered out of the way, and I clambered down a little so I could keep my balance. I turned to see the creature losing its power, as it raised up its arms into the sky and tossed back what I assumed to be its head and screeched like an angry dog on helium.

The whirlwind died to a tiny vortex, leaves fluttering out from it, and branches and twigs crashing down to ground, sending the wargs scattering. At the centre of the vortex, a small red crystal glinted in the firelight. This soon fell into the snapping jaws of a warg, who swallowed it, then whimpered and then scurried away. I took refuge in Salanraja's corridor of spikes, as she spiralled upwards. There, the dragons and the dragon riders were waiting for us, wheeling around the beautiful blue sky.

Olan looked down at Salanraja, and then let out a roar, as if to tell Astravar, wherever he was, that we would not be defeated. The rest of the dragons joined in the chorus.

Then, from a distant hill just at the edge of the Willowed Woods came another roar, ever so faint. Salanraja yanked her head in that direction, and I peered out from my roost at a jet of flame flaring out brightly against the dark rock.

"*Gracious demons,*" Salanraja said. "*Camillan and Shadorow are on that hill.*"

"Who?" I asked.

"*Lars' and Asinda's dragons. We're going there at once.*"

The dragons roared into the sky once again, and they quickly formed an arrowlike formation. Together, we shot off towards the signal.

22

PRISONERS

The signal had come from several miles away, and so it took us a
while to reach the two prefects and their dragons. From far
above the treeline, a bitter wind cut through my fur. I felt even colder
when a grey and gravid cloud occluded the sun.

The pressure in the air pulled on my sinuses. If only I had made it
through the portal after Ta'ra – the weather had looked pleasant in
the Second Dimension, and I had seen no sign of wargs. I was also still
worried about Ta'ra. What was Astravar planning for her, and when
would she finally wake up?

The hill we approached was actually a small cliff made of sharp
black rock that sprang out of the Willowed Woods. It wasn't particularly tall, but still the rock face was devoid of the trees, grass, or leaves
that carpeted the land below. Well, I say devoid, but actually bits of
branches and leaves and other stuff were strewn across the terrain, as
if scattered by floodwater or a terrible storm.

We could see the two dragons on the hill. Asinda's dragon,
Shadorow – a charcoal just like Seramina's dragon, Hallinar – was
well camouflaged against the rock, but Lars' dragon, Camillan, stuck
out like a lemon in a bowl of salmon. A little away from them, a primitive wooden cage structure, constructed of a mass of wiry branches,

contained Prefect Lars and Asinda. We were too high up to see their faces, but I could tell they were sitting down and had little space to move.

"What's wrong with the dragons?" I asked Salanraja.

"They were taken down by a forest golem. Those things, when they're massive enough, can throw tree trunks at dragons and knock them out of the sky."

"So why did they need to signal us? I thought you dragons could communicate across great distances with your minds." Which consequently raised the question of why they didn't tell us where they were in the first place?

"Astravar must have put some magic down to block that," Salanraja explained. "There'll be a dark crystal down there somewhere. Their dragons told me that a crow visited for a moment, whom we suspect was Astravar."

"What's a forest golem, anyway? And where is it now?"

"We just destroyed it. Can't you remember me burning it to a crisp?"

"That was a forest golem?"

"It was – one of the most dangerous golems in the realm."

"But what you did was easy, and they had two dragons. How could that thing defeat them when all they need to do is flame it?"

"It wouldn't have been so easy if the golem had fully formed. Remember what you'd learned about golems in your Magical Creatures primers with Driar Lonamm."

Funnily enough, I'd been asleep through most of them. But interestingly, something came to mind. "Golems gain strength as they gain more and more access to their source material."

"Exactly. Golems at their very essence are just dark magical crystals with a spell cast on them to gather a certain natural resource in a specific way. They get stronger as they gain more of that element, but they also lose speed. Astravar must have ordered that forest golem to lose all its substance when you were stuck up in the tree because he wanted it to catch up to you fast. When it's just leaves and bits of loose wood, it's quite easy to set alight. But forest golems, when they become solid enough, are made of compacted wood and other forest material. They can destroy forests and grow so big they've been known to knock dragons out of the sky with their fists."

"That doesn't explain why Lars' and Asinda's dragons couldn't set it alight."

"Have you ever tried to set fire to a tree with a match?" Salanraja asked.

"I can't say I have," I replied. I'd never even tried to strike a match. It used to fascinate me when the master would rub one against the side of the matchbox to create a flame. But really, I'd never desired to light one myself. Who needs fire when you have humans to cook for you?

"Well, just believe me when I tell you it's not easy. It takes a lot of concentrated fire to fell a fully formed forest golem. Usually, it's better just to fly by, or at least to send someone out to coat the thing in oil first."

"I'm guessing then we brought lots of oil with us, given we knew we'd have to go up against golems?"

"Gracious demons, no. With the amount we'd need to bring, we'd never have made it here so fast."

I groaned, hating how confusing this world was. *"It still doesn't make sense. Those wargs would have beaten me out of the tree, eventually."*

"Or they would have just given up. Wargs are hardly the most patient of creatures."

My head was spinning by this point. There was a reason I always fell asleep in the Driars' lessons. All this stuff was so much to take in. Us cats liked to learn useful things, like how to be stealthy as you padded the ground when hunting a mouse, as they could feel the vibrations beneath them. But when you were near a rabbit, you had to be quick, because they'd smell you before you even smelled them.

Never, though, would I have thought I'd need to contain knowledge about a creature that can suck huge tree parts and compact them into their body, then stomp you into the soil once they were done. Often, I still wondered if all this was just one big dream.

We'd pretty much reached the hill now, and the dragons descended. This time, Salanraja managed a gentle landing. Maybe she'd been listening to me after all.

The bare rock beneath her feet looked hoary, with patches of ice between the cracks. I didn't want to tread on that if I didn't have to. At least from up here, I had Salanraja's dragonfire warming my feet from deep inside her belly.

In fact, it was Ange who was the first to dismount her blue dragon, Quarl. The sapphire dragon first lay down on the ground, allowing Ange to clamber down out of the saddle. The Initiate took her staff off her back and she pointed it at the cage containing Prefect Lars and Prefect Asinda. A beam of green energy shot out of it and it hit the bars and spread out along them, giving the land beneath an eerie green glow. Presently, the bars curled away, leaving an opening at the top for Lars and Asinda to pull themselves out of.

"I guess, when you're going up against a forest golem, it's best to take a leaf magic user with you," I said to Salanraja, proud that I'd finally learned something about this world.

"Are you kidding? That's got to be the worst thing you can do?"

"What? Why?"

"Because leaf magic users are the first who a forest golem will target. It takes an awful lot of leaf magic to dismantle a forest golem, anyway. Only Driar Brigel is rumoured to have ever done so."

"You mean I made a mistake asking Ange to come here?"

"No," Salanraja said. *"Because you at least didn't bring her here alone."*

The two prefects stepped away from the cage, said thank you to Ange with a nod, and then walked over to Aleam and Rine, who were currently examining the fallen dragons. Ange followed them, whilst Seramina stayed in Hallinar's saddle, watching every move I made.

Though I didn't like the look of the sharp and icy ground, I was too curious about what was happening, so I scrambled down Salanraja's tail and went to join the other dragon riders. I looked back at Seramina when I did, wondering why she didn't dismount. But I couldn't stand her intense stare for long. It seemed to diminish the distance between the two of us and made me shudder within my skin.

Aleam was stooped over Camillan's wing, applying some white balm to a red gash that streaked through her thick yellow scales. The dragon groaned as Aleam massaged the wound, but she didn't scream out. "It will be a while until she can fly," Aleam said to Lars as he approached. "You're lucky to have survived this."

Lars bent down so that he could rub Camillan's forehead, causing the dragon to croon.

"How about Shadorow?" Asinda asked. She turned to Ange who was applying a similar balm to the charcoal dragon's wing.

"The wound didn't go as deep," Ange said. "But still, I think she needs to rest. Although Aleam hasn't had a chance to examine her yet."

Aleam shook his head. "You should have retreated, both of you. Two dragons and their riders are no match for a forest golem."

Lars shook his head. "There was nowhere to go. A line of bone dragons cut us off and pushed us right towards the golem. Astravar is in these woods, performing some kind of ceremony. We didn't know we'd be up against so much."

Rine lowered his head. "Astravar's here? But where?"

Prefect Lars pointed into the distance. "Just a few miles in that direction. There were bone dragons, a second forest golem, Manipulators, and a lot of activity until around an hour ago."

I didn't like the sound of that. "Why the whiskers would Astravar keep the bone dragons hidden from us?"

"Because he's planning an ambush," Aleam said, rubbing his chin. He turned to Rine. "There must be a dark magic crystal around here blocking any signals from the dragons. See if you can find it, Rine. Ben, help him out, will you?"

I mewled happily. Hunting things was my forte, although I wish Aleam had sent me chasing after a mouse or bird rather than a crystal. My whiskers detected some strange vibrations in the air, coming from a good hundred spine-spans away. I followed the resonating currents, tracing the crystal like one of those funny machines for finding metal that I'd seen the master and mistress' son using in the back garden of my South Wales home.

It didn't take me long to find it. When I got close enough, I also noticed it emanated a faint whiff of rotten vegetable juice. It stank so much that part of me didn't even want to go near it. But I braved the smell and lifted it up in my mouth, noting it didn't taste the same way it smelled. It didn't taste of anything, in fact, but it did warm my tongue though, as I took it over to Aleam and dropped it by his feet.

"Well, that was easy," Aleam said. He stepped back from it, took his staff off his back, pointed it at the crystal, and then he muttered something in a foreign language to me.

The ancient tongue of the crystals was about the only language I couldn't comprehend here. My crystal had gifted me with the ability to speak the language of all living creatures. But crystals weren't living and weren't creatures.

A single spark leaped out of his staff and hit the crystal, which shattered into what must have been a thousand sharp shards. A wisp of smoke rose from the remains of it, but the magic wasn't over yet. The smoke warped into the shape of Astravar's face, the noxious gas twisting his features and making him look even uglier than he was.

"Well, Aleam," the warlock said faintly. "I thought I'd at least be through the portal before I sent my ambush. But I guess I can't have everything perfect. Regardless, you are already too late." His annoying laughter followed his words, before the smoke dissipated.

In the distance, from the Willowed Woods, came a horrible high-pitched screeching noise that forced my ears down against my head to protect them.

Then, ten bone dragons shot up from the trees and into the sky.

23

SPELLS AND A PORTAL

Though Aleam was an old man, he was still incredibly fast to react to the first sign of danger. He stood up immediately and left the two dragons lying on the ground. "Lars, you jump on Olan with me. Asinda, get on Quarl with Ange."

Ange and Rine were already rushing towards their dragons. The two prefects didn't even hesitate to question Aleam's orders. They immediately took off, leaving their dragons behind, as they ran towards their assigned mounts.

Which, in all honesty, surprised me. *"Didn't you say it was worse than cheating for a rider to mount another dragon?"* I asked Salanraja.

"We don't have time to worry about ethics right now, Bengie. Get on my back." I stalked over to her, and I examined her tail swishing gently against the ground.

"Please tell me we're going to stay in the air," I said. *"I'd feel much safer up there."*

"No, you're all going to fight on the ground while all the dragons battle the bone dragons from above. But we've got to get there first. Now stop wasting time and jump on."

"I don't want to."

"Would you rather I roasted you here and now?"

I growled, as smoke rose from Salanraja's nostrils. Olan had already taken off into the air, and the ground cracked as Ishtkar, Hallinar, and Quarl took off in sync behind her.

"Fine," I said. *"But I'm not going to be the only one fighting the Manipulators this time, am I?"*

"Of course not. Now, you have three seconds before I take off, leaving a smouldering cat on the ground."

I growled again, and then I ran up her tail. I secured myself in place in her corridor of spikes, digging the claws on all four of my feet into her leathery hide as she vaulted into the sky. She didn't seem to care about being gentle this time, but she had to catch up with the other riders after all. Olan led the way, with the other dragons flying right behind her. Salanraja soon caught up to them, and it was a matter of minutes before the bone dragons were upon us.

They came in from the flanks, to which Aleam raised his staff and he whirled it above his head. Sparks flew out in all directions, but they didn't hit us. Instead, they lashed out at the bone dragons, and froze them in place for a moment, leaving them soaring towards the ground, their spiny wings stretched out, with electricity pulsing at their wing tips.

Aleam's spell wouldn't last for long, but it was long enough for the dragons to lower themselves towards the woods.

We headed towards a grassy clearing cut into the trees, where Astravar stood surrounded by maybe twenty Manipulators, who fed the energy into their bone dragons using their ethereal staffs. These wispy creatures floated around Astravar, whilst a massive wooden giant with glowing green eyes and whirlwinds of fire dancing below its midriff, loomed even closer to the warlock. Salanraja had been right – its fists looked almost as large as a dragon, and it was tall enough to knock even Olan out of the sky.

A white glowing portal towered over Astravar, shimmering in the air but not yet open and displaying the world beyond. The warlock fed energy into this from his staff, and he didn't seem worried about any of us being there at all. Between him and the portal, a hollowed-out tree stump contained a purple crystal almost as large as my crystal. This glowed with a faint purple light, and as it made me feel terrible to look at it, as if it had the power to sap out my soul. The demon chimera was there too, walking widdershins around the tree stump and crystal, as if performing some kind of ritual.

I figured Ta'ra was standing on the other side of that portal, with the key to let Astravar in. If only she knew how much trouble she was going to cause. If only I was there with her, I'd find a way to stop her, I was sure.

Salanraja lurched forwards suddenly, and I used the strength in my legs to keep me on her back without flying off. Together the dragons veered towards the ground. All the dragons but Olan landed only briefly, and the Initiates and Prefects rolled off their dragons' saddles in a well-practiced motion. Salanraja landed next, and she lowered her tail, so I could rush down to the bottom.

The wind gusted against me as she lifted back into the sky. The leaves danced around me on the ground, and I peered through them to see Aleam clambering down from Olan's saddle. As soon as he was off of it, the great white dragon lifted into the air. Presently, an ear-piercing screeching came from above. The bone dragons had returned for another pass.

We were still in the woods, surrounded by willow trees with thick boles. The roaring of the magic feeding the bone dragons from the Manipulators and of a waterfall cascading in the distance, made the whole scene seem to brim with fury. Aleam summoned us together, and I didn't hesitate to join him. Everyone, except I, lifted their staffs off the ground, and each one glowed with the magic of their respective colours.

It wasn't fair, really. I was the only one unable to cast magic, and everyone seemed to still expect me to fight. I was half tempted to run away into the woods and never to return to these people. But running away had done me no good last time.

"Go for the Manipulators," Aleam said. "Once they and the bone dragons are down, then the dragons can work on the golem."

Well, that was reassuring. I guess there were now enough dragons here to ignite it with concentrated dragon flame, which meant forest golems weren't invulnerable. Yet still, it looked like we were vastly outnumbered.

"What about me?" I asked. "What should I do?"

No one answered, because Aleam was already screaming out and charging, all the students not far behind him. He sprayed out lightning magic from his staff, which danced across the landscape. One spark latched onto a Manipulator, freezing its action in time. The beam cut off from it, leaving the Manipulator's respective bone dragon open to attack by flame from Salanraja and Olan in tandem.

Meanwhile, Ange pointed her staff at a cluster of leaves and used it to cut off a stream of magic linking a nearby Manipulator with its bone dragon. Above it, Quarl doused the same bone dragon in fire, reducing the skeletal creature to ash.

Rine had ice magic, and he used this to create a massive frozen crystal that floated right in front of a Manipulator's beam. The white light used to feed the bone dragon shone through it and dispersed into a wide rainbow, making the beam useless. Ishtkar could then finish the bone dragon off in the sky.

Asinda was a fire mage, and so she sent out torrents of flame towards another Manipulator, in an attempt to set the ground around it on fire. It seemed to work quite well, and eventually the heat rising from the column of flame became too much for Asinda's ethereal target. The crystal at the centre of the Manipulator fell to the ground, lifeless, and Olan took down another bone dragon.

As for Seramina, I hadn't imagined that she'd be able to fight these things with her mind magic. But strangely, she used her staff to leach all the glowing light away from a Manipulator, sucking it into her staff. Then, she pointed this up into the air, targeting a bone dragon swooping down in pursuit of Hallinar. She let out all the energy that the crystal in her staff had contained, reducing the bone dragon to splinters that tumbled down from the sky.

I'd never actually considered what Prefect Lars' discipline was. He had a white crystal on his staff, which he spun around his body in a complex motion to create a magical shield dome. This surrounded Aleam, the students, and I. Some Manipulators now cast magic at us. They used their staffs to summon hideous Mandragora plants with jaws and thorny tendrils that snapped around us, sending up purple mist as they moved. But nothing could break the shield barrier that protected us.

Behind all this, the forest golem lumbered towards us. But by this time, the bone dragons and Manipulators had all been defeated, and our dragons attacked. The golem swung back at them with its mighty fists, but the dragons hovered around the lumbering beast, unleashing their flames upon it. Salanraja was right, it didn't burn immediately. But the golem's swings were slow, and the dragons were agile.

It was only a matter of time before the massive creation erupted into flames, sending up a roar like that sounded like a thousand scary fireworks – the kind that scream as they whirl into the night and then just explode.

"No!" Seramina screamed out. "He's getting away."

While the battle had raged, Astravar hadn't faltered from his work. Suddenly, the portal flared white, and soon after the light faded until it was only glowing around the rim. The portal now revealed the Second Dimension, that beautiful land where the plants carried a sheen containing every colour of the rainbow. Astravar whistled through two fingers, and his demon chimera Maine Coon bounded up to him. The warlock jumped on his mount's back and the chimera charged. It lowered its goat's head as if ramming something, and the snake tail lashed behind the demon chimera as it went.

Once they were a safe distance inside the other realm, Astravar turned around and pointed his staff at the massive purple crystal in the tree stump. His magic lifted it out of its perch.

The portal cackled with energy, and I knew it was only a matter of time before it would close. On the other side stood the demon chimera, my worst nemesis. But I couldn't let Astravar get away.

"Prefect Lars, lower the shield!" I shouted.

"What?"

"Just do it!"

He seemed to understand what I was getting at, and the shield flickered away.

I swallowed my fears, and I sprinted towards the portal. I dodged out of the way of the crashing, flaming foot of the forest golem as I went. Passing through the barrier between worlds felt like passing through the skin of a fiery bubble. It burned my eyes, and my hair was standing on end when I reached the other side. Then, my skin prickled even more as the portal closed behind me, trapping me in a foreign land.

The first thing I saw in the unknown world was Astravar on the demon chimera, bounding off into a forest of green spruce and fir with that purple crystal floating behind him that he'd carried into this world with his magic.

The second thing – or should I say creature – I saw was Ta'ra.

24

CATFIGHT

It wasn't just the sudden surprise of seeing Ta'ra there that disorientated me, but I'd also stepped from the winter into an intense and humid summer heat. The sun blazed down from an empty sky, and birds chittered all around us. I felt, in a way, I should be out hunting. Part of me wanted to just hide under the shade in this weather as well. But I knew I had to do something about Ta'ra. I couldn't let her get away again.

Ta'ra's eyes were still closed, and she faced me and hissed at me, displaying sharp fangs. I could smell raw meat on her breath, and I wondered if Astravar had hypnotised her into eating a rabbit just like he had with me many moons ago. Ta'ra was the same size as me still, and I worried she might become twice my size or even larger and devour me whole. She expressed anger, much of it, and it took me a moment to realise that this wasn't actually her anger but Astravar, who had taken control of her body.

"Dragoncat," he said through Ta'ra's mouth. "You weren't meant to come here. Everywhere I go, you seem to want to meddle with my plans."

"Just open up a portal back to my home, and you won't have to deal with me anymore."

Ta'ra opened her mouth and cackled in an unnervingly unfeline like way. "Do you really think I'm so stupid, Dragoncat? Our destinies are intertwined, and I need you somewhere I can keep an eye on you. If only you would see the advantages of the power I can give to you. You wouldn't have to go hungry again."

"Everything you want," I said, "is for your own selfish gain, Astravar."

"Coming from a naturally selfish creature himself. How would you behave, I wonder, if you had access to such power? You would never go hungry again."

"I never went hungry in my own world either. Until you yanked me across dimensions and forced me to fend for myself here."

"And I can make it worth your while, one day."

"No. I don't know what you're planning, Astravar. But I won't let you get Ta'ra involved in this."

"But why do you care about her so much?"

"Because she's of my own kin."

"Is she?"

I took a deep breath. "Whatever she was before, she's a cat now."

I was circling Ta'ra, growling at her, and I could feel the fury boiling within me. I was ready to fight for her freedom. It felt odd not to be able to look into her eyes as she bared her teeth at me, but I could imagine them green and glowing underneath her eyelids. Ta'ra was in there somewhere, and I needed to remind her of who she was.

"Very well," she – or rather Astravar – said in a deep growl. "I had hoped there would be a way of turning you over to my side with your soul intact. You'd be much more intelligent that way. Alas, it's not meant to be."

I readied myself to pounce, but Ta'ra beat me to it. As her body sailed towards me, I lifted myself up on my haunches and swiped back at her. I knocked her out of the way, and she whimpered and then turned back to me, a scratch visible on her cheek.

It was now my turn to pounce. I leapt at her, but she turned on her back and kicked me further along my path. When I turned back, growling and snarling, she was twice my size. She charged and knocked me to the ground. I tried to push her off of me, clawing and scrabbling, but she pinned me down by the shoulders.

"Wake up, Ta'ra!" I screamed. "Please, what do I have to do to snap you out of it?"

Still, it was no use. She couldn't hear me. She opened her mouth and leaned in to bite me. But as she did, her grip loosened, and I wriggled out of the way.

I didn't have any chance of waking her while fighting her, I realised. I'd tried it too many times now. So, instead of turning back to face her, I ran towards the spruce forest. I had a plan, and I hoped to cat heaven that it would work.

I had to slide to the side a few times, to stop Ta'ra catching up with me. She was bigger and hence faster than me. But this also made her a little clumsier to turn. I soon found a suitable target, a lonely fir tree, surrounded by a ring of spruces. Gold seemed to shimmer in its needles, and every inch of its bark seemed limned with the colours of the rainbow, like oil on water.

I leapt up the tree, sending Ta'ra crashing against the trunk. She must have hit her head so hard, because she took a while to collect herself. Maybe it had been enough to wake her. But, just in case, I clambered even further up the tree, its sticky sap clinging to my fur, and I leapt down at her from a branch. I used my momentum to swipe at her face with a soft paw.

I hit her, and she groaned in pain. She turned back to look at me with her bright, green, open eyes.

"Ben... What happened? Is this a dream?"

"You ran away and came here," I said. "You were sleepwalking. Or I guess sleep running..."

"I – Where am I?" She sounded a little confused as she turned her head to assess the surroundings. "This looks like home."

"We're in the Second Dimension. The Faerie Realm... Which yes, I guess it is your home."

She didn't quite look like she believed me. "Ben, this is a dream, isn't it?"

"No, Ta'ra. You were dreaming before, but you're not dreaming now. Did you see him in your dreams? Astravar..."

"That warlock? Yes, he was there, and now I'm just in another dream. I'll wake up soon."

She just wasn't getting it… I looked up at the glimmering specks of gold in the tree. The Council of Three had said that these were fairies. Were they up there, watching us from above? If so, why didn't they come down and say anything? Ta'ra surely was one of their own kind.

"Ta'ra… This is serious. It's not a dream, and I'm here in the Faerie Realm with you."

"But then, how did you get here?"

"Because you let me in, and not just me. You also opened the portal for Astravar, and he brought his demon chimera, and a massive purple crystal. I don't know what his plans are, but my crystal predicted the future, and it saw Astravar with an army of Cat Sidhe just like you, and he marched them towards Cimlean, and he turned some of you Cat Sidhe into fairies and made them explode, then he sent the rest of the Cat Sidhe in to destroy the city, and my crystal told me that this is how life, and all the food it brings us, could end."

While Ta'ra had looked incredulous before, she now looked absolutely dumbfounded. "Okay, hang on, hang on. Slow down, okay, Ben? I've just woken up from a terrible dream. I now have a pounding headache, and this is an awful lot to take in."

I mewled, and I rubbed against Ta'ra to comfort her, then I licked the side of her fur. "Okay," I said. "What do you want to know?"

She sat down, and I sat next to her. "Start from the beginning. Tell me exactly what you remember and take it slowly."

So, I did. I told her how she'd run away the first time, and I'd had to chase her until Seramina flew out on Hallinar and woke her up. That part, she said she remembered. She recalled how Captain Onus had locked her in the guard tower with no light in there, Ange cast some wards around the door, and then she went to sleep not knowing what would happen next. I then told her how she'd transformed into a fairy, and she'd said something to me when she was in her human form and then just vanished.

"Astravar made me use one of my lives?" she asked, with bitter undertones in her voice.

"He did…"

I next explained how she'd run away again, and no one knew where she'd gone until we found her bounding through a field of canola. I chased her into the woods, and I couldn't stop her passing through the portal. Then I fought the wargs, and I fought the golem, and I made sure that she understood how brave I was and what a hero I was. Salanraja then burnt the golem, I told her, and we found Asinda and Lars and their injured dragons. Then Astravar sprung an ambush, and we went to fight him too. I even took down a Manipulator of my own – I said – because she didn't need to know the truth of the story. Then, I saw Astravar was about to enter the portal, and I dashed through just before it closed. He ran away into the forest, and I fought Ta'ra, and I woke her up by jumping off this tree.

"Now," I said. "Here we are."

After I'd finished, Ta'ra rolled on the ground, and she started laughing. She tossed and turned as she did, clawing at the air like a maniac. I wondered if it was still Astravar inside her. Maybe he could also dominate her mind when she wasn't asleep.

"Ta'ra, please. Don't let him take control of you again."

She rolled back over and righted herself, her head high in the air. "This is such a wild dream. I must have eaten some funny mushrooms, really. Did you put something in my mackerel, Ben, without telling me about it?"

"I did nothing of the sort, Ta'ra. This is real, you have to believe me!"

"Okay, so let's pretend it is real. Then the next thing I should do is go to Faerini, my home city, and warn everyone. Because if it's all true, they're in a lot of danger."

"And if it's a dream?"

"I should probably do it anyway," she said, wistfully. "Then I'll wake up, of course, and I'll remember that I'll never see them again."

"So, let's go," I said. "And whatever you do, make sure you don't fall asleep again at all costs. Oh, but before we do, grooming time?"

"Sure."

I took some time to lick the pine sap off my fur in an attempt to get myself to smell less like a forest and more like a mighty Bengal again. Given how disgusting that stuff tasted, I knew I could never be dreaming. That's the law of dreams, nothing tastes so revolting in them you want to throw it up again.

We didn't groom ourselves for too long. Though hurrying goes against a cat's nature, we still had to do something about the whole saving the dimensions thing.

Thus, after we felt we'd struck a delicate balance between cleanliness and our mission to save the world, we sprang off into the distance towards Ta'ra's home.

25

REHYDRATION

I t was a long walk to the city, and though we tried to keep a good pace, part of me wanted to collapse against the ground and have a good sleep. I let out a few wide yawns on the way, and I must have almost dozed off while walking. Yet I realised that if I slept, Astravar could find his way inside my dreams again. He hadn't yet controlled me like he had controlled Ta'ra, but that didn't mean he couldn't.

The intense heat of the sun wasn't helping. Everywhere I went, I could hear water trickling, or cascading, or at least swishing. We passed some beautiful lakes, with reflections in which I could see my mighty face, clearer than in the mirror in the master and mistress' bedroom back home. Given the heat, part of me wanted to go for a long and refreshing swim. I don't think Ta'ra would have appreciated it, but like my ancestors, I didn't mind water just so long as it wasn't freezing cold. Some cats do, some cats don't; that's just the way it is.

Both Ta'ra and I were pretty thirsty though, so every now and again we stopped to have a drink of the freshest water I'd tasted in a long while. It tasted even better than the moat water in Dragonsbond Academy, in fact. Almost unnaturally so, as if the freshness had been magicked into it.

We talked about mine and Ta'ra's past, about our likes and dislikes, and about the future. I even asked a question I'd been wondering for an awful long time.

"Is it true, you really don't want to be a cat?"

Ta'ra stopped in her tracks then, and she studied me through the slits in her intense green eyes. "What does that actually mean?"

"Aleam tells me you'd rather return home, sometimes."

Ta'ra shook her head like a human would. Sometimes, her gestures seemed so strange that I wondered if I'd ever shake them out of her. "Of course I do. You don't lose your entire life, have it whisked away from you, and not want to return to it."

"Does that mean that if you were given the chance to change back, you would?" I thought about adding that Aleam thought he had found a cure. But I didn't feel ready to mention that yet.

"What's with the hundred questions, Ben?"

"I just want to know. Will you stay a cat or go back to being a fairy, Ta'ra?"

She turned up her nose and looked towards the lake. "I can't go back. Not for good."

"But if you could, would you?"

"Probably," she said. "So long as I had nothing to hold on to here."

I let out a long, sad mewl. I didn't want to hear that, although I also didn't quite understand why. Ta'ra turned to me, her eyes wide. "How about you, Ben… Would you return to your world, if someone gave you a chance?"

"Of course I would," I said. "I miss my salmon all too much."

"Is it just about the food?" she asked, brushing her nose against my chin.

"I also miss my master and my mistress, and the child too, I guess."

"Do you think they miss you?"

"They must do. I'm too cute not to be missed."

"I see…" Ta'ra lowered her head to the lake and took another lap of water. She turned back to me, the water dripping off her chin. "What if there was someone here who cared about you more than your master and mistress cared about you? Would you leave then?"

"Probably… I've sprayed my territory there."

"And what if there was someone in the First Dimension you cared about more than anyone else? Would you still leave?"

That caused me to pause. I thought about Salanraja, I thought about Ange and Rine, and about Aleam, and then about Ta'ra. How much did I care about them, really? I then thought about the delicious meal of smoked salmon and milk that Astravar had whisked me away from, and my mouth started watering.

"I still want to go home..."

Ta'ra turned away from me. "I see..." She stood up. "I guess we better be going then."

She strolled off around the lake, not looking back. It was almost as if I'd said something to offend her, but I couldn't think what. I let her go a little way, and then I rushed after her. "I thought you said it wasn't far."

"It's not," Ta'ra said, looking up at the sky where floating specks of gold shimmered. "In fact, we're already there."

"What the whiskers are you talking about, Ta'ra?"

She said something in her own language. Probably, if I wasn't able to understand her, I might have thought her language as beautiful. But instead, what she said translated to 'reveal big city before me'.

A glistening superstructure appeared out of nowhere. This wasn't just a city; it was one of the most beautiful things I'd ever seen. A mass of stone rising up out of the lake, with running waterfalls which cascaded down from tall stone towers. The sun glinted off all the running and still water there, glistening as if off the facets of a crystal. Then, there was all the greenery – the wallflowers climbing up the stones, the huts set into trees and rock faces, the massive trees protecting the city underneath their wavering shadows.

Given how hot it was out here and how much shade would be in there, I knew where I wanted to be. But I was also absolutely shocked that a whole city had just appeared in front of my eyes. Was it really there? If I tried stepping onto the stones, would I fall to my death?

Ta'ra was studying me, and she'd clearly noticed my confusion.

"Has no one ever told you about glamour spells?" she asked. "Fairies like to hide things we don't want other people to find. Come on, this city doesn't bite." On that note, she skipped on ahead, and I cautiously followed her into the shaded streets of Faerini.

26

A PLACE OF GLAMOUR

Previously, I'd lived in a village in the Brecon Beacons, in the Welsh wilderness where I could go out exploring whenever I pleased. I tried not to spend too long amidst the nettles and brambles – hating like any living creature to get stung and scratched.

Instead, I preferred using the time after the human tourists had left to explore the ruined castle on the hill. Tourists always left snacks behind, generous as they were. I appreciated the eggs and the bacon in the sandwiches, especially – even though our old neighbourhood Ragamuffin had warned us we shouldn't eat such fatty pork.

Hence, I'd never actually been in a city before. But then why would I want to? I'm a cat and I like my independence, thank you very much. I also don't see the point of trying to find my way through enormous crowds, risking my life every day near busy traffic junctions, and cockroaches and earwigs and the other nasty bugs which converge in such places.

I'd seen cities on television, of course – big ones where you couldn't see the walls, only vast glass and metallic towers stretching out as far as the screen could show. Who'd have thought that the first city I saw in my life wouldn't have been built by humans at all. And fairy cities were so different from human cities. Honestly, it wasn't clear in Faerini whether the forest was growing out of the city or the city was growing out of the forest. Probably, they were both growing out of each other.

Unlike Dragonsbond Academy, there were no gates into this place. But with the fairies' glamour magic, I guess they didn't need gates. They could just make their city disappear whenever they saw invaders on their doorsteps.

I had seen no sign of anything fierce, anyway. No dragons that could toast all the trees. No golems, or wargs, or evil warlocks who would surely love to claim such a magical place as their home. But now they had let one warlock into this realm, and I knew from experience how dangerous this warlock was.

We wandered through leafy streets. The houses were made of colourful planks of wood, sometimes built into the trees, or around the tree, or arranged across the branches in such a way that there was absolutely no way for it to fall. Really, this place made me wonder why I missed home so much. There was so much to explore here. So many trees from which to dash from limb to limb. So many places to hide.

We climbed up some stairs around one tree, ducked under tree roots, then passed over a cobbled passageway behind a rushing waterfall without even getting wet. The air tasted of pollen and good things, and with every step we passed bees carrying honey to and from their hives. A different bird song greeted us at every corner, but I couldn't see the birds and had to wonder if they actually had glamour spells on them too.

Though we passed many houses, nowhere did I see any sign of inhabitants. But I could make out traces of gold dust floating in the air everywhere I looked. It's weird – in a fairy city, I would have expected them to be darting around from tree dwelling to tree dwelling. Instead, I guess they had stopped to stare at a Bengal Cat that they'd never seen in this world.

"If these are little people," I said. "Why do they need such big houses?"

Ta'ra looked at me and laughed. "What would happen to a tiny collection of logs when you light a fire?"

"It would burn?"

"Exactly. Within seconds."

"That doesn't explain why you have such small creatures living in such big places."

"Because," Ta'ra said with a wink, "we can't have small fires when we want to cook. So, we need big cooking pots otherwise they'd get damaged by the fire. A big cooking pot, means we need a bigger fireplace to put it in. And can you imagine what would happen if you had a big fireplace in such a small house – it would burn down instantly."

"Can't you just use magic to cook stuff?"

"We don't have that kind of magic," Ta'ra explained. "Besides, we also like to have big places to have room to fly about. It also gives us plenty of places to hide."

"But you have glamour magic."

"Ah, but we need to be prepared for those times that glamour magic doesn't work."

"And so, everyone is hiding right now? Because I can't see anybody…"

"They're here," Ta'ra said. "But they're scared of us. We rarely see strangers here, and I was already cast out, if you remember my story?"

"But doesn't that mean they'll just cast you out again as soon as they notice you here?"

Ta'ra sniffed at the air and then took a deep breath. "Oh, I'm sure someone's sent an emissary to Prince Ta'lon to announce our arrival. We might see his soldiers at any time now. But until that point, I hope we have time…"

I didn't like the sound of having to deal with fairy soldiers. I know they were only tiny creatures anyway, and if they carried tiny swords, the worst they could do with them is fly up my nostrils and make me sneeze. But Ta'ra had said they could also cast magic, and if they could reveal an entire city out of nowhere, they might even be able to make an army of hippopotami appear in all these pretty ponds. Then we'd be in big trouble.

Ta'ra had now picked up the pace, and it was becoming a chore to keep up with her. I was already tired from almost being eaten by wargs. Meanwhile, Ta'ra had only just slept and she could at least have had some sympathy for my physical state.

"Where are we going?" I asked.

"To see someone." She seemed different all of a sudden. As if she no longer wanted to listen to me.

"Who?"

But Ta'ra didn't answer my question. She stopped outside a door of a hovel with a straw roof and rounded windows made of frosted glass. She lifted herself up on her hind paws, brushed away some dust from the door knocker which was shaped like a deer and made from wood, and she grabbed it in her mouth and released it, letting out a rap. "No metal here."

"Why not?"

She still wasn't listening. Instead, she purred and called out. "Grandfather? Are you in here?"

There was no answer.

"Grandfather?" Ta'ra said again.

Nothing.

Suddenly the door creaked open, and I jumped back, the hackles rising at the back of my neck. Out of the door came the whiff of rotten vegetable juice. Whiskers, Astravar. He must have been around here somewhere, or at least one of his minions.

"Ta'ra, be careful," I said.

But, still ignoring me, she was already pushing through the slight gap in the door. I groaned, and then followed her, expecting to be looking right at Astravar's cracked face. I only saw an empty home.

Everything was one room here, a bare fireplace with a pot over it for cooking, the smell of fruit rising from it. A cot wide enough for three small people to sleep on it – or for one cat to sprawl out across it. A kitchen area with garlic and dried herbs hanging over a window looking outside.

I wasn't looking at that. Rather, I was sniffing out, trying to identify where Astravar could be. It wasn't one of his minions here – it was the warlock himself, somewhere nearby. Yet there was no place in this room where he could hide, or at least he couldn't if he was in human form.

"I don't like this," I said. "We should leave, Ta'ra."

"Shush," Ta'ra said. She was scanning the room, looking for something. She peered under the bed, and then she jumped up on it, and patted down the mattress with her paws.

"Grandfather," she called. "If you're here, it's me, Ta'ra. I know I look different, but where are you hiding? I miss you."

My fur was standing on end at this point. There was something in the air here, and it wasn't just the smell. The crystal in my head was pulling at the bridge of my nose, throbbing there as if it wanted to return to its master. I turned in the direction it led me, looking at an empty doorway. There was nothing there.

"Ta'ra," I said. "Your grandfather's not here. But we need to get out of here, because Astravar is."

"Nonsense, if he was here, I'd smell him. All I can smell is the berry stew, and grandfather has only just cooked it."

I growled. "Ta'ra, how can you not smell him?"

She leaped off the bed and jumped up onto the wooden kitchen worktop. She pawed the garlic and dried herbs as if a fairy could hide there. "Grandfather... Where are you?"

I decided it better to leave, so at least I could keep watch outside. If Astravar wasn't here, he might be in the garden. I made towards the door, but a purple mist seeping out from behind it blocked me in my tracks.

Ta'ra laughed maniacally. I looked at her, thinking she'd gone mad. Next thing I knew, she'd be running around in circles on the floor. The laughter then came in my head and, as the mist gained density, I realised that Astravar's laugh also resounded from behind it.

"Oh, Grandfather, I'll find you eventually," she said. "And I'll find a way for you to lead the rest of the villagers to me willingly, I'm sure."

Whiskers, Astravar had gained control of her again. I backed away into the vacant fireplace and looked up the chimney, wondering if I'd be able to climb up it. Then, I realised the chimney probably wouldn't be the best place for a cat to be when facing off against a warlock, so I jumped up on the cot instead. Besides me, Ta'ra yawned and then started to groom herself on the countertop.

"Ta'ra," I said. "Snap out of it!"

She didn't even seem to hear me now. Astravar's cackling laugh got louder and louder, and he soon stepped in from behind the mist, his blue face seeming to glow slightly. "Ah, Dragoncat, I see you walked right into my trap."

I glanced back at Ta'ra. She had a glazed look in her eyes, and her pupils had become two black pools growing within ponds of green. I looked for a place to run. I could easily get past Astravar right now if he didn't send magic after me. I took a step forward before I heard a growling coming from the doorway.

The beast, my nemesis, stepped through the door. Its fiery tail hissed and lashed around at the air, spitting venom. The goat raised its head and let out a terrifying bleating sound, and then the Maine Coon part of the chimera opened its mouth and gave an incredibly loud and smelly roar. As the sound came out, the cracks in the demon chimera's body glowed, and I could feel the searing heat blazing out from beneath them. The eyes also took on a fire of their own, reminding me of Seramina.

Astravar moved over to the chimera and petted it on the head. "I can convert you to one of these as well, Dragoncat, if you like. All I need is a suitably venomous cobra, a goat, and you can take the part of the lion. Although, I believe you'll have the head of a Bengal, descendant of the great Asian leopard cat. Am I right?"

I didn't like being mocked. I turned around to Ta'ra again, who now had her eyelids shut. Whiskers, this had all been a ruse. She had just pretended to wake up, or Astravar had made her pretend to wake up. But she had always been in that dream.

I searched around the room, looking for a way out. The chimera was edging towards me, baring its teeth, while its snake tail bared even sharper teeth and hissed at me. I arched my back and hissed back. If I had to, I could take it down. I could clench my teeth around the snake and cut it in half. But then I'd surely die of its poison, and I didn't want that.

The demon Maine Coon chimera stalked up to me, and the fire raged in its eyes. "HELLCAT IS NOW EVEN GREATER HELLCAT!" it said, and this time I realised it was talking in the demon language –

the same language that I'd used to command the demon dragon back into its portal. Maybe I had a chance.

Meanwhile, the crystal's lilting voice came back to my head. I remembered what it had told me, *"you must defeat the chimera."* This would be my moment of glory, and I knew exactly what to do.

"HELLCAT, I AM YOUR MASTER," I said. It had worked on the demon dragon, hopefully it would work on this too.

Nothing happened...

"HELLCAT NOT STUPID," the Maine Coon head said back to me. "MY MASTER FEED ME, AND YOU HAVE NO FOOD."

I growled. "What do you want of me, Astravar?"

Astravar let out a long sigh. "Just deal with him, Hellcat; we're wasting valuable time here."

"YES MASTER," the demon chimera replied, and it lowered its goat's head. Three scuffs with its hind hoof, and the thing was charging at me. It rammed the bedframe, which cracked in half, and sent me flying into the air. I landed just by Astravar's feet. He tried to stomp on me, but I rolled out of the way.

I heard the demon scuff its feet against the floor again, but I didn't want to hang around and let it kill me. Fortunately, the demon chimera had tossed me right by the door. I quickly scarpered out, back into the searing heat. As I went, something sharp lanced into my hind paw, and I felt a sudden pain searing through it. But it didn't stop me.

Astravar screamed out "Fool!" from behind me, but I wasn't sure if he was addressing me or his demon minion.

27

BLEARY

The snake head of the chimera had bitten me, and I knew it. I could feel the venom coursing through my muscles, and part of me wanted to just halt and give up. I didn't listen to that part of me.

Instead, I sprinted as fast as I could, maybe even faster than when I'd first left Astravar's tower. I didn't look back to see if the demon chimera was chasing after me. If it was, it would eat me. But if it wasn't, and I was lucky, maybe I'd find a suitable place to hide. I suspected Astravar wouldn't send it after me if he'd realised I'd been bitten. He probably thought I'd die anyway.

My muscles were cramping up from the venom that the snake head had injected me with, but still I ran. Water rushed by nearby, the sound of it hissing in my ears. My eyes had gone blurry, and my head was thumping, and I knew that if I didn't go somewhere soon, I would die here on this path for Astravar to find and do with me whatever he pleased.

Strangely though, Astravar wasn't inside my head. Even so, I felt a sinking feeling in my chest that told me I shouldn't have run. I was meant to be protecting Ta'ra. I'd come into the world to save her, and at the first sight of that demon chimera, I'd bolted. I was nothing more than a coward.

How I would become the hero who defeated Astravar and saved all the worlds from a fate worse than starvation, I had no idea.

It didn't matter, anyway, because I was going to die. The venom inside me was just too strong. But the last thing I wanted was for Astravar to find my body. He'd implied many times that he had a way of bringing me back from the dead. I imagined myself like one of those bone dragons, roaming the earth without a compartment for me to put my food in. Really, I couldn't think of anything worse.

Eventually, I couldn't run anymore, so my legs slowed. The world was spinning and whirling around me, and I found it hard to make out the shapes of anything. I didn't feel any pain anymore. I didn't feel any part of my body at all, in fact. It was as if I had disconnected from it completely. As if a part of me was rising to cat heaven, ready for those delicious meals of whatever they served you there.

But I couldn't let that happen. I was meant to be the hero. I wanted to reach out to Salanraja to ask for help. But she wasn't in this world. Here I would have to survive alone.

I looked around me for the sign of any shapes moving. There was nothing big enough to look like a demon chimera. Nothing had followed me. Yet I didn't really have control of my mind at the time to think that strange.

To my right, or at least I think it was my right, I thought I heard rushing water. It didn't give me a headache now. But it seemed to pull me towards it, and I passed through the cold cascade and found myself in a grotto.

The water sliced against the rock sending up a spray behind me. Seeking dryness and cover, I made my way to the darkest spot I could recognise, and I lay down. When I stopped, I could feel the venom raging through me once again, and I tried to keep my eyes open for as long as I could. Through the shapes, I thought I could see traces of something sparkling – glimmers of gold floating above my head.

Fairies...

"Are you there?" I said, and my words came out slurred. "Please, if you're there, I need your help. Your kin, Ta'ra, she's in trouble. Captured by an evil warlock. Please, if you can hear me, you must help."

I groaned as I mewled out the words. Then, the only bit of clarity in my mind made me realise I'd spoken in the human language. I needed to speak in the fairy tongue.

"Please, if you can hear me," I said in the right language, "you must help."

But no more words formed before my eyes became too heavy and I drifted off into oblivion.

28

BETWEEN TWO WORLDS

I f this was the end, I would no longer have a story to tell, and the future that the crystal had seen would not come to pass. But it wasn't quite the end, because I entered the dream world – that hideous place in the Wastelands where purple gas seeped out from the rents in the ground, and I could see Astravar's blue cracked head everywhere I turned. Purple fluffy clouds whirled around his head as he laughed, and he laughed, and he wouldn't stop.

"It's not over yet, Dragoncat," he said repeatedly. *"Our destinies are intertwined."*

But I was also somewhere else. I had a body in another world. There was a stinging pain in my back foot, and I groaned, and I tossed and turned. I probably had a fever, and I sweated through my paws.

Meanwhile, in the Wastelands, Manipulators rose out of the ground. Several golems also came out of the earth, formed out of hard rock. I coughed and sputtered at the gas that seeped into my lungs. It wanted to consume my life force. It wanted to dry me out to a desolate shell, an empty husk, a shell powered by nothing but dark magic.

Then Astravar, who knew where I was, could take my body and possess it. I'd come back to life without a soul, and I'd wreak carnage on this world together with his demon chimera and Cat Sidhe army.

This couldn't be how it ends. I had to fight it. I had to bring my body back to life. In the true world, I wriggled and squirmed and I did everything I could to wake myself up. My eyelids felt glued together. I tried to lift my head from the ground, pushed up against something solid, but it felt weighted down as if by lead. Alas, I was doomed to live forever in this hideous dream. I probably wouldn't even go to cat heaven. I didn't deserve it after all.

Astravar's magical creations had surrounded me now. There were too many of them to fight, and I had no choice but to back into a deep hollow in the ground. A golem made of the rock of the earth – even bigger than the forest golem that I'd battled with the wargs – now loomed over me. It had a massive fist of rock poised right above my body. It brought it down, ready to crush my bones into the earth as if the hollow was a mortar and its fist a pestle.

But I still had a little strength within me, and I used it to lift my head off the ground and open my impossibly heavy eyelids. My vision flooded with bright light.

29

FAERIE FOLK

I awoke, back in the real world, or at least the fairy world. Given all the glamour spells around here, I didn't actually know whether I was looking at reality or an illusion. An old wrinkly and slight man with a bandana around his head and a scraggly red beard was looking down at me. Something about him didn't look human. It was in his posture, I think – much as a wildcat doesn't behave the same way as a cat.

I backed away from him against the cold and slimy stone wall. It was covered in moss, and so I didn't stay long against it. I arched my back and watched this man or fairy or whatever he was, wide-eyed.

"Don't be scared," he said. "This is a safe place. We've hidden this grotto through glamour magic. Whatever hurt you won't find its way in."

I wanted to tell him that his magic was probably no match for a warlock like Astravar. But I realised if Astravar wanted to find me, he probably would have done so by now.

My back paw still stung a little, but there was also a slight tickle there, as if water was washing over it and soothing the pain. I looked back to see it glowing with a faint yellow light. In fact, my whole fur seemed to be glowing from the skin beneath.

"What did you do to me?" I asked.

"Some of us fairies also know the art of healing," the man said. "At least if we have the fairy dust donated to us from the right crystal. But alas, it's a dying art."

I took a step towards the man and sniffed his foot. He smelled of the berry soup in Ta'ra's home. "You're Ta'ra's grandfather…"

The fairy man waved his hand in front of him a few times and then gave a ridiculously drawn-out bow. "Be'las, at your service. And your name is Ben."

"How do you know?"

"Because I heard my granddaughter call you that when you were walking around outside."

"Then you'll know I'm a descendant of the great Asian wildcat."

"I didn't, but that's all well and good. I'm a fairy of Faerini, weaver of invisible silk and other kinds of magical thread."

Now I was getting the feeling he was pulling my leg. "I didn't see a spinning wheel in your house," I pointed out.

"That's because it's an invisible spinning wheel," Be'las said with a smirk. "How else do you think I weave invisible thread?"

"And who would need invisible thread?"

"Why, anyone who doesn't want to have their clothes noticed. This is fashionable in some parts."

I stalked around the grotto, sniffing out whoever else might have been here. There were certainly others – I could see bits of gold dust floating around in the air. "Why don't your friends show themselves?"

"They're rather shy. I'm the only one bold enough to represent them."

"Then why do you trust me?"

"Because you brought my granddaughter back, despite her hideous form and smell…"

"She looks a lot better than you do, old man!" In fact, I was grateful he wasn't wearing clothes made of his invisible thread.

"Now, now." Be'las stretched his arms out in front of him. "There's no need for that kind of behaviour. Us fairy folk are pleasant people, and we don't like insults."

I groaned. I thought humans were weird. "I thought Ta'ra was banished?"

The fairy man lowered his head. "Doesn't mean some of us didn't want her to stay. Ta'lon threw her out of the kingdom. But I've felt guilty every day since he did. I watched her go, and I did nothing. But now she's back, but she's not in a way, because when I saw you and her, I could tell she was under the warlock's control. That's why I didn't follow her, and we decided instead to hide here. What does Astravar want with us? We've always been a peaceful kingdom."

I rubbed myself against the man's leg, and he flinched and backed away from me. He seemed to think that I might want to do him harm. But then he was bigger than me, or was he? I didn't actually know. Eventually, though, he relaxed. There was a ledge of rock in the grotto, and so I leaped on to it and lay down on it. Then, I told him about my crystal and what it had forecast.

As I narrated, one by one, fairy folk appeared all around me. This should have startled me, but instead, it seemed perfectly natural. Whenever a fairy wanted to appear, the air shimmered around it, and there stood a man or woman – looking human except with funny postures and skin that glittered with specks of gold. They sat down on rocks and tree stumps and ledges scattered around the grotto.

There must have been a good fifty of them by the time I finished my story.

"He wants to turn everyone here into a Cat Sidhe just like Ta'ra," I said. "I ran after her, and everyone at Dragonsbond Academy tried to stop her from opening the portal. But now Astravar is in this world, and he wants to create an army to destroy every dimension. There would be no cats, no butterflies to chase, no salmon to eat from the bowl every morning. Our lives will be ruined."

A woman stepped forward. She wore a colourful dress, striped like the rainbow and flared at the bottom so that it showed her tall legs. Her golden hair spilled over her shoulders where it seemed to froth like waves.

That's when I noticed what was funny about them. These fairies didn't walk like a human or any creature that obeyed gravity should. Normal creatures lifted one foot, then fell on top of another foot, then pushed back against the fall to create continuous motion. But this fairy, and all the fairies as they moved, seemed to glide as if over ice. There seemed no friction between their feet and the ground at all.

"I am Go'na, Prince Ta'lon's sister," she said in an incredibly high-pitched voice that sounded like a cartoon mouse.

I'd already told them my name and ancestry, and so I didn't need to repeat it. "Why do you fairies have such strange names all the time?" I asked instead.

"I'm sorry," Go'na replied. "But I'd rather focus on the task at hand. If what you say is true, then I think Astravar must be heading to the palace now. He wants to use Ta'ra's love for Prince Ta'lon to cast a magic more powerful than anything we've ever imagined before." A tear came down the fairy's porcelain cheek, and she wiped it away.

I wasn't going to let fairy emotions impede the matter at hand – we had seven dimensions to protect. "Just lead me to the palace. Because we need to stop Astravar before it's too late."

Go'na sniffled and turned away. Be'las stepped forward. "Just follow us."

Before I could object, the air shimmered everywhere in the grotto and all I could see were those glistening specks of gold. But now I knew what to look for, I could track them as they floated through the waterfall.

I rushed through the water, and then I followed the fairies towards a massive tree in the centre of Faerini city that towered above everything else. Strangely, I could swear it hadn't been there before.

AN OAKEN PALACE

From a distance, the palace looked like a massive oak tree – kind of odd-looking, offset against all the pines and firs and spruces out here. As we got closer, it took on more of an ornate look. As Ta'ra had said, there was no metal in this world. Instead, it had these intricate woodcarvings etched into the tree bark, the wood of the doors, and decks leading out from the palace. They displayed winged humans in flight, carrying fruit and water, weaving clothes, and planting saplings in the forest. There was no one in battle, as I'd seen in some paintings around Dragonsbond Academy. Rather, the pictures showed the fairies going about their everyday lives.

The fairies – or at least the gold specks in the air representing them – had gathered around the large yellow door, which opened to display a spacious interior. The tree roots lunged out of the ground as if disturbed by massive waves. Once the door had opened, I saw these to be the wings of the palace, the corridors twisting around and up and down unlike any human construction. There was no plaster on the walls, or anything like that. Instead, the walls had a smooth yet unvarnished wooden texture, as if they had been thoroughly sanded down.

A cool breeze circled the interior of the tree, and it smelt glorious to be in here – with a rich natural aroma just like the garden I knew so well in South Wales. I thought it might be great fun to explore, but I knew we didn't have time.

Once we were inside the main atrium – a spacious room with a spiral staircase leading up the trunk, Be'las appeared to me in his human form. "The throne room is at the top," he said.

"All the way up there?" I asked. It led so far up I couldn't see where the staircase ended.

"We tend to fly up…"

"Well, that's all well and good if you can fly."

"Maybe you'll learn one day."

"I don't want to," I growled back. "I'm quite happy being a cat, thank you."

"Suit yourself," Be'las said. "I'll meet you at the top." The air around him shimmered.

"Wait!"

"What?" Be'las said, but he'd already vanished, and I couldn't quite make out which speck of floating gold he was.

"We should all go up the staircase together. What if there are guards?"

"Guards? We don't employ guards."

"What do you mean you don't have guards?"

"Haven't you worked it out yet? Why would we need guards when we have glamour magic? Besides, there's little in this world that's a threat to us, as the only way to enter the Faerie Realm from another dimension is for another fairy to open a portal."

"Or a fae…" I said, remembering how Aleam had told me once that faes were dark fairies.

"Faes don't come home very often. They're manipulated by warlocks to attack the humans who oppose them in the First Dimension. The warlocks have always taken little interest in the Faerie Realm."

"Until now."

"Yes, until now."

"Then let's just go up…" I leaped up the stairs, trying to take them in as large strides as I could. Because I'm an energetic Bengal, I rarely run out of breath, so I thought this would be easy. As I went, the fairies flew around me in circles, as if they wanted to show off that they could fly so much faster than me.

Instinctively, I wanted to reach up and try to bat them out of the way. I found it disturbing with them continuously flitting past my vision when I was trying to get to the top as fast as possible. I resisted though, as I still suspected they could do even worse things with their magic, like turning me into a snail and making the climb even more difficult.

The staircase eventually curled into itself towards the centre of the oak trunk. It led to a large outcropping from the trunk and had a ceiling at the top. Another yellow, closed door stood at the top of the staircase, decorated with wood carvings of fairies flying around various flowers. Whoever was inside had sealed it shut, and it didn't seem to have any door handle to open it with. I tried pushing it, but even with my mighty Bengal strength I couldn't budge it.

I felt the air shift from behind me and then came the smell of ozone. Be'las stood there looking at the door as he shook his head. "It's usually open," he said. "Visitors are meant to be welcome at all times."

"Well, we might not be now," I said. "How do we open it?"

"We can't from here."

"What do you mean, can't?"

"The door can only be opened from the other side."

"Then we're going to have to break it down."

"You can't. It's sealed by protective magic."

Whiskers, I couldn't believe I was hearing this. I moved up to the door and took a deep breath so I could bellow out at the top of my lungs. "Ta'ra," I shouted. "Ta'ra, are you in there?"

No response.

"Prince Ta'lon," I tried. "Prince Ta'lon, I am Ben, a Bengal and descendant of the mighty Asian leopard cat. I also work for Dragonsbond Academy and I'm here to save the Faerie Realm. If you value your kingdom, it's essential you open this door at once."

Still nothing.

I turned back to Be'las, who had a confused frown on his face. "It isn't working," I said. "Maybe we need to say a magic word."

"Magic word?"

"I don't know, like 'open sesame'?" I checked to see if the word had had any effect. It hadn't.

"Why would I want to open a seed?" Be'las asked.

"You don't. You use the phrase to open mystical doors to places." That was one advantage of being taught the language of all creatures, the crystal had given me a whole host of magical words to try in multiple languages.

"Alacazam!" I tried.

Nothing happened.

"Abracadabra!"

Nothing.

"Sim-sala-bim!"

Still nothing.

"Whiskers, Astravar, open this bleeding door!"

Silence ensued. I turned, ready to leave, ready to give up. I had no choice; I'd be stuck in this world forever. But I didn't take a single step before the door creaked from behind me. I spun around to see the door rattle against its hinges a few times.

Then, it swung open, letting out an incredibly warm and putrid draft of air that smelled of – you guessed it – rotten vegetable juice.

Inside, Astravar sat on a throne wrapped in living flowers of all kinds of different colours. The demon chimera sat at the warlock's foot, panting heavily. The purple crystal that Astravar had brought into this world hovered just below the ceiling, infusing its surroundings with a faint purple light. Wooden columns propped up the throne room, each intricately decorated with images that didn't seem to belong here – images of massive cats tearing tiny cities to shreds, throwing towers into the air, and trampling houses and city walls. A purple mist seeped around these columns, and above this stood exactly what had I feared all this time…

An army of Cat Sidhe sat there, hypnotised with their eyelids sealed shut, arranged in neat columns as if ready to march into battle.

Whiskers! We'd arrived too late.

SPRUNG

A shiver ran down my spine and time seemed to stop for a moment, as I took in the contents of the room. Then, slowly, things happened.

The fairies, still golden glitters in the air, had already started floating into the room. They didn't seem to move with a will of their own anymore. Rather, they gravitated towards the crystal, which grew in luminosity as the fairies drew closer.

"Stop!" I shouted. "It's a trap!"

My words did nothing to stop the fairies, as they drifted closer and closer. They didn't even seem to have any fight in them – any will to draw themselves away from the hypnotic spell the crystal was casting on them. Astravar looked across the room with that horrible grin on his face. The demon chimera also lifted its head, and it blinked at me and yawned.

Still, Be'las stood behind me in his human form, his gaze trans-fixed on the crystal and his eyes wide. His expression reminded me of a kitten who'd just seen milk for the first time. Soon enough, the air shimmered around him, and he became a golden speck of dust, floating towards the crystal with his friends.

I glanced from the staircase to Astravar sitting there on the throne, one leg crossed over the other as he leant forward on his staff. My gut told me once again to flee. But last time I did that, the snake tail of the chimera had bitten me, and I'd almost died.

"Oh, come in Dragoncat," Astravar said. "Come on in."

Now he'd mentioned it, I didn't want to obey him either. So, I put my rear down on the ground and groomed myself.

"I said, come in, you impudent cat!"

Suddenly, I felt something grasp hold of my side. Astravar had shot a purple beam right towards me, and he used it to pull me into the room. I screeched, trying to use my front claws to keep purchase on the wooden bark beneath my feet. I held myself there for a while, Astravar's magic trying to tug me into the room. But force was too strong and the pain in my claws became too great. If I didn't let go, they would get torn out of their sockets.

I released my grip and screeched as Astravar magically dragged me across the floor. I skidded to a stop just underneath the crystal. A magical energy ball full of violet light pulsated around me. The only muscles I could move were those in my spine and neck, and so I looked up to see the fairies had now reached the crystal. One by one, each fairy got sucked in towards the surface of it, and then let off a bright spark of light.

They floated like dander to the floor, now bereft of that golden glimmer. As they landed, the mist creeped up to accept them. The purple gas shrouded them in a roughly humanoid shape. Beneath the mist, it looked like the air shimmered a little, and the fairies very faintly took their human glamour forms. Astravar waited until all the specks had fallen and no traces of gold remained in the air.

Then, he lifted himself off the throne, and he cackled loudly as he reached into the pouch on his hip to produce a handful of small glistening crystals. He threw these up at the large purple crystal, and he swung his staff around in one deft motion and shot out a purple beam. The smaller crystals leapt towards the beam like metal to a magnet, and a ball of light formed at the front of the beam, suspended just in front of the crystal.

Soon, Astravar cut off the beam, leaving the glowing ball remaining. The magical ball followed the slow and steady motion of his staff

– the smaller crystals circling around it. The features on Astravar's face tightened into a mask of concentration. He opened his mouth and let out a tremendous yell. The ball shattered, sending the crystals out in many directions at once. Some spun across the floor and came to rest, but there were still enough remaining to shoot right into the foreheads of the fairies, each one creating a blue glowing spot.

I saw Go'na amongst them then, with her pretty wavy hair. Her eyes went from vibrant to white as the glow intensified on her forehead. The mist continued to rise around her, and then it changed shape, and Go'na transformed from human to feline. Her features warped and her clothes melted into her skin, which soon sprouted black fur.

When the transformation had ended, she had become a black cat with a white diamond crest on her chest, much like all the other fairies around her. Astravar lowered his staff.

"Excellent," he said, looking down at me, and he released the magical spell that had had me imprisoned. The violet ball surrounding me dimmed, and I could see clearly once more. I could also now speak.

"Astravar... What have you done?"

"What have I done?" Astravar said. "Oh, my dear servant, you have done this yourself. I only needed to set up the spell. Here, I used your friend Ta'ra to round up half the village. But you endeared the resistance to your cause and brought them to me. You only needed to present yourself to the rest of the villagers as an ally. What a wonderful gift this is, Dragoncat. And my demon chimera here didn't quite inject enough venom into you to kill you, clever minion that he is." He tickled the chimera under its Maine Coon head's chin.

I realised then that when Astravar had called out, "Fool!" before, it had been in fact intended for me. But it wasn't a call of anger. It had been a mocking remark – all a part of his little game.

The Cat Sidhes had now fully taken shape, and they moved into neat columns next to the others. They all had their eyes closed, but every one of them had their heads turned towards me. Remarkably, Astravar could control them all like this, and still function normally.

"You'll never get away with this, Astravar," I said. "Dragonsbond Academy will find a way to stop your schemes."

"Will it now?" Astravar said, his lips stretched into a grin so wide I wondered how his brittle-looking skin didn't crack. "You don't realise what I've just done, do you? I haven't just created an army from fairies, but extracted their magic from them, so I can use it as a reserve. With this," – he pointed up at the massive purple crystal suspended above my head – "I am now powerful enough to tear apart cities with magic alone. They can use my most powerful magic when they use a transformation. I've never realised until now how potent this fairy alteration magic is."

That explained, come to think of it, why in my crystal's vision Astravar had converted them into fairies to attack the dragons. The prediction must have seen them using so much magical power that they couldn't handle it, and so they then fell lifelessly to the floor.

"I shall stop you," I said. I also opened my mouth to tell him all that I'd seen in the crystal. But I thought better of it. Why give him information that he didn't have?

"Yes," Astravar said, his chin resting on steepled hands. "There is that issue of our destinies being intertwined. I can always kill you right now. That might solve my problem."

"Then what are you waiting for?" I asked, with a growl.

"Well," Astravar said, and he pointed his staff at the massive hovering crystal. "You see, I've had a bit of a problem since I brought my Hellcat into this world. When I took my little pet from the Seventh Dimension, I also took on a little debt with Ammit, the crocodile-hippo-lion demon goddess of the Seventh Dimension. And trust me, I don't want to leave a debt of such significance unpaid."

He put his hand underneath the demon chimera's chin and ruffled its mane. The chimera made a purring sound that sounded like rocks grating against each other. As Astravar stroked his pet, a purple beam came out of his staff towards the crystal. It entered it through one face, then emerged refracted on the other side, this time red.

Suddenly, it was as if time stopped. The world fell silent, if just for a moment. Then, a blast of heat came out from behind me, followed by an infernal roar. I looked over my shoulder at the portal that

Astravar had summoned there. It led, I could see, into the fiery landscape of the Seventh Dimension.

"You plan to send me there?" I asked, and I mewled softly as I did
so, because I really didn't want to go.

"Oh, no," Astravar said. "You're going to go willingly."

"Why the whiskers would I go there?"

"Because if you don't, then my demon chimera will rip you apart."
He released his hand from the chimera's mane. "Devour him, Hellcat!"

The demon chimera let out a happy roar. It came out so loud that
it shook the room, I swear. I tried to look around behind the portal,
see if there was a way out from the other side of the room. But the Cat
Sidhe army had each become the size of a panther, and they blocked
the way out. In front of me, the Cat Sidhes also closed in, creating a
corridor for the demon chimera to stalk down. Its snake tail whipped
out at the air, its goat's head bleated at an ear-piercing pitch, and the
Maine Coon's head licked its lips as I moved forward.

Maybe I could fight it. I'd need to attack the snake first. But my
legs trembled as I tried to stay put and muster up the courage to battle
the thing. The crystal can't have been serious, could it? How was I
meant to beat something that was so much bigger than me and had
three heads?

The chimera was now so close to me I could smell its rancid
breath. It readied itself to pounce, and I could see in its eyes that it
intended to eat me very soon. I knew I didn't have a chance against
the demon chimera, and I hoped that in the Seventh Dimension I
might at least live another hour.

Hence, I fled through the raging portal into the searing heat.

32

THE SEVENTH DIMENSION

I skidded to a stop right at the edge of a rock ledge. The ground was so rough, it seemed to tear my skin. I dug in my claws to the ground to stop myself from going over the edge, and then I groaned as I looked at the sea of boiling lava stretching out right to the horizon. It wasn't far beneath me, and bubbles rose from the molten sea, which I was sure would melt me alive.

I spun around, wanting to jump back into the Faerie Realm. Being eaten alive by a chimera might actually have been a better option than boiling to death here. But the portal had already vanished. Astravar had banished me to the Seventh Dimension, and it soon dawned on me that there was no turning back. A nauseous smell of rotten eggs followed me wherever I turned, and I found it hard not to vomit.

Fortunately, I wasn't stuck on an island surrounded by lava. I had just entered the land at what looked like the lowest point. As close as physically possible, in other words, to that bubbling sea.

Most of us cats were made to live in hot places, so in many ways I might have done better in this place than your average dog or human. Our bodies are designed to wash away heat with efficiency, and perhaps that's why I didn't wither to a crisp in the intense heat. But I knew I would if I stayed down here much longer.

I was on a kind of beach which stretched out to my left and right. Behind me the ground rose sharply to a precipice. A narrow path led up there, over a ledge towards a smouldering mountain range. At the top of this, three volcanoes spewed ash and magma into the sky and earth.

I wasn't sure it would be any cooler up there, but I had to take my chances. I took one step, and a massive roar erupted from the sky. Up there, I saw a familiar creature – a demon dragon just like the one I'd defeated in the First Dimension. If it noticed me, I was doomed.

Well, I guess I was doomed anyway – I was in the Seventh Dimension after all.

I made my way across the rocks, keeping my feet as light as possible so I didn't tear my paws on the jagged rocks. I crept away from the boiling lake, and it quietened a little as I progressed. A hot wind came off the boiling sea as I climbed, but it didn't feel like it would kill me anymore. Still, it was hot enough to be uncomfortable; hot enough for me to regret hating the snow.

The passageway up was narrow, and the rockface shot up almost vertically on my right. I hugged this as closely as possible. The earth seemed to sap some heat away from me, and I tried to keep as far away from the lava as I could. Eventually, this wall gave way, forcing me to navigate across a terrifying ridge. I know I'm a cat, and I know I'm excellent at keeping my balance. But the ground underfoot pierced my feet with each step I took, and part of me wanted to just give up and tumble off the side.

Still, I persevered, and I eventually climbed up to a plateau where I could tread a little more readily. The ground was too sharp for lying down, much as my body wanted to do so. But the plateau stretched out far enough to shield me from the heat from below. I knew I needed water, desperately, and I was also ravenously hungry. I hadn't eaten since those sausages last night when fire had actually felt good.

I sniffed the ground for a sign of something, but all I could smell was the sulphur from the molten earth. I tried to detect some movement using my whiskers. But the earth was rumbling so much that I couldn't sense anything. Still, I could see, and I could see well. Something scurried across my path in the distance, and I entered a low crouch to stalk it.

It wasn't long until I recognised the creature from the way it moved. A demon rat – I had hunted many of these before in Astravar's abode. It didn't seem to notice me stalking it, with the roaring coming from the lava below and the rumbling of the earth. But just at the last moment, I readied myself to pounce, and it twitched its nose, turned towards me and scurried off.

I followed it at a pace, knowing that though it wouldn't provide much nutritional value, it would ease my hunger pangs somewhat. It led me over the rough terrain, under a few nefarious looking arch-ways made of craggy rock, and then towards a lake – this time much higher up than the sea – full of smouldering water.

Before I could catch it, it disappeared in a hole in the rock-face. I tried to reach in to fish the demon rat out, but the rock scratched my foreleg, and I yelped out in pain. That was when I sensed something behind me. I don't know if I heard it swishing out of the water, felt its gaze upon me, or sensed the heat coming from the cracks in its skin.

I turned, worried about what beast I could face. Could it be a demon dragon? A demon Maine Coon? A demon chimera? None of these, I admittedly wanted to have to face again, especially in their own realm.

But what I saw before me was much, much, worse. The bulbous and fiery eyes. The huge nostrils that vented steam just like Salanra-ja's. The buck teeth…

It turned out that I was standing face to face with a demon hippopotamus.

33

AMMIT'S SERVANT

The demon hippopotamus was the largest land creature I'd ever seen. Actually, I tell a lie; it didn't quite dwarf the forest golem that I'd battled in the forest back in the land I wished I was back in. But it was larger than the demon Maine Coon, larger than any size Ta'ra had ever grown to, perhaps even as large as an elephant. Well, in all honesty, I'd never seen an elephant, but I'd heard stories about them from the Savannah Cats back home, how they had legs as big as tree trunks that could pancake a cat before it saw what was coming.

This demon hippopotamus had a nose as big as a tree stump, and a head made of sharp grey rock that looked like it could hammer me into the ground. Just like any demon creature I'd seen, it had cracks all over its craggy skin, fire brimming beneath them.

Behind it, the volcanic lake bubbled and boiled, and raged out sulphur into the air. I wondered if there were more demon hippos lying in wait for me there. Maybe they had all sent this one ahead to drag me back into its pond where they could boil me in it until my flesh became tender.

I could only imagine what fate lay in wait for me, but I didn't want to hang around long enough to discover it either. The demon hippopotamus opened its mouth and out came a sound like a thousand pigs playing the trombone. It sent the hackles up on my back. With a dry mouth and my heart pounding against my chest, I turned to flee.

The beast scuffed the ground behind me, and the rock beneath me shuddered and creaked. Hot air rushed towards me. I shrieked and dived out of the way as the massive creature came crashing past. It skidded to a halt, sending up plumes of ash around it.

I backed away, this time realising that I needed to watch the demon hippo carefully to survive this encounter. It turned slowly, snorting and grunting like no pig I'd ever heard before.

I tried shouting out at it in the demon language. "DEMON HIPPOPOTAMUS, I COMMAND YOU TO RETURN TO YOUR LAKE."

But it might have been deaf, or it might have been too stupid to understand me, or maybe in fact it didn't even speak the demon language or any language for that matter.

I tried again. "DEMON HIPPOPOTAMUS. I COMMAND YOU TO LEAVE ME ALONE."

At that, the demon hippopotamus snorted out a laugh. "I OBEY ONLY AMMIT, THE DEVOURER, THE GREAT BRINGER OF DEATH, THE EATER OF HEARTS. YOU CANNOT COMMAND ME."

That didn't sound good, and I groaned, anticipating what might come next. The demon hippo lifted itself up on its stubby legs, kicked the dust up behind it, let out its snorting, bellowing roar and charged at me again.

This time, knowing it was faster than me, I didn't turn my back to it. Rather, I watched in terror as it sped towards me with its buck teeth raised over its wide gaping maw, ready to swallow me whole.

I steeled myself, no matter how much my legs wanted to flee. I measured the distance between that massive gaping mouth as it drew ever closer. I waited until I could see the fires burning at the back of its throat, behind the shadow of a massive tonsil that looked like a bell. The beast had breath that smelled like a salami fished out of the sewers, which made me want to retch. Still, I didn't dare run, at least not yet.

Before it could devour me whole, I ducked to the side, and I leapt onto its back, just as I had with the demon dragon. I thought I might be safer there, but when I saw it was charging right towards that boiling lake, I dived back off again.

The demon skidded to a halt just before the lake. As it turned, I looked around for a way to escape. I could retreat to the ridge, but in the distance, I could see the demon dragon I'd previously seen overhead had perched itself there. The plateau stretched out in most directions for quite a way until it vanished into a shroud of smoke. At one point, the ground rose into a wall of smoothed volcanic rock, jet black save for a slight shine to it, reflecting the red glow from the lava below.

The demon hippopotamus' eyes burned even brighter than before, but this time it didn't charge. Instead, it ambled up towards me, and I had no choice but to back up against that obsidian wall.

I hadn't noticed it before because of the angles, but one side of the wall jutted out in front of the other. This created a corridor wide enough for both me and the hippo to pass through.

I took the chance, and sprinted through the passageway, and found myself on an outcrop of rock, surrounded by a steep drop into the churning lava sea. I felt queasy looking down at it, and I could taste the acrid fumes at the back of my mouth.

The demon hippopotamus emerged from the passageway at its slow, steady pace. "YOU WILL BE A GREAT PRIZE FOR MISTRESS AMMIT. SHE WILL BE PLEASED WITH ME, OH SHE WILL. YOUR HEART SMELLS GOOD, AND I CAN HEAR THE WAY IT BEATS. SO CLEARLY NOW. THE MOST BEAUTIFUL HEART I'VE HEARD FOR A WHILE."

I yelped. I had nowhere to go. The demon had me blocked off completely. My only choice was to jump. I turned away from the hippo and readied myself to leap into the lava sea.

This was the end…

"It is not over yet, young Ben." A voice said in my head, smooth with a lilting Welsh-like accent.

The crystal…

"Have courage, and do not give up until your very last breath."

My crystal... But how was it speaking to me here in the Seventh Dimension?

"Your destiny doesn't lie in the jaws of a demon hippopotamus. Come, this way."

Suddenly, the air in front of me shimmered. Well, actually it was shimmering quite a bit already given the intense heat, but let's just say that it shimmered even more. It also sparkled a little, with a golden sheen, as if made of fairy dust.

The patterns the light played in the air revealed a spiral staircase leading up, with no railings on either side of it. It didn't have any substance, and it looked like my body would pass right through it. But I could feel the furious breath of the hippopotamus so close now. In moments, I'd be toasting within its mouth, and moments later it would deliver me to its mistress Ammit, whoever that was.

"Have courage, Ben. Courage will keep you safe."

I guess I had no choice – if I stepped on this staircase and plummeted into the fires of the earth, it would make no difference. I would have died anyway.

I took the first step, and when I felt it was solid enough underfoot, I dashed up a few steps. The infernal creature beneath me also tested the staircase with its hefty foot, but it couldn't step onto it and almost fell off the cliff. It backed off just in time, which was a shame because I'd wanted to see it fall. The beast made another one of those mighty pig trombone noises – almost loud enough to knock me off through sound alone.

I braced myself and followed the staircase up to wherever it would lead.

34

THE SAME CRYSTAL

The magical staircase led into a dark chamber with three walls, a floor, and a ceiling formed completely of obsidian. It was slightly cooler in here – if that was at all possible in this place – and it would have been completely dark if it weren't for the white light emanating from a giant-size crystal I knew so well. It spun slowly on its vertical axis, showing depictions of me in flight on Salanraja's head with a staff in my mouth, which let off a beam of red energy.

My beam shot out and met a beam of purple energy head on. Alongside me, Astravar flew astride a bone dragon, his staff emitting that second deadly beam which he clearly wanted to kill me with. The crystal had shown me this scene many times, in different variations. It knew many possible threads of the future, but they all seemed to lead towards this ultimate battle between me and Astravar.

The thing the crystal never told me is who would actually win.

It's impossible, I thought. I had to be hallucinating because of the heat. My crystal couldn't possibly be here when it was in the First Dimension, right in Salanraja's chamber where we had left it.

"What is it about my existence that you fail to comprehend?" the crystal – or should I say my hallucination of the crystal – asked me inside my mind.

"You're not here. You cannot be."

"And you do not understand magic well, Ben, for you have slept through your classes. It exists across the dimensions, as does each crystal, including the one you see now."

I took a moment to take that in. Really, my head was spinning so much, and I wanted to faint. No water. No food for hours. Heat exhaustion. I just couldn't think straight. *"Hang on a minute,"* I said after the third time I'd considered the crystal's words. *"Are you telling me you're exactly the same crystal as the one in the First Dimension?"*

"That's exactly what I'm saying. I exist across all seven dimensions."

"Then it was you who saved me from the demon hippopotamus just before it was about to eat me. Whiskers, why did you wait so long?"

"No," my crystal said. *"You saved yourself. I merely provided the tools for you to do so, but you took the leap of faith necessary to survive. That, young Ben, is the lesson you must learn. When and when not to leap."*

As the crystal bathed me in its cooling light, I became less and less fatigued. I still felt so terribly thirsty that I would drink even the foulest reeking swamp water, and my stomach rumbled like an earthquake. But my clarity of mind at least returned to me. I looked over my shoulder at the raging volcanic tempest below, and I wondered if I would have to return to it.

"Can you get me out of here?" I asked.

"Perhaps," the crystal said. *"If you deem yourself worthy."*

"What do you mean?"

"You have already proven yourself ready. The time, Ben, is nigh."

"For what?"

"Your second test. You can now gain your second ability. That is, if you have the strength to do so."

"I thought you said I couldn't gain it until I battled the chimera and won?"

"That's right," the crystal said.

"But I can't fight the chimera. It was bad enough to face the demon Maine Coon when it was just that. But then Astravar turned it into a demon chimera. I don't have a chance against that."

The crystal let out a soft noise that sounded like wind chimes trying to sigh. *"It isn't the chimera without that you must defeat, Ben. It's the chimera within."*

"The chimera within? What nonsense is this?"

"Are you ready for it?"

"I—"

"Are you ready, Ben?"

I hesitated. I guess, in all honesty, I didn't have a choice. It was either fight the chimera within – whatever that meant – get eaten by a demon hippopotamus or be consumed by the Seventh Dimension's boiling sea.

"Fine, I'm ready."

"Very well..." A cooling breeze washed out from the crystal, reminding me of those times the master or mistress would open the boxy freezing machine on a hot day. On the breeze came a scent of lavender that pushed the sulphurous fumes away. As the wind came, the crystal spun faster and faster. The light intensified from it, and the crystal soon was moving so fast that it appeared round.

"Close your eyes, Ben," the lilting voice of the crystal said. *"It's time to face the chimera within."*

I didn't even think twice about disobeying it. The words mesmerized me, and my eyelids felt heavy. They closed on their own accord, and I felt a pressure against my eyelids, soft and not in the least bit painful.

My thoughts became random; my mind became wild. Soon enough, the crystal had woven its spell, transporting me into my world within.

35

THE CHIMERA WITHIN

The crystal dropped me from the scorching heat of the Seventh Dimension into the scorching heat of a desert in the noonday sun, and I didn't appreciate that one bit. The ground was so hot that I had to keep moving so my paws didn't burn. I was thirsty; I was hungry; I knew that if I didn't find what I needed soon, I'd collapse here and die.

But this was all in my imagination, surely? But then maybe my sensations were those of my body in the Seventh Dimension. Maybe the heat and the fumes there were getting to my head. Maybe everything I'd just seen – the crystal, the magical staircase up to the obsidian chamber, the demon hippopotamus – were all hallucinations.

Still, I could physically feel the heat in my paws, and I didn't want to linger long enough to test my theory. I trudged across the sand, lethargy burning in my legs, my tongue as dry as a cactus, my vision hazy, as I tried to see through the bright light reflecting off the sand. There were no plants, no vultures, not even the smell of anything living. A flat, desolate plain of yellow stretched out in all directions, rising to darker dunes behind the distant haze.

"*Believe, Ben,*" the crystal said in my mind. "*Believe and you shall find.*"

Well, if it was going to be like that, I thought I might as well imagine what I wanted, and I wanted water the most of all. I thought of that lake near the invisible Faerini city, where Ta'ra and I had lapped up water. I thought of the moat at Dragonsbond Academy where the water tasted faintly of roses, and where I would often visit for a sneaky drink. I thought of my home in Wales on those days that it rained – admittedly half the year – and how I could step outside after the downpour and drink the water from a puddle.

Low and behold, I spotted a shimmer on the distant ground – closer to me than the horizon. Water, it had to be water. I picked up the pace, bounding towards it at a sprint, forgetting that I should really conserve energy in this heat.

Luckily for me, it wasn't a mirage, and I soon found myself in a glorious oasis with one of the clearest lakes I'd ever seen. I cowered under the shade of a lonely palm tree, and I lapped up the smooth water until I could drink no longer. Then, I tracked the minnows darting around underneath the lake's surface, as I tried to devise a way to fish them out. But I didn't need to, because I suddenly smelled smoked salmon. A meal of it had presented itself in bite-sized chunks in a bowl right at the base of the palm tree.

I mewled in happiness, entirely convinced that I had died and gone straight to cat heaven. Maybe here, bowls of my favourite foods grew on trees and appeared when I most wanted to eat them. I devoured the salmon in what must have been minutes, and then I turned back to the lake, licking my lips.

It finally seemed a good time to have a nap, so I lay down in the sand, appreciating the coolness where the shade covered me from the beating sun. Just as I closed my eyes, a bellowing roar filled my surroundings, accompanied by a terrible stench.

The Savannah Cats back home had told me so many times that the lion's breath smells nastier than rotten salami. When I could finally return home, I looked forwards to telling them that the chimera's breath is ten times worse.

My eyelids shot open, and I spun around to see the lion head's open maw right in front of me. This wasn't the demon chimera, but the same chimera I'd seen in my dream, days ago in Driar Brigel's alteration class. A hissing sound, then the snake's head whipped around the chimera's body, lunging right at me. I dived out of the way just in time. Then, as I bounded away, the goat let out that hideous, ear-piercing bleating noise.

I ran back into the desert, not caring so much now about the scorching earth. Rather, I wanted to get as far away from that beast as possible. I'd had enough dealings with nasty things that could tear me apart for one day. I just wanted a peaceful life. I wanted to go back home.

Salanraja, I said in my mind, wondering if I could reach her. *Salanraja, I need help.*

But there was no answer. Whatever dimension I was in, she wasn't here now. Instead, I was sprinting right towards a form as splendid as a lion, silhouetted against the sun. It had the tail of a snake and horns sticking out of a head from its back.

I stopped in my tracks and checked over my shoulder. How had it found its way around me so fast?

As the beast scuffed its hind hoof against the ground, kicking back the sand in a cloud, I spun around again and sprinted, putting my entire back into it to give me as much speed as I could.

But I realised I was just sprinting towards the sun now getting low and red in the sky. And there was the chimera standing in front of me again.

This isn't real, I told myself. *This is just a dream.*

"The experience isn't real," the crystal said back in my mind. *"But your emotions are, and so are the ways you've trained yourself to react to them. It doesn't matter which world you're in, Ben. You must learn to circumvent instinct."*

While the crystal spoke in my head, I continued to sprint towards the chimera. My body hadn't quite registered that it wasn't running away from the previous chimera. But I stopped myself in my tracks, just before I reached it.

Then I turned to run again.

"Is this what you want, Ben?" the crystal asked. *"To be constantly trapped in a spiral of fear?"*

"I want to go home." I replied in my mind. *"I want life to be easy again."*

"So, take responsibility for your emotions and measure your actions against them. Then, maybe, you'll eventually discover a way."

Whiskers, the crystal was right. I couldn't keep running like this. I had to turn around and face the beast. It was only a product of my imagination after all. It couldn't surely kill me, could it?

I stilled my thoughts, and I stopped my body, and I refused to listen to that part of me that said, 'run'. I turned slowly and stared into the brilliant yellow eyes of the beast. It was only a couple of spine-spans away from me, and I could smell its revolting breath in the warm air.

I held that gaze, and for a moment time seemed to stop between me and the chimera. The snake's head might have hissed, but it remained poised above the lion's head as if charmed. The goat's head also glared at me from a little to the side of the chimera, as if measuring what I would do next.

You have to fight the chimera, the crystal had said to me.

I lowered myself into a crouch. The chimera did the same as if it was my reflection. I hunched myself over my forepaws and the chimera mirrored my very motion. I opened my mouth and let out a hiss. The chimera responded with a tremendous roar.

The thought came to me for a split second to turn and flee. But I pushed it away. I let the beast's roar and its breath wash over me. The snake's head raised itself, as if also poised ready to strike. The goat's head lowered its horns behind the lion's head.

I don't know where I got the strength to do what I did next. It went against every essence of my being. But I let my muscles follow through the same motion I would when hunting a mouse. I leaped into the air, and the chimera also launched itself off its haunches. I readied my paw to swipe at its head, also seeing five sharp extended claws arcing towards me. I kept my eyes open, even though part of me thought I would die.

A sudden coolness washed over my body as I passed right through the chimera as if I'd passed through a waterfall. The sun flared bright white in front of me, and then a wave of calm washed over me.

I turned once more, ready to continue the fight. But the chimera was much more distant from me than it should have been. It didn't look menacing anymore, instead sitting on the sand regarding me. It gave me a humble bow, and then it ran off into the distance, leaving me alone on the cooling sand as the sun plummeted down towards the horizon.

I turned to see that I'd magically been transported back to the oasis. Darkness descended in the sky behind the lake, but the water was still lit by my crystal which emanated a soft and warm white light while spinning suspended in the in air.

"*That was it?*" I asked in my mind. "*I thought I had to actually fight it and win.*"

"*You did win, Ben,*" the crystal said in its beautiful lilting Welsh accent. "*You did what you needed to do. You defeated the chimera within.*"

"*But we didn't even touch each other. It wasn't even there.*"

"*It was there. It's always been there within you and will be until you draw your last breath. You've just never learned how to confront it until now.*"

"*Well, it was easier than I thought,*" I said, and I realised I had my head raised high. I'd regained my normal cat-like stance, standing the way that I'd always stood around my neighbourhood in South Wales.

"*What is easy? Surely you can only do what is in your control.*"

"*You might be right...*" I looked up at the sky, which was clear and now full of twinkling stars. "*So, I guess it's time for my second ability.*"

"*It is...*"

"*What do you have in store for me this time? Will you give me my staff, perhaps?*"

"*You're not ready to wield your staff yet.*"

"*But I defeated the chimera.*"

"*Still, you have many lessons to learn.*"

The crystal started to spin, and I felt an intense pressure on my eyelids. It felt as if someone was sticking two knitting needles into the skin there, but I knew better than to back away. My body felt warm, and my muscles convulsed as they took on a new form. I mewled up to the sky, and then I suddenly felt my face twist, and I roared. My tail hissed back at me, and I could swear that my shoulder blades became horns as my spine bleated.

Then my body went back to normal. Yet my muscles felt stretched, as if I'd been doing that funny human activity called Yoga.

"*What the whiskers was that?*"

"*You now have your second ability,*" the crystal said. "*Congratulations.*"

"*But what is it? I can transform?*"

"*Now, you can bring the chimera within, without. But be careful, Ben. Alteration magic is powerful and if you transform into it too much you will become just like the chimera within – feral and soulless.*"

I thought about Astravar's threats about transforming me into a feral beast. "*I will be careful.*"

"*Good.*" Shimmers of gold appeared on the surface of the lake, and the crystal vanished. Instead, just below it appeared a white portal. It was so bright I couldn't determine where it led. "*Step through, Ben.*"

"*Can this take me back home?*" I asked, hope flaring up in my chest.

"*It will take you where you need to go. Now make haste, before the chance is lost.*"

I didn't question the crystal's motives anymore. As long as it didn't take me back to the Seventh Dimension, with the demon hippopotamus waiting to drag me underneath the boiling waters to its mistress, then I would be better off.

I sprinted right across the solid magical surface overlaying the lake, and through the portal, a chill washing over me as if I'd just passed through an incredibly icy and powerful cascade.

✣ 36 ✣

REJOINING THE TEAM

The crystal's portal took me to where I'd entered the Faerie Realm originally – the clearing where we'd tried to stop Astravar from entering the Second Dimension with his demon chimera and his crystal. It was the place where we'd taken down a load of Manipulators, and fought against a forest golem. I hadn't known what the outcome of the entire battle had been until now.

It was night, and it was absolutely freezing – particularly after having spent the last hours being toasted by lava and then crossing the scorching midday desert floor. But a campfire roared out from a little way away, and I gravitated towards it, letting the heat wash through my fur.

"Well, look what the cat dragged in," a familiar voice said from behind the fire once I reached it. It belonged to Initiate Rine, who peered around the fire, his chin lit red by the flames. All my friends who had travelled with me to the Willowed Woods sat there, save for Ta'ra. I paid them no heed. Rather, I scanned the ground for anything that could wet my tongue and stave off the thirst. I found a puddle of melted snow just by the campfire, and I lapped up the entire thing in several gulps.

As I drank, Aleam, Ange, Rine, Asinda, and Lars all fired a barrage of questions at me. Ange even stood up and walked over to me and stroked me at the back of the neck. But I needed to rehydrate myself before I dealt with trivialities, and so I sought out more puddles and drank to my heart's content. As I did, Seramina glared at me from her seat, in her usual disturbing fashion. Prefect Asinda also watched me with a suspicious frown.

"*Bengie,*" Salanraja said in my mind, and then she roared out from the sky. "*You've returned. What happened? I was so worried about you! I couldn't sense you anywhere.*"

I looked up to see her shadow pass overhead. The dragons weren't nearby, which meant they were probably on some kind of mission. As she spoke to me, the dragon riders stopped asking me questions, as if they knew instinctively I was about to have a conversation with Salanraja.

"*I went on a little adventure,*" I said.

"*I know that. But you just jumped right into the Second Dimension. You should have waited. We thought Astravar would kill you.*"

"*Well, he didn't. Although he almost did…*"

"*Why, what happened?*"

"*He sent me to the Seventh Dimension, and then I had to escape from the boiling lava, and I almost got eaten by a demon hippopotamus, but I got away.*"

Salanraja let out a mighty laugh in my mind. "*Ben, that's impossible. You must be pulling my little dragon foreleg.*"

"*It's true!*"

"*Then how did you get out? There's no way to return from that place unless someone opens a portal from another world.*"

"*Our crystal… I found a version of it in the Seventh Dimension, and it made me battle a chimera, then it told me I could turn into a chimera, and then it sent me back here even though I asked it kindly to send me home.*"

Salanraja hesitated a moment. I felt annoyance rise within her.

"*There you go again,*" she said.

"*What?*"

"*All you seem to ever think about is food and going home. Does our bond mean nothing to you Bengie?*"

"*Well, I'm sorry, but I didn't choose to come into this world.*"

"Suit yourself. But if I'm not important to you, I've got some scouting to do." She flew off and I didn't hear from her for a while.

Ange stood there with her hands on her hips, staring at me. But it wasn't an angry stare. She probably understood that I wanted to talk to my dragon first. Everyone here would understand, really. We were all dragon riders, after all.

Instead of having a civil conversation with my dragon, I'd just come back into this world for Salanraja to complain about my attitude. I would have thought she'd be telling me what a hero I was, and showing a little sympathy for me, and actually explaining to me why the ability to turn into a chimera might be useful.

But no! She'd had to give me a massive guilt trip instead.

Did all dragons treat their riders that way?

I stalked up to Ange and mewled, hoping for a little comfort. I rubbed against her leg, but I still felt a little tender and so I ended up groaning instead.

"Ready to speak now?" Ange asked.

"I think so," I said.

"Then come and tell us all about your adventures," she turned back towards the logs that Driar Aleam, the three Initiates, and the two prefects sat on. They had more sausages on sticks toasting over the campfire.

I jumped up next to Aleam, and mewled, purring. He looked down at me. "I guess you're starving," he said, and he tossed me a sausage from a bag. I devoured it gleefully. I might have had smoked salmon only minutes ago, but I'd only eaten it in my imagination and my stomach knew that.

Aleam tossed me a second sausage, and then a third, and I didn't feel good until I was halfway through that one. Then, I licked my lips, and I sat down and told my story.

When I got to the bit about becoming a demon chimera, everyone there seemed kind of shocked. They looked between themselves, and Seramina stood up and loomed over me. She glared down at me with those burning eyes, and I sensed something rummaging around in my mind, as random thoughts went through it. I hid behind Aleam's back so she wouldn't be able to do what she was planning.

"Did I say something wrong?" I asked from my hiding place.

"No, no," Aleam replied, and I could feel his voice vibrating through his back. "Initiate Seramina, I don't think there is any cause for worry." He shifted over, so Seramina could see me again. She was still glaring, but not as intensely I guess, or at least I didn't have that probing sensation anymore.

"Okay, so what's this about? I would have thought you'd all be happy to see me."

"We are," Ange said. "Believe us, we are. It's just…"

"What?"

Aleam placed his hand over my back and stroked down my fur. "You're different, Ben," he said. "We all know that."

"Of course, I'm different, I'm a cat."

"But you use two kinds of magic," Ange said, her mouth agape.

"What?"

Aleam stood up, and he drew some patterns in the dirt with his staff. "For a long time, no one since dragons and humans bonded, has been able to use more than one kind of magic. When you gained the ability to speak multiple languages, I thought your crystal had chosen you for mind magic. But now you also know alteration magic. We're all just a little surprised, as many of us were equally surprised when we discovered Seramina could use both mind magic and clairvoyance magic."

"But didn't you say that you were a dark magic user once?" I asked Aleam. "So you'd have been able to use lots of different types of magic, just like Astravar."

Aleam shook his head and took a deep breath. "I sacrificed that ability when I found my crystal and bonded with Olan. I lost my abilities, but I also lost the risk that dark magic would eventually consume my soul."

He stared into the flames a moment, as if remembering, and we all shared a moment of silence.

"So, what does this all mean?" Prefect Asinda broke the silence, standing up. She stood next to Seramina and gave me an almost equally unnerving glare. "It could be the crystal Astravar nestled inside him. Maybe it's corrupting him, pushing him towards the dark."

Prefect Lars stood up, took a place next to Asinda and held her hand. He looked down at me for a second, shook his head. "Sorry, Asinda, I can't believe that. Ben has helped us too many times. Surely, we must accept the rules are different now. I mean, no crystal has chosen a cat before as a magic user."

"Exactly..." Ange walked over to me and tickled me under the chin. "I couldn't believe that little Ben here could become an evil warlock. Could you, Ben?"

Rine snorted, and then he spat out some water, angering the flames of the fire.

Asinda turned her harsh gaze on him, then she spun it around on Ange. "Must I remind you, Initiate Ange, that I'm a prefect here, and you should show me some respect."

Ange turned away from her. "Sorry," she muttered under her breath, and she looked down at me. I rolled over on my back, and I let her tickle my tummy for a moment. Then, when it got a little too uncomfortable, I gently pawed her hand away.

"I think Prefect Lars is right," Aleam said, with his hand on his chin. "We have to accept things are a little different with Ben. Not only is he a cat, but he's also from another world. His crystal has already predicted things we'd never even have dreamed of."

"But what if his abilities make the cat turn evil," Asinda said. "What do we do then?"

High Prefect Lars squeezed her hand, and I wasn't sure if it was to encourage her against speaking out of place, or to communicate his support. Really, I thought having Bellari as an enemy was bad enough. But to know that Prefect Asinda wasn't on my side was worrying. With Driar Yila as her auntie, she already knew people in high places.

I wanted to open my mouth and point out that I'd helped save her. And as for Ange, it was she who used her leaf magic to break them out of their prison. She should be grateful for this, and I was just about to tell her so. But before I could get in a word, Aleam cut in.

"I'm sorry, but we have more pressing issues," he said, and he looked up towards the sky.

"What is it, Driar Aleam?" High Prefect Lars asked.

"I've just heard from Olan, and he's spotted Astravar."

"Astravar?" I asked. "Did he leave the Second Dimension?"

"He has his army of Cat Sidhe with him," Aleam said. "Much as your crystal foretold."

"Then we must stop him at once," I said.

"Yes, we must," Aleam said. "Everyone, call back your dragons at once from their scouting locations."

Though I didn't really feel like talking to Salanraja, I thought I would rather go with them than stay in the Willowed Woods alone, where a forest golem could smash me to smithereens. I reached out to call Salanraja back to our location.

Then we all listened as Aleam told us the plan.

37

THE PLAN

R ine, Ange, Lars, and Asinda beat out the fire with nearby
branches as they also turned an ear to what Aleam had to say.
This sapped the heat out of the surroundings and the wind that
buffeted through the willows was icy and cut to the bone. I never
thought I'd say this, but it actually felt good to have a little chill in the
air after coming back from the Seventh Dimension. In the distance, I
heard the howls and gnashes of wargs. But they didn't seem to dare
come anywhere near us magic users – which I guess was a wise
choice.

In a way, listening to the beasts, I wanted to turn into a chimera,
run out and teach them all a lesson. But I remembered what the
crystal had told me about not using the ability too much, and so I
decided it was better not to.

The Initiates and prefects had heard it before, but Aleam said he
wanted to check they completely understood their roles. Aleam also
explained, for my purpose only, how Prefect Lars would use his shield
magic to create a shield, while Aleam, Rine, Asinda, and Ange would
use their elemental magic to help give that shield strength.

Their goal was to protect Seramina in a protective force field, as
she used concentrated mind magic to reverse the spell Astravar had

cast on the crystal. The crystal had not only converted the fairies to Cat Sidhe but had also taken control of their minds. So long as it brimmed with power, every single Cat Sidhe in Astravar's army would be completely under his thrall.

"I still don't get it," I said. "Why do we need to do this reinforcing stuff? With lightning, ice, fire, and leaf magic, surely we have enough power to defeat Astravar."

Aleam shook his head. "Dark magic is a truly wild thing. It has a mind of its own. The warlocks weren't mad at the beginning, but prolonged use of this ruthless magic caused them to lose their minds.

"Astravar has gone so far down that path, that he now has enough power to destroy an unfortified magical barrier, powerful though Lars' shield magic is. If we leave ourselves undefended, we'll open ourselves up for attack from his minions, and the most important thing is for us to guard Seramina so she can take Astravar's crystal down."

"And your elemental magic can make the shield stronger?"

"Now you're getting the hang of it," Aleam said. "It's not actually the warlock we're dealing with, but the magic that has taken over his mind. We need to work as a dedicated team to defeat it. But I'm sure Driar Yila has explained this in classes, Ben. It's first-grade stuff."

I yawned as I thought of Driar Yila trying to explain things. I could swear she spent more time telling people off for things than actually teaching anything valuable. It was always the most trivial things that bothered her, like students drumming their fingers on their table, creaking their chairs against the floor, and sleeping in class.

"I forgot," I said, and I thought I'd better leave it at that.

Aleam rubbed his chin. "I'm sure you did..."

I tried to ignore his lack of confidence in me. "So, after this," I said, instead, "Seramina will break the crystal's magic, and the dragons will fight whatever Astravar throws at us. But we won't hurt the Cat Sidhe, will we? We won't hurt Be'las, and Go'na, and Ta'ra?"

"Not unless we have to," Rine said.

I glared at him. "And what's that meant to mean?"

"It means that we'll do everything in our power to keep the Cat Sidhe safe," Ange said. "That's one of our oaths in Dragonsbond

Academy – to protect non-magical life from those that seek to destroy it."

"I hope that doesn't mean we have to become vegetarian..."

Ange laughed. "I didn't mean it like that..."

A roar cut apart the sky, and Salanraja swept down to land. She'd been the closest to us, given she'd only just gone on scouting duty when I'd come through the portal. Given dragons could only communicate long distances without a rider, Olan had thought it better if she kept watch before I arrived.

She still didn't speak to me though, and that suited me just fine. I was tired and had enough information about magic running around my mind that it was making my head hurt. Seramina sat on the log, right next to the ashes of the fire. She glared at me like always. I remembered what Aleam had said about having to accept people even if they seemed a little odd, and so I decided I should try to connect to Seramina.

So, I went over to her, letting her heady snowdrop perfume wash over me. I sat next to her. For a while, she sat there stock still. Then, she surprised me by reaching out with a soft hand and stroking me gently on the back of the head. I purred – she felt better than I thought she would. Her hand was actually warm.

"I came over," I said, "to check that the Cat Sidhe are going to be in expert hands. Are you up to the task, Seramina? Because I'd do it myself, if I could use magic like yours. Is my friend, Ta'ra, going to be safe?"

"She's more than a friend to you," Seramina said.

"And what's that meant to mean?"

"I mean only what I read. Astravar's destiny isn't the only one intertwined with yours. Ta'ra's is too, as well as my own. The four of us are interconnected, I just wish I knew how."

Aleam turned to Seramina and looked at her with a slight expression of alarm on his face. I don't think she noticed but I did, and I made a mental note to ask the old man about it later.

"You really are odd," I said, as I pushed my nose into her hand.

"That's what people tell me," Seramina said. "But what do you expect of a girl who can manipulate minds and read destinies?"

"But aren't you scared? Because I would be if I were you. You have all that responsibility, and you have to stop Astravar destroying the city."

For the first time, Seramina looked away. "I'm absolutely terrified. But I still need to do it, because this is what my crystal has foretold."

I mewled and rolled over on my back, and she reached over to rub me with a delicate touch. "So, what exactly has your destiny told you?"

Seramina retracted her hand. "That's personal. No one should ask of the destiny of a seer."

"I'm just curious," I said, and I jumped down from the log to watch the other five dragons that flew towards us in a v-formation. Salanraja moved out of the way, to give them plenty of space to land.

"Well," Aleam said, as he dusted off his hands. "I guess it's time to be off then."

"Just one more thing," I shouted back. "You all have roles, but what should I do?"

"Stay out of trouble," Asinda said. "And keep within Lars' shield."

"Yes, ma'am," I said. Really, I was beginning to think she was more bossy than her Auntie Yila. Anyway, maybe I'd find a way to be useful. I had after all gained a new ability, and part of me was itching to try it out.

38

FLIGHT TO BATTLE

S alanraja took off into the sky first, and she wasn't gentle about it.
She beat me against her corridor of spikes as she whirled around
three times in the air. Really, I'd mastered flying so long as it was
gentle, but I hadn't yet toughened my stomach for such extreme
aerobatics.

"*Salanraja, what did I tell you about grace while flying?*" I asked.

"*I just thought I'd start knocking some sense into you... Literally.*"

I found it hard to get my thoughts together with me tumbling
around and around on Salanraja's back. The way she was going, I
thought she was planning to toss me right off her, and then I
wondered if she was going to catch me again. Maybe, she'd decided
that I wasn't useful to her anymore and her life had been so much
better before she'd found me.

I waited until she took a break from spinning around, and had
entered a glide, before I told her what I thought she wanted to hear.
Beside me, I heard Rine crying out in pleasure as Ishtkar did a half
loop-the-loop, followed by a half barrel roll in the air.

"*Fine,*" I said. "*I missed you when I was in the Second Dimension.*"

Salanraja crooned from underneath my feet. "*Do you mean that?*"
she asked.

"No... I'm just saying it, because I don't want your bad flying to cause me to throw up."

"You know," Salanraja said. "I quite enjoy 'flying badly'. Besides, Rine seems to enjoy it, so why don't you?"

"Because I don't have a sadd—"

I didn't have time to finish my thought before she did it again. She entered a corkscrew motion towards the ground, rolling over and over. All I could see was the world spinning below, and it looked for a moment like we were going to crash into the trees. Round and round I went, banging against Salanraja's spikes.

"Stop, Salanraja!"

She levelled out at my command. "Do you have something to say?"

"I can't take this right now. I went through quite a bit of torment in the Second Dimension, you know. Not to mention what happened in the Seventh Dimension after that."

"Fine," Salanraja said, and she pushed herself back up in the air to join the other dragons who had now entered a flying formation. Olan once again was at the front – Aleam looking again like he was moulded into the saddle. The wind whipped against my fur, and I rushed up to Salanraja's head, appreciating the sensation of it.

"This is much better. Now let's fly along pleasantly like this, shall we? We can worry about the fancy stunts if we encounter any of Astravar's bone dragons."

Salanraja laughed into the sky from underneath me. She shook her head a little as she did, but this time she was gentle enough not to risk throwing me off my perch. "I really missed you, Bengie. When you went into the Faerie Realm... I don't know, it's hard to describe. It's as if someone tore a piece of me right off my flesh and took it away forever. As if I'd lost a wing or something."

Strangely, I hadn't felt the same. But then I'd been so worried about Ta'ra, that I'd not really had time to.

"We've not always been together," I pointed out. "We did quite well before we met, don't you think?"

"But didn't you always feel that something was missing?"

"I've never even thought about it. Though now I do, I was quite happy in my world, until Astravar brought me over here."

"Didn't you feel somehow incomplete?"

"No... Did you?"

Salanraja let out a low and pronounced growl, and for a moment I thought she was about to start her bad-flying antics again. But she no longer seemed to have the energy for that, thankfully. *"I wasn't happy before. They said that they'd either have to cut off my spikes or they would force me to be a passenger dragon for King Garmin and his court. I didn't think I had a way out of it, until I found the crystal..."*

"What crystal?"

"It doesn't matter... I shouldn't have said anything."

But cogs were beginning to whirr in my head. *"The crystal?"* I asked. Then it dawned on me. *"You mean our crystal?"*

"I..."

"Salanraja, are you telling me that you knew about our crystal all along?"

Salanraja shook her head slightly, and I held on with my claws to stop myself sliding off.

"It wasn't until you entered the dimension," she said. *"Olan, Aleam, and I stopped Astravar from destroying it. We couldn't believe it at first. But it showed what you were capable of. It showed that you could defeat Astravar and help to save our kingdom."*

"So, you mean that when you met me for the first time, you knew that you were going to bond with me. Why then were you so angry and cruel to me? And why did you almost roast me alive when I was just hungry?" I didn't know how to feel, really. Salanraja had been lying to me all this time.

"What was I meant to say? Hello, you are destined to bond with me and defeat an evil warlock. You would have run away and never come back."

Now, it was me that was growling. *"You could have been a bit nicer to me at the start. There was no need to torture me in your corridor of spikes like you've just done. Admit it Salanraja, you just want to be in control of everything around you. You want to control me."*

"That's not true at all," Salanraja said.

"Then why did you try to scare me when you first met me?"

"Because you weren't the hero I hoped you'd be," Salanraja said, *"and I thought you needed to learn a few lessons in humility."*

"Is there anything wrong with being proud of my heritage?"

"Not if you behave the way your ancestors might have," Salanraja said. *"But it's not just about the food. I could sense that you put on a big show to hide how afraid you were of this world, and I wanted to help teach you how to handle it. How to exhibit true confidence in a situation you know nothing about."*

Part of me wanted to complain more. But then, I remembered how horrible it had been in Astravar's tower when he'd had me trapped there many days ago. I remembered how Salanraja had heard me when I was in trouble and saved me from getting eaten by a spider and its army of serkets. I remembered how she had hunted out so many delicious meals for me to eat.

"Thank you... I do appreciate you Salanraja. Though I wish you'd told me right from the start what I was getting myself into."

"It doesn't matter now, I guess," Salanraja said.

"I guess not..."

My ears twisted towards a sound coming from the distance. Crows. Thousands of them, cawing against the cold swishing wind. *"Do you hear that?"*

"Yes," she said, and it appears that we weren't the only ones who did, because from the centre of our formation, Olan cried out. Together, the dragons joined in the chorus, including Salanraja who tossed her head around as she roared. I scurried back down her neck into the protection of her second ribcage.

Aleam pointed with his staff at a glimmering object on the horizon. I could just make out a faint purple mist rising up around it, and as we got closer, I saw it to be Astravar's purple crystal.

The cawing from the crows intensified, and they scattered in a wide cloud. A cacophony of screeching roars then overtook the cawing, and a dozen bone dragons shot up into the sky. They barrelled towards us, but Olan was already leading our small squadron towards the ground. We swept down so fast, that we got right underneath the bone dragons.

We approached a thicket at the edge of the forest. Salanraja crashed through and touched down lightly. I couldn't see where the other dragons landed – all I could see was purple mist and the dust and leaves that the dragons had whipped up from the ground.

I sprinted down Salanraja's tail, then I looked out for the first Manipulator. It had its white staff pointed up at a bone dragon, leaching energy through the thick canopy through which I could ever so faintly make out the bone dragon wheeling around above. Salanraja took off to pursue the bone dragon, whilst I bounded towards the Manipulator.

I knew how to defeat it now, and I could see the glimmer where its crystal was. Without thinking, I leaped towards the wraith-like formation of spectral light. I took its crystal in my jaws, and then I scurried as fast as I could away from the creation, the crystal's magic burning in my mouth.

From a little way to my left, an ice bolt shot out and hit another Manipulator. To my right, I could see the forest writhing as well, as if being manipulated by leaf magic. Both Rine and Ange were therefore nearby.

Red light flared from overhead, and then a bone dragon came crashing down and shattered into parts when it hit the ground. I dropped the crystal to the floor, satisfied. *"Congratulations, Bengie,"* Salanraja said in my mind. *"Looks like we got the first takedown."*

"I guess we make a good team," I said.

Thunder cracked, then I heard the roar of fire shooting out from nearby. I smelled something charring, then lightning flashed from the sky. Soon after, came a sound like shattering glass, and the smoke in the air mixed with the smell of ozone. Two more bone dragons crashed down through the canopy.

Rine then came rushing towards me. At first, I thought he was pleased to see me. But then, I saw a Manipulator chasing after him. It was sweeping down its spectral staff in a slow arc, and I knew it would only be a matter of time before it fried my friend with its magic.

I put all my strength into my legs, and I rushed towards the ethereal creature. By the time I was upon it, its staff had started to glow, still pointed at Rine. I leaped in and took another crystal in my jaws. I carried it a safe distance away and deposited it on the ground. Then I turned around, and Rine bowed to me as if to say thank you.

Two more bone dragons came crashing through the forest, and I had to dive out of the way of one of them so as not to get crushed. I peered through the dust that the bone dragon had sent up into the air, to see Aleam pushing through the thicket, brushing off his hands. Prefect Lars charged in from the side and Aleam shouted out, "Everyone to me!"

Behind Aleam, a bright purple light pushed through the treeline. I guessed Astravar stood beyond that purple light, and he probably had his army of Cat Sidhe with him, including Ta'ra.

I didn't waste a moment. I bounded up to Aleam, and Rine, Asinda, Ange and Seramina quickly joined us. Once we were in place, Prefect Lars raised his staff to the air, and out shot a fountain of white light. This rose to a central point and then dispersed around us to form a large dome.

It made a terrible buzzing noise – as if we'd just discovered a beehive. I flattened my ears as much as I could to ward off the sound, and that was enough to at least concentrate on what was happening.

Staring at the shield was even more mesmerizing than watching birds through the window. It had a hypnotic effect on the eyes – the way that it sparkled and glowed. The magic seemed to pass over the shield, producing an effect much like rain washing over glass. Honestly, the way it looked, I didn't think it would hold anything out. It looked like even a mouse could pass through it, much like one passes through a waterfall.

I tested the shield by rubbing my nose against it. It let off this electrical stinging sensation, and I immediately backed away. It was definitely solid.

"Everyone ready?" Aleam asked.

Everyone gave their affirmatives.

"Right," Aleam said. "Charge!"

39

THE SHIELD

Though it was a charge, we didn't move particularly fast. We might have done if we didn't have Aleam within the shield. But he was an old man, and he wasn't on his dragon. So, we moved more at his hobbling pace. Prefect Lars also seemed to be moving incredibly slowly as he concentrated on feeding energy into this shield barrier that was meant to protect us. The dragons hovered above us, tracking us as we went.

"Now," Aleam said as we walked. "This is your first team shield. Remember what we talked about. I'll provide the energy first. Then, Asinda, Rine, and Ange you're to fuel the lightning with your elemental magic. Are we ready?"

"Yes, Driar Aleam," Asinda, Rine, and Ange said together.

"Good," Aleam said, and he pointed his staff towards the top of the shield. A yellow beam came out of the crystal at the top of his staff and met with Prefect Lars' beam. The air around me bristled with static, causing my fur to stand on end. Meanwhile, the shield wall took on a yellow hue.

Asinda, Rine, and Ange already had their staffs ready, and they also cast beams of red, blue, and green towards where Aleam's and Lars' beams met. The air around me tamed a little, and the shield took on many more colours, a spectrum washing across it as if someone had taken a rainbow and poured it all over this shield.

It was hot in here, and my mouth felt dry, so I stopped to take another drink of water as we passed a puddle on the ground. But I only managed to get a mouthful down before the shield wall caught up with me. It brushed against my fur, and then I felt a sensation in my side like a sharp static shock ten times magnified. I yelped and scurried away from the shield, and then decided to keep as close to Prefect Lars as possible.

Seramina had her staff poised, and her fiery eyes tracked the purple crystal as we approached it. A smell of fear accompanied her scent of snowdrop perfume, and so I mewled and rubbed against her leg to give her a bit of support. I thought it would be one way to be helpful so that she didn't mess up her task of destroying the crystal and saving Ta'ra.

It must have taken us a good five minutes of this slow hiking, to arrive on the scene. Astravar had set himself up in a hollow, bereft of plant life. But I wasn't sure if this was a natural phenomenon, or if he'd scorched the place with his magic for convenience. That same horrible stench rose from the ground, as always. Fortunately, though, I couldn't smell it now, and so it didn't affect my breathing. The crystal kept the mist out, and I could only smell everyone's sweat, Seramina's, Ange's, and Asinda's perfume, and a thick atmosphere of ozone.

It turned out that the crystal wasn't the only source of light here, but Astravar still had the portal open. Cat Sidhe were flooding out of it, coming out in groups of three, each the size of a panther. There must have been thousands of them, lined up in neat rows like cat soldiers and they were all staring at a point behind the crystal. Well, I say staring, but I was sure that their eyelids were sealed shut.

The lines cut off in the centre to form a circular space, maybe a hundred spine-spans wide. Astravar stood at the centre of this, his long cloak flapping in a wind we couldn't feel behind this shield barrier. The demon chimera stood next to him, grooming itself with its three heads. Fortunately, none of them were faced towards us.

The warlock had his back turned to us, and so he didn't seem to see us or the dragons approaching. Really, that surprised me as this shield was making such a racket that, even with my ears almost fully flattened, I could hardly hear myself think. Added to which, the combination of us and the dragons would have been incredibly easy to spot. Astravar's magic must have required intense concentration, which was probably why he would have sent those Manipulators and bone dragons to deal with us – so we wouldn't interrupt him.

Masses of purple crystals lay on the floor around Astravar and the chimera – no order to how they were arranged. They fed thin streams of light into the crystal on Astravar's staff, which he had raised high. This let out another beam towards the massive dark magic crystal that hovered overhead, much as it had in the fairy's throne room just before he'd banished me to the Seventh Dimension.

"What's he doing?" I asked Aleam.

Aleam was concentrating so much that his reply was slow. "He's charging the purple crystal. Presumably, the more power he can feed into it, the more powerful he'll be when he attacks Cimlean."

"*If* he attacks Cimlean …"

"He will."

"How do you know?"

"Because it's only ten miles in that direction," Aleam said, nodding towards where Astravar and the Cat Sidhe all faced. "Now shush. We need to focus. Seramina, are you ready?"

"Yes, sir," Seramina said, and she lowered her head and tightened her grip on her staff.

Aleam narrowed his eyes, and then looked up as if to double check the shield was sound. "Okay, let's do this," he said.

Seramina nodded, then took a deep breath. I moved in front of her.

"I'm here for you, Seramina," I said. "You can do this." I also gave her a nice, cute meow, to tell her that I really believed in her.

For the first time ever, I saw her smile. It was only for a moment then, immediately after, the lines on her face tightened and her jaw clenched. Her eyes, I could swear, flared bright red and a white beam erupted from her staff. It hit the crystal head on where it blossomed into a wide spot.

That was when Astravar finally noticed our presence. He pivoted around his staff, slowly, and though he was still quite far away his stare felt like he was right here looking at me. He opened his mouth as if to call something out, but with this incessant buzzing I didn't hear what he said.

It was as if an army of statues suddenly sprung to life. The Cat Sidhe all stood up as one, and they stalked towards us. They surrounded us with their fangs bared and their eyelids shut, and a few of them tested the shield with their paws. But their attempts to affect the shield bounded off it. I looked out for Ta'ra – remembering the mark I'd scratched on her cheek. I couldn't find her though.

In front of us, Astravar hunched his shoulders while he twisted his staff slightly. The flow of energy from the crystal to Astravar's staff reversed. Now, both the crystals on the floor and the massive dark crystal fed his staff, which he swung down towards us.

The beam swung with it, and it hit our shield straight on.

Prefect Lars grimaced, and clutched his staff with his second hand, his knuckles whitening. Everyone else took on equally contorted expressions, as the light from their staffs brightened even more.

"Keep it strong," Aleam said. "We can defeat him."

I wanted to do something too, but I felt absolutely powerless. So, I arched my back and hissed at the Cat Sidhe that circled around the shield to communicate that if they did find a way in, then they'd have me to deal with. Behind them all, the crystal had reddened around Seramina's beam, and this red was slowly spreading out across the crystal. It was only a matter of time before she destroyed the thing.

Meanwhile, Astravar seemed to realise that he wouldn't break the shield through his magic alone. So, he decided to change strategy, and his beam of magic switched from purple to blue.

The energy from his beam spilled out over the shield, forming swirling patterns that merged and coalesced into a roughly round shape. The shield buzzed even louder, but another sound started to take its place.

Astravar cackled like he had all the time in my dreams. It wasn't long until we could see his eggshell-skinned face, projected onto the shield, looking down on us with those lifeless grey eyes.

I shrieked, and then I hid behind Aleam. But this time, it wasn't me he had come to talk to. Instead, he went straight to the source...

He seemed to want to talk to Seramina.

40

DISRUPTED

"There you are, girl," the face of Astravar boomed from the shield wall. "At first I thought you were a mere mind-witch. But when I saw your magic, I knew you were something special. Now, I see why. I guess you've always wanted to know who you are."

Aleam turned over his shoulder and looked at her with an expression of alarm. "Remember what we talked about, Seramina. Whatever he says, you can't listen to him. You can't trust anything he says."

"Ah, Aleam," Astravar said, and he had to shout to make himself heard over the roar. "Always the old deceiver. When did you all plan to tell the girl the truth? Seramina, all that time in the orphanage, did you ever wonder why you were there? You lost your mother, but whatever happened to your father?"

"What's he talking about?" Seramina said.

"It doesn't matter for now," Aleam said. "We need to focus on the task at hand."

"Oh, and then what will you do?" Astravar asked. "Kill me? Really, Seramina, do you want to kill your own father?"

Seramina's eyes tightened, and the light went out from them. Her beam lost some of its energy, but she still kept it focused on the point. "You're lying... You can't be..."

"Of course he's lying," I said, and I went back over to her mewling and rubbed against her leg. "Astravar isn't to be trusted. He's a bad man, and he hurts people and cats... Focus, Seramina. Ta'ra's life depends on it."

She didn't seem to be listening to me though. Her eyes flared bright red again, and she turned her fiery gaze on Aleam. "Driar Aleam, what is this about? Is he my father?"

Aleam lowered his head. "I didn't think he would have a chance to talk to you."

"Just tell me the truth," she said through clenched teeth. Her hands were shaking, and I wondered if she was about to drop that staff.

"Seramina, whatever Astravar was, he isn't now. Now, the magic has consumed him. Please, thousands of lives depend on you breaking the magic in that crystal. You can't let him get to you."

Asinda walked over to Seramina and put her hand on her shoulder. "It's okay..." she said.

"Don't touch me," Seramina said, and Asinda backed off. Seramina cut off the white beam coming out of her staff, and she dropped the staff by her side.

"See, that's it..." Astravar said. "Let me do my job, and we'll get this underway. Maybe you'll later want to join me, daughter. Your magic is powerful, and I think you'll make a fine warlock."

But Seramina was shaking her head, tears brimming in her eyes. "Mother dying young, then all that time in the orphanage. Having to fend for myself. She never told me who my father was... No one did!"

"I was always going to come back for you," Astravar said. "Once I gained dominion over this world, there was no way I would let your life go to waste. Not with so much power inside of you."

"No!" Seramina shouted, and she raised her staff again. "I can't let you do this. I don't care who you are, but I grew up in Cimlean. You'll destroy everyone I ever loved."

"Did you really love them?" Astravar said. "The magic coursing within you. Why do you think you're so powerful? And you have destiny magic, I see. So, you already know our fates are intertwined. That magic – all your magic – I gave you a birthright. No one else alive has had such power since birth."

"No!" Seramina shouted again. "You've been corrupted. You might have once been my father, but you're not anymore." A flood of energy came back out of her staff. The crystal took on the same redness as before.

"Seramina, stop!" Aleam said. "You're pushing it too far."

His voice was soon drowned out by Astravar's maniacal laugher. "That's it, my daughter. Let the anger fuel you. Now if I only open a channel between us, I wonder what I might find."

The energy beam coming from her staff intensified, and it took on a slight purple hue. Seramina writhed about on the spot a little, and her face twisted. Her eyes burned ever more brightly, and her brows were furrowed as if in concentration.

"So much power, in there," Astravar said. "So much darkness. You never realized the potential. Now, all you need to do is sleep."

"Don't listen, Seramina," Aleam said. "Control your mind."

But Astravar hummed a deep and sonorous tune, and he managed it so loudly now that I didn't think Seramina could hear Aleam's protests. "Sleep, my darling," Astravar sang between hums. "Worry not about the light. In the darkness there is grace. Fear not my darling. From your fear you can escape."

His song was kind of mesmerizing – so much so that it almost sent me to sleep.

Seramina narrowed her eyes. "I don't care who you are. Just get out of my mind!" The air started to heat up around her, and it was as if a whirlwind erupted within the shield. It buffeted around her, and then I noticed the fire had left her eyes, and instead I could only see the whites of them, glowing with a purple sheen.

That was when the beam from her staff became a deep purple. Her magic lashed over the shield, causing it to crackle, as if someone had just thrown fireworks at it. The shield flickered, and its intensity faded.

"Astravar's possessed her," Aleam shouted. "Somebody do something."

Rine cut off his energy beam, and he edged towards Seramina. He didn't get far before another beam came out of her staff and threw him backwards.

"That's it, daughter," Astravar said, and he cackled maniacally. "Feel the power. You have my blood and can become just as powerful as me. A servant to my cause."

More beams came out of the staff, this time tentacles meant for Prefect Lars. They whipped against his feet and tripped him up. The shield fizzled out.

Above us, the dragons roared, and they went in to attack.

"*Be careful*," I called out to Salanraja in my mind.

She didn't say anything back, and I know what she would have said anyway. If she'd had a chance, she would have told me that fighting Astravar was much more important than her life. Much more important than the bond between us that she held so precious.

But the dragons didn't go far, because Seramina had a massive ball of purple magic glowing above her staff as the whirlwind whipped around her. It drew energy off the massive crystal hovering above Astravar, who had already mounted his demon chimera as if ready to flee.

The ball left Seramina's staff and shot upwards towards where the dragons had gathered. It exploded into one massive shockwave that sent all of them tumbling down from the sky. They crashed into the floor, at such speed that they looked like they must have broken bones.

As they fell, Seramina also fainted to the ground.

"Salanraja!" I screamed out loud. The other dragon riders also called out their dragons' names, and then all fell silent. With my heart thumping in my chest, I thought that our lives would be over then. Astravar would command his army of Cat Sidhe to devour us, and I'd probably get eaten by Ta'ra given how that evil warlock seemed to love irony.

But Astravar didn't seem to want to waste time, and he put two fingers in his mouth and whistled. The Cat Sidhe, who still surrounded us, growling, suddenly jerked upright and turned to face Astravar. Another whistle, and they were off, with Astravar leading them from his mount on the demon chimera, the crystal keeping pace above him.

For a moment, I watched after the Cat Sidhe army, sprinting soullessly after the purple crystal.

"Ta'ra!" I shouted. "Ta'ra..."

I had to stop her. I had to do something.

But I couldn't face them alone. They'd eat me alive. So, instead, I bounded over to Salanraja to check if she was okay.

❧ 41 ❧

TRANSFORMATION

I made a sad mewl when I saw Salanraja lying there on the ground, so helpless. I mean, I'd seen her sleeping, but then I could feel the fire burning in her belly as I slept next to her.

Now, there was no fire inside her. Aleam had told us the dragons weren't dead. But Seramina or Astravar had cast some kind of coma spell on them, and he didn't think they would wake up anytime soon.

I felt guilty. Salanraja had worried about me so much when I'd entered the Faerie Realm. Then, when I'd come back, she'd told me that my departure from this world had torn her apart. Meanwhile, I hadn't even considered Salanraja in the second dimension. I'd thought a lot about Ta'ra, while Salanraja hadn't even crossed my mind.

Now, I could feel that sense of emptiness inside me that Salanraja spoke of. It was as she'd described it – as if a part of me had been ripped away. Like losing my claws, perhaps, or my ears.

Aleam had found some spiky plant that looked a bit like aloe in my world, except with longer spines. He had broken this apart to access the sap inside, and he was walking around administering this to the other dragon riders, who rubbed it into the chest area near their dragon's hearts.

Only Seramina wasn't at work, and that was because she had

passed out. She now lay with her head propped up by her charcoal dragon's, Hallinar's, wing. The spell that she'd cast, Aleam had explained, had absolutely exhausted her.

Aleam had already tended to Olan and Hallinar, and now he came over to Salanraja and placed some salve on her body. It was green, sticky-looking, and smelled like the desert. I moved over to help rub it in.

"Best I do that," Aleam said.

"What, why?" I really wanted to feel helpful here.

"Because you will take half of the sap back away on your fur, and right now it's Salanraja that needs healing."

"Will she wake up?" I asked. "Is that what the salve is for?"

Aleam put his hand to his chin. "We can't apply anything to break the spell. But the salve will help the blood flow more readily."

"But when she wakes up, will she be all right? She took quite a fall. They all did. Maybe they broke some bones."

"Don't worry," Aleam said with a dry chuckle. "Dragons actually have quite a malleable bone structure, which comes as part of their magical make up. They can survive falls from incredible heights, and so yes, I'm sure once the dragons wake up then they'll be flying right back over to us."

"And when will they wake up?"

"It could be a matter of minutes, or it could be a matter of days. There's no way of knowing."

"Whiskers," I said. Meanwhile, we'd let Astravar march on Cimlean, and we had no dragons we could use to catch up with them. Olan had told Aleam that she'd sent out a call for reinforcements tele-pathically to Dragonsbond Academy when she'd discovered Astravar. But it would take them hours to get here, and Astravar would reach the city in an hour, if that. Of course, they also had a good twenty dragons in the city to stand guard. But with what Astravar had at his disposal, Aleam had told me we'd need all the dragons we had.

I was interrupted from my reverie by Seramina letting out a groan as she stirred. I walked up to her as she opened her eyes. She reached out, as if trying to find her staff. But Aleam had placed it in Hallinar's panniers for safekeeping.

Seramina stood up sharply and then moved towards Hallinar.

"Don't you move an inch," Prefect Asinda said, and she stormed over to Seramina and pointed her staff at her. "We need to know first whether you're safe. Who do you serve, Initiate Seramina?"

Ange strolled over to join Asinda. "With all due respect, Prefect Asinda, you can't just burn her with your magic. She's human, and she's probably on our side."

"Oh yeah," Asinda said, and raised her eyebrow at Ange. "Then you do something."

"Fine," Ange said, and turned to Seramina. "Sorry, but this is for everyone's safety." She pointed her staff at the ground. The leaves there stirred, and tree roots broke the soil. They grew quickly, tangling around Seramina's ankles.

Just as Asinda had instructed, Seramina didn't move an inch.

I walked up to her and sniffed her feet, and then I pushed my nose under the hem of her trousers, so I could sniff her skin as well. "She's fine," I said to Ange. "You can release her."

I looked up to her, and she glanced across at Asinda, who glared daggers at me. "You're not to listen to the cat, Initiate. What are you now, Ben? A diviner?"

"No," I said. "I can smell people's emotions."

"And is that some kind of dark magic too?"

"All cats can. Because when you feel things, you release chemicals into the air. And I can tell you that Seramina's scared, and she's stressed, and she feels embarrassed and you have nothing to fear."

Aleam sighed, and then he stood up and walked over to Seramina. He gently took hold of her chin and gazed into her eyes.

"She's fine… You can release her, Initiate Ange."

Ange nodded and pointed her staff at the ground again to loosen the roots' grip on Seramina's ankles. But it didn't seem to matter whether or not she had the bonds, because Seramina remained standing in the same place, her posture as rigid as a broomstick.

"You can move now, Seramina," Aleam said.

Seramina's posture melted. She turned to the old man. I walked around her to keep track of what she was doing with that stare. But her eyes had lost their fire, as if the tears streaming out of them had doused the flames.

"He took control of my mind. I'm sorry. I was weak, and he was so strong in there. I shouldn't have let it happen. I shouldn't have lost control."

Aleam gave Seramina a sympathetic look. "It's easier to beat yourself up about a bad experience than to learn from it. But that doesn't mean it's the best thing to do."

"But he used me. He didn't care about finally meeting his daughter. He just wanted to use my feelings about it to control me. And I let him..."

Aleam lowered his head. "We shouldn't have kept it secret from you. If you'd been prepared for it, he might not have been able to exploit it."

Seramina shuddered, and then she wiped away the tears with the back of her hands. Then she clenched her jaw. "This time, I won't let him get to me. I'll use my magic, and I'll destroy that crystal, and I'll show that warlock how strong I am."

"But how will we get there?" Aleam said, looking over his shoulder at Olan. "We've got no choice but to wait until the other dragons arrive, and by then I fear it will be too late."

"There is another way," I said. I stepped back into the spot where Astravar had previously stood underneath the crystal, and I mustered the power inside me.

Rine, having seen the commotion, had sauntered up over to stand next to Ange. Now, as he watched me, his eyes went wide. "You have to be kidding," he said, obviously understanding what I was getting at. "We ride dragons, not cats, and certainly not chimeras."

But Prefect Asinda seemed concerned for a completely different reason than pride. "Stop that!" She pointed her staff at me, its crystal glowing red and fire brimming at the front of it. "We don't need any more dark magic."

Lars stepped forward, and he pushed down her staff with his hand. "His crystal gave him that magic," he said. "And I think we should trust its judgement. It has everyone's best interest at heart."

Asinda let out a long sigh. "Fine..." she said, and she lowered her staff.

I waited a moment to see if anyone else had any intent of frying me. Satisfied all the dragon riders were now on my side, I began the transformation process.

When the crystal had told me I'd have the ability to turn into a chimera, it had never told me how painful it would actually be. My skin writhed underneath my fur, and my muscles bunched up, making me feel like my entire body would tear apart. My tendons tightened, an enormous lump grew out from my back, and my tail hardened with scales.

At the beginning the pain caused me to yelp and groan, but by the end of it, I was letting out what I imagined to be terrifying roars into the sky. Another part of me bleated, and I felt suddenly as if I had a second mind to use just like my first. Then there came this hissing noise from my tail, and I turned to see a snake poised right above my rear.

Except, it was strange, because I also had the mind of this snake, and I could shift my vision to see my head looking back, as well as my goat's head bleating out in pain. It all looked a little blurry through the snake's eyes, but I could also feel the temperature of everything around me in its glands. I could sense the heat emanating off the dragons and the dragon riders. I could see little mice and voles scurrying through the forest. I could see faint traces of things moving everywhere around me, from the birds in the sky to the earthworms wrestling underneath the soil.

My vision through the goat's head was a little less interesting. Through its eyes I could see normally, except without the colour red. But then, to make up for it, I could see virtually in all directions, as if I had eyes in the back of my head.

Really, I'd never considered how other animals saw before, but now I understood why the old Ragamuffin from back home said to avoid long grass because you never know when an adder is going to strike. With this kind of heat sensing capability, even a cat wouldn't stand a chance in the dark. The old Ragamuffin had also advised that if we ever saw anything with horns – be it a bull or a goat – then the first things we should do was run.

This was why, I guess, Salanraja had always told me to fear the chimera.

"Well," I said. "I hope I'm massive enough, because I feel strong enough to carry you."

Aleam laughed. "You're much bigger than I expected. Big enough for all of us, in fact."

"So, I guess everyone should hop on." Through the senses of all three heads, I could tell clearly where the Cat Sidhe had gone, especially as I smelled their pheromones in the air using my super-sensitive snake tongue – because, weirdly, snakes smell with their tongues and not their noses.

Ange, with her hands folded beneath her waist, looked back nervously at Quarl. "What about the dragons? We can't just leave them behind."

"I'm afraid we have little choice," Aleam said. "Besides, nothing's going to do anything to a dragon, sleeping or not."

"True that," Ange said, and she stepped forward.

"Then what are we waiting for?" I said. "Let's go and defeat Astravar."

Without further hesitation, the dragon riders mounted me. Seramina sat at the front, so she could have a direct view of the crystal in case she needed to attack it in flight. Prefect Lars sat behind her, then Asinda, then Aleam, then Ange, then Rine at the back. I thought they'd all be heavy. But honestly, this chimera transformation must have included super-strength, because I hardly noticed their weight.

"Ready?" I called.

Everyone murmured their consent, and I bounded off over the plains leading to Cimlean, following a scent that I'd come to know all too well.

42

CIMLEAN CITY

I don't know how long it took me to reach Cimlean, but I'm sure it took much less time than I'd thought it would. I used to think that I was fast as a Bengal. But now, with these goat's legs to power my rear and give me a spring to my steps, and my lion paws to keep me stable, I covered the ground faster than I'd ever known. I probably went even faster than the Cat Sidhe.

I stopped on a rise around a mile before the city so we could assess the battlefield. The city looked just as the crystal had shown me in the vision of it getting destroyed. The white walls contrasted against the surrounding snow, giving the whole place an impression of innocence. The golden towers shone out from behind the walls, and archers stood looking out from upon the walls. They had their bows raised waiting, it seemed, for the Cat Sidhe to charge.

These Cat Sidhe sat below, still panther-sized, staring at the city as if awaiting orders from their master who stood at their centre, his demon chimera by his side. Like before, he had a massive circle cleared around him, with the crystal hovering overhead to give him room to cast his magic.

I wondered if the Cat Sidhe could grow large enough to knock down the walls and cause carnage throughout the city. If they could do that here, they could do it anywhere. Who'd have thought that the death of humans wouldn't be caused by famine or plague, but by massive rampaging cats?

Although it wouldn't be caused even by that because we were going to stop him.

Astravar already had his crystals ready from his pouch. He threw these into the air, and purple sparks from the overhead crystal gave them energy. They lit up like comets, and they charged towards the archers. I only saw them ever so faintly, but I knew what was going to happen next.

The magical crystals would burrow themselves in the archers' foreheads. Then, the archers would become possessed by the crystals, much like the Cat Sidhe had. They'd turn their bows on the city, and light their arrows, setting their own houses aflame. Once carnage had been wreaked, the Cat Sidhe would charge in, and the city would soon be Astravar's to claim as his own domain.

I had hoped that the warlock wouldn't have made it this far. But his conquest had already started. Which meant we had to move fast.

"This is it then," I said loud enough for everyone on my back to hear.

"It sure looks like it," Aleam said. I couldn't see him through my cat's eyes, but I could see the back of his head through my snake's eyes. "Everyone dismount, then Lars get the shield ready."

"Should I turn back into a cat?" I asked. One thing I remembered from Driar Brigel's lesson on alteration magic was that if I stayed in any form long enough, then I risked becoming it. Though this chimera had its uses, I didn't want to take it as a permanent form. Honestly, I felt like the other two heads were cramping my style – particularly the one of the goat.

"You should probably hold this for a while, Ben," Aleam replied. "A chimera might have its uses."

"Like what?" I asked. "We'll be inside the shield."

"I don't know," Aleam said. "But I'm sure Astravar has more tricks up his sleeve."

I growled, not so much because I was angry but because it felt good to growl with a lion's voice. High Prefect Lars raised his staff and called out for us to join him. We all gathered together, and Lars cast the shield, which buzzed like a thousand bees all around us. Then Ange, Rine, Asinda, and Aleam cast their elemental magic to strengthen the shield. Meanwhile, Seramina kept her staff ready. I could smell fear in her, but I could also smell anger, and I could see in her expression that she really didn't want to mess this up. The air once again took on that magical scent of ozone.

It took us a good five minutes to get close enough to the crystal for Seramina to do any damage. The crystal hovered in the air, with Astravar standing underneath it. The Cat Sidhe surrounded him in an obedient circle. This time Astravar wasn't casting any magic, and he saw us approach.

He decided this time not to project his face on the sphere. But rather, he spoke out in my mind. Usually, I guess Seramina would have done something to keep him out of there. But she had her eyes focused on the crystal as she readied her staff.

"*Dragoncat,*" he said. "*How fitting. You've gained your second ability. Now, I see you're a chimera.*"

"*Astravar,*" I replied. "*We won't let you take the city.*"

"*Oh, how quaint. It looks like you've learned the virtues of teamwork. But don't you think a team's much better when they're all under your command?*"

"*I think not. They're better when they feed you and look after you and comfort you when you're feeling down.*"

Astravar cackled out in my mind. "*You're still the same old cat. How you can even consider that you can defeat me with such a ridiculous attitude, I don't know.*"

"*I'm not going to defeat you this time...*" I waited for a moment until the mind magic beam erupted out Seramina's staff and hit the crystal dead centre. "*Seramina is.*"

"*Hah, I didn't think she'd come back for another pass. I guess she's strong – she has my blood after all.*"

"*You're not strong. You're weak and you're a coward.*"

"*Really? How so?*"

"*Because you let the dark magic consume you when you could have fought back against it. Now, you're destroying the world, even though there's part of you inside that should try to reconcile with your daughter. You never had the courage to fight the dark magic inside you. Seramina does, though. And, so do I!"*

"Oh yeah," Astravar said. *"Well, maybe I am a coward. But, you know, there's one thing about cowards. They're much better at surviving than heroic fools. Now, dragoncat, I've had enough of your meddling. I thought you'd make a useful minion one day, but I've decided you're better off dead."*

By this point, fissures had spread out across the faces of the crystal, and it looked like it would break apart. If Seramina could rip the thing into pieces, then the spell on the Cat Sidhe would be lifted. All I had to do was keep Astravar talking.

But he wasn't stupid, and he already had plans of his own. He pointed his staff at us and out of it came a purple beam that hit the shield dead on at around knee height. At the same time, his demon chimera tossed its head upwards and let out a roar. I didn't hear it from this side of the shield, with the constant buzzing and humming noises that grated in my ears. But I could feel the anger in it, all the same.

A sudden flash of light spread out around the impact point on the shield. This cloned itself on our side of the shield. The centre of the light evaporated, to create a kind of halo, looking as if Astravar had cut a hole right out of the shield. The sound around us cut off, and time seemed to distort. A sudden cutting breeze washed in through the shield, and I shuddered as it brushed over my skin.

Through that hole, I saw the demon chimera bounding towards us.

43

CLASHING HORNS

"What in the Seventh Dimension?" Aleam said. "A double portal."

"A what?" I asked.

"No time to explain. Brace yourself, Ben. Astravar can only hold the spell for a moment."

I growled, my eyes fixed on the red smouldering eyes of the demon chimera's lion's head. It growled as well as it leapt through the double portal which closed behind it, sealing it in. The demon chimera's eyes weren't on me but Seramina, and it charged towards her. But I moved to block its path. It rammed into me and we tumbled across to the other side of the shield dome.

For a moment, I saw Seramina's tiny shoes, and I thought we'd trip her up. But she side-stepped out of the way just in time.

"Seramina, keep it steady," Aleam said. "Ben will take care of this."

Too right I would. I had the demon chimera pinned down with my paws on its shoulders. It roared at me, and its nauseous, sulphurous breath washed over me. I bit down towards its neck, but it clawed at my face, causing a painful gash that felt like three iron pokers hitting me at the same time.

My goat's head was bleating, and my snake's head was hissing.

Meanwhile, I roared out in pain as well, just as the demon chimera threw me off it. I tumbled across the ground, sending up dirt and dust.

The demon chimera picked itself up again, and it approached Seramina more slowly this time, its snake head raised in the air. She didn't seem to notice it there, but Aleam swung down his staff and sent a bolt of lightning at it. But this didn't seem to harm the beast much. Naturally, I guess – I remembered from my lessons that demons could only be slowed and not harmed by magic.

"I've almost got it," Seramina said. "I just need one more minute."

But she wouldn't have that minute, as I could already see the demon chimera's snake head lurching towards her. I didn't waste a moment. I charged right at it and caught the snake's head in my jaws. I overshot a little and ended up pulling the demon chimera along the ground with me. I grunted as I hit the shield wall, stinging my face. I released my grip, and the demon chimera's snake bit me on the side of my rump. It felt like being stung by a large wasp. I guess I was too massive a beast for the venom to affect me like it had before. Despite that, if I took enough lashes from that thing, it would probably kill me.

Outside the shield, the king's dragons had risen from the city, and they were flying towards Astravar. Astravar and his army of converted archers were now fighting back against the dragons, and so they kept high in the air – probably unsure what to do. A flash of panic shot through me as I thought they might attack the Cat Sidhe army. They might kill Ta'ra. Fortunately, though, Astravar's magic was keeping them at bay.

In front of them, the crystal's fissures now ran deep. White light fizzled underneath the cracks, and the whole thing looked like it would erupt within moments. But if the demon chimera took down Seramina, then I didn't doubt Astravar would win.

It was then that I noticed there weren't as many Cat Sidhe amongst Astravar's ranks as before. Instead, I noticed gold specks glistening in the sky. Whiskers, Astravar was about to send fairies out to sacrifice their lives and bring the king's dragons down. They'd explode, and die, and Ta'ra could be amongst them. But I couldn't do anything but fight the chimera and hope Seramina would break the crystal soon.

Meanwhile, the demon chimera had circled around to face me. It had realised, I guess, that there was no getting to Seramina without going through me first. We circled each other, growling, our gazes locked on each other. The buzzing of the shield seemed to get even louder, and then I saw what the thing was doing. It was trying to back me into the shield so it would fry me. It would be a quick death – I guess – electrocuted, burned, frozen, and warped from the magic that Aleam, Asinda, Rine, and Ange cast against the shield.

But then, I realised it was only a matter of timing. I stopped myself still, facing the demon chimera head on, making myself a target. It seemed to accept the challenge, and it scuffed its back hooves in the ground, and charged, lowering its goat's head, ready to ram me into the shield. I counted to three, then I lowered my goat's head and our horns locked.

The demon chimera had the momentum, and it pushed me back a little, sending my rear into the shield. It burned there, and I felt the intense pain where the chimera's snake had bitten me before. The snake on my tail hissed, and for a moment the pain was so intense that I thought I might as well give up. My snake's vision, my goat vision, and my lion's vision all went hazy, and I was just about ready to quit and die.

This was a demon I was facing, after all. It was far too strong.

"You must defeat the chimera..."

The crystal's voice, I heard it in my head then.

"Not the chimera without, the chimera within."

Suddenly, I realised what it was talking about. Astravar had given up when he'd lost the battle against dark magic and succumbed to it. But Aleam had been a hero and kept his will strong. I also needed to be the hero, because though I faced off against a demon, my chimera was a creation of magic. I only needed to will the strength and I would find it.

I roared from my lion's head, tucked underneath my chest. Meanwhile, my goat's head shrieked, and my snake's tail lashed out. I willed strength into my rear hoofs, and I used my front lion's paws to keep purchase against the ground. I pushed with all my strength, and after a couple of inches, I was free of the shield.

Then, inch by inch, I pushed the demon chimera back. And I continued to push, and though my nemesis struggled against me, it didn't have enough will within it to hold on. I mustered more strength within, imagining myself as a stampede of goats charging at the demon chimera. It bleated, and it growled, and hissed as I backed it into the shield. I pushed it even further until I could smell smouldering rock and the sulphurous fires of the earth.

Soon enough, the beast collapsed on the ground, and the fires underneath its cracks went out.

A bright white light then flared out from in front of the city. This faded, to show the crystal shattering into pieces, shards of it scattering in every direction. Some of these hit the shield, sending up blue sparks on the outside.

The Cat Sidhe remaining on the ground immediately came to life, and they surrounded Astravar with their lips bared in fearsome snarls. They closed in on him and they looked ready to tear the warlock to shreds and eat him for lunch. It was ironic really, given that the fairies had been vegetarians in their own kingdom.

In response, the warlock raised his staff to the sky and a flash of bright purple light shot out of it. This faded, leaving a trail of purple mist surrounding a clump of snow, and a crow flying away towards a large flock awaiting it in the distance.

44

THE CURE

Prefect Lars lowered the shield, and I transformed back into a Bengal, not wanting to listen to the ingratiating hissing of the snake, and the ear-piercing bleating any longer. I'd decided by this point that the three animals that made up a chimera weren't really smart choices. In truth, snakes, lions, and goats hated each other, and it seemed strange to me that the mythical chimera didn't end up eating itself whole.

Meanwhile, the demon chimera I'd just defeated had since turned into a pile of ash. I looked down at it in curiosity, sniffing at the remains. "I thought magic couldn't kill a demon," I said to Aleam.

Aleam shook his head. "Not normal magic, no."

"Then why did this work? Because it looked to me it got destroyed by the shield."

"No," Ange said. "You did that, Ben. Your chimera strength backed it into a place where it had nowhere to go."

"You mean I crushed it."

"Like against a wall," Ange said. "You should have seen yourself, Ben. You were so strong." She pretended to flex a bicep, and then giggled.

I raised my head, pride coursing through my mind. Rine went up to stand by Ange, and Lars went over to stand by Asinda. Seramina, meanwhile, was looking out at the flock of crows in the distance, tears in her eyes. Aleam had found a rock to sit down on, and he rested there, his breathing heavy.

I thought I should leave humans to do human things. So, instead, I went over to find Ta'ra in the army of Cat Sidhe. Part of me wanted to think that Astravar had done something terrible by casting this spell on all these fairies. But then he had also turned them into the greatest creature that had ever lived, and I was sure they'd see the benefits of being a cat soon.

Though they still didn't understand it, because the Cat Sidhe who hadn't yet turned into fairies did so one by one. They didn't take their glamour forms, but instead their golden floating specks floated across the sky, making everything look so pretty and pure. If they were anything like Ta'ra, then they could only transform eight times. Now, they were using their first transformation – probably because they couldn't yet accept who they'd actually become.

Soon, only two black cats with white diamond tufts on their chest remained. I stalked over to them, still with my head held high. One of them I knew just from her smell, it was Ta'ra and it was great to see her again.

Ta'ra turned to me, and she looked at me with her bright green eyes.

"Ben, I'm so sorry… I could see what I was doing. Although it was me when I led you to Faerini city, I thought I had control over myself. But I didn't realise that Astravar could seize my mind at any time."

"It's okay," I said, and I rubbed my face against hers. "Just let me have a little extra of your mackerel next time."

"Oh, so it was you that took it?"

"No… I wouldn't dare. You must have eaten it when possessed. Maybe Astravar was testing his connection to you or something."

Ta'ra looked off into the distance. "I guess." Then she turned to her companion. "By the way, did you ever meet Ta'lon?"

That was something I didn't want to hear. I turned to Ta'lon, and raised my back, hackles shooting out of it. "Ta'lon, your betrothed."

The male Cat Sidhe looked up at me. "Yes," he said. "What of it?"

"You cast her out of your society, and you were horrible to her. How do you think I would have felt if my humans just threw me out on the street?"

Ta'lon lowered his head. "It was years ago that I ordered Ta'ra evicted from our society. For many days since, I've regretted that decision from the bottom of my heart."

"You shouldn't have even done it in the first place," I said, growling at the prince.

"Ben, be civil," Ta'ra said. "And Ta'lon, before you get any smart ideas about fighting Ben, remember that he helped save your skin."

"And I'm a Bengal, descendant of the great Asian leopard cat," I pointed out. "I could probably teach you a thing or two about fighting. At least if I faced you at a fair size."

"I don't want to fight you," Ta'lon said. He yawned in a surprisingly cat-like way. "I'm still getting used to this… form."

"You soon will, and you'll realise it's the greatest form you can have," I said, lowering my back. This Ta'lon guy might have hurt Ta'ra, but otherwise he didn't seem all that bad. Although I still felt threatened by having another tomcat near Ta'ra.

"*See what I mean,*" Salanraja said. "*You like her.*" After Seramina had broken Astravar's spell, the dragons had since woke up and were flying over to our location. They were getting closer now, so I could faintly hear Salanraja inside my mind.

"*Oh, shut up,*" I said.

"*Fine,*" Salanraja said. "*We're almost there now. I can't believe that I missed seeing you as a chimera.*"

"*And I hope you never get to see me that way again.*"

I looked over my shoulder to see that Aleam had lifted himself off his perch. He hobbled over, leaning on his staff and clutching the vial containing the yellow liquid in his free hand.

My heart sank. Whiskers, the cure, I'd completely forgotten about it. All this time to save Ta'ra, and now she'd probably drink the stuff with Ta'lon, and they'd go home together, and I would be a lonely cat in a strange land once again.

Ta'ra blinked at Aleam as he approached. "Is that the cure?"

Aleam looked at her, then at Ta'lon, then back at her again. "It is," he said. "I perfected it with a special ingredient."

"And what was that then?"

"Mandragora root. Enough to reverse the magic in one dose, I think. So long as you haven't used all of your nine transformations. But, unfortunately, there is only enough for one."

I purred and rubbed up against Ta'ra once again, feeling a little sad. "Are you going use it?"

Ta'ra didn't answer the question immediately, as she still had more she wanted to ask Aleam. "Mandragora. That only grows in the far reaches of the Darklands, right?"

"Ruled by the warlocks, with their magical conjurations guarding every mile, it is incredibly risky to obtain."

"And there's only enough for one dose, right?"

Aleam nodded slowly. "Unfortunately so."

"Then," Ta'ra said, turning to Ta'lon. "You should take it, Ta'lon."

"What? No? Ta'ra, I was fool enough to lose you once. I don't want to leave you again."

"But you will always have a place in my heart, my prince," Ta'ra said. "In a way, you were right to cast me out. The fairies would have never accepted me in this form, and it will take them a long time to accept the Cat Sidhe as they now are."

I don't know why, but Ta'ra's professions of affection for Ta'lon made my heart sink even more. Whiskers, it was almost as if I was becoming human. After I'd learned the language and tasted their magic, now I was feeling emotions a cat shouldn't feel.

Ta'lon lowered himself on his haunches. "Then what would you have me do?"

"Return home. Help your father and the other leaders in the Faerie Kingdoms understand that Cat Sidhe are not evil fae. We've not been corrupted, and we can live amongst them. They need to learn how to accept us."

"Or," Ta'lon said. "I can retrieve some Mandragora so that we can make more of the cure."

"No," Ta'ra rubbed her nose against Ta'lon's. "Ta'lon, you cannot fight the warlocks. They've become too strong, and they're becoming stronger. Please, do this for me."

Aleam uncorked the vial, and he approached Ta'lon with it. "Are you sure about this, Ta'ra?" he said. "I did develop it for you."

"I'm sure," Ta'ra said.

Aleam nodded, and he held out the vial towards Ta'lon. Ta'lon looked at Ta'ra with eyes even brighter and greener than hers. He paused a moment, then he lowered his head and approached the vial. Aleam tipped the liquid down the Cat Sidhe's throat, and then he took a step back.

A plume of golden smoke rose around Ta'lon. The cold wind soon blew this away, leaving a golden wisp that floated there for a moment, then glided away.

Ta'ra watched it go.

"What will you do now?" Aleam asked her.

"I'll wait here until the other Cat Sidhe turn back into cats again. Then, I'll help them set up a commune. They'll need to learn how to survive in this world. Because I feel it will be a long time before either we find a cure, or the fairies learn to accept us."

I mewled, sadly. "Can I come with you?" I asked. "I could be your teacher. Everyone can learn how to be a cat from me."

Aleam laughed. "I think you need to finish your studies at Dragonsbond Academy, Ben. But maybe when they've settled somewhere you can visit them."

"I guess," I said. "So, what happens next?"

"Well," Aleam said. "I'm just waiting for the king's guards to ride out of the city. I'm expecting they'll request an audience with us."

"You mean I'll get to meet a king?"

"You will," Aleam said, and he raised an eyebrow, probably because he caught the sarcasm in my voice.

"Big deal," I said. I honestly didn't get the whole monarchy thing. No one ruled over us cats and kept gold in treasuries and told us what to do. We just roamed the land as we pleased.

I turned to see Ange and Rine looking out towards the city. Rine had a hand on Ange's shoulder, and I wondered if this was finally a display of affection from him to her. But when Rine saw me looking at him, he retracted his hand, and his face went red.

Nearby, Prefect Asinda and Prefect Lars held hands, their staffs clutched in their free hands, with the bases resting against the ground and the crystals glowing red and white.

Seramina, meanwhile, sat on the rock where Aleam had been previously staring out into space. Her cheeks were wet with tears. I went over, thinking both that I could provide her comfort and she could provide me some too. I leapt up on her lap, and she reached down and stroked me, but she didn't look at me.

"So that's that then," she said. "I guess I'm truly alone."

I held that thought for a moment. Then I decided otherwise. "No," I said. "I don't think you are. None of us are."

That caused Seramina to look down at me. "How come?"

But I didn't need to answer that question, because from the direction of the Willowed Woods came a loud roar that cut apart the horizon. I remained silent, because Seramina knew, and I knew, and every one of us dragon riders present knew as we turned to face the seven dragons approaching over the horizon.

We would never be alone again because we had our dragons. And I guess I was starting to accept I'd be bonded to Salanraja for life.

EPILOGUE

D rat! Defeated by a cat again! I couldn't believe it. One time was injury, the second was insult. How could I, the mighty Astravar, let such a hopeless creature get in my way? The dragon rider teenagers were bad enough, but for a cat who used to be my minion to take up magic, destroy my beloved demon chimera, and stop me claiming the throne of Cimlean as my own… It caused hate to curdle in my mind.

Part of me wanted to reach out and taunt him using telepathic dark magic. But I couldn't bear the thought of his voice. I had to do something about him. If I couldn't destroy him alone, then I would get help. Anything to get him out of my path.

Then, there was my daughter. Many years ago, I might have felt sad about being rejected by her. But whenever even the slight hint of sadness emerged in me, I felt the magic coursing through my veins, and I remembered that guilt served no purpose in me anymore. Still, now I knew who she was I would have to find a way to convert her to my cause. All this, I would do in due time.

These were the thoughts milling around in my head, as I approached the floating platform. The dragon riders, I believed had their Council, and this was the location of the Council of the

Warlocks. When, that was, we decided it necessary to meet. It must have been at least thirty years since we stood here last.

My crow kin had left me now, and I was flying alone as a crow above the beautiful magical mist that limned the Darklands. Right in the centre of this land hovered the platform on which we held these extremely rare councils. From the sky, it looked like a cog with seven long teeth. Seven crystals held the platform afloat high up in the clouds, each placed right underneath the teeth.

All seven of us had placed magical wards on our sides of the inner circle. To stand on any wards that weren't our own, or even to try and cross them by air would mean instant death. We also had our minions – stone golems – guarding the centre of the platform. We warlocks were paranoid, and I guess naturally so.

The glyph in the centre of one cog-tooth lit up as I flew down towards it. It displayed an image of a crow in flight, and this was the place I should stand. Here, I had to abide by the rules we'd all set. Do not try to cast magic. Do not raise my staff for any purpose whatsoever.

I was the first to arrive, and so I scanned the sky looking for the other warlocks. I'd summoned them through the magical ether – a spell we all knew how to cast and reserved for the most desperate of moments. We all favoured the ability to turn into birds that scavenge. I saw Cala first – a huge white seagull screeching into the air. She landed in her place opposite me, purple mist rising around her.

Her form when she emerged was of a beautiful red-haired woman. This one hadn't lost her looks, but then she'd used her magic to keep them. Junas came down next, a vulture. He was tall and lanky with a hooked nose and bald head. Then came Ritrad, the youngest of the warlocks. He was a buzzard, and his human form was giant and muscular. Lasinta took the condor form, and she was old and frail as a human. Moonz landed as a bald eagle. As a human he looked almost old as Lasinta, but of sturdier build. Finally came Pladana, a hawk. She was small and wiry as a human.

A moment of silence passed between us, as we let ourselves collect our thoughts. It lasted about a minute, before Lasinta called out. She was the oldest, and we'd decided she should always lead the council. Though, I hadn't really had much of a say in this matter.

"We haven't had a Council of the Warlocks for thirty years. What say you, Astravar?" Lasinta asked.

I explained the situation as succinctly as I could. I told the warlocks how Dragonsbond Academy was gaining power. How I'd found myself so close to defeating them, only to have been foiled by their new rising stars. I didn't mention one of them was a cat, nor did I mention another was my long-lost daughter. They didn't need to know those things.

The other six warlocks listened in silence. But I knew they weren't just listening; they were calculating. Working out exactly what I had to give, and how they could use this to gain magical power. I knew the game too well, which was why I was being extra careful not to give anything away.

After I'd finished, I took a deep breath, and we waited again in silence for someone to speak. Eventually, it was Moonz – the oldest male warlock, who'd landed as a hawk – who asked the question they all probably wanted to ask.

"What are you proposing? All you've given us so far is information. But I'm guessing you wouldn't have called us here without a plan."

I steepled my hands in glee. I hadn't thought it would be this easy to get them to listen. But no one yet had asked for anything to trade. They might have wanted crystals, or for me to hand over some of my minions to serve them.

"The dragon riders and the Kingdom of Cimlean are becoming too powerful. If we don't do something now, then they will eventually destroy us."

"Are you suggesting a war?" Moonz asked.

"That's exactly what I'm suggesting. All-out war. If we can combine our forces now, then we can defeat Dragonsbond Academy, and we can wipe out King Garmin's military. After that, we can decide amongst ourselves how to divide the spoils."

Another long silence ensued. I'd delivered the last line on purpose, because everyone here knew what it meant. We would unite to kill our common enemies, then we would turn amongst each other and battle amongst ourselves.

But clearly, given that the cat's destiny and mine were intertwined, I didn't have the power to defeat it. These warlocks were independent from that destiny, and so any of them could sever the link between me and the cat.

"We shall put it to the vote," Lasinta said. "Raise your staff and light it if you want to go to war."

I raised mine immediately to show that I was fully behind my plan. It lit up with a bright purple light, emitting a beam into the clouds above. Pladana raised hers next, and then Cala. Junas, and Ritrad followed. Moonz then raised his, and Lasinta raised hers last.

Soon, seven lights shone up into the sky – beacons for all of our minions down on the surface to see.

"It is so," Lasinta called out.

"Good," I said, as we all lowered our staffs together. "Then I suggest that we take stock of our inventories and then meet back here in three days to discuss our plans."

I didn't wait for an answer. I wanted to show them that I had things to do. So, I let the purple mist rise around me, breathing in its cold, heady scent. I was soon a crow, flying into the Darklands, cawing out my victory to the world.

Finally, the time to destroy the kingdom and start my conquest of the seven dimensions was nigh.

A CAT'S GUIDE TO SAVING THE KINGDOM

DRAGONCAT BOOK 3

CHRIS BEHRSIN

To my brother Tim, and his two cats Raffy and Taffy – three incredibly generous individuals.

DRAGON EGG-AND-SPOON

Purple mist loomed on the horizon. It stretched out from expanse to expanse, and beyond it stood the warlocks and the threat of war. It whipped up a stench in the air, reminiscent of rotten vegetable juice. It brought with it a bitter wind that seeped right through my fur, washing away what should be the warmth of spring.

The warlocks weren't far from Dragonsbond Academy now, and beyond it – so all the Driars said – were thousands and thousands of magical creatures, an army growing by the day. But they would be no match for us, because we had dragons, and we had magic too, and we also had me.

To many, I was just a cat. But to the prophecies, I was a mighty Bengal, descendant of the great Asian leopard cat. The crystals foretold I would defeat the most powerful of warlocks, Astravar. Just as soon as I finally worked out how to get my staff, I could fly out there on Salanraja's back, nestled within her corridor of spikes that served as a natural saddle for cats. Then, with said staff clenched between my strong feline jaws, I would shoot a beam of energy at him. I'd knock him off his bone dragon, and I'd finally be able to rest.

I just wished I could fast forward to that point. Because, right this moment, I wasn't flying towards the mist with a staff in my mouth.

Instead, I had a spoon sticking out of it, with an egg balanced precariously on top of it, and I felt like an absolute fool.

"*Can't I just drop the egg?*" I asked inside my mind to my dragon, Salanraja. "*This is tremendously boring, and my mouth hurts...*"

"*Gracious demons, no,*" Salanraja said. "*We have a chance of winning this, and I want to show the other dragons how magnificent I can be, even with my 'unnatural' spikes.*"

"*But what's the point of it all? Eggs are much better for eating than carrying in your mouth on a spoon.*"

"*Prestige,*" Salanraja said. "*And that is worth all the food in the world.*"

Really, there was no telling my dragon. No matter how much I argued with her, she kept telling me we had to win at least one event on 'Sports Day'. Or at least if we couldn't win, she thought we had to at least try.

It was ridiculous, really. I would much rather sit in Aleam's study by the fireplace, waiting for someone to bring me my staff until Astravar came, and then I could fly out and fulfil the prophecy. But every year there had to be a 'Sports Day', even if war was looming on the horizon. Especially if war is looming on the horizon, Driar Yila had told us one assembly. Because during such times we needed to keep our spirits up and it would help us stay fighting fit for when the warlocks actually marched in. We didn't know where they'd march yet. But we apparently had to be prepared.

So, they'd had me tied to Salanraja's leg, as we stumbled over to the finish line – last. Then they'd had us flying all kinds of stunts, making me dizzy. I felt like I was chasing my tail for ages once I finally returned to the ground. Now, it was the 'dragon egg-and-spoon race', the most pointless activity in the whole wide world. Our goal was to land on the top of the keep tower as fast as possible, making sure that we passed over the designated checkpoints as I, all the while, kept my egg precariously balanced on the spoon.

There came a cry from my right, and I nearly jumped. This almost sent the egg flying, and Salanraja sent out a desultory groan in response.

Rine flew past on his blue dragon, Ishtkar, or should I say they dived together towards the ground so fast that I thought they were going to bore a crater. But right at the last minute, Ishtkar pulled herself back up, and Rine shot up in her saddle, sending out a tail of ice behind him from his staff in his right hand. I wondered how he could keep the egg on his spoon in his left until I noticed the glistens in the ice crystals attached to it.

"*He's cheating!*" I said. "*He's using his magic to keep the egg affixed to his spoon.*"

Salanraja chuckled for a moment, but then she cut off her laughter as if worried her rumbling belly might cause me to drop the egg. "*All's fair in the dragon egg-and-spoon. As long as the magic doesn't end up disrupting the flight of someone else.*"

"*But it does disrupt. It's distracting. They should disqualify him...*"

"*It doesn't matter,*" Salanraja said. "*Because he's not going to win first place flying like that. He knows it though, and he's going for the stunt prize. Now shut up, because we're in the lead and I really need to focus.*"

She was right. I could see a few dragons behind us, but no one yet in front. We only had to fly between the westmost and eastmost towers of Dragonsbond Academy and then land on the keep tower. Then we'd win the race. So long as I didn't drop the egg or spoon, that was, which were together making my mouth feel really sore.

The wind whipped past me, and I could tell that we were going fast. But at least Salanraja was flying steady. After all, this was nowhere near as bad as the dragon stunt show.

"*How long do we have to keep this up for?*" I asked.

"*Just a few minutes. Now just focus. If we win this, we'll be the pride of all the dragons and students in the academy.*"

"Yeah, right." They'd probably tell me I'd cheated. Or that I wasn't a suitable competitor because I was a cat. Or some other nonsense that the humans here liked to spout.

There came a whoosh from beside me, and then a familiar giggling sound. "Here, kitty, kitty," someone called out, and I turned my head to see Ange. Usually, I was more than happy to see her. But this time, in the set of her narrowed eyes, I could tell she wasn't here to play fair.

Just like Rine, she ejected a stream of magic behind her. But instead of pretty patterns of ice, twisting branches shot out from the glowing green crystal on her staff, eventually dissipating into the sky metres behind. They gave her extra propulsion, which was how she had caught up so fast. With her other hand, she held her spoon without shaking it. It wasn't surprising, really, as she'd hardened the skin on her arm to the texture of wood. Green lithe branches sprouted out of her fingertips, twisting around the spoon and fixing the egg in place.

"They're all using magic. This isn't fair."

"Will you just shut up," Salanraja said. *"They're using the magic because they feel they need it. But don't forget, while the other dragons have been lazy because they thought they could rely on their riders' magic, we've trained for this for weeks."*

That was certainly true. Salanraja had taken me out on numerous flights, three times a day, saying that she was respecting my wishes by flying gently – but also at an incredible speed.

"Here kitty, kitty," Ange said again, and she edged her blue dragon, Quarl close enough that I could leap across. "Why don't you come over and sit on my lap?" She laughed.

The offer was tempting, admittedly. Quarl often seemed to me a much smoother flyer than Salanraja.

"Don't you dare," Salanraja said. *"If the rider leaves its mount, we'll be instantly disqualified."*

My dragon's rudeness and chagrin made it even more tempting for me to accept Ange's bait. But, in all honesty, I wanted to win. I'd had enough of the students here thinking that I couldn't do what they could because I was a cat. It didn't matter if I was destined to save the world from Astravar's wrath, everyone here in Dragonsbond Academy seemed to look down on me, as if a primal part of them couldn't quite fathom why I wasn't on permanent rat catching duty.

Even Ange, sometimes…

"I've had enough of this," Salanraja said. *"Hold on to yourself and hold on to that egg."*

"I've nothing to hold on w—"

I didn't have time to finish my thought, as Salanraja lurched to the side suddenly and bashed Quarl aside. The blue dragon let out a roar that cut through the air. I was disorientated for a moment – slightly dizzy – but I kept my focus on the egg and ducked to the side at the last minute to stop it falling off. I came to my senses and peered through a gap within Salanraja's corridor of spikes with one eye.

I mewled in satisfaction as I saw Ange's spoon plummeting to the ground, Quarl diving headlong right after it. Fortunately for her, the egg was still wrapped in the vines and didn't fall off the spoon. Ange and Quarl caught up with it and Ange clutched it within her grasp. But the manoeuvre had turned Quarl around, now flying away from us.

"*Isn't that against the rules? Forget using magic, that's downright dirty of you, Salanraja.*"

"*The rules say we can't use magic against other fliers. But there's nothing about not using pure muscle to bash them out of the way.*"

"It will certainly slow her," I said, and I looked back at Quarl and Ange, now becoming pinpricks on a low layer of grey floating cloud. "*But it wouldn't have been my fault, you know, if you'd sent the egg off towards the ground. That was quite a risk you took, Salanraja.*"

"*I thought you had perfect balance. The grace of the great Asian leopard cat, and all that...*"

"*I'm good at balancing myself, not at balancing things hanging out of my mouth.*"

"*Well, you seem to be doing quite a good job at it,*" Salanraja said. "*Now let me concentrate. I need to get ready for a perfect landing.*"

I wasn't listening to her, because I was focused on a small charcoal dragon gaining on us fast. Its rider was on top of it and hadn't even bothered to draw her staff, instead keeping her body tucked towards the dragon's neck to gain momentum. Her platinum blonde hair whipped back in the wind. Clearly, she didn't need magic, and she had her spoon tucked to her chest underneath her chin, using the dragon's head to shield it from the wind.

"*I don't think we're going to win.*"

"*What do you mean?*" Salanraja asked. "*I'm just about to come in to land on the tower.*"

"*Seramina and Hallinar... They've saved all their energy until this last leg.*"

"Gracious demons," Salanraja said, and she hazarded a quick glance behind her. "*I might have known. That mind-witch is a crafty one.*"

Fortunately, I knew what I had to do to stop her. I only needed to take a leaf out of Ange's book and distract her. If everyone else was allowed to use their magic, I thought I'd use mine too.

"Hang on, Salanraja. I've got this."

"What are you up to, Bengie?"

I didn't answer. Instead, I summoned the beast from within. I closed my eyes and tried to divert my focus away from the pain writhing in my transforming muscles. All the while, I focused on the spoon, on keeping it clenched within my strengthening but expanding jaw.

When I opened my eyes, I felt strong, and I felt complete. I'd only transformed into a chimera a few times since I gained the ability, and though I hated the act of transforming, it felt good to be this beast. I lifted my paw and extended my sharp claws, examining them. But I bit down the instinct to roar, as I wanted to keep that spoon clenched within my mouth. It now felt flimsy and fragile, as if part of a child's play set.

"You idiot, Bengie... Change back," Salanraja said.

"No... Get closer, and I'll scare her."

"You're making me sink, Bengie. You're far too heavy as a chimera."

"Just shut up and get close to her. I can scare her into dropping that spoon."

"It's too late, you moron. Oh, why, Bengie? We would have won. Why did you have to spoil this all now?"

Indeed, Hallinar seemed to be accelerating towards us. But what I didn't realise at the time was that we were actually slowing down. They passed overhead and to the right of us. I thought of turning back, but Hallinar already had her front claws raised, ready to land on the tower. She touched down with a perfectly graceful landing, and a bugle called out from somewhere within the academy walls below.

"We can take second place," I said to Salanraja.

"There is no second place," Salanraja said, her spirits sounding ever so slightly dashed. *"After that, I'm not cooking for you tonight."*

"Fine," I said. But I in all honesty wasn't too happy about it. I groaned softly.

Salanraja crooned beneath my feet sympathetically. She probably felt my intense disappointment about my food and didn't want to let it linger. We were bonded after all. *"Tell you what,"* she said. *"There's a second round of stunt flying coming up, more about choreography to music than sheer aerodynamics. If we can win that, then I'll reconsider letting you feast with me."*

But it wasn't meant to be, because all of a sudden, a second call of bugles came from the wide stone towers of Dragonsbond Academy. On the top of them, prefects with their red cloaks craned their heads to look up at us. The sun glinted off the instruments pressed to their mouths. The tune they sounded had an essence of urgency in their notes. Though the bugles were loud, they were soon drowned out by a roar of dragons coming from those dragons who remained in the towers.

"What's that?" I asked Salanraja.

She growled. *"Sports Day is cancelled,"* she said, this time making it her turn to sound disappointed.

"What, why?"

"I don't know," Salanraja said. *"But Olan just told me we're to return to Dragonsbond Academy at once."*

2

PRIDE AND SUPERFICIALITY

Salanraja scudded down against the ground at the centre of the bailey. Given we would have taken second place if it weren't for the cancellation, we were the first to land on virtually empty ground.

Some guards milled around the closed portcullis though, and many of the serving staff had come out of the doors to the castle, as if waiting for something to happen. The bugle call that cancelled Sports Day had clearly been for something important. Meanwhile, dandelion puffs and grass seeds waltzed gently on the cooling breeze, and I wondered if they'd find any suitable ground to grow from with this whole place stinking of rotten vegetable juice.

"*Get off,*" Salanraja said, and I didn't hesitate to follow her orders. I'd been so long up in the air with her, I was feeling a little queasy. I sprinted down her tail, and she lifted into the air, leaving me standing alone there. She'd been ordered to make room for the other dragons to land, so as not to create any traffic problems. No one had yet told us what the urgency was, but I knew it was a matter of great importance.

I just hoped that the warlocks hadn't decided to march, because I didn't have my staff yet. In all honesty, I was looking forward to clutching it in my teeth and unleashing the power at Astravar. But it wasn't so much the battle itself I was looking forward to. Rather, I was looking forward to the praise and adulation I'd get after the battle.

King Garmin, I was certain, would offer me a grand gift for my efforts in defeating the most powerful warlock in the land. And I would ask for tithes of a house in the countryside outside Cimlean, with lots of room for me and Ta'ra – wherever she was right now – to run around in. I'd let Rine and Ange live with us as well, and Aleam could visit along with Seramina whenever they wanted.

I'd already thought of the problem of feeding our three dragons – Salanraja, Ishtkar, and Quarl – and I'd decided that I'd also ask for a cattle rancher, a shepherd, a fisherman, and a huntsman to be employed on our grounds. They could live in a separate house, of course, and they could each have a cat as long as they kept them away from mine and Ta'ra's territory and treated them well instead of employing them as rat catchers. Of course, the king would have to keep sending us tithes of sheep, chickens, and cattle, but that could be my reward for saving the kingdom. I could live, in other words, like a lord.

My mouth watered at the thought of all the nutritious food I could eat there – much of it roasted by not one, but three dragons. It was only natural, really – I'd had to accept that I probably now had no way of returning to my home in South Wales. Which meant that I had to find an alternative way to make life just as good as it used to be, if not better.

There came a cool gust from above, and the massive shadow of Quarl passed over me. Ange's dragon came into land, with Ishtkar and Rine flying only a short distance behind them. Ange paused a moment to watch Rine land, and then both riders scurried down the sides of their dragons to hit the floor at the same time.

Their dragons took off towards the East Tower. Rine and Ange looked just about to step up to each other, when another dragon blocked their path. A smallish citrine dragon flew right between them and landed, pushing Ange back as if in revolt. Bellari stood up in the dragon's saddle and scanned around her. Her eyes fell on me first, and she frowned. Then she turned to Ange and gave her an even more sour look. Finally, she scurried down her dragon on Rine's side and embraced him in her arms.

"Oh, you were such a fine stuntman up there," she said, brushing Rine's hair away from his cheek. Her dragon lifted off, as Rine planted a prolonged kiss on his girlfriend. I growled, liking this perhaps even less than Ange did. In many ways, Bellari was even more of an enemy to me than Astravar, and I had absolutely no idea of how to stop her from disrupting my plans.

Ange had turned her head away from them and instead was gazing up at her dragon turning in a circle to approach his chamber in the West Tower. I should have been angry with her, really, after how she'd played in the dragon egg-and-spoon.

"*Of course you should be mad at her,*" Salanraja told me. "*For what she pulled, you shouldn't talk to her for at least a week.*"

"*Don't be stupid,*" I said. "*Ange is our friend.*" I walked over to Ange, meowing.

She looked down at me, her eyes wide as if in surprise. "I would have thought you'd be angry at me," she said. "I'm sorry, I can get so competitive sometimes."

I rubbed myself against her bare calf. "All's fair in the dragon egg-and-spoon," I said, reciting Salanraja's exact words during the race.

At that, Ange laughed. "Oh, Ben," she said. "You're becoming more like us every day."

"I hope I'm still retaining my feline mannerisms. Because I'm a descendant of the great Asian Leopard cat, and if my ancestors can see me today from cat heaven, I want them to be proud."

"Don't worry, you're still as cat-like as cats come. Without the talking-like-humans part, of course. Come to think of it, I'd never imagined how a cat would hold an egg-and-spoon before now, but you held it exactly like I would have thought a cat would."

I mewled and rubbed up against her leg once again. Now, I was purring loudly. Ange reached down and picked me up in her warm arms. I looked up into her wide, bright eyes. Meanwhile, another dragon came down to land just a short distance away, and Ange turned her back to it as if to shield me from the stiff wind.

"What's all this commotion about?" I asked. "I thought we'd be flying all day."

"Yes," Ange said, and she glanced at the gates to the academy. "It's such a shame, isn't it?"

"I guess," I said, not quite meaning it. I'd much rather be curled up by Aleam's fireplace right now – even if Ta'ra wasn't here to provide extra warmth anymore. But then, to survive in this place and not be demoted to rat catching duty, I'd learned you needed to show at least a little enthusiasm.

"You don't sound like you mean it," Ange said. "But I understand. You weren't born into this life, after all."

"Neither were you," I pointed out.

"Ah, but I know that every day what I do helps my father, and I also know I'm providing a service to my kingdom."

I yawned and considered jumping back down and getting a drink from the fountain. But I remembered my question remained unanswered. "So, what's all this commotion about, then?"

Ange shook her head as she tickled me under the chin. "Haven't the faintest. But I'm guessing it's something important."

"You think the warlocks are finally going to march? I haven't even got my staff yet."

"I said I don't know, Ben," and she sounded ever so slightly huffy about it. "Why don't you ask Seramina? She has the gift of clairvoyance, right?"

"Sometimes," I said. "When she decides it's worthwhile to use it."

My words didn't quite seem to register with Ange as she was gazing over towards the door of the West Tower where Rine stood with one leg propped up against the stone. He had Bellari in his arms and was holding her very close as he stroked her hair and gazed longingly into her eyes. I smelled a slight whiff of stress coming out of Ange's glands, and I let out a softer meow this time to comfort her.

"Why don't you do something about that?" I asked.

"What?"

"Rine..."

Ange looked down as her grip on me loosened slightly. "Oh, not this again. When are you going to learn, Ben? Rine and I aren't meant to be."

"But you have feelings for him," I said. "And he has feelings for you."

"Do you know that for sure?" Ange said, raising an eyebrow.

"Of course," I said. "I can smell them."

"You can smell them... How do you know they're for me?"

"I just know, okay?"

Ange shook her head and that wistful look returned to her eyes. "Rine's always been so... You, know... Superficial. He's never really been in touch with his feelings, Ben. He doesn't really know what he wants, and I'm not sure he ever will."

"That's why you have to show him," I said. "When I want food, I don't just keep quiet about it. I meow and I meow, and I don't stop until I get what I want."

"Is that how you think love works, Ben?" Ange asks. "You just keep moaning about it until you get it?"

"Why not? It's how you get everything else in this world."

Ange sighed. "You still have a lot to learn about humans. Life is so much more complicated than that." She loosened her grip, so I jumped down before she dropped me on the hard cobblestones beneath.

Virtually as soon as I hit them, there came a roar from the sky. Ange and I both looked up at once, and even Rine and Bellari got a little distracted from their snuggles. At first, I thought it was another dragon coming in to land from the race, making everyone know it had at least got fifth place. But the roar wasn't coming from that direction, but from behind the gate.

A black dragon flew towards it. It wasn't a charcoal like Seramina's dragon, Hallinar, or Prefect Asinda's dragon, Shadorow. More, it was jet black and, I could swear, almost shiny. On it sat a man in a bright red robe, and an equally red, flat hat.

The mist had accumulated in the distance, and I didn't see the other five dragons until a moment later. But behind the jet dragon came a dozen other dragons – two ruby, two citrine, one stone grey, one charcoal, four emerald, and two sapphire blue. It appeared that this man, whoever he was, had decided to fly a little ahead of his flock.

"Well I never," Ange said.

"What?"

"That's Corralsa, Prince Arran's dragon."

"Prince who?"

"Does no one ever tell you anything, Ben? Prince Arran is King Garmin's nephew, and also the air marshal of all the dragon riders in Illumine. He's a very important man, and I've heard he's also incredibly handsome."

"Great," I said. "Another official."

Ange said nothing to that, but I could hear her heart thumping in her chest with my sensitive ears as she watched him with those wide eyes as he came in to land. His dragon thudded down just behind the gate, and Captain Onus of the guards went over to greet him.

"I knew it," Ange said. "So handsome..."

"Does that mean you're not interested in Rine, anymore?" I asked.

"I," Ange looked back at Rine and Bellari. "I never told you I was interested in Rine. But this man – I've heard so much about him..."

The prince clambered down from the saddle of his jet-black dragon, not even looking once at Captain Onus. He strolled in our direction, with his head held high and his hands clasped behind his back. He stopped a moment beside us, then turned to Ange, and gave her a look like she'd just burned his lunch. He then looked down at me without moving his head. "Why, pray tell me, student, is there a cat out from the cattery at this time? We don't fund this academy for raising pets."

Ange looked far too gobsmacked to answer, so I did so for her.

"I – pray tell you – am a Bengal, *direct* descendant of the great Asian leopard cat, and I'm of great importance to this academy. I don't belong, in other words, on rat catching duty."

"Oh, so you're the talking cat," the prince said. "I've heard a lot about your affairs."

"Then you must have heard—" I started.

"Oh, do shut up," the prince said. "I don't care whether you can talk or not. This kingdom will always be run by humans, and animals are meant to serve us, which means your opinion is not important to me. Only your servitude is."

"But he's much more than an animal," Ange said, her nostrils now flared.

"And students do not have a voice here until they're old enough to hold council," the prince said. "Now, if you excuse me, I have important issues to be seeing to." He spun around on his heel and strode off.

"So... You still like the handsome prince?" I asked Ange.

"Beauty is in the eye of the beholder," she replied.

"And why do you think he's here?"

"I don't know," Ange said. "But I'm sure it's the reason for Sports Day being cancelled."

"Then, maybe I'll find out if anyone knows anything," I said.

"Yeah, do that," Ange replied. She no longer seemed her usual buoyant self. Rine and Bellari had since vanished into the West Tower's corridors, probably out of sight of the prince. Ange looked once more over to where they had been, then she huffed, and she stormed off towards the fountain.

I decided it was probably a good idea to leave her alone. Besides, Ange was right. To learn more about this situation, I needed someone with the gift of clairvoyance. So I strolled towards Aleam's study, where Seramina had been staying for the last few months.

3

MEDITATION

Seramina sat on Aleam's mahogany bench with her eyes closed, her legs crossed with both feet resting on her thin thighs, and her hands resting lightly on her knees, palms facing upwards. Motes of dust danced around her like fairies, sparkling in the light coming through Aleam's gauze curtains. Seramina had removed the velvet cushions from the bench, and they instead stood propped up against the wall underneath the window.

Aleam's study always felt kind of empty nowadays, with Ta'ra – my old Cat Sidhe friend – no longer being there. She'd gone to look after the other Cat Sidhe's in the Caldmines Forest. I'd wanted to visit her, but before I'd even had time to do so the warlocks had set up camp outside the castle, and visits to and from Dragonsbond Academy became highly restricted. So, in other words, I hadn't seen her for quite a few months.

Now, only one bowl lay for food on the floor, and only one bowl for water. There was no cat there for me to snuggle against and get warm. But it was the lessons I missed the most. I'd taught Ta'ra a lot about what it's like to be a cat, and she'd taught me a lot about what it's like to be human too, even if she was a fairy.

I guess I had Salanraja, and I had people like Aleam, Ange, Rine, and even Seramina to keep me company. Yet none of them made a suitable replacement for Ta'ra.

I'd tried interacting with the other cats here, but they just didn't seem to understand me. For a long time, I'd felt a foreigner to the humans and had to learn to deal with it. What I hadn't considered so much was that now to my own brethren I was a foreigner too.

So, every time I saw Seramina occupying Ta'ra's spot, I just felt kind of odd. Still, she was a lot kinder than she used to be, and I didn't want to deal with her old, scary self again. So, I made sure to keep in her good graces. As she sat, she took deep breaths, and she didn't seem to notice anything around her at all.

I really didn't enjoy entering the room and not getting the attention I deserved. So, I went up to her and meowed. Seramina ignored me a moment until I jumped on the sofa and rubbed my nose into her belly.

She shuddered, backed up against the sofa, and then looked down at me with those scary fiery eyes that I'd learned to fear. This only lasted for a moment, before her gaze reverted to that usual shade of pale blue-grey.

"Oh, hello, Ben," she said softly. "I'm sorry, I'm trying to stay in control. You must be quiet, by the way. Aleam's sleeping in the next room."

I pushed my nose up to her again, and she raised her head and stroked me. But her movements didn't seem quite real, as if she wasn't completely there or didn't realise I was present. "What do you call this again? This thing that you do?"

"Meditation," Seramina said. "It's something that they taught us to do in mind-school, but I never took it seriously until now. I've heard rumours it didn't come from our world, but our sages actually learned it by studying yours from afar."

"And it calms the mind, soothes the soul, you say?"

"You should try it. I think it would do you good."

"I can't cross my legs like you can," I said. "And I can't sit for that long without sleeping or needing to groom myself."

"I'm sure if you learned to still your mind, you could do it too."

"No," I said. "It's impossible."

Seramina watched me passively. A long time ago, her stare had frightened me so much, I'd not wanted to go anywhere near her. But now – it's strange to say – but when she was calm, after doing this meditation thing, her gaze seemed the most natural in the world.

I pushed myself up against the crook of her elbow, and then I lay down on her lap, purring. She moved slowly to stroke me, and I rolled over on my back to let her rub my belly. It was so relaxing being there, in such calmness, that I almost fell asleep. Maybe I would have, if I hadn't remembered I needed information from Seramina.

"Say, have you heard about the prince's arrival?" I asked.

Seramina raised her eyebrows. "I haven't, no…"

"I just saw him arrive. I was with Ange, and you should have seen the way he treated her."

"And which prince do you mean?"

"Prince Arran, the air marshal. Apparently, I should know who he is."

"Oh," Seramina said, and she looked towards the door which was slightly ajar. Aleam's soft snores emanated from behind it. "I'm sure he has a good reason to be here."

"I'm sure he has, and I was hoping you'd be able to tell me what it is."

Seramina held her breath for a moment. "Ben, I don't do that anymore."

"What?"

"Use my magic willy-nilly. Now Astravar has met me, I'm at just as much risk of him finding his way into my mind as you are of him finding his way into yours. Or if not him, the dark magic… So, I must only use my gifts when absolutely necessary. Unless you have a good reason to need to know why the prince is here, I can't tell you. There's too much at stake."

Come to think of it, Astravar hadn't been visiting my dreams much lately either. It was as if, after defeating his demon chimera that he'd lost interest in me.

"I need to know," I said.

"Why?"

"Because he was rude to Ange and me, and I don't trust him."

"That's not a good enough reason," Seramina said. "You didn't use to trust me either, if you remember. But, with me, you had nothing to fear, and this is probably true with this prince too."

Suddenly, I caught a whiff of smoked trout coming from my bowl on the floor. I groaned, and I stood up shaking my legs, and dropped off the chair. The fish in the bowl was dry, and in another bowl the water was full of fur balls. This meditation thing might have been great for Seramina, but she wasn't doing her duty in replacing the food on time. She still, it seemed, had a lot to learn.

"*If you're hungry, I've just roasted up a whole deer,*" Salanraja said in my mind. Really, I was incredibly glad to hear her voice.

"*Great. Dinnertime,*" I said. "*But I thought you were angry with me and would not let me have any of your meal.*"

I could have eaten in the dining hall. But the food had been pretty bad lately, apparently because of the warlocks cutting off supply routes.

"*I changed my mind,*" Salanraja said. "*Unless you don't want it.*"

"*No, no, I'm on my way,*" I said. I thought about saying goodbye to Seramina, but she already had her eyes closed and was back in her trance, as if she had already forgotten about my visit. I groaned, deeply, and I left the room.

❧ 4 ❧

VENISON

A s I climbed the spiral staircase up to Salanraja's tower, the sweet aroma of the different varieties of meats the dragons had procured and roasted with their own flames seeped out from the entranceways to their chambers. There were aromas of rabbit, mutton, various types of fish, and so many other delicious feasts all melded into one tantalising fragrance.

The dragons' towers were the place to be at dinner time. Due to what they called the 'pre-siege', the kitchens only served soup with a tiny bit of meat in there and lots of disgusting vegetables, and portions of inedible rice, potatoes and bread. Because of this, many riders had taken to eating with their dragons, who flew out specially to get the meat they needed.

When I complained about the poor nutritional quality of the food to Matron Canda, she said that she could serve me up 'cat food' if I wanted. But I knew what that meant. They'd put the worst meat processed in tiny chunks and serve it out to me all mashed up and yucky. My owners back in South Wales had never served me that processed stuff that I'd heard other cats had to endure, and I didn't intend to start eating it now either.

Thus, every time I climbed the spiral staircase of the East Tower, I was tempted to drop into another dragon's chamber and steal their food before I even reached Salanraja. But I also knew trying to take food off a dragon I wasn't bonded to would mean certain death.

I entered Salanraja's chamber soon enough, and the venison she'd promised me lay in the unexposed corner next to the opening to the wider wall. The meat was brown and had that smoky scent to it that I knew and loved all too well.

I chirped a thank you to Salanraja, who looked down at me with her massive yellow eyes, a slight grin stretched across her rubbery lips. Then, I rushed over to the venison and tore off a strip of meat, and I dropped it by the opening to the outer world from which came a nice cooling breeze.

The sun was now getting low in the sky, bringing a pleasant warmth that offset against the breeze. The air didn't smell as fresh as it should either. I couldn't see the purple mist from this side of the castle, but I could smell the rotten vegetable stench of dark magic. I had thought at first it was only Astravar that smelled like that, but it turned out that all warlocks and their creations did.

This is how this whole world would smell if the warlocks took over this world and continued their conquest into the other six dimensions, including my dear home.

Suddenly, a flash of light came from the crystal beside me – a massive, tall, multi-faceted thing that stood unnaturally on the cobblestone floor. It did that sometimes, often when it wanted to tell Salanraja and I something. But now I saw the same old vision of myself as the hero. In the vision, I held the staff in my mouth, with the crystal at the tip of it, glowing blue. I was atop Salanraja, and I knew Astravar was flying nearby on one of his terrifying bone dragons. I'd see him soon in the crystal's vision.

The visions seemed to have been getting more and more frequent lately, which annoyed me. I always saw myself with that staff in my mouth, battling my nemesis. But I had no idea how I was going to obtain that staff and, from what the Driars told us, time was running out.

Salanraja laughed as she saw me watching the crystal. *"It won't* change just by staring at it, you know. It's not going to reveal anything extra to you until it's ready to do so."

"And when will that be?" I asked. "I just want to get Astravar out of the way so I can get back to living a comfortable life."

Salanraja shook her head slowly. "Life will never be comfortable. You're a dragon rider now, and you're meant to work for the kingdom."

"But can't I retire... Like Aleam? He doesn't go flying out on training drills every day and he doesn't have to sit in boring classrooms."

"We'll retire when we're good and old."

I tried to imagine how many years I had left in my life but couldn't fathom it. The crystal had given me the gift of languages, but unfortunately it hadn't thrown in mathematics for good measure.

"The king will let me retire after I save his kingdom. Then we can do what we like."

"Here we go again..." Salanraja lifted one of her forelegs and examined her sharp, long talons.

"What?"

"I'm getting a bit sick of hearing your 'retire in the countryside' fantasies. Have you ever thought about what I might want?"

"I have. I decided to include a large garden in the plans where you, Quarl, and Ishtkar can have plenty of space to roam."

"I'm a dragon, I don't roam in gardens. I roam in the sky."

"Well, you can fly out from there and there'll be ample space for your landings."

Salanraja growled, and for a split second I thought she was also going to breathe fire. "When I grow old, I want to live in the Crystal Mountains with the other dragons. That's where most dragon riders end up, you know? We live like hermits up there. Just us and our riders..."

"What? The mountains. Whiskers, no! It's too cold."

"See what I mean?" Salanraja said. "You don't care do you?"

Now, it was my turn to growl. I walked over to the venison and ripped off another chunk. The taste of it at least brought some solace to this terrible news. I knew from the start that bonding with Salanraja was a bad idea. Now it seemed my doing so had ruined my life. I took my venison back to my spot and chewed into it once again. As I did so, I couldn't help looking back up at the crystal, and the massive, winged creatures, which looked like a cross between a bat and buzzard that I tore out of the sky using magic from my staff.

Behind me, Salanraja let out a loud, breathy sigh. *"You know, when I'd first seen that scene in the crystal, I couldn't quite believe it."*

"Why not?" I asked.

"Well... A cat beating the most powerful warlock alive today. Who'd have thought it possible?"

"But we're mighty creatures... If only you'd seen one of my ancestors, the Great Asian leopard cat."

"Yes, I'm sure I'd be quaking in my skin. And I've still got to meet your mightily scary hippopotamus."

"There's nothing on earth scarier than a hippopotamus. Trust me, I've seen one."

"So you keep telling me," Salanraja said, and she opened her mouth in a wide yawn.

In the crystal, I'd now come face to face with Astravar. The view there had pulled back so I could see myself looking tiny on Salanraja's neck, the staff in my mouth and Astravar atop his bone dragon. A blue beam shot out from my staff, a red from his, and they fused at the centre creating a brilliant purple bulb of energy.

"How am I ever going to do that?" I asked Salanraja.

She turned to the crystal. *"Exactly as you are doing there, I think. You'll hold the staff in your mouth, and you'll shoot out magical energy and defeat Astravar."*

"That's not what I mean..."

"So what do you mean?"

"How am I going to get from this point, stuck here in Dragonsbond Academy, to where I battle Astravar with my staff so I can live in peace again?"

It was a really weird place to be in, this thing that humans called limbo. Cats were not meant to feel the frustration it caused. I mean, when we saw a mouse, or a butterfly, or something worth hunting, we would hunt it when it was there, and then forget about it if it fled out of sight. But this crystal kept reminding me that I had to find this staff. Really, part of me wanted to be out searching for it. But I didn't know where to look.

"Be patient," Salanraja said. *"The crystal will reveal the way when it's*

good and ready. It wouldn't still be showing this vision as a version of the future, if this possibility didn't exist."

"I hope you're right," I said.

Meanwhile, the crystal had now got to my favourite part. The purple bulb at the centre of mine and Astravar's beams had now crept even closer to the warlock, and it was about to knock him off its mount. Just before that happened, there came another roar of bugles that sounded more like hippopotami breaking wind than anything pleasant.

"What is that?" I asked. *"Please don't tell me we have to go back to Sports Day again."*

"No," Salanraja replied. *"I believe it's the call for assembly."*

"Why didn't they ring the bell?"

"I guess they want to tell you this is more important than a regular assembly. This is a military matter."

"Prince Arran... I'd been so wrapped up in my meal, I forgot to ask you if you know why he's here."

"I guess you're about to find out."

"Sounds like it..." I took another piece of venison in my mouth for good luck, then I scurried out of Salanraja's chamber and clambered down towards the bailey.

SCHOOL ASSEMBLY

I'd go as far to say that I was having a terrible day. First, I'd had to carry a spoon in my mouth whilst being tossed around on Salanraja's back for nothing. Then, Bellari had got on my nerves by nuzzling with Rine when he should be with Ange. After that, I'd had to deal with that rude prince, Seramina had ignored me, and that bugle had torn me away from my delicious meal. Now, the day would be topped off with having to listen to the Driars' boring voices in assembly as they waxed lyrical about the wonders of their school.

Hence, I wasn't in the best of moods.

I stormed through the bailey towards the assembly. The dragons that had accompanied Prince Arran on his journey were stationed around the castle – on the tops of the towers and strategic points along the *chemin de ronde*. Around me, students rushed to get to the Council Courtyard. It was so busy I could hardly see where I was going. Whenever a student looked at me, I growled back at them, and I could swear once or twice I even hissed. Still, I reached the courtyard pretty quickly, and passed underneath the archway into a sweaty throng of students.

Most of them were there before me, and I had to navigate through a massive crowd. It was hard to see what was happening on the dais, because so many legs blocked my view like boles in a forest.

No one was yet speaking at the front, and the loud chorus of students surrounded me as they collectively discussed their everyday affairs. I couldn't hear any of the conversation – their heads were too high, and I was too low for that. All I can say is that everyone was making an absolute racket.

Fortunately, being a cat, I didn't need to find my way by sight here. It made much more sense to navigate by smell, and I sought someone familiar. Soon enough, I detected the faint whiff of catnip scented perfume, which I tracked until I was right underneath Ange. I mewled, and I rubbed against her leg, looking up at her. She spotted me, smiled, and then lifted me up in her arms. Though Ange was short, she was close enough to the front of the assembly that I could now see the central stage.

Unusually, the three Driars stood at the back of the dais, rather than at their usual lecterns. The lectern at the centre – usually Driar Lonamm's – now had a red cloth placed over it with some kind of ornate silver statue on top – a white crystal balanced in an open hand.

I still felt a little edgy, but Ange held me tightly and stroked me gently to help calm my instinct to dart away. We were all waiting, I realised, for Prince Arran, and he was clearly late. I could see the annoyance on the tightened faces of each of the Driars. Now I was a little higher, I could also smell tension in the air – stress everywhere. I picked up a few words on the conversations. The students were uttering things like 'war is coming', 'there will be a siege', and 'they will charge'.

All this time, I still didn't have my staff, because if I did I was sure I could just vanquish Astravar and get this whole thing out of the way. Of course, I hadn't even considered the other warlocks as a danger. Part of me, I guess, felt that once Astravar was defeated, the other warlocks would flee from this mighty and dangerous Bengal.

"It will start soon," Ange said.

"It better," I said. "Because I need to get back to my meal."

Ange laughed. "Quarl told me that Salanraja caught a whole deer."

"As she had when I'd first met her," I said, purring.

"I'm envious. We only had fish."

"Nothing wrong with fish," I said, and I waited for Ange to say something else. Instead, the door opened to the keep behind the Driars. Driar Yila raised her staff up high, and the crystal on it glowed red as if to warn that if anyone else spoke, she'd bathe them in fire. The surrounding chattering quickly died down to a whisper, and then nothing.

As before, the prince wore his red robe and red cap, both looking as if made from some kind of velvet material – shiny and dirt-free. He carried a birch staff with a white crystal on it, just like Seramina's.

The prince took his place at Driar Lonamm's desk. He placed a palm on the crystal on the lectern, and both the crystal in his staff and the crystal on the desk glowed. He coughed once, and he held this posture as he addressed the silent courtyard.

"These are trying times, indeed," he said. "Not just for your beloved academy, but for the entire kingdom of Illumine. Unfortunately, it looks like Dragonsbond Academy will get hit first."

This caused a murmur to erupt from the students, and Prince Arran waited as if he had orchestrated this murmur. It didn't die down, and the volume raised in intensity.

"Silence," Driar Yila shouted out from her corner, and the red crystal on her staff let out another burning glow.

Prince Arran glanced at Driar Yila, and then he scanned the crowd with narrowed eyes. "I'm glad to see that your Driars have you well trained," he said after a moment. "Because you have to remember this. You are all servants of the king, and you must always remember your place, particularly in this time of war. If one of you breaks rank, or if one of you disturbs the order that we've built in this kingdom, then our entire operation might fall apart."

I caught sight of High Prefect Lars and Prefect Asinda at the front then. I could see the back of their heads – Lars standing perfectly straight, not moving one bit. Asinda was nodding slowly, one hand on her chin.

"Suffice to say," Arran continued, "time is also of the essence, and so I must keep this speech short. You are all probably wondering the reason for this visit. For days, my dragon riders and dragons have been scouting the land, as we tried to ascertain the exact location the warlocks are likely to target first."

"*What pomposity,*" Salanraja said in my mind. "*Trust that self-righteous fool to call them his dragons. Dragons belong to no one, and the only dominion humans can claim over dragons is that of the bond between rider and dragon. Even with that, no one is really in charge.*"

"*Well, don't you serve his dragon, Corralsa?*" I asked.

"*It's not servitude,*" Salanraja said, sounding slightly annoyed. "*It's a mutual respect whereby we decide to delegate specific decisions to her. If we ever wanted to do our own thing, nothing's stopping us. But dragons are wise enough to know that it's easier to work together sometimes than alone.*"

"*Sounds like you're just using fancy wording to dress up the same idea.*"

"*Believe what you like. Just because you don't understand something, doesn't mean it isn't true.*"

While Salanraja had been explaining, Prince Arran had been telling us more about the importance of Dragonsbond Academy for training dragon riders to enter the king's Dragon Corps. This kind of spiel, we heard every week in droning voices from the Council of Three during our assemblies. But this time, Prince Arran also pointed out many times that he was in fact in charge of the corps. After a while, he paused, as if he was about to deliver an important point.

"War is coming," he said. "And the warlocks have chosen this as the target. They most likely think that striking at the very cradle, so to speak, of our corps will allow them to win, which is why we must fortify this location. We have already called for reinforcements and the White Mages are on their way, although you must understand it will take time for them to arrive. Meanwhile, some of the king's best riders and their dragons will be stationed here."

"The warlocks have strengthened their position over the last few years, and much faster than we expected they would. For a long time, we've feared this day, as we waited for you, students of Dragonsbond Academy, to complete your training before we sent you into battle. We do not know when the warlocks will charge, but our intelligence tells us they are likely to do so soon. When they do, everyone older than sixteen must fight."

He paused, clearly strategically, and another murmur erupted from the crowd, larger than last time. Everyone here knew that there were only two members of Dragonsbond Academy that were under sixteen – Seramina, and I. Both of us, I was sure, would still have to fight.

Driar Yila at the back banged her staff down at the back, screamed out, "Silence!" once again, and passed her basilisk gaze over the students beneath her.

"As I said," Prince Arran said, without looking back at Yila this time. "Order will be required and enforced in this academy. From now on, you are no longer students, but soldiers and you will behave like soldiers. After this meeting, each of you must report directly to your head prefect, who will act like sergeants reporting directly to my stationed officers. For now, this assembly is dismissed. Make sure you leave in an orderly fashion, and don't speak until you're in your private quarters. If anyone disobeys orders or breaks rank, there will be severe consequences."

The crystal on which Prince Arran had placed his hand glowed even brighter, and a stream of white light shot out of his staff towards the crystal above the dais. An eye with a deep blue iris appeared on the crystal of his staff, and the crystal on the ceiling displayed a view of us in the assembly. We were wracked with silence until one student sneezed. The view in the ceiling crystal immediately focused on that student. Then another student mumbled something, but only made it mid-sentence before the view focused on her, cutting off her words.

Then I growled, and I made to clamber down onto the floor, not wanting to be here any longer. But Ange tightened her grasp, and she gave me a chiding look. The view in the crystal immediately focused on me. On the stage, Driar Yila focused her harsh stare on me, and her crystal flared red.

"Shh," Ange said softly, and the crystals view focused on her soft lips. Both of us quietened down together. Meanwhile, at the front, Arran waited patiently, scanning each one of us until not a single whisper emanated from the crowd. All I could now hear was the sounds of birdsongs somewhere in the distance and, even fainter, the cawing of a crow.

"Very well," Arran said. "I see we have work to do. Now, you are dismissed. Except for that talking cat. I wish to see you at once."

Whiskers, I hadn't expected that. Probably he was going to enact one of his 'consequences', all because I'd growled louder than anyone else. Feet scuffed from the ground behind me, and the students started to file out. Still, Ange held me, as if she never wanted to let me go, and I felt safe there.

But I knew this feeling wouldn't last.

6

THE ISSUE AT HAND

S ilence ensued, punctuated only by the soft voices of prefects giving orders. They arranged the students in neat rows and had them file into long trains leading into the bailey. A thick humidity hung in the air, bringing with it a coldness. It wasn't raining yet, but I could sense in my whiskers that it was coming.

Being the youngest class out of the three in Dragonsbond Academy, ours was the last to leave. Rine was there, and Bellari, as well as Seramina, and around one hundred other familiar students. Prefect Calin had been assigned to look after us, which suited me fine because I liked Calin.

He had short, cropped hair, a muscular stature, and he was one of the best sword fighters in Dragonsbond Academy. He arranged us in lines of five, then he walked up to Ange. "You should probably put him down now, Initiate Ange. He needs to stay behind to see the prince."

Ange sighed, then she started to lower me to the floor. But I shrieked, and I clambered further up her chest. I stretched out my claws to tell her that if she dropped me, then I'd tear her clothing.

"Ange is coming with me," I said.

The crystal on the ceiling above the dais focused on me. But the prince had now stopped watching us through it, and rather was talking to the other Driars at the back of the dais. Calin looked at me nervously. Ange smiled at him. Behind us, Bellari scoffed and turned towards the archway that led out of the courtyard. Rine stood close to his girlfriend, his cheeks looking slightly red. A crow flew overhead, cawing, and for a moment I wondered if it was Astravar. But it would have been stupid for him to come alone so close to where we had hundreds of dragons who could scorch him out of the sky.

After a moment, Calin nodded. "Fine," he said. "Everyone else move out."

He led the students towards the courtyard archway in a neat line, leaving Ange and I standing in an unnaturally chilly wind. On it, I caught that whiff of rotten vegetable juice again. I could swear it was getting stronger by the day.

"Can I put you down now?" Ange asked.

"No."

"Why?"

"Because you've proven in the dragon egg-and-spoon that you're not to be trusted. I have no idea if you'd run off as soon as you put me on the ground. As I said, you're coming with me."

Ange huffed, but it was a playful huff. I knew she was a little scared of having to deal with Prince Arran and the potential consequences. But I also remember her also saying that she thought the prince was attractive. I just hoped, at the back of my mind, that she wouldn't end up falling for him rather than Rine. That would be a disaster if I had to spend the rest of my nine lifetimes with this snobbish prince. Then, I would have to cast either Ange or Rine away, because there was no way I could handle both Arran and Bellari for life.

Ange carried me up to the foot of the dais and then stepped cautiously onto it. Usually, students weren't allowed up here, but Arran had called me forward after all. Prince Arran still had that weird-looking eye watching out from the crystal on his staff. As we approached, it looked at us, and then blinked slowly.

"Initiate Ange, I believe," Prince Arran said, without turning to Ange. "So, we meet again."

Ange lowered her head. "You know my name, sir?"

Arran looked back at Driar Yila. "Of course, I learn all the names of those who show signs of insolence. And here you are, disobeying my orders again."

"I didn't have a choice, sir," Ange said. "Ben... Initiate Ben, wouldn't go without me."

"Traitor," I said under my breath, growling. I knew she wasn't to be trusted.

Prince Arran looked down at me with narrowed eyes. I stared back at him, and I kept staring, waiting for him to blink and turn away. One thing these humans never learned is that you can't beat a cat in a staring competition.

"So, you take orders from a cat now, do you?" Prince Arran said. "I've never heard something so ridiculous. What is this establishment coming to?"

Ange looked at Driar Brigel, who shrugged his massive shoulders. Brigel then lowered his head as Prince Arran turned his hard gaze on him. Presently, Arran turned back to Ange.

"Answer me, girl," he said through clenched teeth. "I asked you a question."

Ange shook her head. "It's a fine academy, and I'm proud to be a part of it…. Sir."

"Then you'll do better refraining from molly-coddling this over-spoilt cat, and instead get back to your duties. Go and help the guards fortify our position or something. My dragon riders have been briefed and will have further orders for you soon. And remember, I'm keeping an eye on you."

"Yes, sir," Ange said, and this time she dropped me on the floor so fast I didn't have time to react. She nodded to the prince, curtsied slightly, turned on her heel, and marched off like a true soldier. I made to march after her, but the prince's voice boomed out so loud it caused me to freeze.

"What do you think you're doing, cat?"

I turned back to him. "Going to help the guards fortify your position, as you ordered."

"That order was meant for the girl, not you."

"You didn't specify, sir," I said.

Prince Arran put his hands on his hips and leaned forward until he loomed over me. "Are you really that stupid? I might have expected an inferior species wouldn't be able to understand orders."

"I'm not inferior. I'm a Bengal, descendant of the great Asian leopard cat."

"And I'm a prince, descendant of a long line of royals. I'm also air marshal of King Garmin's dragon riders, which consequently makes me overseer of this academy. Which means, little cat, that I'm your boss and you'll do exactly as you're told."

Behind me, the three Driars were exchanging glances with each other. It seemed that they thought this man as idiotic as I did. I'd seen apes on the television back home, and Prince Arran behaved just like one of those orange ones which swung around on their long arms. Orangutans, I believe they are called.

A roar came from one of the keep towers, and a bitter chill ran through my fur. Behind me, one of Arran's dragons took off from the top of the West Tower, and spiralled round, then landed in one of the chambers where a dragon lived. I guessed the dragons were also enforcing their disciplinary tactics. Salanraja, in particular, wouldn't like that.

Prince Arran snapped his fingers. "Stop dawdling, cat, and pay attention," he said.

"To what?"

He ignored my question. "How exactly are you planning to get the staff?" he asked. "The one that you're destined to use to defeat Astravar. I need timeframes, I need scoping estimates. Anything that I can use to plan our battle strategies moving forwards."

There it was – the question I'd been dreading all this time. "I haven't a clue," I said. "My crystal hasn't told me yet."

Prince Arran turned around to look at the three Driars. Without looking at me, he indicated a point on the ground next to him with a down-turned palm. "Stand here, cat, where I can see you."

I slinked over to the designated position and sat down. I started grooming myself, but the prince didn't seem to notice my intended insolence. Instead, he looked at the three Driars who had now formed a loose circle around him, each resting lightly on their staffs.

"What, pray tell me, is the meaning of this?" he asked them, with a tone as if he was scolding schoolchildren.

Driar Yila spoke out first. "Sir, the truth about the staff is known by Ben's and Salanraja's crystal, and we've been waiting until it's ready to reveal its position. We have the utmost faith that it will provide the answer when we are ready."

"Unacceptable," Prince Arran said.

I heard Driar Lonamm's voice catch in her throat. "Sir, we cannot go against the wishes of the crystal." Her cheeks wobbled as she talked. "That would be sacrilege."

"And that's the problem here..." Arran said, waving his hand. "This superstitious nonsense that you spout. We need to take action now, not to be waiting until we're magically provided a solution."

"But we've worked this way in the past, sir," Driar Brigel said. "Our reliance on the will of the crystals has served us well for many years."

"And never have we had warlocks encroaching on our doorsteps," Prince Arran said. "They've been gaining power for a reason. We need to identify inefficiencies in our system and stamp them out before it's too late."

I was getting sick of all this pointless talk. Really, we were just skirting around the issue.

"We have no idea where to find the staff," I said.

Prince Arran didn't even look down at me. "We have no idea to where to find it, sir. And who gave you permission to speak, cat?"

"Sir..." I said, and I said it as ironically as I could.

"Anyway, back to the issue at hand," Prince Arran said, clearly unaffected by my irony. Boring people are like that, unfortunately. "You could have extracted the information from the crystal using destiny magic. What happened to the mind-witch we sent you? The warlock's daughter?"

"Seramina is off duty for now," Driar Lonamm said. "She could be dangerous. If she uses her magic wrongly..."

Halfway through the sentence, Prince Arran had already turned around and was looking towards the East Tower, which housed Salanraja and about forty other dragons. "Forget this nonsense. I'll do it myself. Cat, lead me to your crystal."

Happily, I thought. I marched that way without permission. *"Kindly toast this arrogant prince for me as soon as we get to your chamber,"* I said to Salanraja in my mind as I went.

She said nothing in response as the five of us all marched together across the bailey to meet my dragon in the flesh.

7

FORCING DESTINY

Aleam was waiting for us in Salanraja's chamber. As he stood, he was hunched even further over his staff, and his face looked sallow and heavily wrinkled. Olan, after she'd heard about the prince's behaviour from the other dragons, had advised Aleam to attend the meeting. The great white dragon had apparently felt that the Council of Three might need his wisdom, or at least his diplomatic skills.

Meanwhile, a thick grey cloud had clustered over the fields outside, and I could taste the ozone in the air, which made a satisfying deviation from the normal sensation of rotten vegetable juice. There was also that thick humidity that told of a coming storm.

The crystal stood by the opening to the outer world, seemingly oblivious to this. It continued to display the same vision of me using my staff of destiny to knock Astravar off his bone dragon perch.

Salanraja had refused to toast Prince Arran. She argued that if she caused any physical damage to the man then Corralsa would cause equal if not greater damage to her. I could understand her fear, really. Corralsa was a big dragon after all.

This fear, however, didn't stop Salanraja growling at Prince Arran as he entered

Arran looked at her and her mighty sharp teeth. He seemed

unfazed as he put his hands on his hips. "I see you're just as insolent as your cat. I guess you're suited for each other. But you still need to learn your place. If you're not careful, I'll get Corralsa to send you over to Bestian Academy."

Driar Yila also looked up at Salanraja, but instead of her usual harsh look, she shook her head as if to tell her not to test this man. Salanraja growled again, and then retreated to the corner where the venison had been before.

"What's Bestian Academy?" I asked her.

The words came out in my mind as if Salanraja didn't particularly want to speak them. *"It's where all of us dragons are trained,"* she replied. *"Every one of us hates it, particularly our trainer, the great grey Matharon. He worked us to exhaustion every day from when we were fledglings until we came of age."*

"You've never talked about this before."

"We dragons don't. We'd rather not remember."

Behind Prince Arran, Driars Yila, Lonamm, and Brigel filed through the entranceway to Salanraja's chamber exceedingly slowly. The three of them walked with their heads low against their chests and their hands folded beneath their waists. Prince Arran didn't pay any heed to their unnatural lethargy, however, for his focus was on the crystal.

He placed the base of his staff down on the ground and widened his legs as he stared at mine and Salanraja's crystal. The smaller crystal on his staff glowed white and a thin, wispy beam floated out of it towards the larger crystal. Static seemed to come off his staff, gently tugging at my fur.

"Prince Arran," Aleam said. "With all due respect, do you really think it's wise to force destiny? We're talking about the threads of the future. Your actions could result in unseen consequences, which might involve losing the war."

"I'm not going to alter anything," Arran said. "I'm simply going to ask it a question."

Aleam raised an eyebrow. "If the crystal had anything to say, it would have done so, don't you think?"

Arran strode over to him and leaned over the old man with his hands on his hips. "Look, Driar Aleam. You're one of the most respected figures in this kingdom, and the king has the dearest respect for you. However, need I remind you of my position? I've been appointed by King Garmin to fight this war using whatever means necessary."

"Including ignoring the counsel of others in knowledgeable positions?"

"That's enough! Silence now, all of you. I need to concentrate." Arran lowered his head and put his free hand on his chin.

"Be careful, Arran," Aleam said. "You must remember what happens if you try to manipulate the will of the crystals."

But Arran didn't seem to be listening. The crystal on his staff grew ever brighter and the wispy beam between it and mine and Salanraja's crystal gained substance. Soon, the images on the crystal grew towards a brilliant white. I had to close my eyelids a little – it was so intense.

A crash of thunder came from outside, accompanied by an icy and heavy wind that had no smell to it. The wind hit me, sending me sliding across the ground, and I had to dig my claws into a crack between the cobblestones to keep purchase. The four elder Driars present widened their stances so they wouldn't get blown over. What-ever this man was up to, the crystal clearly didn't like it.

Salanraja didn't seem to like it either, for she tossed her head upwards and cried out shrilly. Arran turned his head slightly. Then a second beam came from his staff, again white, and it hit the dragon on the bridge of her nose. Salanraja once again whimpered, and she slinked further into the corner.

"*What was all that about?*" I asked Salanraja.

"*This prince is a pompous oaf,*" Salanraja said, growling quietly.

"*I know that already. But what are you so upset about?*"

"*I'm upset because he really shouldn't be behaving like this, despite his title. Arran is the most powerful destiny mage in the kingdom. Even the king's White Mages cannot match his ability.*"

"*So why don't you want him to cast that spell?*"

"*Because it was believed for a long time that you shouldn't interfere with the will of the crystals. It's complicated, Bengie, but let's say Olan*" *doesn't like this either. She's had a word with Corralsa, much to the same effect."*

"Then what's going to happen?"

"I don't know. None of us do. We've never tried this before. But this is how the warlocks got into trouble with dark magic originally. They tried to gain the power they wanted from the crystals, rather than allow the crystals to choose how they want to serve."

"I thought the crystals that the warlocks gained power from were dark crystals. Our crystal is different, surely?"

"No, Bengie. Dark crystals are just normal crystals that have been corrupted over the years through greed and other unfavourable human emotions. For years, the crystals were overused like this, until the warlocks came to power, and humans learned the error of their ways. No creature on this world truly understands the intricacies of these crystals. Gracious demons, I don't want to find out either. But with this pompous prince, we have no choice."

A roar came from outside, followed by a heavy beating of wings. Corralsa appeared at the opening to the outside world. The sun, still fighting to stay in front of the clouds, cast a sharp highlight onto Corralsa's black skin.

The light in the crystal faded back to a subdued grey. Every second or so, it pulsed slightly, and the ground underfoot shook as it did. The wind died down a little, but it still circled and howled around Salanraja's chamber like a yowling wolf.

Then came a familiar lilting voice, speaking out loud. It belonged to the crystal and always sounded to me like it had a Welsh accent. Except this time, this was more like a warrioress Boudica kind of accent – angry with a bite to it. The kind of voice a cat would hide from if it called him in for dinner.

"This is as improper as improper comes," my crystal said. "Who are you to disturb the natural order of magic?"

"I am Prince Arran, cousin of King Garmin IV and appointed air marshal of the Dragon Rider Corps of Illumine Kingdom."

"Your title means nothing in the order of affairs," the crystal said.

"But the situation does," Prince Arran said, "and we need your assistance."

"The situation bears no weight here. Dark ages come when men like you meddle in such unnatural ways. History has proven this time and time again."

"A dark age will come if I don't meddle. Your lack of communication with us leaves us with little choice."

"There is always choice!" the crystal boomed. "There is also patience, a virtue that has taken your people through the darkest times."

"There is no time for patience. We need your help in serving the kingdom. We need to locate the staff that belongs to the cat. And we need, as you well know, to change the future for the better. Tell me, oh crystal. Where can we find that staff?"

The glow from the crystal flickered stochastically. "I can tell you... But I warn you, prince. If you force something that's not due ahead of time, there will always be consequences."

"Our kingdom will pay those consequences united. If we can rid ourselves of the warlocks, there can't be too high a price to pay."

"You know so little, young prince, but you think you know the world through your gift. That is your weakness."

"Just show us where the staff is," Prince Arran said. "And let us be done with this conversation."

Outside, the sky darkened to near pitch. Then lightning cascaded out of the heavy clouds, flooding the landscape white. The crash from the sky was even louder than the last, and I half thought Corralsa would cower away, but she remained hovering in place, both majestic and terrifying.

"I will not be scared down," Prince Arran said. "Reveal the information I wish to know, and I need not disturb you again."

A torrent of rain poured outside, so thick it obscured the view between us and Corralsa. Now, the heavy wind brought upon it a yucky squall. I considered darting into the staircase for shelter, but something in me didn't want to move. If this prince could tell me where this staff was, then I could quest for it, obtain it, then use it to defeat Astravar. This nightmare might then be over sooner than I'd thought.

"Very well," the crystal said, "let your ambition and pride be your undoing."

The sky outside lightened to a sombre grey, whilst the view in the crystal returned to showing its scenes. But this time, underneath the facets, a new dream played out before me. A massive beast, as tall as the sky and wider than ten oak trees, stomped across a thick, dreamy looking wood. The ground looked wet and full of tall mushrooms. The beast's thick wooden legs crushed these under its stumpy feet as it made its way through the forest.

The hackles shot up on the back of my neck, as recognition dawned on me. Just last season, one of these creatures had almost sucked me into its insides and pancaked me to death. Spectral Manipulators and bone dragons surrounded the forest golem, guarding it. But both were dormant at this time.

"A forest golem," Aleam said. "But who..."

"It belongs to Astravar," the crystal said. "He has found and hidden the staff that only the cat can wield."

"That's the Aurorest Forest," Prince Arran said, and he turned to Aleam. "Am I right?"

Aleam nodded. "I know that place well. It's one of the best for gathering medicinal herbs."

"And poisons," Driar Brigel added.

Aleam had told me about this place before. It was so close to the Wastelands – a land full of magical creatures belonging to both the warlocks and the kingdom, that were in constant battle.

But since the warlocks had pushed their front forward, much of the Aurorest Forest now lay in the Wastelands, which had made it increasingly dangerous for Aleam to go there and forage for some of his more potent medicinal supplies.

"And this is where the staff is?" Prince Arran asked, turning back to the crystal. "The one that will save the world?"

"That is up to the decisions of your people," the crystal said. The vision flooded once again with light, which soon faded to a sombre and empty grey. Outside, the sun peeked through the clouds.

"I've seen enough," Prince Arran said, and he cut off the beam from his staff by twisting it sharply. "Driars, prepare the strategy room. We must discuss our plans at once."

He turned on his heel and strode out of the room.

8

DUST AND DISGUST

The strategy room was probably the dustiest room in the entire castle. It had a long oval mahogany table in the centre of it and thick red curtains in front of a single wall inset with full-height windows. Wolf spiders peered out from cracks in the skirting-board, and I couldn't stop sneezing.

Meanwhile, I sat on a velvet padded chair, wood carvings of dragons etched into the long beams across its high back. I had placed myself at one end of the table, licking my fur. Arran sat at the other end, and the three Driars of the Council of Three sat on my left just by the window. Aleam sat next to Arran on the other side, leaving only two chairs empty.

"I don't understand why they didn't hold the rest of the meeting in your chamber," I said to Salanraja. *"It's horrible, and it's dusty, and it's not a good place to be."*

"I'm guessing it's in case there are spies. We can't track every crow and sparrow that enters the castle."

"Or maybe it's because the prince didn't like you," I pointed out.

"I don't think he likes you particularly, either."

"Touché."

As I listened to Prince Arran drone on and on, my stomach started to rumble. It must have been ages since my last meal, and I considered mewling out for food, imagining the tantalising snacks I could be eating right now.

"We will send the cat out alone," Arran said, and hearing that caused the hackles to shoot up on the back of my neck.

Driar Lonamm glanced at me. "I wouldn't recommend that," she said. "Initiate Ben is still inexperienced. He's not fit to fight a forest golem alone."

"We can't spare the resources," Prince Arran said, lifting his head so I could see right up his nostrils.

"But he would probably never return," Driar Brigel said. "Then, we might not even have a staff to fight Astravar with. What will become of us then?"

"That cannot happen. The crystal has already foretold that he will survive getting the staff. He can't defeat Astravar otherwise."

"It's one possible thread of the future," Driar Yila said.

"And," Aleam said, raising his hand. "You've already changed fate by using your magic to alter the essence of time. The crystal told us that there will be consequences for this."

Prince Arran huffed and looked down at the table for a moment, examining it as if looking for flies. He drummed his fingers against the wood there, releasing some of the dust back into the air. "We haven't got time to deliberate... And I would have thought you'd have more faith in your air marshal. I'm the one that can use destiny magic here, and I've been using it for an awfully long time."

No one other than Prince Arran seemed very convinced about this from the look on the Driars' faces. Granted, he might have had powerful abilities to see the future. But something about his behaviour suggested he wasn't telling us everything we needed to know.

"And what does Initiate Ben think?" Driar Aleam asked, turning to me. Driar Yila coughed, Driar Lonamm mumbled something under her breath, and Driar Brigel shifted nervously. A moment of silence ensued.

"Go on then, cat," Prince Arran said. "Say something."

"I…" I stopped myself. I knew whatever I said would get ridiculed, and so I didn't feel like saying anything at all.

"Spit it out… We haven't got all day."

I looked straight at the prince. "I tried to face off against one of those things before, and I have no chance of defeating it. I have no magic, other than the ability to turn into a chimera."

"You'll have your dragon," Prince Arran said.

"A dragon isn't enough to defeat a forest golem," Driar Yila pointed out. "Unless we're very lucky."

"And Ben's crystal has foretold that he will be," Arran said. "We must fortify this castle for the safety of everyone involved. We can't spare a single soul on this quest."

Aleam lowered his head and cupped it in his hands. He shook it slowly and then stood up. "If you'll excuse me, my prince, I've got my own business to be dealing with."

He looked at Driar Yila, gave her a nod, and then walked out of the room. He didn't close the door on the way out. A breeze filtered through, which cleansed the air a little.

I couldn't believe my ears, really. They were going to send me out alone against a forest golem. It would knock Salanraja out of the sky, and then it would crush me under its massive weight. It wouldn't matter then whether the warlocks took the kingdom or not, because I'd be dead. I'd never taste a good meal again.

"*What are we going to do?*" I asked Salanraja. "*We can't head out there on our own because we'll be killed.*"

"*We have no choice,*" Salanraja said. "*We can't break the chain of command, and so we need to do what Prince Arran and Corralsa say.*"

But I wasn't going to listen to this. No one was sticking up for me where they should. Aleam was letting this go ahead. The Council of Three was letting this go ahead. All of them were meant to protect me. I wasn't going to let some stupid prince, whom I had never sworn allegiance to, and had no intention of doing so in the future, dictate when I would die. Death was the greatest threat to my plans of retirement. But this decision would protect nothing but Prince Arran's inflated ego.

So, I made a decision, and I took the opportunity to act on it. I jumped off the chair and I sprinted out the door.

"Stop!" Arran shouted behind me. "That's an order!"

His shouts did nothing to slow me down. In fact, they probably made my legs pump faster. Last time I'd run away from an important meeting like this, Driar Brigel had used his leaf magic to slam the door in front of me. I half expected this to happen again, or for Driar Yila to shoot a fireball in front of me blocking my path, or for Driar Lonamm to freeze me in place with an ice spell.

None of this happened, and I was soon back in the open world. It seemed to stink even more of rotten vegetable juice, but I didn't care as anything was better than that disgusting, dusty room.

9

TANTALISING TEMPTATIONS

Outside, it had got suddenly balmy – the kind of weather you want to be out sleeping in, not dying in an unfair fight against a forest golem. But I didn't have time to think about the weather. Rather, I needed to find a place to hide, and I had little time.

The Council Courtyard wouldn't provide much cover, and so I sprinted across the yard and through the archway into the main bailey.

I considered trying to escape the castle. But everywhere I looked, Prince Arran had posted his dragons. I had no chance of getting past the wall uncharred. Given how nasty this Prince Arran was, I doubted that he'd go easy on me with the punishments. Besides, last time I'd tried to run away, it had resulted in me almost getting eaten by serkets and a giant spider.

With Prince Arran's dragons posted everywhere – on the *chemin de ronde*, by every door, by the portcullis, and atop the towers, I had no option other than to use my favourite hiding place – underneath the stone fountain where Rine and Bellari liked to sit and kiss. I kept myself low, edging as far as I could underneath. From my safehold, I watched feet pass by as prefects shouted out orders, and students filed into neat positions.

"*Bengie, Bengie, what are you doing now?*" Salanraja said in my mind.

"*I'm hiding from the prince. We cannot go over to fight that forest golem alone. It will kill us, and you know it.*"

"*Even if we've never seen such a future happen in the crystal?*"

"*But you heard it yourself, Salanraja. Prince Arran changed the future when he meddled with the affairs of the crystal.*"

"*And you think hiding is going to fix this?*"

"*I don't see any other choice. Just leave me alone, Salanraja.*" She tried to chide me more, but I'd had enough of listening to humans and dragons for one day. So, I mentally refused to translate her words, which became babble at the back of my mind.

I don't know for how long I stayed under the fountain. The very act of zoning out from Salanraja's thoughts made them sound like dream-speak, which probably sent me to sleep. The next thing I knew, a rich clucking sound jostled me awake. Seramina's voice floated down beneath the fountain.

"Oh, Ben," she said. "You do have a habit of getting yourself into a fix, don't you? Why don't you just learn to trust your elders for a change? All the Driars, including Aleam, at least have your best interest at heart."

I growled at her dainty feet, and the tiny toes pointing out of her sandals. Part of me wanted to reach out and scratch them as if they were mice. But I was admittedly still afraid of Seramina and what she might do if I caused her pain. Despite her apparent and recent niceness, she was Astravar's daughter after all.

"I'm not coming out," I said. "I'm going to stay under here forever."

"I don't doubt you might. Unless, of course, I provide a good reason for you not to."

Something small hit the floor, bouncing twice. The sweet aroma of roasted duck assaulted my nostrils. I stared at it, and it seemed to look back at me as if it had eyes. My mouth watered, and I felt the invisible pull towards the appetising food.

"I know what will happen if I come out," I said. "You'll pick me up, then I'll have no choice but to scratch you and hide under here again."

"But it's delicious and tantalising duck. Hallinar caught and roasted this only half an hour ago. Salanraja tells him you've not had duck for an awfully long time. Am I right?"

I knew it – Seramina hadn't changed. Despite her apparent niceness, she was still so cruel. Another morsel of duck fell onto cobblestones, this time less of a chunk and more of a strip. "Just think of all the delicious food you're missing out on, Ben. If you don't come out, you might never have roast duck again." She threw another chunk down on the floor, this time with a delicious amount of skin trailing off of it. I could smell the fat oozing out from the meat, and I wanted it so much.

Whiskers, I had to resist. My life and plans for retirement depended on it. But despite me knowing this, inch by inch I edged towards the base of the fountain. I didn't run for the duck yet, though. Instead, I stood there, staring up at Seramina. She looked back down at me with her pale gaze. She had no staff, no way of using magic. I was safe.

"Here's another one," Seramina said. "Look how delicious it is." Another chunk hit the floor. Whiskers, this was absolute torture. Then I realised. I was a cat, and I would be much faster than her. I only needed to grab a chunk, then I could retreat to safety and munch to my heart's content.

"Put your hands behind your back," I said. "And take two steps back."

"Very well," Seramina said, and she followed my instructions with a faint smile.

I edged forward, watching her every move. Seramina didn't even flinch, and the food drew me towards it. I quickly pounced forward and took the piece with extra skin on it inside my mouth.

It was only at the last minute that I realised something smelled wrong. It wasn't so much the duck, but the surrounding air. The sensation of snowdrop perfume wasn't coming from where I saw Seramina, but to my right.

As the image of Seramina in front of me dissipated, I screeched and turned back towards the fountain. But the real Seramina was too fast. A white beam hit me on the side of the head, tickling only slightly as a warming sensation washed over my skull. I felt suddenly sluggish, frozen in place. Seramina floated over from the right, and she scooped me up in one arm, while she kept the hand of the other wrapped around her staff.

I couldn't move my legs easily. They felt numb, but I could still speak and yowl. "What are you doing?" I asked. "You're such a cruel mind-witch." I screeched out, and I tried to draw attention to myself, hoping that a dragon would stop her long enough that I could return to my hiding place.

The dragon standing on the East Tower turned its head towards us. But before it could spot us, Seramina pointed her staff upwards. It cast a fountain of energy over us. Seramina's arms, and her face, and my paws, and everything else about us vanished from view.

The dragon on the tower roared, and other dragons around it joined in the chorus.

"Will you stop causing such a commotion, Ben?" Seramina asked. "We're on your side."

I wasn't listening. I was growling and screeching at the top of my voice. Even so, I couldn't move my legs to scamper. I couldn't see Seramina beneath me, but I felt her hurrying her pace towards the open door of Aleam's study. Aleam waited there by the doorway, looking from side to side nervously.

Seramina waltzed me inside, and then said, "We're in."

"Good," Aleam said, and he shut the door behind him and bolted it twice.

10

PLANS ARE BORING

R ine and Ange were sitting on the bench where Ta'ra should
have been, when I entered Aleam's study. There was too much
room between them and too much tension as well, hanging there like
an approaching storm. But at that moment, I didn't care too much
about my distant retirement plans with Ange and Rine. I had to
preserve my near future first.

I scanned the room for a place to hide. The door to Aleam's
bedroom was shut, so I couldn't retreat under his bed. That left under
the sofa, or under the desk – both of which were too accessible by
human hands. The window was also closed, so there was no way out
that way.

Seramina gazed at me passively – her eyes looking relaxed, very
unlike they'd been when I first met her. She stood next to Aleam by
the door, with her staff pointed at me, the crystal on it glowing white.
The original paralysis spell she'd cast had worn off. I could move my
legs normally, although they ached a little, as if I'd just been chasing
butterflies for hours. But if I tried any sudden movements, I had no
doubt she'd paralyse me again.

"Gracious demons, sit down, will you, Ben?" Aleam said, a slight whisper in his voice. "Prince Arran is out searching for you. We have little time before they decide to search my quarters too."

Because of Seramina's trickery before, part of me didn't want to trust them. It wasn't just that they'd whisked me here against my will, but Seramina also hadn't given me an adequate portion of roast duck. But I realised that if Prince Arran found me, he'd banish Salanraja and I from Dragonsbond Academy altogether, and only let us back in if I returned with a staff in my mouth and the knowledge of how to use it to defeat Astravar.

Groaning, I made my way over to the sofa and sat between Rine and Ange. Ange put out her hand to stroke me, but I hissed at her and raised a paw with bared claws, so she jerked away quickly. Rine looked at her, then at me, and snorted.

I took a little time to scan the room, and the only thing that was different was a wooden easel against the far wall with a rolled-up scroll affixed to the top of it.

"Now, Ben," Aleam said, sounding slightly annoyed. "Stop blocking off your dragon and reach out to her. She can explain things through thought much faster than we can through words."

I hadn't even realised. That mental shift I'd made before had kept Salanraja still babbling at the back of my mind.

I focused on the words again. *"I'm here,"* I told her.

"Bengie, never, ever do that again!" She didn't sound happy.

"What?"

"You blocked me off, which is one of the worst things you can do to a dragon. Not only is it rude, but if you hold it long enough, you could kill our bond completely."

That sounded, admittedly, ever so slightly appealing. *"Aleam told me you need to explain promptly what's going on. So instead of giving me a lecture, maybe you should do so?"*

I felt Salanraja's frustration boiling in my own chest for a moment before she found the will to suppress it. *"We're going to escape,"* she said. *"The whole of Dragonsbond Academy – including the Council of Three – really doesn't like Prince Arran's idea to send us off into the fray like he discussed, and so we've gathered your most loyal friends to come on the mission with you. There's no way we'll survive facing a forest golem by ourselves."*

"Even if destiny says we must get that staff?"

"Destiny probably dictated Aleam, Seramina, Rine, Ange, and their dragons would go along with you in the first place. The Driars here have always held that you shouldn't treat a crystal's reading as a given, reducing those resources that seem sensible for the mission at hand. That, they believe, is tempting fate. But Prince Arran is young, arrogant and doesn't believe in old wisdom. Hence, we've had to take matters into our own hands."

"So basically no one likes him. Why don't we just tie him up and lock him in the dungeon?"

"Don't be stupid, Bengie. Arran's dragons and dragon riders are completely on his side. He's also a member of the royal family, and so the only person who can give the edict to lock him up is the king."

"Why do we need an edict? We've got enough students and dragons here to overpower him and his forces."

"And with war on the horizon, how do you think the warlocks would react if one of their spies sees mutiny in our ranks?"

"I don't know..."

"Well, I do. They'd use the chaos as an opportunity to charge in and take Dragonsbond Academy as their own. I hope they never ever decide to make you a leader, Bengie. You're clearly a poor strategist."

She was wrong, of course. I was as good a strategist as I needed to be. I knew how to look endearing to people, for example, to get myself a good meal. *"From what you're telling me, it doesn't seem a brilliant strategy to disobey this prince air marshal guy either. We'll just come back, he'll clip your wings and lock me in the cattery or something."*

"We'll sort that out when we return with the staff, after we've defeated the forest golem." Salanraja said.

"If we defeat the forest golem," I pointed out.

"Let's take it one step at a time, shall we..."

While Salanraja and I had been conversing telepathically, Aleam had used his alembic to brew an aromatic cup of tea. The apparatus whistled, shrilly and painfully. Aleam turned off the burner underneath the bulb and then poured out four delicate teacups' worth.

Seramina took two of these over to Ange and Rine, and then she went back to grab a cup for herself.

Aleam turned to me. "Well, Olan tells me you've been fully briefed," he said.

"I wouldn't say fully," I said. "But I've learned enough. And I forgive you, Seramina. Next time, if you try using the food-bait and mind-magic trick on me, I won't fall for it."

"I'm sure you won't," Aleam said with a chuckle, while Seramina shook her head incredulously.

Aleam walked up to the easel on the other side of the room. He unrolled the scroll on it from the top to reveal a hand-drawn map of Dragonsbond Academy, with circles and crosses and other symbols scrawled across it. "Time then for our escape plan," he said. "Is everyone listening?"

Rine, Ange, and Seramina mumbled their agreement, and I groaned. Listening to him would probably send me to sleep, despite the imminent danger. I hated lectures. Plus, there was something about the flowery aroma of that tea that was making me extra tired. I yawned, then I noticed a piece of string dangling from a book on Aleam's high bookshelf. I went over to it, tried to swipe at it, but it was too high up. Instead, I chirped, hoping someone would lower the string so I could use it to keep awake.

"Ben, are you listening?" Aleam asked.

"Of course I'm listening. And I shall do so while focusing intently on this piece of string."

Aleam sighed, then he turned back to his scroll. He droned on and on about an escape plan and something about Seramina using her glamour magic, and for Ange and Rine to get ready to provide support, just in case her concentration lapsed.

"I can help too," I said.

Aleam's jaw dropped, and Rine turned back to me, goggle-eyed. "Whatever you do, don't turn into a chimera," he said. "This is meant to be a stealth operation."

"Fine," I said, and I went to lick the last morsels of smoked trout from the bowl on the floor.

Aleam was tapping nervously on the floor, glancing to the window every now and again. "We better be making a move then. There's no telling when Prince Arran will send his dragon riders to investigate here." He walked up to the door and glanced back at Seramina. "Are you sure you can handle this?"

"I don't think we have a choice," Seramina said, and she took her staff in her hands and walked out the door.

11

WHEN PLANS GO WRONG

I tried to follow Seramina. But Rine's heavy hands grasped me at the back of my belly and jerked me to a halt.

"Don't you dare, Ben," he said. "I thought you'd said you had listened to the plan?"

"I did," I lied. "I just thought it better to follow Seramina, as she has the glamour magic."

Aleam stood shaking his head. "It's going to take a while for her to cause a disruption. She needs time to distract Prince Arran's dragon riders."

"Right," I said, and I jumped up on Rine's legs, purring. Ange reached over to stroke me, and this time I let her. I had a feeling we wouldn't have any moments of comfort like this for a while, and besides, doing this brought Ange closer to Rine. Now, all I had to do was get Rine to hold Ange's hand. I tried to nudge Ange over towards him, but instead he lifted his hand and stroked me on the tail. I growled at him – it wasn't me that needed stroking, it was Ange. But he just didn't seem to get it.

"What?" he asked, shrugging slightly.

I stared at him a moment and then blinked off my frustration. "Have you told Dellari you're going away?"

He snorted. "Bellari? Gracious demons, no. If she knows where I am, then Prince Arran would get the information out of her pretty quickly."

"You don't have to tell her where you've gone."

"Oh, I do. I won't get to tell her I'm going away without telling her where I'm going."

I purred, approving very much of this situation. It meant that when Rine got back, Bellari would be angry with him, consequently increasing the chances that they'd break up and then I could work on getting Rine and Ange together. The only problem was Prince Arran might separate them permanently, and so I'd have to deal with that potential problem too. But, as Salanraja had so succinctly put it, I needed to take things one step at a time.

Aleam now stood at the doorway. After a moment, he turned to the three of us on the sofa, looking alarmed. "It didn't work. We've got Prince Arran with two of his guards coming our way." He closed the door and latched it. Then he backed away and paused, breathing heavily.

A knock came soon after – a heavy rap-rap-rap that sounded like it was produced by metal, not flesh. Either whoever was on the other side had a metal gauntlet, or they were pounding with the haft of a sword.

Aleam glanced over at the cupboard, as if wondering if he could hide me there, then he shook his head and glanced towards the window. "Check no one's outside," he whispered. "Not you, Ben. You stay there."

Ange and Rine stood up together, looked at each other, then Rine moved towards the window. He slid it open from the bottom, and peeked out. "Can't Seramina do—"

"Shh!" Aleam interrupted.

He glanced at the door again, then back to me and shook his head. I turned back to Rine, who signalled a circle with his thumb and fore-finger. The wind from the window whipped his long hair into his face, and he brushed it away.

The knocking came from the door again, this time louder. "Driar

Aleam," Prince Arran said from outside. "Open up. This is the only place left that the cat can be."

"One moment," Aleam called out. Then he turned and whispered, "Go. Now!"

"But Driar Aleam…" Ange whispered, now standing up.

"Escape with Seramina, then we'll work the rest out. She knows to go ahead without me if needs be."

The banging came from the door a third time, this time so loud it shook the shelf and the equipment on the desk. "Driar Aleam. I will not ask a third time. Open the door, or I'll order it broken down."

I didn't need to be prompted further. I stood up on the bench, and I ran the short length between there and the window, then I leaped outside, scratching my hind paws against the window frame as I went. I had been in such a rush, that I hadn't really been watching where I'd been going, because I almost stumbled right into the armoured leg of one of Prince Arran's guards.

I stopped myself and dashed back into a bush underneath Aleam's window. It was rife with brambles, which scratched and stung, but I was so afraid of what might happen next, I didn't care. That was when I realised the guard hadn't even noticed me. He stood staring right at the window with glazed eyes. Meanwhile, Rine, then Ange clambered out of it right under his nose. A door creaked behind me, and I heard Aleam saying something softly.

A white light shone from my side, and I turned to see Seramina's staff, and the girl's platinum blonde hair flailing in the wind. Multiple white beams streaked like continuous bolts of lightning out of this staff, dancing in a zig-zag fashion. Some of these shot out towards the guards that Arran had arranged outside Aleam's abode. An even larger one was focused on the emerald dragon that sat atop the East Tower where Salanraja lived. The dragon faced the courtyard fountain, and it was so still it looked like a statue, or perhaps one of those hideous gargoyle things I once saw when out exploring some church grounds in South Wales.

Seramina looked down at me, this time with her fiery eyes. I backed away slightly.

"I can't hold this forever," she said. "Get over to Salanraja's."

"Salanraja's?"

"*Yes, you moron,*" my dragon said in my mind. "*If you'd been listening, then you'd have realised that we were always going to use this place as the rendezvous.*"

"*I—*"

"*Just get going,*" Salanraja said. "*As the girl said, you don't have much time.*"

Rine had moved closer to the bush, and he had drawn his foot back as if about to kick me. Just as his foot started to swing, I scurried out and towards the tower. I didn't look back at the two guards' legs I passed between, and they didn't seem to notice me either. Rine's and Ange's footsteps pounded behind. As I went, I saw the white light from Seramina's staff dancing around me, casting ethereal glows into the gaps between the cobblestones.

There was something off about that light. It didn't seem as strong as it should be. It wasn't steady, but guttering like candlelight. But I didn't let my fears slow me, and I didn't have time to worry about getting caught.

Dragons roared out all around me, and Seramina cried out. Next there came several shouts from the guards, and a deep rumbling growl of thunder emerged from a suddenly darkening sky. Even brighter flashes crashed around me, shooting into the ground from the gravid clouds above. The stones beneath shook, almost tripping me up.

"Aleam! The traitor…" Prince Arran's voice called out from behind me. "Seize him!"

Presumably with the entire castle focused on Aleam, I reached the East Tower's spiral staircase safely. I sprinted up it so fast that I was out of breath at the top. My burning legs carried me into Salanraja's chamber. She already had her tail lowered, and I rushed onto her, and then nestled myself in a safe place on her back within her corridor of spikes.

She took off, and I peered out from behind to see Rine, Ange, and Seramina standing at the opening of Salanraja's chamber. Their dragons came swooping around from the side of the academy in single file. Quarl came first, and Ange dropped onto him, landing with such grace in the saddle that she could have been a cat herself. Ishtkar followed, and Rine jumped down onto her, a little more clumsily, but he managed to stop himself falling off once he caught the pommel with both hands. Seramina jumped last onto Hallinar so lightly she almost seemed to float.

More flashes of lightning came from the academy, and I saw Aleam standing in the bailey at the centre of a group of Arran's guards, their staffs raised high, the crystals on them glowing in different colours. All the dragons in the castle now had their heads turned to him, and I'm not sure we even needed the cloak of invisibility that Seramina cast around our tight formation.

The prince's dragon riders surrounded Aleam with their crystals glowing on their staffs, and I thought that was it, then. They'd toast Aleam with their magic. But instead, Arran stepped forward, his red cloak trailing behind him. A bright white beam shot out from his staff, and it hit Aleam right on the forehead.

I couldn't see much now from this distance – us cats don't have great eyesight. But Rine later told me that Aleam's legs went wobbly before he collapsed to the ground in a heap.

Another crash of thunder came from the sky, and I took shelter behind Salanraja's neck. Soon, the heavens opened and, oh, did it pour.

12

FLIGHT TO AUROREST

Though the clouds had cleared, trepidation still hung in the air. No one hollered a word from their mounts. No dragons roared into the sky. Even Salanraja remained silent inside my mind. We all flew onwards – Rine, Ange, and Seramina hunched in their saddles. The dragons' wings beat in a slow and steady rhythm, as if part of a rehearsed dance choreographed to help push the clouds and the looming darkness away. Only Seramina cast magic from her staff – a near transparent dome that engulfed our close formation, presumably containing a type of glamour spell to prevent any guard or dragon spotting us from afar. A bitter trailing wind had washed away the scent of ozone and rain.

The castle was now a tiny pinprick, almost invisible behind the low, thin layer of clouds. If Prince Arran and his lackeys could see us at all from there, they'd probably think we were geese or some other large bird. I wondered how long it would be until he noticed we'd left.

All this was my fault. I shouldn't have run away from that pompous idiot, Prince Arran. I should have made it look like I was going along with his plans, stupid as they were. If he'd had nothing to suspect, then the Council of Three would have found a way to sneak out some allies with me. Then, Aleam would be a part of our party.

I now had Ange, Rine, and Seramina with me to protect me against any traps Astravar might have deployed en route. But compared to Aleam, they were nothing. The old man would probably be arrested and thrown in the smelly dungeon that allegedly lay below Dragonsbond Academy and hadn't been used in years.

"*We've got to stop,*" I said to Salanraja.

"*Really, Bengie,*" she replied. "*This isn't a good time for a toilet break.*"

"*I don't need to go,*" I said. "*But we can't face the forest golem without Aleam. We need to go back and rescue him. I can become a chimera, and Seramina can cast her magic, and then Ange can entangle them all in vines while Rine freezes them all to the spot.*"

"*We've already been through this once. I'm not going to repeat it.*"

"*But how can we get the staff without Aleam? And what will they do to him, Salanraja? He might have to go without food for days.*" A deep groan emanated from the pit of my stomach, as I thought about Aleam's potential suffering. Salanraja and I remained silent for a short while.

Soon enough, there came a deep rumbling sound from the direction of the castle. It was the dragons there, roaring, sounding now like distant thunder. Salanraja turned her head back, just as a faint sound of bugles called, sounding like cheap toy horns from this distance.

"*Well, they've probably finally noticed that I and the other dragons are missing,*" Salanraja said.

"*Won't they know where you are automatically? Like when you knew where I was when I ran away and got captured by serkets?*"

"*No, because I and the other dragons aren't bonded. Only with you do I always know of your location.*"

"*But I thought you dragons can communicate long distance…*"

"*The other dragons can call out and we can answer if we choose. Even if we do, they'll have no way of knowing where we are unless we choose to tell them.*"

"*That's a relief,*" I said, and I flattened myself on Salanraja's back, as I watched the sun set behind the distant castle, casting an amber light into the wispy clouds that lingered after the storm.

Uncharacteristically, her flying was so smooth, and the commotion must have made me so tired that I drifted off to sleep. I dreamt of open cans of tuna floating through the clouds, lit by warm sunlight.

My reverie made for a satisfying diversion from this cruel and dark world.

What felt like moments later, the shrill cry of a seagull woke me. I'd learned back home to listen out for those vicious birds. They were one of the few dangers to cats in South Wales – a land that had been rid of horrors such as hippopotami and hyenas. The bird flew really close to Salanraja's tail, and I hissed at it, ready to swipe if it tried landing here. It wasn't until the seagull had flown away that I'd noticed what had been odd about it. Its feathers had a faint green glow to them and smelled of the kind of putrid lake where mosquitoes thrived, as if the bird had just been bathing in algae.

Salanraja laughed inside my mind. *"What are you so scared of, Ben?"*

"Birds," I said.

"I thought you hunted birds?"

"Not the big ones... Besides, this one glows in the dark."

"You really are a scaredy-cat, aren't you, Bengie? Despite being a descendant of the great Asian leopard cat and all that." She certainly sounded in better spirits than before, and admittedly after a little sleep, I felt less gloomy too.

"You still haven't told me much about where we're heading," I said. *"What is the Aurorest Forest, anyway?"*

"It's a forest. You know, a natural habitat with trees arranged close together?"

"I know that... But is it like the Willowed Woods? Do those horrible wargs live there?"

"No. No warg would dare to step into this forest."

I shuddered. *"Why not?"*

Salanraja's body rumbled underfoot, and I don't know if it was because she was laughing or sighing. *"There are things in the Aurorest Forest much worse than wargs. Life there grew so close to the warlocks' magic coming from the Wastelands that this life eventually adapted to contain magic itself. The mushrooms there will send you into a sleep you'll never wake up from, and the warlocks know how to track those spores. I'm sure Astravar will hunt you down pretty quickly if you get left there alone."*

"But would they send you to sleep too? Otherwise, you could just fly me away to safety."

"*They would. Just because dragons are magical, it doesn't mean we're immune to magic. But it's not just the mushrooms we need fear. There are vines that will grow around you and entangle you faster than a mouse can move. Once they have you secured tight, only then do they unleash their thorns. Then there are small creatures that live underground and that nothing alive has ever seen, because rumour has it that when you see them, you're already dead.*"

Another shudder went down my spine, this time almost a spasm. "*Do we have to go?*"

"*Of course. Astravar might have hidden your staff in a dangerous place on purpose, but we can't let that stop us. Once we retrieve it, you can fulfil the crystal's prophecy, and then hopefully this will all be over.*"

"*But if Astravar had the staff, why didn't he hide it in the Wastelands?*"

"*Firstly, the Aurorest Forest is now in the Wastelands. The warlocks have pushed the border forward, remember? As for your question, I don't know the answer to it. But you shouldn't underestimate the forest. No doubt, Astravar's forest golem will be constructed from parts of the forest. And anything that came from the forest, the forest will try to prevent from leaving. It's as if it has its own soul, you see, albeit a very dark one. The forest will fight to protect the forest golem, and so we need to be very careful indeed.*"

"*So it doesn't belong to the warlocks?*"

"*That's what the Wastelands is, remember? A no-man's-land, where battles rage between the magical creatures of King Garmin's White Mages and the dark magical creations of the warlocks.*"

"*But that means we'll have allies in there too.*"

"*I don't think so,*" Salanraja said.

"*Why not?*"

"*It's as I said. The forest is a magical creation of itself. Most creatures that either we or the warlocks send in there won't survive very long. A forest golem is different, because it's made of the forest. As for the Manipulators and bone dragons there that we saw in the crystal, Astravar must have worked some powerful sorcery to keep them there.*"

Salanraja was scaring me so much I wanted to throw up that roast duck Seramina had fed me before. "*I don't want to go there anymore. Let's turn back...*"

"*Nonsense. We're not even going to land in the Aurorest Forest. We'll fight the forest golem from the air. Burn it down until only your staff remains – because magical staffs cannot be burned by dragon fire – then we'll all go home and do what we have to do."*

"I'm never going back to my true home," I said. Then Salanraja growled, because she didn't like to be reminded I wasn't from her world.

The sun was now hidden behind a looming green mist. This didn't smell of rotten vegetable juice like Astravar and the other warlocks. It smelled instead of mould and algae – another scent I wasn't too partial to. I imagined the mushrooms on the ground, and I wondered if they were making me sleepy or if it was just my imagination. There had to be a positive way of looking at this, surely. In the distance I thought I heard running water, and that got me thinking.

"What about food?" I asked. *"Perhaps if the forest has magical qualities, there are good things to eat there as well. Maybe we should at least try to hunt for something. Perhaps, magically, some salmon has found its way into the streams."*

"There's no salmon there," Salanraja said. *"And if it were there, I wouldn't know what it looked like."*

"But it's worth looking for, isn't it? Salanraja, I haven't had salmon in ages."

"Gracious demons, will you just shut up for one moment!" Salanraja snapped.

"Why? What's wrong with salmon?"

"Because we're about to land."

The dragons loosened their formation, and they lowered towards the ground. I could see the mist clearly now behind the darkness, for it glowed like there was a green moon hidden behind it. I imagined I could make out shapes shifting around there – some of them wavering from their roots, others stalking the territory like wargs.

We were heading right for the glowing mist that presumably marked the borders of the forest. The dragons were getting so close to it that if what Salanraja said was true, those things moving inside would eat us alive. A sound emanated out from the forest that at first sounded like a scream. But then, when I listened longer, I noticed the yowling of sad creatures, the hissing of a wind that doesn't want water to stay still, and all the other kinds of sounds I might hear in my nightmares, all singing in a chorus that seemed to say, *stay well away.*

I clambered up Salanraja's neck onto her head, to get as far away from that mist as possible. *"I thought you said we weren't going to land,"* I said.

"Not in the forest, no," Salanraja said. *"The mist marks where it's safe and where it's not."*

"But why do we need to sleep at all?"

"Trust me, you don't want to send four tired dragons up against a forest golem. So long as no one lights a fire, we'll be fine."

Salanraja thudded against the ground, and she bucked her head so hard that she almost sent me tumbling off it. The other three dragons landed around her, and Ange, Rine, and Seramina launched themselves off from their saddles. Rine and Ange then produced two cotton bundles from Ishtkar's and Quarl's panniers. These turned out to be tents.

It took Rine and Ange several minutes to put these up. Soon after, Rine walked over to me and said, "I guess you're sleeping with me tonight, Ben. Without Aleam, we don't need the third tent."

"What, you're not sleeping with—" I almost said it, then I remembered how Seramina had gone back to her old scary self. No, Rine was right. It was better if I left her with Ange.

"Come on," Rine said, "let's get some sleep." He crawled into his tent, and I followed him. I doubted somehow that a thin layer of cotton would protect us from what horrors lay behind that luminous mist. But it was all we had.

13

A COLD NIGHT

I t was much colder than I'd expected in the tent – even with Rine there to provide extra warmth. There was something about this place that leached all the warmth out of the night. Maybe the forest sapped it away, feeding on it and casting a green spooky translucent glow through the tent fabric, the way that sunlight suffuses through skin.

I tried snuggling up as close as possible to Rine. First, I sat in front of his face where his breath could keep me warm, until he pushed me away, mumbling that I stank of fish. Then I stretched outwards towards his belly in an attempt to find the room that a mighty cat like me deserves. But unlike most humans, Rine wouldn't budge when I tried to push him away.

I mean, it was okay for Rine – he had a sleeping bag to keep him warm. All I had was my fur, and a frigid draught crept underneath the tent flap, then stirred around me until finally lurching in to cut through that fur.

It was too much for me. I had to go outside and keep moving. I lifted myself up on my paws and shook off the stiffness in my muscles from the flight. Then I flattened my body and edged underneath the tent flap.

The first thing I smelled when I stepped outside wasn't the rotten vegetable juice that I'd expected, given the Aurorest Forest was now reputedly part of the Wastelands, or that equally putrid algae smell that came from the forest proper. Instead, I smelled snowdrop perfume, and I turned to see Seramina standing in front of her tent, staring out at the green mist. She held her staff horizontally against her thighs. She didn't seem to notice me there until I rubbed up against her calf, purring.

The snores from the dragons and the sounds from the forest seemed to riff off of each other as if part of a performance piece. The noise was even louder than those nights I'd accidentally slept outside in Wales, to be surrounded by crickets. It was no wonder I couldn't get any sleep.

Seramina looked down at me, a glint of green mist catching in her eye. "Oh, Ben... What are you doing here? Shouldn't you be sleeping?"

"Couldn't sleep. But I am nocturnal after all... What about you?"

"Someone has to keep guard," she said with a slight smile, again seeming a little forced.

"I thought that the dangerous creatures that lived in the forest could never leave it." I said. "Don't they need the mist to survive?"

"Oh, but there are also things that live around the forest. This is the wilderness after all, and the fringes of the kingdom also house bandits. You should never assume you're safe." She turned her gaze back from me towards the mist. "You know, it's strange. But it's somewhat beautiful. I'd never have thought that a place like this... It doesn't matter."

I examined the mist, trying to work out what she was talking about. Given humans have inferior hearing to cats, perhaps she couldn't hear the screeches and yowls and sounds of nightmares that came from behind that glowing screen. "I don't know what you're talking about. It smells funny, and it sounds wrong, and I really don't want to go in there tomorrow."

"I guess you've seen the faery realm," Seramina said. "Because in the books, they say it's the most beautiful of the Seven Dimensions."

"Is it really the beauty you're attracted to?" I asked. "Or is it the power contained within the forest?"

"What do you mean?" For a moment, I could swear, some fire sparked in Seramina's eyes. But as soon as it was there, it vanished. "No, I don't want the magic. It's not good for me. I've learned that. I must only use my magic when I need it, and I mustn't embrace anything else. My father... I mean, Astravar, once was good, they say, until dark magic twisted his soul... I could never let that happen to me."

One of the dragons snorted from the darkness, briefly interrupting the harmony of snores. Then there came a rustling from our side and Ange crawled out of the tent flap. She sauntered over to us, stretching and yawning as she moved. "Seramina... You should have woken me. It's surely my turn to keep watch."

Seramina shook her head. "It's okay, you can sleep more. I'm not tired."

"Seramina, really. You can't stay up all night. You've got to sleep sometimes."

"I'm fine," she snapped, her voice raised and the tone of it biting against the wind. She raised her staff, and it started to glow. Fire momentarily burned at the back of her eyes.

Ange took a step back, her arms outstretched. She looked back at her tent, probably at the staff that lay there on the floor next to her fleece sleeping bag. "Seramina... Remember what Aleam told you. Calm your mind."

"I—" Seramina lowered her staff. "I'm sorry. I didn't mean any harm." Though her staff had stopped feeding the night with light, it still emitted a slight afterglow.

"You just thought you'd hypnotise me back to sleep?" Ange had her hands on her hips and her eyebrows raised. "You can't solve your problems with magic, Seramina. But you often can with a good night's rest." She glanced back at her tent.

"I know... But really, I'm not tired."

More rustling came, this time louder and from the other tent.

"What's going on here, then?" Rine said, as he peered out from the tent flap, resting on his elbows and not bothering to lift himself up. He had his staff grasped in his hands, raised at an angle, but it wasn't aglow.

"Nothing," Ange said. "I'm just replacing Seramina on the watch. Unless you've decided to be a gentleman and fill in for me?" She cocked her head like a pretty bird.

Rine shook his head. "I don't know what woke me, the sudden commotion out here or the fact it's so cold. It's freezing, in fact. That magical mist must suck all the heat out of the atmosphere or something. Ben, why did you leave? I was relying on you for warmth."

"I needed to get moving. You weren't warm enough for me, Rine. Look, why don't we light a fire?"

"With what?" Ange asked.

"We have four dragons over there."

Rine snorted. "And you plan to wake them, Ben?"

"Uh, no, I thought one of you might. You're better experienced with these things."

"We're not lighting a fire," Ange said. "It's too dangerous. There's no telling what might be on the surrounding roads."

"Oh, and who put you in charge?" Rine asked.

"I'm the oldest..."

"But not necessarily the wisest."

Ange scowled at Rine. Really, this man wasn't doing himself any favours with the lady he truly loved. I made a mental note to have a word with him about that later.

"I think you'll find she's much wiser than you," Seramina said.

"Well, I don't think it's particularly wise to freeze to death," Rine said. "Come on, we've got three magic users and a cat that can turn into a chimera, as well as four dragons. What can possibly hurt us?"

"Bandits if we're sleeping. Or worse, they could steal our staffs, then what will we fight the forest golem with?" Ange asked.

"Plus, a fire will make it harder for us to see them, and easier for them to see us," Seramina said – trust the girls to stick together.

"So will lighting the place up with that," Rine said, pointing to the crystal on top of Seramina's staff. He pulled in his legs to his chest and then leapt to his feet. "I'll go and get firewood. You want to come, Ben?"

"You mean into the forest?" I asked, and I growled a protest for effect.

Rine laughed. "No, we're not entering the Aurorest until morning. But there's plenty of trees outside the forest. There should be some decent firewood, and you could turn into a chimera to help keep guard against the *bandits*." He put an extra dry undertone on the last words, as if to communicate he didn't believe in such bandits.

"He shouldn't turn into a chimera, Rine," Ange said.

"Why not? We could all do with his strength."

"Because the more he does, the more he risks becoming one for life."

"And wouldn't that be cool?" Rine reached down to stroke me under the chin. "Our own personal chimera."

"Didn't you hear her?" Seramina asked. Her staff was back in her hands, glowing white, and her eyes were afire again. "We're not lighting a fire…"

"Whoa," Rine said.

"Seramina…" Ange said. "Control, remember?"

The mind-witch lowered her head, and the light on her staff guttered out. "I'm sorry… It's just… Aleam. I'm worried. Will he be okay? If my magic was stronger, he would be with us right now."

Ange sidled over to her and put her arm over her shoulder. "He's a tough old man. He'll wriggle his way out of this somehow."

"But what do you think Prince Arran will do to him?"

"I don't know," Ange said. "But it can't be anything too horrible. Prince Arran might be royalty, but he's still subject to the king's law. I'm sure the Council of Three will find a way to release Aleam, and then he'll fly right back out here to help us."

"Right…"

"You should get some sleep, really."

"But you seem so tired as well. I'll be okay," Seramina said through clenched teeth.

"Maybe," Ange yawned and turned to Rine. "I guess if our man here seems awake enough to get firewood, then he'll be well enough also to stand guard."

"No way," Rine said. "I'm getting under the sleeping bag again."

"So, I'll stand guard then," Ange said. "If Rine's too selfish to do so."

"No," Seramina said. "Really, you look exhausted, and I can function without sleep."

"Why don't I keep watch?" I suggested.

Rine guffawed, and Ange turned to me and stared, wide-eyed. "You can't do this, Ben," she said.

"Why not?"

"Because you'll just doze off. Besides, anyone who might have the eye on this camp isn't going to let themselves be deterred by a cat."

"Then I should become a chimera," I said.

"I thought we said that you weren't to become a chimera," Ange said.

But I wasn't listening. The power just felt so good. As I sucked it in, I could swear some thin tendrils of that glowing mist swept towards me, infusing me with the magic of the Aurorest Forest. My muscles writhed and twisted, and I mewled, and then growled and then roared out in pain. Two other heads emerged out of my neck and tail, and I had that sensation of being three animals again, with access to all their sights and hearings, and the ability to taste the world on my snake head's forked tongue.

"There," I said. "Two parts of me can sleep while the other one stays awake. Problem solved."

The three humans stood in place, looking completely gobsmacked. They had also taken several steps away from me and their hands were gripping their staffs, their knuckles white. It seemed they didn't quite trust that this time I might turn feral. But I knew how to keep control.

"*Bengie, I thought we said you weren't going to do that?*" Salanraja said to me, although her voice now sounded muffled, as it often did when I was in chimera form.

"*I thought you were sleeping?*"

"*I was until I felt our bond tensing. You know, if you do that enough, you won't just become feral, but you'll also break the bond between us. Just think what would happen to me then.*"

"*It was necessary!*"

"*What? How?*"

"*They just wouldn't shut up, and Seramina needs to sleep.*"

"*Oh, I knew I would have problems choosing a feline rider. If only our*" *crystal had told me what I'd be getting myself in for. Ah well, what can you do?"* And then, just like that, her thoughts drifted off to oblivion, and I heard her softly mumbling in my mind as if from her dreams.

Meanwhile, back at the campsite and outside the realm of my mind, it was Ange who broke the silence. "Well, I have to admit," she said with a shrug. "I've never seen a goat sleep."

"Yeah, me neither, come to think of it," Rine said. "Say, do goats actually sleep at all?"

Ange had now taken hold of Seramina's hand and was dragging her into the tent. "Come on," she said. "Before it gets bright. You need to get at least a couple of hours of shuteye."

Both girls vanished into the tent. Rine also lowered himself back into his tent. "I guess I'm just going to freeze by myself in here, then," he said, and he let out a yawn that looked almost feline in its vastness.

Funnily enough, the goat part of me didn't feel tired. But I could swear that the snake part and cat part of me caught a few more winks. There was nothing to watch out for though – the whole 'bandits' dilemma had been a complete farce. There weren't any bandits around to fear, and those strange noises from the mist stayed within the mist. Besides, given I had a lion's strength, a snake's venom, and a goat's speed to fight back with, I didn't feel scared of anything.

As I stared off into the darkness, my snake's tongue tasted something in the air. The whiff of rotten vegetable juice floating in faint streams upon the currents that smelled of rotten algae. I'd discovered a trace of more than one dark magical creature in there, and tomorrow I vowed to hunt them down.

❧ 14 ❧

BRO TIME

The next morning, Ange finally allowed us the privilege of lighting a fire.

So, I went with Rine into the surrounding woods that weren't part of the Aurorest Forest and didn't fall under its shroud of glowing mist. Admittedly, it was no longer so cold that we needed a fire, but there was a promise of mutton sausages on the horizon. Rine had already expressed his annoyance to Ange that we had skipped our age-old dragon rider tradition of roasting them on the campfire, all because of her fear of bandits that weren't there. But Ange had said she'd only delayed it and that they would still have the sausages - for breakfast, once the well-rested Initiate proved his worth and gathered the firewood.

We did, of course, need to work out the location of the forest golem. I'd had time to assess the smell, and I could also taste various streams of dark magic on my snake's tongue. Some of them, no doubt, belonged to the bone dragons and Manipulators that we'd seen here in the crystal. But anything could wait for nutritious food, particularly food that had been freshly barbecued on an open fire.

I went with Rine, not so much because I wanted to chop firewood, but because I had work to do in sealing up the rift that had widened between Ange and Rine the previous night.

I was still in chimera form as Rine and I hiked through the woods, and I scanned every single tree we passed – beeches and poplars and silver birches – wondering which of them I'd end up knocking down with my goat horns. Rine would have to weaken the trunk first with his hatchet, of course, but I'd do the hard work of actually felling it.

Rine stopped by a large horizontal trunk of dry silver birch that had already fallen, probably in a storm. He smiled and then unlatched his hatchet from his waist. I went over to sniff the bark and noticed there wasn't anything peculiar about it. It didn't smell of disgusting algae or rotten vegetable juice or anything like that.

"I thought we were going to chop down some trees," I complained. I'd been looking forward to the whole ramming down a tree part. I hadn't used my goat ability since I'd defeated the demon Maine coone.

"Why would we do that, when there's perfectly good firewood on the ground?" Rine asked.

"Well, come to think of it, why would we do any of this searching for firewood when Ange could just generate some using her leaf magic."

Rine laughed. "Have you ever tried to burn wet grass?"

"Can't say I have. Have you ever seen a cat try to burn anything?"

"I guess not." Rine shrugged. "Well, let's just say that Ange can only work with stuff that's alive, which tends to be full of water, meaning it won't burn well." He ran his hand along the branch. "This beauty, on the other hand, has dried out and will make perfect kindling. Which might make a particularly smoky fire, cooking perhaps the best mutton sausages you've ever tasted."

I chirped, liking the sound of that. "So basically, you didn't need me here at all?" I said. "Because it looks like there's nothing I can do to help you chop the firewood."

"I appreciate the company," Rine said, raising his hatchet slowly as he lined up a perfect place to chop the wood. "Besides, aren't you meant to be guarding me in case any bandits attack? I might not be able to get to my staff in time, and I'm not particularly good at throwing an axe."

"There are no bandits. I would have smelled them..."

"I know. It's ridiculous, right? Ah well, girls will be girls."

Rine brought his axe down, slicing right through a large chunk of bark and wood. He nodded, clearly satisfied that his instrument was sharp enough. I watched him for a while, as he worked away at the tree, occasionally stopping to wipe sweat away from his brow with the back of his hand. Eventually it became rather boring, and a passing dragonfly caught my attention. I started after it until I realised that a beast three size the times of a lion was meant to hunt larger things.

So, I turned back to Rine, who had just paused to take a breather, and I focused on the issue at hand. "When are you going to say it to her?" I asked him.

"Say what, and to who?"

"Ange... When are you going to tell her what you truly feel about her?"

Rine looked at me as if he was considering kicking me, but he probably realised I was much bigger and much scarier than him in this form. "Not this again. How many times do I have to tell you, Ben? Ange and I aren't a thing. I'm with Bellari. And that's how I intend it to be for a very long time."

"But not forever," I said.

"I..." Rine looked away. "I didn't say that."

"But you meant it, and do you know why? Because you have feelings for Ange... And if I keep nagging you about them enough, you'll one day act on them. Then, you know what? I think you're going to make a great family."

Rine laughed. "I can't imagine myself having little Ange babies. They'll be so bossy, and they'll think they're the smartest kids in the world. No thanks, Ben. Really."

I barked out a laugh. "Is that what you're scared of? You don't want your kids to be smarter than you? Then tell me, what has Bellari got to offer from the gene pool?"

"It's not that, it's just... Look I can't believe we're having this conversation, Ben. Just shut up. I'm not going to talk about it anymore." He brought down his axe again with such vigour that it looked like he might chop off his hand.

Now, I don't know if being a chimera made me smarter. Perhaps the goat had a bigger brain, or I just had the idiosyncratic cunning of a snake. But I realised through this that I was trying the wrong strategy with Rine. I needed to come in from the side. There was no point telling Rine what his feelings were. I had to make him realise them for himself.

"You know, I've never told you this, but I have regrets."

"What? That you never had another mouthful of that fish, what did you call it, salmon, before you came into this world?" Rine said this with a smile that contained half a mocking sneer.

"No, not that. But I do miss salmon. Now, though, I'm talking about Ta'ra."

Rine stopped a while and looked up at me. "What about her?"

"I never told her about how I really felt before she left us to look after the other Cat Sidhe."

"So why didn't you say anything?" Rine asked.

"Because I wasn't honest with myself about my feelings. Whiskers, I'm not even sure cats are meant to have these kinds of feelings. We're meant to be solitary creatures that look after ourselves, unless we need to eat food, and then someone feeds us, and we go back to looking after ourselves again."

"What are you trying to say, Ben?" Rine cocked his head.

"I'm trying to say that I wish I'd have told her at least how much I wanted her to stay. Because now, I don't know, I might never get to see her again. That's how it is… If we don't seize the opportunities we have when we're presented with them, they don't tend to come up again."

Rine placed his axe down on the trunk and stood up with his hands on his hips, looking me square in the eyes. "And you think it's the same with me and Ange?"

"Oh, I know so," I said, adding a deep rumbling leonine purr of victory to my voice. "You regret getting into that relationship with Bellari and part of you wants to get out and start a relationship with Ange. But you feel too much peer pressure, because your 'friends' are so proud of you for landing such a catch. So you convince yourself that you were 'meant' to be with Bellari all along."

Rine puckered his mouth and sucked air through his tight lips, making a slight whistling sound. "Well, look at you, mister insightful."

"Are you telling me I'm wrong?"

Rine paused and stared into space. "Fine," he said after a moment. "I'm going to tell you what you want to hear, and that will be the end of it. Yes, I feel something for Ange. But of course I do, because she's been my friend all of my life."

"I think it's more than just a 'she's my friend' kind of feeling. You feel more for her than you do for Bellari. Admit it!"

Rine's face had almost gone bright puce, and he looked like he would kick me right now, with no regard for if I was a chimera or not. But when he looked into my eyes, and I yawned, showing him my huge sharp fangs, I guess he came to his senses. "Okay, I feel more for her than I do for Bellari," he said.

"Finally... A confession. So, the next question is, what are you going to do about it?"

"I'm going to do absolutely nothing," Rine said, with a smirk. "And I'll live with those regrets the rest of my life probably, just like you do. I'll be a fallen hero type. I'll complain about it for the rest of my life until I find another girl. I won't marry Bellari in the end, and I know that. I'll eventually, in the wider world, find another girl who isn't Bellari, and isn't Ange, and she'll be beautiful, and then I'll live a very happy life."

I watched Rine as he spoke, my eyes wide, trying to work out if he was serious or just having a jest with me. He waxed lyrical about the type of girl he'd eventually marry. About her upbringing – filthy rich, her hair colour – red like Asinda's, her eyes – a beautiful turquoise green, her measurements. Funnily enough, not once did he mention anything about her personality. Even worse, he hadn't even stopped to consider her quality as a chef. Not that I'm saying a woman needed to be, just I doubted Rine knew his fried eggs from his poached ones.

It seemed as if he would go on and on forever unless I did something about it. "Okay, that's enough," I said. "Go back to chopping firewood, and I might even take another nap."

"A nap? You just slept all night."

"And now it's daytime, a good time for sleeping." I laid my head against the ground and I closed my eyes. But I didn't end up sleeping. Rather, I continued to listen to Rine's chop-chop-chopping of wood, the occasional strand of bark brushing against my whiskers.

Inside, though, I was content. Because despite Rine shining me on, I had made progress. I'd finally made him admit he liked Ange romantically. Now, I had to work out how to break it to her.

15

SAUSAGES

J ust as Ange was the oldest human in our party, Quarl was the oldest dragon, and so the emerald had the honour of lighting the campfire. Everyone stood behind him as he drew back his long neck. A rumbling sound grew in his belly while his nostrils smoked and whistled like a kettle ready to boil. He opened his mouth and out came a jet of amber flame. It hit the neat arrangement of firewood in the centre of the pit, casting out a bright light and long shadows from the ring of stones on the outside that Ange and Seramina had gathered while I was chopping firewood with Rine.

The fire came to life, and its flames shot upwards, reaching into the sky. I watched it for a moment, appreciating the warmth. Then Rine walked over to Ishtkar and took a huge string of sausages out of his panniers. This was so large, he had to place it over his neck before he deposited it in front of the dragons who had gathered in a loose circle. He took another smaller string, separated the links with a pocketknife, then skewered several individual sausages, and started to roast them on the open flame. He sat on a log as he did so, and I watched, mesmerised by both the fat spitting on the sausage and the wonderful aroma it sent up into the air.

Ange joined him on the log. This time she sat next to Rine, a little closer to him. Being a chimera, I was a little too big to sit on a log, and so I curled up by Rine's and Ange's feet as I stared into the flames. Only Seramina didn't sit. Instead, she stood staring into the mist, facing away from us, seemingly uninterested in our feast. Meanwhile, the dragons started to toast their own sausages. All this fire roaring around us cast such an impressive display of light that I forgot momentarily about the glow coming from the Aurorest Forest, and the shadowy shapes that moved within the mist.

"Me first," I said. "Please, Rine, let me have the first sausage."

He looked at me and scoffed. "Turn back into a normal cat, first," he said. "Otherwise, you'll eat more than we can spare."

"No," I said. "I'm staying as a chimera. That way, we have the best bet of defeating the forest golem." From behind me, Salanraja gave a disgruntled snort. But I guess she was so much into roasting her food that she didn't this time bother chiding me.

Ange, however, did. "Ben, this isn't wise," she said. "Remember what happened when you turned into a chimera in the dragon egg-and-spoon? Seramina ended up winning, because you were too heavy for Salanraja to carry."

"She would have won anyway," I pointed out. "Me turning into a chimera gave us the best chance."

I looked up at Seramina, expecting a reaction. She said nothing. She had her staff braced horizontally across her thighs, as the firelight cast pretty patterns over her platinum blonde-hair.

"This isn't the point, and you know it," Ange said. "You'll be far too heavy for Salanraja in your current form. Then, by the time she gets to the forest golem, she'll be too exhausted to fight. Without Olan here, we need all the dragons in tip-top shape. So, as the leader here, I'm ordering you to turn back into a cat."

"I wasn't planning to fly," I said. "I can go by myself through the Aurorest Forest on foot if you want?"

"You've got to be kidding," Rine said. "Great, the cat's being a moron again."

"What?"

Ange was a little more tactful in her approach. "Just because you're a chimera, Ben, doesn't make you invincible. Even in your form the mushrooms will send you to sleep if you try passing through. Then, other creatures in there will emerge and devour you whole. And all that will be before you even get to the forest golem.

"But from the air, I'll lose the trail. If we don't take advantage, we might never find the forest golem. Then, if I don't get the staff, how are we meant to defeat Astravar?"

"A forest golem won't be hard to miss," Rine said.

"Really, and you think we'll be able to see it through that thick mist? Plus, it's got Manipulators and bone dragons guarding it. If we track it on the ground, we reserve the element of surprise."

Ange was shaking her head. "Why don't you ask what your dragon thinks?" she said, her voice slightly raised. "In fact, why don't you ask what all the dragons think?"

I turned back to Salanraja, who had just finished devouring her huge mutton sausage. Still, the scent of it lingered on the air, making me feel even hungrier. I'd much rather be eating than arguing. But I knew we needed the staff as fast as possible. Maybe being part lion gave me extra bravado, but I really needed to make my point.

"*I guess you're going to give me a lecture now,*" I said to Salanraja inside my mind as she turned her head to me.

"*It's not just me,*" Salanraja said. "*Every single one of us dragons thinks you're being idiotic.*"

"*Why? Because I want to take a bit of action around here?*"

"*No, because you're letting your pride impede good old-fashioned common sense. Why don't you listen to people who are wiser than you for once, Ben? Ange, at least, has a good head on her shoulders.*"

"*Because this time I know I'm right. We need to act while we've got the advantage.*"

"*No,*" Salanraja said. "*That's how people like Prince Arran and his dragon Corralsa think. The warlocks will take advantage of such impatience when they notice it. We need to act in a measured way.*"

"*I've thought this through,*" I said. "*I had an entire night to think about it.*"

"*Hah, I never thought I'd meet the day when you think about something first.*"

"*I still let it process in the back of my mind. What do you call that place?*

The subconscious!"

"Did you? Because I don't think you have a clue. Tell me this if you've got such a grand plan. How will you sneak in exactly? What will, in fact, give you the element of surprise?"

"I'll be stealthy."

"What, as a massive chimera beast? You'll stick out like a mouldering talon."

Salanraja's words struck true. A chimera wouldn't be particularly stealthy. For this mission, we needed me in my true form. I could pass through the Aurorest Forest as a Bengal, undetected, much as I'd done many times through the wilderness of my South Wales neighbourhood back home. Besides, Rine and Ange had already started munching on a couple of sausages, and Rine had told me I needed to be a normal cat to eat one.

So, I let the magic seep back into my bones, the way that my crystal had taught me. My muscles gained that stretching sensation – this time due to them shrinking. I roared out in pain, and I continued this way until the roar shrank to a growl, and then a soft chirp. Rine glanced at me, smiled, then he tossed a sausage down on the floor. It smelled delicious as I approached it, and I ripped off a mouthful of tantalising juiciness.

It wasn't until I was delightfully chomping down on it that I realised I couldn't smell rotten vegetable juice anymore. Whiskers, I'd lost my trail. "Great," I said, after I'd swallowed my food. "I can't smell the golem now."

"Salanraja, this is your fault," I added in my mind.

She responded with a loud growl that caused Ange to jump slightly. Ange then gave me a stern look as if to tell me not to aggravate my dragon. Really, it seemed that as soon as she became boss around here I was destined to get on bad terms with her. But then, from the moment I'd encountered authority in this new world, I'd had problems with it.

"So we'll just have to do things the old fashioned way," Rine said with his mouth full. "The way we always did when Aleam was with us. Seramina, do you want a sausage? You've not eaten anything for hours."

But Seramina didn't turn back to us. It was then that I noticed something was off. Her hair was blowing as if moved by a wind that wasn't there, and her staff had a slight glow to it. I still couldn't see her eyes, but I could imagine they were burning like they always did. I wasn't the only one to notice something wasn't quite right, either.

"Seramina?" Ange said.

Ignoring Ange, Seramina took a decisive step forward. In my whiskers I could now feel the breeze picking up and eddying around her.

"I've got this," she said, as if speaking from a dream. "Do not worry. I must take this chance now, or we'll miss it."

She raised her staff, its gem glowing brightly. Then she ran forward, gently, as if almost on tiptoes, but at speed. Her dragon Hallinar tipped back her charcoal head and called out with a shriek, and looked ready to go bounding after her. But Quarl blocked his path, clearly afraid Seramina might do something to her dragon if he interfered.

Seramina continued to run towards the green glowing mist.

"Seramina," Ange called out again. She shook her head and then lifted her staff off her back. The gem at the top of it glowed green for a moment, and then a good dozen twisty stalks shot of it towards Seramina's ankle. Cascades of purple light streamed out of Seramina's staff, falling at the point where Ange's vines were headed. The spells collided head on, and both the vines and the light stream fizzled into nothingness.

"Dark magic," Ange said. "Gracious demons, Seramina!"

But her words couldn't stop the girl, just as her magic couldn't.

"Come on," Ange ran ahead a little, then looked over her shoulder at Rine. "We need to go after her."

Rine shrugged, then unslung his staff from his shoulder and sprinted to catch up with Ange. "Come on, Ben," he screamed without turning around. "And don't turn into a chimera."

I had no choice, really. But before I left, I picked up another mouthful of sausage to keep me going. As I ran, a great thunderous crash boomed out from behind, followed by the flapping of wings as our four dragons lifted into the sky.

16

THROUGH THE FOREST

It took us a matter of minutes to catch up with Seramina, but then she was hardly sprinting. Rather, she sneaked as if stalking a mouse. She had her staff raised up above her head. Purple tentacles of magic whipped out of the crystal on it. Plants veered away from her path, creating a clear route through.

We were well within the forest, and the smell of rotten algae and dirt hung in the air. Around us, yellow clouds floated above nearby clusters of mushrooms. I presumed this to contain the spores that would reputedly send us to sleep. But even the clouds seeped away from Seramina.

"Seramina," Ange called out. "I'm not going to warn you again." She raised her staff to cast another spell, presumably with the aim of tripping Seramina up, or perhaps wresting the staff out of her grasp using magical vines.

I growled, but I didn't have time to warn her not to be so idiotic. Fortunately, Rine also saw sense. He leapt in front of Ange and knocked her staff down to her waist. "Don't!"

"What?" Ange asked, her eyes wide.

"Don't you see? Without her magic, we have no protection. I don't know what kind of magic she's using. But we now have to see how this plays out."

"Fine," Ange said, frowning. "But I really don't like this."

"Neither do I," Rine said. "But we don't have much of a choice, do we?"

Seramina didn't seem to realise we were talking about her. She was in such a trance, with a white glow now floating around her, giving her a spectral appearance. Then I saw why Rine had claimed he had no clue what kind of magic she was using, because there was a white light also coming from her crystal, radiating outwards, presumably casting the protection we needed to make our way through.

"It doesn't matter," I said, stalking as close as I could to Seramina in case I ended up breathing in some of those sleep spores, "because she's leading us to the forest golem."

"How do you know she is?" Rine asked.

"I just have a hunch. Maybe she has the magic to vanquish it without us even having to fight. After all, she is the daughter of Astravar."

"Seramina," Ange said. "Say something, please. At least tell us your plan."

The young teenager stopped and turned around. Ange's jaw dropped, and she gasped. I looked up, and where I'd expected to see fire in her eyes, instead, they had gone pearl white, with a slightly purple glow to them. "You needn't worry." Her voice was flat. "I have it all under control. I'm merely following the trail Ben detected. Keep close and you'll be safe."

Ange frowned. She didn't look convinced. Rine shook his head, then shrugged. I growled at Seramina, not liking that horrible look in her eyes. Seramina turned back and continued onwards, almost floating instead of walking. I looked up to get a view of the dragons. But the green glow made it hard to see far above. I could still hear them, though, or at least their wings beating.

I marched slightly to the side of Seramina so I could see her in profile, and I noticed white lines like lightning bolts streaking across her skin. They were very faint. I remembered how Astravar looked, with his eggshell cracked skin. I'd learned to fear him every time I saw him in my dreams, even if I hadn't seen him much lately. Whiskers, I really hoped that Seramina didn't end up going down the same path as him.

What is Hallinar feeling right now? I wondered.

"Are you talking to me?" Salanraja asked.

"No, just thinking out loud. But maybe... What about Seramina's dragon? Does he like her casting this kind of magic? Something tells me that if I did it, you'd be furious."

"I would," Salanraja said. *"And we need to give Hallinar all the support we can right now. We don't know what Seramina is up to, but something has forced her to cut off her bond to her dragon. Hallinar can't reach her, and he's feeling terribly alone."*

That was all Salanraja said, and so we trudged on silently. As we went, I could hear the heavy beating of Ange's and Rine's hearts, and they kept glancing at Seramina worriedly, unable to do anything. Meanwhile, Seramina's heart sounded deadly still.

It wasn't long until we saw a white glow on the horizon that seemed to push away the ambient green light that surrounded us.

"There they are," Rine said.

"Who?" I asked.

"Manipulators... But usually it's them that sees us first."

"Slow down, Seramina," Ange said. "We must exercise caution now."

"No," Seramina said through clenched teeth, and her hair whipped out in many directions. "I've got this."

"But you have no idea what Astravar put there..."

"Oh, I do," Seramina said. "I do..."

Rine and Ange now had their staffs gripped tightly in their hands, the white of their knuckles showing. Part of me still wanted to turn into a chimera so I could join the fight.

"Don't," Salanraja told me.

"Whiskers, I wish you weren't reading my mind all the time."

"I'm just saying this to protect you. You're better stealthy against a forest golem as a cat than huge and visible as a chimera."

This was one of the rare occasions I knew she was right. Or at least I thought she was...

We continued to follow Seramina, me staying close behind her ankles while Rine and Ange stayed on either side of her. Not long after, the forest golem came into view. It wasn't facing us but looked out towards the direction of the camp as if it thought we were there. The glowing spectral forms of seven Manipulators hovered close to its massive feet, each one having a bone dragon splayed across the ground in front of them.

They didn't seem to see us. In fact, the entire scene was unnaturally still. A bitter wind seeped through the forest, singing out as it whisked past the surrounding strange bulbous plants that leaned away from Seramina as if afraid of what she had become.

"The time is nigh," Seramina said. Then her voice changed, and she spun around to face me. Her eyes went a haunting, glowing purple colour, and those white cracks that I'd seen ever so faintly on her face before shone even brighter.

"Now, young Dragoncat," she said. Her voice was deeper, and I knew it wasn't really Seramina who spoke – I'd seen this kind of magic before. "It is time for you to face your destiny. As for the rest of you, you are fools to bring one of my own blood into my domain. My daughter shall join me soon and share my power. It won't be long until she learns who she truly is."

"Astravar," I hissed, as the hackles shot up on the back of my neck.

The wind picked up around Seramina, sending up a sudden putrid smell of rotten vegetable juice, as if this place didn't smell horrid enough.

She stared back with terrifying, glowing eyes, and I knew well that a battle was nigh.

17

GOLEM BATTLE

S o much happened at once.

There came a great roar from the forest golem, and a creaking sound like wood about to snap. Seramina shrieked out shrilly and spun to face Ange. She thrust her staff forward and cast a purple beam of energy right at Ange. This met a wall of ice that Rine had magicked out of the blue shimmering crystal on his staff.

Ange joined the battle by casting a flurry of vines right out of her green glowing staff. These twisted over Rine's wall like fast-growing wallflowers. They travelled back downwards and crept along the ground at super speed, kicking grey leaves up off the forest floor. Then they gripped Seramina's staff, and the features on the teenager's face contorted into a wicked grin of concentration as purple flames crept along the vines towards Rine's wall of ice.

Meanwhile, the forest golem was glowing green as a powerful wind buffeted around it. The bone dragons screeched as they lifted their necks and they pulled up into the air, and the Manipulators warped into life, their forms shifting until staffs extended from their glowing bodies. From these, they sent up powerful beams that fed the bone dragons with magical energy.

Our dragons crashed through the glowing shroud of mist and

dived at their quarries. Seramina's charcoal dragon, Hallinar came down first, heading straight for the bone dragon closest to us. But the bone dragon had chosen its target like an arrow and hurtled back towards Hallinar. Out of its terrifying jaws came a column of green, gaseous flame. This hit Hallinar on the left wing, and he screeched, and then corkscrewed downwards. He tucked his wings into his body, sending him diving towards the ground so fast that I thought he might hit it. But at the last moment, he opened his wings again, the injured one seeming a little limp, and soared back into the air.

On the ground, the purple flames from Seramina's staff shattered Rine's ice wall, creating a sound like breaking glass. Another more concentrated white beam went straight from the crystal on Seramina's staff towards Ange's forehead. Ange ducked underneath it and she changed tactics. She pointed her staff at the ground just in front of Seramina, whipping up a column of leaves into a vortex. This spun slowly towards Seramina, gaining strength.

"Isn't there anything I can do?" I asked Salanraja, watching as she fled from the bone dragon's acidic flames.

"The Manipulators – take them down, while Rine and Ange work on Seramina."

"It's not Seramina... It's Astravar."

"Bengie, we really don't have time to discuss our enemy's identity!"

I wasn't looking at the Manipulators though, because there was something odd about that forest golem. Last time we'd fought one, it had attempted to smash the dragons out of the air with its fists while, at the same time, it had stomped chaotically with its massive feet in an attempt to trample its enemies to the ground. But this time, it hadn't moved to assault anything.

Instead, it had its fists clutched to its barrelled chest, and was hunched over itself, its head drooping low, its legs stiff and its feet still. The cracks between its joints let out an amber glow that grew in intensity, and the pieces of wood and forest that it had collected resonated with a rapidly increasing frequency. It also let off a loud hum; the pitch sliding up to an ear-piercing intensity.

It was about to blow.

"Watch out!" I screamed, and I was glad I wasn't a chimera,

because I had to dive out of the way of a tree stump that would have flattened me whole if I was any bigger. Other pieces went flying towards Ange and Rine, who cut off their magic so they could flatten themselves against the ground. In the chaos, the debris hit the Manipulators, knocking the crystals out of their centres. The spectral creatures dissipated on the spot while the forest golem remained in place. The golem had transformed into a massive whirlwind, spinning around a red illuminated blurry object that hovered at its centre.

Seramina laughed a wicked and hysterical laugh that clearly didn't belong to her. Her image then split into what must have been twenty versions of her, which danced around her in a second, smaller vortex. "You could also be a powerful warlock," she shouted. "I can see the potential in you. It's such a pity that you'll die so young."

In horror, I realised she was sending both whirlwinds – the forest golem one and the one composed of images of Seramina – towards Ange. I screeched, remembering how recently I'd also been torn apart by a whirlwind-transformed forest golem which tried to lift me off a tree and feed me to wargs. Then, I'd thought it was going to kill me, until Salanraja turned up and scorched it down with her dragon fire. Now, if we did nothing, it would indeed kill Ange.

Quarl and Ishtkar were already on it. Both dragons plunged down through the mist, and they shot towards the forest golem. Out from their mouths came intense gouts of flames, which washed over the vortex of gathered leaves, dancing around that red object – the crystal that powered the golem. The flames converged at a single point, and the crystal within the vortex glowed bright white for a moment. It looked for a moment that the flames would cut the thing off.

Smoke gathered as the dragons flew away, but it was quickly drawn into the larger vortex. The wispy golem form continued onwards unscathed, the smaller whirlwind now getting dangerously close to Ange.

It took me only a moment to see what was going on. A thick white beam came out of the smaller whirlwind towards the larger one. It was hard to see, because of the dozens of images of Seramina spinning around the central point. It seemed that Seramina – or Astravar should I say – powered that golem, much like a Manipulator powers a bone dragon.

"*Gracious demons, that magic is powerful,*" Salanraja said, and I spotted her hovering a safe distance away from the golem, as if getting ready to attack. The glowing mist silhouetted her form, and the spikes on her back curled upwards, the sharp points looking more prominent than usual. But despite her menacing appearance, I knew if Quarl and Ishtkar couldn't bring down the forest golem, there was little she could do. Added to which, there was no time.

It didn't matter, because I was already working up the courage to do what I had to do. This time, I couldn't be afraid, and I couldn't cheat and become a chimera. I needed to be spry old Ben.

"*I'm going in,*" I told Salanraja.

"*Bengie, no!*"

Her words came far too late to stop me, because I was already springing towards the larger whirlwind, my gaze focused on the crystal. It felt like I was entering the embrace of a massive invisible creature as the whirlwind whipped me up into its arms.

I spun around and around, trying to make sense of the rotating world. I saw Ange and Rine lying on the ground, pinned in place. I saw dragons hurtling through the sky. I saw the forest floor and the winding thorny plants that seemed to now be leaning in towards us. I saw the world as if in frames, everything spinning so fast I thought I might throw up. At the same time my legs flailed around, and I felt like a puppet where some huge demon was orchestrating my every movement using huge dangling strings.

But I couldn't give in – I needed to focus. I turned towards the single red crystal. It was like a beacon, calling out to me – my target. I only needed to swipe it out of place. It was also a little easier to focus on, because while the exterior of the whirlwind spun by like the drum of a washing machine, this crystal had a much slower, steadier rotation, remaining fixed in place relative to the vortex as a whole.

I swam like I might swim underwater. The seconds it must have taken to cross that gap felt like minutes. But eventually I managed enough control of my front legs to get nearby and knock at the crystal with my paw. It didn't move, and a paralysing jolt came off the crystal and sent me spinning towards the edge of the whirlwind.

I exited the whirlwind, and my stomach churned as the ground sped towards me. That was it. I was about to get pancaked to the ground. But as if it didn't want me to leave, the whirlwind picked me up again. It carried me up into the air, and I caught a glimpse of Seramina's smaller whirlwind getting ever closer to Ange, who lay supine on the floor. In moments, it would tear her in two.

I turned to the centre, and I focused on the crystal again, squinting my eyes. I clearly needed to be light to stay aloft in this vortex, but I would need to be much stronger to knock the crystal away from its magical perch. I summoned courage once more, and swam towards the crystal, using thin measured strokes to find my way across the eddies. There was a flow to it, I realised, and if I concentrated, I could find the currents that would take me closer to my goal.

I was soon in front of the crystal, spinning around it so fast, but feeling calm inside. I heard a voice then, reaching out to me from a distant land. It had a Welsh accent, and a female soothing voice. *"Remember your destiny, Ben"*, my crystal told me. *"Embrace the chimera within."*

I drew upon the memory of her testing me in that imaginary desert. I had seen my crystal floating above an oasis then – a beautiful transparent lake with fish, all of which had been purely a construct of my mind. I summoned the energy once again to my muscles, and partly transformed into the chimera. But I used only what I needed to build power in my forelegs and swipe at the crystal with all the strength I had within, and then I let go.

It must have been a mighty swipe – the power coming not just from my superior chimera lion strength, but also from the magical energy emitted by the transformation. I hit the crystal, and it shot out of the whirlwind like an arrow and then tumbled across the ground.

I hadn't transformed into a chimera, and I still had my beautifully lithe Bengal body. I stretched myself out so wide that I floated gently down to the ground, like a feather might if suddenly ejected from a hamster wheel. I tracked the smaller whirlwind as I did, terrified that I'd been too late and I was about to lose Ange. But she'd rolled out of the way of the smaller whirlwind while I'd been focusing on the crystal. That whirlwind was also losing momentum. I caught occasional glances of Seramina spinning slowly inside it. The doubled-up images of her had now vanished, and her own eyes had returned to normal. The features on her face looked worn.

I landed on the ground, and I took one more look at Seramina. Her legs buckled, and she fainted. Her staff was no longer aglow, and I could see that mustard yellow mist creeping in – the one with the sleepy spores Salanraja had told me about. Another wind picked up, this time coming off a shock wave that brushed right over me. A blue light flared from behind, and I turned to see a portal had opened up.

Everything seemed to move so much slower. The wind coming out of the portal felt like it was made of treacle. Sound stopped – the silence so dominant it seemed to roar.

Meanwhile, my staff was nowhere to be seen. I could only guess that it was beyond that portal.

Ange had picked herself up now, and words came out of her mouth so slowly they were incomprehensible. But she also pointed at the portal. Clearly, she felt we should enter. The land on the other side of the portal looked kind of dark, with glowing blue outlines around the edges of the rocky, barren terrain. In the distance, a village lay on a hill, also only visible because of its illuminated edges.

In my experience, we only had moments before that portal winked out of existence. But Rine and Ange also seemed to realise what was at stake.

Rine picked himself up, strapped his staff to his back, and took Seramina in his arms. Ange picked up Seramina's staff and strapped it onto her back next to her own. Then, both of them sprinted forward – and I say sprinted, because they did so in such slow motion it wasn't actually sprinting at all. I matched their pace so slowly it felt almost choreographed.

We reached the other side, and time accelerated. Hallinar flew towards us, the other three dragons trailing behind. But I could see they wouldn't make it in time. It wasn't just for the fact that the portal was much too small for them, but also the fact that it was shrinking ever so fast. As predicted, it winked out of existence, leaving us in a world without an aroma.

I felt then the tearing of my soul, much stronger than I'd felt it before. We had just entered another dimension, and I couldn't hear Salanraja in my mind, nor could I feel what she felt, or taste her last meal still lingering upon her tongue. In the pained looked in Rine's and Ange's faces, I could tell they were going through the same.

Rine shook his head. Then he deposited Seramina on the ground. We waited in silence for her to wake.

18

A VACUOUS WORLD

I have no idea how long Seramina took to wake up. The passage of time seemed to go on for hours upon hours, with despair sinking from my heart right down into the pit of my stomach.

I felt despair for being cut off from my dragon, which seemed much worse here than the last time it had happened. I guess because my bond for Salanraja was growing stronger daily. Despair for not finding my staff waiting for me once we defeated the forest golem. Despair for not even knowing what dimension we were in, and not particularly having the will to find out.

Besides, Rine and Ange seemed pretty depressed as well. We just sat on the floor there, Rine and Ange with their legs crossed, me sitting like a cat does. For a long time, we said nothing.

There was something about this place, the bleakness of it, with no natural daylight or moonlight. Just complete darkness with only a faint blue luminescence around the edges of objects to identify shapes by. Even we had glowing outlines that cast only a faint blue light, strong enough to see our faces but not to see our expressions and details. There was no smell. No sound. No taste of anything upon the air. We had, it seemed, entered a vacuous world.

It made me long for the tastes, sounds, and smells back home in

South Wales. The taste of roast chicken straight out of the oven. The scent of catnip drifting upon a warm breeze. The call of the mistress telling me that supper was ready. Such memories made me long for a familiar life. But the worst feeling was not having Salanraja nearby, perhaps never being able to see her again. My connection to her had been severed.

Eventually, Seramina opened her eyes. She didn't look around her yet, but at the three of us sitting nearby. While before I remembered the fire, and then the purple light burning in her eyes, now it seemed to be guilt that burned there. This strengthened when she turned to Ange – the one she'd tried to kill.

"What happened?" Seramina asked. "I—He took control, didn't he?"

Ange reached out and took Seramina's hand in hers. She squeezed it, and I wasn't sure if it was so that she'd be ready to restrain Seramina if she tried anything else, or true empathy.

"Seramina, before you say anything else, I want to know that it's truly you that's with us." I'm surprised she didn't restrain Seramina using her leaf-magic. But then, Ange looked as if she knew what she was doing.

"My fa—" Seramina stopped herself. "Astravar. He tried to kill you, Ange. He—I lost control."

"Seramina, this is important," Ange said, squeezing Seramina's hand even tighter. "Do you know what Astravar was planning? What do you remember?"

"He... I don't know. He wanted Ben to enter this place. And he wanted him to come alone after I'd disposed of the rest of you, including the dragons."

"So he couldn't be here to orchestrate the battle himself," Ange said, shaking her head, "and he took control of his daughter to do his dirty deeds. But why would he want Ben in here?"

"Probably so he could have him locked out of the way, so he can't interfere with Astravar's destiny," Rine said.

"But why not kill him?" Ange said. "After all, Astravar seemed to want us dead. It just doesn't make any sense."

Seramina sat up, then she lowered her head, unable it seemed, to look at any of us. "I don't know. I don't remember that part... But when Astravar took control of me last time he knew he couldn't hold it forever. He knew little about me back then – had hardly known I'd existed. I think he must have implanted a little magic in me, lying dormant until it was time for him to take control.

"Since then, he must have been studying me to gain a stronger grasp on how I tick. That's why I need to keep control of my mind, because I hear him in there sometimes. That's what Aleam's been training me for. So that I can protect myself from him. If only Aleam were here this would have never happened."

"Well, he's not here," Ange said. "You'll need to accept that, Seramina. If you convince yourself that only Aleam can save you, then you'll make yourself more vulnerable to Astravar. You need to learn to rely on your own wits."

Seramina lowered her head and placed her hand on her forehead. She spoke without looking up. "You don't think Driar Aleam will come, do you? Even if he escapes Prince Arran, how will he know where to find us? I really do wish he was here. He'd know exactly what to do now."

"I guess you have to put all this out of your mind for now," Ange said. "Just focus on the present moment and on what we have to do now. That was why he was teaching you to meditate, right? He wanted you to become stronger within."

"It doesn't matter anyway," Rine said. "Astravar won't find us here, unless he's crossed into this dimension. I doubt he's a threat to us anymore."

"And where exactly are we?" I asked.

Ange let go of Seramina's hand, crouched down and stroked me at the back of the neck. I wasn't sure if it was to comfort me, but it sure felt comforting in this strange alien land. "This is the Ghost Realm. The Third Dimension – rumoured to be filled with the souls of the dead. I recognise the pictures from books. It can't be anything else, can it?" She looked at Seramina, as if for confirmation.

"Astravar wanted to trap Ben here forever," Seramina said, "so he could never interfere with the warlock's destiny."

A wind picked up from the hill with the distant village on it. It was strong, and strangely didn't cool or warm as you'd expect wind to do. But it chilled me emotionally, causing a deep wave of depression to sink within me. It howled through the barren landscape, whipping up glowing trails of dust in its wake. Everything around us seemed to shimmer, making me wonder if we were actually standing on solid ground or if it was about to give way and send us plummeting into an abyss full of the tormented souls of hippopotami or something. I shuddered at the thought.

"Do you mean we're dead?" I asked, examining my paw – it looked solid enough, and the claws seemed sharp, as they should be. "I knew it. I shouldn't have gone into the whirlwind. I killed myself, didn't I? And Seramina killed the rest of you."

"I—" Seramina said, and she turned away, looking up towards the glowing village in the distance.

"She did not," Ange said, scowling at me. "We came through the portal, remember? Stop worrying the poor girl."

"What? And you don't think I might be slightly anxious too? We're going to die because it doesn't look like there's any food here. Don't you remember how Seramina attacked you?"

"She wasn't herself," Ange said. "Gracious demons, Ben, you can be so selfish sometimes."

I growled, not expecting to hear this out of Ange of all people. I had thought she would have always sided with the cat, but that shows how wrong I was. Girls would always stick together. I needed Ta'ra here if I was going to have any chance of winning an argument against them. But then, knowing Ta'ra, she'd probably side with the girls too.

Rine stepped in front of me. He had his staff clutched in his hand, which he leaned on as he looked out towards the village. "Look, folks, we've not got any time to be wasting by assigning blame." He stared daggers at me. "Nor have we any time for feeling sorry for ourselves," he then looked at Seramina. This look was softer than it had been with me, but still pretty harsh. "We're in the Ghost Realm, and we need to get out of here fast."

"Is that right, smart Alec?" Ange said with her hands on her hips. "So how do you propose we do that?"

"My guess is that Ben's staff is here. So, if we can find it, then hopefully it has some magic to lift us out of here, or at least Ben's crystal will intervene."

"There's no telling what Ben's crystal can do," Seramina said. "Or any of our crystals. If I'd thought about it earlier, I might have tried to read them, to at least have some idea of our futures. But I was keeping away from the magic. It's all my fault…"

"We can't change what's been done already," Ange said. "But what we can do is start towards that village." She pointed at it, as if none of us had already seen it.

I gazed not at the village but at the darkness beyond it. It seemed to stretch on into infinity, and it gave the impression that there was nothing behind the village, except perhaps a chasm that plummeted into oblivion. Though I knew Ange was right, a huge part of me didn't want to move anywhere in this alien barren land. In many ways, it seemed like a good place to curl up and go to sleep forever.

"What exactly do you expect to find in the village?" I asked.

Rine looked down at me and smiled. "Ghosts I guess. What else would you find in the Ghost Realm?"

I groaned. "I don't want to meet any ghosts…"

"I don't think any of us do," Ange said. "But it's our only chance to get out of here." She looked again at Seramina, as if to check she was okay. I also checked that Seramina's eyes weren't glowing any funny colours, but everything looked normal, fortunately.

Rine grunted, then marched onwards, without looking back. Ange huffed and then trailed after him, with both hers and Seramina's staff swaying with the rhythm of her strides. Seramina followed, but she seemed to want to fall back a little, as if wanting to be alone.

Nobody seemed to care right now if the cat came too, which was odd given it was my staff of destiny we were looking for. In other words, I was the key to getting out of here. But they knew me too well, because it didn't feel right to be left alone here, surrounded by nothing but sheer barrenness. I growled a complaint that no one heard, and then I raced to catch up with Rine and Ange, respecting Seramina's wish to walk alone.

19

INTO THE UNKNOWN

As we climbed, we expended energy. My legs were sore, my tummy rumbled loudly at me, and my throat felt completely dry. I regretted secretly that I hadn't taken a little extra time to eat more sausages at this morning's campfire before taking off after Seramina. If there was food in the village, then it would no doubt be ghost food, which meant that it might have been dead a long time and potentially decaying – in other words completely inedible.

But the more pressing issue was thirst. If we didn't find anything to drink soon, we'd surely die here. Then we'd become ghosts, and we'd be destined to live here forever, roaming this boring place with nothing at all to do.

Seramina still trailed at a distance behind us, but close enough, I noticed, that she could probably hear what we said. I could also hear her footsteps, which was why Ange probably wasn't checking every ten seconds or so to see if she was still there.

"The thing I don't get," Rine said, "is where are all the ghosts? I mean if everyone and everything in all seven dimensions end up here when they die, then there should be millions here, surely."

We were halfway up the hill by that point, and Rine was right. Really, we should have been trudging through wispy stalks of grass, spectral dragonflies, bees, wasps, and butterflies flitting and buzzing around us, cats of all types and ages stalking their prey across rolling meadows. Whiskers, for a moment I wondered if I'd even meet my ancestors here – the great Asian leopard cats of old. But everywhere I looked I saw nothing but darkness with faint glowing lines around its edges. Even the ground I stepped on was pitch black. Fortunately, we could see each other, but only because of those weird glowing outlines around our bodies.

Ange put her hand to her chin as she walked, as if in thought. "Maybe the ghost realm is not quite what we expected it to be. Perhaps we're making a discovery of our own."

"But people must have explored this place, surely?" Rine asked. "I mean what did the books you read say about it? It's not like the Fifth Dimension and Sixth Dimension, is it? We at least understand something about this place, right?"

"Well, if there are ghosts in here," I suggested, "maybe we can't see them. Aren't ghosts meant to be invisible after all?"

"That's not what the books say," Ange said. "There are reports of men and women coming into the Third Dimension, but they don't stay long. The explorers see a village, then they see the ghosts, and then they decide to leave."

"Why would they do that?" Rine asked. "They could learn so much about the place."

"Some reports say it's because of their respect for the dead. They don't want to disturb them. Others claim it's because of their sheer fear of what they see, and so they decide they'd much rather stay in the safety of their own home than face what lives in this place. No one, after all, wants to see a ghost. So they just summon a portal and vanish home."

"You didn't tell me we could summon a portal," I said. "Then let's get out of here. I don't want the staff anymore."

"We can't use portal magic, you idiot," Rine said. "That's done by the White Mages and the warlocks, but never dragon riders. For some reason the crystals never gifted us with that kind of magic."

"Come to think of it, I've never met a White Mage."

"That's because you haven't become a full-fledged dragon rider yet. When you do, you might go on expeditions with them, or you might even fight alongside them in larger battles against the warlocks."

"Then why hasn't the king sent any White Mages to protect us in Dragonsbond Academy?"

"Didn't you listen, Ben," Ange said. "Prince Arran did say that reinforcements were on the way. I guess they're a little late arriving. Perhaps Prince Arran wanted to establish his authority before the rest of the men came in."

"Or they're marching on foot... Travelling by horse carriage, perhaps," Rine said.

"That's a possibility too," Ange said. "I really don't know. Why do you ask?"

"Because I don't know anything about your world. Or at least I didn't until I was forced into it. But at least it's familiar. I really don't like this place, and I don't know what's worse - here or the Seventh Dimension."

"From what you've told me about the Seventh Dimension, I think I'd choose here," Rine said. "At least you don't have, what was that thing, a demon hippopotamus threatening to eat you?"

"I think I'd rather be eaten than die hungry," I said. "Wouldn't you?"

Rine snorted. "No comment," he said. "It's funny how since I've known you you've made everything out to be about food. I would have thought you'd have changed by now, at least a little."

I said nothing back to him, and we were all silent for a moment, the only noise being our footsteps and the soughing of the wind, with Seramina pattering along behind. We were close enough to the village now that I could see the structures within it. The houses looked like the old-fashioned hovels we'd seen in villages back in Salanraja's world. But these buildings completely lacked colour, except for their weird glowing blue outlines that cast a cold light over everything. The village also wasn't showing any signs of movement. No sign of ghosts, whatever they were meant to look like, prowled the streets.

We entered just as that strange wind picked up and rushed through the streets as if it wanted to blow us away. I wondered if these invisible ghosts were calling that wind to push us back from where we came. Perhaps they actually didn't want us treading on their ground, peering into their houses, catching glimpses of their eternal lives.

"I don't like this," Rine said, and he shuddered visibly. I could hear his heart pounding in his chest.

"I don't either," Ange said, her heart pounding too. "It feels as if we really shouldn't be here. No wonder all those scholars turned back." She edged noticeably closer to Rine. But I didn't care at that point. If we were trapped in here, it didn't matter if they got together or not.

"Why do you humans always go around stating the obvious?" I asked. "Sometimes don't you think it's better not to say anything at all?"

Seramina had caught up with us by this point, and her heart wasn't beating as heavily as the other two. I wondered if for a moment Astravar had taken possession of her soul again, because she now seemed a lot more spritely. "I think it's this way," she said, and beckoned us forward.

"Seramina," Ange said, and she reached over her shoulder for her staff.

Seramina frowned at her. "Don't worry, I won't cast any magic. I don't need my staff to detect destiny. I've been reading the possible threads of the future, and how they surround people, all my life."

The young teenager pushed on ahead, and we had no choice but to follow.

Seramina led us over what must have been the main road. Beneath us, the glowing lines running around and over the cobblestones made them look shiny, as if covered with water. But there was no rain.

The outlines weren't the only thing that cast light in here. There were also these strange-looking oil lanterns hanging off rafters that jutted out beneath the eaves of the hovels. They didn't have flames in them, but instead they emitted blue glows as if lit from the inside by crystals.

Seramina turned off into a narrower alleyway, with a lantern shining out so brightly at the end of it, I couldn't see what was behind it. The wind howled loudly, startling me. It came from behind and pushed us down the alleyway, this time seeming to want to edge us towards our target. I screeched and tried to pull away from the light, but the wind came even stronger so that it almost lifted me off the ground.

Seramina opened her arms, and she let the wind carry her towards the light, floating upon it like a stray bin bag caught in a storm. Ange tried to resist the wind like me, but it spun her around and propelled her onwards. Rine ran forwards instead, gaining momentum from the wind. He screamed out in ecstasy, his arms windmilling around him as he went.

Once we'd all accepted there was no turning back, the wind died off. Seramina executed a well-balanced landing, thrusting out her arms and then drawing them back into herself, as if she'd predicted exactly when the wind would stop. But it had carried me high on its currents, and I ended up twisting one of my ankles as I hit the floor. I shrieked out, and rolled over, and then limped forwards towards the light in pain.

I had the sudden sensation of being watched. I turned every which way, expecting at least to see eyes glowering at me from the darkness. They weren't there. But I heard breathing, and whispers in all kinds of languages. Having the gift of languages from my crystal, I understood every word. But as soon as I tried to attach meaning to any sentence, I'd hear more ramblings from another random direction.

These random ideas continued to assault me as if I was on the edge of madness and hearing them in my mind. But I knew these voices weren't in my head. They were out there somewhere.

I shuddered, and I thought it would be saner to focus on the light ahead. Seramina led the way, Rine and Ange slightly behind her. Their figures were framed in silhouettes and cast long shadows well behind me. Not wanting to get left behind, I matched their pace, trying not to get distracted by the voices which got louder with every step I took.

I could hear heavy breathing from the shadows now, and I had this strange itching sensation against my fur. Yet I didn't dare stop to scratch myself – as much as I wanted to.

The light ahead faded slightly, and then a shape seemed to emerge inside it with a slightly darker outline. This continued to gain definition until it took on human form. It wore a cloak that billowed around it, and it had a staff. At first, I thought I was looking at a Manipulator, and I next expected to see bone dragons rise out of nowhere, screeching violently.

But this definitely wasn't a Manipulator. The shape warped even more until I could see the creases on its clothes, the folds underneath its eyes, the cavernous wrinkles in its skin.

Recognition dawned on me. Before me stood Aleam in spectral form.

GHOSTS OF OURSELVES

G host Aleam looked at each of us. First, he studied Rine. Then he turned to look at Ange. Next, he looked down at me. Only last did he turn to Seramina, and then he gave a nod as if in approval.

"Everyone's here, I see," he said. "Just as I've always expected."

His sudden appearance had caused us to freeze in shock. I could see the sides of Rine's and Ange's faces from where I stood, and their mouths were agape. I couldn't see Seramina's face from here, but her straight-backed posture had been replaced with a full slouch.

"Aleam," Seramina said. "This wasn't what I foresaw. You can't be…"

Aleam laughed loudly. "Dead, you mean? We all must pass sometime, you know, and I was getting old. This is one thing that everyone needs to learn to accept."

"No!" Ange said, her face even more blanched of colour than before. "Prince Arran? Did he do this?"

Rine took and squeezed her hand. The outlines of their hands seemed to glow in the light that Aleam emitted.

I walked forward, unable to believe my eyes. Part of me was wondering if ghosts emitted a smell, but there was nothing here.

Strangely, I couldn't even catch whiffs of Seramina's or Ange's perfume, and I longed for the aromas so much. I longed for any aroma, really, for a sense of realism to this world.

The wind picked up again, but this time it pushed me away from Aleam. "Not too close, Ben," he said. "There will be time for that later. For now, our friends are waiting. Will you please follow me?"

He turned slowly, and as he did the light from his body flared up once again. It grew, and seemed to surround him, although ever so faintly did I make out the outline of his form drifting away as if disappearing into the light. "One at a time, now," he said from behind the light. "Don't go too slowly or you'll get left behind."

Rine had let go of Ange's hand. He looked at us in turn as if trying to assess what we all felt. But in all honesty, I've never known a human who can read a feline expression. They all seem to think we're sad when we're happy and happy when we're sad.

"Do you think we can trust him?" he asked, looking again at Ange.

She shook her head and put her hand to her chin but said nothing.

Seramina did though. "We can. I didn't lead you here for nothing. I think I'm beginning to understand." She took a deep breath and walked right into the light.

"Seramina!" Ange called out. "Gah, that girl."

Rine laughed, and then reached out for Seramina's staff on Ange's back, touching it lightly. "Well, her crystal didn't break. So, I guess that means she's okay."

Ange swallowed, then stepped gingerly forward. "I guess we have no choice." She stepped forward and disappeared behind the light.

"My turn," Rine said, and turned back with a cocky smile. He drew his staff from his back, then he charged forward with his shoulder. As he did, he screamed out, "Goblins beware!"

I didn't know what a goblin was, and I wasn't sure I wanted to meet one. If I did, I hoped they were edible, because I was starving. I also knew one thing – I didn't want to be abandoned here, sad and alone. With that thought in mind, a rush of adrenaline coursed through me, and I sprinted forward. As I did, that strange wind without temperature picked up behind me, throwing me forwards.

I hit something cold and wet, and a powerful force pulled me downwards. I couldn't breathe, and whatever was rushing against my fur from above was so cold, I felt paralysed. The next thing I knew I was drowning, my eyeballs bulging so hard I thought they were going to pop out of my sockets.

Sudden dread came over me, as I thought this must have all been a horrible trick. We'd not just seen Aleam, but a Manipulator controlled by Astravar. Annoyed that he'd not killed us with the forest golem, he'd come after us in the Ghost Realm, and used this apparition of our old friend to lead us into a trap.

I was going to die.

Or at least I thought I was, until I tumbled out of the other side, soaking wet but very alive. I sputtered out water, and then a few anchovies flopped out of my throat too and spasmed on the floor a moment before coming to rest. Instinct took over, and I pounced on the anchovies, and I took them into my mouth. I bit down on their crunchy, salty goodness, and then I swallowed them in one bite.

"Those weren't real," Aleam said. "Which means they're absolutely lacking in nutritional value. You realise that don't you, Ben?"

"Yes, but they still tasted so good," I said, and I took some time to look around. We had left the Ghost Realm. Or at least, it seemed that way, because some colour had returned to everything around us. Green verdant hills rolled towards a sun hanging high above. But something about it was off – the sun just didn't seem as bright as it should be given its position in the sky.

Dandelion seeds floated around everywhere, but they lacked definition, as if their fronds weren't separate but instead seemed to be welded together in places. I scanned around looking for butterflies, or birds, or at least something interesting to chase. But I found nothing of interest. I chased after a dandelion seed instead, but I lost it very quickly and that was enough to get bored.

Rine, Ange, and Seramina had already gathered around a campfire – looking kind of blurry from here as if I was looking at a photograph with the background out of focus. Still, I could see my three companions clear as day. I stalked over to them as the light from the campfire got brighter, and the warmth washed over me. Finally, this place had invented heat. The breeze coming off the hills also felt a little cooler. But somehow, the fire didn't feel as warm and the wind as cool as they were meant to be.

You couldn't get too close to a fire, comfortably, without it burning you. But this one felt as if I could step right into it, dance around for a few minutes, and then step out uncharred. I didn't try it though. Every cat knows not to play with fire, and this was no exception.

It was then that I noticed what Rine, Ange and Seramina were looking at.

We also sat on the other side of the campfire, duplicated in blurrier, paler forms. There was a version of Seramina, a version of Ange, a version of Rine, and a version of spry old Ben. Except they all looked slightly paler as if the colours had been bleached out of their hair, skin, and fur. They weren't completely colourless, but somehow everything in this place looked desaturated. They also emitted a faint glow around the outlines, weaker than before but still noticeable.

I wondered if this was like the Faery Realm where everything I saw was made of some kind of glamour spell. If so, this magic was a pale imitation to what those tiny fairies could do.

"How's this possible?" Seramina asked.

"They must be ghosts," Rine said. "Which means we must be dead after all."

"Don't be stupid," Ange said. "If they were ghosts, then we wouldn't be looking at them like this. We'd be the ghosts then."

"Really, and do you know how things work here?" Rine said, his hands on his hips.

I growled, loudly, to let the nascent couple know that I couldn't take another one of their arguments. Aleam made his way over to us using his staff, balanced almost unnaturally on it as if he didn't need it for support at all. He also now had a little colour and emitted a faint glow.

"But they are ghosts, you see," he said. "Just your concept of a ghost isn't what you expect it to be."

Rine looked at him with wide eyes. "Okay, please explain?"

"You need to change your perception of this world," Aleam said. "Ghosts are nothing to fear if you lead a good life. But they are everything to fear if you lead a bad one."

Seramina had leaned in and was watching Aleam with interest. "I can feel something in this place. As if I was meant to be here. The more I study it, the more I recognise things as if I'd known them all along."

"And that is because you are a very gifted child," Aleam said. "You see, the Ghost Realm is the world of the future dead and contains everything that happened in the past and that will happen in the future. It's a timeless place, one which no living creature is wise enough to understand yet. But the crystals understand it, which is how they connect to it to draw off its magic as a source."

"Does that mean you're not dead?" Seramina said, a flash of hope in her eyes.

Aleam gave her a warm smile. "In one version of the future I might be, in another I might not. You know well how this works, girl. After all, destiny magic is your school."

Ange scratched at her forehead and shook her head slowly. She also seemed in better spirits, as if the puzzle of this place had given her energy. "This is the source of magic? Does that mean that this place belongs to the crystals?"

"Not at all," Aleam said. "The crystals learned to project this place onto the world. They are windows, their facets planes that display the essence of existence. What you see in this place are threads of the future, how they might be. You can learn a lot from this place if you have the courage to look through the lens."

"So what you're saying," Ange said, rubbing her chin, "is that anything we see here is a possible thread of the future. Now we're seeing us around the campfire like this, because we might end up there sometime in our lives."

"Or it's already happened," Aleam said. "Don't forget this is a timeless place, so you can gaze across the threads of time."

"Hang on a minute," I said, and stepped towards Aleam and examined him. He emitted a faint Aleam kind of smell now – a combination of sweat and flaky skin. But it wasn't strong enough for me to trust him. "This doesn't make any sense. The visions we saw in the crystals were so vivid. They had lots of colours, and everything here is faded and yucky."

Aleam smiled. "Because you don't put much importance to this," he said. "This vision isn't so strong in your minds, and so you only see it faintly here. But if you use your memories and your imagination to your advantage, the vision will become stronger."

"But how can a vision of the future be in our minds at all, if we've never experienced it?" Ange asked.

"Oh, you have such little faith in this realm. Your mind can transcend time here, if only you let it. Trust the magic of time, and you can see the past and future. Once you learn to do so, then your path here will become clear."

It was then that I realised what ghost Aleam was talking about. Because I recognised the scene, it had only happened this morning after all. We were sitting around the campfire, Rine now cooking sausages. I hadn't noticed the tents yet, because they were so faint. But now they stood there billowing in the wind. I saw the green glow from the Aurorest Forest in the distance, and I smelled that horrible scent of putrid algae coming from it.

The other version of me wasn't a Bengal, I realised, but a chimera. As soon as I recognised this, that version morphed into its expected form. The snake tail had bright yellow and green stripes along its body that I'd never noticed before. Nor had I noticed the deep black around the eyes of the goat's head, creating a stark contrast against its otherwise alabaster coat, fading into a golden colour at the base of its neck. The lion's head had mustard yellow teeth, and its breath absolutely stank.

"I wanted to take you somewhere I knew would be familiar to you," Aleam said. "Now, it's time to explore each of your futures. But I see only one of you is ready." He turned to Seramina. "Shall we begin?"

Seramina shook her head. "I'm not sure I want to see the future. Every time I've used my magic lately, it has ended in disaster."

"And that is the problem we need to work on, young lady." He reached down into a pocket in his cloak, which now was its normal deep brown colour and wasn't glowing at all. From it, he produced a closed pouch, lumpy over its folds, and tied tight at the top. He pulled this back and threw it onto the fire.

For a moment, everything went bright white. Then, the surrounding light faded to reveal Seramina's future.

THE HERMIT

"Just assume, for now, that you've defeated Astravar," the ghost of Aleam said, as the light died down even more. "Because it is not time yet to show you what happens if you don't."

I stood in bright green grass, which looked incredibly vivid compared to how it had looked before. Birds chirped out from the surrounding trees. Some of these trees had lime green leaves with catkins dangling from the winding branches. Others had darker leaves and supported white flowers. The air was heady with pollen, and I saw butterflies and dragonflies dancing around, the way it was meant to be. One butterfly landed nearby and perched itself on the biggest dandelion I'd ever seen in my life. But I was interested in the butterfly and not the flower. I readied myself to pounce on my prey.

I landed on the flower, but the butterfly had already flown away. I chased after it and tried to paw it out of the sky. My blow knocked it aside, but it flapped its wings and fluttered high enough to survive another day.

I growled, then looked up to see a hovel across the field. There was nothing around it, no path leading to it, and it was surrounded by a mystical purple mist that stank of rotten vegetable juice.

"The question is," Aleam continued, "though this place might look beautiful, will you be truly happy here? Or will you become a tormented soul? Seramina, this is your potential future. And, if you ask me, this version of you doesn't seem happy at all."

Aleam pointed with his glowing staff at the porch of the hovel. Behind a rickety wooden balustrade, Seramina's ghost sat on a rocking chair. Her eyes had rolled back in her head so only the whites of them showed. They also had a slight purple tint to them. As she rocked back and forth on her chair, she clutched a staff in her right hand. It had a purple crystal on the top of it, glowing brightly.

"What is this?" the real version of Seramina asked. "Why am I here all alone?"

I didn't like it either, and so I backed away from her, scouring the terrain for butterflies. But everything had run away, and the bird sounds had died down. All that remained was a grating buzzing coming from ghost Seramina's staff.

"You chose this life," Aleam said. "Or rather you lost control, and the dark magic chose it for you. Because you became an even greater enemy to the most powerful in the realm."

"Will become," Seramina corrected. "But, no, I won't. I will never let it happen to me."

"But if you keep hiding from who you really are, you will. You have power, Seramina – it's in your blood. And, if you don't acknowledge that power, then it will consume you whole."

I wasn't the only one who had backed away from the evil version of Seramina. Ange and Rine stood back-to-back, clutching their staffs in front of them. The real Seramina stood close to them. She tapped her fingers against her legs, and she kept glancing at the staff of power in her doppelganger's hands.

"Don't worry," Aleam said. "This is just a vision."

Evil Seramina gazed out at the horizon where a thick carpet of purple clouds loomed. There came a screeching sound from the distance, and then six birds of prey suddenly shot out of the clouds. There was a seagull, a vulture, a buzzard, a condor, a bald eagle, and a hawk. But there was no crow...

Carrion eaters, I thought. All cats knew to stay away from such birds, and if we ever saw one wheeling above or even smelled one nearby, to run and hide. The six birds landed, and greyish purple plumes of smoke billowed around them. These soon dissipated to show six pale skinned figures, in fancy cloaks just like Astravar's.

"That's the other warlocks," Ange said. "What do they want with Seramina?"

One warlock – the one who had been a condor – stepped forward. She was a woman who looked even older than Aleam. She moved with one hand behind her back, the other resting on her staff for support. This staff glowed as she stopped and lifted it into the air. From it came this terrible screeching sound, and two wispy looking purple dragons lurched out of the crystal at the top. They were formed of clouds and circled around the old warlock in a figure-of-eight motion, casting a light across the sky that gave the warlock's silver hair a kind of spectral glow.

Evil Seramina stood up from her chair, whilst the Seramina we knew so well glowered at her but didn't move as if frozen in place.

"What do you want, Lasinta?" evil Seramina said. "All of you... Why do you disturb me? All I've ever wanted is to be left alone."

"Because you hold too much power," the warlock said. "Not only are you a threat to our kind, but you can help us break the treaty with Illumine Kingdom and finish what Astravar started, fool as that man was. This is your last chance. You either join us, or it all ends here."

Evil Seramina narrowed her eyes. She raised her staff high above her head, and it also glowed purple. The ground quaked so hard it sent my cheeks wobbling. I hissed out, crouched, then I dug my claws into the soil to help keep purchase.

Seramina's voice rose in both volume and pitch as she continued to speak. Her words were laced with anger, and an undertone of spite. "I owe you nothing, Lasinta. My father is dead, and you will be soon too if you don't leave this place."

She pointed her staff at Lasinta and out came an intense white beam. Lasinta screamed, and she swung her staff downwards. A vortex shot out of Lasinta's crystal, that sucked in the beam, and the two cloud-shaped dragons spiralled around the vortex as if powered by its circular motion. The other warlocks sprinted into position, clutching their staffs, and casting spells all around them. An incredible light show filled the scene with flashes of purple and white. It reminded me of the scariest night in Wales every year – Bonfire Night when fireworks screech and crash and bang high above tall roaring fires. That used to be the worst night of the year.

For a while, I thought this would be the end of Seramina. Her life would end here, lonelier than she'd ever been. Spells of light and terror whooshed towards the ghost form of the teenager. I saw skulls made of thick glowing fog, thorny purple vines, intense beams of light, and burning purple fireballs.

Some dark magic, or perhaps the magic of the Ghost Realm, also slowed time, meaning I had to wait longer to see who the victor was. Really, given Seramina had turned evil, I didn't know who I wanted to win.

The evil version of Seramina also had tricks up her sleeves. She glowed bright white, just like we'd seen her glowing in the Aurorest Forest, her hair whipping against her face as if stirred by an intense wind. She opened out her arms and her feet lifted off the floor. There she floated as she watched the warlocks' spells approach ever so slowly, her eyes narrow slits and her jaw clenched. Then, she clutched her staff in both her hands and extended it to the sky. Time accelerated back to normal, as Seramina placed all her weight down on the staff, plunging it into the ground.

The whole earth shook, much more violently than last time. I slid across the ground, growling, screeching, and hissing, as it tore at my claws. Around me, the earth had already been torn asunder. Great rents led down into it, leading into enormous pits of boiling magma. Heat raged from beneath, and the smell of rising sulphur reminded me of the time I was in the Seventh Dimension. The earth rocked again, and I slid down towards one of the cracks.

"Ben," Ange shouted. She scrambled over to me, then plunged her staff in the ground. It glowed green, and thorns tore out from her crystal into the earth, rooting her in place.

Just as I was about to slide into a chasm, she scooped me up in her arms and clutched me tightly. She squeezed a little too tight, but I knew it would be stupid to try to claw myself out from her grasp.

Rine had also cast a spell, freezing his feet in place, and he'd done the same to the true version of Seramina.

Meanwhile, evil Seramina still floated in the air, her staff glowing brightly as it fed energy into the ground. From the rents in the earth came great roars, and I saw all manner of creatures rise out of it – all of them incarnations of the Seventh Dimension.

First swarmed out what must have been tens of thousands of demon rats, scurrying as if a lion had just disturbed their nests. Then came swans and cormorants and ravens and other birds as large as giraffes, with gaping cracks in their skin, molten rock glowing underneath. The demon dragons followed them, filling the sky with such a racket it seemed to be crashing down on us. After that flooded out every creature I could imagine, including the terrifying demon hippopotamus. Also, there came a wave of demon salmon, flopping out of the abyss. For a moment I thought I'd never like salmon again.

I knew what would come next, and I hated it. Once the Seventh Dimension had emptied, the First Dimension would become the demons' dominion. They'd flood across into other dimensions, and I doubted very much my old master and mistress in South Wales were equipped to handle them – particularly the demon salmon.

That was enough, I didn't want to see any more. I sealed my eyes shut whilst Ange clutched me in her arms, careening from side to side with the motion of the earth.

A warm light filtered through my eyelids. I opened them to see the entire scene flooded with white light and the vision faded to darkness. We were back in that place without warmth or cold, the glowing outlines rolling over the hills. The village was nowhere to be seen now, and I felt terribly alone. Rine's and Ange's hearts were beating faster than I'd ever heard them beat before, and even Seramina's heart was pounding.

Yet, I couldn't detect a heartbeat in the ghost of Aleam's chest. He didn't smell of anything anymore either. No one smelled of anything.

"I can't do this," Seramina said, this time the good version of her. "Please Aleam, this cannot be my fate."

"But you've seen it yourself," Aleam said. "It comes to you in your dreams. You must learn to take responsibility for your own power.

Eventually, you will become even more powerful than your father. That fact is written in the annals of time. But either you'll learn to take risks upon yourself, or fate will destroy you. Only the first of those will allow you to then use this power for good."

"I can't live up to that," Seramina said. "I'll never be as powerful as him..."

"This place doesn't lie," the ghost of Aleam said. "This is only one possible thread of your destiny. The worst imaginable. I showed it to you because you need to get over your pride."

Seramina cheeks puckered, making a whistling sound as she sucked in air through her teeth. Her eyes were now filled with tears. "Don't you get it? I have no pride. I was born a monster, and I will die a monster. What does this prove?"

Aleam shook his head. "Your pride isn't in what you believe yourself to be, but what you believe others to be compared to you. It's that desire for pride you have to let go of. A desire to belong to a family, a desire to be accepted amongst your peers. You are already great, Seramina. Accept that and then store it in a tiny compartment inside yourself. Only then, will you become strong enough to be who you are destined to be. Once you accept who you are, Astravar can no longer control you like he just did, because you will be complete."

Seramina said nothing, but her gaze had gone distant and tears welled at the bottom of her eyes. She clearly had a lot to think about. Aleam turned to Ange and Rine who had huddled a little closer together. He smiled, and then Ange stepped back from Rine. She looked down at her feet, her cheeks red. She then shook her head hard and glared at Rine as if to warn him away from her.

Rine shook his head and turned his shoulder away from her, just as Aleam turned to look at him.

"Now it's time to see both of your futures," Aleam said with a smile. "What, I ask, might destiny find?"

"Please, no more apocalypses," I said. "I've decided I hate apocalypses."

"Not this time," Aleam said. "To most of you, this one will seem quite mellow in comparison. Although something tells me, young Ben, that you will hate it more."

He raised his staff above his head, and spectral glowing outlines passed over its tip, like water running over its surface during a heavy rainstorm. The ethereal crystal on the staff glowed, intensifying into a blinding white light.

I squinted as the light faded, and I was seeing dots at first, as we entered the vision of Rine's and Ange's future.

A FAILED ROMANCE

We stood on a ledge in the centre of a massive chasm leading down into swirling darkness. It looked like a pool of that gross smelling stuff that the master used to eat in South Wales – I think it was called yeast extract.

The stuff swirled and stank as it flowed towards the horizon. It tainted the bases of the cliff walls that led up on both sides to two houses. Both of these were opulent mansions, with massive gardens. The one to the left had low overhanging gables, crab apple trees surrounding it, and yellow brick walls. The other led to a mansion made of heavy stones, with a slate roof adorned with gemstones and a coniferous hedge with red berries shining out from between the soft needles.

Both gardens looked like two wonderful places that I would love to explore. Only, I couldn't decide which one I'd prefer. I certainly didn't fancy a life where I was trapped on a rock with a steep drop into a pool of yeast extract. This ledge was wide enough for us to walk around a little, but also sheer enough that we could fall to our hideous deaths should we misstep.

"What's with the abyss?" Rine said.

"Visions of the future often use symbolism," Aleam said. "It fills them with rich meaning, and multiple interpretations. This is how soothsayers have always been able to make a living."

"But it's full of that stuff that smells amazing. It's almost as if I could crawl down with a butter knife and spread it upon my toast."

Ange's eyes went wide. "You've got to be kidding me. You'd eat that stuff?"

"What, wouldn't you?"

Aleam laughed an almost bitter laugh. "This food item, once discovered, will spawn divisions across millennia and multiple dimensions. But for now, there's more to see, and what's in the chasm isn't as important as it might seem."

There came a call from the mansion on the right. A female voice that was instantly familiar. Ange stepped out onto the porch, except it was a much older version of Ange, with greying hair and wrinkles under her eyes. She still had that slight squirrelly look to her though, which is how I recognised her.

"Oh Ben," she called out. "Ben, are you out here?"

This caused everyone to smile, including Seramina. The young teenager wiped the tears away from her eyes, but another emerged and dripped from her cheek. She seemed to notice I was looking at her, and so she turned away from me.

"Ben?" The apparition of Ange called again. "Oh, Ben, don't tell me you've gone over to visit Rine again. I—"

Another figure ghosted into view. At first, it looked like a Manipulator, glowing white with every single one of its limbs seeming to warp around its body. But as it moved towards Ange's apparition's doorstep, it gained definition. After a few moments, it took the form of Prince Arran, standing as tall and mighty as that man does, his nose almost higher than his forehead. He wore lush velvet purple attire and a long trailing red cloak. There were other ghostly forms standing nearby, in two sizes – man-size and dragon-size. Presumably they were the guards who had flown in with Arran. But they probably weren't important for this vision, and so they all looked blurred out.

Prince Arran knocked on the door. Ange's apparition turned around and noticed him there, and so she walked over and curtsied slightly. It's strange, while they were so far away, I could see them as if

I was standing right next to them, despite the precipitous chasm that lay between us.

"Driar Ange," Prince Arran said. "Have you completed your target for the day?"

"Yes sir, I've delivered what you expected," Ange said. She reached down to the porch and picked up a small bag. From it, she produced some berries. They had the same colour as the berries on the hedge. "These will produce three times the output of normal crops. I infused them with a little leaf-magic. I believe my research will be quite satisfactory for the king's purposes. Just plant these, and they'll grow into fruitful trees in a good six months. I cannot count on two hands the number of diseases they will prevent."

"Very well," Arran said, accepting the bag. "I'll pass them on. Meanwhile, I don't suppose you've considered my offer of accompanying me to the Royal Gala this year? The king is supposed to be throwing quite a celebration."

From beside me, the true Ange gasped. "Please don't tell me I accept, Aleam," she said. "I would never even consider an offer from that pompous oaf."

"Just watch and see what happens," Aleam said. "Now fate is set in this thread, it will unfold as it was meant to."

I looked up at the real Ange, and then I turned to Rine, as he puffed out some air that he'd been holding between his cheeks. Meanwhile, over the chasm, the apparition of Ange cocked her head as if she was considering a moment.

The prince looked behind him at his guards and dragons. "Please," he said. "I've not got all day for you to consider this. I need an answer now."

That caused the apparition of Ange to immediately straighten her neck. She gave a slight curtsey. It looked lazy, as if she was mocking the prince. "I'm sorry, sir. I'm meant for the fields, doing my work here, and you're meant for higher circles. Somehow, I don't think I would belong at that ball."

Arran shook his head and then turned back to his dragons. He looked over his shoulder for a moment, though I couldn't see from this angle the expression on his face. "Very well, I gave you a chance for a higher life. I guess you're right though. You'll always be meant for a life like this." He placed the pouch to his waist and tied it to his belt. Then, he walked off in his characteristic haughty manner.

Time sped up. The prince walked at a sprinting pace towards his dragons and flew off. Ange scurried about her garden pruning the trees and sprinkling some kind of dust on them that glowed gold.

The sun soon set on her side of the chasm. But strangely, the sun remained up there in the sky over the second house – the one made from yellow bricks on our left. From it came a boisterous laughter, pealing out from inside as the front door swung open.

An older version of Rine emerged on the doorstep. Surprisingly, his features looked edgier on his face, and he'd also bulked up. While when I'd first seen him, he'd been a spotty teenager, now he seemed kind of handsome.

A blonde-haired woman in a free-flowing sequin dress waltzed out the door after Rine's apparition, giggling out in a high-pitched voice. She leaned over to him, gave him a kiss on the lips. Rine took her into his arms and then dipped her down to the ground. She gave a whooping sound as he planted an even longer, firm kiss on her lips. She giggled again.

"Hah," I knew it, the real version of Rine said from our position on the ledge. "I'm a stud."

"I guess blonde is your type," Ange said with a sigh.

"Who cares? She's beautiful, don't you think? I knew it. I guess my time spent with Bellari really paid off. They say you can learn a lot from young love."

The vision of Rine released the woman, and she skipped down the path towards a horse-drawn carriage that was waiting for her. She had a real spring to her step. But Rine's apparition didn't look too happy. As he stared after the girl, he had this long, forlorn expression on his face. Perhaps it was an expression of boredom, or perhaps even loneliness…

Rine's apparition turned towards the chasm, and it looked as if he was almost looking at Ange's house. But he didn't seem to notice anything. Instead, he put his hands to his mouth and hollered out through them.

"Ben," he called. "Ben, where are you now? Don't tell me you've run away again. Ange can't look after you. She doesn't have time. You know you're better here, Ben. You know this is where you belong."

Now my heart was thumping in my chest. I looked up at Aleam, who was glowing and his face had lost form so I could no longer see his wrinkles. "Hang on a minute," I said. "If I'm not at Rine's and I'm not at Ange's, what happened to me? Please Aleam, don't tell me I've died. That would be a sorry end to this story."

Aleam didn't answer me. Instead, he raised his spectral staff to the sky with both hands. Out of it, he cast a light that filled the entire space. It created a beam that split into two and hit both houses on the sides of the walls. The houses folded outwards, so we could see each individual room inside.

Now, both Rine and Ange were in their bedrooms, lying on their beds. Rine had an incredibly opulent four-poster bed, with satin sheets and covers, coloured rose-red. Ange lay on a single bed, with a plain brown blanket. Ange was sobbing, staring at a painted portrait. Rine didn't sob, but he also had a portrait in his hand.

"Let's just stop time there shall we?" Aleam asked.

He clicked his fingers, and everything went silent and eerie around us. Then those two beams latched on to the pictures in Rine's and Ange's hands. They pulled the two portraits towards us, so close that we could see them clearly. They were both the same portrait, an oil painted replica, with only slight variations in the features. On the left side stood Rine in a red cloak and a black flat hat, with his emerald dragon, Ishtkar, peering over his shoulder. On the right stood Ange in the same attire, with her Sapphire, Quarl peering over hers. They both had a scroll in their hands, each wrapped with a red ribbon.

Each picture was set in a wooden frame with a glass pane at the front. And both frames had the glass cracked, forming what looked like a chasm between the couple.

"Our graduation," Ange said. "But why would I break that picture?"

"Yeah," Rine said. "I have no reason to smash that. I mean it's only a paint—"

Aleam cut him off. "Maybe it's time for some introspection. What could the symbolism in this vision actually mean?"

His words fell to silence. Then, Ange turned slowly to Rine and Rine turned slowly to Ange.

"There's no time for that now," Aleam said, and a white light plunged through the surroundings again coming from the staff that he held high above his head. "We are now about to enter the final vision, and this is the most important of them all. Unfortunately, you three must stay behind."

The ground wobbled underfoot, and the scene changed again.

BATTLE FOR THE CLOUDS

The first time I'd flown up on Salanraja's back, I'd felt vertigo like I'd never felt it before. It had made me nauseous, and I'd thought that I'd never fly again. But then, at least we'd taken off from solid ground.

Now, I had suddenly materialised thousands of feet above the ground and flying with nothing underneath us. At first, I thought we were going to plummet. But we continued onwards, as if I stood on an invisible floor. The ghost of Aleam looked at me, and his expression seemed to wonder why I was looking so terrified.

Then he looked down. "Oh, sorry," he said, with a slight chuckle. "Looks like I forgot something."

A light came out of his staff, and a beam leading downwards. It hit something at a point right beneath our feet and spread out into an undefined blob. This took definition – warping into a tangled mass of spikes around us, and a scaly floor beneath our feet. As the vision crystallised further, I noticed myself to be nestled within Salanraja's corridor of spikes. Now, I could hear her inside my mind again.

Yet, it didn't feel good to be connected with her all of a sudden. Because her thoughts were gibberish. "*The hamster. The owl in the bottom of sky dawn. The beauty is oblivion coming to us all.*" She said in the dragon tongue, and more nonsense not worth repeating.

I was alone with her, just as Aleam had promised. No Rine. No Ange. No Seramina. Just Ben, in the sky with an insane dragon not having a clue where he was going. Not even Aleam was there, although I sensed him watching me from nearby, just as I sensed Rine's, Ange's, and Seramina's watchful eyes as they waited for good old Ben to do his stuff. But I couldn't sense where they were watching me from, and I couldn't see their eyes or hear their voices. The thought of it sent my hackles shooting up.

"Where is everyone? Why can't I share this vision with my friends?"

Aleam's voice trickled out of the sky, as if from nowhere. "You will fight this battle in the sky alone, Ben, and none of your friends will mean anything as you battle on the threshold between life and death."

"What does that even mean?" I asked. "Where are you, Aleam? Reveal yourself."

"As I said, you are in this vision alone."

"But what about my ghost? Why can't I see a ghost of myself like Seramina and Rine and Ange did?"

"In this possible thread of time, you don't have a ghost," he said.

"What do you mean I don't have a ghost?" I considered this a moment. "Does that mean I'm going to end up immortal?" Really, I wasn't sure I liked the thought of living forever. After all, one day the world would surely run out of food.

"Because," the haunting voice of Aleam said. "The darkest magic in the universe can obliterate a soul from eternity. If this happens, you wouldn't have a future nor a past."

I tried to fathom that idea. But thinking about it gave me a headache – I just couldn't process all the possibilities.

Salanraja's gibberish continued in her head, and because I was bonded to her, it continued in mine too. "*Night and day and chocolate and treacle. They haven't been invented yet. But my cat, he knows of such things. Dragoncat. The fate of the world belongs to Dragoncat. No one else. Time incarnate, and time existing not at all. There is no time. Time is an illusion. Tick-tock tick-tock boom!*" Really, she sounded like that faint voice you hear just before you go to sleep. If you can focus on it, then sleep comes. But if not, it can drone on for what seems like eternity.

The sky was streaked with wispy clouds and a crimson sunset. Out of the reddening light, another blurry form appeared. A discordant broken sound came out from this, which soon formed into an ear-piercing shriek. Then the shape became two – a glowing dragon, and a glowing humanoid shaped figure perched on top. More time passed until I saw the humanoid carried a staff, glowing purple. Then the sharp bones on the dragon became visible, as well as the white beam that fed it from the staff. As the figure's features gained definition, I recognised the man who carried that staff.

There came a raucous cackling sound of laughter derived purely from evil intent, and I saw Astravar's wicked grin. His eyes glistened purple as he rushed past me, then he wheeled his mount around again, his staff poised ready to knock me off Salanraja with his magic.

"My staff," I screamed out. "Aleam, I need my staff. This isn't fair. I can't fight this battle without it."

"It's not your staff you need right now. You have other lessons to learn."

"No, I need my staff. Give it to me, and all this can be over. I can save the kingdom of Illumine, and I can save all the dimensions. Then, I can retire and live a perfect, happy life."

I stared, hissing and yowling, as Astravar swung round for another pass of taunting me. He was surrounded by these hideous bat-like creatures that I'd seen in other visions. Well, I say bat like, but they actually had sharp beaks that looked like they could pierce through anything.

Astravar swooped around still cackling with laughter, and I remembered from all my dreams how I'd seen his eggshell-skinned face laughing at me in the sky.

"Aleam, help me!" I shouted. "Please, I need my staff!"

Aleam didn't respond. Instead, I heard another voice. A familiar female voice with a lilting near-Welsh accent. The voice of my crystal. *"Initiate Ben, are you not a great warrior, descendant of the great Asian leopard cat? Haven't you always been destined for remarkable things?"*

That's what I'd always told people. And I'd said it over and over again. *"What are you saying?"* I asked.

"You are Dragoncat. Destined for perfection. The most remarkable creature that ever lived. Have I got you right? You don't need your staff. You can do this alone."

Now her words stung so harshly they made me growl. She was right; I was destined for greatness, just as my ancestors were. I imagined them prowling through the jungle, mighty creatures like lions that stalked their prey with ease. Then, it occurred to me – I didn't know what my ancestors looked like at all.

"Answer the questions, Dragoncat. What is it you see in yourself? Who are you? Who must you become? What is your destiny?" Her voice had once again taken on that scary Boudicca quality.

"I don't know!" I screamed, and I'm sure I screamed it out loud at the top of my voice. "I don't know who I am. I don't know who my ancestors were. And I don't know what I'm meant to become."

As if acknowledging the request, my crystal continued the conversation out loud. "Then you have taken the first step towards becoming a hero of legends," she said. Her voice hung for a moment in the air, then it seemed to bounce off the clouds, and the bat-buzzard creatures, and filled the scene with a momentary warmth. "Remember, Ben you must sacrifice yourself to become complete."

Time had stopped for a moment, but it was only going to be for a moment, because soon enough everything accelerated around me. The creatures swooped in to attack Salanraja, and a searing purple beam came shooting out of Astravar's staff.

A jolting searing pain came in my right-paw side, and I wasn't sure if it belonged to Salanraja or myself. Then I smelled something burning – fur, scale, or flesh – and I tumbled down into a bright light that faded into darkness.

The last thing I heard as I fell into the abyss was Salanraja's voice in my mind, still plagued by madness. *"Alas,"* she said. *"This is the end of us all."*

❧ 24 ❧

GHOST TA'RA

I hit hard solid ground. The impact was so strong that I thought I'd broken every single bone in my body. I yowled out in pain, then for a while, I lay there, unable to budge an inch. Again, there was no heat or cold in this place. There was no wind, no sensation of anything other than my muscles throbbing in protest. There were no glowing outlines of objects to see my way by.

Nothing surrounded me but darkness, and a horrible thought came to me. I was dead. Dead, and perhaps even about to be erased from eternity.

I considered turning into a chimera. It could probably take the pain better than I. It was far, far tougher than this fallen Bengal who didn't even know who he was. Whiskers, I couldn't even claim to be like my ancestors, the great Asian leopard cats. I was an imposter – a fraud. There was no way I could live up to their legacy – the great agile beasts that stalked through jungles and caught anything they wanted to eat. I was nothing; I was worthless; and I belonged in this vacuous, dark place.

With such thoughts rolling around my mind, I lay there for a while, pity consuming me. Perhaps this was how you got lost in this place. You first got lost inside your own mind, and then you forgot who you were.

"Get up, Ben." The voice floated over the air to my ears like pollen on a warm breeze. It didn't belong to my crystal, nor did it belong to Aleam. It didn't belong to the mistress who had looked after me in South Wales, either. Yet, it had a sweet familiarity to it. "Ben, you can't lie there forever. But you know that already…"

"I can't move," I said, trying to work out why I knew that voice so well. But my head was throbbing, and I couldn't think straight.

"Of course you can. All injuries in here are only in your mind, and you didn't just really fall from the back of your dragon. It was just a vision, and now that you've experienced it in your mind, I really hope you've learned not to fall like that again. If you ever do, remember, cats always land on their feet. You taught me that, remember? *'Make sure your feet are always facing the ground before you touch down against it… A cat who cannot be graceful doesn't deserve to be called a cat at all.'*"

I blinked in astonishment – slowly because my eyelids still felt incredibly painful to move. "Ta'ra… Is it really you? But that means…"

"Oh, don't worry. I'm still alive in the real world. At least in most of the possible threads of time. You probably won't lose me yet."

I groaned and then rolled over. I grimaced when I felt a sharp sting at my side. Though I couldn't yet see Ta'ra, her familiar smell drifted over to me. She'd never quite smelled completely of cat. She'd always been cleaner, preferring to bathe herself in fresh water and lavender salts whenever she could.

Pain coursed through my legs as I lifted myself up on them. But it wasn't as intense as I'd expected. I stretched, my legs shaking as I did so. The pain felt like the kind of pain you get a couple of weeks after an injury. Still evident slightly on movement, but not strong enough to impede it.

It was almost as if this darkness had an ability to consume you if you let it latch onto you for too long. An ability to weaken the muscles, soften the mind, and numb emotions to the point of despair. But now, Ta'ra's presence was setting me free.

"Ta'ra, where are you?" I asked.

Though I didn't have to because I soon picked up on her scent. I followed it, and the next thing I knew I was brushing against her soft fur. Then I felt her wet nose against mine, and I slid my face across hers, and we rubbed against each other.

A faint light emanated from behind me. I turned to see her blue outline shimmering around the detail of her fur. She'd told me before that Cat Sidhe's were often thought of as ghosts that haunted the night, and now she truly looked like a ghost, with her green eyes and the white crest on her chest shining out from the blackness of her fur. She looked truly spectral – the kind of shade that inspires fairy tales. But I wasn't afraid of her.

"I've so missed you, Ta'ra," I said.

"Don't tell that to me," she said. "For I am now a version of Ta'ra long into the future. Tell it to the Ta'ra in your world, when you see her next. Because, trust me, she longs to hear those words more than anything. And I should know…"

"Oh, I will," I said. "If I ever see her again."

"That is up to you."

I was only half listening to her advice, because really, I didn't care so much about it. This might not have been the version of Ta'ra I wanted to meet, but still it was a version of Ta'ra. I was purring, and I knew I had so much to tell her. "I really thought that I would never see you again. I thought I'd lost you forever."

"And why did you think that?" Ta'ra's ghost asked as she gave me a sidelong look.

"I don't know. Because… I guess I didn't quite believe that we'd win. I didn't think that I'd ever be able to get the staff, and then we'd be stuck in Dragonsbond Academy, unable to leave, and I'd never thought that I'd be able to visit. Meanwhile, you'd be too busy looking after your Cat Sidhe brethren, you wouldn't have time to visit me."

"I thought you wanted me to come and live with you and Rine and Ange in your version of the future. I've talked to versions of you, Ange, and Rine in the Ghost Realm and they've told me everything."

I lowered myself to the ground, stretching my paws against it. But there was nothing there to dig my claws into, as if the ground below was made of incredibly fine sand. "I wanted to believe all of that," I said. "But, whiskers. I never truly believed it. Not deep inside."

The ghost of Ta'ra was now purring. Around her, the atmosphere seemed to sing. At first, the sounds were unrecognisable – a faint unidentified chiming amidst a chorus of what sounded like violins. Lights of all kinds of different colours and shades peeked out of the darkness. They took on angular shapes, displaying smooth polished facets.

I peered at it, trying to work out what I was looking at, as if I was awakening from a pleasant dream and trying to make sense of the real world. Soon enough, it took on enough definition for me to recognise it.

Right after my first flight on Salanraja, she had taken me to the Versta Caverns. In these caverns, I had encountered the crystal that had given me the gift of languages. Without it, I wouldn't have been able to talk to Ta'ra in the first place, as she spoke fairy and not cat. Salanraja had explained that these crystals that glowed from the walls of the caverns were the source of all magic in the first dimension. Now, I could see them as clear as bowl water, displaying visions I'd never imagined possible before I saw the magical creatures of this world for the first time.

In them, I saw humanoid creatures with enormous arms and long legs, so stretchy that they looked like they'd topple over themselves. I saw golems of many shapes and sizes – not just the clay and forest golems I'd encountered, but a golem made of molten metal, a golem made of clouds, a golem made – it seemed – of pure water. I saw dragons aplenty, flying around the stalks of mushrooms which were as tall as trees.

"Ta'ra," I said, looking at her. She'd gained definition now and no longer looked like a creature of the night. "Why did you come to me? And why did you bring me to this place?"

"Don't you think I wanted to see you?" she replied.

"No... I think there's more to it than that. What's in here, Ta'ra?"

She let out a soft, drawn-out chuckle. "You know, there's a cave of crystals like this in every dimension. In your world, so it is said, it was buried deep underground a long time ago, to prevent misuse by rogue monarchs, false theocrats, and eventually corrupt politicians. In the ghost realm, it is only accessible to those the crystals deem worthy of an audience. That's why Astravar could never reach here."

I growled in slight frustration. Not only had she failed to answer my question, but she'd also introduced more questions. "I thought Astravar was controlled by dark magic," I said. "Surely the dark crystals would have let him have access."

"It's not as simple as that," Ta'ra said with a very human shake of the head. "Crystals are always pure at their source. They are forces of nature after all and there's no dichotomy to them – no black and white. Only an intelligent creature can breed essence into the crystals, and then the crystal draws magic from either the darkness in the Ghost Realm or the souls who exist here independent of it.

"Those who use the power for decay will taint the crystals towards darkness, whilst those who use them for growth will steer the crystals towards the light. This is the distinction so few humans understand. The warlocks aren't the only threat to your kingdom, but anyone who binds themselves to dark magic. It's truly a dangerous power, one of which the most powerful should always beware."

"Even dragon riders?" I asked.

"Even dragon riders," Ta'ra said. "As you soon shall learn."

I considered a moment. I was hardly the kind to listen during lectures back at Dragonsbond Academy, and now there was so much to take in. But I felt I had to learn about it, just like I once needed to learn how to hunt. "So, explain something to me," I said. "If crystals don't have will, how can they know what's right and wrong?"

"They don't," Ta'ra said. "But they know what's natural, and they make judgments that work towards preservation of this world."

"Isn't that what I just said."

"It depends on how you look at it," Ta'ra said. "There's always so many perspectives when you study such things." Really, I had never thought she would become this wise. But then I guess looking after a colony of thousands of Cat Sidhe would change her somewhat. Though she was much older than me, I liked this version of Ta'ra. She behaved now a lot more like a cat should, as if she'd never needed my tuition.

"I'm guessing you brought me here to collect my staff," I said. "Is it here?"

"It most certainly is. But I warn you, getting it will not be easy."

"But I thought you said that I'd proven my worth to the crystals. Surely I'm now ready…"

"No," Ta'ra said, and her eyes flared bright green. That strange wind without temperature once again gusted out from behind her. It was almost strong enough to knock me off my feet. "The test is yet to come, Ben. The crystals need to know you're strong enough to pass."

Of course, I thought. There was always going to be a catch. "I'm ready," I said.

Ta'ra's gaze seemed to bore into my mind, as if she knew exactly what I felt within. "Are you?"

"Yes!"

"Well then. I guess we're about to find out. Come…"

Ta'ra stalked away down a narrow passageway leading between rows of neatly stacked glowing crystals. They jutted out from the bottom of the cave walls like the teeth of an invisible beast – a beast that would either swallow me whole, or I'd emerge from its belly victorious.

The outcome, I guessed, was down to fate. With that thought in mind, I followed Ta'ra within.

AN IMPOSSIBLY MIGHTY
STAFF

I only had to get a little way down the passageway when pitch darkness again enveloped me, and I couldn't see a thing. I navigated using Ta'ra's scent, and soon that faded too, along with any sound she emitted. I couldn't even hear her soft footsteps pattering in front of me.

I stopped, wondering if she'd left me alone. But I knew that was stupid. It was just the darkness trying to consume me, and if I lingered too long, I had no doubt it would suck me down into it again.

I carried on, and I soon felt a sharp tearing sensation in the side. It must have been one of the crystals cutting me. I licked my fur there, the sting intensifying. I tasted sticky blood.

But still I pressed on, confident it would do no good to curl up at all and go to sleep in this place. I'd seen enough of it. It wasn't a suitable place to lie down and retire. It was dark, boring, and lacking in both food and water.

My throat was so dry it was sore. I thought I must have been so thirsty, in fact, that I was hallucinating. Maybe Ta'ra and the crystal cave and all the other weird things I'd seen here were just illusions – constructs of my own mind.

Despite my doubts, I still pressed on. It was better to be wrong about this than right. Besides, Ta'ra's ghost had said that the crystals might test me, and this felt a lot like a test.

A faint light coming from in front of me gave me hope. Ta'ra wasn't there, but some crystals were glowing in faint hues from both sides of the dark cavern wall. The passageway had widened out significantly. I turned back to check the cut from earlier, to see if it had gone deep. But I didn't yet have an outline. Then I remembered what Aleam said about having to believe in something to see it. So, I projected an image of my silky fur into my mind, the stripes and leopard-spotted jungle patterns painted over it. Miraculously, my body took form behind me, and I saw that there wasn't a cut there at all. There wasn't any blood either.

My surroundings lit up too. Now, I could see the glowing outlines of a meadow. It had long grass, dandelions, tulips, poppies, lupins, buttercups, and all kinds of other pretty flowers. Bumblebees buzzed around the place, and I thought about chasing one. But then I remembered what had happened the last time, and I didn't want to get stung again. The passageway I'd come from had completely vanished. I wondered for a moment if I was still within the Versta Caverns.

But it was all illusions. I was in the Ghost Realm trying to find light amidst the swirling darkness. I was starting to realise how this place worked.

The surrounding objects continued to warp and coalesce into recognisable shapes. The meadow stretched out in all directions, fields of grass and flowers leading to nothing beyond it except clouds as far as my eyes could see. There was no visible sun either – rather the light came from the blue sky as if from all directions at once. Yet I felt comfortably warm.

An enormous oak tree stood in the centre of it all, massive acorns hanging off its massive boughs and twisty branches. Its bark looked gnarled and whorled by time. There were many owl holes inset into the trunk, and the tree's upper boughs looked gravid with leaves. It cast no shadow, for the light seemed to have no direction here. Yet, the wrinkles in the bark housed deep ambient shadows that seemed to push the light away – making it look as if the tree itself was fighting against the darkness.

Soon, I could sense everything around me in vivid detail. I could smell the grass, and the soil, and the pollen from the flowers. I sensed something watching me from the tree's branches. Growls seemed to come from it, and there was another smell – of cats that had recently sprayed. But this didn't smell of house cats back home in South Wales, or in Dragonsbond Academy for that matter. This smell was muskier – more feral.

I also caught a whiff of the more familiar scent of Ta'ra from behind. I turned to see her approach. She still looked older than the Ta'ra I knew but had now lost her spectral appearance.

"You said my staff was here," I said. "But all I see are flowers and grass and a gigantic tree."

"Then you've found your staff..."

I blinked in confusion. "What, the tree?"

"Precisely," Ta'ra looked up at the tree, with an awfully proud-looking posture. "Your staff is the tree."

"What the whiskers do you mean? I can't go into battle with an oak tree in my mouth. I mean the thing's ginormous."

"You can change its form," Ta'ra said. "Remember, a lot of what exists in this place is to do with belief. A tree donates its spirit to become a magical staff, and then you only need to find the crystal that was meant for it."

I didn't understand. I thought this version of Ta'ra must have been having a joke with me. "So what? I just go up to it and say, excuse me tree, will you turn into a staff for me? This is absurd."

Ta'ra laughed that sweet laugh again. "Not precisely. You will have to defeat its guardians first."

I paused a moment as I took in that foreign scent of cat spray above me. "It's guardians..." I said, my jaw clenched tight with anger.

"Exactly," Ta'ra said. "Behold your ancestors, the great Asian leopard cats..."

I looked at her in astonishment. This really had to be a joke, albeit a very bad one. The older version of Ta'ra was getting her revenge for all the mackerel she thought I'd stolen from her. She'd taken it too far.

Just as I turned away from the tree, ready to find my way to somewhere else, my ears perked up and honed onto some rustling sounds coming from the thick clusters of leaves. Little pink noses emerged first, followed by three pairs of amber eyes.

Three blue shimmering forms stalked along the branches and down the trunk, their bodies seeming to cling to the tree. They found their way to the ground, and then they sprinted towards me.

ANCESTRY

The next thing I knew, I had three cats circling me. They still looked like ghosts, but it didn't take long for their fur and features to gain definition and the glow that outlined them to fade. Soon enough, before me stood three Asian leopard cats, and other than their distinctive oriental look, they looked no different from common house cats.

Disappointment sank into my chest as I took in their size and stature. These were my ancestors, the great Asian leopard cats, and they were hardly great at all. In fact, one of them was even smaller than me. I'd expected the great Asian leopard cat to be a great hunter, like a jaguar or a lion. How was this creature meant to claim any prey it wanted? Your everyday deer would just trample it into the ground.

As a cocktail of confusion and dismay whirled in my mind, I spun around, trying to get glimpses of my ancestors' features. But they moved so fast and seemed so wild it was hard to focus on them for long. Still, I noticed the beautiful markings on their fur. Just like mine, except with more spots and fewer stripes. One of them – a tom cat – had an incredibly long neck, and much of its mass seemed distributed towards the back of its body. Another – a she-cat – had a heavy fur coat, making it look a bit like a Maine coon except much smaller. The third – another tom, and the one that was smaller than me – had a tiny head and massive ears that made it look a bit like a caricatured fox.

"These are my ancestors?" I asked. "The great Asian leopard cat? Then why must I fight them? They're practically family."

Ta'ra wasn't there to answer me. She had disappeared now into the magic of this place. The three cats had one thing in common – their eyes all sloped downwards towards the centre, as if they wore permanent frowns.

"I'll talk to you then," I said to my ancestors, hoping that one would answer. I could, after all, speak their language. "Why must I fight you?"

"You have to prove yourself worthy," the long-necked leopard cat said.

"If you are truly an Asian leopard cat, then you must fight like an Asian leopard cat," the thick furred she-cat said.

"Show us what you're made of, Bengal," the small leopard cat with the large ears said.

Just as the smallest tom cat held my attention, the other male with the long neck pounced on me from behind. Its claws tore into my back, and then it bit through my fur with its teeth, sending a painful shudder up my spine. I shrieked out, and I shook the creature off me. I turned to see it coming at me again with flailing paws. I dived out the way and watched it pass. My heart pounded in my chest, and my breath was so heavy it hurt. I'd never seen a cat move so fast.

While I watched the long-necked cat, something massive leaped out at me from the concealed grass to my side. A fluffy mass of fur sailed towards me, and I turned towards the bared yellow fangs of the female leopard cat. It extended its sharp claws and scraped them across my face. The force of it sent me rolling across the ground, and I tumbled right into the third leopard cat.

I thought this one would be a complete wimp, and I couldn't have been more wrong. Because what it lacked in size, it gained in ferocity. It executed a flurry of movements with its paws and gnashed at me with teeth so sharp I thought they might shred me to fur balls.

I scrambled out of the way, and I hissed and yowled as I ran towards the oak tree. I leapt at the trunk, and I caught myself on the bark with my claws. Hisses and growls came from behind me, and I looked up towards the top of the tree and pulled upwards. The tears in my knotted muscles screamed at me as I went, but I persevered and eventually clambered on to a branch. There, I lay down and watched the leopard cats hissing and growling at me from the bottom of the tree.

It was stupid really because I knew they could also reach me here. They had come down from here to fight me. But they didn't even seem to want to bother coming up. It didn't take me long to realise why.

I looked up to see more leopard cats on the tree, staring at me from higher branches. They wore a variety of coats – some of them in brilliant fiery colours, others in desaturated greys, and others in russet browns. They stalked down the high branches, their fangs bared.

"Come down to the ground, you coward," one of them said.

"Face up to your past," another said.

"Embrace your destiny," said a third.

Still the three Asian leopard cats stalked the bottom of the tree, looking even more ferocious than their brothers and sisters up here. Then I remembered. I had the power to turn into a chimera. I willed the magic into my muscles. But the magic didn't work.

My part of the branch was wide enough to fit three leopard cats side by side. They stalked forward, and I could smell the wildness in their breaths. It wasn't as foul as the breath of the chimera I'd caught a whiff of before, but still it stank of rotten meat.

I never had actually killed an animal and eaten it raw. But these creatures must have done it daily. In other words, they were seasoned killers, and now they were coming to get me. They backed me down the length of the branch until I was right at the edge, the leaves tickling at my shins.

The branch snapped underneath me, and I fell. I yelped out, twisting my body as I fell. Fortunately, I landed on my feet. My heart was pounding, and at first, I thought I was about to taste bitter defeat.

But then, I realised I had no choice. I had to fight. I couldn't run from this. I was a Bengal, a descendant of the great Asian leopard cat. Which meant I must have evolved and adapted to be better than them.

The leopard cats I was meant to face were lying in the grass in wait. As soon as I hit the ground, they charged. The long-necked one pounced first, and I dashed underneath it, swiping up with my claws to scratch underneath its belly. I didn't turn to see it clumsily roll through the grass behind me, but I'd already known from its trajectory that it would.

The small Bengal with the big ears came next. It moved so fast, dashing around me so swiftly that it made me dizzy trying to track it. But still I focused on its small head and the long ears that bobbed over it. When it came in to strike, I was ready. Its flurrying swipes were fast – full of feints and jabs and all kinds of complex manoeuvres. But they were designed to keep larger enemies at bay, and to make the leopard cat seem larger than it actually was.

I pretended I was a goat and lowered my head. I think I even pushed some of the chimera's magic into me, and I charged. I rammed the smaller creature across the ground, and it skidded away.

Finally came the leopard she-cat in the fur coat with the super strong swipes. Without my power as a chimera, I had no chance of defeating her in a paw wrestle. So I ducked the first swipe that it sent at me, darted around the second, then I knocked the leopard cat down from behind. I growled in triumph as I pinned it by the shoulder, and I was just about to bite down on its neck, when I realised something.

Astravar had wanted me all this time to turn feral, which is kind of what dark magic had done to him. It had destroyed his mind, so he didn't care about those who should be close to him. If my lust for this battle won within me, then I'd have lost, because I'd be no different from Astravar.

This was surely the test.

I calmed myself and stepped back off the furry leopard cat. She glared over her shoulder at me, confusion evident on her face.

"This is enough," I said. "I will not fight you."

"What do you mean you won't fight us?" the long-necked leopard cat sputtered back.

"Are you telling us you're weak?" said the small one. "Incapable? Are you a coward?"

"Explain yourself," the thick coated one said.

I took a deep breath and tried my hardest to ignore the adrenaline surging in my legs, shaking in such a way that they compelled me to re-join the fight. "I do not want to win. I only want to save the kingdom, save myself, and to save those I—" The words caught on my tongue, as if I didn't want to admit them to myself. But really, who was I kidding?

"I want to save those that I care about," I said, "including my friends and my dragon. And I'm sure you do too. If you stop me from getting that staff, then all the leopard cats in our world will perish. Is that what you really want?"

The three leopard cats I'd fought remained silent. They stared at me with wide eyes, as if waiting for me to say something. Instead, a loud voice boomed out from the distance. "No," it called out. "That is not what they want."

A cat jumped down off the top of the tree. It wasn't a leopard cat like the others. Instead, it was your typical mongrel tomcat tabby – with a round face and a strong-looking body. One of its eyes was dead, and it looked as if it had been in a lot of fights.

He strode up to me, and then looked me straight in the eyes, recognition painted on his face.

"Who the whiskers are you?" I asked.

He looked a bit taken aback by that reply, but he didn't express this for long. "I'm your father," he said. "And I'm incredibly proud of you, son."

27

THE MIGHTY GEORGE

The old Ragamuffin back home in South Wales had told me it's rare that a cat will ever meet their father. "If you do," he said. "Then you are either incredibly lucky, or you've committed such terrible crimes against cathood that he's spent the rest of his life hunting you down to make you atone for them."

I hadn't committed any crimes – or at least I didn't think I had. But given how battered this cat looked, I didn't quite feel like one of the lucky ones.

I observed him cautiously because I really believed this had to be a trick. At the same time, disappointment bloomed inside me like a toxic flower.

"No," I said, with a bitter laugh. "You can't be my father. I'm a Bengal descendant of the great Asian leopard cat. One of these ghosts is my father, but not you."

As if wanting to wound me, he said it again. "No, Ben. I am your father. Your mother was a Bengal, and her mother before that, and then her father, and her mother, and her mother. You do come from a great line of Bengals, but that doesn't mean your line is pure."

Really, I'd never heard anything so ridiculous in my life. Now, adrenaline was really pumping through me. I felt I should fight this imposter, and then I'd show him not to make up terrible lies.

"If you're really my father, then why are you telling me this? Isn't it better for me to be proud of my heritage, so I don't need to worry about it when fighting Astravar? If I know I'm descended from mongrels, how can I expect to defeat him?"

"That is your problem," my alleged father said. "For a long time, Ben, your pride has been wounding you. It doesn't matter who your ancestors are. All that matters is that you've made it this far, and you have the will to do good."

"How do you know all this? How could you possibly know who my ancestors are?"

"When you live in the ghost realm long enough, you get to trace back your entire family lines. You meet members of your family going generations back, and you learn revealing things about your past you couldn't have possibly learned in the land of the living."

He sounded genuine enough. But I still didn't – or rather I couldn't – believe him.

I stalked over to him, and I sniffed his fur, searching for familiarity. I smelled behind his neck first, and then down his back, all the way to his tail. He had the scent of a normal moggie tomcat – there was nothing special about him.

"There's no way you can be my father," I said. "It's impossible. You don't even smell like me."

"You really think a father and son should smell the same?" the foreign tom cat said, and he cocked his head.

"I mean, you're not even a warrior. You couldn't defeat these great Asian leopard cats."

"Really? Do you want to fight me and test that?" He puffed himself up and arched his back.

"No, it's okay," I replied. I'd really had enough of fighting for one day.

The sun suddenly emerged at the highest point in the sky. Its rays filtered through the blue, limning everything with soft, warm hues and filling me with warmth. It revealed, in this cat's fur coat, familiar markings. The patterns in my fur were made of stripes and spots, and here I saw the stripes.

"*You can trust him,*" a voice said in my head. It was my crystal speaking. "*He has no reason to lie to you.*"

"*But he's not a Bengal,*" I replied in my mind. "*Nor is he a leopard cat.*"

"*Does he need to be?*"

I stopped to consider that for a moment. Though I had no reason to trust this strange cat, I also had no reason not to believe my crystal. It had, after all, guided me through this world and other dimensions, during the times when I was most lost. I turned to the cat. Now, the other leopard cats were nowhere in sight. It was just me and him, standing alone by a massive shimmering oak tree set amongst tall, green grass.

"Father," I said. "Let's say for a moment you are my father... Most cats don't get to meet their fathers, do they?"

"Until they reach the ghost realm," he said. "And yet here you are."

"Then why are you even here in this vision? Surely the entire purpose of this dream – or whatever it is – is for me to get my staff."

My father was purring now – a deep rumbling sound that filled me with comfort.

"I discovered your crystal," he said. "It spoke in this soft Welsh accent, much like the humans back in our home. At first, when it said that I was destined to meet you, I thought that I'd gone crackers. But then, when it showed me visions of you in your litter, with your five brothers and sisters, I was filled with joy. It told me your story – about that evil warlock, and what he tried to do to you. It showed me what he intends to do to the world, including the destruction of my old family home, and all the other little kittens I've fathered, too." He fell silent for a moment.

I meowed at him because I realised he needed a little comfort. I'd never found it easy to watch those visions of Astravar, just as my dreams of him had always spooked me out. I felt grateful that I'd not had to deal with those dreams for a while. Even so, the memories of them remained.

"How many sons and daughters do you have?"

My father laughed. "Oh, I don't know. Hundreds, perhaps. You know, your mother and I knew each other since we were kittens. She really was a beautiful cat."

"And my crystal... What did it tell you to do?"

He turned back to the tree, but it wasn't a tree anymore. I was staring right at my crystal, spinning slowly on its vertical axis. It was showing a vision from my kittenhood. In it I was a kitten when I loved to swipe at pieces of string the mistress' and master's son dangled from a fork. Then when I got the string, he'd hold the fork over my nose, and I'd swipe it out of his tiny fingers. I remember my feeling of pride whenever I did that. But then both me and the child were still young.

The thing that struck me most of all about the vision was my appearance. I still had the long neck and huge ears of an Asian leopard cat. But the markings on my coat were definitely similar to my father's, and my face also had his shape.

The vision of the crystal changed, and it stopped spinning. One of its facets faced us, showing both of us staring forwards, as if at nothing. It took me a moment to realise that this wasn't a vision at all, but my father and I were looking at ourselves in a mirror. Indeed, there were so many similarities, that there was no doubt in my mind who this cat was.

I no longer felt the dismay I'd felt when my father had told me the news. Rather, I felt good to finally have an identity. Now I knew who I really was.

I turned to my father, and I bowed my head. "Father, you never told me your name," I said. "Because I'm going to tell everyone I'm descended from you from now on and be proud."

"George," he said. "I am the great mighty George. Or at least that's what the humans called me."

I laughed. "Much, much better than Bengie. Well, I am Ben, descendant of the great Asian leopard cat and the great mighty George."

"Very well," George said, and he blinked his one good eye, then rubbed his nose against mine. I turned back to the crystal, because it had started to glow white and was spinning once again.

"*Can you accept this, Initiate Ben?*" the crystal said. "*The fabled Drag-*

oncat and descendant not only of the great Asian leopard cat, but many other breeds of cat as well."

"I think so," I said.

"No," the crystal said. "There is no 'think' about it. You either do or you don't."

"Okay," I said. "I accept it, and I accept my destiny. My father is right, it doesn't matter where I come from."

"Then let it be so," my crystal said, glowing as it spoke. "Initiate Ben, the fabled Dragoncat, who will one day be spoken of in legends. Descendant of the great Asian leopard cat and the much-revered George. I must warn you of the powers of this staff, because there is only one other of its kind in existence. It contains dark magic, and we hope and have forecast in most of the possible threads of the future that this dark magic will not corrupt your soul. Can you accept this responsibility?"

"Of course I can," I said.

"Then, it is done. Here is my final gift to you. After this gift, I will only help you if you call on me and you truly need my aid."

The crystal resumed spinning, and it went faster and faster until its facets were completely blurred, and it soon resembled a whirlwind – except this time not a dangerous one. The surrounding light intensified. It got so bright that I saw spots before my eyes.

I couldn't see my father anymore. I couldn't see the great Asian leopard cats around me. Nor could I see Ta'ra, but she had vanished quite a while ago now. The crystal sang like sharp metal blades slicing through the sky. The pitch continued to intensify until it hurt my ears, and it got so loud that I thought my delicate ear drums would rupture.

I lay down and buried my head in the ground as I clutched at my ears with my paws. This shielded me from both the light and the noise. The ground shuddered, and then everything went still.

When I looked up, the crystal, the oak tree, the grass and everything around me had gone. All I saw was a human-sized hand holding a staff with a purple crystal on it. Both hand and staff had that spectral glowing outline to them I'd become used to in this domain. The hand floated around me, as if attached to an invisible body. I tried stepping away from it, but it stayed firm by my side – my new companion.

"The crystals also decided to gift you with a staff-bearer," my crystal said in my mind. *"It will go with you wherever you travel. You will need this, for obvious reasons. Once you call upon the staff, it will place it in your mouth. Only then, can you use it, and you will know instinctively how to do so. But to master its use will require some training."*

I chirped, happily. Finally, I'd got the staff I was destined to retrieve. *"Is that it?"* I asked. *"So now I can return to Dragonsbond Academy, rescue Aleam, defeat Astravar, and end this once and for all."*

"No," said the ghost of Ta'ra, as she was suddenly standing right beside me. I hadn't realised she could hear the voice of my crystal, but I guess everything was possible in the ghost realm. "I think you'll probably want to return to the Caldmines Forest first."

"You mean the place where all the Cat Sidhe are?"

"Yes," ghost Ta'ra said. "Because your friends are in danger, and they urgently need your help."

"What? What's happening to them. Ta'ra?"

She said something in reply, but I didn't quite catch it because her voice and smell were trailing away as the scene filled with white light again.

28

SERAMINA'S SECRET

O nce again, darkness enshrouded me. A haunting silence enveloped everything, so still that for a while I thought myself surrounded by voices. But my mind had created these voices to fill the spaces where sound should have been. I also sensed other things in the darkness – the mistress from South Wales laughing as she called me in for a roast chicken dinner, flames spouting out of Salanraja's mouth onto a raw slice of beef, butterflies and catnip and the warming sun. But none of these really existed. I just longed for them in a darkness that would have consumed me if I didn't hold onto my hope.

Later, the ghost of Ta'ra's words came back to me, now only a memory. *"Your friends are in danger, and they urgently need your help."* Those words echoed around my mind as if they were ball bearings bouncing off the walls of my skull. I wished I knew more. Why hadn't Ta'ra's ghost told me exactly what was wrong?

It could be that they were facing complete annihilation. If that was the danger – Ta'ra had told me nothing. It might be they were bracing against a terrifying flood, or they were stuck in the centre of a raging forest fire, or they'd all been sent to the Seventh Dimension and were stuck on a rock surrounded by glowing, sulphurous magma.

Or Astravar could have sent his lackeys, and the only way to defeat them would be through my staff. Whiskers, for all I knew, Astravar could have left Dragonsbond Academy to fight them. Or maybe he was going to possess them all again so he could use their magic to destroy Dragonsbond Academy.

I imagined a purple mist looming on the horizon, bone dragons flying in from afar, keeping pace over armies of Manipulators, glowing forest golems, and shifting clay golems. Then, in my mind's eye, I saw an image of the Cat Sidhe, their teeth bared and ready for battle. That's all they had for weapons – teeth and claws. And I guess they could also turn into fairies and use their special magic.

Now I had my staff I could now go and help Ta'ra. Yet, I was trapped in this place, surrounded by the darkness that wanted to consume my soul.

As I considered my terrible situation, the darkness and the silence weighed down on me. I growled, I hissed, and I writhed on the floor, clawing at myself to try to get a grasp on reality.

Fortunately, a female voice jerked me out of my downward spiral. It was slightly monotonous, but at least familiar. "Ben," she said. "Is that you?"

I latched on to the smell of snowdrops coming from some place nearby. It was only faint, but strong enough to remember that I still had friends in this lonely place. "Seramina?" The smell intensified. "Seramina, where are you?"

"Here, Ben. I'm right in front of you."

Her voice drifted off into emptiness, and at first, I thought that the silence had returned, and I'd lost her. But then I recognised the roaring of a well-lit fire, crackling and spitting. From my right, a hearth emanated a warm red light. Within a nest of roughly hewn stones, flames lapped up from behind iron bars, stretching up towards a stone chimney. A cloud of soot danced above these, disappearing again into the darkness.

I shivered as the firelight bloomed out and filled the room. I could now see everyone around me. Seramina, Ange, and Rine sat in incredibly comfortably looking armchairs placed around the fire. A fourth armchair lay between Rine and Ange. Both seemed deep in thought as they stared at the fire.

I stepped towards the fireplace. The fire within felt like a real fire. If I was behind those bars, I wouldn't be happy, but here on the comfort of the rug that covered the loose floorboards, I could lie down and have a well-earned nap. I rolled over onto my side so I could feel the warmth of it on my belly. There I lay, purring to the rhythm of the crackles.

"Ben," Rine said, and his eyes lit up when he saw me. I was glad to see some amusement in his eyes. "Here, you might appreciate this."

He pointed his staff, and at first, I thought he was going to freeze me in place. Instead, the blue, frozen beam hit a point on the floorboard next to me. A block of ice sprung out of the ground there. It was as big as my head, and close enough to the fireplace that it immediately started to thaw.

I let out a chirp of appreciation. Then I scrambled over to the ice block and licked off my first drop of water. It tasted amazingly fresh, and I continued to lick away until my tongue was numb. Something shimmered from next to me, and the hand – my staff-bearer – appeared. It had my fabled staff clenched tight between its thumb and fingers, and it glowed blue as a spectral hand should.

Ange also seemed to perk up a little bit when she saw me. I guessed that all three of them had been so worried about me that they had almost become lost in this place. Ange smiled as she looked down at me, then clucked softly. I was about to go over and jump onto her lap when her eyebrows furrowed and her expression twisted to disgust. She wasn't actually looking at me, but at the spectral hand and specifically the purple crystal on the staff that it wielded.

"Ben..." she said through clenched teeth. "Your staff... You have dark magic."

"I do," I said. "The crystals entrusted me with it."

"But how? I was worried when you became the chimera and saw that you could use more than one school of magic. I guess it makes sense, but... You cannot use this staff, Ben. You're not strong enough... The dark magic will taint your soul, and you'll end up just like Astravar."

I blinked at her in surprise. I hadn't expected this from Ange. But then I'd seen how quickly she'd almost turned on Seramina. I guessed she was testing me and wanted to know I still walked in the light. "It's tainted the souls of all humans that have connected with it," I pointed out. "Cats, however, haven't had a chance to try it yet. Maybe we'll be okay."

She shook her head, and then gazed at Seramina, who approached my spectral staff-bearer. Seramina carried her staff in one hand, whilst the other she had cupped over her staff's crystal, which was glowing white.

"Might I suggest something?" she asked. Her hand glowed red as the light suffused from her staff through the skin. She lifted her hand away from the crystal, keeping the palm facing downwards. She carried away a ball of light, hovering just underneath her hand. As it floated across, clinging to her hand like a magnet, it pulsed in a mesmerising way.

Seramina placed the ball over the purple crystal on my staff. It lowered from her palm into the crystal on its own accord, and it touched the crystal, then flared out brilliantly. When the light had faded, all that was left was a white crystal on my staff, just like the one on Seramina's.

"What?" Ange said. "A glamour spell won't change the issue. It's still dark magic."

"Yes," Seramina said. "But no one will have to know now. Ben can just say he's a master of alteration and mind-magic, just as we've always thought." She bit her lip, as if considering something. "Trust me, it worked for me…"

It was as if someone had just smashed a plate in a quiet room. For a moment, Ange seemed stunned into silence. Then her jaw dropped, and she stood up.

"Y-Y-You're a dark magic user as well?"

"I am," Seramina said. "Is that a problem?"

Ange had placed a hand to her temples, and I could sense anger burgeoning inside her. "Well, that makes sense. You had everyone fooled, thinking that you're a mind-witch and destiny-mage when you're actually just as dangerous as the warlocks. That's how Astravar managed to take control of you, and that's why we saw you destroying the world in that vision."

Ange drew her staff off her back as she studied Seramina. She had clearly given Seramina's staff back to her whilst I'd been off fighting the ghosts of my ancestors. Now, her expression said that she thought it had been a mistake to do so.

"I didn't choose my discipline," Seramina said. "I didn't choose what was in my blood, and I didn't choose who my father was." The fire next to Ange flared, and a flame lashed out against the iron bars as if it wanted to escape. At first it seemed Seramina had done this. But then I remembered that this place seemed to feed off our emotions, and the fire was probably all a part of the show.

"And what does the Council of Three think about all this?" Ange asked as she stepped forward and slightly to Seramina's side. "Why would they let you loose in the world if they knew you had the power of a warlock?"

"The Council of Three already knows. I came clean after what happened during the battle with the Cat Sidhe. I'd been hiding it before then. I never knew why I had this power until I learned who my father was. But Aleam and the Council of Three always suspected my powers, and when Aleam saw what I was capable of, he took me under his wing and taught me how to control myself. He knows how to handle dark magic, and he knows how to stop it consuming me."

"But how can you do so without breaking your connection to the dragon? None of this makes any sense."

"I don't know," Seramina said.

Ange took a deep breath, and she turned towards the fireplace and gazed into the flames. "It's not just the warlocks we have to worry about, but the threat of such vile magic consuming us from within our society."

"It's not just me. There are other dark magic users in Dragonsbond Academy. Aleam can still use dark magic. There's also another child of a warlock, I believe."

"What? Who?"

"The way that you're talking about this dark magic, I'm not sure I want to tell you. Anyway, I don't know for sure. I only have my suspicions – and in truth, if I'm right, I don't think she knows either. But you have to understand, we have to keep this a secret. If Prince Arran found out, then there's no telling what he might do. You've seen what he's like."

"So why did you tell me in the first place?" Ange said.

"Because it's about time that people saw who we were," Seramina said.

"But what if it consumes you? What if you become just like the warlocks? You should be stripped of your magic."

Seramina squinted her eyes. "Even if we need it to defeat the warlocks?" she asked. "You've seen Ben's visions, and I've had many of my own as well, that I've kept secret for a long time. Until now, I was even more scared of this power than you are. But Aleam, or at least the future Aleam, made me see sense."

Ange had definitely calmed down, at least a little. She backed away from Seramina and lowered her staff to her legs. As she continued to speak, she no longer sounded angry, but confused, as if she were trying to work out a way to accept this in herself, as if she wanted a way to reason with herself.

"Someone should tell King Garmin," she said. "Why keep it a secret? He would see sense and he could tell Prince Arran that he can't hurt any of you."

Seramina lowered her head. "Not everyone trusts King Garmin. Aleam feels we should keep this a secret from him, and Driar Yila agrees. On the other hand, Driar Brigel and Driar Lonamm think the king could help change things. But everyone agrees – the more people who learn about this, the more at risk our dark magic users become. We think there are many more inside Cimlean City, and if the warlocks learn of this, they will take the opportunity to corrupt those who don't have the power to control their abilities yet. This secret must be guarded closely, Ange and Rine. I'm only telling you this because I just couldn't stand seeing you turning on Ben like that. But I've kept quiet about it because I worry what people might think of me." Her eyes had gone puffy underneath, and her nose was scrunched as if she was about to cry.

Ange lowered her staff, then bent down and placed it down on the ground. She opened out her arms to Seramina. "Come here," she said.

Seramina nodded, then placed her staff down on the ground. She entered Ange's embrace and held her there.

"It must have been hard, keeping this a secret for so long," Ange said.

"It was. But I don't think vanquishing the warlocks will ever be the end of it. Dark magic will always exist in the kingdom in some form."

"We have to do what's right," Ange said. "We've got to fight for a better world. For a better life."

All this time, both Rine and I were happy to take a backseat and watch Ange and Seramina get over their differences. There came a slightly high-pitched buzzing sound from next to Rine, and suddenly the ghost of Aleam stood there. He looked slightly alarmed.

"You've all fulfilled your purposes, I see," he said. "You've reconciled your differences and Ben has got his staff."

Rine stood up from his seat and looked at him, his head askew. "What's wrong?" he said to Aleam.

Aleam looked over his shoulder to where the light from the fire couldn't reach. "You've each encountered the darkness here in various forms, and you've all fought it off in your own ways. That darkness is your enemy – not just the source of dark magic, but the source of dark emotions and dark thoughts. It powers the night, and those who draw magic from it, and it powers the emptiness between spaces. You must use it wisely, Seramina and Ben, but you must fear it and respect it too."

I stood up, and I looked at Aleam with wide eyes. "Aleam?"

He didn't seem to hear me, and he continued to stare onwards. Meanwhile, his ghostly outline was shimmering and seemed to be fading. Even his voice was getting fainter and fainter, though I could still hear what he said.

"Here, in the ghost realm," he continued, "we call it *Cana Dei*, and us ghosts can only travel through it because we exist independent of time. I've held it away from you long enough, and I can't hold it anymore. You must run, or it will consume you." He pointed off towards the darkness – the place I least wanted to go. "In that direction you can find a way out to the Caldmines Forest. Open a portal, Seramina, and get everyone out of here, before it's too late."

THE DARKNESS

"Too late... Too late... Too late..." Aleam's words seemed to echo as if bouncing off the walls of a massive chasm. Meanwhile, the darkness seemed to gain strength. It was as if everything around it seemed to dissolve into it, melting away.

The fireplace went first, the heat from it dissipating instantly. Then went the stonework, then the railing – everything dripping into nothingness as if composed of drops of black liquid. The chairs and the rug went next, followed by the floorboards. The floor felt as if it was made of that horrible yeast extract stuff, and it smelled of it too.

Then I noticed myself sinking ever so slowly into the ground. I lifted my feet, and the act of moving seemed to pull me up again. Even so, I knew if I stayed still long enough, the smelly floor would suck me into the darkness, and I'd become lost forever in its depths.

If I ever got home, I would tell the Savannah Cats that the worst deaths didn't happen underneath the belly of the hippopotamus, as they had claimed. Instead, they happen at the bottom of a pool of yeast extract. A bottomless pit of the stuff that shows no remorse, even to vegetarians.

"Hold on," Rine shouted out. "I've got this." He lifted his staff and its crystal glowed blue. He pointed this at the ground in front of us. A sheet of ice cascaded out to where Aleam had directed us. I turned around to see that the old man had disappeared, and nothing remained of what had been in that warm, cosy room.

Rine stepped onto the sheet, then he yelped out as he went skidding forward. He would have slid off if he wasn't quick enough to cast another spell just next to his foot. This created a block of ice that clung to the sheet and stopped his foot in place.

"Idiot," Ange said. "What will all this be worth if you end up getting killed, Rine?" She cast a spell of her own from her staff. A row of vines sprang out of it, and they quickly crawled along the edges of ice, creating a makeshift balustrade. Rine looked back at Ange and gave her a nod of appreciation. He used the vines to pull himself along his magical sheet of ice, sliding with his feet as he did so.

Seramina stepped forward next, her staff clutched in her hand as she focused on a point at the end of the sheet of ice. She pulled herself along gently with the other hand. Then Ange stepped on, and she kept casting vines that wrapped around the ice, as if to secure it in place.

Meanwhile, I'd forgotten myself while watching Seramina, Ange, and Rine, such that I was up to my knees in the black goo, and I couldn't see my feet. Once I got deep enough in it, I forgot my muscles were even there. In a way, I wanted to sink down all the way into it. Fortunately, I still had that rational part in my brain that told me it wasn't a good idea. The goo hadn't consumed that part yet.

"Come on, Ben," Ange said, turning back to me from her perch on the ice. "You can't stay here." Something also nudged me from behind – my spectral staff-bearer pushing me forwards with its fist.

I summoned my strength and pulled myself out, then I rushed forwards and stepped onto the ice. It was cold against the bottom of my paws – which meant that at least it was real. I slid across it, and I hit a wall of springy vines. I was lucky, really, that Ange had thought to cast vines low enough to support me. I skated after the three teenagers, my feet so cold I thought they might develop frostbite and fall off. I'd said many times that I hated walking on snow, but walking on ice was much, much worse.

Eventually, after what felt like hours of pain travelling along this sheet of ice, with Rine casting the sheet of frozen ground, extending ahead of us, and Ange casting the supporting balustrade and scaffolding, we reached the end of the journey.

Rine stopped first. "What in the Seventh Dimension?" he asked. At first, I noticed the light had gone out on his staff. But then I saw that the darkness had closed around it.

"It's got me too," Ange said. "We can't go any further."

"It doesn't matter," Seramina said. "This is the place, I think."

"You don't sound so sure," Ange said. Her legs were bowed, and her gaze was focused on Seramina's staff, as if she were considering wrenching it from her grasp.

"No, no," Seramina said. "This is it." She raised her staff, and the crystal on it glowed purple. Then, she reached into a pocket, and produced a smaller crystal, again purple and not attached to anything. "Courtesy of Aleam. This should lead us back home."

"You had that all along?" Rine said. "Why didn't you use it?"

"Because Ben needed to find his staff first. Anyway, it doesn't matter now. Just let me concentrate." She closed her eyes and both the crystal on her staff and the crystal in her hand lit up purple. A beam then shot out from her staff into the purple crystal and refracted through it, shining out again into the darkness ahead of us. The faint outline of an oval shimmered there – wide enough for us to pass through it. But there was nothing on the other side to step into yet. There was only an abyss.

I turned back to look at the path from when we'd came. The blackness was edging closer and closer, like water coming in from the sea. It ate away at anything it touched, and it was far too close for comfort. I gave it a matter of seconds before we all fell into it – and this time I doubted we'd be able to crawl our way out of it. If the darkness shrouded our magic, then we'd have nothing left to fight back with.

Strangely, though, it didn't seem to want to cut off the purple crystals. It made sense, I guess. If dark magic fed off this thing, then perhaps it could push it away.

"We've not got much time," I said.

"State the obvious, why don't you, Ben," Rine said. "Seramina, whatever you're doing, you need to hurry."

"Hold it," Seramina said, as a thin film of energy developed over the inside of the oval. "I need just a little longer."

Ange said nothing. Instead, she was wrestling with her staff as if trying to pull it out of the darkness. Still, whatever she did seemed to pull the darkness closer towards her. It had almost reached the bottom of her staff now and would consume her arm.

The light from the portal was growing, but strands of darkness had already crept under our feet, and what used to be ice and vines below us resembled a spiderweb more and more. I clenched my jaw and plucked up some courage. This one was on me.

I glanced at my staff-bearer, that had my staff held tight within it. Just as my crystal had instructed, I reached out mentally and summoned it towards me. It lurched forward, and then it was as instinctive as putting a paw in a hole. It placed the staff in my mouth, and I clenched down on it. Then the crystal on my staff glowed and brimmed with power.

It felt like I had a long pole clenched between my jaws, with the other end wedged underneath a washing machine at the peak of its cycle. It vibrated so hard that part of me wanted to drop it. But still, with such intense power surging through me, I didn't want to let go.

"Ben, no! You're not trained." It was Ange who said it, but her voice seemed so distant now. Instead, I focused on the magic. It was so addictive that part of me wanted to become part of that magic – to lose my mind to it. It felt as if something invisible was reaching out inside me and trying to control my soul.

I had to keep focused. I had to get us all out of there. So, I imagined the most powerful spell I could possibly cast. An explosion that would push the darkness away for miles, revealing the light of the ghost realm that resided underneath it. It would strengthen the ice and vines beneath it and even feed a little magic into the portal. Meanwhile, it would leave Ange, Seramina, Rine, and me unscathed. Plus, it would bring some delicious food with it for good luck.

That was what I hoped for. What happened instead was salmon.

Out of my staff, I shot this tiny pulse of blue light that floated in the darkness for a moment, pushing it away. Just when I expected the explosion that would save us all, the first salmon flopped out, shred-

A CAT'S GUIDE TO SAVING THE KINGDOM

ding the darkness with its sharp teeth as it sailed through it. Then came another, and another. Before I knew it, what must have been thousands of salmon were all leaping out of this magical spell. They flopped at the darkness, pushing it away in swathes. It looked as if they'd tried to leap up a waterfall, but instead of getting to the other side, they'd been dragged through time and space into this world, just as Astravar had done with me. Alas, in this realm, these salmon wouldn't last for long.

"It's done," Seramina called out. "Quickly now."

She beckoned us forward. Ange and Rine stepped through first. I could feel the ground sliding underfoot as well. It seemed that my magical salmon trick hadn't worked for long. I scrambled across the floor, almost losing my footing several times. Just before I went through the portal, I noticed a salmon flopping on the floor. I wanted to drop my staff and pick it up, so I could take it with me.

"Come on, Ben!" Seramina shouted. "There's no time."

The wind without temperature was howling around me now, and I couldn't see anything except what was really close to me – the salmon, Seramina, the portal, and the sparse yet remarkably strong gossamer threads that supported us.

I had no choice but to leave my favourite fish alone here. I sprinted out the portal, and I passed through a cold cascade of what felt like water. I emerged in what seemed a warm and safe world.

I was in forest dense with alders and poplars, birds chirping, the sun shining bright and high in the sky. Then, I caught a whiff of rotten vegetable juice, and dread came over me once again.

30

ALL THAT GLAMOURS

T he smell of rotten vegetable juice was somewhat different than it was at Dragonsbond Academy. It wasn't as potent, and I couldn't smell the distinct variation of Astravar or any of the other warlocks in it. The mist on the northern horizon was also fainter, meaning there probably wasn't a fully equipped army of dark magical creatures waiting behind it. Even so, an army of any size of magical creatures was something to fear.

Despite the looming threat, life thrived in this forest. Blackbirds called out their melodic songs from the high tree branches, and there was a natural mossy aroma to the whole place, quite distinguishable from the smell from the mist. This was what forests should smell like, and I took a breath of fresh air, happy at last to breathe something.

I sniffed around. Cats had definitely been here. They'd sprayed the trees and done their business in the leaf mulch. Unfortunately, I couldn't detect a sign of Ta'ra anywhere. She'd always believed that she shouldn't spray just to leave a scent and mark her territory, much as I'd tried to reason with her.

I continued to follow the scent as I tried to determine where the cats had come from. The trail led me to a hollow with a deer skeleton within it, stripped bare of meat. Around this, some leaves lifted on the breeze and danced around the carcass.

Whatever the Cat Sidhe had been up to, they had been eating well. Rine, Ange, and Seramina didn't follow me, but my staff-bearer did. It floated nearby, wobbling along in a way that looked like the staff might topple out of its hand. I wondered if I could ever lose it or make it invisible. It was so obvious there, glowing all the time, that it would surely ruin my chances of successful hunts.

Seramina had already concealed the colour of the crystal on the staff, using her glamour spell to make it white. Which was fortunate, because in the distance, from behind a thick fog, two golden glowing wisps came into view. They danced around like fireflies, as if searching for something. Then, they must have seen me because they shot right towards me.

They took me by surprise until I remembered this was exactly what fairies looked like. Which meant either they had come from the Fairy Realm, aka the Second Dimension, to visit, or some of the Cat Sidhe had used up one of their transformations. If they had, they would have needed good reasons to do so. Cat Sidhe could only transform eight times in their lives before they would become cats forever. As far as I knew, none of the Cat Sidhe wanted that to happen. They wanted to return to their fairy homes and live amongst their folk again, and they couldn't return to their homeland when they could become cats at any moment. Most fairies don't trust cats, apparently – although I can't imagine for the life of me why.

A plume of golden smoke seeped out of one fairy, as if it had suddenly become a burning ember. This led downwards and soon morphed into a humanoid shape, looking almost like a golden Manipulator. The features formed on this to reveal a familiar figure clad in a short rainbow coloured dress and golden hair. Although, apparently, fairies can display any form they like, they tend to use just one. Most of the time, they liked to be recognisable.

The fairy floated forward in a way that wasn't quite human – her legs crossed like a ballerina's. Once she reached me, she slid to a halt and spoke in a high-pitched voice that, just like last time, reminded me of a cartoon mouse.

"Ben," she said.

I'd seen her last in the fairy realm when I'd first met Ta'ra's grand-father. She'd claimed to be the sister of Ta'ra's ex-betrothed, Prince Ta'lon. But I couldn't for the life of me remember her name.

"I'm sorry, remind me…" I said.

"Remind you what?"

"Your name?"

"Oh…" She put her hand to her mouth and giggled. "I'm Go'na, Prince Ta'lon's sister."

"Yes," I said. "I remember your relationship with the fairy prince. But why are you here and, more importantly, why did you use your transformation? Don't you want to return to your family and once again attend court?" It wasn't that I had any problem with these fairies turning into cats. I just didn't think this fairy woman would make a particularly good one. I guess I was more worried about her ability to survive than anything else.

"We take it in turns to go out and scout," Go'na said. "When we saw the portal emerge from a distance, we decided it was my turn to investigate. None of us want to change forms, really, unless we have to. But anything could have come out of this portal, and we need to stay safe."

"So why not go over as cats?" I asked. "You'd be stealthy and fast in that form."

"Not as stealthy and fast as a fairy in flight. Plus, we can't use magic if we need to, when we're cats. We might need to defend ourselves, you know?"

Her implication that cats couldn't defend themselves sounded ridiculous to me. I turned to see Rine walking over to join us.

"Hello," he said, as he eyed Go'na down then up, as if trying to work her out. Then, when he looked into her eyes, his cheeks went slightly red in a very un-Rine-like way. It was almost as if she'd cast an enchantment spell on him. Whiskers, for all I knew she might have done.

The fairy bowed to Rine, a warm smile on her face. "I'm Go'na, and I was sent here to assist you." She cocked her head rather demurely, her gaze locked on Rine's. "So long as you turned out not to be a threat."

Meanwhile, Seramina studied the fairy from a distance. As a mind-witch, she probably saw right through the glamour. Also, if this fairy knew Seramina's relationship with Astravar, then she would surely consider her one of those threats. So Seramina's caution was wise.

"Knock it off, Rine," Ange said as she approached, and she punched Rine hard on the shoulder, jolting him out of his trance. "Fairies aren't your type, I'm sure..."

He looked away, as if embarrassed to be caught in her enchantment.

"I'm pleased to meet you, Go'na," Ange said, and she stepped forward to shake the fairy's hand. "We all are, in fact. I heard you mention Ta'ra. Is she nearby?"

"She is," Go'na said, looking over her shoulder. "Well, I guess we should take you to her. Come..."

Golden smoke billowed out around her until it concealed her. When it had vanished, she was once again a golden wisp – a ball of light floating in the air. She drifted ahead, circling slightly around the other fairy who hadn't revealed his glamour form.

They shot off through the forest. I was the first to rush after them, excitement brimming in me. After all, I knew that I was once again about to see Ta'ra.

31

THE COMMUNE

I t wasn't cats I first encountered when we reached the Cat Sidhe's new home. Rather, I smelled human sweat, and then I saw a burly man stalking through the forest. I could smell cats, of course – lots of them – their scent getting stronger with each step we took. They just weren't visible yet.

The man sat on a small stool on the porch of a wooden hut. Welcoming firelight glowed out from the open doorway behind him. He had a staff in one hand with a yellow crystal at the top of it, just like Aleam's. On his back, he carried a thick bow and a quiver full of arrows, fletched with peacock feathers. His face sported a full growth grey beard, salt and pepper hair, and intense blue eyes. Behind the man, lay a royal blue dragon, bathing in the patterns of speckled sunlight coming through the canopy.

"You've got to be kidding," Rine said.

"What?" I asked

"That's Driar Reslin."

"You mean, Bellari's father?" Ange asked and she didn't sound happy about it.

"Who else?"

The man watched us approach, his hand on his hips. When he saw

Rine, he let out a loud and hearty laugh, his chest shaking and the sound of his laughter seeming to bounce back from every tree bole.

"Well, look who the cat dragged in?" he said. Then he looked down at me and gave me a nod. "You know, I've been waiting to use that line for so long now, and you finally gave me the chance. Rine, how are you, son? I've not seen you in donkey's years." He barrelled forwards and embraced Rine in a massive bear hug that looked like it would break Rine's body in two. He didn't seem to notice anyone else here.

I shrunk away. If that was how he treated Rine, then I didn't think I'd survive getting picked up by him.

Driar Reslin released Rine from his embrace and stepped back. Then he looked at Ange and Seramina. Go'na had also appeared from a puff of golden smoke, and his eyes finally fell on her. He looked at her as if he'd never seen her before, and probably he never had in this form.

"Well, aren't you going to introduce me to your companions, Rine?"

"I, er..." Rine glanced nervously at Ange.

"Always been one for the ladies, haven't you, son," Driar Reslin said. "You know what I say, don't you? It's okay to have eyes for others of the fairer sex, as long as your heart's always with your true love. Know what I mean? You still have a heart for my Bellari, don't you?" He elbowed Rine in the ribs and laughed raucously once again.

Rine looked as if he didn't know what to say, glancing between Ange and Driar Reslin as if he really wanted to give the game away. Ange had her hands folded beneath her waist and stared at the ground as her foot tapped rapidly against it. The silence was awkward, and I was just about to break it when the other Cat Sidhe did it for me. Rustling sounds came from the trees, and the black cats stalked down from the high boughs where they'd concealed themselves amongst the leaves. One by one, they dropped from their perches, emitting the purrs of a happy and well-fed commune.

I latched on to the familiar scent of Ta'ra nearby, and then I saw her, standing on a catkin carpet next to a beech tree with a thin yet sturdy bole. She was looking at me with her bright green eyes, seeming even brighter as they shone out from her dark fur. The white diamond crest on her chest seemed even larger than the other Cat Sidhe's, and also contrasted sharply against the surrounding fur.

When I returned her gaze, she blinked contentedly. I could hear her purring from here, and I could also smell fish on her breath.

I bounded over to her and then rubbed my body against hers. "Ta'ra… It's been too long. You're okay, and I'm okay. I couldn't have asked for better."

She laughed, then she turned away from me. "Come on," she said, and she glanced back over her shoulder. "Let's go for a walk. The other Cat Sidhe will no doubt have lots of questions for you all. But for now, let's keep this moment just between us two."

She stalked off a little into the forest. I went with her, and as we walked, the surrounding trees got a little thicker, offering better privacy.

"You know," Ta'ra said, "I've been practising since we last parted. See, I can walk even better in a straight line now." She stepped along the ground, her feet landing with absolute precision. Her back paws hit exactly where her front ones had been. She looked graceful, and elegant, very unlike she was when I'd first met her.

Yet, although she'd mastered the first step, she still had a long way to go. "So how well can you climb the trees?" I asked. "And have you mastered jumping yet? If you crouch low enough, you should be able to jump up to six times your height."

Ta'ra cocked her head and blinked heavily as if she couldn't believe she was hearing this. But she had been fishing for compliments. It's well known that proper protocol when a cat does this is to demonstrate how far they have to go. It's the only way you learn.

"Well, I've still got to work all that out, haven't I? But I have learned how to fish, and I've taught the other cats too. Say, we caught some mackerel today, and Driar Reslin here cooked some for us. Would you like some? I remember you liked mackerel."

Now it was me who was purring – loudly. "Mackerel… I'm so hungry. You know I almost brought some salmon for you. I found some in another dimension, but then I tried to take it with me, but I couldn't because I had my staff in my mouth."

"Your staff?" Ta'ra glanced up at my staff-bearer which did a little dance of appreciation in the air. "Ben, you did it! You can now go and defeat Astravar."

"Yes, but I met your ghost, and it told me you were in trouble and then I knew I had to come here first."

"Really, my ghost?"

"Yes, of course. Who else do you think I might meet in the ghost realm? I also met my father, and my ancestors – the great Asian leopard cats. And I fought them, and I won..."

"But what was I like? I mean will I turn out okay?"

"You'll turn out much older than you are now," I said. Then I added, "as a cat." I think that was what she really wanted to know.

Ta'ra turned towards the purple mist that stretched out in the distance. The sun was waning in the sky behind it and was suffusing it with a red glow, making it look like it was burning.

"It's not Astravar," Ta'ra said. "There's no sign of any warlocks. But there are all kinds of different golems and wargs. Every so often we think we detect danger, and so we send two of our own out in fairy form to help. That's how you met Go'na. Whoever sent these creatures, I fear they're trying to get us to use up all our transformations. I heard you're under siege, right? Perhaps they've posted them there to use up all our fairy magic so if you need us, we won't have any magic left to help out with."

"We can fight them," I said. "We can get rid of all the horrible magical monsters over there. I have my staff now, and we've got Seramina and her—" I stopped myself just in time, perhaps because Seramina was staring at me, that burning look behind her eyes. "Mind-magic... And Ange, and Rine, can use their magic too. Our dragons aren't here yet, but they're coming. I can feel them."

Ta'ra looked up at the floating hand hovering near me. At first, she hadn't shown much interest. But now she seemed rather impressed. "You got that from the Ghost Realm?" she said. "I recognise the glowing effect..."

"We did."

"And you got out of there okay?"

"Somehow," I said.

Her eyes went wide as she gazed at me. Her pupils had gone from narrow vertical slits to almost full circles. I knew I was meant to do something at this point. There was something I'd meant to say to her at this point. But I couldn't quite remember what it was.

Meanwhile, I could feel Salanraja trying to tap into my thoughts. Part of me wanted to respond to her, but another part of me was enjoying my private time with Ta'ra and I didn't want anyone – even my dragon – butting in on the moment.

Before I could put any more words to thought, a thundering sound came from the distant south. I spun around and saw four silhouetted forms approaching through the bright sky, looking like geese with jagged wings. They were still quite far away. Another roar came out, but there was nothing threatening about it.

"Your dragons are here," Ta'ra said. "I guess the help you promised is here after all."

But that wasn't all, because I heard Rine call out, and he pointed at something with his staff. Then, as if to drown out the sound of his voice, Reslin called out even louder. "Ahoy!"

All four humans were looking not at our dragons, but at another small flock of them approaching from the west.

They were even nearer than our dragons, and I could see that they were going to land first. I recognised the leading dragon, which was twice the size of the others. Its white scales shimmered in the waning light, and an old man was perched on top of it with his staff's crystal glowing yellow.

"Aleam!" I said. "He made it out. It's a good day for everyone."

He had three other dragons with him. One of them was a charcoal colour, just like Seramina's dragon, Hallinar. The other two were citrines, and I racked my brain to remember who amongst those I knew rode a massive, flying, scaly lemon. High Prefect Lars rode one – his dragon Camillan. Which meant that Asinda must have been with him on her charcoal, Shadorow.

But I couldn't work out who would be on the other dragon. She had her staff lit up, fire drifting out from it, letting off smoke as if to create a signal. Her blonde hair whipped back in the wind, and her face looked almost as red as the crystal on her staff. It seemed like this girl had caught the sun a little.

My heart leapt in my chest. It was Bellari, sitting on her dragon – called Pinacole – with a tremendously haughty posture. Whiskers, I had worried that I might meet Astravar soon, and instead the powers that be had sent me my second worst enemy. And she was here just when Rine and Ange were about to seal the deal.

They were soon almost upon us. The Cat Sidhe cleared out of the way to give them room to land. Meanwhile, our dragons were still pinpricks in the ever-darkening sky. It would take them a while to reach us yet. Salanraja tried to say something in my mind again. But I wasn't interested. Not while everything was going all wrong.

Olan landed first, sending up billows of soil from the ground. Then Camillan came down with Lars, followed by Shadorow with Asinda. Finally, Pinacole hit the ground, and he lowered his neck to let Bellari slide off. Bellari immediately strolled over to where Rine and her father stood. She ignored Rine completely, and she let her father embrace her in a gentle hug.

I perked up my ears to listen in as she spoke.

"Oh, Daddy, how I've missed you," she said. "How many years has it been?"

The loud-mouthed man didn't seem so loud-mouthed with his daughter. He mumbled something in her ear. Rine slinked away from them as they talked.

After a few moments, Bellari broke the hug. Then she spun around and stormed over to Rine, who had been getting closer and closer to Ange as if seeking comfort. I walked up to get a closer look, the hackles rising on the back of my neck.

Bellari glanced at Ange, huffed, and I could only imagine the scornful look she gave her. Her voice was so sharp it hurt my ears.

"Rine," she said. "We need to talk. Now!"

She took hold of Rine's hand and pulled him off into the forest just as our dragons arrived.

32

TALK WITH THE DRAGON

As soon as Salanraja touched down, tossing up a mass of leaves from the forest floor, she let out a roar. It was so loud that it seemed to shake the trees in the forest. The leaves to the side of her and behind her quivered, and those in front of her shot forwards as if propelled by a blast. Many Cat Sidhe arched their backs as they turned towards Salanraja in surprise.

The incident reminded me of the first time I'd met her in her tower. Back then, I'd apparently tried to steal her dinner – because she hadn't understood that food left untended is up for grabs by anyone who discovers it. It's not my rule, it's one of those universal laws that virtually every living creature seems to understand other than humans and dragons. Salanraja had threatened to flame me alive, and I'd believed her, not realising that she would never do that to a poor innocent cat.

Now, she seemed even more angry than before, and I hadn't a clue why. "*You did it again, Bengie,*" she said. "*After me specifically telling you not to.*"

"I did what, sorry?" I asked. "*Oh, and nice to see you, too. It's been so long... I almost died, by the way, not that you seem to care.*"

Salanraja didn't seem to be concerned about any of that later stuff, though. *"You blocked me out of your mind. I wanted to talk to you, and you just shut me away as if you had more important things to do."*

"Well, I had a very important cat to talk to." I looked at Ta'ra, as she gave me that endearing blinking look again.

"And what's that meant to mean? Are you telling me that there's a living creature out there that's more important than your dragon? Do you truly understand what our relationship means?" Smoke rose from her nostrils, and I was glad that I was still a safe distance from her, surrounded by a clowder of Cat Sidhe. In the ghost realm, I really had thought I'd missed my dragon. Now, I wasn't so sure.

"Look, it's like Ange and Rine," I said. *"Though they don't admit it, Ange is the most important to Rine, and Rine is the most important person to Ange. It's like that with me and Ta'ra, or at least it's going that way. Come on, Salanraja. I hadn't seen her in ages. She deserves a bit of my private time."*

"That's what you've never seemed to comprehend, Bengie. There is no private time to dragon riders, or at least as far as your dragon is concerned. We're meant to share everything, so I can protect you, and you when you finally learn how to, can protect me. The most important thing to Rine is Ishtkar, and the most important thing to Ange is Quarl."

"I can't believe that."

"Really? Then who do you suppose is with them every moment of their waking lives? From what I've gathered, I'm not sure Rine and Ange have spent much time together at all. It doesn't seem a good basis for a relationship if you ask me."

"You are so wrong," I said.

"Am I?"

"Yes..."

"And how would you know?"

"Because I've seen it. I've been to the ghost realm, and I've seen their future, and mine, and Seramina's too." I wondered how far I should take this. How would Salanraja react if she knew Seramina was really a warlock? Had she talked to Hallinar about it? Or Olan, perhaps? Whiskers, could she even hear my thoughts right now? Fortunately, it seemed I'd learned to mask them better from her and I wasn't planning on telling her how I was now a budding warlock anytime soon.

"So that's where the portal led," Salanraja said, and she lowered her

head. Her nostrils had stopped smoking, and she seemed to have calmed down a little. *"I'm sorry, Bengie, perhaps I overreacted. You'll learn one day, as you grow stronger. I guess it takes time to become less feline and more..."* She paused briefly, as if to think. *"Human."*

"What? Don't be so ridiculous."

"Of course you are," Salanraja said. *"Who knows, you might even develop opposable thumbs soon. How would you like that? You'd be able to use human tools and cook your own sausages."*

"There's no way I'm getting rid of my claws," I said, and I extended them, admiring their sharpness. One thing that was great about this realm is that the humans didn't bother clipping cat claws. They needed them for a purpose, or perhaps they understood we needed them too.

Salanraja laughed. *"I've missed you, Bengie. You make me complete, you know? I'm so glad you made it out of the ghost realm. I don't know what I would do without you."*

"I've missed you too," I said, and I went up to rub my nose against her massive talon. I turned to see Ta'ra staring after me, as if thinking, *What the whiskers do you think you're doing?*

I'd heard the students say that dragon riders never dated anyone but other dragon riders. Now, I think I understood why.

33

ALEAM'S STORY

After Rine, Ange, Seramina, and I had time to bond with our dragons again – because we needed to after being through such a terrible ordeal – Aleam called us over to Driar Reslin's porch. By 'us', I meant me, Ange, Seramina, Lars, Asinda and Reslin.

The Cat Sidhe had been instructed to stay away, as if the information that Aleam was about to divulge, or at least the implications of it, might scare them. We still couldn't see Bellari and Rine, but I could hear her haughty voice cutting through the forest.

The approaching night brought with it a fresh chill. I could still catch that whiff of rotten vegetable juice upon the breeze every now and again. After being in the ghost realm and having to deal with that wind without warmth or cold, I appreciated this breeze, even if it made me shiver a little. Still, I made sure that I stayed as close as possible to the door and the fire roaring within so I could soak up any warmth that seeped out of the hut. Seramina hung close to me, as if she also wanted to savour the heat too.

"Should we wait for Rine?" Aleam asked, looking to where the voices were coming from.

"Oh, I'm sure he'll hear plenty enough, after Bellari has given him her '*talking to*'," Ange said in a sardonic tone. "That's if he survives."

"Whatever she has to say, I'm sure she has good reason to do so," Reslin said. "One thing I can say for my daughter is that she's a smart lass."

Ange looked at the older man with narrowed eyes and a peculiar frown. "I'm sure she is," she said, her voice dry.

"I can't imagine why my Bellari would be angry with Rine," said Reslin, shaking his head. "He's always seemed such a noble, honest lad. And I can tell he's the type who's great at relationships. I guess it's just her time of the month." He gave a lopsided grin.

Ange nodded slowly, and her jaw looked clenched. She was probably biting her tongue to stop her from saying something unwise. I didn't particularly like this Reslin man either. I wanted to tell him that if Rine was so good at relationships, then he would choose to have one with Ange instead of Bellari. But Aleam had just turned up out of the blue, and he had too much to tell us. I was getting impatient.

"Aleam, what happened?" I asked. "Last I saw, you were throwing thunderbolts at Prince Arran, trying to bring down all his dragon riders like that wizard who helped the king pull the sword out of the stone I saw on the television once."

Seramina kicked me as if to tell me to shut up. But I didn't realise why at first. There was nothing wrong with kings pulling swords out of stones, surely.

"You went up against Arran?" Reslin said, and his hand twitched by his hip.

It suddenly dawned on me that it might not have been so smart to mention this detail in front of a member of one of Prince Arran's dragon corps. Mind you, I never claimed that I was good at human politics. The crystal had never gifted me with that trait.

"I did no such thing," Aleam said. "There was no violence. There was only thunder from the sky, and a bit of lightning flashing around. The worst it hit was a gargoyle."

"You still haven't explained why you needed to do this," Reslin said. He leaned against a pillar on the porch, tapping his foot. As he did, he moved his hand towards his shoulder.

"I did all this to allow Seramina, Ange, and Rine to come here and help Initiate Ben get his staff. Prince Arran would have sent the cat out alone against a verified forest golem and other magical creatures who guarded the staff. And every dragon rider across the realm should know by now that Ben's getting that staff is crucial to Astravar's defeat."

Driar Reslin narrowed his eyes. "That is mutiny," he said. "You went against a direct order from a superior officer. This..." He drew his staff from his back. "I can't allow this."

A rush of air whooshed by me, and some vines sprung out from Ange's staff. These vines shot straight out towards Reslin's staff and wrested it out of his grasp. More wrapped around his shoulders and underneath his armpits, pinning him to the pillar.

"You," Driar Reslin growled. He glared daggers at Ange, and it seemed like he wanted to scream more at her. But he took one look at the glowing green crystal on her staff, and then her cold stare, and he seemed to think better of it.

Seramina also had her staff in her hands, but she hadn't used any magic yet. If she wanted to, she could wipe Reslin's mind or something. He never had to remember Aleam's story. Come to think of it, he never even had to remember that we were here. Maybe if I asked Seramina nicely enough, she could also wipe Bellari and her father's memories of Bellari's relationship with Rine. That would get us all out of an awkward situation very quickly.

"I'm sorry for the sudden surprise, sir," Ange said. "But, with all due respect, who has been loyally serving the king for longer? Aleam or Arran?"

"It doesn't matter," Reslin spat back. "We have chain of command for good reasons."

"Yet he got the position through his royal blood and not his skill at what he does," Aleam said. "It's fair enough that our good King Garmin appointed him to the rank. But when he did so, Garmin intended for Arran to just remain a figurehead. I can't quite understand why the king now has him giving orders on the battlefield. Have you ever thought something is off about this?"

"Are you suggesting a conspiracy?" Reslin said. He seemed much more relaxed now, with his head cocked, as if the idea of a mystery fuelled him with power. He didn't seem to mind being wrapped in vines, almost as if it was a hobby of his.

"I don't know what I'm thinking right now," Aleam said. "I haven't had the time or headspace to investigate this. But believe you me, once this is all over, I will."

The old man looked down at me, then he looked at my staff-bearer. Unlike me, the small human hand seemed rather allergic to the fire coming from the hovel and edged as far away from it as it possibly could. Perhaps it thought the staff would burn if it got too close to the flames.

"Well done, Ben," Aleam said. "So, you finally did it after all. Olan tells me you got the staff from the ghost realm, and you met me, of all people, there. I hope I aged well…"

"You should see what I can do. I can conjure salmon out of my own dimension and use them as a weapon." My tummy rumbled, and I remembered I'd never quite had that mackerel Ta'ra had promised me. "You know, I should do it now. You can finally taste the best fish in the Seven Dimensions."

As I spoke, Aleam was glancing warily at Reslin as if trying to tell me not to reveal too much. But Bellari's father didn't seem to be listening to me. Rather, he had his ears turned towards his daughter's and Rine's voice coming from the forest.

"Okay," Ange said. "We've waited long enough, Driar Aleam. With all due respect, why don't you tell us what happened? Then Driar Reslin can decide if he wants to cooperate or not."

"Very well," Aleam said, and he tugged at the wattles under his neck. "After you left, Prince Arran got worse and worse. I didn't hear his conversations with the Council of Three, being locked up and all. But Lars and Asinda here relayed information to me in my cell underneath Dragonsbond Academy.

"The prince started ruling the castle with an iron fist. He further restricted food rations not because we couldn't spare food, but he reasoned that the hungrier the students were, the more aggressively they'd fight in a battle against the warlocks. He was proposing an all-out charge."

"You've got to be joking," Ange said.

Lars and Asinda shook their heads no.

"He wanted to send every single dragon and dragon rider out there," High Prefect Lars said, his red cloak blowing out behind him in the breeze. "Including Calin's injured dragon, Galludo. But if there's one thing that every Driar and student of Dragonsbond Academy agree on, it's that the warlocks must have a good reason that they've not attacked yet."

"So, what happened?" I asked. "Did you throw that stupid prince in the cell?"

Aleam laughed. "Actually, yes, we did," he said. "Or rather the Council of Three did. After realising Prince Arran wasn't acting in our favour, they locked him up. But they gave him a luxurious bedroom fit for royalty of course, and they locked the door using magic and cast escape-prevention wards on his windows."

"And what about Corralsa?" Seramina asked. "I don't think Arran's dragon would have gone down without a fight."

"It was a shame you weren't there to cast a mind-spell on her," Aleam said. "But we found ways to do it using a little coercion." He glanced at Asinda and then gave Seramina a knowing wink. I guessed either he or Asinda sent the dragon to sleep with their dark magic, now I knew they could use it.

Aleam nodded at Ange. "I think you can release him now."

Ange looked at him with a curious frown. She lowered her staff, and the light went out on the crystal. The vines that had entangled Reslin wilted and dropped to the ground. He stretched his arms and then looked at her. "Never do that again, Initiate. Unless you have a good reason to, of course," he said, but he didn't sound angry. Rather, he said it almost half-heartedly, as if about to deliver the punchline to a joke.

"Yes sir," Ange said.

Reslin turned to Aleam. "Well, old man. I guess you won't get any interference from me on your quest. You seem to know what you're doing." He continued to tell us about the magical creatures stationed nearby and how he'd been trying to work out what to do with them. The fairies had been worried, and he'd told us it had been quite a tense time here in the forest. He also knew that he couldn't defeat all those golems between him and his dragon. But now that they had more dragons and dragon riders, including Aleam – the fabled mage of legends, Reslin thought they might stand a chance.

"Presumably you have a plan," Reslin said after he'd finished his story.

Aleam looked towards the purple mist. "I'm guessing we have no choice but to throw everything we've got at them except the garderobe. I have a feeling we'll need the Cat Sidhe for the ultimate battle, and most of all, this would give Ben time to try out his staff."

I mewled contentedly as I looked at my staff-bearer, hovering slightly above and in front of me now. I was going to show everyone here how powerful Ben the Dragoncat, descendant of the great Asian leopard cat and the great, mighty George could be.

34

ACHOO!

I'd had enough of talking for one day. In all honesty, back home in South Wales, us cats didn't talk much. Occasionally, we'd meet for a couple of minutes and let either the Savannah Cats recount a brief anecdote about beasts that we might face in the Savannah, or perhaps let the old Ragamuffin tell us a wise thought that would help us through the day. One of us might come forward and give a report if a new cat or dog had entered the village that we would need to be cautious of. But we wouldn't convene for long, before sniffing each other to check that we were healthy, and then heading back off to guard our individual patches of territory.

It was a simple life – a pleasant life. I've never been able to get used to how humans seemed so compelled to make everything so complicated.

I went off for a walk, but I found myself gravitating towards Bellari and Rine. Perhaps I wanted to engage in one of my favourite hobbies of taunting her about her 'allergies'. Or perhaps, an even deeper part of me wanted to know how big a threat she was to my dreams of an easy retirement.

I found the couple standing under the boughs of a large beech tree, catkins occasionally falling around them from the high branches.

They were hard to miss, really, given how loud Bellari had been screaming. She had her hands on her hips and her red face thrust out at Rine. She poked her finger into his chest as she spoke, and Rine shrank back from her slightly.

"I can't believe I'm hearing this," Bellari screamed. "You just can't stop humiliating me, can you? It's like a little hobby of yours. Do you know what all the other girls in school have been saying about you? Do you know what they've been saying about *us*? Why do you always have to be so selfish?"

"I'm selfish?" Rine shouted. I liked it when he argued back against Bellari. She deserved nothing less. "You saw me in the forest, and what was the first thing you said? It wasn't, 'hey are you okay, Rine?' Oh, no... You said, 'Rine, we need to talk,' right in front of everyone, as if you really wanted to embarrass me. You didn't think that I might have been in danger here? I could have died out here, you know. But you don't care, do you?"

"Gah! Do you really blame me, Rine? What am I meant to say? Hey, you run off to do what you want, without even warning me. But you know what? It's okay because you almost got yourself killed. So now I forgive you... Really, Rine? How naïve do you think I am?"

Rine took a deep breath. Both of them were so focused on verbally assaulting each other that they didn't notice that I was there. Which was fortunate, because with Bellari's mood and given what she thought of cats, she'd probably kick me to the other side of the forest.

Rine's voice came across a little softer. "Look, Bellari, this relationship isn't what it used to be. When we first met, it was romantic, and you were... Well let's say, decent to me."

"Decent?" Bellari said, her arms flailing about in the air. "You don't think I'm decent anymore?"

"I think you're controlling, and you're a power freak, and you want someone who will do what you command, without question."

"Is that right?" Bellari asked, tapping her foot.

"No, that's not all... Now, it seems that everything you do is to prevent me going near anybody else. You won't even let me breathe, Bellari. Do you know how that makes me feel?"

"And why exactly do you think I'm like this?" She was hoping for something. I could see it. She wanted ammunition. But Rine now seemed well prepared.

"I think you're jealous," Rine said. "And it's changed you. To be honest, I'm not sure I like you anymore. I don't like what you've become."

Now we were talking. This is the kind of talk that I'd been prompting Rine to have for a long time. I just wished that I had my cat snacks with me so I could munch on something while watching this entertainment from a distance. Soon Rine would deliver his coup de grâce, his ultimate conclusion. I could see it boiling within him. All I had to do was wait until Bellari's insults had beaten him so hard that he could take no more.

A rustling sound came from behind me, and I smelled Ta'ra as she approached. "Ben, what are you doing here?" she said, and she brushed her nose up against the side of my chest.

"Shh," I said. "You're going to miss the good stuff, Ta'ra." I'd already lost track of what they were saying.

"Don't you think these two deserve a bit of peace?"

"Not yet... I've been waiting for this moment for ages, and now it's going to happen."

"What moment?"

"Just hang on..." I took a deep breath, inhaling the aromas of the forest. The moss, pollen on the breeze in the distance, the earthy soil, and through it all the smell of rotten vegetable juice, getting stronger I could swear. But I couldn't let my fear of dark magic spoil the occasion.

Bellari was still screaming, her voice getting louder and higher. Really, I'd stopped comprehending what she was saying, and I'm not sure if it was because I couldn't be bothered listening anymore or that she'd just started spouting nonsense. I just caught random words and phrases like 'humiliated', and 'selfish', and 'moron', and 'you just keep going around and doing what you want'.

Meanwhile, Rine looked like he was caught in a battle, bracing himself against an unending volley of arrows. This time, though, he kept his shield up. He stood strong against the barrage, and I could sense him tensing up like the coil of a winding crossbow. Then he executed the all-out assault that I'd been waiting for – a volley of rage so strong that it cut off Bellari in her tracks.

"It's over!" he screamed. His voice twanged through the forest and seemed to bounce back from every direction.

Bellari looked at him, her eyes wide. "What?"

"You heard me. This relationship is over. I'm sick of the lack of respect you give me. I'm sick of you always telling me what I should and should not do. I'm sick of *you*."

I expected even more recoil from Bellari. I expected her to scream back even. But she just narrowed her eyes and glared at him. Heavy, angry breaths rocked her shoulders back and forth. Her next words came out quieter, almost as a whisper, except with a sharp bite to them.

"This is about Ange, isn't it? You have... feelings for her... You've been lying all along, haven't you? Admit it, Rine. This has never been about us."

"No," Rine said. "This *is* about me and you. We aren't compatible, and I don't want to do this... I don't want to do us anymore."

Bellari shook her head slowly, and she turned a moment to gaze at the purple mist. "You know what... You don't get to dump me. I'm going to dump you. It's over Rine! I'll find someone better than you. Someone who 'respects' me for the lady I am. You'll see."

She turned on her heel and stormed off in mine and Ta'ra's direction – her face bright puce. As she passed us, she looked at us. Then, and I could swear this time was deliberate, she let out a horribly loud sneeze.

35

WHAT IS LOVE?

Bellari left the scene under the cover of low sun emerging from beneath a layer of clouds. It sent a warming magical red glow through the forest.

"Well, that was dramatic," Ta'ra said, as she watched the girl go.

"I think it was perfect," I said. "Rine couldn't have performed better."

"Poor girl," Ta'ra said.

"What do you mean, poor girl? You're not telling me you have sympathy for Bellari, do you? She's evil…"

"She's not. Only misguided. And after having worked with her father, I must say, I'm not surprised. He never takes her seriously, and he's always cracking jokes at her expense. If I had a father like that, I don't know how I'd grow up."

I growled. Bellari didn't deserve this sympathy. Not after how horrible she'd always been to me. I changed the subject, as I realised that Ta'ra and I could argue for hours about whether Bellari was 'evil or misguided'.

"Do you reckon I should tell Rine how proud I am of him?" I asked. He hadn't turned to watch Bellari go. He just gazed off at that purple mist that seemed to be getting smellier and smellier. In all honesty, I don't think he even realised that Ta'ra and I were there looking at him.

"No, no," Ta'ra said. "I'd probably leave him be. He needs time to stew – to process it all."

"What's to process? All he needs to do is to go to Ange, profess his love for her, and then they can be together forever – hopefully with you and me by their side."

The sun dropped out of the sky, and twilight befell us. The world suddenly became a cold place again, and I longed for the fire in the hut. But still, I could see that I also needed to close things up with Ta'ra. I just didn't know what I was meant to do.

Ta'ra took a step back from me, and she gave me a discerning look. "If you really think love is that simple, then I'm not sure you really understand it. But, of course, you don't. You're a cat after all. Love is a human emotion... Well, humanoid."

"I know," I said. "It's part of human society. Us cats don't need it. But we do know how to bond."

"Like you bond with your dragon?"

Oh, here we go again, I thought. I was about to have the same lecture with Ta'ra as I'd had with Salanraja. Fortunately, Salanraja was now sleeping off the effect of a long flight alongside the other dragons, and so wouldn't have heard those thoughts.

"Have you got a problem with that bond?"

"No, not at all. I just wonder, if your thoughts are with her all the time, do you ever have space to think about anyone else?"

"Of course I do."

Ta'ra cocked her head and regarded me. Her green eyes seemed to glow, cutting right through the encroaching darkness.

"What? I do!"

Ta'ra said nothing in response. We stood in silence for a while, watching Rine. I still don't think he'd noticed we were there. He made a loud huffing sound – almost a grunt – and he drew his staff. I stood alert, ready to scarper off if he decided to take his anger out on us. It wouldn't have been the first time he'd tried to freeze me using his magic. But instead, he pointed his staff at the high canopy on a tree and sent a massive bolt of ice towards it. The tree quivered, and a cloud of leaves fluttered to the ground.

Rine turned and stormed off, failing to acknowledge Ta'ra and I.

"Can you smell it?" Ta'ra asked as she watched him go.

"What? Rine?"

"No... Not Rine. The magic. It's coming closer, right?"

I took a sniff of the air. "I can smell it... But it's probably just a change in the wind."

"I hope so. But I've sent a couple of fairies out to investigate just in case." We waited for another moment, watching the light fade out of the sky until we couldn't see the mist anymore.

"I never asked you," I said, "what happened to Ta'lon?"

Ta'ra laughed a bitter laugh. "Oh, that fool. His words were just honey on toast. He never came back, you know. He probably went back to court and forgot about us. Even Go'na hasn't heard from him. And she's his sister!"

"Do you think he never loved you?"

"I don't think he does now. He could at least have sent a sign or visited once. But it doesn't matter anymore, I guess."

I growled. I'd known there was something about that fairy as soon as I'd smelt him – both in Cat Sidhe and later fairy form. He wasn't to be trusted, and now he was proving my point. "Couldn't you use your last transformation and visit him? You can turn back into a fairy once more, can't you?"

"Oh, it's not worth using my last transformation for that. I can think of thousands more circumstances much more worth saving it for."

"But that way you can tell him what you feel. Perhaps you can visit his kingdom in fairyland and say to your old fairy prince that the Cat Sidhe are all getting along fine, thank you, and you all want to stay cats forever."

Ta'ra laughed, and she brushed her face gently against my whiskers. "Most of us don't want to stay Cat Sidhe. But, you know, I think I do. Perhaps being a cat isn't so bad after all."

"What do you mean 'isn't so bad'? Come on, you've got to admit it. Being a cat is the best thing in the entire world."

"Sometimes," Ta'ra said, and she chuckled again. "But now at least, I've got to see you, Ben. A good old friend."

"Friend…" The word came out so quietly, it must have drifted off in the breeze.

"Isn't that how you see me? As a friend?"

"I…" Of course I didn't just see her as a friend. But I really didn't know how to say it to her. I mean, it wasn't just that I hadn't practiced bringing out the words, as I'm sure Rine had many times. I was also divided about what my feelings meant. I mean, cats shouldn't have such feelings, should they? Maybe, as Salanraja had said, I was becoming more human, and that thought scared me.

Fortunately, I was cut off from my dilemma by two golden wisps drifting over from the darkness that now concealed the mist. Unlike the first fairies we'd encountered, these weren't darting around without a purpose. They were heading right towards Ta'ra and I, as if following a scent.

The fairies stopped in front of us, and both of them emitted glowing golden clouds of mist. These dissipated to reveal Go'na standing on the right and another male fairy with purple eyes and a rounded face on the left.

Go'na looked alarmed. "It's good I got here in time," she said. "Because I worried I'd turn back into a cat again. It's not long before my time is up, and oh, you should have seen them."

"Go'na," Ta'ra said. "Slow down, please. What did you see?"

"Wargs," she said, and the hackles shot up on the back of my neck. "There must have been hundreds of thousands of them, coming in from nowhere, with slaver dripping from their mouths. They were thin looking, as if they'd charged without food all the way from the Willowed Woods."

"Whiskers," I said. "We're doomed."

"No, we're not," Ta'ra said. "Ben, you must never think that way. Didn't you get your staff so you can fight back after all?" She looked up at my staff-bearer, and it twisted around in the air, so the staff pointed downwards as it gave the Cat Sidhe a thumbs up.

"How long have we got, Go'na?" Ta'ra asked.

"I don't know… Fifteen minutes, maybe. If even that."

"Then we must warn the others. Quickly, get word back to Driar Aleam and the rest of the Cat Sidhe. I'll be right behind you."

Go'na nodded, and the two fairies quickly turned back into their true golden-orb forms. They shot off towards the camp. Without a word, Ta'ra darted after them. It didn't take me long to realise that I didn't fancy hanging around here to get devoured by hundreds of thousands of wargs. So, I promptly followed in her wake.

36

DEFENCES

A s soon as the fairies reached Aleam and told him the news, he sprang into action. The first thing he did was to rouse the dragons. With his alleged school of magic being lightning magic, he could cast a thick cover of clouds over the sky, visible against the rising moonlight. From this he commanded a great bolt of lightning to crash down, accompanied by the loudest thunder I'd ever heard.

I got skittish, and I fled up a tree, which is apparently the worst place to go during a thunderstorm. But then, I never said every single feline instinct makes sense, just as a lot of human ones don't. The lightning was all controlled by Aleam's magic anyway, and the old man wouldn't have let it strike a poor cat – especially a cute Bengal like me.

Olan woke first. She whipped out her head, and she turned her great eyes upon Aleam as if ready to flame him. But she settled down when she realised who had caused the racket. Aleam must have immediately told her about the issue at hand, because she roared, to ensure the other dragons were also awake. One by one, they joined in the angry chorus. Then they all lifted off into the sky, their heavy beating of wings pounding like drums in an orchestra.

But if there were as many wargs as Go'na had claimed, we

wouldn't defeat them by dragon fire alone. Plus, there were all those golems to worry about, who were clearly part of the enemy's offensive strategy.

So, next came the time for setting traps. We probably had about ten minutes left. My ears perked up from my vantage point on the tree, and my hearing latched on to the gnashes and gnarls of approaching beasts. Their feral sounds told me they would take no prisoners on this charge. Ironically, the army that Astravar had created to take Cimlean city would also be destroyed by his creations.

Aleam was on the ground, rushing around giving orders. I'd heard when he'd served as one of the king's dark mages all that time ago, he'd also been one of the king's best military strategists. Right now, he seemed to suit the part.

"We shall dig a trench," he said. "A concealed one. That way, if we can stop the charge of as many wargs as possible, we'll stand a better chance."

"How can we do that quickly?" Driar Reslin asked.

"Glaciation," Aleam replied, and it really didn't take him long to explain the rest and set everyone into action.

It all started with Seramina. She used her staff to cast a beam of mind-magic – or dark magic if you wish to see it that way – straight at Rine's forehead. This was apparently to strengthen Rine's ice spells. Though he was a little slow taking his staff from his back, he seemed to speed up as soon as he cast the first jet of ice, as if the act of casting magic was cathartic to him.

Rine's enhanced stream became a massive wall of ice that seemed to span from one end of the forest to the other. But this wouldn't be enough to stop the golems, as they'd just smash holes in it, still allowing the wargs to stream through.

That's where Lars came in. After Rine's wall of ice was in place, Seramina cast her mind-magic at the high prefect's forehead. Lars then used his blue staff to cast shield magic. This time, though, he didn't cast the spell for protection. Rather, he cast this great shimmering sheet of energy – a long plane of it – designed to repel other magical energy. He brought this downwards, pressing the ice into the ground. There came a crunching and a creaking sound. The earth shook, and the soil parted to make way for the ice, which then compressed the soil on either side, creating a solid ditch.

In all honesty, I didn't have a clue what was going on. All the while, the gnashes and gnarls in the distance became louder, and I spotted the first signs of movement. Trails of dust kicked up by shadows. They would be here soon. Around me, from their perches in the trees, several Cat Sidhe yowled to communicate they'd seen the same.

Meanwhile, it was Bellari's and Asinda's turn to move. They had fire magic, and they cast intense gouts of it to melt the ice. Aleam and Reslin added their lightning to it, as Seramina augmented them with her magic at intervals to strengthen their spells. Bellari didn't look at Rine once during this time, but her magic seemed to flare sometimes as if bouts of anger inside her fed the fire.

After the ice had melted, the four magic users continued to heat it until it was boiling. Then the last part came down to Ange. She took her staff and closed her eyes as she squared her shoulders. She pointed the staff right at the stream, and then she made a humming sound from her lips as vines emerged from the glowing crystal on the staff. They crept across the ground so fast that I thought they belonged to those horrible Mandragoras that I'd fought when I'd first dealt with a Manipulator. The creepers found their way over the ditch full of boiling water, creating a carpet over it. But there were holes in that carpet I saw – holes that led into a ditch full of super-heated water.

"That should do it," Aleam said. "Perhaps we'll quarter their numbers."

"Well done," Reslin said. "You know, Driar Aleam, I'm sorry. I'm sorry to have doubted you, and it's great to work with the all-powerful Aleam." He flexed a bicep. "And Bellari, you did pretty well too. Looks like they've taught you at least something at Dragonsbond Academy."

"Why thank you, Daddy," she said, and she blushed. Then her face twisted into a scowl, which she directed at Rine.

"Oh, oh," Reslin said. "What did you do, Rine?"

"Nothing," he said, and he turned away.

"We've not got time for this," Aleam said, and he looked up over the ditch as a howling sound keened over it. More cries and wails came, sounding like a ferocious war cry.

Then came the wargs. They seemed to materialise out of the night, as if the darkness had created them, and they were charging towards us at breakneck speed.

37

CANNONADE

W here before the night had concealed the mist, now the mist seemed to push back against the night, much like we had pushed back against the dark smelly goo in the ghost realm. It glowed purple from behind the charging wargs, silhouetting their terrible hunched forms and bounding long legs that propelled them forwards. The air smelled of fear, and fury, and rotten vegetable juice.

Between the wargs and the mist, were the golems. There were the forest golems, in whirlwind form, seeming to whip the mist up into spirals. There were the clay golems, shifting and warping over the ground so fast that you only had to blink, and they'd have taken a different shape and position. There were the stone golems – massive blocks of moving rock that looked like they could crush the tallest of trees under their heaving weight. And there was something else – tiny forms that looked like shimmering candle flames, wavering as if upon invisible air currents.

"What in the Seventh Dimension?" Aleam said, peering out from underneath his hand.

"Fire golems," Prefect Lars said, alarm in his voice. He lifted his staff to the sky.

"Everyone to Lars. Now!" Aleam called, just as the burning fire-balls launched towards us, as if fired by distant catapults.

I didn't hesitate. I sprinted right up to Lars' legs and huddled against them. Footsteps followed me, and then there came a flash of white from Lars' staff. The high prefect grunted and widened his legs as the shield dome spread out around him. Ta'ra was there next to me, growling, and many other Cat Sidhe had made it to the shield, as well as Reslin, Bellari, Seramina, Asinda, Ange, Rine, and Aleam. But many of the Cat Sidhe hadn't. We were huddled in so tight that I could feel the heat from the bodies around me. It smelled of sweat in here, and it was stuffy. I knew if we stayed in here for long, we'd run out of oxygen.

The flames came down from the surrounding sky. Then, with a gigantic crashing sound, explosions erupted across the terrain. High Prefect Lars widened his legs, and he grunted even louder; his face contorted. The shield flared out, together with the brilliance from the explosions outside, flooding the surrounding land with bright light.

I thought of all the Cat Sidhe who hadn't made it inside Lars' shield. They wouldn't stand a chance now. As the light continued to fade, Lars took a deep breath, and then the shield dome flickered out. I could breathe again, but the stench of everything outside assaulted me.

Flames spouted all around us, letting out a tremendous roar into the air. The heat raged so hot that it reminded me of that time I'd got trapped amongst lava in the Seventh Dimension. I longed once again to be in the ghost realm, as scary as that place was.

Fortunately, it seemed all the Cat Sidhe who'd been trapped outside the shield had transformed into their fairy form. Golden wisps darted around without purpose. They could use glamour magic, I guessed, but none of them would scare the wargs.

Rine shot large shards of ice at the flames. These hit right at the flames' sources, and then the melting ice suffocated the flames. Lars also started casting little shield bubbles across the landscape. These stayed in place for several seconds and then dissipated. Once gone, the flames underneath them would have also clearly drained of oxygen. Rine and Lars would need to do a lot more to completely quell the fire, and so they continued to work busily away, making a racket as they did so.

"What will those fire golems do, Aleam?" I asked. "Will they attack again?"

"No. They self-destruct as soon as they hit their target." And that was all Aleam said, as he was interrupted by another howling sound coming from in front of us.

The wargs had now stumbled into our trap, and they were stuck in the vines that Ange had woven. Soon, the dragons came down from above and they flamed the carpet of vines, so that the wargs fell in the water. The night filled with the yowls and whimpers of the dying beasts. I could only see their shadows and forms against the encroaching glow, but the sounds they made spoke of their torment.

As the dragons lifted back into the sky, more wargs flooded in, trampling over their dying brothers in the ditch. With angry red eyes, they scoured the terrain for something to attack. In front of them, golden wisps of fog emerged from the sky, and more Cat Sidhe were soon there, transformed back into their feline forms. Ta'ra led their charge into the fray, growing to the size of rhinoceroses as they went.

There were a good two dozen wargs, at least, for every Cat Sidhe. The wargs gnashed at their enemies, and then backed off when the Cat Sidhe lashed out with their claws. The wargs were too fast – much, much faster than the average cat. I wanted to join them in battle, and I felt the impulse to turn into a chimera. I summoned up the energy, and my muscles started to ache.

"*Don't do it, Bengie,*" Salanraja said, her voice stopping me in my tracks.

"*What? Why?*"

"*I might need your magic up here. Olan might not think you're ready yet, but I do.*"

Whiskers, I had forgotten about the staff. The staff-bearer had been floating along behind me, out of view. Or perhaps it was invisible when I wasn't aware of it. I didn't know.

Behind the battle between the Cat Sidhe and wargs, the golems were marching even closer. The ground shook as they came. It pounded, in fact, like a thousand volcanoes were about to spring up around us and add an extra dimension to the battlefield. Those stone golems were massive – five times the size of fully expanded Cat Sidhe. They looked as if they could easily trample the battlefield down to flesh and bone.

"On your dragons!" Aleam called out. "Get ready."

The dragons were already swooping down towards us. Several wargs also approached us, their teeth bared, pink slaver dripping from their mouths. Aleam cast a yellow beam at them, and an orb of bolt-lightning shot out from where it hit at the centre of their formation. The wargs jerked to a halt, convulsing. One by one, their legs seemed to go weak as they collapsed to the ground, allowing room for the dragons to land.

Olan came first and touched down on the ground briefly enough for Aleam to clamber up into the saddle. The dragon roared and took off into the night. Ishtkar and Quarl came next. "Typical," Bellari said, and she glowered at Rine as he ran towards his dragon, aside Ange, who was also sprinting towards hers. They both vaulted onto their mounts. Hallinar landed next alongside Shadorow, allowing Seramina and Asinda to mount and then launch off into the air.

Next came the two yellows – Camillan and Pinacole. Before Lars and Bellari mounted, Bellari turned to Prefect Lars and gave him a wink. "Say," she said. "Maybe we should hang out sometime."

Lars scowled at her. "Focus on the mission, for demon's sake," he said, and he rushed off towards his dragon without another word. Bellari huffed, and then she followed. Immediately after they'd taken off, Reslin's royal blue and Salanraja scudded against the earth. I was immediately upon her and up into the air, with my staff-bearer close by my side.

38

FROM THE DEPTHS

The clouds seemed to gather around us as the golems watched us, waiting for us to charge. The dragons wheeled around above the golems, and the dragon riders studied them, searching for an opening. No one dared to attack yet, and strangely the golems didn't lash out at us either.

I called for my staff, and my staff-bearer closed in. Next thing I knew, the staff was in my mouth, the crystal glowing purple at the end. At that moment, I didn't care if anyone noticed. The world needed my magic now. It was as if I'd become possessed by a force greater than my mind. I was completely in control, and yet I didn't put conscious thought to any of my actions.

It was as if the very act of clenching down on the staff caused something to change within me. Like someone had flicked a switch in my brain and suddenly the lights had come on and made everything clear. I wasn't Bengie the Dragoncat anymore. Instead, I was Ben the warlock, consumer of dark magic. I knew exactly what I had to do.

At that moment, my mind belonged to nothing but the void.

"*Bengie, what are you doing?*" Salanraja asked.

"*Don't worry, I've got this,*" I said.

"*Gracious demons... Not like this, you haven't... I know about the dark magic, Bengie. Olan had warned me about it a long time ago. But don't use it now in front of everyone. There must be another way."*

I wasn't listening to her. I had a different objective. In fact, every muscle in my body had a different objective. There was a pulsing sensation behind my forehead, directing my thoughts, telling me what my next move had to be and what spell I needed to cast.

The wind whipped past me as we flew, and that smell of rotten vegetable juice surrounded me. Yet I wasn't repulsed by it anymore. Rather, I felt like it was a part of me, and I drew it towards me. The mists formed tendrils that gently caressed me as I weaved the magic that would change the world for the better.

Meanwhile, the light at the end of my staff grew brighter and brighter still.

"Bengie, you're out of control," Salanraja said. *"You don't know what you're doing."*

"I know everything," I said, and it was as if something else was speaking through me. Another spirit. *"I am, after all, the incarnation of the seven worlds."*

"What are you—"

"Silence!" My voice shot out in my head, shutting off Salanraja's ramblings. I'd blocked her out again, and it felt good. Salanraja growled, and I could feel the rumbling in her belly underfoot. She careened as if she wanted to throw me off her. Wispy tendrils shot out of my staff, and they wrapped around Salanraja's waist, securing me in place. More mist crowded around us. It wasn't that I was attracting the mist, but it was growing out of me. I was all powerful, the greatest creature that had ever lived.

"You are fools to think you can challenge me." The voice came out of my mouth, but it wasn't me anymore. "Humans, dragons, and now cats... You have always been such fools. Now, I will show you the extent of my power. I will show you how puny you are compared to the force destined to govern all seven worlds."

I felt my body twist around – the muscles moving as if connected to strings dangling from the sky. I saw the golems again – a massive stone fist coming towards Salanraja, but she ducked out of the way. To my right, Ishtkar shot forward, Rine on top of her. She got knocked to the side by the fist of another stone golem. Quarl dove in from the other side to retaliate, but the stone golem also backhanded the sapphire dragon, swiping him away. Soon the mist clouded over again, and I saw nothing except the clouds rolling over each other to form something bigger, something terrifying.

Time seemed to slow as the clouds coalesced into the shape of a massive, bald, blue, male head. The features formed, displaying skin like a cracked eggshell, eyes burning like Seramina's tended to burn. The golems weren't moving, but the dragons were, darting in random directions in confusion. Wherever we flew, we couldn't reach that head. Astravar was always beyond us, watching us with his grey eyes from the clouds.

Soon, we all stopped to face him, all of us hovering in a loose formation. He cackled that horrible cackle that I'd heard so many times in my dreams.

"I hope you like the gift that your crystal gave you, Dragoncat. It's a great power, and now I shall use it for myself. It's time now for you to unlock some of the darkest magic imaginable. Soon, you shall behold the glory and the power of the fifth dimension."

Rine opened his mouth to shout something out, but his voice became lost to the void. Ange tried to cast some magic from her staff at the face, but the light just fizzled out at the top of it. Then, I was swinging around on Salanraja again, commanded by some substantial force.

Out of my staff came a gigantic bolt of white energy, shooting towards the ground. It hit the grass beneath us, where it spread out into a massive portal, lying horizontally. At first, it was pure light, which soon faded to reveal the gateway to another world. A world in rainbow colours, swirling around darkness, looking like a swirling pool of oil. A world where I couldn't even identify the forms that flashed around inside, they moved so fast.

"The thing that none of you ever did," Astravar said, "the claim that no mage ever claimed, was to unlock the secret of the uncharted dimensions. You see, there is a power running through all the dimensions even greater than magic. Once you know it – once you have touched it in every available world, then you can become it. That is the ultimate goal of a warlock. This is truly what it means to become whole."

That's when I noticed the golems were getting sucked towards the gaping hole. Their massive forms sliding towards it as if into quicksand. The portal swallowed the stone golems first, then the clay golems, then the forest golems whirled in last. After that came the wargs – hundreds of thousands of bodies now completely frozen in time like taxidermies. They glided towards the portal as if being dragged upon ice.

"Now, there are four warlocks present, I see," Astravar continued. "One fallen, two the relatives of warlocks, and then you, Dragoncat. According to the prophecies I've seen, you could have been the most powerful of all. Maybe one day I'll use you. If, that is, you can survive in the world I shall create. Oh, it shall be the most beautiful thing imaginable. You have no idea."

As I watched the wargs vanishing into the gaping magical hole in the ground, I realised what was happening. Any creature containing magic was getting sucked towards the vortex. Below, the Cat Sidhe started sliding towards the portal – slower than the wargs – and my heart skipped a beat. I also felt a slight tug against my fur – because I contained magic too.

There came a screeching sound from down beneath us. A sound so high in pitch it seemed to split the sky in two. Time had virtually stopped by this point. I couldn't move an inch. But my staff still fed that portal in the ground with massive energy as forms shot out of the ground. I recognised the creatures as soon as I saw them. They had the sharp beaks of buzzards, squat heads, and long necks leading to bat-like wings. They were larger than I remembered in the vision – around half the size of dragons, perhaps a little larger than that. They lifted into the sky, then whirled around in formation like a hungry flock of crows, ready to tear the world apart.

Meanwhile, Astravar's voice rumbled on. "You feared the demon dragon. But these creatures, are much, much, worse, and you know why? Because there's so many of them. They feed on magic, and the more magic they ingest the more powerful they become. All I need to do is give them a taste of how much of it has grown in this world.

Then they'll come out to do my bidding. Together we shall destroy this world, and then we shall cross dimensions. Only a gift from a crystal can release them, Dragoncat. A measly mongrel like you, it seems, has been given the power."

Astravar's cackles filled the sky, and everything happened in slower and slower motion. This was really the end. The portal had now completely consumed the wargs, and I saw the Cat Sidhe edging closer and closer to the void. I recognised one of them – slightly larger than the rest, with bright green eyes that shone out even from this distance above her.

"Ta'ra," I screamed out. "No!"

The very act of seeing her being dragged towards her fate seemed to break the spell Astravar had on me. It was as if the strings tied to my paws, tail, and head suddenly loosened. I could move again, and the image of Astravar in the purple clouds was fading away – crumbling into tinier clouds.

"That is enough," he said, his voice getting fainter. "You haven't won. I finally have the power we need to destroy everything."

From below came a massive white flare. Then came a sound like the whole earth was shaking. Then came a shockwave pulsing out from the portal below, which converged quickly into a single glowing pinpoint, before guttering out.

My connection to Salanraja didn't return, and as I looked around, the eyes of the dragons had become pure white. Together, all the dragons crashed towards the ground, as the flock of bat-buzzard creatures that Astravar – that *I* had summoned – shot off towards the west.

They were heading straight towards Dragonsbond Academy.

39

BEATEN

I woke up in a puddle of rain, with a terrible headache. I was so thirsty that without even lifting myself, I lapped up some drops of water. It hurt to swallow.

There was a rough sandpaper feeling against my side, and I looked back to see Ta'ra – now normal cat size again – licking my fur. When she saw me stir, she ran forward to stand in front of me.

"Ben," she said, and she rubbed her wet nose against my face. "Ben, I thought I'd lost you."

"What happened?" I asked.

"I don't know... We were fighting thousands of wargs, when all you riders and dragons went up into the sky to fight the golems. There were so many wargs coming at us, trying to tear us apart. We thought we'd lost... But then..." She trailed off.

I stood up, every muscle in my body shaking. I turned to see Salan-raja lying on the ground behind me. Her eyes were closed. I walked up to her, and pushed my head up to her chest, yearning for the warmth of dragonfire boiling within. She was stone cold, and I could detect no sense of her inside my mind, as if she'd blocked me off this time. Now I knew how it felt.

I let out a low and long growl, feeling absolutely terrible.

I'd done this. I'd let Astravar into my mind; I'd walked right into his trap. He'd been waiting until I got the staff, his magic within me probably building power during his period of silence in my mind and dreams. Then, when the moment arrived, he'd used me to unleash whatever terror those things were. Creatures from an unknown dimension. Creatures no one but Astravar – if his account was true – had encountered before.

It made me wonder about what I'd seen in the Ghost Realm. Aleam's ghost, Ta'ra's ghost, all those visions, my father... How much of it was real?

Whiskers, was that even my staff I saw floating nearby? The one my staff-bearer clutched just in front of me, as if it wanted to taunt me. The crystal on it was purple now – no one was making any attempt to hide it anymore. Maybe Astravar had created the staff-bearer and a second staff to trick me. It would have been the perfect way to manipulate destiny – for him to replace my staff with a device of his own that he could use to control me whenever he wished.

I tried swiping out at the hand with my paw, but it ducked away. It clenched its fist and punched the air in front of me as if to warn me off. I shrieked at it and swiped a couple more times until it backed away, keeping a safe distance.

"Ben," Aleam said from behind me, and he grunted as he hobbled over. Clearly, he was aching too. "Ben, you made it."

Even the act of turning towards Aleam sent pain shooting down my side. The other dragon riders stood behind him, looking at me warily. Across the field, I could see the fallen dragons and I couldn't detect any signs of life from them. Cat Sidhe also stalked the terrain, scouting around as if searching for an enemy. But there was no sign of any wargs anywhere.

"Aleam," I said. "I... I did this. Did you see what happened out there?"

"Astravar..." Aleam said, looking up at the clouds. "He must have been building power in that crystal inside you. But somehow, he didn't finish what he started, because he seemed to want to suck all of us into that place. Fortunately, something closed the portal just in time."

I looked up at the clouds where Astravar had been, but there was no sound of him now. "What happened to the wargs?" I asked.

"They all got sucked into the portal," Aleam said. "I'm guessing the stronger the magic inside the beast, the more powerful the pull. Whatever Astravar did, I've never seen anything like it."

"Those creatures... They came out of that portal. I summoned them, didn't I?"

"Yes, and I recognised them. They were the same as the ones as in your vision," Aleam said. "For a long time, I've been trying to work out what they are. No one, to my knowledge, has ever seen them before. Nor have I seen any mention of them in books."

"So, if we don't know what they are, how do we know if we can defeat them?"

"We don't," Aleam said. "It's very worrying indeed."

I bent down to lap up another gulp of water from a puddle. The air pressure was heavy on the sides of my head, and the clouds above were gravid. But it wasn't raining.

The water didn't go down well, and I felt suddenly nauseous. Then I was growling and writhing, as a sharp sensation shot through my head. It seemed to go downwards, past my nose and then towards the back of my throat, as if trying to escape from me.

I retched, and I thought for a moment I was going to suffocate. Was this Astravar's final move? Would he destroy me before I'd even had a chance to fight back? I fought in between retches to breathe, and then something came out of my throat into my mouth. I immediately spat it out.

A blue crystal lay on the floor. It had no light in it – depleted of all its magic. I touched it with my paw to discover it was cold and lifeless.

"What in the Seventh Dimension?" Aleam leaned over the crystal to study it. "Do you recognise this, Ben?" He lifted it up and wiped it against his tunic.

"It's... The golem crystal. The one I swallowed. Back when I first met my crystal."

Aleam stopped for a moment. He put his hand to his chin as if in thought. "So, you defeated it. You've defeated Astravar's control over you. You've finally got him out of your mind..."

"Have I?" I asked, and I looked again at my staff, wondering if it was more Astravar simply no longer needing the crystal inside of me anymore.

Aleam continued to study the crystal, turning it every possible angle and holding it up to the light. "It's completely dry. No magic left in there. Whatever magic Astravar had used on you, he'd finally used up all its power. You're free of him, Ben."

I should have felt a sense of relief at that. But I just felt burning guilt that I'd let Astravar take control of me. When I thought about it, I'd wanted that magic. I'd wanted to use it to beat those creatures, to show everyone what Ben the Bengal, descendant of the great Asian leopard cats and the mighty George could do. I was sure in my mind this was the reason Astravar had taken control of me. Because I wasn't confident about who I was. And because I didn't know, he had defined that image for me – he had used the dark magic inside me to mould me into what he wanted me to be.

"I still destroyed everything," I said. "Because of me, the dragons will die..."

Aleam shook his head. "Oh, don't worry about the dragons. They're magical creatures. A blast of magical energy will knock them out for a while. They shall recover soon."

"But you're not mad at me? You're not angry at what I did?"

Ta'ra came up to me, purring. "You might have released those creatures, but you also saved us. We wouldn't have survived those wargs otherwise. Even as fairies, we hadn't the magic to defeat them. Many of us would have been torn apart by those beasts. Because many Cat Sidhe here can't transform back into fairies – they'll never become fairies again, in fact."

"They won't?"

"Never," Ta'ra said. "Some of us were so dismayed by Ta'lon's lack of communication, that they decided they wanted to embrace the new life. So, they used up their remaining transformations voluntarily."

"And what about you?"

"I'm still holding on to mine. But I don't know for how long I will."

The thought that some of these fairies had chosen to be cats gave me courage. They had accepted who they had become, despite the circumstances handed down to them. I looked at my staff-bearer, and I wondered if I would have to do the same. Fate had changed me. It had wrenched me into an unfamiliar world. It had caused me to bond with a dragon, initiated me into Dragonsbond Academy, and now turned me into a warlock. But I would never win if I couldn't accept who I was.

"So, what now?" I asked, looking up at Aleam. My legs felt bandy beneath me, and I wanted to lie down. My eyelids felt so heavy that I had to blink hard to keep them open. Sleep would be upon me soon.

Aleam turned towards the place where the portal had been. In its place lay a deep crater, and smouldering piles of ash. The earth there was stripped bare, and the rock surface looked smooth, like a polished gemstone.

"We wait for the dragons to awake," Aleam said, "and then we get back to Dragonsbond Academy as soon as possible. Because we need to help them fight those things, whatever they are."

"And what must I do? Will I need to use my staff again?"

"You need to fulfil your prophecy. Embrace the thread of the future that the crystal has predicted. We have no way of knowing if the future where you defeat Astravar is the genuine prediction amongst all the possible threads. But we can only hope…"

"But my staff… Can I trust it? I mean, how do I know it's mine? How do I know it's not some kind of trick that Astravar pulled to help him destroy the world?"

Aleam smiled. "Oh, it's yours alright," he said, and he nodded at the staff-bearer. The conviction in his eyes told me he knew a lot more about this than I could possibly understand.

The exhaustion was really starting to overwhelm me. There was nothing more I could do for now. So, I lay down on the wet ground and I fell into a deep sleep.

40

FLIGHT

I awoke on a carpet of leathery skin, feeling slightly queasy. Heat seeped up from below, and something warm and furry was pressed against my tail. The light, and the heavy wind coming against my face forced my eyelids open. I must have slept through the night.

I was lying on Salanraja's back, flying high in the sky. Below me, fields whirred by – some of them golden, some of them green. Cows and sheep grazed in some fields. Others contained rows upon rows of wheat. The landscape was much more agricultural than the Cald-mines Forest. We must have flown quite a way to get here.

A heavy layer of clouds filled the dark sky. It looked like it wanted to rain but hadn't quite got around to it yet, as if all the heavens needed was that one extra cloud to unleash their load.

I turned to see Ta'ra resting on my tail. She blinked at me, then yawned. My staff-bearer floated just above her, keeping pace despite the wind. It had two fingers and held my staff, pointing it towards the horizon. Probably doing this made it more streamlined for flight. That's what I guessed, anyway – it was going to take me a long time to understand the ways of my magical ally from the ghost realm.

It was such a strange thing to be saddled with. If you'd asked me days before, I'd never have said I'd spend the rest of my life accompanied by a floating human hand. But then, I'd never thought I'd bond with a dragon either, or make friends with a cat who was once a fairy.

"Ben," Ta'ra said. "You made it. I'm so glad to see you're okay. You must have slept for hours."

"How many hours?" I asked, mirroring Ta'ra's contagious yawn.

"I don't know. There's no sun to read the time of day. But I'd say you were out for the entire night and a good portion of the morning – if not some of the afternoon."

I studied Ta'ra. I didn't like the fact she was here. This wasn't part of the plan, or at least it shouldn't have been. It wasn't that I didn't appreciate her company. I just didn't want her to accidentally get zapped by a stray bolt of Astravar's magic.

"Why did you come, anyway, Ta'ra? It's too dangerous up here. You need to be somewhere safe…"

Ta'ra made a low rumbling sound that sounded like a human might sound if they tried to growl like a cat. As I said, she still had a lot to learn. "I came to look after you. We all decided you needed extra support just in case your magic went haywire again."

"But I got rid of the crystal that was controlling my mind. Aleam said that Astravar isn't inside my head anymore. I'm free of him."

"We're just being cautious. Besides, I decided I needed to know if something happened to you. I couldn't bear it if…" She trailed off and turned away to look back at the forest, now a thin line in the distance.

I tugged my tail out from underneath Ta'ra's weight, and I strolled over to Salanraja's neck so I could get a good view of the landscape below. I could see Dragonsbond Academy down there, looking kind of wispy through the layers of clouds. A massive blue magical dome of energy surrounded the fortress, with shimmering pulses of energy cascading over it – shield magic that would hopefully protect anyone within the fortress, because otherwise they wouldn't stand a chance.

The beasts I had released from the Fifth Dimension wheeled around the castle. They seemed attracted to it as a flock of crows would be to an abandoned meal. One beast broke away from its flock and charged straight at the shield. It hit its target, creating a sudden pulse of light. But it couldn't get in and bounced off like a rubber ball bounces off a table.

"It's almost time for me to fight Astravar..." I said "... to fulfil my destiny..." My mouth went dry at the thought. There was a bitter taste on my tongue as I thought about this.

"It's not time yet," Ta'ra called back. "Aleam sent word to Dragonsbond Academy through Olan. Once they knew a powerful force was coming their way, they erected the shield as an extra precaution. But, since I last heard, the warlocks haven't decided to charge yet."

"And how do you know this when you're up here stuck on Salanraja's back?"

"I can talk for real, you know," Salanraja said. I'd never heard her speak out loud while flying before, and her voice came out kind of muffled against the wind. But she was loud enough to be audible. "Just like you, I have sensitive enough hearing to understand when someone addresses me from my back."

Admittedly, it felt so good to hear her voice. Just before I'd passed out, I wondered if I'd ever speak to her again. "Salanraja," I said. "How the whiskers did you wake up faster than me?"

"Maybe because I'm hardier than you? I am, after all, a great mighty dragon." She crooned underfoot, almost as if she were purring. If I was getting more human, I would also say Salanraja was getting more feline day by day.

I took some time to look around us. To the sides of us, the dragons flew in a V formation with Olan at the centre, Aleam stooped over her neck. Ishtkar took one wing of the formation, Quarl the other. We were next to Quarl, with Hallinar between us and Olan. Shadorow and Camillan flew between Olan and Ishtkar.

"Wait," I said, elation rising in me as I realised who was missing. "Where's Bellari and Reslin? Have we lost them for good?"

"They stayed behind to look after the other Cat Sidhe," Ta'ra said. "They might need support from the air, as all of my brothers and sisters here are travelling across Illumine Kingdom to provide support at Dragonsbond Academy. We're going to need all the allies we can get for this battle."

I chirped in amusement. "Bellari is leading the cats into battle. She hates cats. Well, that's justice for you."

"You can be so cruel, Ben," Ta'ra replied. "Besides, Bellari won't have to deal with them if she's on her dragon, will she? I'm guessing she would rather be up there with her father than flying with Rine right now."

"Whatever..." I raised my head to study the horizon.

I could now hear those creatures that I'd summoned from the Fifth Dimension. Their shrill cries seemed to cut the air apart and make it shimmer a little. It hurt my ears so much when I was this far away from them that I couldn't imagine what it would be like facing them in battle. But I was meant to use my staff to knock hundreds of them out of the sky, or at least that's what I'd seen in the vision. I just hoped they didn't tear me to pieces first.

"So why aren't we going straight up against Astravar?" I asked Ta'ra. "I want this to be over with."

She might have answered me, she might not have. I can't remember, because I was interrupted by Salanraja laughing from beneath me. She continued to speak inside my mind, as if she didn't need to share her thoughts with Ta'ra anymore. *"Do you really think you're going to battle the warlocks without support?"*

"Why not? If our crystal's visions are to be believed, then I'll beat him whatever happens, won't I?"

"Now you're thinking like that fool, Prince Arran. Don't forget you saw only one possible thread of the future. Our armies and the Dragon Corps are there to support each other. You may be destined to be our most powerful weapon – a fact that it's taken me a long time to accept, I might add. But powerful weapons are also prime targets. Trust me, we don't want to go out there alone."

"But we don't have any armies."

"They're on their way. The White Mages have been marching from Cimlean for quite a while. They departed when Prince Arran did, didn't you hear him say? But armies move much slower than dragons, you know? Also, didn't Ta'ra just tell you that Reslin and Bellari were coming with the Cat Sidhe? That's two fronts already that we have for support."

"I guess..."

I had so many more questions, and I wished we had all the time in the world to discuss them. But a scream coming from nearby distracted me. It caused such pain in my ears that I flattened them against my head to protect them. I looked up to see the massive beak of a vulture heading towards us, propelled by bat-like wings. Its black feathered head led down to a neck made of brown, rough textured skin, which spanned out into a strong-looking body and massive wings, covered in fur that lacked shine. The thing seemed to suck some of the light away from the day, almost as if that black smelly goo from the ghost realm made up part of its composition.

"*Watch out, Salanraja!*" I called in my mind, and she swept down just in time.

The creature swooped right past us, then it turned as fast as a bat would, sending a massive gust of wind in our direction. The sun glinted off its open beak as it screeched again. The edges of it looked razor sharp, like it could slice through even dragon scales.

More shrieks came from the vicinity, and another four of those creatures swept into view. The dragons responded with a curt roar, including Salanraja, and they shot fire at the unidentified beasts. A jet of flame from Olan hit one on the wing. A shard of ice from Rine's staff hit another beast on the back. But both fire and ice seemed to bounce off from them, and our enemies continued onwards unscathed.

Aleam called out from his mount and gestured everyone inwards with a wide sweep of his arm. Our formation closed inwards. Seramina and Lars fell back a little so that they had a direct line to relay some magic. Seramina then shot a beam of white energy at Lars' forehead, and at the same time, he sent up a massive shield from his staff, surrounding us all in a protective bubble.

"*What's happening, Salanraja?*" I asked.

"*Do you have to ask so many questions? This is a time of crisis.*"

"*But I need to know...*"

"*Fine. We received word from the castle that they're invincible. The only thing that can repel them is shield magic, and we're not sure how long that will last.*"

"*And how do you know all this?*"

"*Because dragons can talk across great distances, remember. We discussed our options with the Council of Three's dragons while you were asleep.*"

"Then we need to get down to Dragonsbond Academy as soon as possible."

"*You think I don't know that?*"

Outside the shield, the hideous bat-buzzard creatures came in again. Each of them had a bulbous protrusion at the top of their beak, as if something was growing inside it. As we flew onwards, they kept charging at our protective barrier, seeming to want to break through using brute force. Their thick necks gave such strength to their black feathered heads that they looked like mallets banging away at the shield.

Fortunately, Dragonsbond Academy was in view. I could see the tall towers of the fortress, and the dragon riders who stood on top of them carrying glowing staffs that fed energy into the shield. "*How are we going to get through? Salanraja, we can't just fly straight at the thing.*"

"*Will you ever get any less annoying, Bengie? You slept through us working all this out, so please now let us get on with the plan.*"

I hissed at her, and Ta'ra came up to me and lay down close to me, as if to calm me down. From our side, Aleam raised his staff, and Lars cut off the shield for a moment. Aleam then cast a bolt of lightning that hit a point just above one tower. I recognised Prefect Calin standing on that tower, and he raised his hand as if to send a signal.

"*Five,*" Salanraja said. We were heading straight at the shield, and we were going to hit it.

"*What does that mean?*"

"*It's a matter of timing...*"

"*What?*"

"*One!*"

Just before we made impact with the shield, it fizzled out for a split second to let us in. The dragons had arranged themselves perfectly, because as soon as they'd entered the shield wall it switched on again, the dragon riders on the towers sending up long beams of energy towards the centre of the shield. Just as it did, some of those bat-buzzards hit the wall, and they shrieked out in anger.

From the inside, the shield looked like the largest waterfall I'd ever seen, except with shimmering energy taking the place of water. I watched it for a while, so mesmerised that I failed to notice Salanraja land.

A sharp female voice calling out from the ground jerked me back to my senses. Driar Yila stepped over the cobblestones towards Olan as Aleam dismounted, and she looked worried.

41

COUNCIL ROOM

As soon as Salanraja had touched down on the ground of the bailey, I dashed down her tail and straight over to Driar Aleam and Driar Yila. I'd missed enough already when I was asleep, and I didn't want to miss any more. I was a big part of this thing, and it was about time that the humans let me in on their plans. It wasn't my fault that I, as a cat, needed a lot more sleep than they did.

Above, the shield added a sombre buzz to the entire tone here. Because of it, there was no wind. In fact, it was unnaturally hot, and I could smell sweat everywhere.

From behind Yila came the sound of clanging swords and students and other dragon riders shouting taunts at each other. The students had been arranged in pairs, sparring against their partner. Each face I saw in the chaos looked long, tired, and afraid of the future to come.

I could hear Driar Gallant, the academy swordmaster, gruffly screaming above all the others, screaming for students to get in line. He bawled out commands as he patrolled the courtyard, supervising the sparring. 'Attack'. 'Parry.' 'Lunge'. 'Thrust'. 'Block'.

"Aleam," Driar Yila said. She had a rather peculiar smile on her face – peculiar because that woman never smiled. "You made it through. I must admit I had my doubts."

"When, Yila, have I ever let you down?" Aleam asked.

Yila shook her head as she chuckled softly. Really, I'd never known her to act so out of character. It was as if the war had softened her a little.

"Come," she said. "Bring everyone to the Council Room. Driar Brigel and Driar Lonamm are there already."

She turned on her heel and marched off. Aleam waited for Lars, Asinda, Ange, and Rine to dismount before he led us after her. I had to weave my way through masses of feet darting forwards, and then retreating in random patterns. I'm surprised, in all honesty, I didn't get kicked.

Fortunately, the Council Courtyard wasn't jam-packed like the bailey. It was empty, in fact. We crossed the lawn, and stepped up onto the dais, passing underneath the ceiling-mounted crystal the Driars often used to augment their magic. It looked cracked and lifeless, as if it hadn't been used for a long time. Or perhaps the Driars had needed to use it so much that they'd broken it. Either way, I didn't want to know.

The double doors of the keep led into a foyer with a mezzanine, underneath which I had once seen Rine and Bellari kissing. We passed through this and then into the meeting room itself.

The first thing I noticed in this next room was how tidy the desks were. Gone were the papers and ornaments that had littered the desks last time I was in here. It was a shame – they had looked like they'd be such fun to knock off their perches.

The only remaining item was on Driar Lonamm's desk – a large parchment that I assumed to be a map. Driar Yila, Driar Lonamm, and Driar Brigel stood stooped over it. Driar Brigel was pointing to something on the map as we walked over, my staff-bearer hovering behind us.

"Let me up," I said. "Someone pick me up. I can't see anything."

Ange did the honours, cuddling me in her warm embrace. She clucked softly as she stroked me under the chin, causing me to purr.

"Me too," Ta'ra said from beneath me, and she sounded just a bit jealous. "I'm a part of this too."

Rine sighed and picked her up. I looked at her, blinked, and then I turned back to the desk.

The map displayed an overhead view of Dragonsbond Academy and the surrounding lands. The thing had been painted ornately. It wasn't one of those weird human maps that looked nothing like the landscape. In fact, this was like an aerial picture of how the terrain looked when I viewed it from Salanraja in the air. I tried to imagine a student sitting on top of their dragon with an easel and a paintbrush, studying the landscape below as they worked out every single intricate detail. But the thought made me queasy.

"The warlocks have set up camp, thirty miles west of here," Driar Lonamm said, pointing to where an ornate red wooden pin with a dragon carved into the top of it lay on the map. "They're stationed under a reinforced shield, but it doesn't matter anyway, because we can't send anyone out with those beasts flying around like they are."

"After we'd set up the shield," Driar Yila said, "we sent three of Arran's dragon riders to fight some of those creatures from the Fifth Dimension. We sent a lightning mage, a fire mage, and an ice mage – a classic elemental trio. But they didn't return." She looked up at the doorway. "I watched the three of them from the towers, being ripped to shreds."

"So basically, we're under siege," Aleam said, and he tugged at the wattle on his neck.

"I wish there was a better way of saying it," Brigel said. "But yes. We have two options: we either fly out and fight, or we stay here and starve."

I shuddered. Since they had started rationing, there really wasn't any food here suitable for cats. I hadn't seen any cats in the bailey or courtyard when we arrived, and I imagined my poor brothers and sisters stuck in the cattery, meowing because they hadn't eaten for days. It made me so sad, really. Given us cats couldn't eat yucky vegetables, we would be the first to die. Of course, it would be this great and mighty Bengal who would save them, and I'd make sure they remembered that for years to come.

Prefect Asinda broke the silence with a heavy sigh. Up to this point, she'd been silent. But I guess being Driar Yila's niece made her feel like she should also take part. "So, what can we do?" she asked, looking at Driar Yila with her cornflower eyes. Driar Yila took a deep breath, and she glanced up at Driar Brigel, as if she was out of options.

"I don't know," Driar Brigel said, and he scratched his massive bald head. "I'm going to be honest with you. None of us know what to do. It seems we have two options, to charge and get destroyed, or to wither under the siege. But I don't know which of those two evils is the lesser one."

"But you have me," I pointed out. "You saw me defeating those things in the visions. I shot purple tentacles out of my staff."

"Yes..." Driar Lonamm said. "But not everything the crystal shows is necessarily true in this thread of the future. You have a mind-magic staff, after all, do you not? It doesn't matter, anyway, because no magic works against those things. We've sent out volleys from the towers, cutting off the shield for very short spurts. Nothing we use can touch them. We're powerless against them."

"Actually, there is a way to defeat them." The pompous voice came from the doorway. Everyone turned towards it, clearly surprised. Because Prince Arran strolled towards us, with Captain Onus and another couple of armoured guards trailing behind.

42

AN UNWELCOME VISITOR

Arran's hands were tied at his front with what looked like some kind of silk, as if not to hurt him. He also didn't have his staff with him.

As he approached, Yila gave Captain Onus a hard stare. I also bristled as I saw Prince Arran, and I was ready to leap right out of Ange's arms and hide in a corner. Or maybe, if he provoked me enough, I might even try scratching him in the face.

"I thought we ordered him locked up?" Driar Yila said.

"You did," Captain Onus said, and he scratched his big, squashed nose. "But Prince Arran insisted he had important information for you. Information, he said, that could save the kingdom."

Yila turned her icy stare on the prince. "Explain?"

Arran scowled at her. "Might I remind you who your commander-in-chief is? Once this is over, the three of you will be court-martialled, believe you me. As well as you, Aleam."

"I think all of us are much more concerned with the matter at hand," Aleam snapped. "What do you know, Arran?"

"I know the shield won't hold forever. And I know what magic you need to defeat those creatures."

"Go on..." Driar Yila said.

Prince Arran turned towards the fireplace. I noticed then that a white staff was leaning against the marble mantlepiece. Arran's staff... He turned to look at me. I didn't particularly take to being stared at by people I didn't like, and so I growled back at him, perhaps with a little hiss in it too.

The prince didn't seem to notice. Instead, his gaze roved even further towards my staff-bearer, which floated behind me. Arran walked up to it and studied the crystal on the staff with intent.

"This crystal is glamoured," he said.

"What?" Aleam said, and he let out a faint cough. "Preposterous."

"I know glamour magic when I see it. This isn't a staff of mind magic."

"What is the point of this, Prince Arran?" Driar Brigel said.

"Yes, you are wasting a lot of time here." Driar Lonamm said.

"Didn't you see the vision in the cat's and his dragon's crystal?" Arran said. "Were any of you paying attention? The cat used dark magic against the flying creatures. He summoned purple tentacles out of his staff to bring the creatures down. These beasts are called *aeriosaurs*, by the way, and do you know how I know that? Because they're recorded in the only account of the Fifth Dimension and Sixth Dimension in the king's inventory. A book kept only for his most trusted advisors, locked deep within his treasury. It's one of his most valuable and most dangerous assets. Because these dimensions are the most dangerous of them all. Anyone who learns of either of them can release terror upon our world."

"But Ben doesn't have a dark magic staff," Driar Yila said. "I can see that."

"As I said," Arran said. "It's glamoured. And *I* would know."

Aleam scratched his chin. "We saw a vision of Astravar when the aeriosaurs were released into this world. He said that he'd explored the Fifth Dimension, and by the sounds of it, the sixth one too."

"And now the force that controls these beasts also controls Astravar," Prince Arran snapped back. "There's a reason he's more powerful than all the other warlocks. That man doesn't have a mind anymore. He has completely lost himself to the darkness, and these beasts are just like Astravar – completely controlled by the dark magic. Now, only the same dark magic can defeat him and these creatures. Nothing else will work."

"So, it's down to the cat?" Driar Yila said. "He'll have to take all those beasts out, and then he'll take out Astravar, and we must support him. Thank you, Prince Arran. Your information has been invaluable. Captain Onus, you may return him to his cell."

"No," Prince Arran said. "He shall have more support than that. Captain Onus, can you hand me my staff please?"

"Err…" Captain Onus said, and he looked askew at the members of the Council of Three in turn.

"Do it," Driar Brigel said. "We have enough of us here to overpower him if he tries something foolish. Cut his ties first, of course."

Captain Onus nodded, then took a dagger from his hip and released Prince Arran from his bonds. He turned towards the fireplace, but Arran raised a hand to stop him. "I'll get it myself. This matter must be handled delicately. I'm sure you understand."

The captain clenched a gauntleted fist by his side, but he said nothing. Meanwhile, the prince strolled over to the staff and clutched it in both of his hands. He closed his eyes and mumbled something under his breath. The crystal on his staff glowed white for a moment, and this light faded to reveal a purple crystal. "This is why the king entrusted me with this role. Because I am now the only user of dark magic still in control of my mind, and we need dark magic so that we can win."

The three members of the Council of Three studied Arran underneath furrowed eyebrows. But they said nothing. Meanwhile, Ange and Rine were looking at each other, both biting their lips. Rine sneaked a glance at Seramina, and then probably realised that he might give too much away and instead lowered his head.

It was Aleam who stepped forward, also clutching his staff. "So, you and the cat want to go in alone?"

"Of course," Arran said. "And everyone else will provide support. It is crucial that I don't die. You realise I could have defeated Astravar without the cat? That is what *I* was destined to do. We didn't need any of this debacle that involved locking me up in a room not even half fit for a prince. This could have all been over by now."

"Except there's one thing you're overlooking," Aleam said, and he raised his staff above his head. This time there came a yellow flash before Aleam broke the glamour on his staff. Now, he had a purple staff as well. "There are more of us than you realise. It's good that you chose to come out of hiding. Because this has been going on for too long."

Arran stared at the tip of Aleam's staff in astonishment. "This—"

"Seramina, Asinda," Aleam said, interrupting Arran. "I think it's time."

Seramina looked at Asinda, who nodded and reached out to hold her hand. Together, they both raised their staffs, Asinda's red, and Seramina's white like Arran's. In a single moment, and behind two bright flashes, they had broken their glamours in much the same way. Prefect Lars looked at Asinda in shock, his face blanched of colour.

The only other person in the room who seemed surprised was Arran...

"I think it will be I who leads this battle," Aleam said. "Talking of experience and all that."

Arran rubbed his brow. "This can't be... The stories say that it was your bond with Olan that completely wiped out your ability to use dark magic. You were too far gone over to the other side. The magic had consumed you – everyone in the royal palace read the reports. If you've been a warlock all along, then... Did you ever change?"

He looked around as if trying to find his guards – or at least someone he could entrust to arrest Aleam. But I also had had my staff-bearer nearby, and if Arran tried anything on Aleam, I would be the first to use my dark magic against him. I'd cover him in a sea of salmon from the North Atlantic so thick that he'd drown. Then we wouldn't need to worry about this idiot anymore. Plus, all the cats would have plenty to eat and the best food they've ever tasted at that.

Alas, I didn't need to do any of that, because Aleam had this well-handled.

"That's where you're wrong," the old man said. "It's sad that no one's been around to teach you the true history, Prince Arran, for you must be descended from a dark magic user yourself.

"Olan bonded with me because she believed she could save me from the dark magic. Then, once King Garmin saw what a dragon could do, he chose to tell the people that I'd been cleansed of dark magic. It was a lie to protect me and others who had once used dark magic in the kingdom. Given how the magic had corrupted us, the crimes we had done, the public couldn't believe there was any turning back. They wanted to see all warlocks – and all dark magic users – as monsters. For them to think I still had access to that power would have caused great civil unrest.

"But with Olan's help – what she taught me all these years ago – I learned to push the dark magic away. It became less like a curse, and more like a resource that I could call on whenever I needed, so long as I was aware how dangerous it is. It's like alteration magic – if we use it too much then we become it. I vouched I would only use it on the rarest occasions, and I'd only use it when there was no other option and I knew it was for the greater good. Dark magic – or whatever force it is that runs across all dimensions – is natural and can be used for good or evil. This is what I've been teaching Seramina and Asinda how to do all this time in private – how to respect such power. Now, it looks like I'll also need to mentor Ben."

Prince Arran's mouth had gone wide, and his face white. He twisted his staff around in his hand as he studied Aleam. Then he looked at Seramina, then at Asinda, and then at me, shaking his head as he did so. The shrieks of those aeriosaurs – as Arran had called them – punctuated the silence, and we could still hear swords clanging outside. Every so often, I heard a loud crashing sound, and a flash of light came from the window as one of the beasts tried to break the shield. I curled up in Ange's arms, appreciative of the warmth, because I knew that this comfort wouldn't last forever.

Out there, one of us could die.

"Might I suggest," Driar Brigel said. "That we work all this out after the battle. We now have those beasts we need to contend with."

"Yes," Arran said. "And yes, Aleam, you should lead this battle. But if anything happens to you, command transfers to me. Is that understood?"

"I understand," Aleam said, his head lowered.

Driar Yila stepped forward. "Captain Onus, order the buglers to call an assembly. It's time to go to war."

43

SPEECHES

The only residents of Dragonsbond Academy who didn't attend the assembly were the shield mages responsible for feeding the massive dome that protected us. The towers those shield mages stood on housed the dragons, and I could only imagine the anticipation of the great beasts. Though Salanraja was silent in my mind, I could sense her need to fight. She didn't seem scared so much but, like me, she seemed to just want to get this over with.

Once we defeated the aeriosaurs, we could vanquish the warlocks once and for all. I would shoot Astravar out of the sky, just as I was destined to do. Then, either I got to retire or perhaps someone would finally offer to open a portal for me to return home. Now, with Ta'ra, Rine, Ange, Seramina, and Aleam in my life, I would much prefer to stay here. But I still craved a life of comfort. Cats should enjoy nothing but lives of comfort.

I stood on the dais behind the three lecterns as I gazed at the mesmerising effect of the buzzing, glowing beams of ozone cast by the shield mages into the sky. Seramina and Asinda stood close to me, and my staff-bearer hovered right in front of me, holding the staff erect as if it was proud of it. For now, mine and Seramina's staffs were white, and Asinda's staff was red, all three looking like they normally did.

Prince Arran and Aleam stood at the centre of the dais, in front of the lecterns. Both men's staffs also had their glamours on them – Arran's white and Aleam's his characteristic yellow. The three Driars of the Council of Three stood just behind Aleam and Arran, as if ready to provide support if needed.

But the prince and the old man were to run the show.

On the lawn below us, stood the members of Prince Arran's Dragon Corps, the Driars behind them, then the Prefects, then the Initiates, then the support staff and guards at the back. I could smell tension everywhere, and the students murmured in funereal tones. I didn't hear anyone laughing from the crowd. Nor did I see anyone jostling their friends, or playing games, or behaving like teenage dragon riders like to behave.

Because everyone here knew what that final call of the bugle had meant. There were no pretences anymore.

"Silence!" Driar Yila's voice cut through the noise, and it hung there for a moment as the surrounding voices faded to emptiness. Driar Lonamm let out a loud cough to help still the noise, and Driar Brigel put out his hand, palm down, pressing against the air.

This gave Arran room to deliver his speech.

"The king has appointed you to—" he said. Yada, yada, yada. I just couldn't listen to that stupid, pompous voice without yawning. He might have accepted us now as dark mages who would fight alongside him. But still, he had one of the most uninspiring voices I'd ever heard. I caught snippets, of course.

"By law, everyone over the age of sixteen must fight..." Which meant everyone here, except Seramina and me, and we had to fight, anyway.

"Your deeds will be remembered and go down in history. Your names will be carved on tablets in King Garmin's hallways. Whatever the outcome today, you will go down in history as heroes." Now I was there thinking, is that what people here really wanted? If so, they were crazy. I certainly didn't get into this dragon rider business to have my name carved on a tablet. Besides, if someone scribed my name there, it would be a name that humans had chosen for me. My feline name, and the name that really mattered to me, couldn't be represented by any symbols from the human languages.

Arran then described the plan. Of course, he had to show off as he did so. As he was speaking, and without even telling anyone he was going to do so, he raised his staff and with a flash of light, erased the glamour from it. The white glow faded, to be replaced by a purple one that Arran held there for a moment.

A murmur erupted from the crowd again. Then, as if they were being pushed by a powerful ocean wave, they backed away from the dais.

"Do not be scared," Aleam called out. He raised his staff next. One moment it looked like he was about to cast his lightning magic over the entire crowd, the next he also stood with a glowing purple crystal.

Then, Seramina and Asinda raised their staffs above their heads and removed the glamours on them, and I also commanded my staff to do the same. The three of us, and my staff-bearer stepped forward, as the Council of Three parted to make way for us. We stood together, our staffs high above our heads as mumblings of terror and consternation enveloped the crowd.

"Silence!" Driar Yila called out again with her cutting voice, even louder than before. This time, it completely stunned the crowd into submission.

"Oh, for demon's sake." Prince Arran mumbled.

"At least we now have their attention," Aleam pointed out.

"We do…" Arran said softly, and then he raised his voice to address the assembly once again. "I am only choosing to reveal this to you, because dark magic is the only way to conquer the beasts called aeriosaurs that fly around this castle, as well as Astravar himself. Now, we five are your unexpected allies, as well as an army of Cat Sidhe that is approaching from the east."

More angry murmurs came from the crowd. Prince Arran turned to Aleam and shrugged his shoulders. From the side, I could see his raised eyebrows, and his expression told me he wanted Aleam to take control. Aleam smiled at Arran and gave him a conciliatory nod.

Arran took a step back, and Aleam took a step forward. About time, I thought. Aleam would know what to do.

"I said, silence!" Driar Yila screamed. Her cry didn't do much this time, though. Everyone was too scared.

Arran turned to Aleam. "I've had enough. You handle this, Aleam."

Aleam let out a cough, and he raised his hand. Then, with his voice at a volume that belied his age, he continued the speech. He didn't even need to tell the crowd to shut up. His voice commanded such power that all heads eventually turned up to him. The assembly watched him in awe as if they were studying fish in a tank.

"I know you're all afraid," Aleam said. "And I don't blame you, because I would also be afraid in your shoes. But I have lived for eighty good years plus some, and all those years I've had to deal with a lot of change. I saw dark magic being used in its very infancy, and through all this time I've learned that it isn't the dark magic that's bad. It's the greed that causes people to consume and hoard until they forget the value of what they're consuming and hoarding.

"I was once a man with too much of that pride, and I wanted far more of it. Until I met Olan, my dragon, who I'm sure you all know well, and she taught me the value of humility. She is a far wiser soul than I can ever be, and she taught me that I didn't need the dark magic. So, instead I learned how to use the lightning magic that my crystal gifted me with when I bonded with Olan. Through Olan's guidance, I resisted using the dark magic that always remained available to me, and eventually the spell it had on me went away.

"All this time, the stories you've heard about me are true. King Garmin never lied about me, and I never lied either. Olan cured me during those three years I spent in the crystal mountains, learning the ways of the dragons, and at the same time learning what it truly means to be alive. She taught me how to be complete. She taught me, how to be more human.

"Remember, the warlocks were once just men and women like us. We are not fighting these warlocks – we are fighting the forces that seek to destroy us. Day by day, we fight such forces, and as we grow, we learn better to overcome them.

"So do not be afraid of us who need to use dark magic to vanquish the warlocks, because we will only do so when we absolutely have to. Also, do not be afraid of the warlocks. Be afraid instead of what might happen if we let these dark forces consume our kingdom.

"At the end of the day, it does not matter whose name is written on the tablet. What truly matters is how we fought. Because do you want to live in a world where we are scared of who we are? Such worlds spawn the type of false pride we need to be wary of.

"So go out and fight the battle you must fight. Be true to yourself and what you believe in deep inside, and we shall prevail. Because that's the grandest lesson that Olan has taught me – truth always wins in the end."

Aleam stopped speaking with his head held high, and his staff raised even higher above his head, the crystal a dull purple. Beneath him, everyone listened in deferential silence, allowing him to speak. I could see his long grey hair falling behind his shoulders, and he didn't look like stooped old Aleam from this angle. He looked like a leader. Someone you want to follow. Someone you could trust to look after your dinner while you go and do your business.

"So will you fight with us, despite our choice of magic?" he shouted.

"Yes!" the crowd roared back.

"Will you fight for your kingdom?"

"Always!"

"And will you fight for your true selves?"

"Forever!"

"Then let's go out and conquer, because this day will be remembered forever."

A roar came back from the crowd, growing in intensity as they raised their arms and chanted, "For the kingdom! For the kingdom!" I didn't like loud noises, and I wanted to shrink into a corner somewhere with my ears flattened against my head until it was over.

Soon, the dragons joined in the chorus, making this cacophony even louder. But then there came another roar of voices from the crowd, and I don't know who started it. Rine, perhaps. Yeah, it was probably Rine.

"For Ben," they said. "For Ben! For Ben! For Ben!" Because

everyone here by now, even if they hadn't seen the vision, knew what I had to do.

I stepped to the front of the dais, and I stalked across the edge with the perfect grace of a cat. I could swear someone even threw rose petals over me and I basked in the adulation for as long as I could before the battle commenced.

44

AERIOSAURS

The shield mages needed to work even harder to expand the shield so that the dragons could emerge from their towers. A few of the senior dragons – namely Driar Yila's ruby dragon, Farago, Driar Lonamm's sapphire dragon, Flue, Driar Brigel's emerald dragon Plishk, and Olan – flew around the inside wall of the shield to supervise the operation. The other dragons came out of their towers in twos, and soon hundreds of dragons were arranged on the cobblestones of the bailey, ready to launch into the air.

Those that had to stay in the academy did so behind locked doors, barred tightly shut from the other side. This included the support staff, the guards, and anyone who hadn't been trained to ride a dragon. Also, many of the shield mages weren't going to come with us – even if their dragons would join the battle unmanned. These dragon riders needed to stay behind to keep up the shield. If the warlocks got into Dragonsbond Academy, then most thought we wouldn't have a chance of getting it back. The land around would become the new Darklands – the territory of the warlocks – and our enemy would continue to expand their dominion, using Dragonsbond Academy as a strategic point, until there was no non-magical life left in this kingdom.

Despite my erratic path, my staff-bearer stayed close. Whenever a dragon lurched into position, almost blocking its path, it twisted skilfully in the air as if it was a martial artist trained in the use of the quarterstaff.

"*Salanraja, where are you?*" I asked in my mind as I weaved my way between two scaly legs, each as wide as tree stumps. "*There are too many dragons. How am I meant to find you in this mess?*"

"*I thought you could navigate by smell,*" Salanraja said, her tone of voice amused.

"*I can when there aren't so many conflicting smells. But what do you expect in this heat? It's suffocating. I can't wait to get out of the shield.*"

"*Well, you'll have to wait until we're in formation. We can't hurry these things, you know. Meanwhile, navigate using your mind. You should instinctively know how to find me by now.*"

I growled. I was so tired from my adventures that I couldn't bear to do this 'navigating with my mind' stuff. It took concentration. Fortunately, I didn't need to, because I ducked around another dragon leg, almost getting trampled, and I saw Salanraja, or rather I saw her peculiar arrangement of spikes. Once upon a time, the dragons used to mock her because these spikes prevented her from bearing a saddle. Now, with her being bonded to the famous descendant of the great Asian leopard cat, they apparently all respected her.

"*Very good, Bengie,*" Salanraja said in my mind.

"*When are you going to stop calling me that?*"

"*Never. It's a fine and mighty name.*"

"*Whatever.*"

Just as I reached Salanraja's tail and was ready to leap up onto her back, I heard a meowing sound from nearby. Ta'ra had found her way towards me, and she looked at me with angry eyes. "Please don't tell me you were thinking of leaving without me, Ben," she said.

"Didn't I tell you once? It's too dangerous up there."

"You tried to tell me, yes, but I didn't listen. You need someone to keep you in check. Salanraja can't be watching your every move when she's focusing on navigating through the clouds."

"I'm bonded to Salanraja. She knows exactly what I'm thinking at any point, and she'll notice at the first sign of trouble. Our bond is designed to protect me."

"That didn't stop you doing what you did last time, Ben. I'm coming with you and that's the end of it."

I growled at her, but I couldn't be bothered arguing anymore. Salanraja didn't seem to object, either. For all I knew, it could have been my dragon's idea.

Soon, I was on Salanraja's back, and Ta'ra wasn't far behind me. "If anything happens to you," I said to her, "then I can't be held responsible."

"I'll take responsibility for my own life, thank you very much. Besides, if I'm falling through the clouds, I can always become a fairy. I have one transformation left, remember?"

"So, you take responsibility for my life, but you don't let me take responsibility for yours?"

"It's not like that," Ta'ra said.

"Really, then how is it?"

"Oh, why do you have to be so…"

"So, what?"

"So… I don't know, irascible? You've got a lot on your shoulders right now, and surely it's better to have someone to help you through this."

"Fine," I said, and I didn't have the time to object any more, because a bugle sounded, and Salanraja immediately lifted off. Once she got high enough, I could feel the shield pulling on my hair as if someone had blown up and charged a massive balloon with static electricity up there.

There were so many flying dragons, that at first it was hard to recognise my friends. But after a moment of searching, I spotted Rine sitting upon his great emerald, Ishtkar and Ange upon her sapphire, Quarl. They were flying not far from each other, gazing into each other's eyes, sharing some kind of moment. Things really were going well between them. So long as we got through this, everything was going according to plan.

I found Arran, standing upon the weirdly shiny, jet black dragon Corralsa. No dragon I'd ever seen looked like that. I saw Shadorow with Asinda and Camillan with Lars, slowly hovering around each other in circles. Then there was Seramina aboard Hallinar, and Aleam on Olan – both of whom had their staffs clutched in their hands, their purple crystal in full view for everyone to see.

From up here, I could see the camp of the warlocks below. They had already drained the land of life, and the terrain surrounding them looked purple, windswept, and dry. They had a shield dome over their white tents, which must have been even larger than ours. A ring of Manipulators fed this shield, sending white beams into it. They stood on the outside of the camp, with bone dragons lying dormant nearby.

All manner of magical creatures waited outside the shield. I noticed the different types of golems that I'd seen outside the Cald-mines Forest – except maybe around ten times the amount of them. At the back of the formation, stone golems towered so high they looked like they could knock down the walls of Dragonsbond Academy and reduce it to rubble. Clay golems morphed across the ground near the front, and in front of them too stood a line of fully formed forest golems. I had to squint to see them, but I also saw flames on the horizon – no doubt those dangerous fire golems.

One thing was for sure. If we lost that shield, then Dragonsbond Academy was doomed.

Meanwhile, the aeriosaurs plugged away at the shield. They were relentless – not seeming to injure or tire, as if they thought they could break their way in. I had a feeling they'd manage if they tried for long enough. More and more sparks lashed out of the shield, each time making almighty bangs that were even louder than fireworks. My ears were in so much pain.

We waited until all the dragons were aloft – still protected by the shield. Then, we slowly filtered outwards, facing the shield, leaving Corralsa and Olan at the centre. The bugles called out again from below.

"This is going to be a delicate operation," Salanraja told me. She was flapping her wings slowly, to keep herself aloft. "Hold on to your horses —or should I say dragon..."

"I have no intention ever to ride a horse..." I couldn't think of anything more ridiculous.

"Must you be so literal? Now call your staff-bearer. We need you and Seramina to take out the aeriosaurs."

I did exactly what she suggested, knowing that if I didn't, the aeriosaurs would tear Salanraja and me to shreds pretty quickly. I reached out in my mind, and my staff-bearer swung forward so fast I thought it would club me off Salanraja. But it slowed just at the last moment and placed my staff gently in my mouth.

Suddenly, a different kind of sensation washed over me.

The muscles all over my body hummed, and power surged through me. I felt strong, and I felt complete. But this time, I would not let the magic consume me. I could see the aeriosaurs in slow motion, swooping by at the speed that feathers swoop when caught upon the wind. I wasn't Ben the Bengal anymore; I was a Dragoncat – a powerful mage.

The bugles cried out again, and the shield fizzled out. Salanraja charged so fast that I felt myself sliding down her back. But I was in complete control, and I quickly dug my claws into her scales to secure myself in place.

I looked over my shoulder to check Ta'ra was okay. She'd grown in size a little, and she'd secured herself by sticking one strong paw between two of Salanraja's spikes. Behind her, the shield had released a wave of dragons – everyone except Olan and Corralsa.

The shield turned back on immediately, letting only several aeriosaurs inside the perimeter. But Aleam and Arran were already there to attack them with beams of dark magic. They reduced the aeriosaurs to dust, and then they flew out towards the shield wall.

I turned back to the matter at hand. We were out into the open, and the aeriosaurs swooped in – coming at me in slow motion. Or at least that's how it appeared from my magically augmented perspective. I summoned up the energy inside me, putting all my focus into the staff. It warmed up in my mouth, and out of the crystal came thousands of tentacles. They whipped at the aeriosaurs, just as I'd seen in the vision, soon lashing across their bodies and cutting them in two like a chef chopping fruit. As each tentacle hit the enemy, the creature flashed purple and then crumbled to dust.

Meanwhile, other dragons flew around me, their riders casting all manner of spells. These hit the aeriosaurs, not seeming to scathe them, but still distracting and confusing them.

It was chaos. Yet I was completely in control, as Salanraja flew across the sky, and I eliminated anything that crossed my path. I felt all powerful – as if I could conquer anything Astravar might throw at me.

But a roar ten times louder than thunder coming from the distance brought me back to reality. I recognised that sound, and that recognition jerked me out of my trance and set a shudder down my spine. Underlying this noise came gnashes and yowls and yaps from the horizon, getting louder fast.

I saw the wargs first, charging towards the shield that would keep Dragonsbond Academy safe. But not for long, because something even more terrifying came through the sky. A dragon ten times the size of Olan, with skin like rock, rents within it leading to pools of burning magma.

I'd fought one of these creatures a while ago and sent it back to the Seventh Dimension through language alone.

But now I had no chance of controlling it. Because Astravar piloted this demon dragon, his staff in his hand. Before we could react, he flew right at Dragonsbond Academy. Then the demon dragon opened its mouth and let out a roar so powerful that through demon magic alone it destroyed the shield. This opened up the castle for the wargs to flood in, an army of golems trailing in their wake.

❧ 45 ❧

TENTACLES

I watched the demon dragon in shock as it turned away from where the shield had once been over Dragonsbond Academy. For a moment, the sky smelled less of rotten vegetable juice and more of sulphur. It smelled as if the world beneath was about to erupt, bathing the ground in magma and leaving no place left to land.

This wasn't how it was meant to be. The crystal had never shown us fighting a demon dragon in the visions. Astravar was always on top of a bone dragon and me on top of Salanraja. But then, I'd never seen Ta'ra in any of those visions of the ultimate battle either.

Beneath us, the shield mages had retreated into the towers, and the wargs hungrily stalked the bailey and the Council Courtyard, looking for prey. Fortunately, the support staff and the castle guards remained safely inside, while the shield mages had also found their way back into the towers. They would be defenceless, standing out in the open against an army of hungry, oversized wolves. If we had the dragons, we could wipe the bailey and courtyard clean, but all the dragons were up here fighting the aeriosaurs.

Arrows sailed out of the embrasures near the bottom of the towers. Some of these hit wargs, battering them down to the ground. Meanwhile, other wargs flooded towards the doorways. They took it in turns to charge at the doors with all their strength, trying to ram them to splinters as they tore at loose pieces of wood with their mighty jaws.

If we didn't do something about them soon, then Dragonsbond Academy wouldn't survive – especially after the stone and forest golems had charged in and knocked down the walls with their mighty strength. Those golems were moving slowly but surely. Meanwhile, the clay golems moved much faster, morphing along the ground in their characteristic way. Only the fire golems stayed behind as if waiting for a target to catapult their kamikaze fireballs at.

But we still had thousands of aeriosaurs to deal with up the air, and that wasn't all. The shield blinked out above the warlocks' camp, just long enough for the Manipulators and bone dragons to flood out. The bone dragons joined the swarm of aeriosaurs, sailing every which way through the sky, whilst the Manipulators fed them with magical energy from the ground.

Astravar sat atop his demon dragon as he searched the sky for a target. Waves of aeriosaurs and bone dragons wheeled close to him, blocking our own dragons from getting near him. He had his staff raised up high above his head, and the crystal on it was glowing bright purple. He seemed to spot me, and the demon dragon bucked in the air and turned towards me. I called energy to my staff, the magic coursing through my veins, my muscles thrumming as before.

"It's show time," I said to Salanraja. "Charge!"

"Wait," she replied.

"What for? This is our moment. This'll be even bigger than winning the dragon egg-and-spoon."

"Look behind you. We're a team, remember."

I checked over my shoulder. Ta'ra was already near the base of Salanraja's tail, staring out into the distance. Behind her, Olan, Corralsa, Hallinar, and Shadorow approached in formation, with their riders on board. They were much closer to us than the demon dragon was. Within seconds they had arranged themselves to either side of me – Arran and Asinda on one side, Aleam and Seramina on the other. Aleam put his hand on his head in salute. I raised a paw to salute back.

Then, there came another mighty roar from the sky, and Astravar was amongst us.

He charged right at me first. As the demon dragon came, it opened its great gaping mouth and let out a vortex of energy. Last time this had happened, it had almost knocked Salanraja out of the sky. But this time, I was ready for it, or at least my instinct knew what to do. My throat tasted dry, and my tongue had a slightly metallic tang on it.

I summoned energy to my staff and out came what looked like a ball of bolt lightning. This travelled through the air and met the vortex head on. Both flashed together, and the ball shrank to the size of a ping pong ball, encasing the vortex within its folds. Together, both magical spells dissipated into nothing.

Unfortunately, this didn't stop the demon dragon in its tracks. Still, it barrelled right at us, and Salanraja had to veer sharply to dive out of its way. The demon beast overshot its target and let out a mighty roar that not only would have shaken the ground, but also seemed to try to shake every single dragon out of the sky. Astravar's manic laughter pealed through the air as he turned to face us, and we turned around to face him too. It wasn't just his staff that glowed purple, but his eyes did, too. They cut through the gathering purple mist around him, which also gathered around me and the other dark mages.

I expected to hear Astravar in my mind then, or to see his face upon the clouds or something. But his golem's crystal was no longer lodged in my brain, so he couldn't control me. His demon dragon hovered a safe distance from us as his staff gained power. The crystal on it glowed brighter and brighter, the colour now verging towards white.

Our dragons fanned out around us as more aeriosaurs flooded in. I pushed power to my staff again, whipping our enemies out of the sky with another load of tentacles. They didn't just shoot out of my staff, but Aleam's, Seramina's, Asinda's, and Arran's too. I hadn't been trained to use this magic, and I guessed Seramina and Asinda had never handled such power before, either. But the magic seemed to just fill me with knowledge as if as soon as I'd picked up that staff, I'd automatically memorised an entire grimoire of spells.

Thousands of aeriosaurs got cut out of the sky. Then a good swarm of bone dragons charged in, and the magic took them out too. Bone dragons might have been invincible to normal magic, but it seemed dark magic could still destroy them. The white energy that the Manipulators fed them with meant nothing against our flashing purple tentacles.

As one bone dragon crumbled into bone dust, I saw Quarl and Ishtkar flash past. Rine shot down a bolt of ice at a Manipulator on the ground, then Ange used some vines to whip up the crystal into the air and then another tangle of vines to crush it into shards.

But I couldn't focus on the battle for too long, because Astravar's magic was now ready. He shot a red beam out from his staff, and I responded in kind by shooting a blue beam from mine.

BEAMS

This was the moment I'd been waiting for all this time – happening just as my crystal had foreseen. Two beams of magic meeting straight on – Astravar's red, mine blue. They fused in the middle, in a display of bright purple light, with that terrible mist gathering around it. If that light hit me, then I knew I'd die. If that light hit Astravar, then he would die.

It was a game governed by simple rules – a battle of two beams. I could swear that I'd seen something similar on television – in those cartoons the mistress' and master's son liked to watch.

But Astravar was too strong for me. I might have had a magical staff, but I wasn't practised in battling the most powerful warlock of all time. Slowly, that purple light crept towards me, and even with all the concentration in the world, I couldn't keep it away. Sweat welled from the glands in my paws, and my fur itched. I put even more mental power into it, but no matter how much I tried, the light crept ever closer. Powerful static tugged on every single strand of fur in my body, causing intense pain.

I hadn't a chance in the world. The game would soon be over, and I would die.

Fortunately, I wasn't fighting Astravar alone. After Aleam had wiped away another wave of incoming aeriosaurs, he turned Olan to face Astravar. From a pouch on his hip, he took into his hand a fist-sized crystal. It was purple, and almost as shiny as a diamond. He threw this right at the beam, and it latched on inside the magic and held in place. It hovered just in front of where the purple fusion of light crept towards me. Astravar's red beam thus split in several directions, sending out searing jets of energy into the clouds.

Aleam flew into the path of one of these jets and met it with a beam from his staff, which he directed towards the crystal. Arran flew into another beam, and he also cast some energy at the crystal from his staff. Seramina latched on to another beam and Asinda another. Once all the dragons were in place, five of us fed energy into the crystal, pushing it back towards Astravar. His expression had gone from one of arrogance to abject fear, and his face twisted as he pushed more and more magic into the spell.

Yet we continued to push the crystal back, our strength combined. Astravar might have stood a chance against any of us alone, maybe even two of us. But now the crystal gained speed, and soon it was shooting towards Astravar.

Just before it hit him, his demon dragon roared again, sounding like the crack of ten thunderbolts in unison. Astravar also bellowed out something at the top of his voice. He had such power in his lungs, probably through years of being augmented by magic. Then, there came a blinding flash of light from his staff, and the crystal shattered.

For a moment I only saw spots, and things moving in the spaces between those spots. Behind it all, more aeriosaurs flooded in, and it took all my concentration to track their motion. More tentacles whipped out around us, and we became surrounded in purple mist.

Once I could see clearly again, Astravar had vanished.

"Ben, behind you!" Ta'ra shouted out.

But she didn't need to, because soon Astravar's crazy laughter resounded from behind us, and I spun around sharply to see him on our tail. Except there wasn't one Astravar this time. There were five of him, each of them sitting on top of a demon dragon.

"Gracious demons," Salanraja said. *"He's split."*

"Is it a glamour?" I asked.

"Neither Aleam nor Arran think so... There are five Astravars. What kind of sorcery is this?"

Each version of Astravar shot out a red beam at each of us. I didn't see what the other dragons were up to before Salanraja swooped downwards, then entered a loop-the-loop. It made my stomach churn, but I tried not to let it get to me. I also I hoped Salanraja's crazy flying tactics wouldn't throw Ta'ra off her back. She wasn't as acquainted with her aerobatics as I was.

Once we reached the top of her trajectory, Salanraja corrected herself with a half barrel roll, so we were facing towards Astravar's red beam. It swept up towards us, and I immediately hit it with a beam of my own – a brilliant blue one full of dragon fire or something. The purple fusion of light danced at the centre of our two beams once again. In my peripheral vision, I could see the other beams searing through the air, met by beams from my allies' staffs. But I knew it wouldn't be wise to check to see which of them were winning.

Instead, I applied all my concentration towards that focal point where the two beams met. Not only did I need to will as much magic as possible from my staff to counter Astravar's, but I also needed to focus on this image or doppelgänger or whatever it was, reading its every move so it didn't cut around my beam. It wasn't just a matter of watching it. I could feel the movements, great swings in the field of magical energy that I had to adjust to, using micro-movements in the muscles in my neck and mouth.

It was like that elaborate sport that the humans in my world called fencing. Except the length of the swords seemed to stretch out to infinity, and they were constructed from pure energy.

I'd hoped that Astravar, having split his form, would have significantly weakened his strength. Yet he seemed even stronger than before, fuelled either by rage or abject fear. Again, the white light that separated the two beams was getting ever closer to me. In a matter of seconds, it would fry me to a crisp.

I had lost...

"Ben," Ta'ra said from behind me. "I'm sorry. We don't have a choice Ben..."

"Ta'ra, what are you—"

"Don't say anything. Just remember. I love you."

"What?" But I couldn't put many more words to thought, nor did I dare turn around to see what she was talking about. Yet this soon became obvious, because a golden wisp floated out underneath the beam, heading straight at Astravar.

Whiskers, she'd used her last transformation. But I couldn't worry about it. I couldn't worry about her. I needed to focus on keeping that light away from me. I willed as much energy as I could into the staff as I clenched my jaws tight around it. My muscles hummed like I was sitting on a washing machine at the peak of its cycle. The light between mine and Astravar's staff grew so bright it almost blinded.

Meanwhile, I could see that golden glow getting ever fainter as it flew towards Astravar. The warlock didn't even seem to notice. Out of everything he was fighting today, he probably had never thought his greatest threat would be a stray fairy.

The golden glow that was Ta'ra got in front of Astravar, and she swept upwards into Astravar's beam in one swift motion that caused my heart to lurch in my chest. Whatever she did there was powerful enough to cut off Astravar's beam, and I felt my beam being released from Astravar's grasp. My magic hit Astravar in the chest.

Then, there came a flash of brilliance, accompanied by a tremendous bang. A bright golden flare filled the sky. As the light faded, it left behind a glowing cloud – also golden. From it, I noticed a tiny golden flake fluttering towards the ground, shimmering in a thin beam of sunlight that had just emerged from the clouds.

I saw everything else in slow motion. Astravar had completely vanished. No sign of him or the demon dragon was to be seen. Instead, around the golden glow, four fist-sized obsidian-coloured crystals seemed to hover in the air, as if someone had thrown them straight up and they'd just reached their apex. Meanwhile, a stone golem had just rammed its fist through the West Tower of Dragonsbond Academy.

Time seemed to return to normal as simultaneously the four crystals and the rubble from the top of the tower plummeted to the ground.

47

VANQUISHED

I didn't know what to feel. One moment Astravar had been there on his demon dragon, and then both had vanished into whiskers knows what dimension. One moment, Ta'ra had been sitting behind me, providing that 'support' that she'd said she'd provide. Then she'd exploded into a golden flash of light.

She had been lying to me all along. She hadn't come along to support me at all. She'd known this was going to happen. Everyone must have discussed this when I'd been asleep.

She couldn't be dead, could she? Somehow, I doubted she could have downed both Astravar and a demon dragon with whatever fairy magic she used and survived.

Had one of the crystals shown her something that I didn't know? Had this been part of the plan? My dark magic – everything I had fought for all this time – was always going to end like this. No matter how much I tried, I couldn't convince myself otherwise.

Whiskers, I felt like such a fool.

But it didn't matter anyway, because Ta'ra was gone...

Even the last golden flake that I assumed was once part of fairy Ta'ra had vanished from the sky. There was no trace of her left to be seen. It felt so cold now, up here against the icy wind. As we flew, more and more purple mist developed around us – and it now seemed to be becoming part of the clouds.

We were still losing. The six warlocks stood safely behind their shield, watching from afar, not even having to cast any magic. Despite Astravar having been defeated, those infernal aeriosaurs still flocked around us. They seemed to come in from all directions at once, and I felt rage surge to me whenever any of them got close. Out of my staff came great flashes of purple light, creating a display like fireworks that would have made the humans back home proud.

The Manipulators below floated across the purple land, feeding more bone dragons with energy. From there, great crashing sounds seemed to split the clouds apart. Stone tumbled down from the towers that had once been vast. They fell like that game my mistress and master liked to play when they invited friends around – the one where you only needed to remove a single block, and everything would collapse. More wargs came from behind the warlocks' shield in the meantime – filling up the courtyard now like water fills up a dammed lake. Meanwhile, the fire golems launched themselves at the high towers. They hit their targets bathing the parapets in flame. In time, those fires would roast the people and cats inside and force them out into the open. They didn't stand a chance.

Above it all, the sky was filled with the shrieks and cries of beasts, and no matter how we tried, our enemy wouldn't let us anywhere near Dragonsbond Academy to save them from their fate.

Now, Ta'ra was dead, and soon we all would die.

"Come on, Bengie," Salanraja said. "Pull yourself together."

She said this just as more aeriosaurs flooded in, and I let out my rage at them, whipping them out of the sky with my magic.

"It's okay for you to say. You haven't lost your..." My voice trailed off inside my mind. What had Ta'ra been to me? Really, I didn't want to think about that now.

"It's hard, I know," Salanraja said. "I've lost loved ones in my life too. But dwell later. Now, you need to fight."

She swooped down underneath a bone dragon coming from her tail, and I shot out a beam of energy at the Manipulator that fed energy into it, sending its crystal spinning across the ground. Salanraja caught up with the bone dragon and flamed it to bonemeal as it shrieked out its dying call.

I watched it wither underneath Salanraja's searing flame, and I stopped feeling the will to fight. It didn't matter anymore. I'd done my duty here. I'd defeated Astravar, and I'd fulfilled my destiny, just as my crystal had foreseen it. I didn't want to live through to see the end of all of this. I just couldn't...

I called my staff-bearer onwards in my mind, ready to return my staff. I wanted no more to do it. I wanted to die a cat, not a dark mage. Hovering several metres away, it clenched a fist at me, but I gave it a mental nudge to tell it that it didn't have a choice. It pushed forward, slowly, just as Salanraja dived out of its way.

"*Knock it off, Bengie,*" she said. "*More aeriosaurs inbound.*"

I couldn't stop myself. The will to destroy was too strong. More tentacles whipped out, disintegrating the vile beasts into purple dust. One moment there were thousands; then there were none.

But I didn't want such power anymore. So, my jaw went slack, and the staff fell out of it and spun towards the ground.

"*Bengie,*" Salanraja said. "*You moron! Stop this. We cannot lose.*"

She went after the staff, the staff-bearer charging alongside her. She accelerated at such a pace that she got underneath the staff. She tossed it upwards with her head, and the staff-bearer caught it in a tight grip. Olan, Corralsa, Hallinar, and Shadorow meanwhile streaked across the sky in random motions, as the four allied dark mages knocked more aeriosaurs out of the sky.

Nevertheless, we wouldn't stand a chance against those golems. Around us, everyone looked beaten. The dragons' wings beat slower than normal, and the riders atop them swung their staffs with far less vigour. Meanwhile Dragonsbond Academy was crumbling like Welsh cheese – it was beginning to look like that ruined castle I liked to explore on the hill in South Wales. It wouldn't be long until the wargs flooded into the corridors and tore the place apart.

I stared out at the clouds, at the ever-thickening purple mist, as I remembered that flash of light – Ta'ra sacrificing herself, but for what? But then, a voice came in my head. Her own words. "I love you,

Ben," she'd said. As I remembered, I felt a little strength surge up in me. I turned towards to my staff-bearer, reconsidering...

Suddenly, a call of bugles came out from Dragonsbond Academy. The dragons responded with an almighty roar, and the dragon riders cheered out a triumphant cry that for a moment silenced the shrieks of any aeriosaurs or bone dragons left in the sky.

"*Gracious demons,*" Salanraja said. "*Take hold of your staff now, Ben, and fight. Our reinforcements have arrived.*"

"What? Who?"

She didn't need to answer that, because coming from the east I saw a massive gathering dust mound. A yellow and a royal blue dragon came out of the clouds, with presumably Bellari and Reslin mounted on top of them. Next came the Cat Sidhe – giant beasts charging with purpose, as if they knew about the death of their beloved leader.

But they weren't the only reinforcements, because from the north came the sound of thousands of whickering horses and trampling hooves. The great white horses that emerged seemed to shimmer with a radiant glow, as if each of them had burning stars inside their hearts that pumped light through their veins. Mages in white cloaks with white staffs rode on top of these – and by white, I mean both the crystal and staff shone like glowing diamonds. But what seemed most unusual, as the horses came closer, was that each of them had a horn on its head.

"*What the whiskers are they?*" I asked Salanraja, forgetting the whole situation with Ta'ra for a moment.

"*King Garmin's White Mages,*" Salanraja said. "*Help at last has come.*"

"No, I mean the horses. Why do they have massive horns on their heads?"

"*Because they're magical. They're called unicorns... I can't believe you don't know that. They are to the White Mages what dragons are to dragon riders.*"

"How weird..."

"*More aeriosaurs inbound, Bengie.*"

I didn't hesitate to call my staff back to me. The new arrival had seeded an inkling of hope that was quickly growing in power. As I summoned more tentacles, using my staff, I put all my will into the fight. I fought for my owners back in South Wales that had looked after me. I fought for Aleam, and Seramina, and Rine, and Ange, all of whom had the kindness to guide me through this world, despite its prejudices. I fought for all the dragon riders, and the kingdom, and most of all, I fought for Ta'ra, because she'd almost certainly wanted me to live.

After I'd lashed those beasts down, no more remained in the sky. There were no more bone dragons, either. I could see now, with the vast numbers of Cat Sidhe and unicorns and White Mages that cascaded across the fields, the warlocks didn't stand a chance.

More creatures came from behind these unicorns. Magnificent birds as big as dragons, with massive beaks and their huge wings which were covered in fire. Wispy looking dragons that soared through the sky – their bodies so long that they almost looked like serpents and their bodies seeming to be formed of clouds. And chimera – an entire regiment of them. This time, fortunately, they weren't demon chimera, but valiant looking creatures, with impressive manes that waved in the wind as they charged.

Some wargs had, in the meantime, ripped open the double doors of the Dragonsbond Academy keep, and it looked like they were about to flood inside. But out charged a large charcoal dragon, blocking the wargs' path. I recognised the rider – Prefect Calin, who carried a sword in one hand and a glowing yellow staff in the other. That meant the charging dragon must have been his injured dragon, Galludo.

We had won; I realised that now. The warlocks also seemed to realise it, because the warlocks' shield went down and out of it six birds emerged into the sky. I couldn't see what type of birds they were from here, but they all looked like birds of prey, or some kind of carrion eaters at least. They retreated towards the purple mist that still lingered on the horizon – back towards the Darklands, where the warlocks belonged.

48

TRANSFORMATION

After we'd defeated the last of the wargs and golems, I asked Salanraja to deposit me down on the ground. I didn't want to face anyone yet, nor did I want to return to Dragonsbond Academy. I needed to find her – or at least I needed to try. Whether she had fallen as a Cat Sidhe or fairy, I needed to at least see her with my own eyes. Otherwise, I'd never be able to believe.

Salanraja deposited me by a massive husk of smouldering rock on the ground. It smelled of sulphur, and after a brief inspection, I saw the great teeth and the closed stone eyelid. This had been the demon dragon – the invincible creature that we could never defeat. Yet we had.

Some purple clouds remained in the sky, but they slowly dissipated, and the sun's rays filtered through them, making everything look magical. Dandelion seeds and motes of dust danced around, and sometimes with the way they reflected the light, I could almost imagine them to be fairies. Perhaps Ta'ra waltzed amongst them. But who was I kidding?

My staff-bearer hovered nearby. It moved in front of me, and bowed with its staff, as if wanting to offer sympathy. But it just reminded me of the version of Ta'ra in the ghost realm who had led me to the staff. I didn't want to remember her in that form.

"Just go away," I said, and I willed as much with my mind. To my surprise, the staff-bearer immediately vanished. I didn't need to have it follow me around, I realised. It was a ghost, after all. I could summon it when needed, and then command it to hide when not.

Two more dragons came down from the sky and landed close to me. They were Ishtkar and Quarl. Rine and Ange hopped off their mounts, and Rine stepped towards Ange, looking at her with intent. But Ange turned her head and saw me.

I turned away.

"Rine, wait," Ange said. "Just a moment." I heard her scuffle towards me through the long, dry grass. Then she reached down and stroked me on the neck. I flinched, and I backed away. I really didn't want to be comforted now.

"Wait, Ben," Ange said. "Where's Ta'ra? She went up with you, didn't she?"

I growled deeply. "Gone... She killed Astravar, and she..." I couldn't finish it. I just didn't want to say it. Not until I saw it.

"Are you sure?"

"I'm going to find her. I need to know..."

Ange nodded. Rine walked up behind her, looking kind of pleased with himself. But his expression fell when he turned to Ange, and he noticed her concerned expression. Tears had welled at the bottom of her eyes as if she was about to cry. If only I could cry like she could. Humans often told me it made them feel so much better.

I turned, and I searched for her scent. She smelled so often of lavender as a cat, because of those weird baths she used to take. Still there was that lingering miasma of rotten vegetable juice, but this was fading with each minute, and instead, many distinct aromas of pollen floated upon the breeze.

It wasn't the scent of lavender that I latched on to first, but a flash of white. It seemed as if one of the sun's rays coming down through the sky had focused on it – a beam highlighting where I was meant to go. I rushed towards it, as the clouds broke even more, letting an even thicker beam onto this target. It filled the land with warmth, pushing the last vestiges of purple mist away.

Then, I caught the scent of lavender, and once I found it, I scouted her out pretty fast. She lay in the grass, tinier than I ever remembered her. She was so small that I had to push away blades of grass with my nose to see her in full.

She had dark skin and straight raven hair whisked up like foamy water around her cheeks. Her dress was pure white and short enough to accentuate her slender thighs and calves. Her eyes were still green, but behind them, there wasn't any life left in them. I couldn't bear to look at them, and so I tried to close her eyelids with my nose. But she was far too small, and they seemed so delicate I thought I might damage them. So, I decided to leave them alone.

The sunlight coming down from the sky seemed to be getting warmer – almost searing, in fact. It felt as if the sun was concentrating its energy on this one spot. But it had to be an illusion, surely. I'd been freezing cold up there, which is why down here the sun felt unnaturally warm.

I took one last look at Ta'ra, sad I'd not seen her in cat form. Then I turned away. I didn't want to go to Rine and Ange. I didn't want to go to Salanraja, or Dragonsbond Academy, for that matter. I turned towards the purple mist, wanting nothing but a good long walk.

It was as if the magic happened when I wasn't looking. As if the sun filled her with new life, healing her as might one of Aleam's cures. Her voice came from behind me, stopping me in my tracks for a moment. "You know, I always heard it said that cats have nine lives."

It was Ta'ra's voice. It couldn't have been anything else. Yet I had to be hallucinating, surely. I was hearing what I wanted to hear. I growled and continued on my way.

"For whisker's sake, Ben, look at me when I'm talking to you."

I wasn't going to listen to the delusions. So, I didn't turn around.

"Dearie me. Must I do everything myself?" A scuffling sound came from behind me, and I knew it to be Ta'ra before she even bounded in front of me. I stopped, and I looked at her, and I blinked the dust out of my eyes.

It couldn't be, surely. "Ta'ra... How?"

"I don't know," Ta'ra said, examining herself. "I thought I was using my last transformation, but I guess my last was always going to be turning back into a cat. I must have still had that one last life left." She cocked her head. "It makes sense, right?"

"No..." I really wasn't sure it did. It didn't matter, I guess, because either this was all a dream, or I was experiencing a miracle. I didn't know what else to say. I was just so happy to see her. I sprung up to her and rubbed my nose against hers.

"Oh, Ben, you..." She lowered herself on her haunches and pounced. She landed over me, and we played swiping at each other – without claws of course – tumbling over each other. Being the stronger and greater of the species, I ended up on top of her.

Ange's voice floated over from the other side of the meadow. "Look Rine... It's Ta'ra. She survived. Will you look at that?"

I looked up, purring, as the familiar smell of Ta'ra's breath washed over me. Ange had a wide smile on her face, and Rine's eyes seemed to glisten in the light. Then, as if to celebrate, he took hold of Ange's hand – exactly as I'd told him to do so, all this time.

EPILOGUE

Respect is why the warlocks had chosen me to sign the treaty. That is why I came to the palace today.

I stood in the king's throne room. King Garmin sat on the throne a safe distance away from I, the revered Lasinta. It didn't matter, anyway. I'd left my staff behind to come here, and they'd searched me from wrinkled head to toe for any rogue crystals.

The king wore his celebratory red silk robe. Over his well-groomed blonde hair sat a diamond crown that I would one day knock off his head and claim as my own. But that would take time, because the only way to gain respect is through unerring patience. I had lived many years, and I had many more to come.

That was Astravar's undoing – he didn't have that patience and he certainly didn't have that respect. He'd tried to take over the world alone, rather than attempting to commandeer the service of loyal allies and subjects. Which was why we warlocks had watched him fly to his fate from our safehold in our protective shield as he foolishly tried to change the tides of destiny.

We'd waited, happily. Then we'd retreated, happily. It was all a part of the plan.

The king had two guards posted by the doors to the throne room and two guards posted by his throne, each of them wielding halberds that rested on their shoulder nearest to the door or throne. The only other person in the room was the king's trusted nephew – Prince Arran – commander of their Dragon Corps. I knew him well, and he knew me well, but no one else in the palace knew that. He was just one of many in my web of influence.

Of course, everyone in this palace knows my name – Lasinta, the great condor, the queen of the skies, the warlock who the other five remaining look up to the most. Age is a great asset, you see. It's one of the most powerful catalysts for respect. That's why I never tell anyone my true age, not just because I don't want them to take advantage, but because none of them would believe me.

A cooling draught filtered through the palace, coming from the open windows and gently caressing the red curtains. The sun shone through one window, but not a speck of dust was to be seen dancing in its rays. Marble arches spanned across either side of the throne room, adding to the cooling effect, much appreciated on this warm spring day.

In front of me stood a reading lectern with a leather-bound black book placed on it. Right now, it was closed, and the title shone out at me in gilt letters. "Treaty between the Warlocks and the Kingdom of Illumine." Next to this lay a spoon containing sealing wax and a lit candle in a holder.

Once my seal was placed, there would be a time of peace between the kingdoms. A time for the king's people to feel a sense of security. A time for us warlocks to weave through the kingdom, recruiting allies, plotting our way to usurp the throne.

Astravar never understood this, you see. Treaties and times of peace can be incredibly useful things.

I flicked through the pages of the book, every one of them crisp, the ink neatly pressed into them. I scanned the text for any warning signs, but the king wouldn't be foolish enough to include laws that we would likely break. I found the last page of the book, and I ran my finger over the king's seal – the unicorn and dragon imprinted in the puddle of dried wax.

I took the ring from my finger. I also took hold of the spoon and rested it over the candle. An aroma of fresh pine and cinnamon wafted upwards from the sealing wax – all a part of the ceremony handed down across ages of kings.

Once ready, I dripped the hot wax from the spoon, and I printed my seal, leaving an impression of a condor in mid-flight, its broad wings stretched out from tip to tip. I raised my head and spoke to the king.

"It is done," I said.

He nodded but said nothing. Too much blood had been shed in the names of the warlocks, and I would never gain his respect. But I did have the respect of Prince Arran, who stepped forward with his two hands wrapped around a scroll. "Here is the deed of treaty. You can sign it when you return home."

"Thank you, Prince Arran," I said out loud for everyone to hear, and I studied his grey eyes to check that his respect was still there, and that it hadn't dwindled - because if it had we might need to send an assassin in the night.

It was there, all right. He lowered his head and spoke under his breath so that only I could hear. "No, thank you, Grandmother. We shall all be together, eventually."

"That we shall," I whispered as I took the deed out of his hand. Then, without another word, I turned on my heel and strode out of the throne room, my work here complete.

Once outside, I ignored the guards staring at me and transformed into a condor underneath a plume of glorious purple smoke. I sailed over the fields – the lands that were part of the Kingdom of Illumine. Farmers in those fields would gaze up in the sky and watch in awe at the great condor, the largest bird in the realm. That was how it should be, because one day Illumine would be mine.

It was only a matter of patience, because I had all the time in the world.

ACKNOWLEDGMENTS

Thank you to my editor Wayne M. Scace, Carol Brandon for rigorous proofreading, my friends and family, and my dear wife Ola.

Also thank you to everyone on my ARC team, for all the feedback and support you've given me through this series and my other books.

Last but not least, thank you to all readers of my works. I appreciate everything that you do for indie authors.

ABOUT THE AUTHOR

When Chris Behrsin isn't out exploring the world, he's behind a keyboard writing tales of dragons and magical lands. He was born into the genre through a steady diet of Terry Pratchett. His fiction fuses a love for fantasy and whimsical plots with philosophy and voyages into the worlds of dreams.

You can learn more about him and download two free books at his website, www.chrisbehrsin.com.

facebook.com/chrisbehrsin
twitter.com/chrisbehrsin

Made in the USA
Monee, IL
25 November 2023

47309206R00378